THE ILLUSTRATED BEN-HUR

TWO VOLUMES IN ONE

BY

LEW. WALLACE

ILLUSTRATED WITH DRAWINGS BY
WILLIAM MARTIN JOHNSON
AND PHOTOGRAPHS

BONANZA BOOKS
NEW YORK

Formerly published as *Ben-Hur* in two volumes.

Special material copyright © MCMLXXIX by Crown Publishers, Inc.
Copyright © MDCCCXCI by Harper & Brothers
Copyright © MDCCCXCIX by Harper & Brothers

This edition is published by Bonanza Books,
a division of Crown Publishers, Inc.
b c d e f g h
BONANZA BOOKS
1978 Edition

Library of Congress Cataloging in Publication Data
Wallace, Lewis, 1827–1905.
The illustrated Ben-Hur.
Reprint of the 1901 issue of the ed. first
published in 1899 by Harper & Bros., New York,
under title: Ben-Hur.
1. Jesus Christ—Fiction. I. Title.
PZ3.W154Il 1978 [PS3124] 813'.4 78–17956
ISBN 0-517-25948-6

Dear General

I have, this morn-
ing, finished reading
"Ben-Hur" and I
must thank you
for the pleasure it
has given me –

The theme was dif
ficult; but you have
handled it with great
delicacy and power.

Several of the scenes

Such as the wise
men in the desert —
the Sea fight — the
chariot race — will
I am sure take a
permanent and high
place in literature.

With this beautiful
and reverent book
You have lightened
the burden of my
daily life — and re-
newed our acquain-
tance which began
at Shiloh —

Very truly Your
J. A. Garfield

Gov. Lew Wallace
Santa Fe. N.M.

GENERAL LEW. WALLACE

FOREWORD TO THE 1978 EDITION

We have come to know Lewis Wallace (1827-1905) simply as Lew. This is odd for a man who was a lawyer, congressman, and general. But Wallace was a man who loved people and wanted them to know it, a sort of nineteenth-century Jimmy Carter. Also, like President Carter, he was a deeply religious man.

Born in Brookville, Indiana, Wallace spent his early years as an adventurous fellow, often playing the truant. Adolescence brought an awakening of intellectual curiosity and the beginnings of his lifelong love of literature, art, and music, which was later to become the center of his life. But his career as a writer had to wait until his thirst for adventure had been sated.

Lew Wallace was admitted to the bar in Indiana in 1849, and he was elected to the Indiana state senate in 1856. When the Civil War broke out, he became an officer in the Union army, and quickly rose to the rank of Major-General in 1862. He was an extremely successful commander; his relationship with his troops was such that they would do anything for him. His greatest military achievement came in 1863 when he saved Cincinnati from capture by Confederate forces.

After the war, he returned to Indiana to practice law, and he remained there until he was appointed governor of New Mexico in 1878. It was around this time that Wallace underwent an experience that changed his life. On a train ride with the freethinker Robert Ingersoll, their discussion turned to God, Christ, and the afterlife. Ingersoll must have challenged Wallace's vague religious leanings, because Wallace realized that he had never seriously confronted his own religious beliefs. A few years earlier he had written a short article on

the three Wise Men and Christ's birth, and he now returned to this piece and more thoroughly researched the customs and beliefs of Judea at the time of Christ. As a result, he became convinced of the divinity of Christ.

Out of this experience grew *Ben-Hur,* a novel that traces the growth of the fame of Jesus as a backdrop for the life of Judah Ben-Hur, a Judean aristocrat. Judah Ben-Hur is a man of tremendous integrity and spirituality, and his search for truth culminates at Christ's crucifixion. Wallace's research on Judea and the Roman Empire is evident in the richness of historical detail.

SOLOMON J. SCHEPPS

VOLUME ONE

TABLE OF CONTENTS

VOLUME I

BOOK FIRST

BOOK SECOND

BOOK THIRD

BOOK FOURTH

FULL-PAGE ILLUSTRATIONS

VOLUME I

THE ILLUSTRATED BEN-HUR

BOOK FIRST

"
The flashes come and go;
All heaven bursts her starry floors,
And strews her lights below,
And deepens on and up!..."
—TENNYSON.

the passing of the stately brute. The charm is not in the figure, which not even love can make beautiful; nor in the movement, the noiseless stepping, or the broad career. As is the kindness of the sea to a ship, so is that of the desert to its creature. It clothes him with all its mysteries; in such manner, too, that while we are looking at him we are thinking of them: therein is the wonder. The animal which now came out of the wady might well have claimed the customary homage. Its color and height; its breadth of foot, its bulk of body, not fat, but overlaid with muscle, its long, slender neck, of swan-like curvature; the head, wide between the eyes, and tapering to a muzzle which a lady's bracelet might have almost clasped, its motion, step long and elastic, tread sure and soundless—all certified its Syrian blood, old as the days of Cyrus, and absolutely priceless. There was the usual bridle, covering the forehead with scarlet fringe, and garnishing the throat with pendent brazen chains, each ending with a tinkling silver bell; but to the bridle there was neither rein for the rider nor strap for a driver. The furniture perched on the back was an invention which with any other people than of the East would have made the inventor renowned. It consisted of two wooden boxes, scarce four feet in length, balanced so that one hung at each side; the inner space, softly lined and carpeted, was arranged to allow the master to sit or lie half reclined; over it all was stretched a green awning. Broad back and breast straps, and

23

girths, secured with countless knots and ties, held the device in place. In such manner the ingenious sons of Cush had contrived to make comfortable the sunburned ways of the wilderness, along which lay their duty as often as their pleasure.

When the dromedary lifted itself out of the last break of the wady, the traveller had passed the boundary of El Belka, the ancient Ammon. It was morning-time. Before him was the sun, half curtained in fleecy mist; before him also spread the desert; not the realm of drifting sands, which was farther on, but the region where the herbage began to dwarf; where the surface is strewn with bowlders of granite, and gray and brown stones, interspersed with languishing acacias and tufts of camel-grass. The oak, bramble, and arbutus lay behind, as if they had come to a line, looked over into the well-less waste, and crouched with fear.

And now there was an end of path or road. More than ever the camel seemed insensibly driven, it lengthened and quickened its pace, its head pointed straight towards the horizon; through the wide nostrils it drank the wind in great draughts. The litter swayed, and rose and fell like a boat in the waves. Dried leaves in occasional beds rustled underfoot. Sometimes a perfume like absinthe sweetened all the air. Lark and chat and rock-swallow leaped to wing, and white partridges ran whistling and clucking out of the way. More rarely a fox or a hyena quickened his gallop, to

24

study the intruders at a safe distance. Off to
the right rose the hills of the Jebel, the pearl-
gray veil resting upon them changing mo-
mentarily into a purple which the sun would
make matchless a little later. Over their
highest peaks a vulture sailed on broad wings
into widening circles. But of all these things
the tenant under the green tent saw nothing,
or, at least, made no sign of recognition. His
eyes were fixed and dreamy. The going of
the man, like that of the animal, was as one
being led.

For two hours the dromedary swung for-
ward, keeping the trot steadily and the line
due east. In that time the traveller never
changed his position, nor looked to the right
or left. On the desert, distance is not meas-
ured by miles or leagues, but by the saat, or
hour, and the manzil, or halt: three and a half
leagues fill the former, fifteen or twenty-five
the latter; but they are the rates for the com-
mon camel. A carrier of the genuine Syrian
stock can make three leagues easily. At full
speed he overtakes the ordinary winds. As
one of the results of the rapid advance, the face
of the landscape underwent a change. The
Jebel stretched along the western horizon, like
a pale-blue ribbon. A tell, or hummock of
clay and cemented sand, arose here and there.
Now and then basaltic stones lifted their round
crowns, outposts of the mountain against the
forces of the plain; all else, however, was
sand, sometimes smooth as the beaten beach,
then heaped in rolling ridges; here chopped

waves, there long swells. So, too, the condition of the atmosphere changed. The sun, high risen, had drunk his fill of dew and mist, and warmed the breeze that kissed the wanderer under the awning; far and near he was tinting the earth with faint milk-whiteness, and shimmering all the sky.

Two hours more passed without rest or deviation from the course. Vegetation entirely ceased. The sand, so crusted on the surface that it broke into rattling flakes at every step, held undisputed sway. The Jebel was out of view, and there was no landmark visible. The shadow that before followed had now shifted to the north, and was keeping even race with the objects which cast it; and as there was no sign of halting, the conduct of the traveller became each moment more strange.

No one, be it remembered, seeks the desert for a pleasure-ground. Life and business traverse it by paths along which the bones of things dead are strewn as so many blazons. Such are the roads from well to well, from pasture to pasture. The heart of the most veteran sheik beats quicker when he finds himself alone in the pathless tracts. So the man with whom we are dealing could not have been in search of pleasure; neither was his manner that of a fugitive; not once did he look behind him. In such situations fear and curiosity are the most common sensations; he was not moved by them. When men are lonely, they stoop to any companion-

ship; the dog becomes a comrade, the horse a friend, and it is no shame to shower them with caresses and speeches of love. The camel received no such token, not a touch, not a word.

Exactly at noon the dromedary, of its own will, stopped, and uttered the cry or moan, peculiarly piteous, by which its kind always protest against an overload, and sometimes crave attention and rest. The master thereupon bestirred himself, waking, as it were, from sleep. He threw the curtains of the houdah up, looked at the sun, surveyed the country on every side long and carefully, as if to identify an appointed place. Satisfied with the inspection, he drew a deep breath and nodded, much as to say, "At last, at last!" A moment after, he crossed his hands upon his breast, bowed his head, and prayed silently. The pious duty done, he prepared to dismount. From his throat proceeded the sound heard doubtless by the favorite camels of Job—Ikh! ikh!—the signal to kneel. Slowly the animal obeyed, grunting the while. The rider then put his foot upon the slender neck, and stepped upon the sand.

CHAPTER II
MEETING OF THE WISE MEN

HE man as now revealed was of admirable proportions, not so tall as powerful. Loosening the silken rope which held the kufiyeh on his head, he brushed the fringed folds back until his face was bare—a strong face, almost negro in color; yet the low, broad forehead, aquiline nose, the outer corners of the eyes turned slightly upward, the hair profuse, straight, harsh, of metallic lustre, and falling to the shoulder in many plaits, were signs of origin impossible to disguise. So looked the Pharaohs and the later Ptolemies; so looked Mizraim, father of the Egyptian race. He wore the kamis, a white cotton shirt, tight-sleeved, open in front, extending to the ankles and embroidered down the collar and breast, over which was thrown a brown woollen cloak, now, as in all probability it was then, called the aba, an outer garment with long skirt and short sleeves, lined inside with stuff of mixed cotton and silk, edged all round with a margin of clouded yellow. His feet were protected by sandals, attached by thongs of soft leather. A sash held the kamis to his waist. What was very noticeable, considering he was alone, and that the desert was the haunt of leopards and lions, and men quite as wild, he carried

lesser joints, one within another, which, when united together, formed a centre pole higher than his head. When the pole was planted, and the rods set around it, he spread the cloth over them, and was literally at home—a home much smaller than the habitations of emir and sheik, yet their counterpart in all other respects. From the litter again he brought a carpet or square rug, and covered the floor of the tent on the side from the sun. That done, he went out, and once more, and with greater care and more eager eyes, swept the encircling country. Except a distant jackal, galloping across the plain, and an eagle flying towards the Gulf of Akaba, the waste below, like the blue above it, was lifeless.

He turned to the camel, saying low, and in a tongue strange to the desert, " We are far from home, O racer with the swiftest winds— we are far from home, but God is with us. Let us be patient."

Then he took some beans from a pocket in the saddle, and put them in a bag made to hang below the animal's nose; and when he saw the relish with which the good servant took to the food, he turned and again scanned the world of sand, dim with the glow of the vertical sun.

" They will come," he said, calmly. " He that led me is leading them. I will make ready."

From the pouches which lined the interior of the cot, and from a willow basket which was part of its furniture, he brought forth ma-

no arms, not even the crooked stick used for guiding camels; wherefore we may at least infer his errand peaceful, and that he was either uncommonly bold or under extraordinary protection.

The traveller's limbs were numb, for the ride had been long and wearisome; so he rubbed his hands and stamped his feet, and walked round the faithful servant, whose lustrous eyes were closing in calm content with the cud he had already found. Often, while making the circuit, he paused, and, shading his eyes with his hands, examined the desert to the extremest verge of vision; and always, when the survey was ended, his face clouded with disappointment, slight, but enough to advise a shrewd spectator that he was there expecting company, if not by appointment; at the same time, the spectator would have been conscious of a sharpening of the curiosity to learn what the business could be that required transaction in a place so far from civilized abode.

However disappointed, there could be little doubt of the stranger's confidence in the coming of the expected company. In token thereof, he went first to the litter, and, from the cot or box opposite the one he had occupied in coming, produced a sponge and a small gurglet of water, with which he washed the eyes, face, and nostrils of the camel; that done, from the same depository he drew a circular cloth, red-and-white-striped, a bundle of rods, and a stout cane. The latter, after some manipulation, proved to be a cunning device of

terials for a meal: platters close-woven of the
fibres of palms; wine in small gurglets of skin;
mutton dried and smoked; stoneless shami,
or Syrian pomegranates; dates of El Shelebei,
wondrous rich and grown in the nakhil, or
palm orchards, of Central Arabia; cheese, like
David's "slices of milk;" and leavened bread
from the city bakery — all which he carried
and set upon the carpet under the tent. As
the final preparation, about the provisions he
laid three pieces of silk cloth, used among re-
fined people of the East to cover the knees of
guests while at table—a circumstance signifi-
cant of the number of persons who were to
partake of his entertainment—the number he
was awaiting.

All was now ready. He stepped out: lo!
in the east a dark speck on the face of the
desert. He stood as if rooted to the ground;
his eyes dilated; his flesh crept chilly, as if
touched by something supernatural. The
speck grew; became large as a hand; at length
assumed divine proportions. A little later,
full into view swung a duplication of his own
dromedary, tall and white, and bearing a hou-
dah, the travelling litter of Hindostan. Then
the Egyptian crossed his hands upon his
breast, and looked to heaven.

"God only is great!" he exclaimed, his eyes
full of tears, his soul in awe.

The stranger drew nigh—at last stopped.
Then he, too, seemed just waking. He beheld
the kneeling camel, the tent, and the man
standing prayerfully at the door. He crossed

his hands, bent his head, and prayed silently; after which, in a little while, he stepped from his camel's neck to the sand, and advanced towards the Egyptian, as did the Egyptian towards him. A moment they looked at each other; then they embraced—that is, each threw his right arm over the other's shoulder, and the left round the side, placing his chin first upon the left, then upon the right breast.

"Peace be with thee, O servant of the true God!" the stranger said.

"And to thee, O brother of the true faith! —to thee peace and welcome," the Egyptian replied, with fervor.

The new-comer was tall and gaunt, with lean face, sunken eyes, white hair and beard, and a complexion between the hue of cinnamon and bronze. He, too, was unarmed. His costume was Hindostani; over the skull-cap a shawl was wound in great folds, forming a turban; his body garments were in the style of the Egyptian's, except that the aba was shorter, exposing wide flowing breeches gathered at the ankles. In place of sandals, his feet were clad in half-slippers of red leather, pointed at the toes. Save the slippers, the costume from head to foot was of white linen. The air of the man was high, stately, severe. Visvamitra, the greatest of the ascetic heroes of the Iliad of the East, had in him a perfect representative. He might have been called a Life drenched with the wisdom of Brahma— Devotion Incarnate. Only in his eyes was there proof of humanity; when he lifted his face from the

Egyptian's breast, they were glistening with tears.

"God only is great!" he exclaimed, when the embrace was finished.

"And blessed are they that serve him!" the Egyptian answered, wondering at the paraphrase of his own exclamation. "But let us wait," he added, "let us wait; for see, the other comes yonder!"

They looked to the north, where, already plain to view, a third camel, of the whiteness of the others, came careening like a ship. They waited, standing together—waited until the new-comer arrived, dismounted, and advanced towards them.

"Peace to you, O my brother!" he said, while embracing the Hindoo.

And the Hindoo answered, "God's will be done!"

The last comer was all unlike his friends: his frame was slighter; his complexion white; a mass of waving light hair was a perfect crown for his small but beautiful head; the warmth of his dark-blue eyes certified a delicate mind, and a cordial, brave nature. He was bareheaded and unarmed. Under the folds of the Tyrian blanket which he wore with unconscious grace appeared a tunic, short-sleeved and low-necked, gathered to the waist by a band, and reaching nearly to the knee, leaving the neck, arms, and legs bare. Sandals guarded his feet. Fifty years, probably more, had spent themselves upon him, with no other effect, apparently, than to tinge his demeanor

with gravity and temper his words with fore-thought. The physical organization and the brightness of soul were untouched. No need to tell the student from what kindred he was sprung; if he came not himself from the groves of Athené, his ancestry did.

When his arms fell from the Egyptian, the latter said, with a tremulous voice, " The Spirit brought me first; wherefore I know myself chosen to be the servant of my brethren. The tent is set, and the bread is ready for the breaking. Let me perform my office."

Taking each by the hand, he led them within, and removed their sandals and washed their feet, and he poured water upon their hands, and dried them with napkins.

Then, when he had laved his own hands, he said, " Let us take care of ourselves, brethren, as our service requires, and eat, that we may be strong for what remains of the day's duty. While we eat we will each learn who the others are, and whence they come, and how they are called."

He took them to the repast, and seated them so that they faced each other. Simultaneously their heads bent forward, their hands crossed upon their breasts, and, speaking together, they said aloud this simple grace :

" Father of all—God !—what we have here is of thee ; take our thanks and bless us, that we may continue to do thy will."

With the last word they raised their eyes, and looked at each other in wonder. Each had spoken in a language never before heard

34

TOWER OF DAVID, JERUSALEM

by the others; yet each understood perfectly what was said. Their souls thrilled with divine emotion; for by the miracle they recognized the Divine Presence.

CHAPTER III
THE ATHENIAN SPEAKS—FAITH

TO speak in the style of the period, the meeting just described took place in the year of Rome 747. The month was December, and winter reigned over all the regions east of the Mediterranean. Such as ride upon the desert in this season go not far until smitten with a keen appetite. The company under the little tent were not exceptions to the rule. They were hungry, and ate heartily; and, after the wine, they talked.

"To a wayfarer in a strange land nothing is so sweet as to hear his name on the tongue of a friend," said the Egyptian, who assumed to be president of the repast. "Before us lie many days of companionship. It is time we knew each other. So, if it be agreeable, he who came last shall be first to speak."

Then, slowly at first, like one watchful of himself, the Greek began:

"What I have to tell, my brethren, is so strange that I hardly know where to begin or what I may with propriety speak. I do not yet understand myself. The most I am sure of is that I am doing a Master's will, and that the service is a constant ecstasy. When I

think of the purpose I am sent to fulfil, there
is in me a joy so inexpressible that I know the
will is God's."

The good man paused, unable to proceed,
while the others, in sympathy with his feelings,
dropped their gaze.

"Far to the west of this," he began again,
"there is a land which may never be forgot-
ten; if only because the world is too much its
debtor, and because the indebtedness is for
things that bring to men their purest pleasures.
I will say nothing of the arts, nothing of phi-
losophy, of eloquence, of poetry, of war : O my
brethren, hers is the glory which must shine
forever in perfected letters, by which He we
go to find and proclaim will be made known
to all the earth. The land I speak of is
Greece. I am Gaspar, son of Cleanthes the
Athenian.

"My people," he continued, "were given
wholly to study, and from them I derived the
same passion. It happens that two of our
philosophers, the very greatest of the many,
teach, one the doctrine of a Soul in every man,
and its Immortality; the other the doctrine of
One God, infinitely just. From the multitude
of subjects about which the schools were dis-
puting, I separated them, as alone worth the
labor of solution ; for I thought there was a
relation between God and the soul as yet un-
known. On this theme the mind can reason
to a point, a dead, impassable wall; arrived
there, all that remains is to stand and cry
aloud for help. So I did ; but no voice came

36

to me over the wall. In despair, I tore myself from the cities and the schools."

At these words a grave smile of approval lighted the gaunt face of the Hindoo.

"In the northern part of my country—in Thessaly," the Greek proceeded to say, "there is a mountain famous as the home of the gods, where Theus, whom my countrymen believe supreme, has his abode; Olympus is its name. Thither I betook myself. I found a cave in a hill where the mountain, coming from the west, bends to the southeast; there I dwelt, giving myself up to meditation—no, I gave myself up to waiting for what every breath was a prayer—for revelation. Believing in God, invisible yet supreme, I also believed it possible so to yearn for him with all my soul that he would take compassion and give me answer."

"And he did—he did!" exclaimed the Hindoo, lifting his hands from the silken cloth upon his lap.

"Hear me, brethren," said the Greek, calming himself with an effort. "The door of my hermitage looks over an arm of the sea, over the Thermaic Gulf. One day I saw a man flung overboard from a ship sailing by. He swam ashore. I received and took care of him. He was a Jew, learned in the history and laws of his people; and from him I came to know that the God of my prayers did indeed exist, and had been for ages their lawmaker, ruler, and king. What was that but the Revelation I dreamed of? My faith had not been fruitless; God answered me!"

37

"As he does all who cry to him with such faith," said the Hindoo.

"But, alas!" the Egyptian added, "how few are there wise enough to know when he answers them!"

"That was not all," the Greek continued. "The man so sent to me told me more. He said the prophets who, in the ages which followed the first revelation, walked and talked with God, declared he would come again. He gave me the names of the prophets, and from the sacred books quoted their very language. He told me, further, that the second coming was at hand—was looked for momentarily in Jerusalem."

The Greek paused, and the brightness of his countenance faded.

"It is true," he said, after a little—"it is true the man told me that as God and the revelation of which he spoke had been for the Jews alone, so it would be again. He that was to come should be King of the Jews. 'Had he nothing for the rest of the world?' I asked. 'No,' was the answer, given in a proud voice—'No, we are his chosen people.' The answer did not crush my hope. Why should such a God limit his love and benefaction to one land, and, as it were, to one family?· I set my heart upon knowing. At last I broke through the man's pride, and found that his fathers had been merely chosen servants to keep the Truth alive, that the world might at last know it and be saved. When the Jew was gone, and I was alone again, I chastened my soul with a new

prayer—that I might be permitted to see the King when he was come, and worship him. One night I sat by the door of my cave trying to get nearer the mysteries of my existence, knowing which is to know God; suddenly, on the sea below me, or rather in the darkness that covered its face, I saw a star begin to burn; slowly it arose and drew nigh, and stood over the hill and above my door, so that its light shone full upon me. I fell down, and slept, and in my dream I heard a voice say:

"'O Gaspar! Thy faith hath conquered! Blessed art thou! With two others, come from the uttermost parts of the earth, thou shalt see Him that is promised, and be a witness for him, and the occasion of testimony in his behalf. In the morning arise, and go meet them, and keep trust in the Spirit that shall guide thee.'

"And in the morning I awoke with the Spirit as a light within me surpassing that of the sun. I put off my hermit's garb, and dressed myself as of old. From a hiding-place I took the treasure which I had brought from the city. A ship went sailing past. I hailed it, was taken aboard, and landed at Antioch. There I bought the camel and his furniture. Through the gardens and orchards that enamel the banks of the Orontes, I journeyed to Emesa, Damascus, Bostra, and Philadelphia; thence hither. And so, O brethren, you have my story. Let me now listen to you."

CHAPTER IV
SPEECH OF THE HINDOO—LOVE

THE Egyptian and the Hindoo looked at each other; the former waved his hand; the latter bowed, and began:
"Our brother has spoken well. May my words be as wise."

He broke off, reflected a moment, then resumed:

"You may know me, brethren, by the name of Melchior. I speak to you in a language which, if not the oldest in the world, was at least the soonest to be reduced to letters—I mean the Sanscrit of India. I am a Hindoo by birth. My people were the first to walk in the fields of knowledge, first to divide them, first to make them beautiful. Whatever may hereafter befall, the four Vedas must live, for they are the primal fountains of religion and useful intelligence. From them were derived the Upa-Vedas, which, delivered by Brahma, treat of medicine, archery, architecture, music, and the four-and-sixty mechanical arts; the Ved-Angas, revealed by inspired saints, and devoted to astronomy, grammar, prosody, pronunciation, charms and incantations, religious rites and ceremonies; the Up-Angas, written by the sage Vyasa, and given to cosmogony, chronology, and geography; therein also are the Ramayâna and the Mahabhârata, heroic poems,

40

designed for the perpetuation of our gods and dèmi-gods. Such, O brethren, are the Great Shastras, or books of sacred ordinances. They are dead to me now; yet through all time they will serve to illustrate the budding genius of my race. They were promises of quick perfection. Ask you why the promises failed? Alas! the books themselves closed all the gates of progress. Under pretext of care for the creature, their authors imposed the fatal principle that a man must not address himself to discovery or invention, as Heaven had provided him all things needful. When that condition became a sacred law, the lamp of Hindoo genius was let down a well, where ever since it has lighted narrow walls and bitter waters.

"These allusions, brethren, are not from pride, as you will understand when I tell you that the Shastras teach a Supreme God called Brahm; also, that the Purânas, or sacred poems of the Up-Angas, tell us of Virtue and Good Works, and of the Soul. So, if my brother will permit the saying"—the speaker bowed deferentially to the Greek—"ages before his people were known, the two great ideas, God and the Soul, had absorbed all the forces of the Hindoo mind. In further explanation, let me say that Brahm is taught, by the same sacred books, as a Triad—Brahma, Vishnu, and Shiva. Of these, Brahma is said to have been the author of our race; which, in course of creation, he divided into four castes. First, he peopled the worlds below and the heavens

above; next, he made the earth ready for terrestrial spirits; then from his mouth proceeded the Brahman caste, nearest in likeness to himself, highest and noblest, sole teachers of the Vedas, which at the same time flowed from his lips in finished state, perfect in all useful knowledge. From his arms next issued the Kshatriya, or warriors; from his breast, the seat of life, came the Vaisya, or producers—shepherds, farmers, merchants; from his foot, in sign of degradation, sprang the Sudra, or serviles, doomed to menial duties for the other classes—serfs, domestics, laborers, artisans. Take notice, further, that the law, so born with them, forbade a man of one caste becoming a member of another; the Brahman could not enter a lower order; if he violated the laws of his own grade, he became an outcast, lost to all but outcasts like himself."

At this point, the imagination of the Greek, flashing forward upon all the consequences of such a degradation, overcame his eager attention, and he exclaimed, " In such a state, O brethren, what mighty need of a loving God !"

" Yes," added the Egyptian, " of a loving God like ours."

The brows of the Hindoo knit painfully; when the emotion was spent, he proceeded, in a softened voice.

" I was born a Brahman. My life, consequently, was ordered down to its least act, its last hour. My first draught of nourishment; the giving me my compound name; taking me out the first time to see the sun; investing me

42

with the triple thread by which I became one
of the twice-born; my induction into the first
order — were all celebrated with sacred texts
and rigid ceremonies. I might not walk, eat,
drink, or sleep without danger of violating a
rule. And the penalty, O brethren, the penal-
ty was to my soul! According to the degrees
of omission, my soul went to one of the heav-
ens—Indra's the lowest, Brahma's the highest;
or it was driven back to become the life of a
worm, a fly, a fish, or a brute. The reward for
perfect observance was Beatitude, or absorp-
tion into the being of Brahm, which was not
existence as much as absolute rest."

The Hindoo gave himself a moment's
thought; proceeding, he said: "The part of a
Brahman's life called the first order is his stu-
dent life. When I was ready to enter the sec-
ond order—that is to say, when I was ready to
marry and become a householder — I ques-
tioned everything, even Brahm; I was a her-
etic. From the depths of the well I had dis-
covered a light above, and yearned to go up
and see what all it shone upon. At last—ah,
with what years of toil!—I stood in the per-
fect day, and beheld the principle of life, the
element of religion, the link between the soul
and God—Love!"

The shrunken face of the good man kindled
visibly, and he clasped his hands with force.
A silence ensued, during which the others
looked at him, the Greek through tears. At
length he resumed:

"The happiness of love is in action; its test

is what one is willing to do for others. I could not rest. Brahm had filled the world with so much wretchedness. The Sudra appealed to me; so did the countless devotees and victims. The island of Ganga Lagor lies where the sacred waters of the Ganges disappear in the Indian Ocean. Thither I betook myself. In the shade of the temple built there to the sage Kapila, in a union of prayers with the disciples whom the sanctified memory of the holy man keeps around his house, I thought to find rest. But twice every year came pilgrimages of Hindoos seeking the purification of the waters. Their misery strengthened my love. Against its impulse to speak I clenched my jaws; for one word against Brahm or the Triad or the Shastras would doom me; one act of kindness to the outcast Brahmans who now and then dragged themselves to die on the burning sands—a blessing said, a cup of water given—and I became one of them, lost to family, country, privileges, caste. The love conquered! I spoke to the disciples in the temple; they drove me out. I spoke to the pilgrims, they stoned me from the island. On the highways I attempted to preach; my hearers fled from me, or sought my life. In all India, finally, there was not a place in which I could find peace or safety—not even among the outcasts; for, though fallen, they were still believers in Brahm. In my extremity, I looked for a solitude in which to hide from all but God. I followed the Ganges to its source, far up in the Himalayas. When I entered the pass

at Hurdwar, where the river, in unstained purity, leaps to its course through the muddy lowlands, I prayed for my race, and thought myself lost to them forever. Through gorges, over cliffs, across glaciers, by peaks that seemed star-high, I made my way to the Lang Tso, a lake of marvellous beauty, asleep at the feet of the Tise Gangri, the Gurla, and the Kailas Parbot, giants which flaunt their crowns of snow everlastingly in the face of the sun. There, in the centre of the earth, where the Indus, Ganges, and Brahmapootra rise to run their different courses; where mankind took up their first abode, and separated to replete the world, leaving Balk, the mother of cities, to attest the great fact; where Nature, gone back to its primeval condition, and secure in its immensities, invites the sage and the exile, with promise of safety to the one and solitude to the other—there I went to abide alone with God, praying, fasting, waiting for death."

Again the voice fell, and the bony hands met in a fervent clasp.

"One night I walked by the shores of the lake, and spoke to the listening silence, 'When will God come and claim his own? Is there to be no redemption?' Suddenly a light began to glow tremulously out on the water; soon a star arose, and moved towards me, and stood overhead. The brightness stunned me. While I lay upon the ground, I heard a voice of infinite sweetness say, 'Thy love hath conquered. Blessed art thou, O son of India! The redemption is at hand. With two others,

from far quarters of the earth, thou shalt see the Redeemer, and be a witness that he hath come. In the morning arise, and go meet them; and put all thy trust in the Spirit which shall guide thee.'

"And from that time the light has stayed with me; so I knew it was the visible presence of the Spirit. In the morning I started to the world by the way I had come. In a cleft of the mountain I found a stone of vast worth, which I sold in Hurdwar. By Lahore, and Cabool, and Yezd, I came to Ispahan. There I bought the camel, and thence was led to Bagdad, not waiting for caravans. Alone I travelled, fearless, for the Spirit was with me, and is with me yet. What glory is ours, O brethren! We are to see the Redeemer—to speak to him—to worship him? I am done."

CHAPTER V

THE EGYPTIAN'S STORY—GOOD WORKS

THE vivacious Greek broke forth in expressions of joy and congratulations; after which the Egyptian said, with characteristic gravity:

"I salute you, my brother. You have suffered much, and I rejoice in your triumph. If you are both pleased to hear me, I will now tell you who I am, and how I came to be called. Wait for me a moment."

He went out and tended the camels; coming back, he resumed his seat.

"Your words, brethren, were of the Spirit," he said, in commencement; "and the Spirit gives me to understand them. You each spoke particularly of your countries; in that there was a great object, which I will explain; but to make the interpretation complete, let me first speak of myself and my people. I am Balthasar the Egyptian."

The last words were spoken quietly, but with so much dignity that both listeners bowed to the speaker.

"There are many distinctions I might claim for my race," he contined; "but I will content myself with one. History began with us. We were the first to perpetuate events by records kept. So we have no traditions; and instead of poetry, we offer you certainty. On the façades of palaces and temples, on obelisks, on the inner walls of tombs, we wrote the names of our kings, and what they did; and to the delicate papyri we intrusted the wisdom of our philosophers and the secrets of our religion— all the secrets but one, whereof I will presently speak. Older than the Vedas of Para-Brahm or the Up-Angas of Vyasa, O Melchior; older than the songs of Homer or the metaphysics of Plato, O my Gaspar; older than the sacred books or kings of the people of China, or those of Siddârtha, son of the beautiful Maya; older than the Genesis of Moschè the Hebrew — oldest of human records are the writings of Menes, our first king." Pausing an instant, he fixed his large eyes kindly upon the Greek, saying, "In the youth of Hel-

47

las, who, O Gaspar, were the teachers of her teachers?"

The Greek bowed, smiling.

"By those records," Balthasar continued, "we know that when the fathers came from the far East, from the region of the birth of the three sacred rivers, from the centre of the earth — the Old Iran of which you spoke, O Melchior—came bringing with them the history of the world before the Flood, and of the Flood itself, as given to the Aryans by the sons of Noah, they taught God, the Creator and the Beginning, and the Soul, deathless as God. When the duty which calls us now is happily done, if you choose to go with me, I will show you the sacred library of our priesthood; among others, the Book of the Dead, in which is the ritual to be observed by the soul after Death has despatched it on its journey to judgment. The ideas — God and the Immortal Soul — were borne to Mizraim over the desert, and by him to the banks of the Nile. They were then in their purity, easy of understanding, as what God intends for our happiness always is; so, also, was the first worship—a song and a prayer natural to a soul joyous, hopeful, and in love with its Maker."

Here the Greek threw up his hands, exclaiming, "Oh! the light deepens within me!"

"And in me!" said the Hindoo, with equal fervor.

The Egyptian regarded them benignantly, then went on, saying, "Religion is merely the

law which binds man to his Creator: in purity it has but these elements—God, the Soul, and their Mutual Recognition; out of which, when put in practice, spring Worship, Love, and Reward. This law, like all others of divine origin —like that, for instance, which binds the earth to the sun—was perfected in the beginning by its Author. Such, my brothers, was the religion of the first family; such was the religion of our father Mizraim, who could not have been blind to the formula of creation, nowhere so discernible as in the first faith and the earliest worship. Perfection is God; simplicity is perfection. The curse of curses is that men will not let truths like these alone."

He stopped, as if considering in what manner to continue.

"Many nations have loved the sweet waters of the Nile," he said next; "the Ethiopian, the Pali-Putra, the Hebrew, the Assyrian, the Persian, the Macedonian, the Roman—of whom all, except the Hebrew, have at one time or another been its masters. So much coming and going of peoples corrupted the old Mizraimic faith. The Valley of Palms became a Valley of Gods. The Supreme One was divided into eight, each personating a creative principle in nature, with Ammon-Re at the head. Then Isis and Osiris, and their circle, representing water, fire, air, and other forces, were invented. Still the multiplication went on until we had another order, suggested by human qualities, such as strength, knowledge, love, and the like."

"In all which there was the old folly!" cried the Greek, impulsively. "Only the things out of reach remain as they came to us."

The Egyptian bowed, and proceeded:

"Yet a little further, O my brethren, a little further, before I come to myself. What we go to will seem all the holier of comparison with what is and has been. The records show that Mizraim found the Nile in possession of the Ethiopians, who were spread thence through the African desert; a people of rich, fantastic genius, wholly given to the worship of nature. The poetic Persian sacrificed to the sun, as the completest image of Ormuzd, his God; the devout children of the far East carved their deities out of wood and ivory; but the Ethiopian, without writing, without books, without mechanical faculty of any kind, quieted his soul by the worship of animals, birds, and insects, holding the cat sacred to Re, the bull to Isis, the beetle to Pthah. A long struggle against their rude faith ended in its adoption as the religion of the new empire. Then rose the mighty monuments that cumber the river-bank and the desert — obelisk, labyrinth, pyramid, and tomb of king, blent with tomb of crocodile. Into such deep debasement, O brethren, the sons of the Aryan fell!"

Here, for the first time, the calmness of the Egyptian forsook him: though his countenance remained impassive, his voice gave way.

"Do not too much despise my countrymen," he began again. "They did not all forget

God. I said awhile ago, you may remember, that to papyri we intrusted all the secrets of our religion except one; of that I will now tell you. We had as king once a certain Pharaoh, who lent himself to all manner of changes and additions. To establish the new system, he strove to drive the old entirely out of mind. The Hebrews then dwelt with us as slaves. They clung to their God; and when the persecution became intolerable, they were delivered in a manner never to be forgotten. I speak from the records now. Mosché, himself a Hebrew, came to the palace, and demanded permission for the slaves, then millions in number, to leave the country. The demand was in the name of the Lord God of Israel. Pharaoh refused. Hear what followed. First, all the water, that in the lakes and rivers, like that in the wells and vessels, turned to blood. Yet the monarch refused. Then frogs came up and covered all the land. Still he was firm. Then Mosché threw ashes in the air, and a plague attacked the Egyptians. Next, all the cattle, except of the Hebrews, were struck dead. Locusts devoured the green things of the valley. At noon the day was turned into a darkness so thick that lamps would not burn. Finally, in the night all the first-born of the Egyptians died; not even Pharaoh's escaped. Then he yielded. But when the Hebrews were gone he followed them with his army. At the last moment the sea was divided, so that the fugitives passed it dry-shod. When the pursuers drove in after

them, the waves rushed back and drowned
horse, foot, charioteers, and king. You spoke
of revelation, my Gaspar—"

The blue eyes of the Greek sparkled.

"I had the story from the Jew," he cried.
"You confirm it, O Balthasar!"

"Yes, but through me Egypt speaks, not
Mosché. I interpret the marbles. The priests
of that time wrote in their way what they
witnessed, and the revelation has lived. So
I come to the one unrecorded secret. In my
country, brethren, we have, from the day of
the unfortunate Pharaoh, always had two re-
ligions—one private, the other public; one of
many gods, practised by the people; the other
of one God, cherished only by the priesthood.
Rejoice with me, O brothers! All the trampl-
ing by the many nations, all the harrowing by
kings, all the inventions of enemies, all the
changes of time, have been in vain. Like a
seed under the mountains waiting its hour,
the glorious Truth has lived; and this—this is
its day!"

The wasted frame of the Hindoo trembled
with delight, and the Greek cried aloud,

"It seems to me the very desert is singing."

From a gurglet of water near by the Egyp-
tian took a draught, and proceeded:

"I was born at Alexandria, a prince and a
priest, and had the education usual to my class.
But very early I became discontented. Part
of the faith imposed was that after death, upon
the destruction of the body, the soul at once
began its former progression from the lowest

52

up to humanity, the highest and last existence; and that without reference to conduct in the mortal life. When I heard of the Persian's Realm of Light, his Paradise across the bridge Chinevat, where only the good go, the thought haunted me; insomuch that in the day, as in the night, I brooded over the comparative ideas Eternal Transmigration and Eternal Life in Heaven. If, as my teacher taught, God was just, why was there no distinction between the good and the bad? At length it became clear to me, a certainty, a corollary of the law to which I reduced pure religion, that death was only the point of separation at which the wicked are left or lost, and the faithful rise to a higher life; not the nirvana of Buddha, or the negative rest of Brahma, O Melchior; nor the better condition in hell, which is all of Heaven allowed by the Olympic faith, O Gaspar; but life—life active, joyous, everlasting— LIFE WITH GOD! The discovery led to another inquiry. Why should the Truth be longer kept a secret for the selfish solace of the priesthood? The reason for the suppression was gone. Philosophy had at least brought us toleration. In Egypt we had Rome instead of Rameses. One day, in the Brucheium, the most splendid and crowded quarter of Alexandria, I arose and preached. The East and West contributed to my audience. Students going to the Library, priests from the Serapeion, idlers from the Museum, patrons of the race-course, countrymen from the Rhacotis— a multitude—stopped to hear me. I preached

God, the Soul, Right and Wrong, and Heaven, the reward of a virtuous life. You, O Melchior, were stoned; my auditors first wondered, then laughed. I tried again; they pelted me with epigrams, covered my God with ridicule, and darkened my Heaven with mockery. Not to linger needlessly, I fell before them."

The Hindoo here drew a long sigh, as he said, "The enemy of man is man, my brother."

Balthasar lapsed into silence.

" I gave much thought to finding the cause of my failure, and at last succeeded," he said, upon beginning again. " Up the river, a day's journey from the city, there is a village of herdsmen and gardeners. I took a boat and went there. In the evening I called the people together, men and women, the poorest of the poor. I preached to them exactly as I had preached in the Brucheium. They did not laugh. Next evening I spoke again, and they believed and rejoiced, and carried the news abroad. At the third meeting a society was formed for prayer. I returned to the city then. Drifting down the river, under the stars, which never seemed so bright and so near, I evolved this lesson : To begin a reform, go not into the places of the great and rich ; go rather to those whose cups of happiness are empty —to the poor and humble. And then I laid a plan and devoted my life. As a first step, I secured my vast property, so that the income would be certain, and always at call for the relief of the suffering. From that day, O brethren, I travelled up and down the Nile, in the

villages, and to all the tribes, preaching One God, a righteous life, and reward in Heaven. I have done good—it does not become me to say how much. I also know that part of the world to be ripe for the reception of Him we go to find.

A flush suffused the swarthy cheek of the speaker; but he overcame the feeling, and continued:

"The years so given, O my brothers, were troubled by one thought—When I was gone, what would become of the cause I had started? Was it to end with me? I had dreamed many times of organization as a fitting crown for my work. To hide nothing from you, I had tried to effect it, and failed. Brethren, the world is now in the condition that, to restore the old Mizraimic faith, the reformer must have a more than human sanction; he must not merely come in God's name, he must have the proofs subject to his word; he must demonstrate all he says, even God. So preoccupied is the mind with myths and systems; so much do false deities crowd every place—earth, air, sky; so have they become of everything a part, that return to the first religion can only be along bloody paths, through fields of persecution; that is to say, the converts must be willing to die rather than recant. And who in this age can carry the faith of men to such a point but God himself? To redeem the race—I do not mean to destroy it—to redeem the race, he must make himself once more manifest; HE MUST COME IN PERSON."

Intense emotion seized the three.

"Are we not going to find him?" exclaimed the Greek.

"You understand why I failed in the attempt to organize," said the Egyptian, when the spell was past. "I had not the sanction. To know that my work must be lost made me intolerably wretched. I believed in prayer; and to make my appeals pure and strong, like you, my brethren, I went out of the beaten ways, I went where man had not been, where only God was. Above the fifth cataract, above the meeting of rivers in Sennar, up the Bahr el Abiad, into the far unknown of Africa, I went. There, in the morning, a mountain blue as the sky flings a cooling shadow wide over the western desert, and, with its cascades of melted snow, feeds a broad lake nestling at its base on the east. The lake is the mother of the great river. For a year and more the mountain gave me a home. The fruit of the palm fed my body, prayer my spirit. One night I walked in the orchard close by the little sea. 'The world is dying. When wilt thou come? Why may I not see the redemption, O God?' So I prayed. The glassy water was sparkling with stars. One of them seemed to leave its place, and rise to the surface, where it became a brilliancy burning to the eyes. Then it moved towards me, and stood over my head, apparently in hand's reach. I fell down and hid my face. A voice, not of the earth, said, 'Thy good works have conquered. Blessed art thou, O son of Mizraim! The redemption cometh. With two

others, from the remoteness of the world, thou shalt see the Saviour, and testify for him. In the morning arise, and go meet them. And when ye have all come to the holy city of Jerusalem, ask of the people, Where is he that is born King of the Jews? for we have seen his star in the East, and are sent to worship him. Put all thy trust in the Spirit which will guide thee.'

"And the light became an inward illumination not to be doubted, and has stayed with me, a governor and a guide. It led me down the river to Memphis, where I made ready for the desert. I bought my camel, and came hither without rest, by way of Suez and Kufileh, and up through the lands of Moab and Ammon. God is with us, O my brethren!"

He paused, and thereupon, with a prompting not their own, they all arose, and looked at each other.

"I said there was a purpose in the particularity with which we described our peoples and their histories," so the Egyptian proceeded. "He we go to find was called 'King of the Jews;' by that name we are bidden to ask for him. But, now that we have met, and heard from each other, we may know him to be the Redeemer, not of the Jews alone, but of all the nations of the earth. The patriarch who survived the Flood had with him three sons, and their families, by whom the world was repeopled. From the old Aryana-Vaêjo, the well-remembered Region of Delight in the heart of Asia, they parted. India and the far East

57

received the children of the first; the descendants of the youngest, through the North, streamed into Europe; those of the second overflowed the deserts about the Red Sea, passing into Africa; and though most of the latter are yet dwellers in shifting tents, some of them became builders along the Nile."

By a simultaneous impulse the three joined hands.

"Could anything be more divinely ordered?" Balthasar continued. "When we have found the Lord, the brothers, and all the generations that have succeeded them, will kneel to him in homage with us. And when we part to go our separate ways, the world will have learned a new lesson—that Heaven may be won, not by the sword, not by human wisdom, but by Faith, Love, and Good Works."

There was silence, broken by sighs and sanctified with tears; for the joy that filled them might not be stayed. It was the unspeakable joy of souls on the shores of the River of Life, resting with the Redeemed in God's presence.

Presently their hands fell apart, and together they went out of the tent. The desert was still as the sky. The sun was sinking fast. The camels slept.

A little while after, the tent was struck, and, with the remains of the repast, restored to the cot; then the friends mounted, and set out single file, led by the Egyptian. Their course was due west, into the chilly night. The camels swung forward in steady trot, keeping the line and the intervals so exactly that those

following seemed to tread in the tracks of the leader. The riders spoke not once.

By-and-by the moon came up. And as the three tall white figures sped, with soundless tread, through the opalescent light, they appeared like spectres flying from hateful shadows. Suddenly, in the air before them, not farther up than a low hill-top, flared a lambent flame; as they looked at it, the apparition contracted into a focus of dazzling lustre. Their hearts beat fast; their souls thrilled; and they shouted as with one voice, "The Star! the Star! God is with us!"

CHAPTER VI
THE JOPPA GATE

ON an aperture of the western wall of Jerusalem hang the "oaken valves" called the Bethlehem or Joppa Gate. The area outside of them is one of the notable places of the city. Long before David coveted Zion there was a citadel there. When at last the son of Jesse ousted the Jebusite, and began to build, the site of the citadel became the north-west corner of the new wall, defended by a tower much more imposing than the old one. The location of the gate, however, was not disturbed, for the reasons, most likely, that the roads which met and merged in front of it could not well be transferred to any other point, while the area outside had become a recognized market-place.

59

In Solomon's day there was great traffic at the locality, shared in by traders from Egypt and the rich dealers from Tyre and Sidon. Nearly three thousand years have passed, and yet a kind of commerce clings to the spot. A pilgrim wanting a pin or a pistol, a cucumber or a camel, a house or a horse, a loan or a lentil, a date or a dragoman, a melon or a man, a dove or a donkey, has only to inquire for the article at the Joppa Gate. Sometimes the scene is quite animated, and then it suggests, What a place the old market must have been in the days of Herod the Builder! And to that period and that market the reader is now to be transferred.

Following the Hebrew system, the meeting of the wise men described in the preceding chapters took place in the afternoon of the twenty-fifth day of the third month of the year; that is to say, on the twenty-fifth day of December. The year was the second of the 193d Olympiad, or the 747th of Rome; the sixty-seventh of Herod the Great, and the thirty-fifth of his reign; the fourth before the beginning of the Christian era. The hours of the day, by Judean custom, begin with the sun, the first hour being the first after sunrise; so, to be precise, the market at the Joppa Gate during the first hour of the day stated was in full session, and very lively. The massive valves had been wide open since dawn. Business, always aggressive, had pushed through the arched entrance into a narrow lane and court, which, passing by the walls of the great

tower, conducted on into the city. As Jerusalem is in the hill country, the morning air on this occasion was not a little crisp. The rays of the sun, with their promise of warmth, lingered provokingly far up on the battlements and turrets of the great piles about, down from which fell the crooning of pigeons and the whir of the flocks coming and going.

As a passing acquaintance with the people of the Holy City, strangers as well as residents, will be necessary to an understanding of some of the pages which follow, it will be well to stop at the gate and pass the scene in review. Better opportunity will not offer to get sight of the populace who will after a while go forward in a mood very different from that which now possesses them.

The scene is at first one of utter confusion —confusion of action, sounds, colors, and things. It is especially so in the lane and court. The ground there is paved with broad unshaped flags, from which each cry and jar and hoof-stamp arises to swell the medley that rings and roars up between the solid impending walls. A little mixing with the throng, however, a little familiarity with the business going on, will make analysis possible.

Here stands a donkey, dozing under panniers full of lentils, beans, onions, and cucumbers, brought fresh from the gardens and terraces of Galilee. When not engaged in serving customers, the master, in a voice which only the initiated can understand, cries his stock. Nothing can be simpler than his cos-

tume—sandals, and an unbleached, undyed blanket, crossed over one shoulder and girt round the waist. Near-by, and far more imposing and grotesque, though scarcely as patient as the donkey, kneels a camel, raw-boned, rough, and gray, with long shaggy tufts of fox-colored hair under its throat, neck, and body, and a load of boxes and baskets curiously arranged upon an enormous saddle. The owner is an Egyptian, small, lithe, and of a complexion which has borrowed a good deal from the dust of the roads and the sands of the desert. He wears a faded tarbooshe, a loose gown, sleeveless, unbelted, and dropping from the neck to the knee. His feet are bare. The camel, restless under the load, groans and occasionally shows his teeth; but the man paces indifferently to and fro, holding the driving-strap, and all the time advertising his fruits fresh from the orchards of the Kedron—grapes, dates, figs, apples, and pomegranates.

At the corner where the lane opens out into the court, some women sit with their backs against the gray stones of the wall. Their dress is that common to the humbler classes of the country—a linen frock extending the full length of the person, loosely gathered at the waist, and a veil or wimple broad enough, after covering the head, to wrap the shoulders. Their merchandise is contained in a number of earthen jars, such as are still used in the East for bringing water from the wells, and some leathern bottles. Among the jars and bottles, rolling upon the stony floor, regardless of the

crowd and cold, often in danger but never hurt, play half a dozen half-naked children, their brown bodies, jetty eyes, and thick black hair attesting the blood of Israel. Sometimes, from under the wimples, the mothers look up, and in the vernacular modestly bespeak their trade: in the bottles "honey of grapes," in the jars "strong drink." Their entreaties are usually lost in the general uproar, and they fare illy against the many competitors: brawny fellows with bare legs, dirty tunics, and long beards, going about with bottles lashed to their backs, and shouting "Honey of wine! Grapes of En-Gedi!" When a customer halts one of them, round comes the bottle, and, upon lifting the thumb from the nozzle, out into the ready cup gushes the deep-red blood of the luscious berry.

Scarcely less blatant are the dealers in birds —doves, ducks, and frequently the singing bulbul, or nightingale, most frequently pigeons; and buyers, receiving them from the nets, seldom fail to think of the perilous life of the catchers, bold climbers of the cliffs; now hanging with hand and foot to the face of the crag, now swinging in a basket far down the mountain fissure.

Blent with peddlers of jewelry—sharp men cloaked in scarlet and blue, top-heavy under prodigious white turbans, and fully conscious of the power there is in the lustre of a ribbon and the incisive gleam of gold, whether in bracelet or necklace, or in rings for the finger or the nose—and with peddlers of household

utensils, and with dealers in wearing-apparel, and with retailers of unguents for anointing the person, and with hucksters of all articles, fanciful as well as of need, hither and thither, tugging at halters and ropes, now screaming, now coaxing, toil the venders of animals—donkeys, horses, calves, sheep, bleating kids, and awkward camels; animals of every kind except the outlawed swine. All these are there; not singly, as described, but many times repeated; not in one place, but everywhere in the market.

Turning from this scene in the lane and court, this glance at the sellers and their commodities, the reader has need to give attention, in the next place, to visitors and buyers, for which the best studies will be found outside the gates, where the spectacle is quite as varied and animated; indeed, it may be more so, for there are superadded the effects of tent, booth, and sook, greater space, larger crowd, more unqualified freedom, and the glory of the Eastern sunshine.

CHAPTER VII
TYPICAL CHARACTERS AT THE JOPPA GATE

ET us take our stand by the gate, just out of the edge of the currents—one flowing in, the other out—and use our eyes and ears a while.

In good time! Here come two men of a most noteworthy class.

"Gods! How cold it is!" says one of them, a powerful figure in armor; on his head a brazen helmet, on his body a shining breastplate and skirts of mail. "How cold it is! Dost thou remember, my Caius, that vault in the Comitium at home which the flamens say is the entrance to the lower world? By Pluto! I could stand there this morning, long enough, at least to get warm again!"

The party addressed drops the hood of his military cloak, leaving bare his head and face, and replies, with an ironic smile, "The helmets of the legions which conquered Mark Antony were full of Gallic snow; but thou—ah, my poor friend!—thou hast just come from Egypt, bringing its summer in thy blood."

And with the last word they disappear through the entrance. Though they had been silent, the armor and the sturdy step would have published them Roman soldiers.

From the throng a Jew comes next, meagre of frame, round-shouldered, and wearing a

65

coarse brown robe; over his eyes and face, and down his back hangs a mat of long uncombed hair. He is alone. Those who meet him laugh, if they do not worse; for he is a Nazarite, one of a despised sect which rejects the books of Moses, devotes itself to abhorred vows, and goes unshorn while the vows endure.

As we watch his retiring figure, suddenly there is a commotion in the crowd, a parting quickly to the right and left, with exclamations sharp and decisive. Then the cause comes— a man, Hebrew in feature and dress. The mantle of snow-white linen, held to his head by cords of yellow silk, flows free over his shoulders; his robe is richly embroidered; a red sash with fringes of gold wraps his waist several times. His demeanor is calm; he even smiles upon those who, with such rude haste, make room for him. A leper? No, he is only a Samaritan. The shrinking crowd, if asked, would say he is a mongrel—an Assyrian— whose touch of the robe is pollution; from whom, consequently, an Israelite, though dying, might not accept life. In fact, the feud is not of blood. When David set his throne here on Mount Zion, with only Judah to support him, the ten tribes betook themselves to Shechem, a city much older, and, at that date, infinitely richer in holy memories. The final union of the tribes did not settle the dispute thus begun. The Samaritans clung to their tabernacle on Gerizim, and, while maintaining its superior sanctity, laughed at the irate doctors in Jerusalem. Time brought no assuage-

ment of the hate. Under Herod, conversion
to the faith was open to all the world except
the Samaritans; they alone were absolutely
and forever shut out from communion with
Jews.

As the Samaritan goes in under the arch of
the gate, out come three men so unlike all
whom we have yet seen that they fix our gaze,
whether we will or not. They are of unusual
stature and immense brawn; their eyes are
blue, and so fair is their complexion that the
blood shines through the skin like blue pen-
cilling; their hair is light and short; their
heads, small and round, rest squarely upon
necks columnar as the trunks of trees. Wool-
len tunics, open at the breast, sleeveless and
loosely girt, drape their bodies, leaving bare
arms and legs of such development that they
at once suggest the arena; and when thereto
we add their careless, confident, insolent man-
ner, we cease to wonder that the people give
them way, and stop after they have passed to
look at them again. They are gladiators—
wrestlers, runners, boxers, swordsmen; pro-
fessionals unknown in Judea before the com-
ing of the Roman; fellows who, what time
they are not in training, may be seen strolling
through the king's gardens or sitting with the
guards at the palace gates; or possibly they
are visitors from Cæsarea, Sebaste, or Jericho;
in which Herod, more Greek than Jew, and
with all a Roman's love of games and bloody
spectacles, has built vast theatres, and now
keeps schools of fighting-men, drawn, as is the

custom, from the Gallic provinces or the Slavic tribes on the Danube.

"By Bacchus!" says one of them, drawing his clinched hand to his shoulder, "their skulls are not thicker than egg-shells."

The brutal look which goes with the gesture disgusts us, and we turn happily to something more pleasant.

Opposite us is a fruit-stand. The proprietor has a bald head, a long face, and a nose like the beak of a hawk. He sits upon a carpet spread upon the dust; the wall is at his back; overhead hangs a scant curtain; around him, within hand's reach, and arranged upon little stools, lie osier boxes full of almonds, grapes, figs, and pomegranates. To him now comes one at whom we cannot help looking, though for another reason than that which fixed our eyes upon the gladiators: he is really beautiful—a beautiful Greek. Around his temples, holding the waving hair, is a crown of myrtle, to which still cling the pale flowers and half-ripe berries. His tunic, scarlet in color, is of the softest woollen fabric; below the girdle of buff leather, which is clasped in front by a fantastic device of shining gold, the skirt drops to the knee in folds heavy with embroidery of the same royal metal; a scarf, also woollen, and of mixed white and yellow, crosses his throat and falls trailing at his back; his arms and legs, where exposed, are white as ivory, and of the polish impossible except by perfect treatment with bath, oil, brushes, and pincers.

The dealer, keeping his seat, bends forward,

and throws his hands up until they meet in front of him, palm downward and fingers extended.

"What hast thou, this morning, O son of Paphos?" says the young Greek, looking at the boxes rather than at the Cypriote. "I am hungry. What hast thou for breakfast?"

"Fruits from the Pedius—genuine—such as the singers of Antioch take of mornings to restore the waste of their voices," the dealer answers, in a querulous nasal tone.

"A fig, but not one of thy best, for the singers of Antioch!" says the Greek. "Thou art a worshipper of Aphrodite, and so am I, as the myrtle I wear proves; therefore I tell thee their voices have the chill of a Caspian wind. Seest thou this girdle?—a gift of the mighty Salome—"

"The king's sister!" exclaims the Cypriote, with another salaam.

"And of royal taste and divine judgment. And why not? She is more Greek than the king. But—my breakfast! Here is thy money—red coppers of Cyprus. Give me grapes, and—"

"Wilt thou not take the dates also?"

"No, I am not an Arab."

"Nor figs?"

"That would be to make me a Jew. No, nothing but the grapes. Never waters mixed so sweetly as the blood of the Greek and the blood of the grape."

The singer in the grimed and seething market, with all his airs of the court, is a vision

not easily shut out of mind by such as see him;
as if for the purpose, however, a person follows
him challenging all our wonder. He comes
up the road slowly, his face towards the
ground; at intervals he stops, crosses his
hands upon his breast, lengthens his counte-
nance, and turns his eyes towards heaven, as
if about to break into prayer. Nowhere, ex-
cept in Jerusalem, can such a character be
found. On his forehead, attached to the band
which keeps the mantle in place, projects a
leathern case, square in form; another similar
case is tied by a thong to the left arm; the
borders of his robe are decorated with deep
fringe; and by such signs—the phylacteries,
the enlarged borders of the garment, and the
savor of intense holiness pervading the whole
man—we know him to be a Pharisee, one of
an organization (in religion a sect, in politics
a party) whose bigotry and power will shortly
bring the world to grief.

The densest of the throng outside the gate
covers the road leading off to Joppa. Turn-
ing from the Pharisee, we are attracted by
some parties who, as subjects of study, oppor-
tunely separate themselves from the motley
crowd. First among them a man of very no-
ble appearance — clear, healthful complexion;
bright black eyes; beard long and flowing, and
rich with unguents; apparel well-fitting, cost-
ly, and suitable for the season. He carries a
staff, and wears, suspended by a cord from his
neck, a large golden seal. Several servants at-
tend him, some of them with short swords

stuck through their sashes; when they address
him, it is with the utmost deference. The rest
of the party consists of two Arabs of the pure
desert stock; thin, wiry men, deeplv bronzed,
and with hollow cheeks, and eyes of almost
evil brightness; on their heads red tarbooshes;
over their abas, and wrapping the left shoul-
der and the body so as to leave the right arm
free, brown woollen haicks, or blankets. There
is loud chaffering; for the Arabs are leading
horses and trying to sell them; and in their
eagerness they speak in high, shrill voices.
The courtly person leaves the talking mostly
to his servants; occasionally he answers with
much dignity; directly, seeing the Cypriote, he
stops and buys some figs. And when the whole
party has passed the portal, close after the
Pharisee, if we betake ourselves to the dealer
in fruits, he will tell, with a wonderful salaam,
that the stranger is a Jew, one of the princes of
the city, who has travelled, and learned the dif-
ference between the common grapes of Syria
and those of Cyprus, so surpassingly·rich with
the dews of the sea.

And so, till towards noon, sometimes later,
the steady currents of business habitually flow
in and out of the Joppa Gate, carrying with
them every variety of character; including rep-
resentatives of all the tribes of Israel, all the
sects among whom the ancient faith has been
parcelled and refined away, all the religious
and social divisions, all the adventurous rabble
who, as children of art and ministers of pleas-
ure, riot in the prodigalities of Herod, and all

the peoples of note at any time compassed by the Cæsars and their predecessors, especially those dwelling within the circuit of the Mediterranean.

In other words, Jerusalem, rich in sacred history, richer in connection with sacred prophecies — the Jerusalem of Solomon, in which silver was as stones, and cedars as the sycamores of the vale—had come to be but a copy of Rome, a centre of unholy practices, a seat of pagan power. A Jewish king one day put on priestly garments, and went into the Holy of Holies of the first temple to offer incense, and he came out a leper; but in the time of which we are reading, Pompey entered Herod's temple and the same Holy of Holies, and came out without harm, finding but an empty chamber, and of God not a sign.

CHAPTER VIII
JOSEPH AND MARY GOING TO BETHLEHEM

THE reader is now besought to return to the court described as part of the market at the Joppa Gate. It was the third hour of the day, and many of the people had gone away; yet the press continued without apparent abatement. Of the new-comers, there was a group over by the south wall, consisting of a man, a woman, and a donkey, which requires extended notice.

The man stood by the animal's head, holding a leading-strap, and leaning upon a stick

which seemed to have been chosen for the
double purpose of goad and staff. His dress
was like that of the ordinary Jews around him,
except that it had an appearance of newness.
The mantle dropping from his head, and the
robe or frock which clothed his person from
neck to heel, were probably the garments he
was accustomed to wear to the synagogue on
Sabbath days. His features were exposed,
and they told of fifty years of life, a surmise
confirmed by the gray that streaked his other-
wise black beard. He looked around him with
the half-curious, half-vacant stare of a stranger
and provincial.

The donkey ate leisurely from an armful of
green grass, of which there was an abundance
in the market. In its sleepy content, the brute
did not admit of disturbance from the bustle
and clamor about; no more was it mindful of
the woman sitting upon its back in a cush-
ioned pillion. An outer robe of dull woollen
stuff completely covered her person, while a
white wimple veiled her head and neck.
Once in a while, impelled by curiosity to see
or hear something passing, she drew the wim-
ple aside, but so slightly that the face remained
invisible.

At length the man was accosted.

"Are you not Joseph of Nazareth?"

The speaker was standing close by.

"I am so called," answered Joseph, turning
gravely around. "And you — ah, peace be
unto you! my friend, Rabbi Samuel!"

"The same give I back to you." The Rabbi

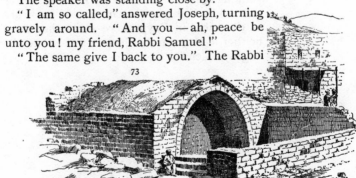

paused, looking at the woman, then added, "To you, and unto your house and all your helpers, be peace."

With the last word, he placed one hand upon his breast, and inclined his head to the woman, who, to see him, had by this time withdrawn the wimple enough to show the face of one but a short time out of girlhood. Thereupon the acquaintances grasped right hands, as if to carry them to their lips; at the last moment, however, the clasp was let go, and each kissed his own hand, then put its palm upon his forehead.

"There is so little dust upon your garments," the Rabbi said, familiarly, "that I infer you passed the night in this city of our fathers."

"No," Joseph replied; "as we could only make Bethany before the night came, we stayed in the khan there, and took the road again at daybreak."

"The journey before you is long, then—not to Joppa, I hope."

"Only to Bethlehem."

The countenance of the Rabbi, theretofore open and friendly, became lowering and sinister, and he cleared his throat with a growl instead of a cough.

"Yes, yes—I see," he said. "You were born in Bethlehem, and wend thither now, with your daughter, to be counted for taxation, as ordered by Cæsar. The children of Jacob are as the tribes in Egypt were—only they have neither a Moses nor a Joshua. How are the mighty fallen!"

74

Joseph answered, without change of posture or countenance,

"The woman is not my daughter."

But the Rabbi clung to the political idea; and he went on, without noticing the explanation, "What are the Zealots doing down in Galilee?"

"I am a carpenter, and Nazareth is a village," said Joseph, cautiously. "The street on which my bench stands is not a road leading to any city. Hewing wood and sawing plank leave me no time to take part in the disputes of parties."

"But you are a Jew," said the Rabbi, earnestly. "You are a Jew, and of the line of David. It is not possible you can find pleasure in the payment of any tax except the shekel given by ancient custom to Jehovah."

Joseph held his peace.

"I do not complain," his friend continued, "of the amount of the tax—a denarius is a trifle. Oh no! The imposition of the tax is the offence. And, besides, what is paying it but submission to tyranny? Tell me, is it true that Judas claims to be the Messiah? You live in the midst of his followers."

"I have heard his followers say he was the Messiah," Joseph replied.

At this point the wimple was drawn aside, and for an instant the whole face of the woman was exposed. The eyes of the Rabbi wandered that way, and he had time to see a countenance of rare beauty, kindled by a look of intense interest; then a blush overspread

her cheeks and brow, and the veil was returned to its place.

The politician forgot his subject.

"Your daughter is comely," he said, speaking lower.

"She is not my daughter," Joseph repeated.

The curiosity of the Rabbi was aroused; seeing which, the Nazarene hastened to say further, "She is the child of Joachim and Anna of Bethlehem, of whom you have at least heard; for they were of great repute—"

"Yes," remarked the Rabbi, deferentially, "I know them. They were lineally descended from David. I knew them well."

"Well, they are dead now," the Nazarene proceeded. "They died in Nazareth. Joachim was not rich, yet he left a house and garden to be divided between his daughters Marian and Mary. This is one of them; and to save her portion of the property, the law required her to marry her next of kin. She is now my wife."

"And you were—"

"Her uncle."

"Yes, yes! And as you were both born in Bethlehem, the Roman compels you to take her there with you to be also counted."

The Rabbi clasped his hands, and looked indignantly to heaven, exclaiming, "The God of Israel still lives! The vengeance is his!"

With that he turned and abruptly departed. A stranger near by, observing Joseph's amazement, said, quietly, "Rabbi Samuel is a zealot. Judas himself is not more fierce."

Joseph, not wishing to talk with the man, appeared not to hear, and busied himself gathering in a little heap the grass which the donkey had tossed abroad; after which he leaned upon his staff again, and waited.

In another hour the party passed out the gate, and, turning to the left, took the road to Bethlehem. The descent into the valley of Hinnom was quite broken, garnished here and there with straggling wild olive-trees. Carefully, tenderly, the Nazarene walked by the woman's side, leading-strap in hand. On their left, reaching to the south and east round Mount Zion, rose the city wall, and on their right the steep prominences which form the western boundary of the valley.

Slowly they passed the Lower Pool of Gihon, out of which the sun was fast driving the lessening shadow of the royal hill; slowly they proceeded, keeping parallel with the aqueduct from the Pools of Solomon, until near the site of the country-house on what is now called the Hill of Evil Counsel; there they began to ascend to the plain of Rephaim. The sun streamed garishly over the stony face of the famous locality, and under its influence Mary, the daughter of Joachim, dropped the wimple entirely, and bared her head. Joseph told the story of the Philistines surprised in their camp there by David. He was tedious in the narrative, speaking with the solemn countenance and lifeless manner of a dull man. She did not always hear him.

Wherever on the land men go, and on the

sea ships, the face and figure of the Jew are
familiar. The physical type of the race has al-
ways been the same; yet there have been some
individual variations. "Now he was ruddy,
and withal of a beautiful countenance, and
goodly to look to." Such was the son of Jesse
when brought before Samuel. The fancies of
men have been ever since ruled by the de-
scription. Poetic license has extended the
peculiarities of the ancestor to his notable de-
scendants. So all our ideal Solomons have
fair faces, and hair and beard chestnut in
the shade, and of the tint of gold in the sun.
Such, we are also made believe, were the locks
of Absalom the beloved. And, in the absence
of authentic history, tradition has dealt no less
lovingly by her whom we are now following
down to the native city of the ruddy king.

She was not more than fifteen. Her form,
voice, and manner belonged to the period of
transition from girlhood. Her face was per-
fectly oval, her complexion more pale than
fair. The nose was faultless; the lips, slightly
parted, were full and ripe, giving to the lines
of the mouth warmth, tenderness, and trust;
the eyes were blue and large, and shaded by
drooping lids and long lashes; and, in har-
mony with all, a flood of golden hair, in the
style permitted to Jewish brides, fell uncon-
fined down her back to the pillion on which
she sat. The throat and neck had the downy
softness sometimes seen which leaves the ar-
tist in doubt whether it is an effect of contour
or color. To these charms of feature and per-

son were added others more indefinable—an
air of purity which only the soul can impart,
and of abstraction natural to such as think
much of things impalpable. Often, with trem-
bling lips, she raised her eyes to heaven, itself
not more deeply blue; often she crossed her
hands upon her breast, as in adoration and
prayer; often she raised her head like one
listening eagerly for a calling voice. Now and
then, midst his slow utterances, Joseph turned
to look at her, and, catching the expression
kindling her face as with light, forgot his theme,
and with bowed head, wondering, plodded on.

So they skirted the great plain, and at length
reached the elevation Mar Elias; from which,
across a valley, they beheld Bethlehem, the old,
old House of Bread, its white walls crowning a
ridge, and shining above the brown scumbling
of leafless orchards. They paused there, and
rested, while Joseph pointed out the places of
sacred renown; then they went down into the
valley to the well which was the scene of one
of the marvellous exploits of David's strong
men. The narrow space was crowded with
people and animals. A fear came upon Joseph
—a fear lest, if the town were so thronged,
there might not be house-room for the gentle
Mary. Without delay, he hurried on, past the
pillar of stone marking the tomb of Rachel,
up the gardened slope, saluting none of the
many persons he met on the way, until he
stopped before the portal of the khan that
then stood outside the village gates, near a
junction of roads.

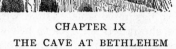

CHAPTER IX
THE CAVE AT BETHLEHEM

TO understand thoroughly what happened to the Nazarene at the khan, the reader must be reminded that Eastern inns were different from the inns of the Western world. They were called khans, from the Persian, and, in simplest form, were fenced enclosures, without house or shed, often without a gate or entrance. Their sites were chosen with reference to shade, defence, or water. Such were the inns that sheltered Jacob when he went to seek a wife in Padan-Aram. Their like may be seen at this day in the stopping-places of the desert. On the other hand, some of them, especially those on the roads between great cities, like Jerusalem and Alexandria, were princely establishments, monuments to the piety of the kings who built them. In ordinary, however, they were no more than the house or possession of a sheik, in which, as in headquarters, he swayed his tribe. Lodging the traveller was the least of their uses; they were markets, factories, forts; places of assemblage and residence for merchants and artisans quite as much as places of shelter for belated and wandering wayfarers. Within their walls, all the year round, occurred the multiplied daily transactions of a town.

The singular management of these hostelries

was the feature likely to strike a Western mind with most force. There was no host or hostess; no clerk, cook, or kitchen; a steward at the gate was all the assertion of government or proprietorship anywhere visible. Strangers arriving stayed at will without rendering account. A consequence of the system was that whoever came had to bring his food and culinary outfit with him, or buy them of dealers in the khan. The same rule held good as to his bed and bedding, and forage for his beasts. Water, rest, shelter, and protection were all he looked for from the proprietor, and they were gratuities. The peace of synagogues was sometimes broken by brawling disputants, but that of the khans never. The houses and all their appurtenances were sacred: a well was not more so.

The khan at Bethlehem, before which Joseph and his wife stopped, was a good specimen of its class, being neither very primitive nor very princely. The building was purely Oriental; that is to say, a quadrangular block of rough stones, one story high, flat-roofed, externally unbroken by a window, and with but one principal entrance—a doorway, which was also a gateway, on the eastern side, or front. The road ran by the door so near that the chalk dust half covered the lintel. A fence of flat rocks, beginning at the north-eastern corner of the pile, extended many yards down the slope to a point from whence it swept westwardly to a limestone bluff; making what was in the highest degree essential to a respectable khan —a safe enclosure for animals.

In a village like Bethlehem, as there was but
one sheik, there could not well be more than
one khan; and, though born in the place, the
Nazarene, from long residence elsewhere, had
no claim to hospitality in the town. More-
over, the enumeration for which he was com-
ing might be the work of weeks or months;
Roman deputies in the provinces were pro-
verbially slow; and to impose himself and
wife for a period so uncertain upon acquaint-
ances or relations was out of the question. So,
before he drew nigh the great house, while he
was yet climbing the slope, in the steep places
toiling to hasten the donkey, the fear that he
might not find accommodations in the khan
became a painful anxiety; for he found the
road thronged with men and boys who, with
great ado, were taking their cattle, horses, and
camels to and from the valley, some to water,
some to the neighboring caves. And when he
was come close by, his alarm was not allayed
by the discovery of a crowd investing the
door of the establishment, while the enclos-
ure adjoining, broad as it was, seemed already
full.

"We cannot reach the door," Joseph said,
in his slow way. "Let us stop here, and learn,
if we can, what has happened."

The wife, without answering, quietly drew
the wimple aside. The look of fatigue at first
upon her face changed to one of interest. She
found herself at the edge of an assemblage
that could not be other than a matter of curi-
osity to her, although it was common enough

WITHIN THE JAFFA GATE, JERUSALEM

at the khans on any of the highways which
the great caravans were accustomed to trav-
erse. There were men on foot, running hith-
er and thither, talking shrilly and in all the
tongues of Syria; men on horseback scream-
ing to men on camels; men struggling doubt-
fully with fractious cows and frightened sheep;
men peddling bread and wine; and among the
mass a herd of boys apparently in chase of
a herd of dogs. Everybody and everything
seemed to be in motion at the same time.
Possibly the fair spectator was too weary to
be long attracted by the scene; in a little
while she sighed, and settled down on the
pillion, and, as if in search of peace and rest,
or in expectation of some one, looked off to
the south, and up to the tall cliffs of the Mount
of Paradise, then faintly reddening under the
setting sun.

While she was thus looking, a man pushed
his way out of the press, and, stopping close by
the donkey, faced about with an angry brow.
The Nazarene spoke to him.

"As I am what I take you to be, good friend
—a son of Judah—may I ask the cause of this
multitude?"

The stranger turned fiercely; but, seeing the
solemn countenance of Joseph, so in keeping
with his deep, slow voice and speech, he raised
his hand in half-salutation, and replied,

"Peace be to you, Rabbi! I am a son of
Judah, and will answer you. I dwell in Beth-
Dagon, which, you know, is in what used to be
the land of the tribe of Dan."

83

"On the road to Joppa from Modin," said Joseph.

"Ah, you have been in Beth-Dagon," the man said, his face softening yet more. "What wanderers we of Judah are! I have been away from the ridge—old Ephrath, as our father Jacob called it—for many years. When the proclamation went abroad requiring all Hebrews to be numbered at the cities of their birth— That is my business here, Rabbi."

Joseph's face remained stolid as a mask, while he remarked, "I have come for that also —I and my wife."

The stranger glanced at Mary and kept silence. She was looking up at the bald top of Gedor. The sun touched her upturned face, and filled the violet depths of her eyes; and upon her parted lips trembled an aspiration which could not have been to a mortal. For the moment, all the humanity of her beauty seemed refined away: she was as we fancy they are who sit close by the gate in the transfiguring light of Heaven. The Beth-Dagonite saw the original of what, centuries after, came as a vision of genius to Sanzio the divine, and left him immortal.

"Of what was I speaking? Ah! I remember. I was about to say that when I heard of the order to come here, I was angry. Then I thought of the old hill, and the town, and the valley falling away into the depths of Cedron; of the vines and orchards, and fields of grain, unfailing since the days of Boaz and Ruth; of the familiar mountains—Gedor here, Gibeah

84

yonder, Mar Elias there—which, when I was a boy, were the walls of the world to me; and I forgave the tyrants and came—I, and Rachel, my wife, and Deborah and Michal, our roses of Sharon."

The man paused again, looking abruptly at Mary, who was now looking at him and listening. Then he said, "Rabbi, will not your wife go to mine? You may see her yonder with the children, under the leaning olive-tree at the bend of the road. I tell you "—he turned to Joseph and spoke positively—"I tell you the khan is full. It is useless to ask at the gate."

Joseph's will was slow, like his mind; he hesitated, but at length replied, "The offer is kind. Whether there be room for us or not in the house, we will go see your people. Let me speak to the gate-keeper myself. I will return quickly."

And, putting the leading-strap in the stranger's hand, he pushed into the stirring crowd.

The keeper sat on a great cedar block outside the gate. Against the wall behind him leaned a javelin. A dog squatted on the block by his side.

"The peace of Jehovah be with you," said Joseph, at last confronting the keeper.

"What you give, may you find again; and, when found, be it many times multiplied to you and yours," returned the watchman, gravely, though without moving.

"I am a Bethlehemite," said Joseph, in his most deliberate way. "Is there not room for—"

"There is not."

"You may have heard of me—Joseph of Nazareth. This is the house of my fathers. I am of the line of David."

These words held the Nazarene's hope. If they failed him, further appeal was idle, even that of the offer of many shekels. To be a son of Judah was one thing—in the tribal opinion a great thing; to be of the house of David was yet another; on the tongue of a Hebrew there could be no higher boast. A thousand years and more had passed since the boyish shepherd became the successor of Saul and founded a royal family. Wars, calamities, other kings, and the countless obscuring processes of time had, as respects fortune, lowered his descendants to the common Jewish level; the bread they ate came to them of toil never more humble; yet they had the benefit of history sacredly kept, of which genealogy was the first chapter and the last; they could not become unknown; while, wherever they went in Israel, acquaintance drew after it a respect amounting to reverence.

If this were so in Jerusalem and elsewhere, certainly one of the sacred line might reasonably rely upon it at the door of the khan of Bethlehem. To say, as Joseph said, "This is the house of my fathers," was to say the truth most simply and literally; for it was the very house Ruth ruled as the wife of Boaz; the very house in which Jesse and his ten sons, David the youngest, were born; the very house in which Samuel came seeking a king, and

found him; the very house which David gave
to the son of Barzillai, the friendly Gileadite;
the very house in which Jeremiah, by prayer,
rescued the remnant of his race flying before
the Babylonians.

The appeal was not without effect. The
keeper of the gate slid down from the cedar
block, and, laying his hand upon his beard,
said, respectfully, " Rabbi, I cannot tell you
when this door first opened in welcome to the
traveller, but it was more than a thousand
years ago; and in all that time there is no
known instance of a good man turned away,
save when there was no room to rest him in.
If it has been so with the stranger, just cause
must the steward have who says no to one of
the line of David. Wherefore, I salute you
again; and, if you care to go with me, I will
show you that there is not a lodging-place left
in the house; neither in the chambers, nor in
the lewens, nor in the court—not even on the
roof. May I ask when you came ?"

" But now."

The keeper smiled.

" ' The stranger that dwelleth with you shall
be as one born among you, and thou shalt
love him as thyself.' Is not that the law,
Rabbi ?"

Joseph was silent.

" If it be the law, can I say to one a long
time come, ' Go thy way; another is here to
take thy place ?' "

Yet Joseph held his peace.

" And, if I said so, to whom would the place

belong? See the many that have been wait-
ing, some of them since noon."

"Who are all these people?" asked Joseph,
turning to the crowd. "And why are they
here at this time?"

"That which doubtless brought you, Rabbi
—the decree of the Cæsar"—the keeper threw
an interrogative glance at the Nazarene, then
continued—"brought most of those who have
lodging in the house. And yesterday the car-
avan passing from Damascus to Arabia and
Lower Egypt arrived. These you see here be-
long to it—men and camels."

Still Joseph persisted.

"The court is large," he said.

"Yes, but it is heaped with cargoes—with
bales of silk, and pockets of spices, and goods
of every kind."

Then for a moment the face of the appli-
cant lost its stolidity; the lustreless, staring
eyes dropped. With some warmth he next
said, "I do not care for myself, but I have with
me my wife, and the night is cold—colder on
these heights than in Nazareth. She cannot
live in the open air. Is there not room in the
town?"

"These people"—the keeper waved his hand
to the throng before the door—"have all be-
sought the town, and they report its accom-
modations all engaged."

Again Joseph studied the ground, saying,
half to himself, "She is so young! if I make
her bed on the hill, the frosts will kill her."

Then he spoke to the keeper again.

"It may be you knew her parents, Joachim and Anna, once of Bethlèhem, and, like myself, of the line of David."

"Yes, I knew them. They were good people. That was in my youth."

This time the keeper's eyes sought the ground in thought. Suddenly he raised his head.

"If I cannot make room for you," he said, "I cannot turn you away. Rabbi, I will do the best I can for you. How many are of your party?"

Joseph reflected, then replied, "My wife and a friend with his family, from Beth-Dagon, a little town over by Joppa; in all, six of us."

"Very well. You shall not lie out on the ridge. Bring your people, and hasten; for, when the sun goes down behind the mountain, you know the night comes quickly, and it is nearly there now."

"I give you the blessing of the houseless traveller; that of the sojourner will follow."

So saying, the Nazarene went back joyfully to Mary and the Beth-Dagonite. In a little while the latter brought up his family, the women mounted on donkeys. The wife was matronly, the daughters were images of what she must have been in youth; and as they drew nigh the door, the keeper knew them to be of the humble class.

"This is she of whom I spoke," said the Nazarene; "and these are our friends."

Mary's veil was raised.

"Blue eyes and hair of gold," muttered the

steward to himself, seeing but her. "So looked the young king when he went to sing before Saul."

Then he took the leading-strap from Joseph and said to Mary, "Peace to you, O daughter of David!" Then to the others, "Peace to you all!" Then to Joseph, "Rabbi, follow me."

The party were conducted into a wide passage paved with stone, from which they entered the court of the khan. To a stranger the scene would have been curious; but they noticed the lewens that yawned darkly upon them from all sides, and the court itself, only to remark how crowded they were. By a lane reserved in the stowage of the cargoes, and thence by a passage similar to the one at the entrance, they emerged into the enclosure adjoining the house, and came upon camels, horses, and donkeys, tethered and dozing in close groups; among them were the keepers, men of many lands; and they, too, slept or kept silent watch. They went down the slope of the crowded yard slowly, for the dull carriers of the women had wills of their own. At length they turned into a path running towards the gray limestone bluff overlooking the khan on the west.

"We are going to the cave," said Joseph, laconically.

The guide lingered till Mary came to his side.

"The cave to which we are going," he said to her, "must have been a resort of your ancestor David. From the field below us, and

from the well down in the valley, he used to
drive his flocks to it for safety; and afterwards,
when he was king, he came back to the old
house here for rest and health, bringing great
trains of animals. The mangers yet remain as
they were in his day. Better a bed upon the
floor where he has slept than one in the court-
yard or out by the road-side. Ah, here is the
house before the cave!"

This speech must not be taken as an apol-
ogy for the lodging offered. There was no
need of apology. The place was the best then
at disposal. The guests were simple folks, by
habits of life easily satisfied. To the Jew of
that period, moreover, abode in caverns was a
familiar idea, made so by every-day occur-
rences, and by what he heard of Sabbaths in
the synagogues. How much of Jewish history,
how many of the most exciting incidents in
that history, had transpired in caves! Yet
further, these people were Jews of Bethlehem,
with whom the idea was especially common-
place; for their locality abounded with caves
great and small, some of which had been dwell-
ing-places from the time of the Emim and Ho-
rites. No more was there offence to them in
the fact that the cavern to which they were
being taken had been, or was, a stable. They
were the descendants of a race of herdsmen,
whose flocks habitually shared both their hab-
itations and wanderings. In keeping with a
custom derived from Abraham, the tent of the
Bedawin yet shelters his horses and children
alike. So they obeyed the keeper cheerfully,

and gazed at the house, feeling only a natural curiosity. Everything associated with the history of David was interesting to them.

The building was low and narrow, projecting but a little from the rock to which it was joined at the rear, and wholly without a window. In its blank front there was a door, swung on enormous hinges, and thickly daubed with ochreous clay. While the wooden bolt of the lock was being pushed back, the women were assisted from their pillions. Upon the opening of the door, the keeper called out, "Come in!"

The guests entered, and stared about them. It became apparent immediately that the house was but a mask or covering for the mouth of a natural cave or grotto, probably forty feet long, nine or ten high, and twelve or fifteen in width. The light streamed through the doorway, over an uneven floor, falling upon piles of grain and fodder, and earthen-ware and household property, occupying the centre of the chamber. Along the sides were mangers, low enough for sheep, and built of stones laid in cement. There were no stalls or partitions of any kind. Dust and chaff yellowed the floor, filled all the crevices and hollows, and thickened the spider-webs, which dropped from the ceiling like bits of dirty linen; otherwise the place was cleanly, and, to appearance, as comfortable as any of the arched lewens of the khan proper. In fact, a cave was the model and first suggestion of the lewen.

"Come in!" said the guide. "These piles

upon the floor are for travellers like your-
selves. Take what of them you need."

Then he spoke to Mary.

"Can you rest here?"

"The place is sanctified," she answered.

"I leave you then. Peace be with you all!"

When he was gone, they busied themselves
making the cave habitable.

CHAPTER X

THE LIGHT IN THE SKY

T a certain hour in the evening the
shouting and stir of the people in
and about the khan ceased; at the
same time, every Israelite, if not al-
ready upon his feet, arose, solemnized his face,
looked towards Jerusalem, crossed his hands
upon his breast, and prayed; for it was the sa-
cred ninth hour, when sacrifices were offered in
the temple on Moriah, and God was supposed
to be there. When the hands of the worship-
pers fell down, the commotion broke forth
again; everybody hastened to bread, or to
make his pallet. A little later, the lights were
put out, and there was silence, and then sleep.

.

About midnight some one on the roof cried
out, "What light is that in the sky? Awake,
brethren, awake and see!"

The people, half asleep, sat up and looked;
then they became wide awake, though wonder-
struck. And the stir spread to the court be-

93

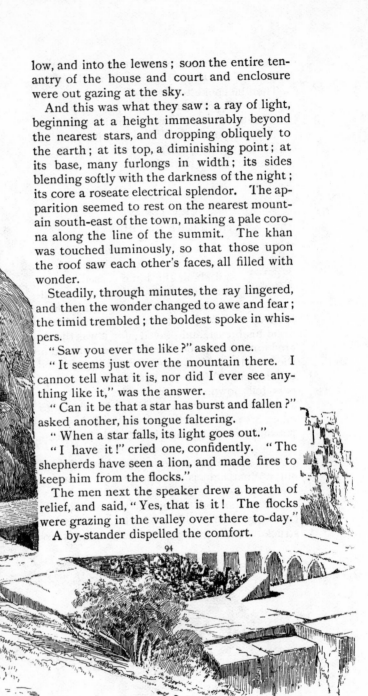

low, and into the lewens; soon the entire tenantry of the house and court and enclosure were out gazing at the sky.

And this was what they saw: a ray of light, beginning at a height immeasurably beyond the nearest stars, and dropping obliquely to the earth; at its top, a diminishing point; at its base, many furlongs in width; its sides blending softly with the darkness of the night; its core a roseate electrical splendor. The apparition seemed to rest on the nearest mountain south-east of the town, making a pale corona along the line of the summit. The khan was touched luminously, so that those upon the roof saw each other's faces, all filled with wonder.

Steadily, through minutes, the ray lingered, and then the wonder changed to awe and fear; the timid trembled; the boldest spoke in whispers.

"Saw you ever the like?" asked one.

"It seems just over the mountain there. I cannot tell what it is, nor did I ever see anything like it," was the answer.

"Can it be that a star has burst and fallen?" asked another, his tongue faltering.

"When a star falls, its light goes out."

"I have it!" cried one, confidently. "The shepherds have seen a lion, and made fires to keep him from the flocks."

The men next the speaker drew a breath of relief, and said, "Yes, that is it! The flocks were grazing in the valley over there to-day."

A by-stander dispelled the comfort.

"No, no! Though all the wood in all the valleys of Judah was brought together in one pile and fired, the blaze would not throw a light so strong and high."

After that there was silence on the housetop, broken but once again while the mystery continued.

"Brethren!" exclaimed a Jew of venerable mien, "what we see is the ladder our father Jacob saw in his dream. Blessed be the Lord God of our fathers!"

CHAPTER XI
CHRIST IS BORN

A MILE and a half, it may be two miles, south-east of Bethlehem, there is a plain separated from the town by an intervening swell of the mountain. Besides being well sheltered from the north winds, the vale was covered with a growth of sycamore, dwarf-oak, and pine-trees, while in the glens and ravines adjoining there were thickets of olive and mulberry; all at this season of the year invaluable for the support of sheep, goats, and cattle, of which the wandering flocks consisted.

At the side farthest from the town, close under a bluff, there was an extensive mârâh, or sheepcot, ages old. In some long-forgotten foray, the building had been unroofed and almost demolished. The enclosure attached to it remained intact, however, and that was of

95

more importance to the shepherds who drove
their charges thither than the house itself.
The stone wall around the lot was high as a
man's head, yet not so high but that some-
times a panther or a lion, hungering from the
wilderness, leaped boldly in. On the inner
side of the wall, and as an additional security
against the constant danger, a hedge of the
rhamnus had been planted, an invention so
successful that now a sparrow could hardly
penetrate the overtopping branches, armed as
they were with great clusters of thorns hard
as spikes.

The day of the occurrences which occupy
the preceding chapters, a number of shepherds,
seeking fresh walks for their flocks, led them
up to this plain; and from early morning the
groves had been made ring with calls, and the
blows of axes, the bleating of sheep and goats,
the tinkling of bells, the lowing of cattle, and
the barking of dogs. When the sun went
down, they led the way to the mârâh, and by
nightfall had everything safe in the field; then
they kindled a fire down by the gate, partook
of their humble supper, and sat down to rest
and talk, leaving one on watch.

There were six of these men, omitting the
watchman; and afterwhile they assembled in
a group near the fire, some sitting, some lying
prone. As they went bareheaded habitually,
their hair stood out in thick, coarse, sunburnt
shocks; their beard covered their throats, and
fell in mats down the breast; mantles of the
skin of kids and lambs, with the fleece on,

wrapped them from neck to knee, leaving the
arms exposed; broad belts girthed the rude
garments to their waists; their sandals were
of the coarsest quality; from their right shoul-
ders hung scrips containing food and selected
stones for slings, with which they were armed;
on the ground near each one lay his crook, a
symbol of his calling and a weapon of offence.

Such were the shepherds of Judea! In ap-
pearance, rough and savage as the gaunt dogs
sitting with them around the blaze; in fact,
simple-minded, tender-hearted: effects due, in
part, to the primitive life they led, but chiefly
to their constant care of things lovable and
helpless.

They rested and talked; and their talk was
all about their flocks, a dull theme to the
world, yet a theme which was all the world to
them. If in narrative they dwelt long upon af-
fairs of trifling moment; if one of them omit-
ted nothing of detail in recounting the loss of
a lamb, the relation between him and the un-
fortunate should be remembered: at birth it
became his charge, his to keep all its days, to
help over the floods, to carry down the hol-
lows, to name and train; it was to be his com-
panion, his object of thought and interest, the
subject of his will; it was to enliven and share
his wanderings; in its defence he might be
called on to face the lion or robber—to die.

The great events, such as blotted out na-
tions and changed the mastery of the world,
were trifles to them, if perchance they came
to their knowledge. Of what Herod was do-

97

ing in this city or that, building palaces and gymnasia, and indulging forbidden practices, they occasionally heard. As was her habit in those days, Rome did not wait for people slow to inquire about her; she came to them. Over the hills along which he was leading his lagging herd, or in the fastnesses in which he was hiding them, not unfrequently the shepherd was startled by the blare of trumpets, and, peering out, beheld a cohort, sometimes a legion, in march; and when the glittering crests were gone, and the excitement incident to the intrusion over, he bent himself to evolve the meaning of the eagles and gilded globes of the soldiery, and the charm of a life so the opposite of his own.

Yet these men, rude and simple as they were, had a knowledge and a wisdom of their own. On Sabbaths they were accustomed to purify themselves, and go up into the synagogues, and sit on the benches farthest from the ark. When the chazzan bore the Torah round, none kissed it with greater zest; when the sheliach read the text, none listened to the interpreter with more absolute faith; and none took away with them more of the elder's sermon, or gave it more thought afterwards. In a verse of the Shema they found all the learning and all the law of their simple lives—that their Lord was One God, and that they must love him with all their souls. And they loved him, and such was their wisdom, surpassing that of kings.

While they talked, and before the first watch

was over, one by one the shepherds went to
sleep, each lying where he had sat.

The night, like most nights of the winter
season in the hill country, was clear, crisp, and
sparkling with stars. There was no wind. The
atmosphere seemed never so pure, and the
stillness was more than silence; it was a holy
hush, a warning that heaven was stooping low
to whisper some good thing to the listening
earth.

By the gate, hugging his mantle close, the
watchman walked; at times he stopped, at-
tracted by a stir among the sleeping herds, or
by a jackal's cry off on the mountain-side. The
midnight was slow coming to him; but at last
it came. His task was done; now for the
dreamless sleep with which labor blesses its
wearied children! He moved towards the
fire, but paused; a light was breaking around
him, soft and white, like the moon's. He
waited breathlessly. The light deepened;
things before invisible came to view; he saw
the whole field, and all it sheltered. A chill
sharper than that of the frosty air—a chill of
fear—smote him. He looked up; the stars
were gone; the light was dropping as from
a window in the sky; as he looked, it became
a splendor; then, in terror, he cried,

"Awake, awake!"

Up sprang the dogs, and, howling, ran away.
The herds rushed together bewildered.

The men clambered to their feet, weapons
in hand.

"What is it?" they asked, in one voice.

"See!" cried the watchman, "the sky is on fire!"

Suddenly the light became intolerably bright, and they covered their eyes, and dropped upon their knees; then, as their souls shrank with fear, they fell upon their faces blind and fainting, and would have died had not a voice said to them,

"Fear not!"

And they listened.

"Fear not: for behold, I bring you tidings of great joy, which shall be to all people."

The voice, in sweetness and soothing more than human, and low and clear, penetrated all their being, and filled them with assurance. They rose upon their knees, and, looking worshipfully, beheld in the centre of a great glory the appearance of a man, clad in a robe intensely white; above its shoulders towered the tops of wings, shining and folded; a star over its forehead glowed with steady lustre, brilliant as Hesperus; its hands were stretched towards them in blessing; its face was serene and divinely beautiful.

They had often heard, and, in their simple way, talked, of angels; and they doubted not now, but said, in their hearts, The glory of God is about us, and this is he who of old came to the prophet by the river of Ulai.

Directly the angel continued:

"For unto you is born this day, in the city of David, a Saviour, which is Christ the Lord!"

Again there was a rest, while the words sank into their minds.

"And this shall be a sign unto you," the annunciator said next. "Ye shall find the babe, wrapped in swaddling-clothes, lying in a manger."

The herald spoke not again; his good tidings were told; yet he stayed a while. Suddenly the light, of which he seemed the centre, turned roseate and began to tremble; then up, far as the men could see, there was flashing of white wings, and coming and going of radiant forms, and voices as of a multitude chanting in unison,

"Glory to God in the highest, and on earth peace, good-will towards men!"

Not once the praise, but many times.

Then the herald raised his eyes as seeking approval of one far off; his wings stirred, and spread slowly and majestically, on their upper side white as snow, in the shadow vari-tinted, like mother-of-pearl; when they were expanded many cubits beyond his stature, he arose lightly, and, without effort, floated out of view, taking the light up with him. Long after he was gone, down from the sky fell the refrain in measure mellowed by distance, "Glory to God in the highest, and on earth peace, good-will towards men!"

When the shepherds came fully to their senses, they stared at each other stupidly, until one of them said, "It was Gabriel, the Lord's messenger unto men."

None answered.

"Christ the Lord is born; said he not so?"

Then another recovered his voice, and replied, "That is what he said."

"And did he not also say, in the city of David, which is our Bethlehem yonder? And that we should find him a babe in swaddling-clothes?"

"And lying in a manger."

The first speaker gazed into the fire thoughtfully, but at length said, like one possessed of a sudden resolve, "There is but one place in Bethlehem where there are mangers; but one, and that is in the cave near the old khan. Brethren, let us go see this thing which has come to pass. The priests and doctors have been a long time looking for the Christ. Now he is born, and the Lord has given us a sign by which to know him. Let us go up and worship him."

"But the flocks!"

"The Lord will take care of them. Let us make haste." Then they all arose and left the mârâh.

.

Around the mountain and through the town they passed, and came to the gate of the khan, where there was a man on watch.

"What would you have?" he asked.

"We have seen and heard great things to-night," they replied.

"Well, we, too, have seen great things, but heard nothing. What did you hear?"

"Let us go down to the cave in the enclosure, that we may be sure; then we will tell you all. Come with us, and see for yourself."

"It is a fool's errand."

"No, the Christ is born."

"The Christ! How do you know?"

"Let us go and see first."

The man laughed scornfully.

"The Christ indeed! How are you to know him?"

"He was born this night, and is now lying in a manger, so we were told; and there is but one place in Bethlehem with mangers."

"The cave?"

"Yes. Come with us."

They went through the court-yard without notice, although there were some up even then talking about the wonderful light. The door of the cavern was open. A lantern was burning within, and they entered unceremoniously.

"I give you peace," the watchman said to Joseph and the Beth-Dagonite. "Here are people looking for a child born this night, whom they are to know by finding him in swaddling-clothes and lying in a manger."

For a moment the face of the stolid Nazarene was moved; turning away, he said, "The child is here."

They were led to one of the mangers, and there the child was. The lantern was brought, and the shepherds stood by mute. The little one made no sign; it was as others just born.

"Where is the mother?" asked the watchman.

One of the women took the baby, and went to Mary, lying near, and put it in her arms. Then the by-standers collected about the two.

"It is the Christ!" said a shepherd, at last.

"The Christ!" they all repeated, falling upon

their knees in worship. One of them repeated several times over,

"It is the Lord, and his glory is above the earth and heaven."

And the simple men, never doubting, kissed the hem of the mother's robe, and with joyful faces departed. In the khan, to all the people aroused and pressing about them, they told their story; and through the town, and all the way back to the mârâh, they chanted the refrain of the angels, "Glory to God in the highest, and on earth peace, good - will towards men !"

The story went abroad, confirmed by the light so generally seen; and the next day, and for days thereafter, the cave was visited by curious crowds, of whom some believed, though the greater part laughed and mocked.

CHAPTER XII
THE WISE MEN ARRIVE AT JERUSALEM

THE eleventh day after the birth of the child in the cave, about mid-afternoon, the three wise men approached Jerusalem by the road from Shechem. After crossing Brook Cedron, they met many people, of whom none failed to stop and look after them curiously.

Judea was of necessity an international thoroughfare; a narrow ridge, raised, apparently, by the pressure of the desert on the east, and the sea on the west, was all she could claim

to be; over the ridge, however, nature had stretched the line of trade between the east and the south; and that was her wealth. In other words, the riches of Jerusalem were the tolls she levied on passing commerce. Nowhere else, consequently, unless in Rome, was there such constant assemblage of so many people of so many different nations; in no other city was a stranger less strange to the residents than within her walls and purlieus. And yet these three men excited the wonder of all whom they met on the way to the gates.

A child belonging to some women sitting by the road-side opposite the Tombs of the Kings saw the party coming; immediately it clapped its hands, and cried, "Look, look! What pretty bells! What big camels!"

The bells were silver; the camels, as we have seen, were of unusual size and whiteness, and moved with singular stateliness; the trappings told of the desert and of long journeys thereon, and also of ample means in possession of the owners, who sat under the little canopies exactly as they appeared at the rendezvous beyond the Jebel. Yet it was not the bells or the camels, or their furniture, or the demeanor of the riders, that were so wonderful; it was the question put by the man who rode foremost of the three.

The approach to Jerusalem from the north is across a plain which dips southward, leaving the Damascus Gate in a vale or hollow. The road is narrow, but deeply cut by long use, and in places difficult on account of the cobbles

left loose and dry by the washing of the rains. On either side, however, there stretched, in the old time, rich fields and handsome olive-groves, which must, in luxurious growth, have been beautiful, especially to travellers fresh from the wastes of the desert. In this road the three stopped before the party in front of the Tombs.

"Good people," said Balthasar, stroking his plaited beard, and bending from his cot, "is not Jerusalem close by?"

"Yes," answered the woman into whose arms the child had shrunk. "If the trees on yon swell were a little lower you could see the towers on the market-place."

Balthasar gave the Greek and the Hindoo a look, then asked,

"Where is he that is born King of the Jews?"

The women gazed at each other without reply.

"You have not heard of him?"

"No."

"Well, tell everybody that we have seen his star in the east, and are come to worship him."

Thereupon the friends rode on. Of others they asked the same question, with like result. A large company whom they met going to the Grotto of Jeremiah were so astonished by the inquiry and the appearance of the travellers that they turned about and followed them into the city.

So much were the three occupied with the idea of their mission that they did not care for

the view which presently rose before them in
the utmost magnificence: for the village first
to receive them on Bezetha; for Mizpah and
Olivet, over on their left; for the wall behind
the village, with its forty tall and solid towers,
superadded partly for strength, partly to grat-
ify the critical taste of the kingly builder; for
the same towered wall bending off to the right,
with many an angle, and here and there an em-
battled gate, up to the three great white piles
Phasælus, Mariamne, and Hippicus; for Zion,
tallest of the hills, crowned with marble pal-
aces, and never so beautiful; for the glittering
terraces of the temple on Moriah, admittedly
one of the wonders of the earth; for the regal
mountains rimming the sacred city round
about until it seemed in the hollow of a
mighty bowl.

They came, at length, to a tower of great
height and strength, overlooking the gate
which, at that time, answered to the present
Damascus Gate, and marked the meeting-place
of the three roads from Shechem, Jericho, and
Gibeon. A Roman guard kept the passage-
way. By this time the people following the
camels formed a train sufficient to draw the
idlers hanging about the portal; so that when
Balthasar stopped to speak to the sentinel, the
three became instantly the centre of a close
circle eager to hear all that passed.

"I give you peace," the Egyptian said, in a
clear voice.

The sentinel made no reply.

"We have come great distances in search of

one who is born King of the Jews. Can you tell us where he is?"

The soldier raised the visor of his helmet, and called loudly. From an apartment at the right of the passage an officer appeared.

"Give way," he cried, to the crowd which now pressed closer in; and as they seemed slow to obey, he advanced twirling his javelin vigorously, now right, now left; and so he gained room.

"What would you?" he asked of Balthasar, speaking in the idiom of the city.

And Balthasar answered in the same,

"Where is he that is born King of the Jews?"

"Herod?" asked the officer, confounded.

"Herod's kingship is from Cæsar; not Herod."

"There is no other King of the Jews."

"But we have seen the star of him we seek, and come to worship him."

The Roman was perplexed.

"Go farther," he said, at last. "Go farther. I am not a Jew. Carry the question to the doctors in the Temple, or to Hannas the priest, or, better still, to Herod himself. If there be another King of the Jews, he will find him."

Thereupon he made way for the strangers, and they passed the gate. But, before entering the narrow street, Balthasar lingered to say to his friends, "We are sufficiently proclaimed. By midnight the whole city will have heard of us and of our mission. Let us to the khan now."

CHAPTER XIII
THE WITNESSES BEFORE HEROD

THAT evening, before sunset, some women were washing clothes on the upper step of the flight that led down into the basin of the Pool of Siloam. They knelt each before a broad bowl of earthen-ware. A girl at the foot of the steps kept them supplied with water, and sang while she filled the jar. The song was cheerful, and no doubt lightened their labor. Occasionally they would sit upon their heels, and look up the slope of Ophel, and round to the summit of what is now the Mount of Offence, then faintly glorified by the dying sun.

While they plied their hands, rubbing and wringing the clothes in the bowls, two other women came to them, each with an empty jar upon her shoulder.

"Peace to you," one of the new-comers said.

The laborers paused, sat up, wrung the water from their hands, and returned the salutation.

"It is nearly night—time to quit."

"There is no end to work," was the reply.

"But there is a time to rest, and—"

"To hear what may be passing," interposed another.

"What news have you?"

"Then you have not heard?"

"No."

"They say the Christ is born," said the news-monger, plunging into her story.

It was curious to see the faces of the laborers brighten with interest; on the other side down came the jars, which, in a moment, were turned into seats for their owners.

"The Christ!" the listeners cried.

"So they say."

"Who?"

"Everybody; it is common talk."

"Does anybody believe it?"

"This afternoon three men came across Brook Cedron on the road from Shechem," the speaker replied, circumstantially, intending to smother doubt. "Each one of them rode a camel spotless white, and larger than any ever before seen in Jerusalem."

The eyes and mouths of the auditors opened wide.

"To prove how great and rich the men were," the narrator continued, "they sat under awnings of silk; the buckles of their saddles were of gold, as was the fringe of their bridles; the bells were of silver, and made real music. Nobody knew them; they looked as if they had come from the ends of the world. Only one of them spoke, and of everybody on the road, even the women and children, he asked this question—'Where is he that is born King of the Jews?' No one gave them answer—no one understood what they meant; so they passed on, leaving behind them this saying: 'For we have seen his star in the east, and are come to worship him.' They put the question

to the Roman at the gate; and he, no wiser than the simple people on the road, sent them up to Herod."

"Where are they now?"

"At the khan. Hundreds have been to look at them already, and hundreds more are going."

"Who are they?"

"Nobody knows. They are said to be Persians — wise men who talk with the stars — prophets, it may be, like Elijah and Jeremiah."

"What do they mean by King of the Jews?"

"The Christ, and that he is just born."

One of the women laughed, and resumed her work, saying, "Well, when I see him I will believe."

Another followed her example: "And I — well, when I see him raise the dead, I will believe."

A third said quietly, "He has been a long time promised. It will be enough for me to see him heal one leper."

And the party sat talking until the night came, and, with the help of the frosty air, drove them home.

Later in the evening, about the beginning of the first watch, there was an assemblage in the palace on Mount Zion, of probably fifty persons, who never came together except by order of Herod, and then only when he had demanded to know some one or more of the deeper mysteries of the Jewish law and history. It was, in short, a meeting of the teach-

ers of the colleges, of the chief priests, and of
the doctors most noted in the city for learning
—the leaders of opinion, expounders of the
different creeds; princes of the Sadducees;
Pharisaic debaters; calm, soft-spoken, stoical
philosophers of the Essene socialists.

The chamber in which the session was held
belonged to one of the interior court-yards of
the palace, and was quite large and Roman-
esque. The floor was tessellated with marble
blocks; the walls, unbroken by a window, were
frescoed in panels of saffron-yellow; a divan
occupied the centre of the apartment, covered
with cushions of bright-yellow cloth, and fash-
ioned in form of the letter U, the opening tow-
ards the door-way; in the arch of the divan,
or, as it were, in the bend of the letter, there
was an immense bronze tripod, curiously in-
laid with gold and silver, over which a chan-
delier dropped from the ceiling, having seven
arms, each holding a lighted lamp. The divan
and the lamp were purely Jewish.

The company sat upon the divan after the
style of Orientals, in costume singularly uni-
form, except as to color. They were mostly
men advanced in years; immense beards cov-
ered their faces; to their large noses were
added the effects of large black eyes, deeply
shaded by bold brows; their demeanor was
grave, dignified, even patriarchal. In brief,
their session was that of the Sanhedrim.

He who sat before the tripod, however, in
the place which may be called the head of the
divan, having all the rest of his associates on

his right and left, and, at the same time, before him, evidently president of the meeting, would have instantly absorbed the attention of a spectator. He had been cast in large mould, but was now shrunken and stooped to ghastliness; his white robe dropped from his shoulders in folds that gave no hint of muscle or anything but an angular skeleton. His hands, half-concealed by sleeves of silk, white and crimson striped, were clasped upon his knees. When he spoke, sometimes the first finger of the right hand extended tremulously; he seemed incapable of other gesture. But his head was a splendid dome. A few hairs, whiter than fine-drawn silver, fringed the base; over a broad, full-sphered skull the skin was drawn close, and shone in the light with positive brilliance; the temples were deep hollows, from which the forehead beetled like a wrinkled crag; the eyes were wan and dim; the nose was pinched; and all the lower face was muffled in a beard flowing and venerable as Aaron's. Such was Hillel the Babylonian! The line of prophets, long extinct in Israel, was now succeeded by a line of scholars, of whom he was first in learning—a prophet in all but the divine inspiration! At the age of one hundred and six, he was still Rector of the Great College.

On the table before him lay out-spread a roll or volume of parchment inscribed with Hebrew characters; behind him, in waiting, stood a page richly habited.

There had been discussion, but at this mo-

ment of introduction the company had reached a conclusion; each one was in an attitude of rest, and the venerable Hillel, without moving, called the page.

"Hist!"

The youth advanced respectfully.

"Go tell the king we are ready to give him answer."

The boy hurried away.

After a time two officers entered and stopped, one on each side the door; after them slowly followed a most striking personage—an old man clad in a purple robe bordered with scarlet, and girt to his waist by a band of gold linked so fine that it was pliable as leather; the latchets of his shoes sparkled with precious stones; a narrow crown wrought in filigree shone outside a tarbooshe of softest crimson plush, which, encasing his head, fell down the neck and shoulders, leaving the throat and neck exposed. Instead of a seal, a dagger dangled from his belt. He walked with a halting step, leaning heavily upon a staff. Not until he reached the opening of the divan did he pause or look up from the floor; then, as for the first time conscious of the company, and roused by their presence, he raised himself, and looked haughtily round, like one startled and searching for an enemy—so dark, suspicious, and threatening was the glance. Such was Herod the Great—a body broken by diseases, a conscience seared with crimes, a mind magnificently capable, a soul fit for brotherhood with the Cæsars; now seven-and-sixty

years old, but guarding his throne with a jealousy never so vigilant, a power never so despotic, and a cruelty never so inexorable.

There was a general movement on the part of the assemblage—a bending forward in salaam by the more aged, a rising-up by the more courtierly, followed by low genuflections, hands upon the beard or breast.

His observations taken, Herod moved on until at the tripod opposite the venerable Hillel, who met his cold glance with an inclination of the head, and a slight lifting of the hands.

"The answer!" said the king, with imperious simplicity, addressing Hillel, and planting his staff before him with both hands. "The answer!"

The eyes of the patriarch glowed mildly, and, raising his head, and looking the inquisitor full in the face, he answered, his associates giving him closest attention:

"With thee, O king, be the peace of God, of Abraham, Isaac, and Jacob!"

His manner was that of invocation; changing it, he resumed:

"Thou hast demanded of us where the Christ should be born."

The king bowed, though the evil eyes remained fixed upon the sage's face.

"That is the question."

"Then, O king, speaking for myself, and all my brethren here, not one dissenting, I say, in Bethlehem of Judea."

Hillel glanced at the parchment on the tri-

pod; and, pointing with his tremulous finger, continued, "In Bethlehem of Judea, for thus it is written by the prophet, 'And thou, Bethlehem, in the land of Judea, art not the least among the princes of Judah; for out of thee shall come a governor that shall rule my people Israel.'"

Herod's face was troubled, and his eyes fell upon the parchment while he thought. Those beholding him scarcely breathed; they spoke not, nor did he. At length he turned about and left the chamber.

"Brethren," said Hillel, "we are dismissed."

The company then arose, and in groups departed.

"Simeon," said Hillel again.

A man, quite fifty years old, but in the hearty prime of life, answered and came to him.

"Take up the sacred parchment, my son; roll it tenderly."

The order was obeyed.

"Now lend me thy arm; I will to the litter."

The strong man stooped; with his withered hands the old man took the offered support, and, rising, moved feebly to the door.

So departed the famous Rector, and Simeon, his son, who was to be his successor in wisdom, learning, and office.

.

Yet later in the evening the wise men were lying in a lewen of the khan awake. The stones which served them as pillows raised their heads so they could look out of the open arch into the depths of the sky; and as they

watched the twinkling of the stars, they thought
of the next manifestation. How would it come?
What would it be? They were in Jerusalem
at last; they had asked at the gate for Him
they sought; they had borne witness of his
birth; it remained only to find him; and as to
that, they placed all trust in the Spirit. Men
listening for the voice of God, or waiting a sign
from Heaven, cannot sleep.

While they were in this condition, a man
stepped in under the arch, darkening the lewen.

"Awake!" he said to them; "I bring you a
message which will not be put off."

They all sat up.

"From whom?" asked the Egyptian.

"Herod the king."

Each one felt his spirit thrill.

"Are you not the steward of the khan?"
Balthasar asked next.

"I am."

"What would the king with us?"

"His messenger is without; let him answer."

"Tell him, then, to abide our coming."

"You were right, O my brother!" said the
Greek, when the steward was gone. "The
question put to the people on the road, and to
the guard at the gate, has given us quick no-
toriety. I am impatient; let us up quickly."

They arose, put on their sandals, girt their
mantles about them, and went out.

"I salute you, and give you peace, and pray
your pardon; but my master, the king, has sent
me to invite you to the palace, where he would
have speech with you privately."

117

Thus the messenger discharged his duty.

A lamp hung in the entrance, and by its light they looked at each other, and knew the Spirit was upon them. Then the Egyptian stepped to the steward, and said, so as not to be heard by the others, "You know where our goods are stored in the court, and where our camels are resting. While we are gone, make all things ready for our departure, if it should be needful."

"Go your way assured; trust me," the steward replied.

"The king's will is our will," said Balthasar to the messenger. "We will follow you."

The streets of the Holy City were narrow then as now, but not so rough and foul; for the great builder, not content with beauty, enforced cleanliness and convenience also. Following their guide, the brethren proceeded without a word. Through the dim starlight, made dimmer by the walls on both sides, sometimes almost lost under bridges connecting the house-tops, out of a low ground they ascended a hill. At last they came to a portal reared across the way. In the light of fires blazing before it in two great braziers, they caught a glimpse of the structure, and also of some guards leaning motionlessly upon their arms. They passed into a building unchallenged. Then by passages and arched halls; through courts, and under colonnades not always lighted; up long flights of stairs, past innumerable cloisters and chambers, they were conducted into a tower of great height. Suddenly the

118

guide halted, and, pointing through an open door, said to them,

"Enter. The king is there."

The air of the chamber was heavy with the perfume of sandal-wood, and all the appointments within were effeminately rich. Upon the floor, covering the central space, a tufted rug was spread, and upon that a throne was set. The visitors had but time, however, to catch a confused idea of the place—of carved and gilt ottomans and couches; of fans and jars and musical instruments; of golden candlesticks glittering in their own lights; of walls painted in the style of the voluptuous Grecian school, one look at which had made a Pharisee hide his head with holy horror. Herod, sitting upon the throne to receive them, clad as when at the conference with the doctors and lawyers, claimed all their minds.

At the edge of the rug, to which they advanced uninvited, they prostrated themselves. The king touched a bell. An attendant came in, and placed three stools before the throne.

"Seat yourselves," said the monarch, graciously.

"From the North Gate," he continued, when they were at rest, "I had this afternoon report of the arrival of three strangers, curiously mounted, and appearing as if from far countries. Are you the men?"

The Egyptian took the sign from the Greek and the Hindoo, and answered, with the profoundest salaam, "Were we other than we are, the mighty Herod, whose fame is as incense to

the whole world, would not have sent for us.
We may not doubt that we are the strangers."

Herod acknowledged the speech with a wave
of the hand.

"Who are you? Whence do you come?"
he asked, adding significantly, "Let each speak
for himself."

In turn they gave him account, referring sim-
ply to the cities and lands of their birth, and
the routes by which they came to Jerusalem.
Somewhat disappointed, Herod plied them
more directly.

"What was the question you put to the offi-
cer at the gate?"

"We asked him, 'Where is he that is born
King of the Jews?'"

"I see now why the people were so curious.
You excite me no less. Is there another King
of the Jews?"

The Egyptian did not blanch.

"There is one newly born."

An expression of pain knit the dark face of
the monarch, as if his mind were swept by a
harrowing recollection.

"Not to me, not to me!" he exclaimed.

Possibly the accusing images of his mur-
dered children flitted before him; recovering
from the emotion, whatever it was, he asked,
steadily, "Where is the new king?"

"That, O king, is what we would ask."

"You bring me a wonder—a riddle surpass-
ing any of Solomon's," the inquisitor said next.
"As you see, I am in the time of life when cu-
riosity is as ungovernable as it was in child-

hood, when to trifle with it is cruelty. Tell me further, and I will honor you as kings honor each other. Give me all you know about the newly-born, and I will join you in the search for him; and when we have found him, I will do what you wish; I will bring him to Jerusalem, and train him in kingcraft; I will use my grace with Cæsar for his promotion and glory. Jealousy shall not come between us, so I swear. But tell me first how, so widely separated by seas and deserts, you all came to hear of him."

"I will tell you truly, O king."

"Speak on," said Herod.

Balthasar raised himself erect, and said, solemnly,

"There is an Almighty God."

Herod was visibly startled.

"He bade us come hither, promising that we should find the Redeemer of the World; that we should see and worship him, and bear witness that he was come; and, as a sign, we were each given to see a star. His Spirit stayed with us. O king, his Spirit is with us now!"

An overpowering feeling seized the three. The Greek with difficulty restrained an outcry. Herod's gaze darted quickly from one to the other; he was more suspicious and dissatisfied than before.

"You are mocking me," he said. "If not, tell me more. What is to follow the coming of the new king?"

"The salvation of men."

"From what?"

"Their wickedness."

"How?"

"By the divine agencies—Faith, Love, and Good Works."

"Then"—Herod paused, and from his look no man could have said with what feeling he continued—"you are the heralds of the Christ. Is that all?"

Balthasar bowed low.

"We are your servants, O king."

The monarch touched a bell, and the attendant appeared.

"Bring the gifts," the master said.

The attendant went out, but in a little while returned, and, kneeling before the guests, gave to each one an outer robe or mantle of scarlet and blue, and a girdle of gold. They acknowledged the honors with Eastern prostrations.

"A word further," said Herod, when the ceremony was ended. "To the officer of the gate, and but now to me, you spoke of seeing a star in the east."

"Yes," said Balthasar, "his star, the star of the newly born."

"What time did it appear?"

"When we were bidden come hither."

Herod arose, signifying the audience was over. Stepping from the throne towards them, he said, with all graciousness,

"If, as I believe, O illustrious men, you are indeed the heralds of the Christ just born, know that I have this night consulted those wisest in things Jewish, and they say with one voice he should be born in Bethlehem of Ju-

dea. I say to you, go thither; go and search diligently for the young child; and when you have found him bring me word again, that I may come and worship him. To your going there shall be no let or hinderance. Peace be with you!"

And, folding his robe about him, he left the chamber.

Directly the guide came, and led them back to the street, and thence to the khan, at the portal of which the Greek said, impulsively, "Let us to Bethlehem, O brethren, as the king has advised."

"Yes," cried the Hindoo. "The Spirit burns within me."

"Be it so," said Balthasar, with equal warmth. "The camels are ready."

They gave gifts to the steward, mounted into their saddles, received directions to the Joppa Gate, and departed. At their approach the great valves were unbarred, and they passed out into the open country, taking the road so lately travelled by Joseph and Mary. As they came up out of Hinnom, on the plain of Rephaim, a light appeared, at first wide-spread and faint. Their pulses fluttered fast. The light intensified rapidly; they closed their eyes against its burning brilliance: when they dared look again, lo! the star, perfect as any in the heavens, but low down and moving slowly before them. And they folded their hands, and shouted, and rejoiced with exceeding great joy.

"God is with us! God is with us!" they re-

123

peated, in frequent cheer, all the way, until the star, rising out of the valley beyond Mar Elias, stood still over a house up on the slope of the hill near the town.

<p style="text-align:center">CHAPTER XIV</p>

<p style="text-align:center">THE WISE MEN FIND THE CHILD</p>

T was now the beginning of the third watch, and at Bethlehem the morning was breaking over the mountains in the east, but so feebly that it was yet night in the valley. The watchman on the roof of the old khan, shivering in the chilly air, was listening for the first distinguishable sounds with which life, awakening, greets the dawn, when a light came moving up the hill towards the house. He thought it a torch in some one's hand; next moment he thought it a meteor; the brilliance grew, however, until it became a star. Sore afraid, he cried out, and brought everybody within the walls to the roof. The phenomenon, in eccentric motion, continued to approach; the rocks, trees, and roadway under it shone as in a glare of lightning; directly its brightness became blinding. The more timid of the beholders fell upon their knees, and prayed, with their faces hidden; the boldest, covering their eyes, crouched, and now and then snatched glances fearfully. Afterwhile the khan and everything thereabout lay under the intolerable radiance. Such as dared look beheld the star standing

<p style="text-align:center">124</p>

still directly over the house in front of the cave where the Child had been born.

In the height of this scene, the wise men came up, and at the gate dismounted from their camels, and shouted for admission. When the steward so far mastered his terror as to give them heed, he drew the bars and opened to them. The camels looked spectral in the unnatural light, and, besides their outlandishness, there were in the faces and manner of the three visitors an eagerness and exaltation which still further excited the keeper's fears and fancy; he fell back, and for a time could not answer the question they put to him.

"Is not this Bethlehem of Judea?"

But others came, and by their presence gave him assurance.

"No, this is but the khan; the town lies farther on."

"Is there not here a child newly born?"

The by-standers turned to each other marvelling, though some of them answered, "Yes, yes."

"Show us to him!" said the Greek, impatiently.

"Show us to him!" cried Balthasar, breaking through his gravity; "for we have seen his star, even that which ye behold over the house, and are come to worship him."

The Hindoo clasped his hands, exclaiming, "God indeed lives! Make haste, make haste! The Saviour is found. Blessed, blessed are we above men!"

The people from the roof came down and

followed the strangers as they were taken
through the court and out into the enclosure;
at sight of the star yet above the cave, though
less candescent than before, some turned back
afraid; the greater part went on. As the
strangers neared the house, the orb arose;
when they were at the door, it was high up
overhead vanishing; when they entered, it
went out lost to sight. And to the witnesses
of what then took place came a conviction
that there was a divine relation between the
star and the strangers, which extended also
to at least some of the occupants of the cave.
When the door was opened, they crowded in.

The apartment was lighted by a lantern
enough to enable the strangers to find the
mother, and the child awake in her lap.

"Is the child thine?" asked Balthasar of
Mary.

And she who had kept all the things in the
least affecting the little one, and pondered them
in her heart, held it up in the light, saying,

"He is my son!"

And they fell down and worshipped him.

They saw the child was as other children:
about its head was neither nimbus nor materi-
al crown; its lips opened not in speech; if it
heard their expressions of joy, their invoca-
tions, their prayers, it made no sign whatever,
but, baby-like, looked longer at the flame in
the lantern than at them.

In a little while they arose, and, returning to
the camels, brought gifts of gold, frankincense,
and myrrh, and laid them before the child,

abating nothing of their worshipful speeches; of which no part is given, for the thoughtful know that the pure worship of the pure heart was then what it is now, and has always been, an inspired song.

And this was the Saviour they had come so far to find!

Yet they worshipped without a doubt.

Why?

Their faith rested upon the signs sent them by him whom we have since come to know as the Father; and they were of the kind to whom his promises were so all-sufficient that they asked nothing about his ways. Few there were who had seen the signs and heard the promises — the Mother and Joseph, the shepherds, and the Three — yet they all believed alike; that is to say, in this period of the plan of salvation, God was all and the Child nothing. But look forward, O reader! A time will come when the signs will all proceed from the Son. Happy they who then believe in him!

Let us wait that period.

BOOK SECOND

" There is a fire
And motion of the soul which will
 not dwell
In its own narrow being, but aspire
Beyond the fitting medium of desire;
And, but once kindled, quenchless
 evermore,
Preys upon high adventure, nor can
 tire
Of aught but rest."
 —CHILDE HAROLD.

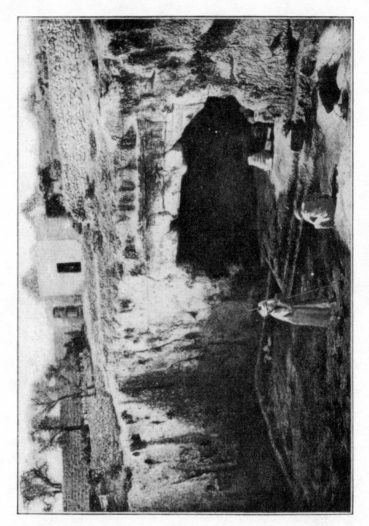

TOMBS OF THE KINGS, JERUSALEM

CHAPTER I

JERUSALEM UNDER THE ROMANS

T is necessary now to carry the reader
forward twenty-one years, to the
beginning of the administration of
Valerius Gratus, the fourth imperial
governor of Judea—a period which will be re-
membered as rent by political agitations in
Jerusalem, if, indeed, it be not the precise time
of the opening of the final quarrel between the
Jew and the Roman.

In the interval Judea had been subjected to
changes affecting her in many ways, but in
nothing so much as her political status. Herod
the Great died within one year after the birth
of the Child—died so miserably that the Chris-
tian world had reason to believe him overtaken
by the divine wrath. Like all great rulers
who spend their lives in perfecting the power
they create, he dreamed of transmitting his
throne and crown—of being the founder of a
dynasty. With that intent, he left a will di-
viding his territories between his three sons,
Antipas, Philip, and Archelaus, of whom the
last was appointed to succeed to the title.
The testament was necessarily referred to Au-
gustus, the emperor, who ratified all its pro-
visions with one exception : he withheld from
Archelaus the title of king until he proved
his capacity and loyalty; in lieu thereof, he

created him ethnarch, and as such permitted him to govern nine years, when, for misconduct and inability to stay the turbulent elements that grew and strengthened around him, he was sent into Gaul as an exile.

Cæsar was not content with deposing Archelaus; he struck the people of Jerusalem in a manner that touched their pride, and keenly wounded the sensibilities of the haughty habitués of the Temple. He reduced Judea to a Roman province, and annexed it to the prefecture of Syria. So, instead of a king ruling royally from the palace left by Herod on Mount Zion, the city fell into the hands of an officer of the second grade, an appointee called procurator, who communicated with the court in Rome through the Legate of Syria, residing in Antioch. To make the hurt more painful, the procurator was not permitted to establish himself in Jerusalem; Cæsarea was his seat of government. Most humiliating, however, most exasperating, most studied, Samaria, of all the world the most despised—Samaria was joined to Judea as a part of the same province! What ineffable misery the bigoted Separatists or Pharisees endured at finding themselves elbowed and laughed at in the procurator's presence in Cæsarea by the devotees of Gerizim!

In this rain of sorrows, one consolation, and one only, remained to the fallen people: the high-priest occupied the Herodian palace in the market-place, and kept the semblance of a court there. What his authority really was is

a matter of easy estimate. Judgment of life and death was retained by the procurator. Justice was administered in the name and according to the decretals of Rome. Yet more significant, the royal house was jointly occupied by the imperial exciseman, and all his corps of assistants, registrars, collectors, publicans, informers, and spies. Still, to the dreamers of liberty to come, there was a certain satisfaction in the fact that the chief ruler in the palace was a Jew. His mere presence there day after day kept them reminded of the covenants and promises of the prophets, and the ages when Jehovah governed the tribes through the sons of Aaron; it was to them a certain sign that he had not abandoned them: so their hopes lived, and served their patience, and helped them wait grimly the son of Judah who was to rule Israel.

Judea had been a Roman province eighty years and more—ample time for the Cæsars to study the idiosyncrasies of the people—time enough, at least, to learn that the Jew, with all his pride, could be quietly governed if his religion were respected. Proceeding upon that policy, the predecessors of Gratus had carefully abstained from interfering with any of the sacred observances of their subjects. But he chose a different course: almost his first official act was to expel Hannas from the high-priesthood, and give the place to Ishmael, son of Fabus.

Whether the act was directed by Augustus, or proceeded from Gratus himself, its impolicy

became speedily apparent. The reader shall
be spared a chapter on Jewish politics; a few
words upon the subject, however, are essential
to such as may follow the succeeding narra-
tion critically. At this time, leaving origin
out of view, there were in Judea the party
of the nobles and the Separatist or popular
party. Upon Herod's death, the two united
against Archelaus; from temple to palace,
from Jerusalem to Rome, they fought him
sometimes with intrigue, sometimes with the
actual weapons of war. More than once the
holy cloisters on Moriah resounded with the
cries of fighting men. Finally, they drove him
into exile. Meantime throughout this strug-
gle the allies had their diverse objects in view.
The nobles hated Joazar, the high-priest; the
Separatists, on the other hand, were his zeal-
ous adherents. When Herod's settlement
went down with Archelaus, Joazar shared the
fall. Hannas, the son of Seth, was selected by
the nobles to fill the great office; thereupon the
allies divided. The induction of the Sethian
brought them face to face in fierce hostility.

In the course of the struggle with the un-
fortunate ethnarch, the nobles had found it
expedient to attach themselves to Rome. Dis-
cerning that when the existing settlement was
broken up some form of government must
needs follow, they suggested the conversion of
Judea into a province. The fact furnished the
Separatists an additional cause for attack;
and, when Samaria was made part of the prov-
ince, the nobles sank into a minority, with

age justified any assumption. In the terrible wars between the first Cæsar and his great enemies, a Messala had been the friend of Brutus. After Philippi, without sacrifice of his honor, he and the conqueror became reconciled. Yet later, when Octavius disputed for the empire, Messala supported him. Octavius, as the Emperor Augustus, remembered the service, and showered the family with honors. Among other things, Judea being reduced to a province, he sent the son of his old client or retainer to Jerusalem, charged with the receipt and management of the taxes levied in that region; and in that service the son had since remained, sharing the palace with the high-priest. The youth just described was his son, whose habit it was to carry about with him all too faithfully a remembrance of the relation between his grandfather and the great Romans of his day.

The associate of the Messala was slighter in form, and his garments were of fine white linen and of the prevalent style in Jerusalem; a cloth covered his head, held by a yellow cord, and arranged so as to fall away from the forehead down low over the back of the neck. An observer skilled in the distinctions of race, and studying his features more than his costume, would have soon discovered him to be of Jewish descent. The forehead of the Roman was high and narrow, his nose sharp and aquiline, while his lips were thin and straight, and his eyes cold and close under the brows. The front of the Israelite, on the other hand, was low and

nothing to support them but the imperial court and the prestige of their rank and wealth; yet for fifteen years—down, indeed, to the coming of Valerius Gratus—they managed to maintain themselves in both palace and Temple.

Hannas, the idol of his party, had used his power faithfully in the interest of his imperial patron. A Roman garrison held the Tower of Antonia; a Roman guard kept the gates of the palace; a Roman judge dispensed justice, civil and criminal; a Roman system of taxation, mercilessly executed, crushed both city and country; daily, hourly, and in a thousand ways, the people were bruised and galled, and taught the difference between a life of independence and a life of subjection; yet Hannas kept them in comparative quiet. Rome had no truer friend; and he made his loss instantly felt. Delivering his vestments to Ishmael, the new appointee, he walked from the courts of the Temple into the councils of the Separatists, and became the head of a new combination, Bethusian and Sethian.

Gratus, the procurator, left thus without a party, saw the fires which in the fifteen years, had sunk into sodden smoke begin to glow with returning life. A month after Ishmael took the office, the Roman found it necessary to visit him in Jerusalem. When from the walls, hooting and hissing him, the Jews beheld his guard enter the north gate of the city and march to the Tower of Antonia, they understood the real purpose of the visit—a

full cohort of legionaries was added to the former garrison, and the keys of their yoke could now be tightened with impunity. If the procurator deemed it important to make an example, alas for the first offender!

CHAPTER II
BEN-HUR AND MESSALA

WITH the foregoing explanation in mind, the reader is invited to look into one of the gardens of the palace on Mount Zion. The time was noonday in the middle of July, when the heat of summer was at its highest.

The garden was bounded on every side by buildings, which in places arose two stories, with verandas shading the doors and windows of the lower story, while retreating galleries, guarded by strong balustrades, adorned and protected the upper. Here and there, moreover, the structures fell into what appeared low colonnades, permitting the passage of such winds as chanced to blow, and allowing other parts of the house to be seen, the better to realize its magnitude and beauty. The arrangement of the ground was equally pleasant to the eye. There were walks, and patches of grass and shrubbery, and a few large trees, rare specimens of the palm, grouped with the carob, apricot, and walnut. In all directions the grade sloped gently from the centre, where there was a reservoir, or deep marble basin,

136

broken at intervals by little gates which, when raised, emptied the water into sluices bordering the walks—a cunning device for the rescue of the place from the aridity too prevalent elsewhere in the region.

Not far from the fountain, there was a small pool of clear water nourishing a clump of cane and oleander, such as grow on the Jordan and down by the Dead Sea. Between the clump and the pool, unmindful of the sun shining full upon them in the breathless air, two boys, one about nineteen, the other seventeen, sat engaged in earnest conversation.

They were both handsome, and, at first glance, would have been pronounced brothers. Both had hair and eyes black; their faces were deeply browned; and, sitting, they seemed of a size proper for the difference in their ages.

The elder was bareheaded. A loose tunic, dropping to the knees, was his attire complete, except sandals and a light-blue mantle spread under him on the seat. The costume left his arms and legs exposed, and they were brown as the face; nevertheless, a certain grace of manner, refinement of features, and culture of voice decided his rank. The tunic, of softest woollen, gray-tinted, at the neck, sleeves, and edge of the skirt bordered with red, and bound to the waist by a tasselled silken cord, certified him the Roman he was. And if in speech he now and then gazed haughtily at his companion and addressed him as an inferior, he might almost be excused, for he was of a family noble even in Rome—a circumstance which in that

137

broad ; his nose long, with expanded nostrils ; his upper lip, slightly shading the lower one, short and curving to the dimpled corners, like a Cupid's bow ; points which, in connection with the round chin, full eyes, and oval cheeks reddened with a wine-like glow, gave his face the softness, strength, and beauty peculiar to his race. The comeliness of the Roman was severe and chaste, that of the Jew rich and voluptuous.

"Did you not say the new procurator is to arrive to-morrow ?"

The question proceeded from the younger of the friends, and was couched in Greek, at the time, singularly enough, the language everywhere prevalent in the politer circles of Judea ; having passed from the palace into the camp and college , thence, nobody knew exactly when or how, into the Temple itself, and, for that matter, into precincts of the Temple far beyond the gates and cloisters—precincts of a sanctity intolerable for a Gentile.

"Yes, to-morrow," Messala answered.

"Who told you ?"

"I heard Ishmael, the new governor in the palace—you call him high-priest—tell my father so last night. The news had been more credible, I grant you, coming from an Egyptian, who is of a race that has forgotten what truth is, or even from an Idumæan, whose people never knew what truth was ; but, to make quite certain, I saw a centurion from the Tower this morning, and he told me preparations were going on for the reception ; that the

armorers were furbishing the helmets and
shields, and regilding the eagles and globes;
and that apartments long unused were being
cleansed and aired as if for an addition to the
garrison — the body-guard, probably, of the
great man."

A perfect idea of the manner in which the
answer was given cannot be conveyed, as its
fine points continually escape the power be-
hind the pen. The reader's fancy must come
to his aid; and for that he must be reminded
that reverence as a quality of the Roman mind
was fast breaking down, or, rather, it was be-
coming unfashionable. The old religion had
nearly ceased to be a faith; at most it was a
mere habit of thought and expression, cherish-
ed principally by the priests who found service
in the Temple profitable, and the poets who,
in the turn of their verses, could not dispense
with the familiar deities . there are singers of
this age who are similarly given. As philoso-
phy was taking the place of religion, satire was
fast substituting reverence; insomuch that in
Latin opinion it was to every speech, even to
the little diatribes of conversation, as salt to
viands, or aroma to wine. The young Messala,
educated in Rome, but lately returned, had
caught the habit and manner · the scarce per-
ceptible movement of the outer corner of the
lower eyelid, the decided curl of the corre-
sponding nostril, and a languid utterance af-
fected as the best vehicle to convey the idea
of general indifference, but more particularly
because of the opportunities it afforded for

certain rhetorical pauses thought to be of prime importance to enable the listener to take the happy conceit or receive the virus of the stinging epigram. Such a stop occurred in the answer just given, at the end of the allusion to the Egyptian and Idumæan. The color in the Jewish lad's cheeks deepened, for he remained silent, looking absently into the depths of the pool.

"Our farewell took place in this garden. 'The peace of the Lord go with you!'—your last words. 'The gods keep you!' I said. Do you remember? How many years have passed since then?"

"Five," answered the Jew, gazing into the water.

"Well, you have reason to be thankful to—whom shall I say? The gods? No matter. You have grown handsome; the Greeks would call you beautiful—happy achievement of the years! If Jupiter would stay content with one Ganymede, what a cup-bearer you would make for the emperor! Tell me, my Judah, how the coming of the procurator is of such interest to you."

Judah bent his large eyes upon the questioner; the gaze was grave and thoughtful, and caught the Roman's, and held it while he replied, "Yes, five years. I remember the parting; you went to Rome; I saw you start, and cried, for I loved you. The years are gone, and you have come back to me accomplished and princely—I do not jest; and yet—yet—I wish you were the Messala you went away."

The fine nostril of the satirist stirred, and he put on a longer drawl as he said, " No, no ; not a Ganymede—an oracle, my Judah. A few lessons from my teacher of rhetoric hard by the Forum—I will give you a letter to him when you become wise enough to accept a suggestion which I am reminded to make you —a little practice of the art of mystery, and Delphi will receive you as Apollo himself. At the sound of your solemn voice, the Pythia will come down to you with her crown. Seriously, O my friend, in what am I not the Messala I went away ? I once heard the greatest logician in the world. His subject was Disputation. One saying I remember—' Understand your antagonist before you answer him.' Let me understand you."

The lad reddened under the cynical look to which he was subjected ; yet he replied, firmly, " You have availed yourself, I see, of your opportunities ; from your teachers you have brought away much knowledge and many graces. You talk with the ease of a master ; yet your speech carries a sting. My Messala, when he went away, had no poison in his nature ; not for the world would he have hurt the feelings of a friend."

The Roman smiled as if complimented, and raised his patrician head a toss higher.

" O my solemn Judah, we are not at Dodona or Pytho. Drop the oracular, and be plain. Wherein have I hurt you ?"

The other drew a long breath, and said, pulling at the cord about his waist, " In the five

years, I, too, have learned somewhat. Hillel may not be the equal of the logician you heard, and Simeon and Shammai are, no doubt, inferior to your master hard by the Forum. Their learning goes not out into forbidden paths; those who sit at their feet arise enriched simply with knowledge of God, the law, and Israel; and the effect is love and reverence for everything that pertains to them. Attendance at the Great College, and study of what I heard there, have taught me that Judea is not as she used to be. I know the space that lies between an independent kingdom and the petty province Judea is. I were meaner, viler, than a Samaritan not to resent the degradation of my country. Ishmael is not lawfully high-priest, and he cannot be while the noble Hannas lives; yet he is a Levite; one of the devoted who for thousands of years have acceptably served the Lord God of our faith and worship. His—"

Messala broke in upon him with a biting laugh.

"Oh, I understand you now. Ishmael, you say, is a usurper, yet to believe an Idumæan sooner than Ishmael is to sting like an adder. By the drunken son of Semele, what it is to be a Jew! All men and things, even heaven and earth, change; but a Jew never. To him there is no backward, no forward; he is what his ancestor was in the beginning. In this sand I draw you a circle—there! Now tell me what more a Jew's life is? Round and round, Abraham here, Isaac and Jacob yonder, God

143

in the middle. And the circle—by the master of all thunders! the circle is too large. I draw it again—" He stopped, put his thumb upon the ground, and swept the fingers about it. "See, the thumb-spot is the Temple, the finger-lines Judea. Outside the little space is there nothing of value? The arts! Herod was a builder; therefore he is accursed. Painting, sculpture! to look upon them is sin. Poetry you make fast to your altars. Except in the synagogue, who of you attempts eloquence? In war all you conquer in the six days you lose on the seventh. Such your life and limit; who shall say no if I laugh at you? Satisfied with the worship of such a people, what is your God to our Roman Jove, who lends us his eagles that we may compass the universe with our arms? Hillel, Simeon, Shammai, Abtalion — what are they to the masters who teach that everything is worth knowing that can be known?"

The Jew arose, his face much flushed.

"No, no; keep your place, my Judah, keep your place," Messala cried, extending his hand.

"You mock me."

"Listen a little further. Directly"—the Roman smiled derisively—"directly Jupiter and his whole family, Greek and Latin, will come to me, as is their habit, and make an end of serious speech. I am mindful of your goodness in walking from the old house of your fathers to welcome me back and renew the love of our childhood—if we can. 'Go,' said my teacher, in his last lecture—'Go, and,

to make your lives great, remember Mars reigns and Eros has found his eyes.' He meant love is nothing, war everything. It is so in Rome. Marriage is the first step to divorce. Virtue is a tradesman's jewel. Cleopatra, dying, bequeathed her arts, and is avenged; she has a successor in every Roman's house. The world is going the same way; so, as to our future, down Eros, up Mars! I am to be a soldier; and you, O my Judah, I pity you; what can you be?"

The Jew moved nearer the pool; Messala's drawl deepened.

"Yes, I pity you, my fine Judah. From the college to the synagogue; then to the Temple; then—oh, a crowning glory!—the seat in the Sanhedrim. A life without opportunities; the gods help you! But I—"

Judah looked at him in time to see the flush of pride that kindled in his haughty face as he went on.

"But I—ah, the world is not all conquered. The sea has islands unseen. In the north there are nations yet unvisited. The glory of completing Alexander's march to the Far East remains to some one. See what possibilities lie before a Roman."

Next instant he resumed his drawl.

"A campaign into Africa; another after the Scythian; then—a legion! Most careers end there; but not mine. I—by Jupiter! what a conception!—I will give up my legion for a prefecture. Think of life in Rome with money—money, wine, women, games—poets at the

banquet, intrigues in the court, dice all the year round. Such a rounding of life may be—a fat prefecture, and it is mine. O my Judah, here is Syria! Judea is rich; Antioch a capital for the gods. I will succeed Cyrenius, and you—shall share my fortune."

The sophists and rhetoricians who thronged the public resorts of Rome, almost monopolizing the business of teaching her patrician youth, might have approved these sayings of Messala, for they were all in the popular vein; to the young Jew, however, they were new, and unlike the solemn style of discourse and conversation to which he was accustomed. He belonged, moreover, to a race whose laws, modes, and habits of thought forbade satire and humor; very naturally, therefore, he listened to his friend with varying feelings: one moment indignant, then uncertain how to take him. The superior airs assumed had been offensive to him in the beginning; soon they became irritating, and at last an acute smart. Anger lies close by this point in all of us; and that the satirist evoked in another way. To the Jew of the Herodian period patriotism was a savage passion scarcely hidden under his common humor, and so related to his history, religion, and God that it responded instantly to derision of them. Wherefore it is not speaking too strongly to say that Messala's progress down to the last pause was exquisite torture to his hearer; at that point the latter said, with a forced smile,

"There are a few, I have heard, who can af-

ford to make a jest of their future; you convince me, O my Messala, that I am not one of them."

The Roman studied him; then replied, "Why not the truth in a jest as well as a parable? The great Fulvia went fishing the other day; she caught more than all the company besides. They said it was because the barb of her hook was covered with gold."

"Then you were not merely jesting?"

"My Judah, I see I did not offer you enough," the Roman answered, quickly, his eyes sparkling. "When I am prefect, with Judea to enrich me, I—will make you high-priest."

The Jew turned off angrily.

"Do not leave me," said Messala.

The other stopped irresolute.

"Gods, Judah, how hot the sun shines!" cried the patrician, observing his perplexity. "Let us seek a shade."

Judah answered, coldly,

"We had better part. I wish I had not come. I sought a friend and find a—"

"Roman," said Messala, quickly.

The hands of the Jew clinched, but controlling himself again, he started off. Messala arose, and, taking the mantle from the bench, flung it over his shoulder, and followed after; when he gained his side, he put his hand upon his shoulder and walked with him.

"This is the way—my hand thus—we used to walk when we were children. Let us keep it as far as the gate."

Apparently Messala was trying to be serious

and kind, though he could not rid his countenance of the habitual satirical expression. Judah permitted the familiarity.

"You are a boy; I am a man; let me talk like one."

The complacency of the Roman was superb. Mentor lecturing the young Telemachus could not have been more at ease.

"Do you believe in the Parcæ? Ah, I forgot, you are a Sadducee: the Essenes are your sensible people; they believe in the sisters. So do I. How everlastingly the three are in the way of our doing what we please! I sit down scheming. I run paths here and there. Perpol! Just when I am reaching to take the world in hand, I hear behind me the grinding of scissors. I look, and there she is, the accursed Atropos! But, my Judah, why did you get mad when I spoke of succeeding old Cyrenius? You thought I meant to enrich myself plundering your Judea. Suppose so; it is what some Roman will do. Why not I?"

Judah shortened his step.

"There have been strangers in mastery of Judea before the Roman," he said, with lifted hand. "Where are they, Messala? She has outlived them all. What has been will be again."

Messala put on his drawl.

"The Parcæ have believers outside the Essenes. Welcome, Judah, welcome to the faith!"

"No, Messala, count me not with them. My faith rests on the rock which was the foundation of the faith of my fathers back further

148

than Abraham—on the covenants of the Lord God of Israel."

"Too much passion, my Judah, How my master would have been shocked had I been guilty of so much heat in his presence! There were other things I had to tell you, but I fear to now."

When they had gone a few yards, the Roman spoke again.

"I think you can hear me now, especially as what I have to say concerns yourself. I would serve you, O handsome as Ganymede; I would serve you with real good-will. I love you—all I can. I told you I meant to be a soldier. Why not you also? Why not you step out of the narrow circle which, as I have shown, is all of noble life your laws and customs allow?"

Judah made no reply.

"Who are the wise men of our day?" Messala continued. "Not they who exhaust their years quarrelling about dead things; about Baals, Joves, and Jehovahs; about philosophies and religions. Give me one great name, O Judah; I care not where you go to find it—to Rome, Egypt, the East, or here in Jerusalem— Pluto take me if it belong not to a man who wrought his fame out of the material furnished him by the present; holding nothing sacred that did not contribute to the end, scorning nothing that did! How was it with Herod? How with the Maccabees? How with the first and second Cæsars? Imitate them. Begin now. At hand see—Rome, as ready to help you as she was the Idumæan Antipater."

The Jewish lad trembled with rage; and, as the garden-gate was close by, he quickened his steps, eager to escape.

"O Rome, Rome!" he muttered.

"Be wise," continued Messala. "Give up the follies of Moses and the traditions; see the situation as it is. Dare look the Parcæ in the face, and they will tell you, Rome is the world. Ask them of Judea, and they will answer, She is what Rome wills."

They were now at the gate. Judah stopped, and took the hand gently from his shoulder, and confronted Messala, tears trembling in his eyes.

"I understand you, because you are a Roman; you cannot understand me—I am an Israelite. You have given me suffering to-day by convincing me that we can never be the friends we have been—never! Here we part. The peace of the God of my fathers abide with you!"

Messala offered him his hand; the Jew walked on through the gate-way. When he was gone, the Roman was silent a while; then he, too, passed through, saying to himself, with a toss of the head,

"Be it so. Eros is dead, Mars reigns!"

150

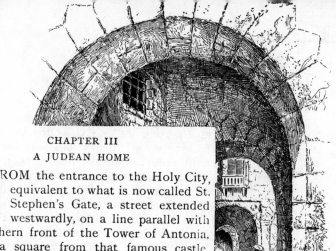

CHAPTER III
A JUDEAN HOME

FROM the entrance to the Holy City, equivalent to what is now called St. Stephen's Gate, a street extended westwardly, on a line parallel with the northern front of the Tower of Antonia, though a square from that famous castle. Keeping the course as far as the Tyropœon Valley, which it followed a little way south, it turned and again ran west until a short distance beyond what tradition tells us was the Judgment Gate, from whence it broke abruptly south. The traveller or the student familiar with the sacred locality will recognize the thoroughfare described as part of the Via Dolorosa—with Christians of more interest, though of a melancholy kind, than any street in the world. As the purpose in view does not at present require dealing with the whole street, it will be sufficient to point out a house standing in the angle last mentioned as marking the change of direction south, and which, as an important centre of interest, needs somewhat particular description.

The building fronted north and west, probably four hundred feet each way, and, like most pretentious Eastern structures, was two stories in height, and perfectly quadrangular. The street on the west side was about twelve

feet wide, that on the north not more than ten; so that one walking close to the walls, and looking up at them, would have been struck by the rude, unfinished, uninviting, but strong and imposing, appearance they presented; for they were of stone laid in large blocks, undressed—on the outer side, in fact, just as they were taken from the quarry. A critic of this age would have pronounced the house fortelesque in style, except for the windows, with which it was unusually garnished, and the ornate finish of the door-ways or gates. The western windows were four in number, the northern only two, all set on the line of the second story in such manner as to overhang the thoroughfares below. The gates were the only breaks of wall externally visible in the first story; and, besides being so thickly riven with iron bolts as to suggest resistance to battering-rams, they were protected by cornices of marble, handsomely executed, and of such bold projection as to assure visitors well informed of the people that the rich man who resided there was a Sadducee in politics and creed.

Not long after the young Jew parted from the Roman at the palace up on the Market-place, he stopped before the western gate of the house described, and knocked. The wicket (a door hung in one of the valves of the gate) was opened to admit him. He stepped in hastily, and failed to acknowledge the low salaam of the porter.

To get an idea of the interior arrangement

of the structure, as well as to see what more
befell the youth, we will follow him.

The passage into which he was admitted
appeared not unlike a narrow tunnel with pan-
elled walls and pitted ceiling. There were
benches of stone on both sides, stained and
polished by long use. Twelve or fifteen steps
carried him into a court-yard, oblong north
and south, and in every quarter, except the
east, bounded by what seemed the fronts of
two-story houses; of which the lower floor
was divided into lewens, while the upper was
terraced and defended by strong balustrading.
The servants coming and going along the ter-
races; the noise of millstones grinding; the
garments fluttering from ropes stretched from
point to point; the chickens and pigeons in
full enjoyment of the place; the goats, cows,
donkeys, and horses stabled in the lewens; a
massive trough of water, apparently for the
common use, declared this court appurtenant
to the domestic management of the owner.
Eastwardly there was a division-wall broken
by another passage-way in all respects like the
first one.

Clearing the second passage, the young man
entered a second court, spacious, square, and
set with shrubbery and vines, kept fresh and
beautiful by water from a basin erected near a
porch on the north side. The lewens here
were high, airy, and shaded by curtains striped
alternate white and red. The arches of the
lewens rested on clustered columns. A flight
of steps on the south ascended to the terraces

of the upper story, over which great awnings were stretched as a defence against the sun. Another stair-way reached from the terraces to the roof, the edge of which, all around the square, was defined by a sculptured cornice, and a parapet of burned-clay tiling, sexangular and bright red. In this quarter, moreover, there was everywhere observable a scrupulous neatnesss, which, allowing no dust in the angles, not even a yellow leaf upon a shrub, contributed quite as much as anything else to the delightful general effect; insomuch that a visitor, breathing the sweet air, knew, in advance of introduction, the refinement of the family he was about calling upon.

A few steps within the second court, the lad turned to the right, and, choosing a walk through the shrubbery, part of which was in flower, passed to the stair-way, and ascended to the terrace — a broad pavement of white and brown flags closely laid, and much worn. Making way under the awning to a door-way on the north side, he entered an apartment which the dropping of the screen behind him returned to darkness. Nevertheless, he proceeded, moving over a tiled floor to a divan, upon which he flung himself, face downward, and lay at rest, his forehead upon his crossed arms.

About nightfall a woman came to the door and called; he answered, and she went in.

"Supper is over, and it is night. Is not my son hungry?" she asked,

"No," he replied,

"Are you sick?"

"I am sleepy."

"Your mother has asked for you."

"Where is she?"

"In the summer-house on the roof."

He stirred himself, and sat up.

"Very well. Bring me something to eat."

"What do you want?"

"What you please, Amrah. I am not sick, but indifferent. Life does not seem as pleasant as it did this morning. A new ailment, O my Amrah; and you who know me so well, who never failed me, may think of the things now that answer for food and medicine. Bring me what you choose."

Amrah's questions, and the voice in which she put them—low, sympathetic, and solicitous —were significant of an endeared relation between the two. She laid her hand upon his forehead; then, as satisfied, went out, saying, "I will see."

After a while she returned, bearing on a wooden platter a bowl of milk, some thin cakes of white bread broken, a delicate paste of brayed wheat, a bird broiled, and honey and salt. On one end of the platter there was a silver goblet full of wine, on the other a brazen hand-lamp lighted.

The room was then revealed: its walls smoothly plastered; the ceiling broken by great oaken rafters, brown with rain-stains and time; the floor of small diamond-shaped white and blue tiles, very firm and enduring; a few stools with legs carved in imitation of the legs of

lions; a divan raised a little above the floor, trimmed with blue cloth, and partially covered by an immense striped woollen blanket or shawl—in brief, a Hebrew bedroom.

The same light also gave the woman to view. Drawing a stool to the divan, she placed the platter upon it, then knelt close by ready to serve him. Her face was that of a woman of fifty, dark-skinned, dark-eyed, and at the moment softened by a look of tenderness almost maternal. A white turban covered her head, leaving the lobes of the ear exposed, and in them the sign that settled her condition— an orifice bored by a thick awl. She was a slave, of Egyptian origin, to whom not even the sacred fiftieth year could have brought freedom; nor would she have accepted it, for the boy she was attending was her life. She had nursed him through babyhood, tended him as a child, and could not break the service. To her love he could never be a man.

He spoke but once during the meal.

"You remember, O my Amrah," he said, "the Messala who used to visit me here days at a time."

"I remember him."

"He went to Rome some years ago, and is now back. I called upon him to-day."

A shudder of disgust seized the lad.

"I knew something had happened," she said, deeply interested. "I never liked the Messala. Tell me all."

But he fell into musing, and to her repeated inquiries only said, "He is much changed,

and I shall have nothing more to do with him."

When Amrah took the platter away, he also went out, and up from the terrace to the roof.

The reader is presumed to know somewhat of the uses of the house-top in the East. In the matter of customs, climate is a lawgiver everywhere. The Syrian summer day drives the seeker of comfort into the darkened lewen; night, however, calls him forth early, and the shadows deepening over the mountain-sides seem veils dimly covering Circean singers; but they are far off, while the roof is close by, and raised above the level of the shimmering plain enough for the visitation of cool airs, and sufficiently above the trees to allure the stars down closer, down at least into brighter shining. So the roof became a resort—became play-ground, sleeping-chamber, boudoir, rendezvous for the family, place of music, dance, conversation, reverie, and prayer.

The motive that prompts the decoration, at whatever cost, of interiors in colder climes suggested to the Oriental the embellishment of his house-top. The parapet ordered by Moses became a potter's triumph; above that, later, arose towers, plain and fantastic; still later, kings and princes crowned their roofs with summer-houses of marble and gold. When the Babylonian hung gardens in the air, extravagance could push the idea no further.

The lad whom we are following walked slowly across the house-top to a tower built

over the north-west corner of the palace. Had
he been a stranger, he might have bestowed
a glance upon the structure as he drew nigh
it, and seen all the dimness permitted — a
darkened mass, low, latticed, pillared, and
domed. He entered, passing under a half-
raised curtain. The interior was all darkness,
except that on four sides there were arched
openings like door-ways, through which the
sky, lighted with stars, was visible. In one of
the openings, reclining against a cushion from
a divan, he saw the figure of a woman, indis-
tinct even in white floating drapery. At the
sound of his steps upon the floor, the fan in
her hand stopped, glistening where the star-
light struck the jewels with which it was
sprinkled, and she sat up, and called his name.

"Judah, my son!"

"It is I, mother," he answered, quickening
his approach.

Going to her, he knelt, and she put her arms
around him, and with kisses pressed him to
her bosom.

CHAPTER IV

THE STRANGE THINGS BEN-HUR WANTS TO KNOW

THE mother resumed her easy position against the cushion, while the son took place on the divan, his head in her lap. Both of them, looking out of the opening, could see a stretch of lower house-tops in the vicinity, a bank of blue blackness over in the west which they knew to be mountains, and the sky, its shadowy depths brilliant with stars. The city was still. Only the winds stirred.

"Amrah tells me something has happened to you," she said, caressing his cheek. "When my Judah was a child, I allowed small things to trouble him, but he is now a man. He must not forget "— her voice became very soft — "that one day he is to be my hero."

She spoke in the language almost lost in the land, but which a few—and they were always as rich in blood as in possessions—cherished in its purity, that they might be more certainly distinguished from Gentile peoples—the language in which the loved Rebekah and Rachel sang to Benjamin.

The words appeared to set him thinking anew; after a while, however, he caught the hand with which she fanned him, and said, "To-day, O my mother, I have been made to

159

think of many things that never had place in my mind before. Tell me, first, what am I to be?"

"Have I not told you? You are to be my hero."

He could not see her face, yet he knew she was in play. He became more serious.

"You are very good, very kind, O my mother. No one will ever love me as you do."

He kissed the hand over and over again.

"I think I understand why you would have me put off the question," he continued. "Thus far my life has belonged to you. How gentle, how sweet, your control has been! I wish it could last forever. But that may not be. It is the Lord's will that I shall one day become owner of myself—a day of separation, and therefore a dreadful day to you. Let us be brave and serious. I will be your hero, but you must put me in the way. You know the law—every son of Israel must have some occupation. I am not exempt, and ask now, shall I tend the herds? or till the soil? or drive the saw? or be a clerk or a lawyer? What shall I be? Dear, good mother, help me to an answer."

"Gamaliel has been lecturing to-day," she said, thoughtfully.

"If so, I did not hear him."

"Then you have been walking with Simeon, who, they tell me, inherits the genius of his family."

"No, I have not seen him. I have been up

on the Market-place, not to the Temple. I
visited the young Messala."

A certain change in his voice attracted the
mother's attention. A presentiment quickened
the beating of her heart; the fan became mo-
tionless again.

"The Messala!" she said. "What could he
say to so trouble you?"

"He is very much changed."

"You mean he has come back a Roman."

"Yes."

"Roman!" she continued, half to herself.
"To all the world the word means master.
How long has he been away?"

"Five years."

She raised her head, and looked off into the
night.

"The airs of the Via Sacra are well enough
in the streets of the Egyptian and in Babylon;
but in Jerusalem—our Jerusalem—the cove-
nant abides."

And, full of the thought, she settled back
into her easy place. He was first to speak.

"What Messala said, my mother, was sharp
enough in itself; but, taken with the manner,
some of the sayings were intolerable."

"I think I understand you. Rome, her po-
ets, orators, senators, courtiers, are mad with
affectation of what they call satire."

"I suppose all great peoples are proud," he
went on, scarcely noticing the interruption;
"but the pride of that people is unlike all
others; in these latter days it is so grown the
gods barely escape it."

161

"The gods escape!" said the mother, quickly. "More than one Roman has accepted worship as his divine right."

"Well, Messala always had his share of the disagreeable quality. When he was a child, I have seen him mock strangers whom even Herod condescended to receive with honors; yet he always spared Judea. For the first time, in conversation with me to-day, he trifled with our customs and God. As you would have had me do, I parted with him finally. And now, O my dear mother, I would know with more certainty if there be just ground for the Roman's contempt. In what am I his inferior? Is ours a lower order of people? Why should I, even in Cæsar's presence, feel the shrinking of a slave? Tell me especially why, if I have the soul, and so choose, I may not hunt the honors of the world in all its fields? Why may not I take sword and indulge the passion of war? As a poet, why may not I sing of all themes? I can be a worker in metals, a keeper of flocks, a merchant, why not an artist like the Greek? Tell me, O my mother—and this is the sum of my trouble—why may not a son of Israel do all a Roman may?"

The reader will refer these questions back to the conversation in the Market-place; the mother, listening with all her faculties awake, from something which would have been lost upon one less interested in him—from the connections of the subject, the pointing of the questions, possibly his accent and tone—was

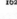

not less swift in making the same reference. She sat up, and in a voice quick and sharp as his own, replied, " I see, I see ! From association Messala, in boyhood, was almost a Jew ; had he remained here, he might have become a proselyte, so much do we all borrow from the influences that ripen our lives ; but the years in Rome have been too much for him. I do not wonder at the change ; yet "—her voice fell—" he might have dealt tenderly at least with you. It is a hard, cruel nature which in youth can forget its first loves."

Her hand dropped lightly upon his forehead, and the fingers caught in his hair and lingered there lovingly, while her eyes sought the highest stars in view. Her pride responded to his, not merely in echo, but in the unison of perfect sympathy. She would answer him ; at the same time, not for the world would she have had the answer unsatisfactory : an admission of inferiority might weaken his spirit for life. She faltered with misgivings of her own powers.

" What you propose, O my Judah, is not a subject for treatment by a woman. Let me put its consideration off till to-morrow, and I will have the wise Simeon—"

" Do not send me to the Rector," he said, abruptly.

" I will have him come to us."

" No, I seek more than information ; while he might give me that better than you, O my mother, you can do better by giving me what he cannot—the resolution which is the soul of a man's soul."

She swept the heavens with a rapid glance, trying to compass all the meaning of his questions.

"While craving justice for ourselves, it is never wise to be unjust to others. To deny valor in the enemy we have conquered is to underrate our victory; and if the enemy be strong enough to hold us at bay, much more to conquer us"—she hesitated—"self-respect bids us seek some other explanation of our misfortunes than accusing him of qualities inferior to our own."

Thus, speaking to herself rather than to him, she began:

"Take heart, O my son. The Messala is nobly descended; his family has been illustrious through many generations. In the days of Republican Rome—how far back I cannot tell—they were famous, some as soldiers, some as civilians. I can recall but one consul of the name; their rank was senatorial, and their patronage always sought because they were always rich. Yet if to-day your friend boasted of his ancestry, you might have shamed him by recounting yours. If he referred to the ages through which the line is traceable, or to deeds, rank, or wealth—such allusions, except when great occasion demands them, are tokens of small minds—if he mentioned them in proof of his superiority, then without dread, and standing on each particular, you might have challenged him to a comparison of records."

Taking a moment's thought, the mother proceeded:

"One of the ideas of fast hold now is that time has much to do with the nobility of races and families. A Roman boasting his superiority on that account over a son of Israel will always fail when put to the proof. The founding of Rome was his beginning; the very best of them cannot trace their descent beyond that period; few of them pretend to do so; and of such as do, I say not one could make good his claim except by resort to tradition. Messala certainly could not. Let us look now to ourselves. Could we better?"

A little more light would have enabled him to see the pride that diffused itself over her face.

"Let us imagine the Roman putting us to the challenge. I would answer him, neither doubting nor boastful."

Her voice faltered; a tender thought changed the form of the argument.

"Your father, O my Judah, is at rest with his fathers; yet I remember, as though it were this evening, the day he and I, with many rejoicing friends, went up into the Temple to present you to the Lord. We sacrificed the doves, and to the priest I gave your name, which he wrote in my presence—'Judah, son of Ithamar, of the House of Hur.' The name was then carried away, and written in a book of the division of records devoted to the saintly family.

"I cannot tell you when the custom of registration in this mode began. We know it prevailed before the flight from Egypt. I have

heard Hillel say Abraham caused the record
to be first opened with his own name, and the
names of his sons, moved by the promises of
the Lord which separated him and them from
all other races, and made them the highest and
noblest, the very chosen of the earth. The
covenant with Jacob was of like effect. ' In
thy seed shall all the nations of the earth be
blessed '—so said the angel to Abraham in the
place Jehovah-jireh. ' And the land whereon
thou liest, to thee will I give it, and to thy
seed '—so the Lord himself said to Jacob asleep
at Bethel on the way to Haran. Afterwards
the wise men looked forward to a just division
of the land of promise; and, that it might be
known in the day of partition who were en-
titled to portions, the Book of Generations
was begun. But not for that alone. The
promise of a blessing to all the earth through
the patriarch reached far into the future. One
name was mentioned in connection with the
blessing—the benefactor might be the hum-
blest of the chosen family, for the Lord our
God knows no distinctions of rank or riches.
So, to make the performance clear to men of
the generation who were to witness it, and
that they might give the glory to whom it be-
longed, the record was required to be kept
with absolute certainty. Has it been so kept?"

The fan played to and fro, until, becoming
impatient, he repeated the question, " Is the
record absolutely true?"

" Hillel said it was, and of all who have lived
no one was so well-informed upon the subject.

Our people have at times been heedless of some parts of the law, but never of this part. The good rector himself has followed the Books of Generations through three periods—from the promises to the opening of the Temple; thence to the Captivity; thence, again, to the present. Once only were the records disturbed, and that was at the end of the second period; but when the nation returned from the long exile, as a first duty to God, Zerubbabel restored the Books, enabling us once more to carry the lines of Jewish descent back unbroken fully two thousand years. And now—"

She paused as if to allow the hearer to measure the time comprehended in the statement.

"And now," she continued, "what becomes of the Roman boast of blood enriched by ages? By that test, the sons of Israel watching the herds on old Rephaim yonder are nobler than the noblest of the Marcii."

"And I, mother—by the Books, who am I?"

"What I have said thus far, my son, had reference to your question. I will answer you. If Messala were here, he might say, as others have said, that the exact trace of your lineage stopped when the Assyrian took Jerusalem, and razed the Temple, with all its precious stores; but you might plead the pious action of Zerubbabel, and retort that all verity in Roman genealogy ended when the barbarians from the West took Rome, and camped six months upon her desolated site. Did the Government keep family histories? If so, what

167

became of them in those dreadful days? No,
no; there is verity in our Books of Genera-
tions; and, following them back to the Cap-
tivity, back to the foundation of the first Tem-
ple, back to the march from Egypt, we have
absolute assurance that you are lineally sprung
from Hur, the associate of Joshua. In the
matter of descent sanctified by time, is not the
honor perfect? Do you care to pursue fur-
ther? If so, take the Torah, and search the
Book of Numbers, and of the seventy-two gen-
erations after Adam you can find the very
progenitor of your house."

There was silence for a time in the chamber
on the roof.

"I thank you, O my mother," Judah next
said, clasping both her hands in his; "I thank
you with all my heart. I was right in not hav-
ing the good rector called in; he could not
have satisfied me more than you have. Yet
to make a family truly noble, is time alone
sufficient?"

"Ah, you forget, you forget; our claim rests
not merely upon time; the Lord's preference
is our especial glory."

"You are speaking of the race, and I, moth-
er, of the family—our family. In the years
since Father Abraham, what have they achiev-
ed? What have they done? What great
things to lift them above the level of their fel-
lows?"

She hesitated, thinking she might all this
time have mistaken his object. The informa-
tion he sought might have been for more than

satisfaction of wounded vanity. Youth is but
the painted shell within which, continually
growing, lives that wondrous thing the spirit
of a man, biding its moment of apparition,
earlier in some than in others. She trembled
under a perception that this might be the
supreme moment come to him ; that as chil-
dren at birth reach out their untried hands
grasping for shadows, and crying the while, so
his spirit might, in temporary blindness, be
struggling to take hold of its impalpable future.
They to whom a boy comes asking, Who am
I, and what am I to be? have need of ever so
much care. Each word in answer may prove
to the after-life what each finger-touch of the
artist is to the clay he is modelling.

"I have a feeling, O my Judah," she said,
patting his cheek with the hand he had been
caressing—"I have the feeling that all I have
said has been in strife with an antagonist more
real than imaginary. If Messala is the enemy,
do not leave me to fight him in the dark.
Tell me all he said."

THE young Israelite proceeded then, and rehearsed his conversation with Messala, dwelling with particularity upon the latter's speeches in contempt of the Jews, their customs, and muchpent round of life.

Afraid to speak the while, the mother listened, discerning the matter plainly. Judah had gone to the palace on the Market-place, allured by love of a playmate whom he thought to find exactly as he had been at the parting years before ; a man met him, and, in place of laughter and references to the sports of the past, the man had been full of the future, and talked of glory to be won, and of riches and power. Unconscious of the effect, the visitor had come away hurt in pride, yet touched with a natural ambition ; but she, the jealous mother, saw it, and, not knowing the turn the aspiration might take, became at once Jewish in her fear. What if it lured him away from the patriarchal faith ? In her view, that consequence was more dreadful than any or all others. She could discover but one way to avert it, and she set about the task, her native power reinforced by love to such degree that her speech took a masculine strength and at times a poet's fervor.

"There never has been a people," she began, "who did not think themselves at least equal to any other; never a great nation, my son, that did not believe itself the very superior. When the Roman looks down upon Israel and laughs, he merely repeats the folly of the Egyptian, the Assyrian, and the Macedonian; and as the laugh is against God, the result will be the same."

Her voice became firmer.

"There is no law by which to determine the superiority of nations; hence the vanity of the claim, and the idleness of disputes about it. A people risen, run their race, and die either of themselves or at the hands of another, who, succeeding to their power, take possession of their place, and upon their monuments write new names; such is history. If I were called upon to symbolize God and man in the simplest form, I would draw a straight line and a circle; and of the line I would say, 'This is God, for he alone moves forever straightforward;' and of the circle, 'This is man—such is his progress.' I do not mean that there is no difference between the careers of nations; no two are alike. The difference, however, is not, as some say, in the extent of the circle they describe or the space of earth they cover, but in the sphere of their movement, the highest being nearest God.

"To stop here, my son, would be to leave the subject where we began. Let us go on. There are signs by which to measure the height of the circle each nation runs while in its course.

By them let us compare the Hebrew and the Roman.

"The simplest of all the signs is the daily life of the people. Of this I will only say, Israel has at times forgotten God, while the Roman never knew him; consequently comparison is not possible.

"Your friend, or your former friend, charged, if I understood you rightly, that we have had no poets, artists, or warriors; by which he meant, I suppose, to deny that we have had great men, the next most certain of the signs. A just consideration of this charge requires a definition at the commencement. A great man, O my boy, is one whose life proves him to have been recognized, if not called, by God. A Persian was used to punish our recreant fathers, and he carried them into captivity; another Persian was selected to restore their children to the Holy Land; greater than either of them, however, was the Macedonian through whom the desolation of Judea and the Temple was avenged. The special distinction of the men was that they were chosen by the Lord, each for a divine purpose; and that they were Gentiles does not lessen their glory. Do not lose sight of this definition while I proceed.

"There is an idea that war is the most noble occupation of men, and that the most exalted greatness is the growth of battle-fields. Because the world has adopted the idea, be not you deceived. That we must worship something is a law which will continue as long as there is anything we cannot understand. The

prayer of the barbarian is a wail of fear addressed to Strength, the only divine quality he can clearly conceive; hence his faith in heroes. What is Jove but a Roman hero? The Greeks have their great glory because they were the first to set Mind above Strength. In Athens the orator and philosopher were more revered than the warrior. The charioteer and the swiftest runner are still idols of the arena; yet the immortelles are reserved for the sweetest singer. The birthplace of one poet was contested by seven cities. But was the Hellene the first to deny the old barbaric faith? No. My son, that glory is ours; against brutalism our fathers erected God; in our worship, the wail of fear gave place to the Hosanna and the Psalm. So the Hebrew and the Greek would have carried all humanity forward and upward. But, alas! the government of the world presumes war as an eternal condition; wherefore, over Mind and above God, the Roman has enthroned his Cæsar, the absorbent of all attainable power, the prohibition of any other greatness.

"The sway of the Greek was a flowering time for genius. In return for the liberty it then enjoyed, what a company of thinkers the Mind led forth? There was a glory for every excellence, and a perfection so absolute that in everything but war even the Roman has stooped to imitation. A Greek is now the model of the orators in the Forum; listen, and in every Roman song you will hear the rhythm of the Greek; if a Roman opens his mouth

speaking wisely of moralities, or abstractions, or of the mysteries of nature, he is either a plagiarist or the disciple of some school which had a Greek for its founder. In nothing but war, I say again, has Rome a claim to originality. Her games and spectacles are Greek inventions, dashed with blood to gratify the ferocity of her rabble; her religion, if such it may be called, is made up of contributions from the faiths of all other peoples; her most venerated gods are from Olympus—even her Mars, and, for that matter, the Jove she much magnifies. So it happens, O my son, that of the whole world our Israel alone can dispute the superiority of the Greek, and with him contest the palm of original genius.

"To the excellences of other peoples the egotism of a Roman is a blindfold, impenetrable as his breastplate. Oh, the ruthless robbers! Under their trampling the earth trembles like a floor beaten with flails. Along with the rest we are fallen—alas that I should say it to you, my son! They have our highest places, and the holiest, and the end no man can tell; but this I know—they may reduce Judea as an almond broken with hammers, and devour Jerusalem, which is the oil and sweetness thereof; yet the glory of the men of Israel will remain a light in the heavens overhead out of reach; for their history is the history of God, who wrote with their hands, spake with their tongues, and was himself in all the good they did, even the least; who dwelt with them, a Lawgiver on Sinai, a Guide in the

wilderness, in war a Captain, in government a King; who once and again pushed back the curtains of the pavilion which is his resting-place, intolerably bright, and, as a man speaking to men, showed them the right, and the way to happiness, and how they should live, and made them promises binding the strength of his Almightiness with covenants sworn to everlastingly. O my son, could it be that they with whom Jehovah thus dwelt, an awful familiar, derived nothing from him?—that in their lives and deeds the common human qualities should not in some degree have been mixed and colored with the divine? that their genius should not have in it, even after the lapse of ages, some little of heaven?"

For a time the rustling of the fan was all the sound heard in the chamber.

"In the sense which limits art to sculpture and painting, it is true," she next said, "Israel has had no artists."

The admission was made regretfully, for it must be remembered she was a Sadducee, whose faith, unlike that of the Pharisees, permitted a love of the beautiful in every form, and without reference to its origin.

"Still he who would do justice," she proceeded, "will not forget that the cunning of our hands was bound by the prohibition, 'Thou shall not make unto thee any graven image, or any likeness of anything;' which the Sopherim wickedly extended beyond its purpose and time. Nor should it be forgotten that long before Dædalus appeared in Attica and with

175

his wooden statues so transformed sculpture
as to make possible the schools of Corinth and
Ægina, and their ultimate triumphs the Pœ-
cile and Capitolium—long before the age of
Dædalus, I say, two Israelites, Bezaleel and
Aholiab, the master-builders of the first taber-
nacle, said to have been skilled 'in all manner
of workmanship,' wrought the cherubim of the
mercy - seat above the ark. Of gold beaten,
not chiselled, were they; and they were statues
in form both human and divine. 'And they
shall stretch forth their wings on high, . . .
and their faces shall look one to another.' Who
will say they were not beautiful? or that they
were not the first statues?"

"Oh, I see now why the Greek outstripped
us," said Judah, intensely interested. "And
the ark; accursed be the Babylonians who de-
stroyed it!"

"Nay, Judah, be of faith. It was not de-
stroyed, only lost, hidden away too safely in
some cavern of the mountains. One day—
Hillel and Shammai both say so — one day,
in the Lord's good time, it will be found and
brought forth, and Israel dance before it, sing-
ing as of old. And they who look upon the
faces of the cherubim then, though they have
seen the face of the ivory Minerva, will be
ready to kiss the hand of the Jew from love
of his genius, asleep through all the thousands
of years."

The mother, in her eagerness, had risen into
something like the rapidity and vehemence of
a speech-maker; but now, to recover herself,

or to pick up the thread of her thought, she rested a while.

"You are so good, my mother," he said, in a grateful way. "And I will never be done saying so. Shammai could not have talked better, nor Hillel. I am a true son of Israel again."

"Flatterer!" she said. "You do not know that I am but repeating what I heard Hillel say in an argument he had one day in my presence with a sophist from Rome."

"Well, the hearty words are yours."

Directly all her earnestness returned.

"Where was I? Oh, yes, I was claiming for our Hebrew fathers the first statues. The trick of the sculptor, Judah, is not all there is of art, any more than art is all there is of greatness. I always think of great men marching down the centuries in groups and goodly companies, separable according to nationalities; here the Indian, there the Egyptian, yonder the Assyrian; above them the music of trumpets and the beauty of banners; and on their right hand and left, as reverent spectators, the generations from the beginning, numberless. As they go, I think of the Greek, saying, 'Lo! the Hellene leads the way.' Then the Roman replies, 'Silence! what was your place is ours now; we have left you behind as dust trodden on.' And all the time, from the far front back over the line of march, as well as forward into the furthest future, streams a light of which the wranglers know nothing, except that it is forever leading them on—the Light of Reve-

lation! Who are they that carry it? Ah,
the old Judean blood! How it leaps at the
thought! By the light we know them. Thrice
blessed, O our fathers, servants of God, keepers
of the covenants! Ye are the leaders of men,
the living and the dead. The front is thine;
and though every Roman were a Cæsar, ye
shall not lose it!"

Judah was deeply stirred.

"Do not stop, I pray you," he cried. "You
give me to hear the sound of timbrels. I wait
for Miriam and the women who went after
her dancing and singing."

She caught his feeling, and, with ready wit,
wove it into her speech.

"Very well, my son. If you can hear the
timbrel of the prophetess, you can do what I
was about to ask; you can use your fancy, and
stand with me, as if by the way-side, while the
chosen of Israel pass us at the head of the
procession. Now they come—the patriarchs
first; next the fathers of the tribes. I almost
hear the bells of their camels and the lowing
of their herds. Who is he that walks alone be-
tween the companies? An old man, yet his
eye is not dim, nor his natural force abated.
He knew the Lord, face to face! Warrior, poet,
orator, law-giver, prophet, his greatness is as
the sun at morning, its flood of splendor
quenching all other lights, even that of the
first and noblest of the Cæsars. After him
the judges. And then the kings—the son of
Jesse, a hero in war, and a singer of songs eter-
nal as that of the sea; and his son, who, pass-

THE DEAD SEA

ing all other kings in riches and wisdom, and while making the Desert habitable, and in its waste places planting cities, forgot not Jerusalem which the Lord had chosen for his seat on earth. Bend lower, my son! These that come next are the first of their kind, and the last. Their faces are raised, as if they heard a voice in the sky and were listening. Their lives were full of sorrows. Their garments smell of tombs and caverns. Hearken to a woman among them — 'Sing ye to the Lord, for he hath triumphed gloriously.' Nay, put your forehead in the dust before them! They were tongues of God, his servants, who looked through heaven, and, seeing all the future, wrote what they saw, and left the writing to be proven by time. Kings turned pale as they approached them, and nations trembled at the sound of their voices. The elements waited upon them. In their hands they carried every bounty and every plague. See the Tishbite and his servant Elisha! See the sad son of Hilkiah, and him, the seer of visions, by the river of Chebar! And of the three children of Judah who refused the image of the Babylonian, lo! that one who, in the feast to the thousand lords, so confounded the astrologers. And yonder—O my son, kiss the dust again!—yonder the gentle son of Amoz, from whom the world has its promise of the Messiah to come!"

In this passage the fan had been kept in rapid play; it stopped now, and her voice sank low.

"You are tired," she said.

"No," he replied, "I was listening to a new song of Israel."

The mother was still intent upon her purpose, and passed the pleasant speech.

"In such light as I could, my Judah, I have set our great men before you—patriarchs, legislators, warriors, singers, prophets. Turn we to the best of Rome. Against Moses place Cæsar, and Tarquin against David; Sylla against either of the Maccabees; the best of the consuls against the judges; Augustus against Solomon, and you are done: comparison ends there. But think then of the prophets—greatest of the great."

She laughed scornfully.

"Pardon me. I was thinking of the soothsayer who warned Caius Julius against the ides of March, and fancied him looking for the omens of evil which his master despised in the entrails of a chicken. From that picture turn to Elijah sitting on the hill-top on the way to Samaria, amid the smoking bodies of the captains and their fifties, warning the son of Ahab of the wrath of our God. Finally, O my Judah — if such speech be reverent— how shall we judge Jehovah and Jupiter unless it be by what their servants have done in their names? And as for what you shall do—"

She spoke the latter words slowly, and with a tremulous utterance.

"As for what you shall do, my boy—serve the Lord, the Lord God of Israel, not Rome. For a child of Abraham there is no glory ex-

cept in the Lord's ways, and in them there is
much glory."

"I may be a soldier then?" Judah asked.

"Why not? Did not Moses call God a man
of war?"

There was then a long silence in the summer
chamber.

"You have my permission," she said, finally;
"if only you serve the Lord instead of Cæsar."

He was content with the condition, and by-
and-by fell asleep. She arose then, and put the
cushion under his head, and, throwing a shawl
over him and kissing him tenderly, went away.

CHAPTER VI
THE ACCIDENT TO GRATUS

HE good man, like the bad, must die;
but, remembering the lesson of our
faith, we say of him and the event,
"No matter, he will open his eyes in
heaven." Nearest this in life is the waking
from healthful sleep to a quick consciousness
of happy sights and sounds.

When Judah awoke, the sun was up over the
mountains; the pigeons were abroad in flocks,
filling the air with the gleams of their white
wings; and off south-east he beheld the Temple,
an apparition of gold in the blue of the sky.
These, however, were familiar objects, and they
received but a glance; upon the edge of the di-
van, close by him, a girl scarcely fifteen sat sing-
ing to the accompaniment of a nebel, which she

rested upon her knee, and touched gracefully. To her he turned, listening; and this was what she sang:

THE SONG.

"Wake not, but hear me, love!
 Adrift, adrift on slumber's sea,
 Thy spirit call to list to me.
Wake not, but hear me, love!
 A gift from Sleep, the restful king,
 All happy, happy dreams I bring.

"Wake not, but hear me, love!
 Of all the world of dreams 'tis thine
 This once to choose the most divine.
So choose, and sleep, my love!
 But ne'er again in choice be free,
 Unless, unless—thou dream'st of me."

She put the instrument down, and, resting her hands in her lap, waited for him to speak. And as it has become necessary to tell somewhat of her, we will avail ourselves of the chance, and add such particulars of the family into whose privacy we are brought as the reader may wish to know.

The favors of Herod had left surviving him many persons of vast estate. Where this fortune was joined to undoubted lineal descent from some famous son of one of the tribes, especially Judah, the happy individual was accounted a Prince of Jerusalem—a distinction which sufficed to bring him the homage of his less-favored countrymen, and the respect, if nothing more, of the Gentiles with whom business and social circumstance brought him into

dealing. Of this class none had won in private
or public life a higher regard than the father
of the lad whom we have been following. With
a remembrance of his nationality which never
failed him, he had yet been true to the king,
and served him faithfully at home and abroad.
Some offices had taken him to Rome, where his
conduct attracted the notice of Augustus, who
strove without reserve to engage his friend-
ship. In his house, accordingly, were many
presents, such as had gratified the vanity of
kings—purple togas, ivory chairs, golden pa-
teræ—chiefly valuable on account of the im-
perial hand which had honorably conferred
them. Such a man could not fail to be rich;
yet his wealth was not altogether the largess
of royal patrons. He had welcomed the law
that bound him to some pursuit; and, instead
of one, he entered into many. Of the herds-
men watching flocks on the plains and hill-
sides, far as old Lebanon, numbers reported to
him as their employer; in the cities by the
sea, and in those inland, he founded houses
of traffic; his ships brought him silver from
Spain, whose mines were then the richest
known; while his caravans came twice a year
from the East, laden with silks and spices. In
faith he was a Hebrew, observant of the law
and every essential rite; his place in the syn-
agogue and Temple knew him well; he was
thoroughly learned in the Scriptures; he de-
lighted in the society of the college-masters,
and carried his reverence for Hillel almost to
the point of worship. Yet he was in no sense

a Separatist; his hospitality took in strangers
from every land; the carping Pharisees even
accused him of having more than once enter-
tained Samaritans at his table. Had he been
a Gentile, and lived, the world might have
heard of him as the rival of Herodes Atticus:
as it was, he perished at sea some ten years be-
fore this second period of our story, in the
prime of life, and lamented everywhere in Ju-
dea. We are already acquainted with two
members of his family—his widow and son;
the only other was a daughter—she whom we
have seen singing to her brother.

Tirzah was her name, and as the two look-
ed at each other, their resemblance was plain.
Her features had the regularity of his, and
were of the same Jewish type; they had also
the charm of childish innocency of expression.
Home-life and its trustful love permitted the
negligent attire in which she appeared. A
chemise buttoned upon the right shoulder,
and passing loosely over the breast and back
and under the left arm, but half concealed her
person above the waist, while it left the arms
entirely nude. A girdle caught the folds of
the garment, marking the commencement of
the skirt. The coiffure was very simple and
becoming—a silken cap, Tyrian-dyed; and
over that a striped scarf of the same material,
beautifully embroidered, and wound about in
thin folds so as to show the shape of the head
without enlarging it; the whole finished by a
tassel dropping from the crown point of the
cap. She had rings, ear and finger; anklets

and bracelets, all of gold; and around her neck there was a collar of gold, curiously garnished with a net-work of delicate chains, to which were pendants of pearl. The edges of her eyelids were painted, and the tips of her fingers stained. Her hair fell in two long plaits down her back. A curled lock rested upon each cheek in front of the ear. Altogether it would have been impossible to deny her grace, refinement, and beauty.

"Very pretty, my Tirzah, very pretty!" he said, with animation.

"The song?" she asked.

"Yes—and the singer, too. It has the conceit of a Greek. Where did you get it?"

"You remember the Greek who sang in the theatre last month? They said he used to be a singer at the court for Herod and his sister Salome. He came out just after an exhibition of wrestlers, when the house was full of noise. At his first note everything became so quiet that I heard every word. I got the song from him."

"But he sang in Greek."

"And I in Hebrew."

"Ah, yes. I am proud of my little sister. Have you another as good?"

"Very many. But let them go now. Amrah sent me to tell you she will bring you your breakfast, and that you need not come down. She should be here by this time. She thinks you sick—that a dreadful accident happened you yesterday. What was it? Tell me, and I will help Amrah doctor you. She knows

the cures of the Egyptians, who were always a stupid set; but I have a great many recipes of the Arabs, who—"

"Are even more stupid than the Egyptians," he said, shaking his head.

"Do you think so? Very well, then," she replied, almost without pause, and putting her hands to her left ear. "We will have nothing to do with any of them. I have here what is much surer and better—the amulet which was given to some of our people—I cannot tell when, it was so far back—by a Persian magician. See, the inscription is almost worn out."

She offered him the ear-ring, which he took, looked at, and handed back, laughing.

"If I were dying, Tirzah, I could not use the charm. It is a relic of idolatry, forbidden every believing son and daughter of Abraham. Take it, but do not wear it any more."

"Forbidden! Not so," she said. "Our father's mother wore it I do not know how many Sabbaths in her life. It has cured I do not know how many people—more than three, anyhow. It is approved—look, here is the mark of the rabbis."

"I have no faith in amulets."

She raised her eyes to his in astonishment.

"What would Amrah say?"

"Amrah's father and mother tended sakiyeh for a garden on the Nile."

"But Gamaliel!"

"He says they are godless inventions of unbelievers and Shechemites."

Tirzah looked at the ring doubtfully.

"What shall I do with it?"

"Wear it, my little sister. It becomes you —it helps make you beautiful, though I think you that without help."

Satisfied, she returned the amulet to her ear just as Amrah entered the summer chamber, bearing a platter, with wash-bowl, water, and napkins.

Not being a Pharisee, the ablution was short and simple with Judah. The servant then went out, leaving Tirzah to dress his hair. When a lock was disposed to her satisfaction, she would unloose the small metallic mirror which, as was the fashion among her fair countrywomen, she wore at her girdle, and give it to him, that he might see the triumph, and how handsome it made him. Meanwhile they kept up their conversation.

"What do you think, Tirzah?—I am going away."

She dropped her hands with amazement.

"Going away! When? Where? For what?"

He laughed.

"Three questions, all in a breath! What a body you are!" Next instant he became serious. "You know the law requires me to follow some occupation. Our good father set me an example. Even you would despise me if I spent in idleness the results of his industry and knowledge. I am going to Rome."

"Oh, I will go with you."

"You must stay with mother. If both of us leave her she will die."

The brightness faded from her face.

187

"Ah, yes, yes! But—must you go? Here in Jerusalem you can learn all that is needed to be a merchant—if that is what you are thinking of."

"But that is not what I am thinking of. The law does not require the son to be what the father was."

"What else can you be?"

"A soldier," he replied, with a certain pride of voice.

Tears came into her eyes.

"You will be killed."

"If God's will, be it so. But, Tirzah, the soldiers are not all killed."

She threw her arms around his neck, as if to hold him back.

"We are so happy! Stay at home, my brother."

"Home cannot always be what it is. You yourself will be going away before long."

"Never!"

He smiled at her earnestness.

"A prince of Judah, or some other of one of the tribes, will come soon and claim my Tirzah, and ride away with her, to be the light of another house. What will then become of me?"

She answered with sobs.

"War is a trade," he continued, more soberly. "To learn it thoroughly, one must go to school, and there is no school like a Roman camp."

"You would not fight for Rome?" she asked, holding her breath.

"And you—even you hate her. The whole world hates her. In that, O Tirzah, find the reason of the answer I give you— Yes, I will fight for her, if, in return, she will teach me how one day to fight against her."

"When will you go?"

Amrah's steps were then heard returning.

"Hist!" he said. "Do not let her know of what I am thinking."

The faithful slave came in with breakfast, and placed the waiter holding it upon a stool before them; then, with white napkins upon her arm, she remained to serve them. They dipped their fingers in a bowl of water, and were rinsing them, when a noise arrested their attention. They listened, and distinguished martial music in the street on the north side of the house.

"Soldiers from the Prætorium! I must see them," he cried, springing from the divan, and running out.

In a moment more he was leaning over the parapet of tiles which guarded the roof at the extreme north-east corner, so absorbed that he did not notice Tirzah by his side, resting one hand upon his shoulder.

Their position—the roof being the highest one in the locality—commanded the house-tops eastward as far as the huge, irregular Tower of Antonia, which has been already mentioned as a citadel for the garrison and military headquarters for the governor. The street, not more than ten feet wide, was spanned here and there by bridges, open and covered,

which, like the roofs along the way, were beginning to be occupied by men, women, and children, called out by the music. The word is used, though it is hardly fitting; what the people heard when they came forth was rather an uproar of trumpets and the shriller litui so delightful to the soldiers.

The array after a while came into view of the two upon the house of the Hurs. First, a vanguard of the light-armed—mostly slingers and bowmen — marching with wide intervals between their ranks and files; next a body of heavy-armed infantry, bearing large shields, and hastæ longæ, or spears identical with those used in the duels before Ilium; then the musicians; and then an officer riding alone, but followed closely by a guard of cavalry; after them again, a column of infantry, also heavy-armed, which, moving in close order, crowded the street from wall to wall, and appeared to be without end.

The brawny limbs of the men; the cadenced motion from right to left of the shields; the sparkle of scales, buckles, and breastplates and helms, all perfectly burnished; the plumes nodding above the tall crests; the sway of ensigns and iron-shod spears; the bold, confident step, exactly timed and measured; the demeanor, so grave, yet so watchful; the machine-like unity of the whole moving mass—made an impression upon Judah, but as something felt rather than seen. Two objects fixed his attention—the eagle of the legion first—a gilded effigy perched on a tall shaft, with wings

out-spread until they met above its head. He
knew that, when brought from its chamber in
the Tower, it had been received with divine
honors.

The officer riding alone in the midst of the
column was the other attraction. His head
was bare; otherwise he was in full armor. At
his left hip he wore a short sword; in his
hand, however, he carried a truncheon, which
looked like a roll of white paper. He sat upon
a purple cloth instead of a saddle, and that,
and a bridle with a forestall of gold and reins
of yellow silk broadly fringed at the lower
edge, completed the housings of the horse.

While the man was yet in the distance, Ju-
dah observed that his presence was sufficient
to throw the people looking at him into an-
gry excitement. They would lean over the
parapets or stand boldly out, and shake their
fists at him; they followed him with loud cries,
and spit at him as he passed under the bridges;
the women even flung their sandals, sometimes
with such good effect as to hit him. When
he was nearer, the yells became distinguish-
able — "Robber, tyrant, dog of a Roman!
Away with Ishmael! Give us back our Han-
nas!"

When quite near, Judah could see that, as
was but natural, the man did not share the
indifference so superbly shown by the soldiers;
his face was dark and sullen, and the glances he
occasionally cast at his persecutors were full
of menace; the very timid shrank from them.

Now the lad had heard of the custom, bor-

rowed from a habit of the first Cæsar, by which chief commanders, to indicate their rank, appeared in public with only a laurel vine upon their heads. By that sign he knew this officer —VALERIUS GRATUS, THE NEW PROCURATOR OF JUDEA!

To say truth now, the Roman under the unprovoked storm had the young Jew's sympathy; so that when he reached the corner of the house, the latter leaned yet farther over the parapet to see him go by, and in the act rested a hand upon a tile which had been a long time cracked and allowed to go unnoticed. The pressure was strong enough to displace the outer piece, which started to fall. A thrill of horror shot through the youth. He reached out to catch the missile. In appearance the motion was exactly that of one pitching something from him. The effort failed—nay, it served to push the descending fragment farther out over the wall. He shouted with all his might. The soldiers of the guard looked up; so did the great man, and that moment the missile struck him, and he fell from his seat as dead.

The cohort halted; the guards leaped from their horses, and hastened to cover the chief with their shields. On the other hand, the people who witnessed the affair, never doubting that the blow had been purposely dealt, cheered the lad as he yet stooped in full view over the parapet, transfixed by what he beheld, and by anticipation of the consequences flashed all too plainly upon him.

A mischievous spirit flew with incredible speed from roof to roof along the line of march, seizing the people, and urging them all alike. They laid hands upon the parapets and tore up the tiling and the sunburnt mud of which the house-tops were for the most part made, and with blind fury began to fling them upon the legionaries halted below. A battle then ensued. Discipline, of course, prevailed. The struggle, the slaughter, the skill of one side, the desperation of the other, are alike unnecessary to our story. Let us look rather to the wretched author of it all.

He arose from the parapet, his face very pale.

"O Tirzah, Tirzah! What will become of us?"

She had not seen the occurrence below, but was listening to the shouting and watching the mad activity of the people in view on the houses. Something terrible was going on, she knew; but what it was, or the cause, or that she or any of those dear to her were in danger, she did not know.

"What has happened? What does it all mean?" she asked, in sudden alarm.

"I have killed the Roman governor. The tile fell upon him."

An unseen hand appeared to sprinkle her face with the dust of ashes—it grew white so instantly. She put her arm around him, and looked wistfully, but without a word, into his eyes. His fears had passed to her, and the sight of them gave him strength.

"I did not do it purposely, Tirzah—it was an accident," he said, more calmly.

"What will they do?" she asked.

He looked off over the tumult momentarily deepening in the street and on the roofs, and thought of the sullen countenance of Gratus. If he were not dead, where would his vengeance stop? And if he were dead, to what height of fury would not the violence of the people lash the legionaries? To evade an answer, he peered over the parapet again, just as the guard were assisting the Roman to remount his horse.

"He lives, he lives, Tirzah! Blessed be the Lord God of our fathers!"

With that outcry, and a brightened countenance, he drew back and replied to her question.

"Be not afraid, Tirzah. I will explain how it happened, and they will remember our father and his services, and not hurt us."

He was leading her to the summer-house when the roof jarred under their feet, and a crash of strong timbers being burst away, followed by a cry of surprise and agony, arose apparently from the court-yard below. He stopped and listened. The cry was repeated; then came a rush of many feet, and voices lifted in rage blent with voices in prayer; and then the screams of women in mortal terror. The soldiers had beaten in the north gate, and were in possession of the house The terrible sense of being hunted smote him. His first impulse was to fly: but where? Nothing but wings

would serve him. Tirzah, her eyes wild with fear, caught his arm.

"O Judah, what does it mean?"

The servants were being butchered—and his mother! Was not one of the voices he heard hers? With all the will left him, he said, "Stay here, and wait for me, Tirzah. I will go down and see what is the matter, and come back to you."

His voice was not steady as he wished. She clung closer to him.

Clearer, shriller, no longer a fancy, his mother's cry arose. He hesitated no longer.

"Come, then, let us go."

The terrace or gallery at the foot of the steps was crowded with soldiers. Other soldiers with drawn swords ran in and out of the chambers. At one place a number of women on their knees clung to each other or prayed for mercy. Apart from them, one with torn garments, and long hair streaming over her face, struggled to tear loose from a man all whose strength was tasked to keep his hold. Her cries were shrillest of all; cutting through the clamor, they had risen distinguishably to the roof. To her Judah sprang—his steps were long and swift, almost a winged flight—"Mother, mother!" he shouted. She stretched her hands towards him; but when almost touching them he was seized and forced aside. Then he heard some one say, speaking loudly,

"That is he!"

Judah looked, and saw—Messala.

"What, the assassin—that?" said a tall man,

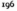

in legionary armor of beautiful finish. "Why, he is but a boy."

"Gods!" replied Messala, not forgetting his drawl. "A new philosophy! What would Seneca say to the proposition that a man must be old before he can hate enough to kill? You have him; and that is his mother; yonder his sister. You have the whole family."

For love of them, Judah forgot his quarrel.

"Help them, O my Messala! Remember our childhood and help them. I—Judah—pray you."

Messala affected not to hear.

"I cannot be of further use to you," he said to the officer. "There is richer entertainment in the street. Down Eros, up Mars!"

With the last words he disappeared. Judah understood him, and, in the bitterness of his soul, prayed to Heaven.

"In the hour of thy vengeance, O Lord," he said, "be mine the hand to put it upon him!"

By great exertion, he drew nearer the officer.

"O sir, the woman you hear is my mother. Spare her, spare my sister yonder. God is just, he will give you mercy for mercy."

The man appeared to be moved.

"To the Tower with the women!" he shouted, "but do them no harm. I will demand them of you." Then to those holding Judah, he said, "Get cords and bind his hands, and take him to the street. His punishment is reserved."

The mother was carried away. The little Tirzah, in her home attire, stupefied with fear,

went passively with her keepers. Judah gave each of them a last look, and covered his face with his hands, as if to possess himself of the scene fadelessly. He may have shed tears, though no one saw them.

There took place in him then what may be justly called the wonder of life. The thoughtful reader of these pages has ere this discerned enough to know that the young Jew in disposition was gentle even to womanliness —a result that seldom fails the habit of loving and being loved. The circumstances through which he had come had made no call upon the harsher elements of his nature, if such he had. At times he had felt the stir and impulses of ambition, but they had been like the formless dreams of a child walking by the sea and gazing at the coming and going of stately ships. But now, if we can imagine an idol, sensible of the worship it was accustomed to, dashed suddenly from its altar, and lying amid the wreck of its little world of love, an idea may be had of what had befallen the young Ben-Hur, and of its effect upon his being. Yet there was no sign, nothing to indicate that he had undergone a change, except that when he raised his head, and held his arms out to be bound, the bend of the Cupid's bow had vanished from his lips. In that instant he had put off childhood and become a man.

A trumpet sounded in the court-yard. With the cessation of the call, the gallery was cleared of the soldiery; many of whom, as they

dared not appear in the ranks with visible plunder in their hands, flung what they had upon the floor, until it was strewn with articles of richest virtù. When Judah descended, the formation was complete, and the officer waiting to see his last order executed.

The mother, daughter, and entire household were led out of the north gate, the ruins of which choked the passage-way. The cries of the domestics, some of whom had been born in the house, were most pitiable. When, finally, the horses and all the dumb tenantry of the place were driven past him, Judah began to comprehend the scope of the procurator's vengeance. The very structure was devoted. Far as the order was possible of execution, nothing living was to be left within its walls. If in Judea there were others desperate enough to think of assassinating a Roman governor, the story of what befell the princely family of Hur would be a warning to them, while the ruin of the habitation would keep the story alive.

The officer waited outside while a detail of men temporarily restored the gate.

In the street the fighting had almost ceased. Upon the houses here and there clouds of dust told where the struggle was yet prolonged. The cohort was, for the most part, standing at rest; its splendor, like its ranks, in nowise diminished. Borne past the point of care for himself, Judah had heart for nothing in view but the prisoners, among whom he looked in vain for his mother and Tirzah.

Suddenly, from the earth where she had been lying, a woman arose and started swiftly back to the gate. Some of the guards reached out to seize her, and a great shout followed their failure. She ran to Judah, and, dropping down, clasped his knees, the coarse black hair powdered with dust veiling her eyes.

"O Amrah, good Amrah," he said to her, "God help you; I cannot."

She could not speak.

He bent down, and whispered, "Live, Amrah, for Tirzah and my mother. They will come back, and—"

A soldier drew her away; whereupon she sprang up and rushed through the gate-way and passage into the vacant court-yard.

"Let her go," the officer shouted. "We will seal the house, and she will starve."

The men resumed their work, and when it was finished there, passed round to the west side. That gate was also secured, after which the palace of the Hurs was lost to use.

The cohort at length marched back to the Tower, where the procurator stayed to recover from his hurts and dispose of his prisoners. On the tenth day following he visited the Market-place.

CHAPTER VII
A GALLEY-SLAVE

EXT day a detachment of legionaries went to the desolated palace, and, closing the gates permanently, plastered the corners with wax, and at the sides nailed a notice in Latin :

" THIS IS THE PROPERTY OF
THE EMPEROR."

In the haughty Roman idea, the sententious announcement was thought sufficient for the purpose—and it was.

The day after that again, about noon, a decurion with his command of ten horsemen approached Nazareth from the south — that is, from the direction of Jerusalem. The place was then a straggling village, perched on a hill-side, and so insignificant that its one street was little more than a path well beaten by the coming and going of flocks and herds. The great plain of Esdraelon crept close to it on the south, and from the height on the west a view could be had of the shores of the Mediterranean, the region beyond the Jordan, and Hermon. The valley below, and the country on every side, were given to gardens, vineyards, orchards, and pasturage. Groves of palm-trees Orientalized the landscape. The

200

houses, in irregular assemblage, were of the humbler class—square, one-story, flat-roofed, and covered with bright-green vines. The drought that had burned the hills of Judea to a crisp, brown and lifeless, stopped at the boundary line of Galilee.

A trumpet, sounded when the cavalcade drew near the village, had a magical effect upon the inhabitants. The gates and front doors cast forth groups eager to be the first to catch the meaning of a visitation so unusual.

Nazareth, it must be remembered, was not only aside from any great highway, but within the sway of Judas of Gamala; wherefore it should not be hard to imagine the feelings with which the legionaries were received. But when they were up and traversing the street, the duty that occupied them became apparent, and then fear and hatred were lost in curiosity, under the impulse of which the people, knowing there must be a halt at the well in the north-eastern part of the town, quit their gates and doors, and closed in after the procession.

A prisoner whom the horsemen were guarding was the object of curiosity. He was afoot, bareheaded, half naked, his hands bound behind him. A thong fixed to his wrists was looped over the neck of a horse. The dust went with the party when in movement, wrapping him in yellow fog, sometimes in a dense cloud. He dropped forward, foot-sore and faint. The villagers could see he was young.

At the well the decurion halted, and, with most of the men, dismounted. The prisoner sank down in the dust of the road, stupefied, and asking nothing: apparently he was in the last stage of exhaustion. Seeing, when they came near, that he was but a boy, the villagers would have helped him had they dared.

In the midst of their perplexity, and while the pitchers were passing among the soldiers, a man was descried coming down the road from Sepphoris. At sight of him a woman cried out: "Look! Yonder comes the carpenter. Now we will hear something."

The person spoken of was quite venerable in appearance. Thin white locks fell below the edge of his full turban, and a mass of still whiter beard flowed down the front of his coarse gray gown. He came slowly, for, in addition to his age, he carried some tools—an axe, a saw, and a drawing-knife, all very rude and heavy—and had evidently travelled some distance without rest.

He stopped close by to survey the assemblage.

"O Rabbi, good Rabbi Joseph!" cried a woman, running to him. "Here is a prisoner; come ask the soldiers about him, that we may know who he is, and what he has done, and what they are going to do with him."

The rabbi's face remained stolid; he glanced at the prisoner, however, and presently went to the officer.

"The peace of the Lord be with you!" he said, with unbending gravity.

"And that of the gods with you," the decurion replied.

"Are you from Jerusalem?"

"Yes."

"Your prisoner is young."

"In years, yes."

"May I ask what he has done?"

"He is an assassin."

The people repeated the word in astonishment, but Rabbi Joseph pursued his inquest.

"Is he a son of Israel?"

"He is a Jew," said the Roman, dryly.

The wavering pity of the by-standers came back.

"I know nothing of your tribes, but can speak of his family," the speaker continued. "You may have heard of a prince of Jerusalem named Hur—Ben-Hur, they called him. He lived in Herod's day."

"I have seen him," Joseph said.

"Well, this is his son."

Exclamations became general, and the decurion hastened to stop them.

"In the streets of Jerusalem, day before yesterday, he nearly killed the noble Gratus by flinging a tile upon his head from the roof of a palace—his father's, I believe."

There was a pause in the conversation during which the Nazarenes gazed at the young Ben-Hur as at a wild beast.

"Did he kill him?" asked the rabbi.

"No."

"He is under sentence?"

"Yes—the galleys for life."

"The Lord help him!" said Joseph, for once moved out of his stolidity.

Thereupon a youth who came up with Joseph, but had stood behind him unobserved, laid down an axe he had been carrying, and, going to the great stone standing by the well, took from it a pitcher of water. The action was so quiet that before the guard could interfere, had they been disposed to do so, he was stooping over the prisoner, and offering him drink.

The hand laid kindly upon his shoulder awoke the unfortunate Judah, and, looking up, he saw a face he never forgot—the face of a boy about his own age, shaded by locks of yellowish bright chestnut hair; a face lighted by dark-blue eyes, at the time so soft, so appealing, so full of love and holy purpose, that they had all the power of command and will. The spirit of the Jew, hardened though it was by days and nights of suffering, and so imbittered by wrong that its dreams of revenge took in all the world, melted under the stranger's look, and became as a child's. He put his lips to the pitcher, and drank long and deep. Not a word was said to him, nor did he say a word.

When the draught was finished, the hand that had been resting upon the sufferer's shoulder was placed upon his head, and stayed there in the dusty locks time enough to say a blessing; the stranger then returned the pitcher to its place on the stone, and, taking his axe again, went back to Rabbi Joseph. All eyes went

with him, the decurion's as well as those of
the villagers.

This was the end of the scene at the well.
When the men had drunk, and the horses, the
march was resumed. But the temper of the
decurion was not as it had been; he himself
raised the prisoner from the dust, and helped
him on a horse behind a soldier. The Naza-
renes went to their houses—among them Rabbi
Joseph and his apprentice.

And so, for the first time, Judah and the son
of Mary met and parted.

BOOK THIRD

"CLEOPATRA.... *Our size of sorrow,*
Proportion'd to our cause, must be as great
As that which makes it.—

Enter, below, DIOMEDES.

How now? is he dead?
DIOMEDES. *His death's upon him, but not dead.*"

—ANTONY AND CLEOPATRA
(Act iv., sc. xiii.).

CHAPTER I

QUINTUS ARRIUS GOES TO SEA

THE city of Misenum gave name to the promontory which it crowned, a few miles south-west of Naples. An account of ruins is all that remains of it now; yet in the year of our Lord 24—to which it is desirable to advance the reader —the place was one of the most important on the western coast of Italy.*

In the year mentioned, a traveller coming to the promontory to regale himself with the view there offered, would have mounted a wall, and, with the city at his back, looked over the bay of Neapolis, as charming then as now; and then, as now, he would have seen the matchless shore, the smoking cone, the sky and waves so softly, deeply blue, Ischia here and Capri yonder; from one to the other and back again, through the purpled air, his gaze would have sported; at last—for the eyes do weary of the beautiful as the palate with sweets—at last it would have dropped upon a spectacle which the modern tourist cannot see—half the reserve navy of Rome astir or at anchor below him. Thus regarded, Misenum

* The Roman government, it will be remembered, had two harbors in which great fleets were constantly kept—Ravenna and Misenum.

was a very proper place for three masters to meet, and at leisure parcel the world among them.

In the old time, moreover, there was a gateway in the wall at a certain point fronting the sea—an empty gate-way forming the outlet of a street which, after the exit, stretched itself, in the form of a broad mole, out many stadia into the waves.

The watchman on the wall above the gate-way was disturbed, one cool September morning, by a party coming down the street in noisy conversation. He gave one look, then settled into his drowse again.

There were twenty or thirty persons in the party, of whom the greater number were slaves with torches, which flamed little and smoked much, leaving on the air the perfume of the Indian nard. The masters walked in advance, arm-in-arm. One of them, apparently fifty years old, slightly bald, and wearing over his scant locks a crown of laurel, seemed, from the attentions paid him, the central object of some affectionate ceremony. They all sported ample togas of white wool broadly bordered with purple. A glance had sufficed the watchman. He knew, without question, they were of high rank, and escorting a friend to ship after a night of festivity. Further explanation will be found in the conversation they carried on.

"No, my Quintus," said one, speaking to him with the crown, "it is ill of Fortune to take thee from us so soon. Only yesterday thou didst return from the seas beyond the

Pillars. Why, thou hast not even got.back thy land legs."

"By Castor! if a man may swear a woman's oath," said another, somewhat worse of wine, "let us not lament. Our Quintus is but going to find what he lost last night. Dice on a rolling ship is not dice on shore—eh, Quintus?"

"Abuse not Fortune!" exclaimed a third. "She is not blind or fickle. At Antium, where our Arrius questions her, she answers him with nods, and at sea she abides with him holding the rudder. She takes him from us, but does she not always give him back with a new victory?"

"The Greeks are taking him away," another broke in. "Let us abuse them, not the gods. In learning to trade they forgot how to fight."

With these words, the party passed the gateway, and came upon the mole, with the bay before them beautiful in the morning light. To the veteran sailor the plash of the waves was like a greeting. He drew a long breath, as if the perfume of the water were sweeter than that of the nard, and held his hand aloft.

"My gifts were at Præneste, not Antium—and see! Wind from the west. Thanks, O Fortune, my mother!" he said, earnestly.

The friends all repeated the exclamation, and the slaves waved their torches.

"She comes—yonder!" he continued, pointing to a galley outside the mole. "What need has a sailor for other mistress? Is your Lucrece more graceful, my Caius?"

He gazed at the coming ship, and justified

his pride. A white sail was bent to the low
mast, and the oars dipped, arose, poised a mo-
ment, then dipped again, with wing-like action,
and in perfect time.

"Yes, spare the gods," he said, soberly, his
eyes fixed upon the vessel. "They send us
opportunities. Ours the fault if we fail. And
as for the Greeks, you forget, O my Lentulus,
the pirates I am going to punish are Greeks.
One victory over them is of more account
than a hundred over the Africans."

"Then thy way is to the Ægean?"

The sailor's eyes were full of his ship.

"What grace, what freedom! A bird hath
not less care for the fretting of the waves.
See!" he said, but almost immediately added,
"Thy pardon, my Lentulus. I am going to
the Ægean; and as my departure is so near,
I will tell the occasion—only keep it under the
rose. I would not that you abuse the duum-
vir when next you meet him. He is my friend.
The trade between Greece and Alexandria, as
ye may have heard, is hardly inferior to that
between Alexandria and Rome. The people
in that part of the world forgot to celebrate
the Cerealia, and Triptolemus paid them with
a harvest not worth the gathering. At all
events, the trade is so grown that it will not
brook interruption a day. Ye may also have
heard of the Chersonesan pirates, nested up in
the Euxine; none bolder, by the Bacchæ! Yes-
terday word came to Rome that, with a fleet,
they had rowed down the Bosphorus, sunk the
galleys off Byzantium and Chalcedon, swept

the Propontis, and, still unsated, burst through into the Ægean. The corn-merchants who have ships in the East Mediterranean are frightened. They had audience with the Emperor himself, and from Ravenna there go to-day a hundred galleys, and from Misenum "— he paused as if to pique the curiosity of his friends, and ended with an emphatic—" one."

"Happy Quintus! We congratulate thee!"

"The preferment forerunneth promotion. We salute thee duumvir; nothing less."

"Quintus Arrius, the duumvir, hath a better sound than Quintus Arrius, the tribune."

In such manner they showered him with congratulations.

"I am glad with the rest," said the bibulous friend, "very glad; but I must be practical, O my duumvir; and not until I know if promotion will help thee to knowledge of the tesseræ will I have an opinion as to whether the gods mean thee ill or good in this—this business."

"Thanks, many thanks!" Arrius replied, speaking to them collectively. "Had ye but lanterns, I would say ye were augurs. Perpol! I will go further, and show what master diviners ye are! See—and read."

From the folds of his toga he drew a roll of paper, and passed it to them, saying, "Received while at table last night from — Sejanus."

The name was already a great one in the Roman world; great, and not so infamous as it afterwards became.

"Sejanus!" they exclaimed, with one voice, closing in to read what the minister had written.

"Sejanus to C. Cæcilius Rufus, Duumvir.
 "ROME, XIX. Kal. Sept.

"Cæsar hath good report of Quintus Arrius, the tribune. In particular he hath heard of his valor, manifested in the western seas; insomuch that it is his will that the said Quintus be transferred instantly to the East.

"It is our Cæsar's will, further, that you cause a hundred triremes, of the first class, and full appointment, to be despatched without delay against the pirates who have appeared in the Ægean, and that Quintus be sent to command the fleet so despatched.

"Details are thine, my Cæcilius.

"The necessity is urgent, as thou wilt be advised by the reports enclosed for thy perusal and the information of the said Quintus. SEJANUS."

Arrius gave little heed to the reading. As the ship drew more plainly out of the perspective, she became more and more an attraction to him. The look with which he watched her was that of an enthusiast. At length he tossed the loosened folds of his toga in the air; in reply to the signal, over the aplustre, or fanlike fixture at the stern of the vessel, a scarlet flag was displayed; while several sailors appeared upon the bulwarks, and swung themselves hand over hand up the ropes to the antenna, or yard, and furled the sail. The bow was put round, and the time of the oars increased one-half; so that at racing speed she bore down directly towards him and his friends. He observed the manœuvring with a percepti-

ble brightening of the eyes. Her instant answer to the rudder, and the steadiness with which she kept her course, were especially noticeable as virtues to be relied upon in action.

" By the Nymphæ !" said one of the friends, giving back the roll, " we may not longer say our friend will be great; he is already great. Our love will now have famous things to feed upon. What more hast thou for us ?"

" Nothing more," Arrius replied, " What ye have of the affair is by this time old news in Rome, especially between the palace and the Forum. The duumvir is discreet ; what I am to do, where go to find my fleet, he will tell on the ship, where a sealed package is waiting me. If, however, ye have offerings for any of the altars to-day, pray the gods for a friend plying oar and sail somewhere in the direction of Sicily. But she is here, and will come to," he said, reverting to the vessel. " I have interest in her masters ; they will sail and fight with me. It is not an easy thing to lay ship side on a shore like this ; so let us judge their training and skill."

" What, is she new to thee ?"

" I never saw her before ; and, as yet, I know not if she will bring me one acquaintance."

" Is that well ?"

" It matters but little. We of the sea come to know each other quickly ; our loves, like our hates, are born of sudden dangers."

The vessel was of the class called naves liburnicæ—long, narrow, low in the water, and modelled for speed and quick manœuvre. The

bow was beautiful. A jet of water spun from its foot as she came on, sprinkling all the prow, which rose in graceful curvature twice a man's stature above the plane of the deck. Upon the bending of the sides were figures of Tritons blowing shells. Below the bow, fixed to the keel, and projecting forward under the water-line, was the rostrum, or beak, a device of solid wood, reinforced and armed with iron, in action used as a ram. A stout moulding extended from the bow the full length of the ship's sides, defining the bulwarks, which were taste-fully crenellated; below the moulding, in three rows, each covered with a cap or shield of bull-hide, were the holes in which the oars were worked—sixty on the right, sixty on the left. In further ornamentation, caducei leaned against the lofty prow. Two immense ropes passing across the bow marked the number of anchors stowed on the foredeck.

The simplicity of the upper works declared the oars the chief dependence of the crew. A mast, set a little forward of midship, was held by fore and back stays and shrouds fixed to rings on the inner side of the bulwarks. The tackle was that required for the management of one great square sail and the yard to which it was hung. Above the bulwarks the deck was visible.

Save the sailors who had reefed the sail, and yet lingered on the yard, but one man was to be seen by the party on the mole, and he stood by the prow helmeted and with a shield.

The hundred and twenty oaken blades, kept

white and shining by pumice and the constant
wash of the waves, rose and fell as if operated
by the same hand, and drove the galley for-
ward with a speed rivalling that of a modern
steamer.

So rapidly, and apparently so rashly, did she
come that the landsmen of the tribune's party
were alarmed. Suddenly the man by the prow
raised his hand with a peculiar gesture; where-
upon all the oars flew up, poised a moment in
the air, then fell straight down. The water
boiled and bubbled about them; the galley
shook in every timber, and stopped as if scared.
Another gesture of the hand, and again the
oars arose, feathered, and fell; but this time
those on the right, dropping towards the
stern, pushed forward; while those on the left,
dropping towards the bow, pulled backward.
Three times the oars thus pushed and pulled
against each other. Round to the right the
ship swung as upon a pivot; then, caught by
the wind, she settled gently broadside to the
mole.

The movement brought the stern to view,
with all its garniture—Tritons like those at the
bow; name in large raised letters; the rudder
at the side; the elevated platform upon which
the helmsman sat, a stately figure in full ar-
mor, his hand upon the rudder-rope; and the
aplustre, high, gilt, carved, and bent over the
helmsman like a great runcinate leaf.

In the midst of the rounding-to, a trumpet
was blown brief and shrill, and from the hatch-
ways out poured the marines, all in superb

equipment, brazen helms, burnished shields and javelins. While the fighting-men thus went to quarters as for action, the sailors proper climbed the shrouds and perched themselves along the yard. The officers and musicians took their posts. There was no shouting or needless noise. When the oars touched the mole, a bridge was sent out from the helmsman's deck. Then the tribune turned to his party and said, with a gravity he had not before shown:

"Duty now, O my friends."

He took the chaplet from his head and gave it to the dice-player.

"Take thou the myrtle, O favorite of the tesseræ!" he said. "If I return, I will seek my sestertii again; if I am not victor, I will not return. Hang the crown in thy atrium."

To the company he opened his arms, and they came one by one and received his parting embrace.

"The gods go with thee, O Quintus!" they said.

"Farewell," he replied.

To the slaves waving their torches he waved his hand; then he turned to the waiting ship, beautiful with ordered ranks and crested helms and shields and javelins. As he stepped upon the bridge, the trumpets sounded, and over the aplustre rose the vexillum purpureum, or pennant of a commander of a fleet.

CHAPTER II
AT THE OAR

HE tribune, standing upon the helms-man's deck with the order of the duumvir open in his hand, spoke to the chief of the rowers.*

"What force hast thou?"

"Of oarsmen, two hundred and fifty-two: ten supernumeraries."

"Making reliefs of—"

"Eighty-four."

"And thy habit?"

"It has been to take off and put on every two hours."

The tribune mused a moment.

"The division is hard, and I will reform it, but not now. The oars may not rest day or night."

Then to the sailing-master he said:

"The wind is fair. Let the sail help the oars."

When the two thus addressed were gone, he turned to the chief pilot.†

"What service hast thou had?"

"Two-and-thirty years."

"In what seas chiefly?"

"Between our Rome and the East."

"Thou art the man I would have chosen."

* Called hortator. † Called rector.

219

The tribune looked at his orders again.

"Past the Camponellan cape, the course will be to Messina. Beyond that, follow the bend of the Calabrian shore till Melito is on thy left, then— Knowest thou the stars that govern in the Ionian Sea?"

"I know them well."

"Then from Melito course eastward for Cythera. The gods willing, I will not anchor until in the Bay of Antemona. The duty is urgent. I rely upon thee."

A prudent man was Arrius—prudent, and of the class which, while enriching the altars at Præneste and Antium, was of opinion, nevertheless, that the favor of the blind goddess depended more upon the votary's care and judgment than upon his gifts and vows. All night as master of the feast he had sat at table drinking and playing; yet the odor of the sea returned him to the mood of the sailor, and he would not rest until he knew his ship. Knowledge leaves no room for chances. Having begun with the chief of the rowers, the sailing-master, and the pilot, in company with the other officers—the commander of the marines, the keeper of the stores, the master of the machines, the overseer of the kitchen or fires—he passed through the several quarters. Nothing escaped his inspection. When he was through, of the community crowded within the narrow walls he alone knew perfectly all there was of material preparation for the voyage and its possible incidents; and, finding the preparation complete, there was left him but one thing

further—thorough knowledge of the person-
nel of his command. As this was the most
delicate and difficult part of his task, requiring
much time, he set about it his own way.

At noon that day the galley was skimming
the sea off Pæstum. The wind was yet from
the west, filling the sail to the master's con-
tent. The watches had been established. On
the foredeck the altar had been set and sprin-
kled with salt and barley, and before it the
tribune had offered solemn prayers to Jove and
to Neptune and all the Oceanidæ, and, with
vows, poured the wine and burned the in-
cense. And now, the better to study his men
he was seated in the great cabin, a very mar-
tial figure.

The cabin, it should be stated, was the cen-
tral compartment of the galley, in extent quite
sixty-five by thirty feet, and lighted by three
broad hatchways. A row of stanchions ran
from end to end, supporting the roof, and near
the centre the mast was visible, all bristling
with axes and spears and javelins. To each
hatchway there were double stairs descending
right and left, with a pivotal arrangement at
the top to allow the lower ends to be hitched
to the ceiling; and, as these were now raised,
the compartment had the appearance of a sky-
lighted hall.

The reader will understand readily that this
was the heart of the ship, the home of all
aboard — eating-room, sleeping-chamber, field
of exercise, lounging-place off duty — uses
made possible by the laws which reduced life

there to minute details and a routine relentless as death.

At the after-end of the cabin there was a platform, reached by several steps. Upon it the chief of the rowers sat; in front of him a sounding-table, upon which, with a gavel, he beat time for the oarsmen; at his right a clepsydra, or water-clock, to measure the reliefs and watches. Above him, on a higher platform, well guarded by gilded railing, the tribune had his quarters, overlooking everything, and furnished with a couch, a table, and a cathedra, or chair, cushioned, and with arms and high back —articles which the imperial dispensation permitted of the utmost elegance.

Thus at ease, lounging in the great chair, swaying with the motion of the vessel, the military cloak half draping his tunic, sword in belt, Arrius kept watchful eye over his command, and was as closely watched by them. He saw critically everything in view, but dwelt longest upon the rowers. The reader would doubtless have done the same : only he would have looked with much sympathy, while, as is the habit with masters, the tribune's mind ran forward of what he saw, inquiring for results.

The spectacle was simple enough of itself. Along the sides of the cabin, fixed to the ship's timbers, were what at first appeared to be three rows of benches; a closer view, however, showed them a succession of rising banks, in each of which the second bench was behind and above the first one, and the third above and

222

behind the second. To accommodate the sixty rowers on a side, the space devoted to them permitted nineteen banks separated by intervals of one yard, with a twentieth bank divided so that what would have been its upper seat or bench was directly above the lower seat of the first bank. The arrangement gave each rower when at work ample room, if he timed his movements with those of his associates, the principle being that of soldiers marching with cadenced step in close order. The arrangement also allowed a multiplication of banks, limited only by the length of the galley.

As to the rowers, those upon the first and second benches sat, while those upon the third, having longer oars to work, were suffered to stand. The oars were loaded with lead in the handles, and near the point of balance hung to pliable thongs, making possible the delicate touch called feathering, but, at the same time, increasing the need of skill, since an eccentric wave might at any moment catch a heedless fellow and hurl him from his seat. Each oar-hole was a vent through which the laborer opposite it had his plenty of sweet air. Light streamed down upon him from the grating which formed the floor of the passage between the deck and the bulwark over his head. In some respects, therefore, the condition of the men might have been much worse. Still, it must not be imagined that there was any pleasantness in their lives. Communication between them was not allowed. Day after day they filled their places without speech; in

hours of labor they could not see each other's
faces; their short respites were given to sleep
and the snatching of food. They never laugh-
ed; no one ever heard one of them sing. What
is the use of tongues when a sigh or a groan
will tell all men feel while, perforce, they think
in silence? Existence with the poor wretches
was like a stream underground sweeping slow-
ly, laboriously on to its outlet, wherever that
might chance to be.

O Son of Mary! The sword has now a
heart—and thine the glory! So now; but, in
the days of which we are writing, for captivity
there was drudgery on walls, and in the streets
and mines, and the galleys both of war and
commerce were insatiable. When Druilius won
the first sea-fight for his country, Romans plied
the oars, and the glory was to the rower not
less than the marine. These benches which now
we are trying to see as they were testified to
the change come with conquest, and illustrat-
ed both the policy and the prowess of Rome.
Nearly all the nations had sons there, mostly
prisoners of war, chosen for their brawn and
endurance. In one place a Briton; before him
a Libyan; behind him a Crimean. Elsewhere
a Scythian, a Gaul, and a Thebasite. Roman
convicts cast down to consort with Goths and
Longobardi, Jews, Ethiopians, and barbarians
from the shores of Mæotis. Here an Athenian,
there a red-haired savage from Hibernia, yon-
der blue-eyed giants of the Cimbri.

In the labor of the rowers there was not
enough art to give occupation to their minds,

224

rude and simple as they were. The reach forward, the pull, the feathering the blade, the dip, were all there was of it; motions most perfect when most automatic. Even the care forced upon them by the sea outside grew in time to be a thing instinctive rather than of thought. So, as the result of long service, the poor wretches became imbruted—patient, spiritless, obedient—creatures of vast muscle and exhausted intellects, who lived upon recollections generally few but dear, and at last lowered into the semiconscious alchemic state wherein misery turns to habit, and the soul takes on incredible endurance.

From right to left, hour after hour, the tribune, swaying in his easy-chair, turned with thought of everything rather than the wretchedness of the slaves upon the benches. Their motions, precise, and exactly the same on both sides of the vessel, after a while became monotonous; and then he amused himself singling out individuals. With his stylus he made note of objections, thinking, if all went well, he would find among the pirates of whom he was in search better men for the places.

There was no need of keeping the proper names of the slaves brought to the galleys as to their graves; so, for convenience, they were usually identified by the numerals painted upon the benches to which they were assigned. As the sharp eyes of the great man moved from seat to seat on either hand, they came at last to number sixty, which, as has been said, belonged properly to the last bank on the left-

hand side, but, wanting room aft, had been fixed above the first bench of the first bank. There they rested.

The bench of number sixty was slightly above the level of the platform, and but a few feet away. The light glinting through the grating over his head gave the rower fairly to the tribune's view — erect, and, like all his fellows, naked, except a cincture about the loins. There were, however, some points in his favor. He was very young, not more than twenty. Furthermore, Arrius was not merely given to dice; he was a connoisseur of men physically, and when ashore indulged a habit of visiting the gymnasia to see and admire the most famous athletæ. From some professor, doubtless, he had caught the idea that strength was as much of the quality as the quantity of the muscle, while superiority in performance required a certain mind as well as strength. Having adopted the doctrine, like most men with a hobby, he was always looking for illustrations to support it.

The reader may well believe that while the tribune, in the search for the perfect, was often called upon to stop and study, he was seldom perfectly satisfied—in fact, very seldom held as long as on this occasion.

In the beginning of each movement of the oar, the rower's body and face were brought into profile view from the platform; the movement ended with the body reversed, and in a pushing posture. The grace and ease of the action at first suggested a doubt of the honesty

HOUSE OF SAINT VERONICA, JERUSALEM

of the effort put forth; but it was speedily dismissed; the firmness with which the oar was held while in the reach forward, its bending under the push, were proofs of the force applied; not that only, they as certainly proved the rower's art, and put the critic in the great arm-chair in search of the combination of strength and cleverness which was the central idea of his theory.

In course of the study, Arrius observed the subject's youth; wholly unconscious of tenderness on that account, he also observed that he seemed of good height, and that his limbs, upper and nether, were singularly perfect. The arms, perhaps, were too long, but the objection was well hidden under a mass of muscle, which, in some movements, swelled and knotted like kinking cords. Every rib in the round body was discernible; yet the leanness was the healthful reduction so strained after in the palæstræ. And altogether there was in the rower's action a certain harmony which, besides addressing itself to the tribune's theory, stimulated both his curiosity and general interest.

Very soon he found himself waiting to catch a view of the man's face in full. The head was shapely and balanced upon a neck broad at the base, but of exceeding pliancy and grace. The features in profile were of Oriental outline, and of that delicacy of expression which has always been thought a sign of blood and sensitive spirit. With these observations, the tribune's interest in the subject deepened.

227

"By the gods," he said to himself, "the fellow impresses me! He promises well. I will know more of him."

Directly the tribune caught the view he wished—the rower turned and looked at him.

"A Jew! and a boy!"

Under the gaze then fixed steadily upon him, the large eyes of the slave grew larger—the blood surged to his very brows—the blade lingered in his hands. But instantly, with an angry crash, down fell the gavel of the hortator. The rower started, withdrew his face from the inquisitor, and, as if personally chidden, dropped the oar half feathered. When he glanced again at the tribune, he was vastly more astonished—he was met with a kindly smile.

Meantime the galley entered the Strait of Messina, and, skimming past the city of that name, was after a while turned eastward, leaving the cloud over Ætna in the sky astern.

Often as Arrius returned to his platform in the cabin he returned to study the rower, and he kept saying to himself, "The fellow hath a spirit. A Jew is not a barbarian. I will know more of him."

CHAPTER III

ARRIUS AND BEN-HUR ON DECK

THE fourth day out, and the Astræa—
so the galley was named—speeding
through the Ionian Sea. The sky
was clear, and the wind blew as if
bearing the good-will of all the gods.

As it was possible to overtake the fleet be-
fore reaching the bay east of the island of Cy-
thera, designated for assemblage, Arrius, some-
what impatient, spent much time on deck. He
took note diligently of matters pertaining to
his ship, and as a rule was well pleased. In
the cabin, swinging in the great chair, his
thought continually reverted to the rower on
number sixty.

"Knowest thou the man just come from yon
bench?" he at length asked of the hortator.

A relief was going on at the moment.

"From number sixty?" returned the chief.

"Yes."

The chief looked sharply at the rower then
going forward.

"As thou knowest," he replied, "the ship is
but a month from the maker's hand, and the
men are as new to me as the ship."

"He is a Jew," Arrius remarked, thought-
fully.

"The noble Quintus is shrewd."

"He is very young," Arrius continued.

229

"But our best rower," said the other. "I have seen his oar bend almost to breaking."

"Of what disposition is he?"

"He is obedient; further I know not. Once he made request of me."

"For what?"

"He wished me to change him alternately from the right to the left."

"Did he give a reason?"

"He had observed that the men who are confined to one side become misshapen. He also said that some day of storm or battle there might be sudden need to change him, and he might then be unserviceable."

"Perpol! The idea is new. What else hast thou observed of him?"

"He is cleanly above his companions."

"In that he is Roman," said Arrius, approvingly. "Have you nothing of his history?"

"Not a word."

The tribune reflected a while, and turned to go to his own seat.

"If I should be on deck when his time is up," he paused to say, "send him to me. Let him come alone."

About two hours later Arrius stood under the aplustre of the galley; in the mood of one who, seeing himself carried swiftly towards an event of mighty import, has nothing to do but wait—the mood in which philosophy vests an even-minded man with the utmost calm, and is ever so serviceable. The pilot sat with a hand upon the rope by which the rudder paddles, one on each side of the vessel, were man-

aged. In the shade of the sail some sailors
lay asleep, and up on the yard there was a look-
out. Lifting his eyes from the solarium set
under the aplustre for reference in keeping the
course, Arrius beheld the rower approaching.

"The chief called thee the noble Arrius, and
said it was thy will that I should seek thee
here. I have come."

Arrius surveyed the figure, tall, sinewy, glis-
tening in the sun, and tinted by the rich red
blood within—surveyed it admiringly, and with
a thought of the arena; yet the manner was
not without effect upon him: there was in the
voice a suggestion of life at least partly spent
under refining influences; the eyes were clear
and open, and more curious than defiant. To
the shrewd, demanding, masterful glance bent
upon it, the face gave back nothing to mar its
youthful comeliness—nothing of accusation or
sullenness or menace, only the signs which a
great sorrow long borne imprints as time mel-
lows the surface of pictures. In tacit acknowl-
edgment of the effect, the Roman spoke as an
older man to a younger, not as a master to a
slave.

"The hortator tells me thou art his best
rower."

"The hortator is very kind," the rower an-
swered.

"Hast thou seen much service?"

"About three years."

"At the oars?"

"I cannot recall a day of rest from them."

"The labor is hard; few men bear it a year

231

without breaking, and thou — thou art but a boy."

"The noble Arrius forgets that the spirit hath much to do with endurance. By its help the weak sometimes thrive, when the strong perish."

"From thy speech, thou art a Jew."

"My ancestors further back than the first Roman were Hebrews."

"The stubborn pride of thy race is not lost in thee," said Arrius, observing a flush upon the rower's face.

"Pride is never so loud as when in chains."

"What cause hast thou for pride?"

"That I am a Jew."

Arrius smiled.

"I have not been to Jerusalem," he said; "but I have heard of its princes. I knew one of them. He was a merchant, and sailed the seas. He was fit to have been a king. Of what degree art thou?"

"I must answer thee from the bench of a galley. I am of the degree of slaves. My father was a prince of Jerusalem, and, as a merchant, he sailed the seas. He was known and honored in the guest-chamber of the great Augustus."

"His name?"

"Ithamar, of the house of Hur."

The tribune raised his hand in astonishment.

"A son of Hur—thou?"

After a silence, he asked,

"What brought thee here?"

Judah lowered his head, and his breast labored hard. When his feelings were sufficiently mastered, he looked the tribune in the face, and answered,

"I was accused of attempting to assassinate Valerius Gratus, the procurator."

"Thou!" cried Arrius, yet more amazed, and retreating a step. "Thou that assassin! All Rome rang with the story. It came to my ship in the river by Lodinum."

The two regarded each other silently.

"I thought the family of Hur blotted from the earth," said Arrius, speaking first.

A flood of tender recollections carried the young man's pride away; tears shone upon his cheeks.

"Mother—mother! And my little Tirzah! Where are they? O tribune, noble tribune, if thou knowest anything of them"—he clasped his hands in appeal—"tell me all thou knowest. Tell me if they are living—if living, where are they? and in what condition? Oh, I pray thee, tell me!"

He drew nearer Arrius, so near that his hands touched the cloak where it dropped from the latter's folded arms.

"The horrible day is three years gone," he continued—"three years, O tribune, and every hour a whole lifetime of misery—a lifetime in a bottomless pit with death, and no relief but in labor—and in all that time not a word from any one, not a whisper. Oh, if, in being forgotten, we could only forget! If only I could hide from that scene—my sister torn

from me, my mother's last look! I have felt the plague's breath, and the shock of ships in battle; I have heard the tempest lashing the sea, and laughed, though others prayed: death would have been a riddance. Bend the oar—yes, in the strain of mighty effort trying to escape the haunting of what that day occurred. Think what little will help me. Tell me they are dead, if no more, for happy they cannot be while I am lost. I have heard them call me in the night; I have seen them on the water walking. Oh, never anything so true as my mother's love! And Tirzah—her breath was as the breath of white lilies. She was the youngest branch of the palm—so fresh, so tender, so graceful, so beautiful! She made my day all morning. She came and went in music. And mine was the hand that laid them low! I—"

"Dost thou admit thy guilt?" asked Arrius, sternly.

The change that came upon Ben-Hur was wonderful to see, it was so instant and extreme. The voice sharpened; the hands arose tight-clinched; every fibre thrilled; his eyes inflamed.

"Thou hast heard of the God of my fathers," he said; "of the infinite Jehovah. By his truth and almightiness, and by the love with which he hath followed Israel from the beginning, I swear I am innocent!"

The tribune was much moved.

"O noble Roman!" continued Ben-Hur, "give me a little faith, and into my darkness, deeper darkening every day, send a light!"

Arrius turned away, and walked the deck.

"Didst thou not have a trial?" he asked, stopping suddenly.

"No!"

The Roman raised his head, surprised.

"No trial—no witnesses! Who passed judgment upon thee?"

Romans, it should be remembered, were at no time such lovers of the law and its forms as in the ages of their decay.

"They bound me with cords, and dragged me to a vault in the Tower. I saw no one. No one spoke to me. Next day soldiers took me to the sea-side. I have been a galley-slave ever since."

"What couldst thou have proven?"

"I was a boy, too young to be a conspirator. Gratus was a stranger to me. If I had meant to kill him, that was not the time or the place. He was riding in the midst of a legion, and it was broad day. I could not have escaped. I was of a class most friendly to Rome. My father had been distinguished for his services to the emperor. We had a great estate to lose. Ruin was certain to myself, my mother, my sister. I had no cause for malice, while every consideration — property, family, life, conscience, the Law — to a son of Israel as the breath of his nostrils—would have stayed my hand, though the foul intent had been ever so strong. I was not mad. Death was preferable to shame; and, believe me, I pray, it is so yet.'

"Who was with thee when the blow was struck?"

235

"I was on the house-top—my father's house.
Tirzah was with me—at my side—the soul of
gentleness. Together we leaned over the par-
apet to see the legion pass. A tile gave way
under my hand, and fell upon Gratus. I
thought I had killed him. Ah, what horror I
felt!"

"Where was thy mother?"

"In her chamber below."

"What became of her?"

Ben-Hur clinched his hands, and drew a
breath like a gasp.

"I do not know. I saw them drag her
away—that is all I know. Out of the house
they drove every living thing, even the dumb
cattle, and they sealed the gates. The pur-
pose was that she should not return. I, too,
ask for her. Oh for one word! She, at least,
was innocent. I can forgive—but I pray thy
pardon, noble tribune! A slave like me should
not talk of forgiveness or of revenge. I am
bound to an oar for life."

Arrius listened intently. He brought all his
experience with slaves to his aid. If the feel-
ing shown in this instance were assumed, the
acting was perfect; on the other hand, if it were
real, the Jew's innocence might not be doubt-
ed; and if he were innocent, with what blind
fury the power had been exercised! A whole
family blotted out to atone an accident! The
thought shocked him.

There is no wiser providence than that our
occupations, however rude or bloody, cannot
wear us out morally; that such qualities as

justice and mercy, if they really possess us, continue to live on under them, like flowers under the snow. The tribune could be inexorable, else he had not been fit for the usages of his calling; he could also be just; and to excite his sense of wrong was to put him in the way to right the wrong. The crews of the ships in which he served came after a time to speak of him as the good tribune. Shrewd readers will not want a better definition of his character.

In this instance there were many circumstances certainly in the young man's favor, and some to be supposed. Possibly Arrius knew Valerius Gratus without loving him. Possibly he had known the elder Hur. In the course of his appeal, Judah had asked him of that; and, as will be noticed, he had made no reply.

For once the tribune was at loss, and hesitated. His power was ample. He was monarch of the ship. His prepossessions all moved him to mercy, His faith was won. Yet, he said to himself, there was no haste—or, rather, there was haste to Cythera; the best rower could not then be spared; he would wait; he would learn more; he would at least be sure this was the prince Ben-Hur, and that he was of a right disposition. Ordinarily, slaves were liars.

"It is enough," he said aloud. "Go back to thy place."

Ben-Hur bowed; looked once more into the master's face, but saw nothing for hope. He turned away slowly, looked back, and said,

"If thou dost think of me again, O tribune,
let it not be lost in thy mind that I prayed
thee only for word of my people — mother,
sister."

He moved on.

Arrius followed him with admiring eyes.

"Perpol!" he thought. "With teaching,
what a man for the arena! What a runner!
Ye gods! what an arm for the sword or the
cestus!—Stay!" he said, aloud.

Ben-Hur stopped, and the tribune went to
him.

"If thou wert free, what wouldst thou do?"

"The noble Arrius mocks me!" Judah said,
with trembling lips.

"No; by the gods, no!"

"Then I will answer gladly. I would give
myself to duty the first of life. I would know
no other. I would know no rest until my
mother and Tirzah were restored to home. I
would give every day and hour to their hap-
piness. I would wait upon them; never a slave
more faithful. They have lost much, but, by
the God of my fathers, I would find them
more!"

The answer was unexpected by the Roman.
For a moment he lost his purpose.

"I spoke to thy ambition," he said, recover-
ing. "If thy mother and sister were dead, or
not to be found, what wouldst thou do?"

A distinct pallor overspread Ben-Hur's face,
and he looked over the sea. There was a
struggle with some strong feeling; when it was
conquered, he turned to the tribune.

238

"What pursuit would I follow?" he asked.

"Yes."

"Tribune, I will tell thee truly. Only the night before the dreadful day of which I have spoken, I obtained permission to be a soldier. I am of the same mind yet; and, as in all the earth there is but one school of war, thither I would go."

"The palæstra!" exclaimed Arrius.

"No; a Roman camp."

"But thou must first acquaint thyself with the use of arms."

Now a master may never safely advise a slave. Arrius saw his indiscretion, and, in a breath, chilled his voice and manner.

"Go now," he said, "and do not build upon what has passed between us. Perhaps I do but play with thee. Or "—he looked away musingly—"or, if thou dost think of it with any hope, choose between the renown of a gladiator and the service of a soldier. The former may come of the favor of the emperor; there is no reward for thee in the latter. Thou art not a Roman. Go!"

A short while after Ben-Hur was upon his bench again.

A man's task is always light if his heart is light. Handling the oar did not seem so toilsome to Judah. A hope had come to him, like a singing bird. He could hardly see the visitor or hear its song; that it was there, though, he knew; his feelings told him so. The caution of the tribune — "Perhaps I do but play with thee"—was dismissed often as it recurred

to his mind. That he had been called by the
great man and asked his story was the bread
upon which he fed his hungry spirit. Surely
something good would come of it. The light
about his bench was clear and bright with
promises, and he prayed.

"O God! I am a true son of the Israel thou
hast so loved! Help me, I pray thee!"

CHAPTER IV
"NO. 60"

ON the bay of Antemona, east of Cythe-
ra the island, the hundred galleys
assembled. There the tribune gave
one day to inspection. He sailed
then to Naxos, the largest of the Cyclades,
midway the coasts of Greece and Asia, like a
great stone planted in the centre of a highway,
from which he could challenge everything that
passed; at the same time, he would be in posi-
tion to go after the pirates instantly, whether
they were in the Ægean or out on the Medi-
terranean.

As the fleet, in order, rowed in towards the
mountain-shores of the island, a galley was
descried coming from the north. Arrius went
to meet it: she proved to be a transport just
from Byzantium, and from her commander he
learned the particulars of which he stood in
most need.

The pirates were from all the farther shores
of the Euxine. Even Tanais, at the mouth of

240

the river which was supposed to feed Palus
Mæotis, was represented among them. Their
preparations had been with the greatest se-
crecy. The first known of them was their ap-
pearance off the entrance to the Thracian Bos-
phorus, followed by the destruction of the fleet
in station there. Thence to the outlet of the
Hellespont everything afloat had fallen their
prey. There were quite sixty galleys in the
squadron, all well manned and supplied. A
few were biremes, the rest stout triremes. A
Greek was in command, and the pilots, said to
be familiar with all the Eastern seas, were
Greek. The plunder had been incalculable.
The panic, consequently, was not on the sea
alone; cities, with closed gates, sent their peo-
ple nightly to the walls. Traffic had almost
ceased.

Where were the pirates now?

To this question, of most interest to Arrius,
he received answer.

After sacking Hephæstia, on the island of
Lemnos, the enemy had coursed across to the
Thessalian group, and, by last account, disap-
peared in the gulfs between Eubœa and Hel-
las.

Such were the tidings.

Then the people of the island, drawn to the
hill-tops by the rare spectacle of a hundred
ships careering in united squadron, beheld the
advance division suddenly turn to the north,
and the others follow, wheeling upon the same
point like cavalry in a column. News of the
piratical descent had reached them, and now,

watching the white sails until they faded from
sight up between Rhene and Syros, the thought-
ful among them took comfort, and were grate-
ful. What Rome seized with strong hand she
always defended : in return for their taxes, she
gave them safety.

The tribune was more than pleased with
the enemy's movements ; he was doubly thank-
ful to Fortune. She had brought swift and
sure intelligence, and had lured his foes into
the waters where, of all others, destruction was
most assured. He knew the havoc one galley
could play in a broad sea like the Mediterra-
nean, and the difficulty of finding and over-
hauling her ; he knew, also, how those very
circumstances would enhance the service and
glory if, at one blow, he could put a finish to
the whole piratical array.

If the reader will take a map of Greece and
the Ægean, he will notice the island of Eubœa
lying along the classic coast like a rampart
against Asia, leaving a channel between it and
the continent quite a hundred and twenty
miles in length, and scarcely an average of eight
in width. The inlet on the north had admit-
ted the fleet of Xerxes, and now it received
the bold raiders from the Euxine. The towns
along the Pelasgic and Meliac gulfs were rich
and their plunder seductive. All things con-
sidered, therefore, Arrius judged that the rob-
bers might be found somewhere below Ther-
mopylæ. Welcoming the chance, he resolved
to enclose them north and south, to do which
not an hour could be lost ; even the fruits and

wines and women of Naxos must be left behind. So he sailed away without stop or tack until, a little before nightfall, Mount Ocha was seen upreared against the sky, and the pilot reported the Eubœan coast.

At a signal the fleet rested upon its oars. When the movement was resumed, Arrius led a division of fifty of the galleys, intending to take them up the channel, while another division, equally strong, turned their prows to the outer or seaward side of the island, with orders to make all haste to the upper inlet, and descend sweeping the waters.

To be sure, neither division was equal in number to the pirates; but each had advantages in compensation, among them, by no means least, a discipline impossible to a lawless horde, however brave. Besides, it was a shrewd count on the tribune's side, if, peradventure, one should be defeated, the other would find the enemy shattered by his victory, and in condition to be easily overwhelmed.

Meantime Ben-Hur kept his bench, relieved every six hours. The rest in the Bay of Antemona had freshened him, so that the oar was not troublesome, and the chief on the platform found no fault.

People, generally, are not aware of the ease of mind there is in knowing where they are, and where they are going. The sensation of being lost is a keen distress; still worse is the feeling one has in driving blindly into unknown places. Custom had dulled the feeling with Ben-Hur, but only measurably. Pulling

away hour after hour, sometimes days and
nights together, sensible all the time that the
galley was gliding swiftly along some of the
many tracks of the broad sea, the longing to
know where he was, and whither going, was
always present with him; but now it seemed
quickened by the hope which had come to new
life in his breast since the interview with the
tribune. The narrower the abiding-place hap-
pens to be, the more intense is the longing;
and so he found. He seemed to hear every
sound of the ship in labor, and listened to each
one as if it were a voice come to tell him
something; he looked to the grating overhead,
and through it into the light of which so
small a portion was his, expecting, he knew not
what; and many times he caught himself on
the point of yielding to the impulse to speak
to the chief on the platform, than which no
circumstance of battle would have astonished
that dignitary more.

In his long service, by watching the shifting
of the meagre sunbeams upon the cabin floor
when the ship was under way, he had come to
know, generally, the quarter into which she
was sailing. This, of course, was only of clear
days like those good-fortune was sending the
tribune. The experience had not failed him
in the period succeeding the departure from
Cythera. Thinking they were tending tow-
ards the old Judean country, he was sensitive
to every variation from the course. With a
pang, he had observed the sudden change
northward which, as has been noticed, took

place near Naxos : the cause, however, he could not even conjecture ; for it must be remembered that, in common with his fellow-slaves, he knew nothing of the situation, and had no interest in the voyage. His place was at the oar, and he was held there inexorably, whether at anchor or under sail. Once only in three years had he been permitted an outlook from the deck. The occasion we have seen. He had no idea that, following the vessel he was helping drive, there was a great squadron close at hand and in beautiful order ; no more did he know the object of which it was in pursuit.

When the sun, going down, withdrew his last ray from the cabin, the galley still held northward. Night fell, yet Ben-Hur could discern no change. About that time the smell of incense floated down the gangways from the deck.

"The tribune is at the altar," he thought. "Can it be we are going into battle ?"

He became observant.

Now he had been in many battles without having seen one. From his bench he had heard them above and about him, until he was familiar with all their notes, almost as a singer with a song. So, too, he had become acquainted with many of the preliminaries of an engagement, of which, with a Roman as well as a Greek, the most invariable was the sacrifice to the gods. The rites were the same as those performed at the beginning of a voyage, and to him, when noticed, they were always an admonition.

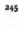

A battle, it should be observed, possessed for him and his fellow-slaves of the oar an interest unlike that of the sailor and marine; it came, not of the danger encountered, but of the fact that defeat, if survived, might bring an alteration of condition—possibly freedom—at least a change of masters, which might be for the better.

In good time the lanterns were lighted and hung by the stairs, and the tribune came down from the deck. At his word the marines put on their armor. At his word again, the machines were looked to, and spears, javelins, and arrows, in great sheaves, brought and laid upon the floor, together with jars of inflammable oil, and baskets of cotton balls wound loose like the wicking of candles. And when, finally, Ben-Hur saw the tribune mount his platform and don his armor, and get his helmet and shield out, the meaning of the preparations might not be any longer doubted, and he made ready for the last ignominy of his service.

To every bench, as a fixture, there was a chain with heavy anklets. These the hortator proceeded to lock upon the oarsmen, going from number to number, leaving no choice but to obey, and, in event of disaster, no possibility of escape.

In the cabin, then, a silence fell, broken at first, only by the sough of the oars turning in 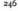 the leathern cases. Every man upon the benches felt the shame, Ben-Hur more keenly than his companions. He would have put it

246

away at any price. Soon the clanking of the
fetters notified him of the progress the chief
was making in his round. He would come to
him in turn; but would not the tribune inter-
pose for him?

The thought may be set down to vanity or
selfishness, as the reader pleases; it certainly,
at that moment, took possession of Ben-Hur.
He believed the Roman would interpose; any-
how, the circumstance would test the man's
feelings. If, intent upon the battle, he would
but think of him, it would be proof of his
opinion formed—proof that he had been tac-
itly promoted above his associates in misery
—such proof as would justify hope.

Ben-Hur waited anxiously. The interval
seemed like an age. At every turn of the oar
he looked towards the tribune, who, his simple
preparations made, lay down upon the couch
and composed himself to rest; whereupon num-
ber sixty chid himself, and laughed grimly, and
resolved not to look that way again.

The hortator approached. Now he was at
number one—the rattle of the iron links sound-
ed horribly. At last number sixty! Calm
from despair, Ben-Hur held his oar at poise,
and gave his foot to the officer. Then the trib-
une stirred—sat up—beckoned to the chief.

A strong revulsion seized the Jew. From
the hortator, the great man glanced at him;
and when he dropped his oar all the section
of the ship on his side seemed aglow. He
heard nothing of what was said; enough that
the chain hung idly from its staple in the

bench, and that the chief, going to his seat, began to beat the sounding - board. The notes of the gavel were never so like music. With his breast against the leaded handle, he pushed with all his might—pushed until the shaft bent as if about to break.

The chief went to the tribune, and, smiling, pointed to number sixty.

"What strength!" he said.

"And what spirit!" the tribune answered. "Perpol! He is better without the irons. Put them on him no more."

So saying, he stretched himself upon the couch again.

The ship sailed on hour after hour under the oars in water scarcely rippled by the wind. And the people not on duty slept, Arrius in his place, the marines on the floor.

Once—twice—Ben-Hur was relieved; but he could not sleep. Three years of night, and through the darkness a sunbeam at last! At sea adrift and lost, and now land! Dead so long, and lo! the thrill and stir of resurrection. Sleep was not for such an hour. Hope deals with the future; now and the past are but servants that wait on her with impulse and suggestive circumstance. Starting from the favor of the tribune, she carried him forward indefinitely. The wonder is, not that things so purely imaginative as the results she points us to can make us so happy, but that we can receive them as so real. They must be as gorgeous poppies under the influence of which, under the crimson and purple and gold, reason

lies down the while, and is not. Sorrows assuaged; home and the fortunes of his house restored; mother and sister in his arms once more—such were the central ideas which made him happier that moment than he had ever been. That he was rushing, as on wings, into horrible battle had, for the time, nothing to do with his thoughts. The things thus in hope were unmixed with doubts—they were. Hence his joy so full, so perfect, there was no room in his heart for revenge. Messala, Gratus, Rome, and all the bitter, passionate memories connected with them, were as dead plagues—miasms of the earth above which he floated, far and safe, listening to singing stars.

The deeper darkness before the dawn was upon the waters, and all things going well with the Astræa, when a man, descending from the deck, walked swiftly to the platform where the tribune slept, and awoke him. Arrius arose, put on his helmet, sword, and shield, and went to the commander of the marines.

"The pirates are close by. Up and ready!" he said, and passed to the stairs, calm, confident, insomuch that one might have thought, "Happy fellow! Apicius has set a feast for him."

CHAPTER V

THE SEA-FIGHT

VERY soul aboard, even the ship, awoke. Officers went to their quarters. The marines took arms, and were led out, looking in all respects like legionaries. Sheaves of arrows and armfuls of javelins were carried on deck. By the central stairs the oil-tanks and fire-balls were set ready for use. Additional lanterns were lighted. Buckets were filled with water. The rowers in relief assembled under guard in front of the chief. As Providence would have it, Ben-Hur was one of the latter. Overhead he heard the muffled noise of the final preparations — of the sailors furling sail, spreading the nettings, unslinging the machines, and hanging the armor of bull-hide over the side. Presently quiet settled about the galley again; quiet full of vague dread and expectation, which, interpreted, means ready.

At a signal passed down from the deck, and communicated to the hortator by a petty officer stationed on the stairs, all at once the oars stopped.

What did it mean?

Of the hundred and twenty slaves chained to the benches, not one but asked himself the question. They were without incentive. Patriotism, love of honor, sense of duty, brought

them no inspiration. They felt the thrill common to men rushed helpless and blind into danger. It may be supposed the dullest of them, poising his oar, thought of all that might happen, yet could promise himself nothing ; for victory would but rivet his chains the firmer, while the chances of the ship were his ; sinking or on fire, he was doomed to her fate.

Of the situation without they might not ask. And who were the enemy ? And what if they were friends, brethren, countrymen ? The reader, carrying the suggestion forward, will see the necessity which governed the Roman when, in such emergencies, he locked the hapless wretches to their seats.

There was little time, however, for such thought with them. A sound like the rowing of galleys astern attracted Ben-Hur, and the Astræa rocked as if in the midst of countering waves. The idea of a fleet at hand broke upon him—a fleet in manœuvre—forming probably for attack. His blood started with the fancy.

Another signal order came down from deck. The oars dipped, and the galley started imperceptibly. No sound from without, none from within, yet each man in the cabin instinctively poised himself for a shock ; the very ship seemed to catch the sense, and hold its breath, and go crouched, tiger-like.

In such a situation time is inappreciable ; so that Ben-Hur could form no judgment of distance gone. At last there was a sound of trumpets on deck, full, clear, long-blown. The

chief beat the sounding-board until it rang;
the rowers reached forward full-length, and,
deepening the dip of their oars, pulled sud-
denly with all their united force. The galley,
quivering in every timber, answered with a
leap. Other trumpets joined in the clamor—
all from the rear, none forward—from the lat-
ter quarter only a rising sound of voices in
tumult heard briefly. There was a mighty
blow; the rowers in front of the chief's plat-
form reeled, some of them fell; the ship bound-
ed back, recovered, and rushed on more irre-
sistibly than before. Shrill and high arose
the shrieks of men in terror; over the blare
of trumpets, and the grind and crash of the
collision, they arose; then under his feet,
under the keel, pounding, rumbling, breaking
to pieces, drowning, Ben-Hur felt something
overridden. The men about him looked at
each other afraid. A shout of triumph from
the deck—the beak of the Roman had won!
But who were they whom the sea had drunk?
Of what tongue, from what land were they?

No pause, no stay! Forward rushed the As-
træa; and, as it went, some sailors ran down,
and, plunging the cotton-balls into the oil-
tanks, tossed them dripping to comrades at
the head of the stairs: fire was to be added to
other horrors of the combat.

Directly the galley heeled over so far that
the oarsmen on the uppermost side with dif-
ficulty kept their benches. Again the hearty
Roman cheer, and with it despairing shrieks.
An opposing vessel, caught by the grappling-

hooks of the great crane swinging from the prow, was being lifted into the air that it might be dropped and sunk.

The shouting increased on the right hand and on the left; before, behind, swelled an indescribable clamor. Occasionally there was a crash, followed by sudden peals of fright, telling of other ships ridden down, and their crews drowned in the vortexes.

Nor was the fight all on one side. Now and then a Roman in armor was borne down the hatchway, and laid bleeding, sometimes dying, on the floor.

Sometimes, also, puffs of smoke, blended with steam, and foul with the scent of roasting human flesh, poured into the cabin, turning the dimming light into yellow murk. Gasping for breath the while, Ben-Hur knew they were passing through the cloud of a ship on fire, and burning up with the rowers chained to the benches.

The Astræa all this time was in motion Suddenly she stopped. The oars forward were dashed from the hands of the rowers, and the rowers from their benches. On deck, then, a furious trampling, and on the sides a grinding of ships afoul of each other. For the first time the beating of the gavel was lost in the uproar. Men sank on the floor in fear or looked about seeking a hiding-place. In the midst of the panic a body plunged or was pitched headlong down the hatchway, falling near Ben-Hur. He beheld the half-naked carcass, a mass of hair blackening the face, and under it

a shield of bull-hide and wicker-work—a bar-
barian from the white-skinned nations of the
North whom death had robbed of plunder and
revenge. How came he there? An iron hand
had snatched him from the opposing deck?—
no, the Astræa had been boarded! The Ro-
mans were fighting on their own deck? A
chill smote the young Jew: Arrius was hard
pressed—he might be defending his own life.
If he should be slain! God of Abraham fore-
fend! The hopes and dreams so lately come,
were they only hopes and dreams? Mother
and sister—house—home—Holy Land—was
he not to see them, after all? The tumult
thundered above him; he looked around; in
the cabin all was confusion—the rowers on the
benches paralyzed; men running blindly hith-
er and thither; only the chief on his seat im-
perturbable, vainly beating the sounding-board,
and waiting the order of the tribune—in the
red murk illustrating the matchless discipline
which had won the world.

The example had a good effect upon Ben-
Hur. He controlled himself enough to think.
Honor and duty bound the Roman to the plat-
form; but what had he to do with such motives
then? The bench was a thing to run from;
while, if he were to die a slave, who would be
the better of the sacrifice? With him living
was duty, if not honor. His life belonged to
his people. They arose before him never more
real: he saw them, their arms out-stretched;
he heard them imploring him. And he would
go to them. He started—stopped. Alas! a

Roman judgment held him in doom. While it endured, escape would be profitless. In the wide, wide earth there was no place in which he would be safe from the imperial demand; upon the land none, nor upon the sea. Whereas he required freedom according to the forms of law, so only could he abide in Judea and execute the filial purpose to which he would devote himself: in other land he would not live. Dear God! How he had waited and watched and prayed for such a release! And how it had been delayed! But at last he had seen it in the promise of the tribune. What else the great man's meaning? And if the benefactor so belated should now be slain! The dead come not back to redeem the pledges of the living. It should not be—Arrius should not die. At least, better perish with him than survive a galley-slave.

Once more Ben-Hur looked around. Upon the roof of the cabin the battle yet beat; against the sides the hostile vessels yet crushed and grinded. On the benches, the slaves struggled to tear loose from their chains, and, finding their efforts vain, howled like madmen; the guards had gone up-stairs; discipline was out, panic in. No, the chief kept his chair, unchanged, calm as ever—except the gavel, weaponless. Vainly with his clangor he filled the lulls in the din. Ben-Hur gave him a last look, then broke away—not in flight, but to seek the tribune.

A very short space lay between him and the stairs of the hatchway aft. He took it with a

leap, and was half-way up the steps—up far enough to catch a glimpse of the sky blood-red with fire, of the ships alongside, of the sea covered with ships and wrecks, of the fight closed in about the pilot's quarter, the assail-ants many, the defenders few—when suddenly his foothold was knocked away, and he pitch-ed backward. The floor, when he reached it, seemed to be lifting itself and breaking to pieces; then, in a twinkling, the whole after-part of the hull broke asunder, and, as if it had all the time been lying in wait, the sea, hissing and foaming, leaped in, and all became dark-ness and surging water to Ben-Hur.

It cannot be said that the young Jew help-ed himself in this stress. Besides his usual strength, he had the indefinite extra force which nature keeps in reserve for just such perils to life; yet the darkness, and the whirl and roar of water, stupefied him. Even the holding his breath was involuntary.

The influx of the flood tossed him like a log forward into the cabin, where he would have drowned but for the refluence of the sinking motion. As it was, fathoms under the surface the hollow mass vomited him forth, and he arose along with the loosed débris. In the act of rising, he clutched something, and held to it. The time he was under seemed an age longer than it really was; at last he gained the top; with a great gasp he filled his lungs afresh, and, tossing the water from his hair and eyes, climbed higher upon the plank he held, and looked about him.

Death had pursued him closely under the waves; he found it waiting for him when he was risen—waiting multiform.

Smoke lay upon the sea like a semitransparent fog, through which here and there shone cores of intense brilliance. A quick intelligence told him that they were ships on fire. The battle was yet on; nor could he say who was victor. Within the radius of his vision now and then ships passed, shooting shadows athwart lights. Out of the dun clouds farther on he caught the crash of other ships colliding. The danger, however, was closer at hand. When the Astræa went down, her deck, it will be recollected, held her own crew, and the crews of the two galleys which had attacked her at the same time, all of whom were ingulfed. Many of them came to the surface together, and on the same plank or support of whatever kind continued the combat, begun possibly in the vortex fathoms down. Writhing and twisting in deadly embrace, sometimes striking with sword or javelin, they kept the sea around them in agitation, at one place inky-black, at another aflame with fiery reflections. With their struggles he had nothing to do; they were all his enemies: not one of them but would kill him for the plank on which he floated. He made haste to get away.

About that time he heard oars in quickest movement, and beheld a galley coming down upon him. The tall prow seemed doubly tall, and the red light playing upon its gilt and carving gave it an appearance of snaky life.

Under its foot the water churned to flying foam.

He struck out, pushing the plank, which was very broad and unmanageable. Seconds were precious—half a second might save or lose him. In the crisis of the effort, up from the sea, within arm's reach, a helmet shot like a gleam of gold. Next came two hands with fingers extended—large hands were they, and strong—their hold once fixed, might not be loosed. Ben-Hur swerved from them appalled. Up rose the helmet and the head it encased —then two arms, which began to beat the water wildly—the head turned back, and gave the face to the light. The mouth gaping wide; the eyes open, but sightless, and the bloodless pallor of a drowning man—never anything more ghastly! Yet he gave a cry of joy at the sight, and as the face was going under again, he caught the sufferer by the chain which passed from the helmet beneath the chin, and drew him to the plank.

The man was Arrius, the tribune.

For a while the water foamed and eddied violently about Ben-Hur, taxing all his strength to hold to the support and at the same time keep the Roman's head above the surface. The galley had passed, leaving the two barely outside the stroke of its oars. Right through the floating men, over heads, helmeted as well as heads bare, she drove, in her wake nothing but the sea sparkling with fire. A muffled crash, succeeded by a great outcry, made the rescuer look again from his charge. A certain

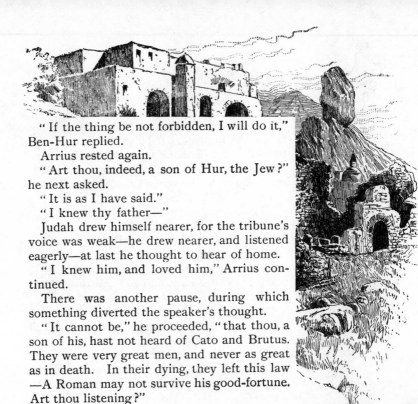

"If the thing be not forbidden, I will do it,"
Ben-Hur replied.

Arrius rested again.

"Art thou, indeed, a son of Hur, the Jew?"
he next asked.

"It is as I have said."

"I knew thy father—"

Judah drew himself nearer, for the tribune's
voice was weak—he drew nearer, and listened
eagerly—at last he thought to hear of home.

"I knew him, and loved him," Arrius con-
tinued.

There was another pause, during which
something diverted the speaker's thought.

"It cannot be," he proceeded, "that thou, a
son of his, hast not heard of Cato and Brutus.
They were very great men, and never as great
as in death. In their dying, they left this law
—A Roman may not survive his good-fortune.
Art thou listening?"

"I hear."

"It is a custom of gentlemen in Rome to
wear a ring. There is one on my hand. Take
it now."

He held the hand to Judah, who did as he
asked.

"Now put it on thine own hand."

Ben-Hur did so.

"The trinket hath its uses," said Arrius next.
"I have property and money. I am accounted
rich even in Rome. I have no family. Show
the ring to my freedman, who hath control in
my absence; you will find him in a villa near
Misenum. Tell him how it came to thee, and

ask anything, or all he may have; he will not refuse the demand. If I live, I will do better by thee. I will make thee free, and restore thee to thy home and people; or thou mayst give thyself to the pursuit that pleaseth thee most. Dost thou hear?"

"I could not choose but hear."

"Then pledge me. By the gods—"

"Nay, good tribune, I am a Jew."

"By thy God, then, or in the form most sacred to those of thy faith—pledge me to do what I tell thee now, and as I tell thee; I am waiting, let me have thy promise."

"Noble Arrius, I am warned by thy manner to expect something of gravest concern. Tell me thy wish first."

"Wilt thou promise then?"

"That were to give the pledge, and— Blessed be the God of my fathers! yonder cometh a ship!"

"In what direction?"

"From the north."

"Canst thou tell her nationality by outward signs?"

"No. My service hath been at the oars."

"Hath she a flag?"

"I cannot see one."

Arrius remained quiet some time, apparently in deep reflection.

"Does the ship hold this way yet?" he at length asked.

"Still this way."

"Look for the flag now."

"She hath none."

"Nor any other sign?"

"She hath a sail set, and is of three banks, and cometh swiftly—that is all I can say of her."

"A Roman in triumph would have out many flags. She must be an enemy. Hear now," said Arrius, becoming grave again, "hear, while yet I may speak. If the galley be a pirate, thy life is safe; they may not give thee freedom; they may put thee to the oar again; but they will not kill thee. On the other hand, I—"

The tribune faltered.

"Perpol!" he continued, resolutely. "I am too old to submit to dishonor. In Rome let them tell how Quintus Arrius, as became a Roman tribune, went down with his ship in the midst of the foe. This is what I would have thee do. If the galley prove a pirate, push me from the plank and drown me. Dost thou hear? Swear thou wilt do it."

"I will not swear," said Ben-Hur, firmly; "neither will I do the deed. The Law, which is to me most binding, O tribune, would make me answerable for thy life. Take back the ring"—he took the seal from his finger—"take it back, and all thy promises of favor in the event of delivery from this peril. The judgment which sent me to the oar for life made me a slave, yet I am not a slave; no more am I thy freedman. I am a son of Israel, and this moment, at least, my own master. Take back the ring."

Arrius remained passive.

"Thou wilt not?" Judah continued. "Not in anger, then, nor in any despite, but to free myself from a hateful obligation, I will give thy gift to the sea. See, O tribune!"

He tossed the ring away. Arrius heard the splash where it struck and sank, though he did not look.

"Thou hast done a foolish thing," he said; "foolish for one placed as thou art. I am not dependent upon thee for death. Life is a thread I can break without thy help; and, if I do, what will become of thee? Men determined on death prefer it at the hands of others, for the reason that the soul which Plato giveth us is rebellious at the thought of self-destruction; that is all. If the ship be a pirate, I will escape from the world. My mind is fixed. I am a Roman. Success and honor are all in all. Yet I would have served thee; thou wouldst not. The ring was the only witness of my will available in this situation. We are both lost. I will die regretting the victory and glory wrested from me; thou wilt live to die a little later, mourning the pious duties undone because of this folly. I pity thee."

Ben-Hur saw the consequences of his act more distinctly than before, yet he did not falter.

"In the three years of my servitude, O tribune, thou wert the first to look upon me kindly. No, no! There was another." The voice dropped, the eyes became humid, and he saw plainly as if it were then before him the face of the boy who helped him to a drink by the

old well at Nazareth. "At least," he proceeded, "thou wert the first to ask me who I was; and if, when I reached out and caught thee, blind and sinking the last time, I, too, had thought of the many ways in which thou couldst be useful to me in my wretchedness, still the act was not all selfish; this I pray you to believe. Moreover, seeing as God giveth me to now, the ends I dream of are to be wrought by fair means alone. As a thing of conscience, I would rather die with thee than be thy slayer. My mind is firmly set as thine; though thou wert to offer me all Rome, O tribune, and it belonged to thee to make the gift good, I would not kill thee. Thy Cato and Brutus were as little children compared to the Hebrew whose law a Jew must obey."

"But my request. Hast—"

"Thy command would be of more weight, and that would not move me. I have said."

Both became silent, waiting.

Ben-Hur looked often at the coming ship. Arrius rested with closed eyes, indifferent.

"Art thou sure she is an enemy?" Ben-Hur asked.

"I think so," was the reply.

"She stops, and puts a boat over the side."

"Dost thou see her flag?"

"Is there no other sign by which she may be known if Roman?"

"If Roman, she hath a helmet over the mast's top."

"Then be of cheer, I see the helmet."

Still Arrius was not assured.

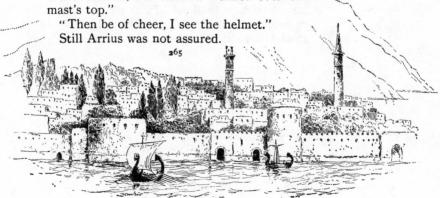

"The men in the small boat are taking in the people afloat. Pirates are not humane."

"They may need rowers," Arrius replied, recurring, possibly, to times when he had made rescues for the purpose.

Ben-Hur was very watchful of the actions of the strangers.

"The ship moves off," he said.

"Whither?"

"Over on our right there is a galley which I take to be deserted. The new-comer heads towards it. Now she is alongside. Now she is sending men aboard."

Then Arrius opened his eyes and threw off his calm.

"Thank thou thy God," he said to Ben-Hur, after a look at the galleys, "thank thou thy God, as I do my many gods. A pirate would sink, not save, yon ship. By the act and the helmet on the mast I know a Roman. The victory is mine. Fortune hath not deserted me. We are saved. Wave thy hand—call to them—bring them quickly. I shall be duumvir, and thou! I knew thy father, and loved him. He was a prince indeed. He taught me a Jew was not a barbarian. I will take thee with me. I will make thee my son. Give thy God thanks, and call the sailors. Haste! The pursuit must be kept. Not a robber shall escape. Hasten them!"

Judah raised himself upon the plank, and waved his hand, and called with all his might; at last he drew the attention of the sailors in the small boat, and they were speedily taken up.

Arrius was received on the galley with all the honors due a hero so the favorite of Fortune. Upon a couch on the deck he heard the particulars of the conclusion of the fight. When the survivors afloat upon the water were all saved and the prize secured, he spread his flag of commandant anew, and hurried northward to rejoin the fleet and perfect the victory. In due time the fifty vessels coming down the channel closed in upon the fugitive pirates, and crushed them utterly; not one escaped. To swell the tribune's glory, twenty galleys of the enemy were captured.

Upon his return from the cruise, Arrius had warm welcome on the mole at Misenum. The young man attending him very early attracted the attention of his friends there; and to their questions as to who he was the tribune proceeded in the most affectionate manner to tell the story of his rescue and introduce the stranger, omitting carefully all that pertained to the latter's previous history. At the end of the narrative he called Ben-Hur to him, and said, with a hand resting affectionately upon his shoulder:

"Good friends, this is my son and heir, who, as he is to take my property—if it be the will of the gods that I leave any—shall be known to you by my name. I pray you all to love him as you love me."

Speedily as opportunity permitted, the adoption was formally perfected. And in such manner the brave Roman kept his faith with Ben-Hur, giving him happy introduction into the

imperial world. The month succeeding Arrius's return, the armilustrium was celebrated with the utmost magnificence in the theatre of Scaurus. One side of the structure was taken up with military trophies; among which by far the most conspicuous and most admired were twenty prows, complemented by their corresponding aplustra, cut bodily from as many galleys; and over them, so as to be legible to the eighty thousand spectators in the seats, was this inscription:

TAKEN FROM
THE PIRATES IN THE GULF OF EURIPUS,
BY
QUINTUS ARRIUS,
DUUMVIR.

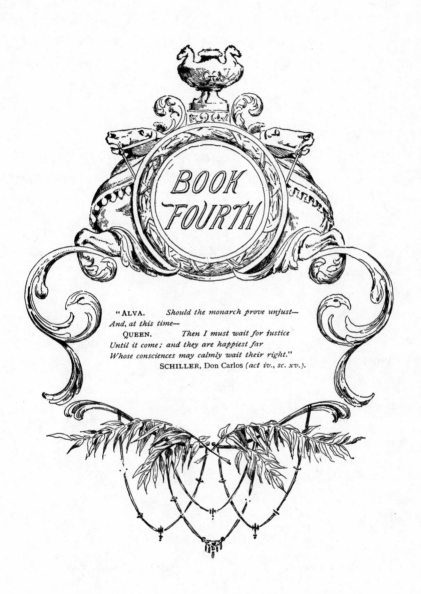

BOOK FOURTH

"ALVA. Should the monarch prove unjust—
And, at this time—
QUEEN. Then I must wait for justice
Until it come; and they are happiest far
Whose consciences may calmly wait their right."
SCHILLER, Don Carlos (act iv., sc. xv.).

CHAPTER I

BEN-HUR RETURNS EAST

THE month to which we now come is July, the year that of our Lord 29, and the place Antioch, then Queen of the East, and next to Rome the strongest, if not the most populous, city in the world.

There is an opinion that the extravagance and dissoluteness of the age had their origin in Rome, and spread thence throughout the empire; that the great cities but reflected the manners of their mistress on the Tiber. This may be doubted. The reaction of the conquest would seem to have been upon the morals of the conqueror. In Greece she found a spring of corruption; so also in Egypt; and the student, having exhausted the subject, will close the books assured that the flow of the demoralizing river was from the East westwardly, and that this very city of Antioch, one of the oldest seats of Assyrian power and splendor, was a principal source of the deadly stream.

A transport galley entered the mouth of the river Orontes from the blue waters of the sea. It was in the forenoon. The heat was great, yet all on board who could avail themselves of the privilege were on deck—Ben-Hur among others.

The five years had brought the young Jew to perfect manhood. Though the robe of white linen in which he was attired somewhat masked his form, his appearance was unusually attractive. For an hour and more he had occupied a seat in the shade of the sail, and in that time several fellow-passengers of his own nationality had tried to engage him in conversation, but without avail. His replies to their questions had been brief, though gravely courteous, and in the Latin tongue. The purity of his speech, his cultivated manners, his reticence, served to stimulate their curiosity the more. Such as observed him closely were struck by an incongruity between his demeanor, which had the ease and grace of a patrician, and certain points of his person. Thus, his arms were disproportionately long; and when, to steady himself against the motion of the vessel, he took hold of anything near by, the size of his hands and their evident power compelled remark; so the wonder who and what he was mixed continually with a wish to know the particulars of his life. In other words, his air cannot be better described than as a notice —This man has a story to tell.

The galley, in coming, had stopped at one of the ports of Cyprus, and picked up a Hebrew of most respectable appearance, quiet, reserved, paternal. Ben-Hur ventured to ask him some questions; the replies won his confidence, and resulted finally in an extended conversation.

It chanced, also, that as the galley from Cy-

prus entered the receiving bay of the Orontes, two other vessels which had been sighted out in the sea met it and passed into the river at the same time; and as they did so both the strangers threw out small flags of brightest yellow. There was much conjecture as to the meaning of the signals. At length a passenger addressed himself to the respectable Hebrew for information upon the subject.

"Yes, I know the meaning of the flags," he replied; "they do not signify nationality — they are merely marks of ownership."

"Has the owner many ships?"

"He has."

"You know him?"

"I have dealt with him."

The passengers looked at the speaker as if requesting him to go on. Ben-Hur listened with interest.

"He lives in Antioch," the Hebrew continued, in his quiet way. "That he is vastly rich has brought him into notice, and the talk about him is not always kind. There used to be in Jerusalem a prince of very ancient family named Hur."

Judah strove to be composed, yet his heart beat quicker.

"The prince was a merchant, with a genius for business. He set on foot many enterprises, some reaching far East, others West. In the great cities he had branch houses. The one in Antioch was in charge of a man said by some to have been a family servant called Simonides, Greek in name, yet an Israelite.

273

The master was drowned at sea. His business, however, went on, and was scarcely less prosperous. After a while misfortune overtook the family. The prince's only son, nearly grown, tried to kill the procurator Gratus in one of the streets of Jerusalem. He failed by a narrow chance, and has not since been heard of. In fact, the Roman's rage took in the whole house—not one of the name was left alive. Their palace was sealed up, and is now a rookery for pigeons; the estate was confiscated; everything that could be traced to the ownership of the Hurs was confiscated. The procurator cured his hurt with a golden salve."

The passengers laughed.

"You mean he kept the property," said one of them.

"They say so," the Hebrew replied; "I am only telling a story as I received it. And, to go on, Simonides, who had been the prince's agent here in Antioch, opened trade in a short time on his own account, and in a space incredibly brief became the master-merchant of the city. In imitation of his master, he sent caravans to India; and on the sea at present he has galleys enough to make a royal fleet. They say nothing goes amiss with him. His camels do not die, except of old age; his ships never founder; if he throw a chip into the river, it will come back to him gold."

"How long has he been going on thus?"

"Not ten years."

"He must have had a good start."

"Yes, they say the procurator took only the

A PALANQUIN OF THE DESERT

prince's property ready at hand—his horses, cattle, houses, land, vessels, goods. The money could not be found, though there must have been vast sums of it. What became of it has been an unsolved mystery."

"Not to me," said a passenger, with a sneer.

"I understand you," the Hebrew answered. "Others have had your idea. That it furnished old Simonides his start is a common belief. The procurator is of that opinion—or he has been—for twice in five years he has caught the merchant, and put him to torture."

Judah griped the rope he was holding with crushing force.

"It is said," the narrator continued, "that there is not a sound bone in the man's body. The last time I saw him he sat in a chair, a shapeless cripple, propped against cushions."

"So tortured!" exclaimed several listeners in a breath.

"Disease could not have produced such a deformity. Still the suffering made no impression upon him. All he had was his lawfully, and he was making lawful use of it—that was the most they wrung from him. Now, however, he is past persecution. He has a license to trade signed by Tiberius himself."

"He paid roundly for it, I warrant."

"These ships are his," the Hebrew continued, passing the remark. "It is a custom among his sailors to salute each other upon meeting by throwing out yellow flags, the sight of which is as much as to say, 'We have had a fortunate voyage.'"

The story ended there.

When the transport was fairly in the channel of the river, Judah spoke to the Hebrew.

"What was the name of the merchant's master?"

"Ben-Hur, Prince of Jerusalem."

"What became of the prince's family?"

"The boy was sent to the galleys. I may say he is dead. One year is the ordinary limit of life under that sentence. The widow and daughter have not been heard of; those who know what became of them will not speak. They died doubtless in the cells of cne of the castles which spot the way-sides of Judea."

Judah walked to the pilot's quarter. So absorbed was he in thought that he scarcely noticed the shores of the river, which from sea to city were surpassingly beautiful with orchards of all the Syrian fruits and vines, clustered about villas rich as those of Neapolis. No more did he observe the vessels passing in an endless fleet, nor hear the singing and shouting of the sailors, some in labor, some in merriment. The sky was full of sunlight, lying in hazy warmth upon the land and the water; nowhere except over his life was there a shadow.

Once only he awoke to a momentary interest, and that was when some one pointed out the Grove of Daphne, discernible from a bend in the river.

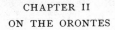

CHAPTER II

ON THE ORONTES

HEN the city came into view, the passengers were on deck, eager that nothing of the scene might escape them. The respectable Jew already introduced to the reader was the principal spokesman.

"The river here runs to the west," he said, in the way of general answer. "I remember when it washed the base of the walls; but as Roman subjects we have lived in peace, and, as always happens in such times, trade has had its will; now the whole river front is taken up with wharves and docks. Yonder"—the speaker pointed southward—"is Mount Caius, or, as these people love to call it, the Mountains of Orontes, looking across to its brother Amnus in the north; and between them lies the Plain of Antioch. Farther on are the Black Mountains, whence the Ducts of the Kings bring the purest water to wash the thirsty streets and people; yet they are forests in a wilderness state, dense, and full of birds and beasts."

"Where is the lake?" one asked.

"Over north there. You can take horse, if you wish to see it—or, better, a boat, for a tributary connects it with the river."

"The Grove of Daphne!" he said, to a third

inquirer. "Nobody can describe it; only beware! It was begun by Apollo, and completed by him. He prefers it to Olympus. People go there for one look — just one — and never come away. They have a saying which tells it all—'Better be a worm and feed on the mulberries of Daphne than a king's guest.'"

"Then you advise me to stay away from it?"

"Not I! Go you will. Everybody goes, cynic philosopher, virile boy, women, and priests —all go. So sure am I of what you will do that I assume to advise you. Do not take quarters in the city—that will be loss of time; but go at once to the village in the edge of the grove. The way is through a garden, under the spray of fountains. The lovers of the god and his Penæan maid built the town; and in its porticos and paths and thousand retreats you will find characters and habits and sweets and kinds elsewhere impossible. But the wall of the city! there it is, the masterpiece of Xeræus, the master of mural architecture."

All eyes followed his pointing finger.

"This part was raised by order of the first of the Seleucidæ. Three hundred years have made it part of the rock it rests upon."

The defence justified the encomium. High, solid, and with many bold angles, it curved southwardly out of view.

"On the top there are four hundred towers, each a reservoir of water," the Hebrew continued. "Look now! Over the wall, tall as it is, see in the distance two hills, which you may know as the rival crests of Sulpius. The struct-

278

ure on the farthest one is the citadel, garrisoned all the year round by a Roman legion. Opposite it this way rises the Temple of Jupiter, and under that the front of the legate's residence—a palace full of offices, and yet a fortress against which a mob would dash harmlessly as a south wind."

At this point the sailors began taking in sail, whereupon the Hebrew exclaimed, heartily, 'See! you who hate the sea, and you who have vows, get ready your curses and your prayers. The bridge yonder, over which the road to Seleucia is carried, marks the limit of navigation. What the ship unloads for further transit, the camel takes up there. Above the bridge begins the island upon which Calinicus built his new city, connecting it with five great viaducts so solid time has made no impression upon them, nor floods nor earthquakes. Of the main town, my friends, I have only to say you will be happier all your lives for having seen it."

As he concluded, the ship turned and made slowly for her wharf under the wall, bringing even more fairly to view the life with which the river at that point was possessed. Finally the lines were thrown, the oars shipped, and the voyage was done. Then Ben-Hur sought the respectable Hebrew.

"Let me trouble you a moment before saying farewell."

The man bowed assent.

"Your story of the merchant has made me curious to see him. You called him Simonides?"

279

"Yes. He is a Jew with a Greek name."

"Where is he to be found?"

The acquaintance gave a sharp look before he answered,

"I may save you mortification. He is not a money-lender."

"Nor am I a money-borrower," said Ben-Hur, smiling at the other's shrewdness.

The man raised his head and considered an instant.

"One would think," he then replied, "that the richest merchant in Antioch would have a house for business corresponding to his wealth; but if you would find him in the day, follow the river to yon bridge, under which he quarters in a building that looks like a buttress of the wall. Before the door there is an immense landing, always covered with cargoes come and to go. The fleet that lies moored there is his. You cannot fail to find him."

"I give you thanks."

"The peace of our fathers go with you."

"And with you."

With that they separated.

Two street-porters, loaded with his baggage, received Ben-Hur's orders upon the wharf.

"To the citadel," he said; a direction which implied an official military connection.

Two great streets, cutting each other at right angles, divided the city into quarters. A curious and immense structure, called the Nymphæum, arose at the foot of the one running north and south. When the porters turned

south there, the new-comer, though fresh from Rome, was amazed at the magnificence of the avenue. On the right and left there were palaces, and between them extended indefinitely double colonnades of marble, leaving separate ways for footmen, beasts, and chariots; the whole under shade, and cooled by fountains of incessant flow.

Ben-Hur was not in mood to enjoy the spectacle. The story of Simonides haunted him. Arrived at the Omphalus — a monument of four arches wide as the streets, superbly illustrated, and erected to himself by Epiphanes, the eighth of the Seleucidæ — he suddenly changed his mind.

"I will not go to the citadel to-night," he said to the porters. "Take me to the khan nearest the bridge on the road to Seleucia."

The party faced about, and in good time he was deposited in a public-house of primitive but ample construction, within stone's-throw of the bridge under which old Simonides had his quarters. He lay upon the house-top through the night. In his inner mind lived the thought, "Now—now I will hear of home —and mother—and the dear little Tirzah. If they are on earth, I will find them."

CHAPTER III
THE DEMAND ON SIMONIDES

NEXT day early, to the neglect of the city, Ben-Hur sought the house of Simonides. Through an embattled gate-way he passed to a continuity of wharves; thence up the river midst a busy press, to the Seleucian Bridge, under which he paused to take in the scene.

There, directly under the bridge, was the merchant's house, a mass of gray stone, un-hewn, referable to no style, looking, as the voyager had described it, like a buttress of the wall against which it leaned. Two immense doors in front communicated with the wharf. Some holes near the top, heavily barred, serv-ed as windows. Weeds waved from the crev-ices, and in places black moss splotched the otherwise bald stones.

The doors were open. Through one of them business went in; through the other it came out; and there was hurry, hurry in all its movements.

On the wharf there were piles of goods in every kind of package, and groups of slaves, stripped to the waist, going about in the aban-don of labor.

Below the bridge lay a fleet of galleys, some loading, others unloading. A yellow flag blew out from each mast-head. From fleet and

wharf, and from ship to ship, the bondmen of
traffic passed in clamorous counter-currents.

Above the bridge, across the river, a wall
rose from the water's edge, over which tower-
ed the fanciful cornices and turrets of an im-
perial palace, covering every foot of the island
spoken of in the Hebrew's description. But,
with all its suggestions, Ben-Hur scarcely no-
ticed it. Now, at last, he thought to hear of
his people—this, certainly, if Simonides had
indeed been his father's slave. But would the
man acknowledge the relation? That would
be to give up his riches and the sovereignty of
trade so royally witnessed on the wharf and
river. And what was of still greater conse-
quence to the merchant, it would be to forego
his career in the midst of amazing success, and
yield himself voluntarily once more a slave.
Simple thought of the demand seemed a mon-
strous audacity. Stripped of diplomatic ad-
dress, it was to say, You are my slave; give
me all you have, and—yourself.

Yet Ben-Hur derived strength for the inter-
view from faith in his rights and the hope
uppermost in his heart. If the story to which
he was yielding were true, Simonides belong-
ed to him, with all he had. For the wealth, be
it said in justice, he cared nothing. When he
started to the door determined in mind, it was
with a promise to himself—" Let him tell me
of mother and Tirzah, and I will give him his
freedom without account."

He passed boldly into the house.

The interior was that of a vast depot where,

in ordered spaces, and under careful arrangement, goods of every kind were heaped and pent. Though the light was murky and the air stifling, men moved about briskly; and in places he saw workmen with saws and hammers making packages for shipments. Down a path between the piles he walked slowly, wondering if the man of whose genius there were here such abounding proofs could have been his father's slave? If so, to what class had he belonged? If a Jew, was he the son of a servant? Or was he a debtor or a debtor's son? Or had he been sentenced and sold for theft? These thoughts, as they passed, in nowise disturbed the growing respect for the merchant of which he was each instant more and more conscious. A peculiarity of our admiration for another is that it is always looking for circumstances to justify itself.

At length a man approached and spoke to him.

"What would you have?"

"I would see Simonides, the merchant."

"Will you come this way?"

By a number of paths left in the stowage, they finally came to a flight of steps; ascending which, he found himself on the roof of the depot, and in front of a structure which cannot be better described than as a lesser stone house built upon another, invisible from the landing below, and out west of the bridge under the open sky. The roof, hemmed in by a low wall, seemed like a terrace, which, to his astonishment, was brilliant with flowers; in

the rich surrounding, the house sat squat, a plain square block, unbroken except by a doorway in front. A dustless path led to the door, through a bordering of shrubs of Persian rose in perfect bloom. Breathing a sweet attar-perfume, he followed the guide.

At the end of a darkened passage within, they stopped before a curtain half-parted. The man called out,

"A stranger to see the master."

A clear voice replied, "In God's name, let him enter."

A Roman might have called the apartment into which the visitor was ushered his atrium. The walls were panelled; each panel was comparted like a modern office - desk, and each compartment crowded with labelled folios all filemot with age and use. Between the panels, and above and below them, were borders of wood once white, now tinted like cream, and carved with marvellous intricacy of design. Above a cornice of gilded balls, the ceiling rose in pavilion style until it broke into a shallow dome set with hundreds of panes of violet mica, permitting a flood of light deliciously reposeful. The floor was carpeted with gray rugs so thick that an invading foot fell half-buried and soundless.

In the midlight of the room were two persons—a man resting in a chair high-backed, broad-armed, and lined with pliant cushions; and at his left, leaning against the back of the chair, a girl well forward into womanhood. At sight of them Ben-Hur felt the blood red-

den his forehead; bowing, as much to recover himself as in respect, he lost the lifting of the hands, and the shiver and shrink with which the sitter caught sight of him—an emotion as swift to go as it had been to come. When he raised his eyes the two were in the same position, except the girl's hand had fallen and was resting lightly upon the elder's shoulder; both of them were regarding him fixedly.

"If you are Simonides, the merchant, and a Jew"—Ben-Hur stopped an instant—"then the peace of the God of our father Abraham upon you and—yours."

The last word was addressed to the girl.

"I am the Simonides of whom you speak, by birthright a Jew," the man made answer, in a voice singularly clear. "I am Simonides, and a Jew; and I return you your salutation, with prayer to know who calls upon me."

Ben-Hur looked as he listened, and where the figure of the man should have been in healthful roundness, there was only a formless heap sunk in the depths of the cushions, and covered by a quilted robe of sombre silk. Over the heap shone a head royally proportioned— the ideal head of a statesman and conqueror —a head broad of base and dome-like in front, such as Angelo would have modelled for Cæsar. White hair dropped in thin locks over the white brows, deepening the blackness of the eyes shining through them like sullen lights. The face was bloodless, and much puffed with folds, especially under the chin. In other words, the head and face were those of

a man who might move the world more readily than the world could move him—a man to be twice twelve times tortured into the shapeless cripple he was, without a groan, much less a confession; a man to yield his life, but never a purpose or a point; a man born in armor, and assailable only through his loves. To him Ben-Hur stretched his hands, open and palm up, as he would offer peace at the same time he asked it.

"I am Judah, son of Ithamar, late head of the House of Hur, and a prince of Jerusalem."

The merchant's right hand lay outside the robe—a long, thin hand, articulate to deformity with suffering. It closed tightly; otherwise there was not the slightest expression of feeling of any kind on his part; nothing to warrant an inference of surprise or interest; nothing but this calm answer,

"The princes of Jerusalem, of the pure blood, are always welcome in my house; you are welcome. Give the young man a seat, Esther."

The girl took an ottoman near by, and carried it to Ben-Hur. As she arose from placing the seat, their eyes met. "The peace of our Lord with you," she said, modestly. "Be seated and at rest."

When she resumed her place by the chair, she had not divined his purpose. The powers of woman go not so far; if the matter is of finer feeling, such as pity, mercy, sympathy, that she detects; and therein is a difference between her and man which will endure as long as she remains, by nature, alive to such

feelings. She was simply sure he brought some wound of life for healing.

Ben-Hur did not take the offered seat, but said, deferentially, "I pray the good master Simonides that he will not hold me an intruder. Coming up the river yesterday, I heard he knew my father."

"I knew the Prince Hur. We were associated in some enterprises lawful to merchants who find profit in lands beyond the sea and the desert. But sit, I pray you—and, Esther, some wine for the young man. Nehemiah speaks of a son of Hur who once ruled the half part of Jerusalem; an old house; very old, by the faith! In the days of Moses and Joshua even some of them found favor in the sight of the Lord, and divided honors with those princes among men. It can hardly be that their descendant, lineally come to us, will refuse a cup of wine-fat of the genuine vine of Sorek, grown on the south hill-sides of Hebron."

By the time of the conclusion of this speech, Esther was before Ben-Hur with a silver cup filled from a vase upon a table a little removed from the chair. She offered the drink with downcast face. He touched her hand gently to put it away. Again their eyes met; whereat he noticed that she was small, not nearly to his shoulder in height; but very graceful, and fair and sweet of face, with eyes black and inexpressibly soft. She is kind and pretty, he thought, and looks as Tizrah would were she living. Poor Tirzah! Then he said aloud,

"No, thy father—if he is thy father?"—he paused.

"I am Esther, the daughter of Simonides," she said, with dignity.

"Then, fair Esther, thy father, when he has heard my further speech, will not think worse of me if yet I am slow to take his wine of famous extract; nor less I hope not to lose grace in thy sight. Stand thou here with me a moment!"

Both of them, as in common cause, turned to the merchant. "Simonides!" he said, firmly, "my father, at his death, had a trusted servant of thy name, and it has been told me that thou art the man!"

There was a sudden start of the wrenched limbs under the robe, and the thin hand clinched.

"Esther, Esther!" the man called, sternly; "here, not there, as thou art thy mother's child and mine—here, not there, I say!"

The girl looked once from father to visitor; then she replaced the cup upon the table, and went dutifully to the chair. Her countenance sufficiently expressed her wonder and alarm.

Simonides lifted his left hand and gave it into hers, lying lovingly upon his shoulder, and said, dispassionately, "I have grown old in dealing with men—old before my time. If he who told thee that whereof thou speakest was a friend acquainted with my history, and spoke of it not harshly, he must have persuaded thee that I could not be else than a man distrustful of my kind. The God of Israel help him who,

at the end of life, is constrained to acknowl-
edge so much! My loves are few, but they
are. One of them is a soul which "—he car-
ried the hand holding his to his lips, in man-
ner unmistakable—" a soul which to this time
has been unselfishly mine, and such sweet com-
fort that, were it taken from me, I would die."

Esther's head drooped until her cheek touch-
ed his.

"The other love is but a memory; of which
I will say further that, like a benison of the
Lord, it hath a compass to contain a whole
family, if only "—his voice lowered and trem-
bled—" if only I knew where they were."

Ben-Hur's face suffused, and, advancing a
step, he cried, impulsively, "My mother and
sister! Oh, it is of them you speak!"

Esther, as if spoken to, raised her head; but
Simonides returned to his calm, and answered,
coldly, "Hear me to the end. Because I am
that I am, and because of the loves of which
I have spoken, before I make return to thy
demand touching my relations to the Prince
Hur, and as something which of right should
come first, do thou show me proofs of who
thou art. Is thy witness in writing? Or com-
eth it in person?"

The demand was plain, and the right of it
indisputable. Ben-Hur blushed, clasped his
hands, stammered, and turned away at loss.
Simonides pressed him.

"The proofs, the proofs, I say! Set them
before me—lay them in my hands!"

Yet Ben-Hur made no answer. He had **not**

anticipated the requirement; and, now that it was made, to him as never before came the awful fact that the three years in the galley had carried away all the proofs of his identity; mother and sister gone, he did not live in the knowledge of any human being. Many there were acquainted with him, but that was all. Had Quintus Arrius been present, what could he have said more than where he found him, and that he believed the pretender to be the son of Hur? But, as will presently appear in full, the brave Roman sailor was dead. Judah had felt the loneliness before; to the core of life the sense struck him now. He stood, hands clasped, face averted, in stupefaction. Simonides respected his suffering, and waited in silence.

"Master Simonides," he said, at length, "I can only tell my story; and I will not that unless you stay judgment so long, and with goodwill deign to hear me."

"Speak," said Simonides, now, indeed, master of the situation—"speak, and I will listen the more willingly that I have not denied you to be the very person you claim yourself."

Ben-Hur proceeded then, and told his life hurriedly, yet with the feeling which is the source of all eloquence; but as we are familiar with it down to his landing at Misenum, in company with Arrius, returned victorious from the Ægean, at that point we will take up the words.

"My benefactor was loved and trusted by the emperor, who heaped him with honorable

rewards. The merchants of the East contributed magnificent presents, and he became doubly rich among the rich of Rome. May a Jew forget his religion? or his birthplace, if it were the Holy Land of our fathers? The good man adopted me his son by formal rites of law; and I strove to make him just return: no child was ever more dutiful to father than I to him. He would have had me a scholar; in art, philosophy, rhetoric, oratory, he would have furnished me the most famous teacher. I declined his insistence, because I was a Jew, and could not forget the Lord God, or the glory of the prophets, or the city set on the hills by David and Solomon. Oh, ask you why I accepted any of the benefactions of the Roman? I loved him; next place, I thought I could, with his help, array influences which would enable me one day to unseal the mystery close-locking the fate of my mother and sister; and to these there was yet another motive, of which I shall not speak except to say it controlled me so far that I devoted myself to arms, and the acquisition of everything deemed essential to thorough knowledge of the art of war. In the palæstræ and circuses of the city I toiled, and in the camps no less; and in all of them I have a name, but not that of my fathers. The crowns I won—and on the walls of the villa by Misenum there are many of them— all came to me as the son of Arrius, the duumvir. In that relation only am I known among Romans. . . . In steadfast pursuit of my secret aim, I left Rome for Antioch, intending to ac-

company the Consul Maxentius in the cam-
paign he is organizing against the Parthians.
Master of personal skill in all arms, I seek now
the higher knowledge pertaining to the con-
duct of bodies of men in the field. The con-
sul has admitted me one of his military family.
But yesterday, as our ship entered the Orontes,
two other ships sailed in with us flying yellow
flags. A fellow-passenger and countryman
from Cyprus explained that the vessels be-
longed to Simonides, the master-merchant of
Antioch; he told us, also, who the merchant
was; his marvellous success in commerce; of
his fleets and caravans, and their coming and
going; and, not knowing I had interest in the
theme beyond my associate listeners, he said
Simonides was a Jew, once the servant of the
Prince Hur; nor did he conceal the cruelties
of Gratus, or the purpose of their infliction."

At this allusion Simonides bowed his head,
and, as if to help him conceal his feelings and
her own deep sympathy, the daughter hid her
face on his neck. Directly he raised his eyes,
and said, in a clear voice, "I am listening."

"O good Simonides!" Ben-Hur then said, ad-
vancing a step, his whole soul seeking expres-
sion, "I see thou art not convinced, and that
yet I stand in the shadow of thy distrust."

The merchant held his features fixed as mar-
ble, and his tongue as still.

"And not less clearly, I see the difficulties
of my position," Ben-Hur continued. "All
my Roman connection I can prove; I have
only to call upon the consul, now the guest of

the governor of the city; but I cannot prove the particulars of thy demand upon me. I cannot prove I am my father's son. They who could serve me in that — alas! they are dead or lost."

He covered his face with his hands; whereupon Esther arose, and taking the rejected cup to him, said, "The wine is of the country we all so love. Drink, I pray thee!"

The voice was sweet as that of Rebekah offering drink at the well near Nahor the city; he saw there were tears in her eyes, and he drank, saying, "Daughter of Simonides, thy heart is full of goodness; and merciful art thou to let the stranger share it with thy father. Be thou blessed of our God! I thank thee."

Then he addressed himself to the merchant again:

"As I have no proof that I am my father's son, I will withdraw that I demanded of thee, O Simonides, and go hence to trouble you no more; only let me say I did not seek thy return to servitude nor account of thy fortune; in any event, I would have said, as now I say, that all which is product of thy labor and genius is thine; keep it in welcome. I have no need of any part thereof. When the good Quintus, my second father, sailed on the voyage which was his last, he left me his heir, princely rich. If, therefore, thou dost think of me again, be it with remembrance of this question, which, as I do swear by the prophets and Jehovah, thy God and mine, was the chief purpose of my coming here: What dost thou

know—what canst thou tell me—of my mother and Tirzah, my sister—she who should be in beauty and grace even as this one, thy sweetness of life, if not thy very life? Oh! what canst thou tell me of them?"

The tears ran down Esther's cheeks; but the man was wilful; in a clear voice, he replied,

"I have said I knew the Prince Ben-Hur. I remember hearing of the misfortune which overtook his family. I remember the bitterness with which I heard it. He who wrought such misery to the widow of my friend is the same who, in the same spirit, hath since wrought upon me. I will go further, and say to you, I have made diligent quest concerning the family, but—I have nothing to tell you of them. They are lost."

Ben-Hur uttered a great groan.

"Then—then it is another hope broken!" he said, struggling with his feelings. "I am used to disappointments. I pray you pardon my intrusion; and if I have occasioned you annoyance, forgive it because of my sorrow. I have nothing now to live for but vengeance. Farewell."

At the curtain he turned, and said, simply, "I thank you both."

"Peace go with you," the merchant said.

Esther could not speak for sobbing.

And so he departed.

CHAPTER IV

SIMONIDES AND ESTHER

SCARCELY was Ben-Hur gone, when Simonides seemed to wake as from sleep; his countenance flushed; the sullen light of his eyes changed to brightness; and he said, cheerily,

"Esther, ring—quick!"

She went to the table, and rang a service-bell.

One of the panels in the wall swung back, exposing a door-way which gave admittance to a man who passed round to the merchant's front, and saluted him with a half-salaam.

"Malluch, here—nearer—to the chair," the master said, imperiously. "I have a mission which shall not fail though the sun should. Hearken! A young man is now descending to the storeroom — tall, comely, and in the garb of Israel; follow him, his shadow not more faithful; and every night send me report of where he is, what he does, and the company he keeps; and if, without discovery, you overhear his conversations, report them word for word, together with whatever will serve to expose him, his habits, motives, life. Understand you? Go quickly! Stay, Malluch: if he leave the city, go after him—and, mark you, Malluch, be as a friend. If he bespeak you, tell him what you will to the occasion most

suited, except that you are in my service; of that, not a word. Haste—make haste!"

The man saluted as before, and was gone.

Then Simonides rubbed his wan hands together, and laughed.

"What is the day, daughter?" he said, in the midst of the mood. "What is the day? I wish to remember it for happiness come. See, and look for it laughing, and laughing tell me, Esther."

The merriment seemed unnatural to her; and, as if to entreat him from it, she answered, sorrowfully, "Woe's me, father, that I should ever forget this day!"

His hands fell down the instant, and his chin, dropping upon his breast, lost itself in the muffling folds of flesh composing his lower face.

"True, most true, my daughter!" he said, without looking up. "This is the twentieth day of the fourth month. To-day, five years ago, my Rachel, thy mother, fell down and died. They brought me home broken as thou seest me, and we found her dead of grief. Oh, to me she was a cluster of camphire in the vineyards of En-Gedi! I have gathered my myrrh with my spice. I have eaten my honey-comb with my honey. We laid her away in a lonely place—in a tomb cut in the mountain; no one near her. Yet in the darkness she left me a little light, which the years have increased to a brightness of morning." He raised his hand and rested it upon his daughter's head. "Dear Lord, I thank thee that now in my Esther my lost Rachel liveth again!"

Directly he lifted his head, and said, as with a sudden thought, "Is it not clear day outside?"

"It was, when the young man came in."

"Then let Abimelech come and take me to the garden, where I can see the river and the ships, and I will tell thee, dear Esther, why but now my mouth filled with laughter, and my tongue with singing, and my spirit was like to a roe or to a young hart upon the mountains of spices."

In answer to the bell a servant came, and at her bidding pushed the chair, set on little wheels for the purpose, out of the room to the roof of the lower house, called by him his garden. Out through the roses, and by beds of lesser flowers, all triumphs of careful attendance, but now unnoticed, he was rolled to a position from which he could view the palace-tops over against him on the island, the bridge in lessening perspective to the farther shore, and the river below the bridge crowded with vessels, all swimming amidst the dancing splendors of the early sun upon the rippling water. There the servant left him with Esther.

The much shouting of laborers, and their beating and pounding, did not disturb him any more than the tramping of people on the bridge-floor almost overhead, being as familiar to his ear as the view before him to his eye, and therefore unnoticeable, except as suggestions of profits in promise.

Esther sat on the arm of the chair nursing his hand, and waiting his speech, which came

298

at length in the calm way, the mighty will having carried him back to himself.

"When the young man was speaking, Esther, I observed thee, and thought thou wert won by him."

Her eyes fell as she replied,

"Speak you of faith, father, I believed him."

"In thy eyes, then, he is the lost son of the Prince Hur?"

"If he is not—" She hesitated.

"And if he is not, Esther?"

"I have been thy handmaiden, father, since my mother answered the call of the Lord God; by thy side I have heard and seen thee deal in wise ways with all manner of men seeking profit, holy and unholy; and now I say, if indeed the young man be not the prince he claims to be, then before me falsehood never played so well the part of righteous truth."

"By the glory of Solomon, daughter, thou speakest earnestly. Dost thou believe thy father his father's servant?"

"I understood him to ask of that as something he had but heard."

For a time Simonides' gaze swam among his swimming ships, though they had no place in his mind.

"Well, thou art a good child, Esther, of genuine Jewish shrewdness, and of years and strength to hear a sorrowful tale. Wherefore give me heed, and I will tell you of myself, and of thy mother, and of many things pertaining to the past not in thy knowledge or thy dreams —things withheld from the persecuting Ro-

mans for a hope's sake, and from thee that thy
nature should grow towards the Lord straight
as the reed to the sun.... I was born in a tomb
in the valley of Hinnom, on the south side of
Zion. My father and mother were Hebrew
bond-servants, tenders of the fig and olive trees
growing, with many vines, in the King's Garden
hard by Siloam ; and in my boyhood I helped
them. They were of the class bound to serve
forever. They sold me to the Prince Hur, then,
next to Herod the King, the richest man in
Jerusalem. From the garden he transferred
me to his storehouse in Alexandria of Egypt,
where I came of age. I served him six years,
and in the seventh, by the law of Moses, I went
free."

Esther clapped her hands lightly.

" Oh, then, thou art not his father's servant !"

" Nay, daughter, hear. Now, in those days
there were lawyers in the cloisters of the Tem-
ple who disputed vehemently, saying the chil-
dren of servants bound forever took the con-
dition of their parents ; but the Prince Hur
was a man righteous in all things, and an in-
terpreter of the law after the straitest sect,
though not of them. He said I was a Hebrew
servant bought, in the true meaning of the
great law-giver, and, by sealed writings, which
I yet have, he set me free."

" And my mother?" Esther asked.

"Thou shalt hear all, Esther ; be patient.
Before I am through thou shalt see it were
easier for me to forget myself than thy mother.
... At the end of my service, I came up to

300

Jerusalem to the Passover. My master enter-
tained me. I was in love with him already,
and I prayed to be continued in his service.
He consented, and I served him yet another
seven years, but as a hired son of Israel. In
his behalf I had charge of ventures on the sea
by ships, and of ventures on land by caravans
eastward to Susa and Persepolis, and the lands
of silk beyond them. Perilous passages were
they, my daughter; but the Lord blessed all
I undertook. I brought home vast gains for
the prince, and richer knowledge for myself,
without which I could not have mastered the
charges since fallen to me. . . . One day I
was a guest in his house in Jerusalem. A serv-
ant entered with some sliced bread on a plat-
ter. She came to me first. It was then I saw
thy mother, and loved her, and took her away
in my secret heart. After a while a time came
when I sought the prince to make her my
wife. He told me she was bond-servant for-
ever; but if she wished, he would set her free
that I might be gratified. She gave me love
for love, but was happy where she was, and re-
fused her freedom. I prayed and besought,
going again and again after long intervals.
She would be my wife, she all the time said, if
I would become her fellow in servitude. Our
father Jacob served yet other seven years for
his Rachel. Could I not as much for mine?
But thy mother said I must become as she, to
serve forever. I came away, but went back.
Look, Esther, look here."

He pulled out the lobe of his left ear.

"See you not the scar of the awl?"

"I see it," she said; "and, oh, I see how thou didst love my mother!"

"Love her, Esther! She was to me more than the Shulamite to the singing king, fairer, more spotless; a fountain of gardens, a well of living waters, and streams from Lebanon. The master, even as I required him, took me to the judges, and back to his door, and thrust the awl through my ear into the door, and I was his servant forever. So I won my Rachel. And was ever love like mine?"

Esther stooped and kissed him, and they were silent, thinking of the dead.

"My master was drowned at sea, the first sorrow that ever fell upon me," the merchant continued. "There was mourning in his house, and in mine here in Antioch, my abiding-place at the time. Now, Esther, mark you! When the good prince was lost, I had risen to be his chief steward, with everything of property belonging to him in my management and control. Judge you how much he loved and trusted me! I hastened to Jerusalem to render account to the widow. She continued me in the stewardship. I applied myself with greater diligence. The business prospered, and grew year by year. Ten years passed; then came the blow which you heard the young man tell about—the accident, as he called it, to the Procurator Gratus. The Roman gave it out an attempt to assassinate him. Under that pretext, by leave from Rome, he confiscated to his own use the immense fortune of the wid-

ow and children. Nor stopped he there. That there might be no reversal of the judgment, he removed all the parties interested. From that dreadful day to this the family of Hur have been lost. The son, whom I had seen as a child, was sentenced to the galleys. The widow and daughter are supposed to have been buried in some of the many dungeons of Judea, which, once closed upon the doomed, are like sepulchres sealed and locked. They passed from the knowledge of men as utterly as if the sea had swallowed them unseen. We could not hear how they died—nay, not even that they were dead."

Esther's eyes were dewy with tears.

"Thy heart is good, Esther, good as thy mother's was; and I pray it have not the fate of most good hearts—to be trampled upon by the unmerciful and blind. But hearken further. I went up to Jerusalem to give help to my benefactress, and was seized at the gate of the city and carried to the sunken cells of the Tower of Antonia; why, I knew not, until Gratus himself came and demanded of me the moneys of the House of Hur, which he knew, after our Jewish custom of exchange, were subject to my draft in the different marts of the world. He required me to sign to his order. I refused. He had the houses, lands, goods, ships, and movable property of those I served; he had not their moneys. I saw, if I kept favor in the sight of the Lord, I could rebuild their broken fortunes. I refused the tyrant's demands. He put me to torture; my

303

will held good, and he set me free, nothing gained. I came home and began again, in the name of Simonides of Antioch, instead of the Prince Hur of Jerusalem. Thou knowest, Esther, how I have prospered; that the increase of the millions of the prince in my hands was miraculous; thou knowest how, at the end of three years, while going up to Cæsarea, I was taken and a second time tortured by Gratus to compel a confession that my goods and moneys were subject to his order of confiscation; thou knowest he failed as before. Broken in body, I came home and found my Rachel dead of fear and grief for me. The Lord our God reigned, and I lived. From the emperor himself I bought immunity and license to trade throughout the world. To-day — praised be He who maketh the clouds his chariot and walketh upon the winds! — to-day, Esther, that which was in my hands for stewardship is multiplied into talents sufficient to enrich a Cæsar."

He lifted his head proudly; their eyes met; each read the other's thought. "What shall I with the treasure, Esther?" he asked, without lowering his gaze.

"My father," she answered, in a low voice, "did not the rightful owner call for it but now?"

Still his look did not fail.

"And thou, my child; shall I leave thee a beggar?"

"Nay, father, am not I, because I am thy child, his bond-servant? And of whom was

it written. 'Strength and honor are her cloth-
ing, and she shall rejoice in time to come?'"

A gleam of ineffable love lighted his face
as he said, " The Lord hath been good to me
in many ways ; but thou, Esther, art the sov-
ereign excellence of His favor."

He drew her to his breast and kissed her
many times.

" Hear now," he said, with clearer voice—
"hear now why I laughed this morning. The
young man faced me the apparition of his fa-
ther in comely youth. My spirit arose to
salute him. I felt my trial-days were over and
my labors ended. Hardly could I keep from
crying out. I longed to take him by the hand
and show the balance I had earned, and say,
' Lo, 'tis all thine ! and I am thy servant, ready
now to be called away.' And so I would have
done, Esther, so I would have done, but that
moment three thoughts rushed to restrain
me. I will be sure he is my master's son—
such was the first thought ; if he is my master's
son, I will learn somewhat of his nature. Of
those born to riches, bethink you, Esther, how
many there are in whose hands riches are but
breeding curses "—he paused, while his hands
clutched, and his voice shrilled with passion—
" Esther, consider the pains I endured at the
Roman's hands ; nay, not Gratus's alone : the
merciless wretches who did his bidding the
first time and the last were Romans, and they
all alike laughed to hear me scream. Consider
my broken body, and the years I have gone
shorn of my stature ; consider thy mother yon-

305

der in her lonely tomb, crushed of soul as I of
body; consider the sorrows of my master's
family if they are living, and the cruelty of
their taking-off if they are dead; consider all,
and, with Heaven's love about thee, tell me,
daughter, shall not a hair fall or a red drop run
in expiation? Tell me not, as the preachers
sometimes do—tell me not that vengeance is
the Lord's. Does He not work His will harm-
fully as well as in love by agencies? Has He
not His men of war more numerous than His
prophets? Is not His the law, Eye for eye,
hand for hand, foot for foot? Oh, in all these
years I have dreamed of vengeance, and prayed
and provided for it, and gathered patience from
the growing of my store, thinking and prom-
ising, as the Lord liveth, it will one day buy
me punishment of the wrong-doers! And
when, speaking of his practice with arms, the
young man said it was for a nameless purpose,
I named the purpose even as he spoke—ven-
geance! and that, Esther, that it was — the
third thought which held me still and hard
while his pleading lasted, and made me laugh
when he was gone."

Esther caressed the faded hands, and said,
as if her spirit with his were running for-
ward to results, "He is gone. Will he come
again?"

"Aye, Malluch the faithful goes with him,
and will bring him back when I am ready."

"And when will that be, father?"

"Not long, not long. He thinks all his wit-
nesses dead. There is one living who will not

fail to know him, if he be, indeed, my master's
son."

" His mother ?"

" Nay, daughter, I will set the witness before
him ; till then let us rest the business with the
Lord. I am tired. Call Abimelech."

Esther called the servant, and they returned
into the house.

CHAPTER V
THE GROVE OF DAPHNE

HEN Ben-Hur sallied from the great
warehouse, it was with the thought
that another failure was to be added
to the many he had already met in
the quest for his people ; and the idea was de-
pressing exactly in proportion as the objects
of his quest were dear to him ; it curtained
him round about with a sense of utter loneli-
ness on earth, which, more than anything else,
serves to eke from a soul cast down its remain-
ing interest in life.

Through the people, and the piles of goods,
he made way to the edge of the landing, and
was tempted by the cool shadows darkening
the river's depth. The lazy current seemed
to stop and wait for him. In counteraction of
the spell, the saying of the voyager flashed into
memory—" Better be a worm, and feed upon
the mulberries of Daphne, than a king's guest."
He turned, and walked rapidly down the land-
ing and back to the khan.

" The road to Daphne !" the steward said,

surprised at the question Ben-Hur put to him.
"You have not been here before? Well, count
this the happiest day of your life. You can-
not mistake the road. The next street to the
left, going south, leads straight to Mount Sul-
pius, crowned by the altar of Jupiter and the
Amphitheatre; keep it to the third cross street,
known as Herod's Colonnade; turn to your
right there, and hold the way through the old
city of Seleucus to the bronze gates of Epiph-
anes. There the road to Daphne begins—and
may the gods keep you!"

A few directions respecting his baggage, and
Ben-Hur set out.

The Colonnade of Herod was easily found;
thence to the brazen gates, under a continuous
marble portico, he passed with a multitude
mixed of people from all the trading nations of
the earth.

It was about the fourth hour of the day when
he passed out the gate, and found himself one
of a procession apparently interminable, mov-
ing to the famous Grove. The road was di-
vided into separate ways for footmen, for men
on horses, and men in chariots; and those
again into separate ways for outgoers and in-
comers. The lines of division were guarded
by low balustrading, broken by massive pedes-
tals, many of which were surmounted with
statuary. Right and left of the road extended
margins of sward perfectly kept, relieved at in-
tervals by groups of oak and sycamore trees,
and vine-clad summer-houses for the accom-
modation of the weary, of whom, on the re-

turn side, there were always multitudes. The ways of the footmen were paved with red stone, and those of the riders strewn with white sand compactly rolled, but not so solid as to give back an echo to hoof or wheel. The number and variety of fountains at play were amazing, all gifts of visiting kings, and called after them. Out south-west to the gates of the Grove, the magnificent thoroughfare stretched a little over four miles from the city.

In his wretchedness of feeling, Ben-Hur barely observed the royal liberality which marked the construction of the road. Nor more did he at first notice the crowd going with him. He treated the processional displays with like indifference. To say truth, besides his self-absorption, he had not a little of the complacency of a Roman visiting the provinces fresh from the ceremonies which daily eddied round and round the golden pillar set up by Augustus as the centre of the world. It was not possible for the provinces to offer anything new or superior. He rather availed himself of every opportunity to push forward through the companies in the way, and too slow-going for his impatience. By the time he reached Heracleia, a suburban village intermediate the city and the Grove, he was somewhat spent with exercise, and began to be susceptible of entertainment. Once a pair of goats led by a beautiful woman, woman and goats alike brilliant with ribbons and flowers, attracted his attention. Then he stopped to look at a bull of mighty girth, and snowy-

white, covered with vines freshly cut, and bearing on its broad back a naked child in a basket, the image of a young Bacchus, squeezing the juice of ripened berries into a goblet, and drinking with libational formulas. As he resumed his walk, he wondered whose altars would be enriched by the offerings. A horse went by with clipped mane, after the fashion of the time, his rider superbly dressed. He smiled to observe the harmony of pride between the man and the brute. Often after that he turned his head at hearing the rumble of wheels and the dull thud of hoofs; unconsciously he was becoming interested in the styles of chariots and charioteers, as they rustled past him going and coming. Nor was it long until he began to make notes of the people around him. He saw they were of all ages, sexes, and conditions, and all in holiday attire. One company was uniformed in white, another in black; some bore flags, some smoking censers; some went slowly, singing hymns; others stepped to the music of flutes and tabrets. If such were the going to Daphne every day in the year, what a wondrous sight Daphne must be! At last there was a clapping of hands, and a burst of joyous cries; following the pointing of many fingers, he looked and saw upon the brow of a hill the templed gate of the consecrated Grove. The hymns swelled to louder strains; the music quickened time; and, borne along by the impulsive current, and sharing the common eagerness, he passed in, and, Romanized in taste as he was, fell to worshipping the place.

Rearward of the structure which graced the entrance-way—a purely Grecian pile—he stood upon a broad esplanade paved with polished stone; around him a restless exclamatory multitude, in gayest colors, relieved against the iridescent spray flying crystal-white from fountains; before him, off to the south-west, dustless paths radiated out into a garden, and beyond that into a forest, over which rested a veil of pale-blue vapor. Ben-Hur gazed wistfully, uncertain where to go. A woman that moment exclaimed,

"Beautiful! But where to now?"

Her companion, wearing a chaplet of bays, laughed and answered, "Go to, thou pretty barbarian! The question implies an earthly fear; and did we not agree to leave all such behind in Antioch with the rusty earth? The winds which blow here are respirations of the gods. Let us give ourselves to waftage of the winds."

"But if we should get lost?"

"O thou timid! No one was ever lost in Daphne, except those on whom her gates close forever."

"And who are they?" she asked, still fearful.

"Such as have yielded to the charms of the place and chosen it for life and death. Hark! Stand we here, and I will show you of whom I speak."

Upon the marble pavement there was a skurry of sandalled feet; the crowd opened, and a party of girls rushed about the speaker and his fair friend, and began singing and dancing

311

to the tabrets they themselves touched. The woman, scared, clung to the man, who put an arm about her, and, with kindled face, kept time to the music with the other hand overhead. The hair of the dancers floated free, and their limbs blushed through the robes of gauze which scarcely draped them. Words may not be used to tell of the voluptuousness of the dance. One brief round, and they darted off through the yielding crowd lightly as they had come.

"Now what think you?" cried the man to the woman.

"Who are they?" she asked.

"Devadasi—priestesses devoted to the Temple of Apollo. There is an army of them. They make the chorus in celebrations. This is their home. Sometimes they wander off to other cities, but all they make is brought here to enrich the house of the divine musician. Shall we go now?"

Next minute the two were gone.

Ben-Hur took comfort in the assurance that no one was ever lost in Daphne, and he, too, set out—where, he knew not.

A sculpture reared upon a beautiful pedestal in the garden attracted him first. It proved to be the statue of a centaur. An inscription informed the unlearned visitor that it exactly represented Chiron, the beloved of Apollo and Diana, instructed by them in the mysteries of hunting, medicine, music, and prophecy. The inscription also bade the stranger look out at a certain part of the heavens, at a certain

hour of the clear night, and he would behold
the dead alive among the stars, whither Jupi-
ter had transferred the good genius.

The wisest of the centaurs continued, never-
theless, in the service of mankind. In his hand
he held a scroll, on which, graven in Greek,
were paragraphs of a notice:

"O Traveller!
"Art thou a stranger?
"I. Hearken to the singing of the brooks, and fear
not the rain of the fountains; so will the Naiades
learn to love thee.
"II. The invited breezes of Daphne are Zephyrus
and Auster; gentle ministers of life, they will gather
sweets for thee; when Eurus blows, Diana is else-
where hunting; when Boreas blusters, go hide, for
Apollo is angry.
"III. The shades of the Grove are thine in the
day; at night they belong to Pan and his Dryades.
Disturb them not.
"IV. Eat of the Lotus by the brook-sides sparing-
ly, unless thou wouldst have surcease of memory,
which is to become a child of Daphne.
"V. Walk thou round the weaving spider—'tis
Arachne at work for Minerva.
"VI. Wouldst thou behold the tears of Daphne,
break but a bud from a laurel bough—and die.
"Heed thou!
"And stay and be happy."

Ben-Hur left the interpretation of the mys-
tic notice to others fast enclosing him, and
turned away as the white bull was led by. The
boy sat in the basket, followed by a procession;
after them again, the woman with the goats;
and behind her the flute and tabret players,
and another procession of gift-bringers.

"Whither go they?" asked a by-stander.

Another made answer, "The bull to Father Jove; the goat—"

"Did not Apollo once keep the flocks of Admetus?"

"Aye, the goat to Apollo!"

The goodness of the reader is again besought in favor of an explanation. A certain facility of accommodation in the matter of religion comes to us after much intercourse with people of a different faith; gradually we attain the truth that every creed is illustrated by good men who are entitled to our respect, but whom we cannot respect without courtesy to their creed. To this point Ben-Hur had arrived. Neither the years in Rome nor those in the galley had made any impression upon his religious faith: he was yet a Jew. In his view, nevertheless, it was not an impiety to look for the beautiful in the Grove of Daphne.

The remark does not interdict the further saying, if his scruples had been ever so extreme, not improbably he would at this time have smothered them. He was angry; not as the irritable, from chafing of a trifle; nor was his anger like the fool's, pumped from the wells of nothing, to be dissipated by a reproach or a curse; it was the wrath peculiar to ardent natures rudely awakened by the sudden annihilation of a hope—dream, if you will—in which the choicest happinesses were thought to be certainly in reach. In such case nothing intermediate will carry off the passion—the quarrel is with Fate.

314

Let us follow the philosophy a little further, and say to ourselves, it were well in such quarrels if Fate were something tangible, to be despatched with a look or a blow, or a speaking personage with whom high words were possible; then the unhappy mortal would not always end the affair by punishing himself.

In ordinary mood, Ben-Hur would not have come to the Grove alone, or, coming alone, he would have availed himself of his position in the consul's family, and made provision against wandering idly about, unknowing and unknown; he would have had all the points of interest in mind, and gone to them under guidance, as in the despatch of business; or, wishing to squander days of leisure in the beautiful place, he would have had in hand a letter to the master of it all, whoever he might be. This would have made him a sight-seer, like the shouting herd he was accompanying; whereas he had no reverence for the deities of the Grove, nor curiosity; a man in the blindness of bitter disappointment, he was adrift, not waiting for Fate, but seeking it as a desperate challenger.

Every one has known this condition of mind, though, perhaps, not all in the same degree; every one will recognize it as the condition in which he has done brave things with apparent serenity; and every one reading will say, Fortunate for Ben-Hur if the folly which now catches him is but a friendly harlequin with whistle and painted cap, and not some Violence with a pointed sword pitiless.

EN-HUR entered the woods with the
processions. He had not interest
enough at first to ask where they
were going; yet, to relieve him from
absolute indifference, he had a vague impres-
sion that they were in movement to the tem-
ples, which were the central objects of the
Grove, supreme in attractions.

Presently, as singers dreamfully play with a
flitting chorus, he began repeating to himself,
" Better be a worm, and feed on the mulber-
ries of Daphne, than a king's guest." Then of
the much repetition arose questions importu-
nate of answer. Was life in the Grove so very
sweet? Wherein was the charm? Did it lie
in some tangled depth of philosophy? Or was
it something in fact, something on the sur-
face, discernible to every-day wakeful senses?
Every year thousands, forswearing the world,
gave themselves to service here. Did they find
the charm? And was it sufficient, when found,
to induce forgetfulness profound enough to
shut out of mind the infinitely diverse things
of life? those that sweeten and those that
imbitter? hopes hovering in the near future
as well as sorrows born of the past? If the
Grove were so good for them, why should it
not be good for him? He was a Jew; could

316

it be that the excellences were for all the world but children of Abraham? Forthwith he bent all his faculties to the task of discovery, unmindful of the singing of the gift-bringers and the quips of his associates.

In the quest, the sky yielded him nothing; it was blue, very blue, and full of twittering swallows—so was the sky over the city.

Farther on, out of the woods at his right hand, a breeze poured across the road, splashing him with a wave of sweet smells, blended of roses and consuming spices. He stopped, as did others, looking the way the breeze came.

"A garden over there?" he said, to a man at his elbow.

"Rather some priestly ceremony in performance — something to Diana, or Pan, or a deity of the woods."

The answer was in his mother-tongue. Ben-Hur gave the speaker a surprised look.

"A Hebrew?" he asked him.

The man replied, with a deferential smile,

"I was born within a stone's-throw of the market-place in Jerusalem."

Ben-Hur was proceeding to further speech, when the crowd surged forward, thrusting him out on the side of the walk next the woods, and carrying the stranger away. The customary gown and staff, a brown cloth on the head tied by a yellow rope, and a strong Judean face to avouch the garments of honest right, remained in the young man's mind, a kind of summary of the man.

This took place at a point where a path into

the woods began, offering a happy escape from
the noisy processions. Ben-Hur availed him-
self of the offer.

He walked first into a thicket which, from
the road, appeared in a state of nature, close,
impenetrable, a nesting-place for wild birds.
A few steps, however, gave him to see the
master's hand even there. The shrubs were
flowering or fruit-bearing; under the bending
branches the ground was pranked with bright-
est blooms; over them the jasmine stretched
its delicate bonds. From lilac and rose and
lily and tulip, from oleander and strawberry-
tree, all old friends in the gardens of the val-
leys about the city of David, the air, lingering
or in haste, loaded itself with exhalations day
and night; and that nothing might be wanting
to the happiness of the nymphs and naiads,
down through the flower-lighted shadows of
the mass a brook went its course gently, and
by many winding ways.

Out of the thicket, as he proceeded, on his
right and left, issued the cry of the pigeon and
the cooing of turtle-doves; blackbirds waited
for him, and bided his coming close; a night-
ingale kept its place fearless, though he passed
in arm's-length; a quail ran before him at his
feet, whistling to the brood she was leading,
and as he paused for them to get out of his
way, a figure crawled from a bed of honeyed
musk brilliant with balls of golden blossoms.
Ben-Hur was startled. Had he, indeed, been
permitted to see a satyr at home? The creat-
ure looked up at him, and showed in its teeth

a hooked pruning-knife; he smiled at his own
scare, and, lo! the charm was evolved! Peace
without fear—peace a universal condition—
that it was!

He sat upon the ground beneath a citron-
tree, which spread its gray roots sprawling to
receive a branch of the brook. The nest of a
titmouse hung close to the bubbling water,
and the tiny creature looked out of the door
of the nest into his eyes. "Verily, the bird is
interpreting to me," he thought. "It says, 'I
am not afraid of you, for the law of this happy
place is Love.'"

The charm of the Grove seemed plain to
him; he was glad, and determined to render
himself one of the lost in Daphne. In charge
of the flowers and shrubs, and watching the
growth of all the dumb excellences everywhere
to be seen, could not he, like the man with the
pruning-knife in his mouth, forego the days of
his troubled life—forego them forgetting and
forgotten?

But by-and-by his Jewish nature began to
stir within him.

The charm might be sufficient for some peo-
ple. Of what kind were they?

Love is delightful—ah! how pleasant as a
successor to wretchedness like his. But was
it all there was of life? All?

There was an unlikeness between him and
those who buried themselves contentedly here.
They had no duties—they could not have had;
but he—

"God of Israel!" he cried aloud, springing

319

to his feet, with burning cheeks — "Mother! Tirzah! Cursed be the moment, cursed the place, in which I yield myself happy in your loss!"

He hurried away through the thicket, and came to a stream flowing with the volume of a river between banks of masonry, broken at intervals by gated sluice-ways. A bridge carried the path he was traversing across the stream; and, standing upon it, he saw other bridges, no two of them alike. Under him the water was lying in a deep pool, clear as a shadow; down a little way it tumbled with a roar over rocks; then there was another pool, and another cascade; and so on, out of view; and bridges and pools and resounding cascades said, plainly as inarticulate things can tell a story, the river was running by permission of a master, exactly as the master would have it, tractable as became a servant of the gods.

Forward from the bridge he beheld a landscape of wide valleys and irregular heights, with groves and lakes and fanciful houses linked together by white paths and shining streams. The valleys were spread below, that the river might be poured upon them for refreshment in days of drought, and they were as green carpets figured with beds and fields of flowers, and flecked with flocks of sheep white as balls of snow; and the voices of shepherds following the flocks were heard afar. As if to tell him of the pious inscription of all he beheld, the altars out under the open sky seemed countless, each with a white-gowned figure

320

attending it, while processions in white went slowly hither and thither between them ; and the smoke of the altars, half-risen, hung collected in pale clouds over the devoted places.

Here, there, happy in flight, intoxicated in pause, from object to object, point to point, now in the meadow, now on the heights, now lingering to penetrate the groves and observe the processions, then lost in efforts to pursue the paths and streams which trended mazily into dim perspectives to end finally in— Ah, what might be a fitting end to scene so beautiful ! What adequate mysteries were hidden behind an introduction so marvellous ! Here and there, the speech was beginning, his gaze wandered, so he could not help the conviction, forced by the view, and as the sum of it all, that there was peace in the air and on the earth, and invitation everywhere to come and lie down here and be at rest.

Suddenly a revelation dawned upon him— the Grove was, in fact, a temple—one far-reaching, wall-less temple !

Never anything like it !

The architect had not stopped to pother about columns and porticos, proportions or interiors, or any limitation upon the epic he sought to materialize : he had simply made a servant of Nature—art can go no further. So the cunning son of Jupiter and Callisto built the old Arcadia; and in this, as in that, the genius was Greek.

From the bridge Ben-Hur went forward into the nearest valley.

He came to a flock of sheep. The shepherd was a girl, and she beckoned him, "Come!"

Farther on, the path was divided by an altar—a pedestal of black gneiss capped with a slab of white marble deftly foliated, and on that a brazier of bronze holding a fire. Close by it, a woman, seeing him, waved a wand of willow, and as he passed called him, "Stay!" And the temptation in her smile was that of passionate youth.

On yet farther, he met one of the processions; at its head a troop of little girls, nude except as they were covered with garlands, piped their shrill voices into a song; then a troop of boys, also nude, their bodies deeply sun-browned, came dancing to the song of the girls; behind them the procession, all women, bearing baskets of spices and sweets to the altars—women clad in simple robes, careless of exposure. As he went by they held their hands to him, and said, "Stay, and go with us." One, a Greek, sang a verse from Anacreon:

> "For to-day I take or give;
> For to-day I drink and live;
> For to-day I beg or borrow;
> Who knows about the silent morrow?"

But he pursued his way indifferent, and came next to a grove luxuriant, in the heart of the vale at the point where it would be most attractive to the observing eye. As it came close to the path he was travelling, there was a seduction in its shade, and through the foli-

322

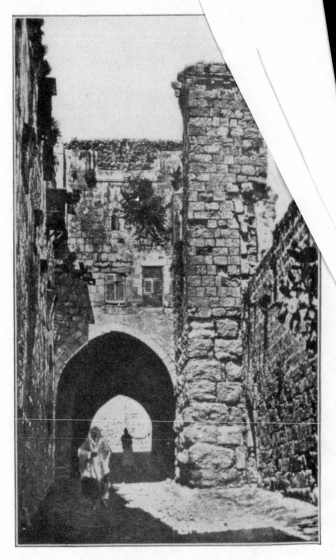

TOWER OF ANTONIA

age he caught the shining of what appeared a pretentious statue; so he turned aside, and entered the cool retreat.

The grass was fresh and clean. The trees did not crowd each other; and they were of every kind native to the East, blended well with strangers adopted from far quarters; here grouped in exclusive companionship palm-trees plumed like queens; there sycamores, overtopping laurels of darker foliage; and evergreen oaks rising verdantly, with cedars vast enough to be kings on Lebanon; and mulberries; and terebinths so beautiful it is not hyperbole to speak of them as blown from the orchards of Paradise.

The statue proved to be a Daphne of wondrous beauty. Hardly, however, had he time to more than glance at her face: at the base of the pedestal a girl and a youth were lying upon a tiger's skin asleep in each other's arms; close by them the implements of their service —his axe and sickle, her basket—flung carelessly upon a heap of fading roses.

The exposure startled him. Back in the hush of the perfumed thicket he discovered, as he thought, that the charm of the great Grove was peace without fear, and almost yielded to it; now, in this sleep in the day's broad glare—this sleep at the feet of Daphne —he read a further chapter to which only the vaguest allusion is sufferable. The law of the place was Love, but Love without Law.

And this was the sweet peace of Daphne! This the life's end of her ministers!

For this kings and princes gave of their revenues!

For this a crafty priesthood subordinated Nature—her birds and brooks and lilies, the river, the labor of many hands, the sanctity of altars, the fertile power of the sun!

It would be pleasant now to record that as Ben-Hur pursued his walk assailed by such reflections, he yielded somewhat to sorrow for the votaries of the great out-door temple; especially for those who, by personal service, kept it in a state so surpassingly lovely. How they came to the condition was not any longer a mystery; the motive, the influence, the inducement, were before him. Some there were, no doubt, caught by the promise held out to their troubled spirits of endless peace in a consecrated abode, to the beauty of which, if they had not money, they could contribute their labor; this class implied intellect peculiarly subject to hope and fear; but the great body of the faithful could not be classed with such. Apollo's nets were wide, and their meshes small; and hardly may one tell what all his fishermen landed: this less for that they cannot be described than because they ought not to be. Enough that the mass were of the sybarites of the world, and of the herds in number vaster and in degree lower—devotees of the unmixed sensualism to which the East was almost wholly given. Not to any of the exaltations—not to the singing-god, or his unhappy mistress; not to any philosophy requiring for its enjoyment the calm of retirement

gride of wheels, and the prospect of diversion excite me. I have some skill in the exercises. In the palæstræ of Rome I am not unknown. Let us to the course."

Malluch lingered to say, quickly, "The duumvir was a Roman, yet I see his son in the garments of a Jew."

"The noble Arrius was my father by adoption," Ben-Hur answered.

"Ah! I see, and beg pardon."

Passing through the belt of forest, they came to a field with a track laid out upon it, in shape and extent exactly like those of the stadia. The course, or track proper, was of soft earth, rolled and sprinkled, and on both sides defined by ropes, stretched loosely upon upright javelins. For the accommodation of spectators, and such as had interests reaching forward of the mere practice, there were several stands shaded by substantial awnings, and provided with seats in rising rows. In one of the stands the two new-comers found places.

Ben-Hur counted the chariots as they went by—nine in all.

"I commend the fellows," he said, with goodwill. "Here in the East, I thought they aspired to nothing better than the two; but they are ambitious, and play with royal fours. Let us study their performance."

Eight of the fours passed the stand, some walking, others on the trot, and all unexceptionally handled; then the ninth one came on the gallop. Ben-Hur burst into exclamation.

"I have been in the stables of the emperor,

Malluch, but, by our father Abraham of blessed memory! I never saw the like of these."

The last four was then sweeping past. All at once they fell into confusion. Some one on the stand uttered a sharp cry. Ben-Hur turned, and saw an old man half-risen from an upper seat, his hands clinched and raised, his eyes fiercely bright, his long white beard fairly quivering. Some of the spectators nearest him began to laugh.

"They should respect his beard at least. Who is he?" asked Ben-Hur.

"A mighty man from the Desert, somewhere beyond Moab, and owner of camels in herds, and horses descended, they say, from the racers of the first Pharaoh—Sheik Ilderim by name and title."

Thus Malluch replied.

The driver meanwhile exerted himself to quiet the four, but without avail. Each ineffectual effort excited the sheik the more.

"Abaddon seize him!" yelled the patriarch, shrilly. "Run! fly! do you hear, my children?" The question was to his attendants, apparently of the tribe. "Do you hear? They are Desertborn, like yourselves. Catch them—quick!"

The plunging of the animals increased.

"Accursed Roman!" and the sheik shook his fist at the driver. "Did he not swear he could drive them—swear it by all his brood of bastard Latin gods? Nay, hands off me—off, I say! They should run swift as eagles, and with the temper of hand-bred lambs, he swore. Cursed be he—cursed the mother of liars who

calls him son! See them, the priceless! Let him touch one of them with a lash, and "—the rest of the sentence was lost in a furious grinding of his teeth. "To their heads, some of you, and speak them—a word, one is enough, from the tent-song your mothers sang you. Oh, fool, fool that I was to put trust in a Roman!"

Some of the shrewder of the old man's friends planted themselves between him and the horses. An opportune failure of breath on his part helped the stratagem.

Ben-Hur, thinking he comprehended the sheik, sympathized with him. Far more than mere pride of property—more than anxiety for the result of the race—in his view it was within the possible for the patriarch, according to his habits of thought and his ideas of the inestimable, to love such animals with a tenderness akin to the most sensitive passion.

They were all bright bays, unspotted, perfectly matched, and so proportioned as to seem less than they really were. Delicate ears pointed small heads; the faces were broad and full between the eyes; the nostrils in expansion disclosed membrane so deeply red as to suggest the flashing of flame; the necks were arches, overlaid with fine mane so abundant as to drape the shoulders and breast, while in happy consonance the forelocks were like ravellings of silken veils; between the knees and the fetlocks the legs were flat as an open hand, but above the knees they were rounded with mighty muscles, needful to upbear the shapely close-knit bodies; the hoofs were like cups of

polished agate; and in rearing and plunging they whipped the air, and sometimes the earth, with tails glossy-black and thick and long. The sheik spoke of them as the priceless, and it was a good saying.

In this second and closer look at the horses, Ben-Hur read the story of their relation to their master. They had grown up under his eyes, objects of his special care in the day, his visions of pride in the night, with his family at home in the black tent out on the shadeless bosom of the desert, as his children beloved. That they might win him a triumph over the haughty and hated Roman, the old man had brought his loves to the city, never doubting they would win, if only he could find a trusty expert to take them in hand; not merely one with skill, but of a spirit which their spirits would acknowledge. Unlike the colder people of the West, he could not protest the driver's inability, and dismiss him civilly; an Arab and a sheik, he had to explode, and rive the air about him with clamor.

Before the patriarch was done with his expletives, a dozen hands were at the bits of the horses, and their quiet assured. About that time, another chariot appeared upon the track; and, unlike the others, driver, vehicle, and racers were precisely as they would be presented in the Circus the day of final trial. For a reason which will presently be more apparent, it is desirable now to give this turnout plainly to the reader.

There should be no difficulty in understand-

ing the carriage known to us all as the chariot of classical renown. One has but to picture to himself a dray with low wheels and broad axle, surmounted by a box open at the tail-end. Such was the primitive pattern. Artistic genius came along in time, and, touching the rude machine, raised it into a thing of beauty—that, for instance, in which Aurora, riding in advance of the dawn, is given to our fancy.

The jockeys of the ancients, quite as shrewd and ambitious as their successors of the present, called their humblest turnout a two, and their best in grade a four; in the latter, they contested the Olympics and the other festal shows founded in imitation of them.

The same sharp gamesters preferred to put their horses to the chariot all abreast; and for distinction they termed the two next the pole yoke-steeds, and those on the right and left outside trace-mates. It was their judgment, also, that, by allowing the fullest freedom of action, the greatest speed was attainable; accordingly, the harness resorted to was peculiarly simple; in fact, there was nothing of it save a collar round the animal's neck, and a trace fixed to the collar, unless the lines and a halter fall within the term. Wanting to hitch up, the masters pinned a narrow wooden yoke, or cross-tree, near the end of the pole, and, by straps passed through rings at the end of the yoke, buckled the latter to the collar. The traces of the yoke-steeds they hitched to the axle; those of the trace-mates to the top rim of the chariot-bed. There remained then but

331

the adjustment of the lines, which, judged by the modern devices, was not the least curious part of the method. For this there was a large ring at the forward extremity of the pole ; securing the ends to that ring first, they parted the lines so as to give one to each horse, and proceeded to pass them to the driver, slipping them separately through rings on the inner side of the halters at the mouth.

With this plain generalization in mind, all further desirable knowledge upon the subject can be had by following the incidents of the scene occurring.

The other contestants had been received in silence ; the last comer was more fortunate. While moving towards the stand from which we are viewing the scene, his progress was signalized by loud demonstrations, by clapping of hands and cheers, the effect of which was to centre attention upon him exclusively. His yoke-steeds, it was observed, were black, while the trace-mates were snow-white. In conformity to the exacting canons of Roman taste, they had all four been mutilated; that is to say, their tails had been clipped, and, to complete the barbarity, their shorn manes were divided into knots tied with flaring red and yellow ribbons.

In advancing, the stranger at length reached a point where the chariot came into view from the stand, and its appearance would of itself have justified the shouting. The wheels were very marvels of construction. Stout bands of burnished bronze reinforced the hubs, other-

wise very light; the spokes were sections of ivory tusks, set in with the natural curve outward to perfect the dishing, considered important then as now; bronze tires held the fellies, which were of shining ebony. The axle, in keeping with the wheels, was tipped with heads of snarling tigers done in brass, and the bed was woven of willow wands gilded with gold.

The coming of the beautiful horses and resplendent chariot drew Ben-Hur to look at the driver with increased interest.

Who was he?

When Ben-Hur asked himself the question first, he could not see the man's face, or even his full figure; yet the air and manner were familiar, and pricked him keenly with a reminder of a period long gone.

Who could it be?

Nearer now, and the horses approaching at a trot. From the shouting and the gorgeousness of the turnout, it was thought he might be some official favorite or famous prince. Such an appearance was not inconsistent with exalted rank. Kings often struggled for the crown of leaves which was the prize of victory. Nero and Commodus, it will be remembered, devoted themselves to the chariot. Ben-Hur arose and forced a passage down nearly to the railing in front of the lower seat of the stand. His face was earnest, his manner eager.

And directly the whole person of the driver was in view. A companion rode with him, in classic description a Myrtilus, permitted men of high estate indulging their passion for the

333

race - course. Ben - Hur could see only the driver, standing erect in the chariot, with the reins passed several times round his body—a handsome figure, scantily covered by a tunic of light-red cloth; in the right hand a whip; in the other, the arm raised and lightly extended, the four lines. The pose was exceedingly graceful and animated. The cheers and clapping of hands were received with statuesque indifference. Ben-Hur stood transfixed —his instinct and memory had served him faithfully—the driver was Messala.

By the selection of horses, the magnificence of the chariot, the attitude, and display of person — above all, by the expression of the cold, sharp, eagle features, imperialized in his countrymen by sway of the world through so many generations, Ben-Hur knew Messala unchanged as haughty, confident, and audacious as ever, the same in ambition, cynicism, and mocking insouciance.

CHAPTER VIII
THE FOUNTAIN OF CASTALIA

 S Ben-Hur descended the steps of the stand, an Arab arose upon the last one at the foot, and cried out,

"Men of the East and West — hearken! The good Sheik Ilderim giveth greeting. With four horses, sons of the favorites of Solomon the Wise, he hath come up against the best. Needs he most a mighty man to

334

drive them. Whoso will take them to his satisfaction, to him he promiseth enrichment forever. Here — there — in the city and in the Circuses, and wherever the strong most do congregate, tell ye this his offer. So saith my master, Sheik Ilderim the Generous."

The proclamation awakened a great buzz among the people under the awning. By night it would be repeated and discussed in all the sporting circles of Antioch. Ben-Hur, hearing it, stopped and looked hesitatingly from the herald to the sheik. Malluch thought he was about to accept the offer, but was relieved when he presently turned to him and asked, " Good Malluch, where to now?"

The worthy replied, with a laugh, " Would you liken yourself to others visiting the Grove for the first time, you will straightway to hear your fortune told."

" My fortune, said you? Though the suggestion has in it a flavor of unbelief, let us to the goddess at once."

" Nay, son of Arrius, these Apollonians have a better trick than that. Instead of speech with a Pythia or a Sibyl, they will sell you a plain papyrus leaf, hardly dry from the stalk, and bid you dip it in the water of a certain fountain, when it will show you a verse in which you may hear of your future."

The glow of interest departed from Ben-Hur's face.

" There are people who have no need to vex themselves about their future," he said, gloomily.

335

"Then you prefer to go to the temples?"

"The temples are Greek, are they not?"

"They call them Greek."

"The Hellenes were masters of the beautiful in art; but in architecture they sacrificed variety to unbending beauty. Their temples are all alike. How call you the fountain?"

"Castalia."

"Oh! it has repute throughout the world. Let us thither."

Malluch kept watch on his companion as they went, and saw that for the moment, at least, his good spirits were out. To the people passing he gave no attention; over the wonders they came upon there were no exclamations; silently, even sullenly, he kept a slow pace.

The truth was, the sight of Messala had set Ben-Hur to thinking. It seemed scarce an hour ago that the strong hands had torn him from his mother, scarce an hour ago that the Roman had put seal upon the gates of his father's house. He recounted how, in the hopeless misery of the life — if such it might be called—in the galleys, he had had little else to do, aside from labor, than dream dreams of vengeance, in all of which Messala was the principal. There might be, he used to say to himself, escape for Gratus, but for Messala — never! And to strengthen and harden his resolution, he was accustomed to repeat over and over, Who pointed us out to the persecutors? And when I begged him for help— not for myself —who mocked me, and went

336

away laughing? And always the dream had the same ending. The day I meet him, help me, thou good God of my people!—help me to some fitting special vengeance!

And now the meeting was at hand.

Perhaps, if he had found Messala poor and suffering, Ben-Hur's feeling had been different; but it was not so. He found him more than prosperous; in the prosperity there was a dash and glitter—gleam of sun on gilt of gold.

So it happened that what Malluch accounted a passing loss of spirit was pondering when the meeting should be, and in what manner he could make it most memorable.

They turned after a while into an avenue of oaks, where the people were going and coming in groups; footmen here, and horsemen; there women in litters borne by slaves; and now and then chariots rolled by thunderously.

At the end of the avenue the road, by an easy grade, descended into a lowland, where, on the right hand, there was a precipitous facing of gray rock, and on the left an open meadow of vernal freshness. Then they came in view of the famous Fountain of Castalia.

Edging through a company assembled at the point, Ben-Hur beheld a jet of sweet water pouring from the crest of a stone into a basin of black marble, where, after much boiling and foaming, it disappeared as through a funnel.

By the basin, under a small portico cut in the solid wall, sat a priest, old, bearded, wrinkled, cowled—never being more perfectly eremitish. From the manner of the people pres-

ent, hardly might one say which was the attraction, the fountain, forever sparkling, or the priest, forever there. H : heard, saw, was seen, but never spoke. Occasionally a visitor extended a hand to him with a coin in it. With a cunning twinkle of the eyes, he took the money, and gave the party in exchange a leaf of papyrus.

The receiver made haste to plunge the papyrus into the basin ; then, holding the dripping leaf in the sunlight, he would be rewarded with a versified inscription upon its face ; and the fame of the fountain seldom suffered loss by poverty of merit in the poetry. Before Ben-Hur could test the oracle, some other visitors were seen approaching across the meadow, and their appearance piqued the curiosity of the company, his not less than theirs.

He saw first a camel, very tall and very white, in leading of a driver on horseback. A houdah on the animal, besides being unusually large, was of crimson and gold. Two other horsemen followed the camel with tall spears in hand.

"What a wonderful camel!" said one of the company.

"A prince from afar," another one suggested.

"More likely a king."

"If he were on an elephant, I would say he was a king."

A third man had a very different opinion.

"A camel—and a white camel!" he said, authoritatively.

" By Apollo, friends, they who come yonder
— you can see there are two of them — are
neither kings nor princes ; they are women !"

In the midst of the dispute the strangers
arrived.

The camel seen at hand did not belie his
appearance afar. A taller, statelier brute of
his kind no traveller at the fountain, though
from the remotest parts, had ever beheld.
Such great black eyes ! such exceedingly fine
white hair ! feet so contractile when raised, so
soundless in planting, so broad when set !—no-
body had ever seen the peer of this camel.
And how well he became his housing of silk,
and all its frippery of gold in fringe and gold
in tassel ! The tinkling of silver bells went be-
fore him, and he moved lightly, as if unknow-
ing of his burden.

But who were the man and woman under
the houdah ?

Every eye saluted them with the inquiry.

If the former were a prince or a king, the
philosophers of the crowd might not deny the
impartiality of Time. When they saw the thin,
shrunken face buried under an immense tur-
ban, the skin of the hue of a mummy, making
it impossible to form an idea of his national-
ity, they were pleased to think the limit of life
was for the great as well as the small. They
saw about his person nothing so enviable as
the shawl which draped him.

The woman was seated in the manner of the
East, amid veils and laces of surpassing fine-
ness. Above her elbows she wore armlets fash-

339

ioned like coiled asps, and linked to bracelets
at the wrists by strands of gold; otherwise the
arms were bare and of singular natural grace,
complemented with hands modelled daintily as
a child's. One of the hands rested upon the
side of the carriage, showing tapered fingers
glittering with rings, and stained at the tips
till they blushed like the pink of mother-of-
pearl. She wore an open caul upon her head,
sprinkled with beads of coral, and strung with
coin-pieces called sunlets, some of which were
carried across her forehead, while others fell
down her back, half-smothered in the mass of
her straight, blue-black hair, of itself an incom-
parable ornament, not needing the veil which
covered it, except as a protection against sun
and dust. From her elevated seat she looked
upon the people calmly, pleasantly, and appar-
ently so intent upon studying them as to be
unconscious of the interest she herself was ex-
citing; and, what was unusual—nay, in violent
contravention of the custom among women of
rank in public—she looked at them with an
open face.

It was a fair face to see; quite youthful; in
form, oval; complexion not white, like the
Greek; nor brunette, like the Roman; nor blond,
like the Gaul; but rather the tinting of the sun
of the Upper Nile upon a skin of such trans-
parency that the blood shone through it on
cheek and brow with nigh the ruddiness of
lamplight. The eyes, naturally large, were
touched along the lids with the black paint
immemorial throughout the East. The lips

were slightly parted, disclosing, through their
scarlet lake, teeth of glistening whiteness. To
all these excellences of countenance the reader
is finally besought to superadd the air derived
from the pose of a small head, classic in shape,
set upon a neck long, drooping, and graceful—
the air, we may fancy, happily described by the
word queenly.

As if satisfied with the survey of people and
locality, the fair creature spoke to the driver—
an Ethiopian of vast brawn, naked to the waist
—who led the camel nearer the fountain, and
caused it to kneel; after which he received from
her hand a cup, and proceeded to fill it at the
basin. That instant the sound of wheels and
the trampling of horses in rapid motion broke
the silence her beauty had imposed, and, with
a great outcry, the by-standers parted in every
direction, hurrying to get away.

"The Roman has a mind to ride us down.
Look out!" Malluch shouted to Ben-Hur, set-
ting him at the same time an example of hasty
flight.

The latter faced to the direction the sounds
came from, and beheld Messala in his chariot
pushing the four straight at the crowd. This
time the view was near and distinct.

The parting of the company uncovered the
camel, which might have been more agile than
his kind generally; yet the hoofs were almost
upon him, and he resting with closed eyes,
chewing the endless cud with such sense of se-
curity as long favoritism may be supposed to
have bred in him. The Ethiopian wrung his

hands afraid. In the houdah, the old man moved to escape; but he was hampered with age, and could not, even in the face of danger, forget the dignity which was plainly his habit. It was too late for the woman to save herself. Ben-Hur stood nearest them, and he called to Messala,

"Hold! Look where thou goest! Back, back!"

The patrician was laughing in hearty good-humor; and, seeing there was but one chance of rescue, Ben-Hur stepped in, and caught the bits of the left yoke-steed and his mate. "Dog of a Roman! Carest thou so little for life?" he cried, putting forth all his strength. The two horses reared, and drew the others round; the tilting of the pole tilted the chariot; Messala barely escaped a fall, while his complacent Myrtilus rolled back like a clod to the ground. Seeing the peril past, all the by-standers burst into derisive laughter.

The matchless audacity of the Roman then manifested itself. Loosing the lines from his body, he tossed them to one side, dismounted, walked round the camel, looked at Ben-Hur, and spoke partly to the old man and partly to the woman.

"Pardon, I pray you — I pray you both. I am Messala," he said; "and, by the old Mother of the earth, I swear I did not see you or your camel! As to these good people — perhaps I trusted too much to my skill. I sought a laugh at them—the laugh is theirs. Good may it do them!"

The good-natured, careless look and gesture he threw the by-standers accorded well with the speech. To hear what more he had to say, they became quiet. Assured of victory over the body of the offended, he signed his companion to take the chariot to a safer distance, and addressed himself boldly to the woman.

"Thou hast interest in the good man here, whose pardon, if not granted now, I shall seek with the greatest diligence hereafter; his daughter, I should say."

She made him no reply.

"By Pallas, thou art beautiful! Beware Apollo mistake thee not for his lost love. I wonder what land can boast herself thy mother. Turn not away. A truce! a truce! There is the sun of India in thine eyes; in the corners of thy mouth, Egypt hath set her love-signs. Perpol! Turn not to that slave, fair mistress, before proving merciful to this one. Tell me, at least, that I am pardoned."

At this point she broke in upon him.

"Wilt thou come here?" she asked, smiling, and with gracious bend of the head to Ben-Hur.

"Take the cup and fill it, I pray thee," she said to the latter. "My father is thirsty."

"I am thy most willing servant!"

Ben-Hur turned about to do the favor, and was face to face with Messala. Their glances met; the Jew's defiant; the Roman's sparkling with humor.

"O stranger, beautiful as cruel!" Messala said, waving his hand to her. "If Apollo get

343

thee not, thou shalt see me again. Not knowing thy country, I cannot name a god to commend thee to ; so, by all the gods, I will commend thee to—myself !"

Seeing the Myrtilus had the four composed and ready, he returned to the chariot. The woman looked after him as he moved away, and whatever else there was in her look, there was no displeasure. Presently she received the water ; her father drank ; then she raised the cup to her lips, and leaning down, gave it to Ben-Hur ; never action more graceful and gracious.

"Keep it, we pray of thee ! It is full of blessings—all thine !"

Immediately the camel was aroused, and on his feet, and about to go, when the old man called,

"Stand thou here."

Ben-Hur went to him respectfully.

"Thou hast served the stranger well to-day. There is but one God. In His holy name I thank thee. I am Balthasar, the Egyptian. In the Great Orchard of Palms, beyond the village of Daphne, in the shade of the palms, Sheik Ilderim the Generous abideth in his tents, and we are his guests. Seek us there. Thou shalt have welcome sweet with the savor of the grateful."

Ben-Hur was left in wonder at the old man's clear voice and reverend manner. As he gazed after the two departing, he caught sight of Messala going as he had come, joyous, indifferent, and with a mocking laugh.

344

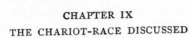

CHAPTER IX
THE CHARIOT-RACE DISCUSSED

AS a rule, there is no surer way to the
dislike of men than to behave well
where they have behaved badly. In
this instance, happily, Malluch was
an exception to the rule. The affair he had
just witnessed raised Ben-Hur in his estima-
tion, since he could not deny him courage and
address; could he now get some insight into
the young man's history, the results of the
day would not be all unprofitable to good mas-
ter Simonides.

On the latter point, referring to what he
had as yet learned, two facts comprehended it
all—the subject of his investigation was a Jew,
and the adopted son of a famous Roman. An-
other conclusion which might be of impor-
tance was beginning to formulate itself in the
shrewd mind of the emissary; between Mes-
sala and the son of the duumvir there was a
connection of some kind. But what was it?
—and how could it be reduced to assurance?
With all his sounding, the ways and means of
solution were not at call. In the heat of the
perplexity, Ben-Hur himself came to his help.
He laid his hand on Malluch's arm and drew
him out of the crowd, which was already going
back to its interest in the gray old priest and
the mystic fountain.

345

"Good Malluch," he said, stopping, "may a man forget his mother?"

The question was abrupt and without direction, and therefore of the kind which leaves the person addressed in a state of confusion. Malluch looked into Ben-Hur's face for a hint of meaning, but saw, instead, two bright-red spots, one on each cheek, and in his eyes traces of what might have been repressed tears; then he answered, mechanically, "No!" adding, with fervor, "never;" and a moment after, when he began to recover himself, "If he is an Israelite, never!" And when at length he was completely recovered—"My first lesson in the synagogue was the Shema; my next was the saying of the son of Sirach, 'Honor thy father with thy whole soul, and forget not the sorrows of thy mother.'"

The red spots on Ben-Hur's face deepened.

"The words bring my childhood back again; and, Malluch, they prove you a genuine Jew. I believe I can trust you."

Ben-Hur let go the arm he was holding, and caught the folds of the gown covering his own breast, and pressed them close, as if to smother a pain, or a feeling there as sharp as a pain.

"My father," he said, "bore a good name, and was not without honor in Jerusalem, where he dwelt. My mother, at his death, was in the prime of womanhood; and it is not enough to say of her she was good and beautiful: in her tongue was the law of kindness, and her works were the praise of all in the gates, and she smiled at days to come. I had a little sister,

346

and she and I were the family, and we were so happy that I, at least, have never seen harm in the saying of the old rabbi, 'God could not be everywhere, and, therefore, he made mothers.' One day an accident happened to a Roman in authority as he was riding past our house at the head of a cohort; the legionaries burst the gate and rushed in and seized us. I have not seen my mother or sister since. I cannot say they are dead or living. I do not know what became of them. But, Malluch, the man in the chariot yonder was present at the separation; he gave us over to the captors; he heard my mother's prayer for her children, and he laughed when they dragged her away. Hardly may one say which graves deepest in memory, love or hate. To-day I knew him afar—and, Malluch—"

He caught the listener's arm again.

"And, Malluch, he knows and takes with him now the secret I would give my life for: he could tell if she lives, and where she is, and her condition; if she—no, they—much sorrow has made the two as one—if they are dead, he could tell where they died, and of what, and where their bones await my finding."

"And will he not?"

"No."

"Why?"

"I am a Jew, and he is a Roman."

"But Romans have tongues, and Jews, though ever so despised, have methods to beguile them."

"For such as he? No; and, besides, the se-

cret is one of state. All my father's property
was confiscated and divided."

Malluch nodded his head slowly, much as
to admit the argument; then he asked anew,
"Did he not recognize you?"

"He could not. I was sent to death in life,
and have been long since accounted of the
dead."

"I wonder you did not strike him," said Mal-
luch, yielding to a touch of passion.

"That would have been to put him past serv-
ing me forever. I would have had to kill him,
and Death, you know, keeps secrets better
even than a guilty Roman."

The man who, with so much to avenge, could
so calmly put such an opportunity aside must
be confident of his future or have ready some
better design, and Malluch's interest changed
with the thought; it ceased to be that of an
emissary in duty bound to another. Ben-Hur
was actually asserting a claim upon him for his
own sake. In other words, Malluch was pre-
paring to serve him with good heart and from
downright admiration.

After brief pause, Ben-Hur resumed speaking.

"I would not take his life, good Malluch;
against that extreme the possession of the se-
cret is for the present, at least, his safeguard;
yet I may punish him, and so you give me help,
I will try."

"He is a Roman," said Malluch, without
hesitation; "and I am of the tribe of Judah.
I will help you. If you choose, put me under
oath — under the most solemn oath."

"Give me your hand, that will suffice."

As their hands fell apart, Ben-Hur said, with lightened feeling, "That I would charge you with is not difficult, good friend; neither is it dreadful to conscience. Let us move on."

They took the road which led to the right across the meadow spoken of in the description of the coming to the fountain. Ben-Hur was the first to break the silence.

"Do you know Sheik Ilderim the Generous?"

"Yes."

"Where is his Orchard of Palms? or, rather, Malluch, how far is it beyond the village of Daphne?"

Malluch was touched by a doubt; he recalled the prettiness of the favor shown him by the woman at the fountain, and wondered if he who had the sorrows of a mother in mind was about to forget them for a lure of love; yet he replied, "The Orchard of Palms lies beyond the village two hours by horse, and one by a swift camel."

"Thank you; and to your knowledge once more. Have the games of which you told me been widely published? and when will they take place?"

The questions were suggestive; and if they did not restore Malluch his confidence, they at least stimulated his curiosity.

"Oh yes, they will be of ample splendor. The prefect is rich, and could afford to lose his place; yet, as is the way with successful men, his love of riches is nowise diminished; and to gain a friend at court, if nothing more,

349

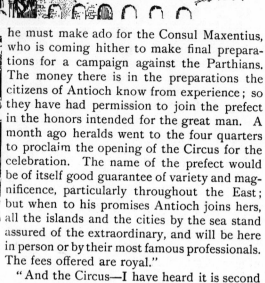

he must make ado for the Consul Maxentius, who is coming hither to make final preparations for a campaign against the Parthians. The money there is in the preparations the citizens of Antioch know from experience; so they have had permission to join the prefect in the honors intended for the great man. A month ago heralds went to the four quarters to proclaim the opening of the Circus for the celebration. The name of the prefect would be of itself good guarantee of variety and magnificence, particularly throughout the East; but when to his promises Antioch joins hers, all the islands and the cities by the sea stand assured of the extraordinary, and will be here in person or by their most famous professionals. The fees offered are royal."

"And the Circus—I have heard it is second only to the Maximus."

"At Rome, you mean. Well, ours seats two hundred thousand people, yours seats seventy-five thousand more; yours is of marble, so is ours; in arrangement they are exactly the same."

"Are the rules the same?"

Malluch smiled.

"If Antioch dared be original, son of Arrius, Rome would not be the mistress she is. The laws of the Circus Maximus govern except in one particular: there but four chariots may start at once, here all start without reference to number."

"That is the practice of the Greeks," said Ben-Hur.

"Yes, Antioch is more Greek than Roman."

"So then, Malluch, I may choose my own chariot?"

"Your own chariot and horses. There is no restriction upon either."

While replying, Malluch observed the thoughtful look on Ben-Hur's face give place to one of satisfaction.

"One thing more now, O Malluch. When will the celebration be?"

"Ah! your pardon," the other answered. "To-morrow—and the next day," he said, counting aloud, "then, to speak in the Roman style, if the sea-gods be propitious, the consul arrives. Yes, the sixth day from this we have the games."

"The time is short, Malluch, but it is enough." The last words were spoken decisively. "By the prophets of our old Israel! I will take to the reins again. Stay! a condition; is there assurance that Messala will be a competitor?"

Malluch saw now the plan, and all its opportunities for the humiliation of the Roman; and he had not been true descendant of Jacob if, with all his interest wakened, he had not rushed to a consideration of the chances. His voice actually trembled as he said, "Have you the practice?"

"Fear not, my friend. The winners in the Circus Maximus have held their crowns these three years at my will. Ask them—ask the best of them—and they will tell you so. In the last great games the emperor himself offered

351

me his patronage if I would take his horses in hand and run them against the entries of the world."

"But you did not?"

Malluch spoke eagerly.

"I—I am a Jew"—Ben-Hur seemed shrinking within himself as he spoke—"and, though I wear a Roman name, I dared not do professionally a thing to sully my father's name in the cloisters and courts of the Temple. In the palæstræ I could indulge practice which, if followed into the Circus, would become an abomination; and if I take to the course here, Malluch, I swear it will not be for the prize or the winner's fee."

"Hold—swear not so!" cried Malluch. "The fee is ten thousand sestertii—a fortune for life!"

"Not for me, though the prefect trebled it fifty times. Better than that, better than all the imperial revenues from the first year of the first Cæsar—I will make this race to humble my enemy. Vengeance is permitted by the law."

Malluch smiled and nodded as if saying, "Right, right—trust me a Jew to understand a Jew."

"The Messala will drive," he said, directly. "He is committed to the race in many ways —by publication in the streets, and in the baths and theatres, the palace and barracks; and, to fix him past retreat, his name is on the tablets of every young spendthrift in Antioch."

"In wager, Malluch?"

" Yes, in wager; and every day he comes ostentatiously to practise, as you saw him."

' Ah! and that is the chariot, and those the horses, with which he will make the race? Thank you, thank you, Malluch! You have served me well already. I am satisfied. Now be my guide to the Orchard of Palms, and give me introduction to Sheik Ilderim the Generous."

" When?"

" To-day. His horses may be engaged to-morrow."

" You like them, then?"

Ben-Hur answered with animation,

" I saw them from the stand an instant only, for Messala then drove up, and I might not look at anything else; yet I recognized them as of the blood which is the wonder as well as the glory of the deserts. I never saw the kind before, except in the stables of Cæsar; but once seen, they are always to be known. To-morrow, upon meeting, I will know you, Malluch, though you do not so much as salute me; I will know you by your face, by your form, by your manner; and by the same signs I will know them, and with the same certainty. If all that is said of them be true, and I can bring their spirit under control of mine, I can—"

" Win the sestertii!" said Malluch, laughing.

" No," answered Ben-Hur, as quickly. " I will do what better becomes a man born to the heritage of Jacob—I will humble mine enemy in a most public place. But," he added, im-

patiently, "we are losing time. How can we most quickly reach the tents of the sheik?"

Malluch took a moment for reflection.

"It is best we go straight to the village, which is fortunately near by; if two swift camels are to be had for hire there, we will be on the road but an hour."

"Let us about it, then."

The village was an assemblage of palaces in beautiful gardens, interspersed with khans of princely sort. Dromedaries were happily secured, and upon them the journey to the famous Orchard of Palms was begun.

CHAPTER X
BEN-HUR HEARS OF CHRIST

BEYOND the village the country was undulating and cultivated; in fact, it was the garden-land of Antioch, with not a foot lost to labor. The steep faces of the hills were terraced; even the hedges were brighter of the trailing vines which, besides the lure of shade, offered passers-by sweet promises of wine to come, and grapes in clustered purple ripeness. Over melon-patches, and through apricot and fig-tree groves, and groves of oranges and limes, the whitewashed houses of the farmers were seen; and everywhere Plenty, the smiling daughter of Peace, gave notice by her thousand signs that she was at home, making the generous traveller merry at heart, until he was even disposed to give

Rome her dues. Occasionally, also, views were had of Taurus and Lebanon, between which, a separating line of silver, the Orontes placidly pursued its way.

In course of their journey the friends came to the river, which they followed with the windings of the road, now over bold bluffs, and then into vales, all alike allotted for country-seats; and if the land was in full foliage of oak and sycamore and myrtle, and bay and arbutus, and perfuming jasmine, the river was bright with slanted sunlight, which would have slept where it fell but for ships in endless procession, gliding with the current, tacking for the wind, or bounding under the impulse of oars—some coming, some going, and all suggestive of the sea, and distant peoples, and famous places, and things coveted on account of their rarity. To the fancy there is nothing so winsome as a white sail seaward blown, unless it be a white sail homeward bound, its voyage happily done. And down the shores the friends went continuously till they came to a lake fed by backwater from the river, clear, deep, and without current. An old palm-tree dominated the angle of the inlet; turning to the left at the foot of the tree, Malluch clapped his hands and shouted,

"Look, look! The Orchard of Palms!"

The scene was nowhere else to be found unless in the favored oases of Arabia or the Ptolemæan farms along the Nile; and to sustain a sensation new as it was delightful, Ben-Hur was admitted into a tract of land apparently

without limit and level as a floor. All under foot was fresh grass, in Syria the rarest and most beautiful production of the soil; if he looked up, it was to see the sky palely blue through the groinery of countless date-bearers, very patriarchs of their kind, so numerous and old, and of such mighty girth, so tall, so serried, so wide of branch, each branch so perfect with fronds, plumy and waxlike and brilliant, they seemed enchanters enchanted. Here was the grass coloring the very atmosphere; there the lake, cool and clear, rippling but a few feet under the surface, and helping the trees to their long life in old age. Did the Grove of Daphne excel this one? And the palms, as if they knew Ben-Hur's thought, and would win him after a way of their own, seemed, as he passed under their arches, to stir and sprinkle him with dewy coolness.

The road wound in close parallelism with the shore of the lake; and when it carried the travellers down to the water's edge, there was always on that side a shining expanse limited not far off by the opposite shore, on which, as on this one, no tree but the palm was permitted.

"See that," said Malluch, pointing to a giant of the place. "Each ring upon its trunk marks a year of its life. Count them from root to branch, and if the sheik tells you the grove was planted before the Seleucidæ were heard of in Antioch, do not doubt him."

One may not look at a perfect palm-tree but that, with a subtlety all its own, it assumes a presence for itself, and makes a poet of the be-

holder. This is the explanation of the honors it has received, beginning with the artists of the first kings, who could find no form in all the earth to serve them so well as a model for the pillars of their palaces and temples; and for the same reason Ben-Hur was moved to say,

"As I saw him at the stand to-day, good Malluch, Sheik Ilderim appeared to be a very common man. The rabbis in Jerusalem would look down upon him, I fear, as a son of a dog of Edom. How came he in possession of the Orchard? And how has he been able to hold it against the greed of Roman governors?"

"If blood derives excellence from time, son of Arrius, then is old Ilderim a man, though he be an uncircumcised Edomite."

Malluch spoke warmly.

"All his fathers before him were sheiks. One of them—I shall not say when he lived or did the good deed—once helped a king who was being hunted with swords. The story says he loaned him a thousand horsemen, who knew the paths of the wilderness and its hiding-places as shepherds know the scant hills they inhabit with their flocks; and they carried him here and there until the opportunity came, and then with their spears they slew the enemy, and set him upon his throne again. And the king, it is said, remembered the service, and brought the son of the Desert to this place, and bade him set up his tent and bring his family and his herds, for the lake and trees, and all the land from the river to the nearest mountains, were his and his children's forever. And they

357

have never been disturbed in the possession. The rulers succeeding have found it policy to keep good terms with the tribe, to whom the Lord has given increase of men and horses, and camels and riches, making them masters of many highways between cities; so that it is with them any time they please to say to commerce, 'Go in peace,' or 'Stop, and what they say shall be done. Even the prefect in the citadel overlooking Antioch thinks it happy day with him when Ilderim, surnamed the Generous on account of good deeds done unto all manner of men, with his wives and children, and his trains of camels and horses, and his belongings of sheik, moving as our fathers Abraham and Jacob moved, comes up to exchange briefly his bitter wells for the pleasantness you see about us."

"How is it, then?" said Ben-Hur, who had been listening unmindful of the slow gait of the dromedaries. "I saw the sheik tear his beard while he cursed himself that he had put trust in a Roman. Cæsar, had he heard him, might have said, 'I like not such a friend as this; put him away.'"

"It would be but shrewd judgment," Malluch replied, smiling. "Ilderim is not a lover of Rome; he has a grievance. Three years ago the Parthians rode across the road from Bozra to Damascus, and fell upon a caravan laden, among other things, with the incoming tax-returns of a district over that way. They slew every creature taken, which the censors in Rome could have forgiven if the imperial

treasure had been spared and forwarded. The farmers of the taxes, being chargeable with the loss, complained to Cæsar, and Cæsar held Herod to payment, and Herod, on his part, seized property of Ilderim, whom he charged with treasonable neglect of duty. The sheik appealed to Cæsar, and Cæsar has made him such answer as might be looked for from the unwinking sphinx. The old man's heart has been aching sore ever since, and he nurses his wrath, and takes pleasure in its daily growth."

"He can do nothing, Malluch."

"Well," said Malluch, " that involves another explanation, which I will give you, if we can draw nearer. But see!—the hospitality of the sheik begins early—the children are speaking to you."

The dromedaries stopped, and Ben-Hur looked down upon some little girls of the Syrian peasant class, who were offering him their baskets filled with dates. The fruit was freshly gathered, and not to be refused; he stooped and took it, and as he did so a man in the tree by which they were halted cried, " Peace to you, and welcome!"

Their thanks said to the children, the friends moved on at such gait as the animals chose.

"You must know," Malluch continued, pausing now and then to dispose of a date, "that the merchant Simonides gives me his confidence, and sometimes flatters me by taking me into counsel; and as I attend him at his house, I have made acquaintance with many of his friends, who, knowing my footing with the host,

359

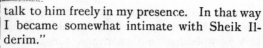

talk to him freely in my presence. In that way
I became somewhat intimate with Sheik Il-
derim."

For a moment Ben-Hur's attention wandered.
Before his mind's eye there arose the image,
pure, gentle, and appealing, of Esther, the mer-
chant's daughter. Her dark eyes bright with
the peculiar Jewish lustre met his in modest
gaze; he heard her step as when she ap-
proached him with the wine, and her voice as
she tendered him the cup; and he acknowl-
edged to himself again all the sympathy she
manifested for him, and manifested so plainly
that words were unnecessary, and so sweetly
that words would have been but a detraction.
The vision was exceeding pleasant, but upon
his turning to Malluch, it flew away.

"A few weeks ago," said Malluch, continu-
ing, "the old Arab called on Simonides, and
found me present. I observed he seemed much
moved about something, and, in deference,
offered to withdraw, but he himself forbade
me. 'As you are an Israelite,' he said, 'stay,
for I have a strange story to tell.' The em-
phasis on the word Israelite excited my curi-
osity. I remained, and this is in substance his
story—I cut it short because we are drawing
nigh the tent, and I leave the details to the
good man himself. A good many years ago,
three men called at Ilderim's tent, out in the
wilderness. They were all foreigners, a Hin-
doo, a Greek, and an Egyptian; and they had
come on camels, the largest he had ever seen,
and all white. He welcomed them, and gave

360

them rest. Next morning they arose and prayed a prayer new to the sheik—a prayer addressed to God and his son—this with much mystery besides. After breaking fast with him, the Egyptian told who they were, and whence they had come. Each had seen a star, out of which a voice had bidden them go to Jerusalem and ask, 'Where is he that is born King of the Jews?' They obeyed. From Jerusalem they were led by a star to Bethlehem, where, in a cave, they found a child newly born, which they fell down and worshipped ; and after worshipping it, and giving it costly presents, and bearing witness of what it was, they took to their camels, and fled without pause to the sheik, because if Herod—meaning him surnamed the Great—could lay hands upon them, he would certainly kill them. And, faithful to his habit, the sheik took care of them, and kept them concealed for a year, when they departed, leaving with him gifts of great value, and each going a separate way."

"It is, indeed, a most wonderful story," Ben-Hur exclaimed at its conclusion. "What did you say they were to ask at Jerusalem?"

"They were to ask, 'Where is he that is born King of the Jews?'"

"Was that all?"

"There was more to the question, but I cannot recall it."

"And they found the child?"

"Yes, and worshipped him."

"It is a miracle, Malluch."

"Ilderim is a grave man, though excitable,

as all Arabs are. A lie on his tongue is impossible."

Malluch spoke positively. Thereupon the dromedaries were forgotten, and, quite as unmindful of their riders, they turned off the road to the growing grass.

"Has Ilderim nothing more of the three men?" asked Ben-Hur. "What became of them?"

"Ah, yes, that was the cause of his coming to Simonides the day of which I was speaking. Only the night before that day the Egyptian reappeared to him."

"Where?"

"Here at the door of the tent to which we are coming."

"How knew he the man?"

"As you knew the horses to-day—by face and manner."

"By nothing else?"

"He rode the same great white camel, and gave him the same name—Balthasar, the Egyptian."

"It is a wonder of the Lord's!"

Ben-Hur spoke with excitement.

And Malluch, wondering, asked "Why so?"

"Balthasar, you said?"

"Yes. Balthasar, the Egyptian."

"That was the name the old man gave us at the fountain to-day."

Then, at the reminder, Malluch became excited.

"It is true," he said; "and the camel was the same—and you saved the man's life."

"And the woman," said Ben-Hur, like one speaking to himself—"the woman was his daughter."

He fell to thinking; and even the reader will say he was having a vision of the woman, and that it was more welcome than that of Esther, if only because it stayed longer with him; but no—

"Tell me again," he said, presently. "Were the three to ask, 'Where is he that is to be King of the Jews?'"

"Not exactly. The words were 'born to be King of the Jews.' Those were the words as the old sheik caught them first in the desert, and he has ever since been waiting the coming of the king; nor can any one shake his faith that he will come."

"How—as king?"

"Yes, and bringing the doom of Rome—so says the sheik."

Ben-Hur kept silent a while, thinking and trying to control his feeling.

"The old man is one of many millions," he said, slowly—"one of many millions each with a wrong to avenge; and this strange faith, Malluch, is bread and wine to his hope; for who but a Herod may be King of the Jews while Rome endures? But, following the story, did you hear what Simonides said to him?"

"If Ilderim is a grave man, Simonides is a wise one," Malluch replied. "I listened, and he said— But hark! Some one comes overtaking us."

The noise grew louder, until presently they

363

heard the rumble of wheels mixed with the beating of horse-hoofs—a moment later Sheik Ilderim himself appeared on horseback followed by a train, among which were the four wine-red Arabs drawing the chariot. The sheik's chin, in its muffling of long white beard, was drooped upon his breast. Our friends had out-travelled him; but at sight of them he raised his head and spoke kindly.

"Peace to you!—Ah, my friend Malluch! Welcome! And tell me you are not going, but just come; that you have something for me from the good Simonides — may the Lord of his fathers keep him in life for many years to come! Aye, take up the straps, both of you, and follow me. I have bread and leben, or, if you prefer it, arrack, and the flesh of young kid. Come!"

They followed after him to the door of the tent, in which, when they were dismounted, he stood to receive them, holding a platter with three cups filled with creamy liquor just drawn from a great smoke-stained skin bottle, pendent from the central post.

"Drink," he said, heartily, "drink, for this is the fear-naught of the tentmen."

They each took a cup, and drank till but the foam remained.

"Enter now, in God's name."

And when they were gone in, Malluch took the sheik aside, and spoke to him privately; after which he went to Ben-Hur and excused himself.

"I have told the sheik about you, and he

will give you the trial of his horses in the morning. He is your friend. Having done for you all I can, you must do the rest, and let me return to Antioch. There is one there who has my promise to meet him to-night. I have no choice but to go. I will come back to-morrow prepared, if all goes well in the mean time, to stay with you until the games are over."

With blessings given and received, Malluch set out in return.

CHAPTER XI

THE WISE SERVANT AND HIS DAUGHTER

WHAT time the lower horn of a new moon touched the castellated piles on Mount Sulpius, and two-thirds of the people of Antioch were out on their house-tops comforting themselves with the night breeze when it blew, and with fans when it failed, Simonides sat in the chair which had come to be a part of him, and from the terrace looked down over the river, and his ships a-swing at their moorings. The wall at his back cast its shadow broadly over the water to the opposite shore. Above him the endless tramp upon the bridge went on. Esther was holding a plate for him containing his frugal supper — some wheaten cakes, light as wafers, some honey, and a bowl of milk, into which he now and then dipped the wafers after dipping them into the honey.

"Malluch is a laggard to-night," he said. showing where his thoughts were.

"Do you believe **he will come?**" Esther asked.

"Unless he has taken to the sea or the desert, and is yet following on, he will come."

Simonides spoke with quiet confidence.

"He may write," she said.

"Not so, Esther. He would have despatched a letter when he found he could not return, and told me so; because I have not received such a letter, I know he can come, and will."

"I hope so," she said, very softly.

Something in the utterance attracted his attention; it might have been the tone, it might have been the wish. The smallest bird cannot light upon the greatest tree without sending a shock to its most distant fibre; every mind is at times no less sensitive to the most trifling words.

"You wish him to come, Esther?" he asked.

"Yes," she said, lifting her eyes to his.

"Why? Can you tell me?" he persisted.

"Because"—she hesitated, then began again—"because the young man is—" The stop was full.

"Our master. Is that the word?"

"Yes."

"And you still think I should not suffer him to go away without telling him to come, if he chooses, and take us—and all we have—all, Esther—the goods, the shekels, the ships, the slaves, and the mighty credit, which is a mantle of cloth of gold and finest silver spun for me by the greatest of the angels of men—Success."

She made no answer.

"Does that move you nothing? No?" he said, with the slightest taint of bitterness. "Well, well, I have found, Esther, the worst reality is never unendurable when it comes out from behind the clouds through which we at first see it darkly—never—not even the rack. I suppose it will be so with death. And by that philosophy the slavery to which we are going must afterwhile become sweet. It pleases me even now to think what a favored man our master is. The fortune cost him nothing—not an anxiety, not a drop of sweat, not so much as a thought; it attaches to him undreamed of, and in his youth. And, Esther, let me waste a little vanity with the reflection; he gets what he could not go into the market and buy with all the pelf in a sum—thee, my child, my darling; thou blossom from the tomb of my lost Rachel!"

He drew her to him, and kissed her twice —once for herself, once for her mother.

"Say not so," she said, when his hand fell from her neck. "Let us think better of him; he knows what sorrow is, and will set us free."

"Ah, thy instincts are fine, Esther; and thou knowest I lean upon them in doubtful cases where good or bad is to be pronounced of a person standing before thee as he stood this morning. But—but"—his voice rose and hardened—"these limbs upon which I cannot stand—this body drawn and beaten out of human shape—they are not all I bring him of myself. Oh no, no! I bring him a soul which

367

has triumphed over torture and Roman malice keener than any torture — I bring him a mind which has eyes to see gold at a distance farther than the ships of Solomon sailed, and power to bring it to hand — aye, Esther, into my palm here for the fingers to grip and keep lest it take wings at some other's word — a mind skilled at scheming " — he stopped and laughed — " Why, Esther, before the new moon which in the courts of the Temple on the Holy Hill they are this moment celebrating passes into its next quartering I could ring the world so as to startle even Cæsar ; for know you, child, I have that faculty which is better than any one sense, better than a perfect body, better than courage and will, better than experience, ordinarily the best product of the longest lives—the faculty divinest of men, but which " — he stopped, and laughed again, not bitterly, but with real zest — " but which even the great do not sufficiently account, while with the herd it is a non-existent—the faculty of drawing men to my purpose and holding them faithfully to its achievement, by which, as against things to be done, I multiply myself into hundreds and thousands. So the captains of my ships plough the seas, and bring me honest returns ; so Malluch follows the youth, our master, and will " — just then a footstep was heard upon the terrace — " Ha, Esther ! said I not so ? He is here, and we will have tidings. For thy sake, sweet child—my lily just budded —I pray the Lord God, who has not forgotten his wandering sheep of Israel, that they be

good and comforting. Now we will know if he will let thee go with all thy beauty, and me with all my faculties."

Malluch came to the chair.

"Peace to you, good master," he said, with a low obeisance — "and to you, Esther, most excellent of daughters."

He stood before them deferentially, and the attitude and the address left it difficult to define his relation to them; the one was that of a servant, the other indicated the familiar and friend. On the other side, Simonides, as was his habit in business, after answering the salutation went straight to the subject.

"What of the young man, Malluch?"

The events of the day were told quietly and in the simplest words, and until he was through there was no interruption; nor did the listener in the chair so much as move a hand during the narration; but for his eyes, wide open and bright, and an occasional long-drawn breath, he might have been accounted an effigy.

"Thank you, thank you, Malluch," he said, heartily, at the conclusion; "you have done well — no one could have done better. Now what say you of the young man's nationality?"

"He is an Israelite, good master, and of the tribe of Judah."

"You are positive?"

"Very positive."

"He appears to have told you but little of his life."

"He has somewhere learned to be prudent. I might call him distrustful. He baffled all my

attempts upon his confidence until we started from the Castalian fount going to the village of Daphne."

"A place of abomination! Why went he there?"

"I would say from curiosity, the first motive of the many who go; but, very strangely, he took no interest in the things he saw. Of the Temple, he merely asked if it were Grecian. Good master, the young man has a trouble of mind from which he would hide, and he went to the Grove, I think, as we go to sepulchres with our dead—he went to bury it."

"That were well, if so," Simonides said, in a low voice; then louder, "Malluch, the curse of the time is prodigality. The poor make themselves poorer as apes of the rich, and the merely rich carry themselves like princes. Saw you signs of the weakness in the youth? Did he display moneys—coin of Rome or Israel?"

"None, none, good master."

"Surely, Malluch, where there are so many inducements to folly—so much, I mean, to eat and drink—surely he made you generous offer of some sort. His age, if nothing more, would warrant that much."

"He neither ate nor drank in my company."

"In what he said or did, Malluch, could you in anywise detect his master-idea? You know they peep through cracks close enough to stop the wind."

"Give me to understand you," said Malluch, in doubt.

PILGRIMS ENTERING BETHLEHEM, CHRISTMAS

"Well, you know we nor speak nor act, much less decide grave questions concerning ourselves, except as we be driven by a motive. In that respect, what made you of him?"

"As to that, Master Simonides, I can answer with much assurance. He is devoted to finding his mother and sister—that first. Then he has a grievance against Rome; and as the Messala of whom I told you had something to do with the wrong, the great present object is to humiliate him. The meeting at the fountain furnished an opportunity, but it was put aside as not sufficiently public."

"The Messala is influential," said Simonides, thoughtfully.

"Yes; but the next meeting will be in the Circus."

"Well—and then?"

"The son of Arrius will win."

"How know you?"

Malluch smiled.

"I am judging by what he says."

"Is that all?"

"No; there is a much better sign—his spirit."

"Aye; but, Malluch, his idea of vengeance—what is its scope? Does he limit it to the few who did him the wrong, or does he take in the many? And more—is his feeling but the vagary of a sensitive boy, or has it the seasoning of suffering manhood to give it endurance? You know, Malluch, the vengeful thought that has root merely in the mind is but a dream of idlest sort which one clear day will dissipate; while revenge the passion is a disease of the

heart which climbs up, up to the brain, and feeds itself on both alike."

In this question, Simonides for the first time showed signs of feeling; he spoke with rapid utterance, and with clinched hands and the eagerness of a man illustrating the disease he described?

"Good my master," Malluch replied, "one of my reasons for believing the young man a Jew is the intensity of his hate. It was plain to me he had himself under watch, as was natural, seeing how long he has lived in an atmosphere of Roman jealousy; yet I saw it blaze— once when he wanted to know Ilderim's feeling towards Rome, and again when I told him the story of the sheik and the wise man, and spoke of the question, 'Where is he that is born King of the Jews?'"

Simonides leaned forward quickly.

"Ah, Malluch, his words—give me his words; let me judge the impression the mystery made upon him."

"He wanted to know the exact words. Were they 'to be' or 'born to be?' It appeared he was struck by a seeming difference in the effect of the two phrases."

Simonides settled back into his pose of listening judge.

"Then," said Malluch, "I told him Ilderim's view of the mystery—that the king would come with the doom of Rome. The young man's blood rose over his cheeks and forehead, and he said earnestly, 'Who but a Herod can be king while Rome endures?'"

372

"Meaning what?"

"That the empire must be destroyed before there could be another rule."

Simonides gazed for a time at the ships and their shadows slowly swinging together in the river; when he looked up, it was to end the interview.

"Enough, Malluch," he said. "Get you to eat, and make ready to return to the Orchard of Palms; you must help the young man in his coming trial. Come to me in the morning. I will send a letter to Ilderim." Then, in an undertone, as if to himself, he added, "I may attend the Circus myself."

When Malluch after the customary benediction given and received was gone, Simonides took a deep draught of milk, and seemed refreshed and easy of mind.

"Put the meal down, Esther," he said; "it is over."

She obeyed.

"Here now."

She resumed her place upon the arm of the chair close to him.

"God is good to me, very good," he said, fervently. "His habit is to move in mystery, yet sometimes he permits us to think we see and understand him. I am old, dear, and must go; but now, in this eleventh hour, when my hope was beginning to die, he sends me this one with a promise, and I am lifted up. I see the way to a great part in a circumstance itself so great that it shall be as a new birth to the whole world. And I see a reason for the gift

373

of my great riches, and the end for which they were designed. Verily, my child, I take hold on life anew."

Esther nestled closer to him, as if to bring his thoughts from their far-flying.

"The king has been born," he continued, imagining he was still speaking to her, "and he must be near the half of common life. Balthasar says he was a child on his mother's lap when he saw him, and gave him presents and worship; and Ilderim holds it was twenty-seven years ago last December when Balthasar and his companions came to his tent asking a hiding-place from Herod. Wherefore the coming cannot now be long delayed. To-night—to-morrow it may be. Holy fathers of Israel, what happiness in the thought! I seem to hear the crash of the falling of old walls and the clamor of a universal change—aye, and for the uttermost joy of men, the earth opens to take Rome in, and they look up and laugh and sing that she is not, while we are;" then he laughed at himself. "Why, Esther, heard you ever the like? Surely, I have on me the passion of a singer, the heat of blood and the thrill of Miriam and David. In my thoughts, which should be those of a plain worker in figures and facts, there is a confusion of cymbals clashing and harp-strings loud beaten, and the voices of a multitude standing around a new-risen throne. I will put the thinking by for the present; only, dear, when the king comes he will need money and men, for as he was a child born of woman he will be but a man after all,

bound to human ways as you and I are. And
for the money he will have need of getters and
keepers, and for the men leaders. There, there!
See you not a broad road for my walking, and
the running of the youth our master?—and at
the end of it glory and revenge for us both?—
and—and "—he paused, struck with the selfish-
ness of a scheme in which she had no part or
good result; then added, kissing her, "And
happiness for thy mother's child."

She sat still, saying nothing. Then he re-
membered the difference in natures, and the
law by which we are not permitted always to
take delight in the same cause or be equally
afraid of the same thing. He remembered she
was but a girl.

"Of what are you thinking, Esther?" he said,
in his common home-like way. "If the thought
have the form of a wish, give it me, little one,
while the power remains mine. For power,
you know, is a fretful thing, and hath its wings
always spread for flight."

She answered, with a simplicity almost
childish,

"Send for him, father. Send for him to-
night, and do not let him go into the Circus."

"Ah!" he said, prolonging the exclamation;
and again his eyes fell upon the river, where
the shadows were more shadowy than ever,
since the moon had sunk far down behind Sul-
pius, leaving the city to the ineffectual stars.
Shall we say it, reader? He was touched by a
twinge of jealousy. If she should really love
the young master! Oh no! That could not

be; she was too young. But the idea had fast grip, and directly held him still and cold. She was sixteen. He knew it well. On the last natal day he had gone with her to the ship-yard where there was a launch, and the yellow flag which the galley bore to its bridal with the waves had on it "Esther;" so they celebrated the day together. Yet the fact struck him now with the force of a surprise. There are realizations which come to us all painfully; mostly, however, such as pertain to ourselves; that we are growing old, for instance; and, more terrible, that we must die. Such a one crept into his heart, shadowy as the shadows, yet substantial enough to wring from him a sigh which was almost a groan. It was not sufficient that she should enter upon her young womanhood a servant, but she must carry to her master her affections, the truth and tenderness and delicacy of which he, the father, so well knew, because to this time they had all been his own undividedly. The fiend whose task it is to torture us with fears and bitter thoughts seldom does his work by halves. In the pang of the moment, the brave old man lost sight of his new scheme, and of the miraculous king its subject. By a mighty effort, however, he controlled himself, and asked, calmly, "Not go into the Circus, Esther? Why, child?"

"It is not a place for a son of Israel, father."

"Rabbinical, rabbinical, Esther! Is that all?"

The tone of the inquiry was searching, and

went to her heart, which began to beat loudly
—so loudly she could not answer. A con-
fusion new and strangely pleasant fell upon
her.

"The young man is to have the fortune,"
he said, taking her hand, and speaking more
tenderly; "he is to have the ships and the
shekels—all, Esther, all. Yet I did not feel
poor, for thou wert left me, and thy love so
like the dead Rachel's. Tell me, is he to have
that too?"

She bent over him, and laid her cheek against
his head.

"Speak, Esther. I will be the stronger of
the knowledge. In warning there is strength."

She sat up then, and spoke as if she were
Truth's holy self.

"Comfort thee, father. I will never leave
thee; though he take my love, I will be thy
handmaid ever as now."

And, stooping, she kissed him.

"And more," she said, continuing, "he is
comely in my sight, and the pleading of his
voice drew me to him, and I shudder to think
of him in danger. Yes, father, I would be more
than glad to see him again. Still, the love that
is unrequited cannot be perfect love, where-
fore I will wait a time, remembering I am thy
daughter and my mother's."

"A very blessing of the Lord art thou, Es-
ther! A blessing to keep me rich, though all
else be lost. And by his holy name and ever-
lasting life, I swear thou shalt not suffer."

At his request, a little later, the servant came

and rolled the chair into the room, where he sat for a time thinking of the coming of the king, while she went off and slept the sleep of the innocent.

CHAPTER XII
A ROMAN ORGIE

THE palace across the river nearly opposite Simonides' place is said to have been completed by the famous Epiphanes, and was all such a habitation can be imagined; though he was a builder whose taste ran to the immense rather than the classical, now so called—an architectural imitator, in other words, of the Persians instead of the Greeks.

The wall enclosing the whole island to the water's edge, and built for the double purpose of bulwark against the river and defence against the mob, was said to have rendered the palace unfit for constant occupancy, insomuch that the legates abandoned it and moved to another residence erected for them on the western ridge of Mount Sulpius, under the Temple of Jupiter. Persons were not wanting, however, who flatly denied the bill against the ancient abode. They said, with shrewdness, at least, that the real object of the removal of the legates was not a more healthful locality, but the assurance afforded them by the huge barracks, named, according to the prevalent style, citadel, situated just over the way on the eastern ridge of the mount. And the opinion had

plausible showing. Among other pertinent things, it was remarked that the palace was kept in perpetual readiness for use ; and when a consul, general of the army, king, or visiting potentate of any kind arrived at Antioch, quarters were at once assigned him on the island.

As we have to do with but one apartment in the old pile, the residue of it is left to the reader's fancy ; and as pleases him, he may go through its gardens, baths, halls, and labyrinth of rooms to the pavilions on the roof, all furnished as became a house of fame in a city which was more nearly Milton's "gorgeous East" than any other in the world.

At this age the apartment alluded to would be termed a saloon. It was quite spacious, floored with polished marble slabs, and lighted in the day by skylights in which colored mica served as glass. The walls were broken by Atlantes, no two of which were alike, but all supporting a cornice wrought with arabesques exceedingly intricate in form, and more elegant on account of superadditions of color—blue, green, Tyrian purple, and gold. Around the room ran a continuous divan of Indian silks and wool of Cashmere. The furniture consisted of tables and stools of Egyptian patterns grotesquely carved. We have left Simonides in his chair perfecting his scheme in aid of the miraculous king, whose coming he has decided is so close at hand. Esther is asleep ; and now, having crossed the river by the bridge, and made way through the lion-guarded gate and

a number of Babylonian halls and courts, let us enter the gilded saloon.

There are five chandeliers hanging by sliding bronze chains from the ceiling—one in each corner, and in the centre one—enormous pyramids of lighted lamps, illuminating even the demoniac faces of the Atlantes and the complex tracery of the cornice. About the tables, seated or standing, or moving restlessly from one to another, there are probably a hundred persons, whom we must study at least for a moment.

They are all young, some of them little more than boys. That they are Italians and mostly Romans is past doubt. They all speak Latin in purity, while each one appears in the in-door dress of the great capital on the Tiber; that is, in tunics short of sleeve and skirt, a style of vesture well adapted to the climate of Antioch, and especially comfortable in the too close atmosphere of the saloon. On the divan here and there togas and lacernæ lie where they have been carelessly tossed, some of them significantly bordered with purple. On the divan also lie sleepers stretched at ease; whether they were overcome by the heat and fatigue of the sultry day or by Bacchus we will not pause to inquire.

The hum of voices is loud and incessant. Sometimes there is an explosion of laughter, sometimes a burst of rage or exultation; but over all prevails a sharp, prolonged rattle, at first somewhat confusing to the non-familiar. If we approach the tables, however, the mystery solves itself. The company is at the favor-

ite games, draughts and dice, singly or together, and the rattle is merely of the tesseræ, or ivory cubes, loudly shaken, and the moving of the hostes on the checkered boards.

Who are the company?

"Good Flavius," said a player, holding his piece in suspended movement, "thou seest yon lacerna; that one in front of us on the divan. It is fresh from the shop, and hath a shoulder-buckle of gold broad as a palm."

"Well," said Flavius, intent upon his game, "I have seen such before; wherefore thine may not be old, yet, by the girdle of Venus, it is not new! What of it?"

"Nothing. Only I would give it to find a man who knows everything."

"Ha, ha! For something cheaper I will find thee here several with purple who will take thy offer. But play."

"There — check!"

"So, by all the Jupiters! Now, what sayest thou? Again?"

"Be it so."

"And the wager?"

"A sestertium."

Then each drew his tablets and stilus and made a memorandum; and, while they were resetting the pieces, Flavius returned to his friend's remark.

"A man who knows everything! Hercle! the oracles would die. What wouldst thou with such a monster?"

"Answer to one question, my Flavius; then, perpol! I would cut his throat."

381

"And the question?"

"I would have him tell me the hour— Hour, said I?—nay, the minute—Maxentius will arrive to-morrow."

"Good play, good play! I have you! And why the minute?"

"Hast thou ever stood uncovered in the Syrian sun on the quay at which he will land? The fires of the Vesta are not so hot; and, by the Stator of our father Romulus, I would die, if die I must, in Rome. Avernus is here; there, in the square before the Forum, I could stand, and, with my hand raised thus, touch the floor of the gods. Ha, by Venus, my Flavius, thou didst beguile me! I have lost. O Fortune!"

"Again?"

"I must have back my sestertium."

"Be it so."

And they played again and again; and when day, stealing through the skylights, began to dim the lamps, it found the two in the same places at the same table, still at the game. Like most of the company, they were military attachés of the consul, awaiting his arrival and amusing themselves meantime.

During this conversation a party entered the room, and, unnoticed at first, proceeded to the central table. The signs were that they had come from a revel just dismissed. Some of them kept their feet with difficulty. Around the leader's brow was a chaplet which marked him master of the feast, if not the giver. The wine had made no impression upon him un-

less to heighten his beauty, which was of the most manly Roman style; he carried his head high raised; the blood flushed his lips and cheeks brightly; his eyes glittered; though the manner in which, shrouded in a toga spotless white and of ample folds, he walked was too nearly imperial for one sober and not a Cæsar. In going to the table, he made room for himself and his followers with little ceremony and no apologies; and when at length he stopped and looked over it and at the players, they all turned to him, with a shout like a cheer.

"Messala! Messala!" they cried.

Those in distant quarters, hearing the cry, re-echoed it where they were. Instantly there were dissolutions of groups, and breaking-up of games, and a general rush towards the centre.

Messala took the demonstration indifferently, and proceeded presently to show the ground of his popularity.

"A health to thee, Drusus, my friend," he said to the player next at his right; "a health —and thy tablets a moment."

He raised the waxen boards, glanced at the memoranda of wagers, and tossed them down.

"Denarii, only denarii—coin of cartmen and butchers!" he said, with a scornful laugh. "By the drunken Semele, to what is Rome coming, when a Cæsar sits o' nights waiting a turn of fortune to bring him but a beggarly denarius!"

The scion of the Drusi reddened to his brows, but the by-standers broke in upon his reply

by surging closer around the table, and shouting, "The Messala! the Messala!"

"Men of the Tiber," Messala continued, wresting a box with the dice in it from a hand near by, "who is he most favored of the gods? A Roman. Who is he law-giver of the nations? A Roman. Who is he, by sword right, the universal master?"

The company were of the easily inspired, and the thought was one to which they were born; in a twinkling they snatched the answer from him.

"A Roman, a Roman!" they shouted.

"Yet—yet"—he lingered to catch their ears "yet there is a better than the best of Rome."

He tossed his patrician head and paused, as if to sting them with his sneer.

"Hear ye?" he asked. "There is a better than the best of Rome."

"Aye—Hercules!" cried one.

"Bacchus!" yelled a satirist.

"Jove—Jove!" thundered the crowd.

"No," Messala answered, "among men."

"Name him, name him!" they demanded.

"I will," he said, the next lull. "He who to the perfection of Rome hath added the perfection of the East; who to the arm of conquest, which is Western, hath also the art needful to the enjoyment of dominion, which is Eastern."

"Perpol! His best is a Roman, after all," some one shouted; and there was a great laugh, and long clapping of hands—an admission that Messala had the advantage.

384

"In the East," he continued, "we have no gods, only Wine, Women, and Fortune, and the greatest of them is Fortune; wherefore our motto, 'Who dareth what I dare?'—fit for the senate, fit for battle, fittest for him who, seeking the best, challenges the worst."

His voice dropped into an easy, familiar tone, but without relaxing the ascendency he had gained.

"In the great chest up in the citadel I have five talents coin current in the markets, and here are the receipts for them."

From his tunic he drew a roll of paper, and, flinging it on the table, continued, amid breathless silence, every eye having him in view fixed on his, every ear listening:

"The sum lies there the measure of what I dare. Who of you dares so much? You are silent. Is it too great? I will strike off one talent. What! still silent? Come, then, throw me once for these three talents—only three; for two; for one—one at least—one for the honor of the river by which you were born — Rome East against Rome West! — Orontes the barbarous against Tiber the sacred!"

He rattled the dice overhead while waiting.

"The Orontes against the Tiber!" he repeated, with an increase of scornful emphasis.

Not a man moved; then he flung the box upon the table, and, laughing, took up the receipts.

"Ha, ha, ha! By the Olympian Jove, I know now ye have fortunes to make or to mend;

therefore are ye come to Antioch. Ho, Cecilius!"

"Here, Messala!" cried a man behind him; "here am I, perishing in the mob, and begging a drachma to settle with the ragged ferryman. But, Pluto take me! these new ones have not so much as an obolus among them."

The sally provoked a burst of laughter, under which the saloon rang and rang again. Messala alone kept his gravity.

"Go, thou," he said to Cecilius, "to the chamber whence we came, and bid the servants bring the amphoræ here, and the cups and goblets. If these our countrymen, looking for fortune, have not purses, by the Syrian Bacchus, I will see if they are not better blessed with stomachs! Haste thee!"

Then he turned to Drusus, with a laugh heard throughout the apartment.

"Ha, ha, my friend! Be thou not offended because I levelled the Cæsar in thee down to the denarii. Thou seest I did but use the name to try these fine fledglings of our old Rome. Come, my Drusus, come!" He took up the box again and rattled the dice merrily. "Here, for what sum thou wilt, let us measure fortunes."

The manner was frank, cordial, winsome. Drusus melted in a moment.

"By the Nymphæ, yes!" he said, laughing. "I will throw with thee, Messala—for a denarius."

A very boyish person was looking over the table watching the scene. Suddenly Messala turned to him.

"Who art thou?" he asked.

The lad drew back.

"Nay, by Castor! and his brother, too! I meant not offence. It is a rule among men, in matters other than dice, to keep the record closest when the deal is least. I have need of a clerk. Wilt thou serve me?"

The young fellow drew his tablets ready to keep the score: the manner was irresistible.

"Hold, Messala, hold!" cried Drusus. "I know not if it be ominous to stay the poised dice with a question; but one occurs to me, and I must ask it though Venus slap me with her girdle."

"Nay, my Drusus, Venus with her girdle off is Venus in love. To thy question—I will make the throw and hold it against mischance. Thus—"

He turned the box upon the table and held it firmly over the dice.

And Drusus asked, "Did you ever see one Quintus Arrius?"

"The duumvir?"

"No—his son?"

"I knew not he had a son."

"Well, it is nothing," Drusus added, indifferently; "only, my Messala, Pollux was not more like Castor than Arrius is like thee."

The remark had the effect of a signal: twenty voices took it up.

"True, true! His eyes—his face," they cried.

"What!" answered one, disgusted. "Messala is a Roman; Arrius is a Jew."

"Thou sayest right," a third exclaimed.

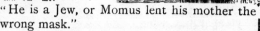

"He is a Jew, or Momus lent his mother the
wrong mask."

There was promise of a dispute; seeing
which, Messala interposed. "The wine is not
come, my Drusus; and, as thou seest, I have
the freckled Pythias as they were dogs in
leash. As to Arrius, I will accept thy opinion
of him, so thou tell me more about him."

"Well, be he Jew or Roman — and, by the
great god Pan, I say it not in disrespect of thy
feelings, my Messala!—this Arrius is hand-
some and brave and shrewd. The emperor
offered him favor and patronage, which he re-
fused. He came up through mystery, and
keepeth distance as if he felt himself better
or knew himself worse than the rest of us. In
the palæstræ he was unmatched; he played
with the blue-eyed giants from the Rhine and
the hornless bulls of Sarmatia as they were
willow wisps. The duumvir left him vastly
rich. He has a passion for arms, and thinks
of nothing but war. Maxentius admitted him
into his family, and he was to have taken ship
with us, but we lost him at Ravenna. Never-
theless he arrived safely. We heard of him
this morning. Perpol! Instead of coming to
the palace or going to the citadel, he dropped
his baggage at the khan, and hath disappeared
again."

At the beginning of the speech Messala lis-
tened with polite indifference; as it proceeded,
he became more attentive; at the conclusion,
he took his hand from the dice-box, and called
out, "Ho, my Caius! Dost thou hear?"

A youth at his elbow—his Myrtilus, or com-
rade, in the day's chariot practice—answered,
much pleased with the attention, "Did I not,
my Messala, I were not thy friend."

"Dost thou remember the man who gave
thee the fall to-day?"

"By the love-locks of Bacchus, have I not a
bruised shoulder to help me keep it in mind?"
and he seconded the words with a shrug that
submerged his ears.

"Well, be thou grateful to the Fates—I have
found thy enemy. Listen."

Thereupon Messala turned to Drusus.

"Tell us more of him—perpol!—of him who
is both Jew and Roman—by Phœbus, a com-
bination to make a Centaur lovely! What gar-
ments doth he affect, my Drusus?"

"Those of the Jews."

"Hearest thou, Caius?" said Messala. "The
fellow is young—one; he hath the visage of a
Roman—two; he loveth best the garb of a Jew
—three; and in the palæstræ fame and fortune
come of arms to throw a horse or tilt a chariot,
as the necessity may order—four. And, Dru-
sus, help thou my friend again. Doubtless this
Arrius hath tricks of language; otherwise he
could not so confound himself, to-day a Jew,
to-morrow a Roman; but of the rich tongue
of Athene—discourseth he in that as well?"

"With such purity, Messala, he might have
been a contestant in the Isthmia."

"Art thou listening, Caius?" said Messala.
"The fellow is qualified to salute a woman—
for that matter Aristomache herself—in the

Greek; and as I keep the count, that is five. What sayest thou?"

"Thou hast found him, my Messala," Caius answered; "or I am not myself."

"Thy pardon, Drusus—and pardon of all—for speaking in riddles thus," Messala said, in his winsome way. "By all the decent gods, I would not strain thy courtesy to the point of breaking, but now help thou me. See!"—he put his hand on the dice-box again, laughing—"See how close I hold the Pythias and their secret! Thou didst speak, I think, of mystery in connection with the coming of the son of Arrius. Tell me of that."

"'Tis nothing, Messala, nothing," Drusus replied; "a child's story. When Arrius, the father, sailed in pursuit of the pirates, he was without wife or family; he returned with a boy—him of whom we speak—and next day adopted him."

"Adopted him?" Messala repeated. "By the gods, Drusus, thou dost, indeed, interest me! Where did the duumvir find the boy? And who was he?"

"Who shall answer thee that, Messala? who but the young Arrius himself? Perpol! in the fight the duumvir—then but a tribune—lost his galley. A returning vessel found him and one other—all of the crew who survived—afloat upon the same plank. I give you now the story of the rescuers, which hath this excellence at least—it hath never been contradicted. They say, the duumvir's companion on the plank was a Jew—"

"A Jew!" echoed Messala.

"And a slave."

"How Drusus? A slave?"

"When the two were lifted to the deck, the duumvir was in his tribune's armor, and the other in the vesture of a rower."

Messala arose from leaning against the table.

"A galley"—he checked the debasing word, and looked around, for once in his life at loss. Just then a procession of slaves filed into the room, some with great jars of wine, others with baskets of fruits and confections, others again with cups and flagons, mostly silver. There was inspiration in the sight. Instantly Messala climbed upon a stool.

"Men of the Tiber," he said, in a clear voice, "let us turn this waiting for our chief into a feast of Bacchus. Whom choose ye for master?"

Drusus arose.

"Who shall be master but the giver of the feast?" he said. "Answer, Romans."

They gave their reply in a shout.

Messala took the chaplet from his head, gave it to Drusus, who climbed upon the table, and, in the view of all, solemnly replaced it, making Messala master of the night.

"There came with me into the room," he said, "some friends just risen from table. That our feast may have the approval of sacred custom, bring hither that one of them most overcome by wine."

A din of voices answered, "Here he is, here he is!"

And from the floor where he had fallen, a youth was brought forward, so effeminately beautiful he might have passed for the drinking-god himself — only the crown would have dropped from his head, and the thyrsus from his hand.

"Lift him upon the table," the master said.

It was found he could not sit.

"Help him, Drusus, as the fair Nyone may yet help thee."

Drusus took the inebriate in his arms.

Then, addressing the limp figure, Messala said, amid profound silence, "O Bacchus! greatest of the gods, be thou propitious tonight. And for myself, and these thy votaries, I vow this chaplet" — and from his head he raised it reverently — "I vow this chaplet to thy altar in the Grove of Daphne."

He bowed, replaced the crown upon his locks, then stooped and uncovered the dice, saying, with a laugh, "See, my Drusus, by the ass of Silenus, the denarius is mine!"

There was a shout that set the floor to quaking, and the grim Atlantes to dancing, and the orgies began.

A DRIVER FOR ILDERIM'S ARABS

HEIK ILDERIM was a man of too much importance to go about with a small establishment. He had a reputation to keep with his tribe, such as became a prince and patriarch of the greatest following in all the Desert east of Syria; with the people of the cities he had another reputation, which was that of one of the richest personages not a king in all the East; and, being rich in fact — in money as well as in servants, camels, horses, and flocks of all kinds — he took pleasure in a certain state, which, besides magnifying his dignity with strangers, contributed to his personal pride and comfort. Wherefore the reader must not be misled by the frequent reference to his tent in the Orchard of Palms. He had there really a respectable dowar; that is to say, he had there three large tents — one for himself, one for visitors, one for his favorite wife and her women; and six or eight lesser ones, occupied by his servants and such tribal retainers as he had chosen to bring with him as a body-guard —strong men of approved courage, and skilful with bow, spear, and horses.

To be sure, his property of whatever kind was in no danger at the Orchard; yet as the habits of a man go with him to town not less

than the country, and as it is never wise to slip the bands of discipline, the interior of the dowar was devoted to his cows, camels, goats, and such property in general as might tempt a lion or a thief.

To do him full justice, Ilderim kept well all the customs of his people, abating none, not even the smallest; in consequence his life at the Orchard was a continuation of his life in the Desert; nor that alone, it was a fair reproduction of the old patriarchal modes—the genuine pastoral life of primitive Israel.

Recurring to the morning the caravan arrived at the Orchard—"Here, plant it here," he said, stopping his horse, and thrusting a spear into the ground. "Door to the south; the lake before it thus; and these, the children of the Desert, to sit under at the going-down of the sun."

At the last words he went to a group of three great palm-trees, and patted one of them as he would have patted his horse's neck, or the cheek of the child of his love.

Who but the sheik could of right say to the caravan, Halt! or of the tent, Here be it pitched? The spear was wrested from the ground, and over the wound it had riven in the sod the base of the first pillar of the tent was planted, marking the centre of the front door. Then eight others were planted—in all, three rows of pillars, three in a row. Then, at call, the women and children came, and unfolded the canvas from its packing on the camels. Who might do this but the women? Had

they not sheared the hair from the brown goats of the flock? and twisted it into thread? and woven the thread into cloth? and stitched the cloth together, making the perfect roof, dark brown in fact, though in the distance black as the tents of Kedar? And, finally, with what jests and laughter, and pulls altogether, the united following of the sheik stretched the canvas from pillar to pillar, driving the stakes and fastening the cords as they went! And when the walls of open reed matting were put in place—the finishing-touch to the building after the style of the Desert—with what hush of anxiety they waited the good man's judgment! When he walked in and out, looking at the house in connection with the sun, the trees, and the lake, and said. rubbing his hands with might of heartiness, "Well done! Make the dowar now as ye well know, and to-night we will sweeten the bread with arrack, and the milk with honey, and at every fire there shall be a kid. God with ye! Want of sweet water there shall not be, for the lake is our well; neither shall the bearers of burden hunger, or the least of the flock, for here is green pasture also. God with you all, my children! Go."

And, shouting, the many happy went their ways then to pitch their own habitations. A few remained to arrange the interior for the sheik; and of these the men-servants hung a curtain to the central row of pillars, making two apartments; the one on the right sacred to Ilderim himself, the other sacred to his horses—his jewels of Solomon—which they led

in, and with kisses and love-taps set at liberty. Against the middle pillar they then erected the arms-rack and filled it with javelins and spears, and bows, arrows, and shields; outside of them hanging the master's sword, modelled after the new moon; and the glitter of its blade rivalled the glitter of the jewels bedded in its grip. Upon one end of the rack they hung the housings of the horses, gay some of them as the livery of a king's servant, while on the other end they displayed the great man's wearing-apparel—his robes woollen and robes linen, his tunics and trousers, and many-colored kerchiefs for the head. Nor did they give over the work until he pronounced it well.

Meantime the women drew out and set up the divan, more indispensable to him than the beard down-flowing over his breast, white as Aaron's. They put a frame together in shape of three sides of a square, the opening to the door, and covered it with cushions and base curtains, and the cushions with a changeable spread striped brown and yellow; at the corners they placed pillows and bolsters sacked in cloth blue and crimson; then around the divan they laid a margin of carpet, and the inner space they carpeted as well; and when the carpet was carried from the opening of the divan to the door of the tent, their work was done; whereupon they again waited until the master said it was good. Nothing remained then but to bring and fill the jars with water, and hang the skin bottles of arrack ready for the hand—to-morrow the leben. Nor might

an Arab see why Ilderim should not be both
happy and generous—in his tent by the lake of
sweet waters, under the palms of the Orchard
of Palms.

Such was the tent at the door of which we
left Ben-Hur.

Servants were already waiting the master's
direction. One of them took off his sandals;
another unlatched Ben-Hur's Roman shoes;
then the two exchanged their dusty outer gar-
ments for fresh ones of white linen.

"Enter—in God's name, enter, and take thy
rest," said the host, heartily, in the dialect of
the Market-place of Jerusalem; forthwith he
led the way to the divan.

"I will sit here," he said next, pointing; "and
there the stranger."

A woman—in the old time she would have
been called a handmaid—answered, and dex-
terously piled the pillows and bolsters as rests
for the back; after which they sat upon the
side of the divan, while water was brought
fresh from the lake, and their feet bathed and
dried with napkins.

"We have a saying in the Desert," Ilderim
began, gathering his beard, and combing it with
his slender fingers, "that a good appetite is
the promise of a long life. Hast thou such?"

"By that rule, good sheik, I will live a hun-
dred years. I am a hungry wolf at thy door,"
Ben-Hur replied.

"Well, thou shalt not be sent away like a
wolf. I will give thee the best of the flocks."

Ilderim clapped his hands.

"Seek the stranger in the guest-tent, and say I, Ilderim, send him a prayer that his peace may be as incessant as the flowing of waters."

The man in waiting bowed.

"Say, also," Ilderim continued, "that I have returned with another for breaking of bread; and, if Balthasar the wise careth to share the loaf, three may partake of it, and the portion of the birds be none the less."

The second servant went away.

"Let us take our rest now."

Thereupon Ilderim settled himself upon the divan, as at this day merchants sit on their rugs in the bazaars of Damascus; and when fairly at rest, he stopped combing his beard, and said, gravely, "That thou art my guest, and hast drunk my leben, and art about to taste my salt, ought not to forbid a question: Who art thou?"

"Sheik Ilderim," said Ben-Hur, calmly enduring his gaze, "I pray thee not to think me trifling with thy just demand; but was there never a time in thy life when to answer such a question would have been a crime to thyself?"

"By the splendor of Solomon, yes!" Ilderim answered. "Betrayal of self is at times as base as the betrayal of a tribe."

"Thanks, thanks, good sheik!" Ben-Hur exclaimed. "Never answer became thee better. Now I know thou dost but seek assurance to justify the trust I have come to ask, and that such assurance is of more interest to thee than the affairs of my poor life."

The sheik in his turn bowed, and Ben-Hur hastened to pursue his advantage.

"So it please thee then," he said, "first, I am not a Roman, as the name given thee as mine implieth."

Ilderim clasped the beard overflowing his breast, and gazed at the speaker with eyes faintly twinkling through the shade of the heavy, close-drawn brows.

"In the next place," Ben-Hur continued, "I am an Israelite of the tribe of Judah."

The sheik raised his brows a little.

"Nor that merely. Sheik, I am a Jew with a grievance against Rome compared with which thine is not more than a child's trouble."

The old man combed his beard with nervous haste, and let fall his brows until even the twinkle of the eyes went out.

"Still further: I swear to thee, Sheik Ilderim —I swear by the covenant the Lord made with my fathers—so thou but give me the revenge I seek, the money and the glory of the race shall be thine."

Ilderim's brows relaxed; his head arose; his face began to beam; and it was almost possible to see the satisfaction taking possession of him.

"Enough!" he said. "If at the roots of thy tongue there is a lie in coil, Solomon himself had not been safe against thee. That thou art not a Roman—that as a Jew thou hast a griev-ance against Rome, and revenge to compass, I believe; and on that score enough. But as to thy skill. What experience hast thou in racing with chariots? And the horses—canst

thou make them creatures of thy will?—to know thee? to come at call? to go, if thou sayest it, to the last extreme of breath and strength? and then, in the perishing moment, out of the depths of thy life thrill them to one exertion the mightiest of all? The gift, my son, is not to every one. Ah, by the splendor of God! I knew a king who governed millions of men, their perfect master, but could not win the respect of a horse. Mark! I speak not of the dull brutes whose round it is to slave for slaves—the debased in blood and image—the dead in spirit; but of such as mine here—the kings of their kind; of a lineage reaching back to the broods of the first Pharaoh; my comrades and friends, dwellers in tents, whom long association with me has brought up to my plane; who to their instincts have added our wits and to their senses joined our souls, until they feel all we know of ambition, love, hate, and contempt; in war, heroes; in trust, faithful as women. Ho, there!"

A servant came forward.

"Let my Arabs come!"

The man drew aside part of the division curtain of the tent, exposing to view a group of horses, which lingered a moment where they were as if to make certain of the invitation.

"Come!" Ilderim said to them. "Why stand ye there? What have I that is not yours? Come, I say!"

They stalked slowly in.

"Son of Israel," the master said, "thy Moses was a mighty man, but—ha, ha, ha!—I must

laugh when I think of his allowing thy fathers the plodding ox and the dull, slow-natured ass, and forbidding them property in horses. Ha, ha, ha! Thinkest thou he would have done so had he seen that one—and that—and this?" At the word he laid his hand upon the face of the first to reach him, and patted it with infinite pride and tenderness.

"It is a misjudgment, sheik, a misjudgment," Ben-Hur said, warmly. "Moses was a warrior as well as a law-giver beloved by God; and to follow war—ah, what is it but to love all its creatures—these among the rest?"

A head of exquisite turn—with large eyes, soft as a deer's, and half hidden by the dense forelock, and small ears, sharp-pointed and sloped well forward—approached then quite to his breast, the nostrils open, and the upper lip in motion. "Who are you?" it asked, plainly as ever man spoke. Ben-Hur recognized one of the four racers he had seen on the course, and gave his open hand to the beautiful brute.

"They will tell you, the blasphemers!—may their days shorten as they grow fewer!"—the sheik spoke with the feeling of a man repelling a personal defamation—"they will tell you, I say, that our horses of the best blood are derived from the Nesæan pastures of Persia. God gave the first Arab a measureless waste of sand, with some treeless mountains, and here and there a well of bitter waters; and said to him, 'Behold thy country!' And when the poor man complained, the Mighty One pitied

him, and said again, 'Be of cheer! for I will
twice bless thee above other men.' The Arab
heard, and gave thanks, and with faith set out
to find the blessings. He travelled all the
boundaries first, and failed; then he made a
path into the desert, and went on and on—and
in the heart of the waste there was an island
of green very beautiful to see; and in the
heart of the island, lo! a herd of camels, and
another of horses! He took them joyfully
and kept them with care for what they were
—best gifts of God. And from that green isle
went forth all the horses of the earth; even to
the pastures of Nesæa they went; and north-
ward to the dreadful vales perpetually thresh-
ed by blasts from the Sea of Chill Winds.
Doubt not the story; or if thou dost, may nev-
er amulet have charm for an Arab again. Nay,
I will give thee proof."

He clapped his hands.

" Bring me the records of the tribe," he said
to the servant who responded.

While waiting, the sheik played with the
horses, patting their cheeks, combing their
forelocks with his fingers, giving each one a
token of remembrance. Presently six men
appeared with chests of cedar re-enforced by
bands of brass, and hinged and bolted with
brass.

" Nay," said Ilderim, when they were all set
down by the divan, " I meant not all of them;
only the records of the horses—that one. Open
it and take back the others."

The chest was opened, disclosing a mass of

ivory tablets strung on rings of silver wire; and as the tablets were scarcely thicker than wafers, each ring held several hundreds of them.

"I know," said Ilderim, taking some of the rings in his hand—" I know with what care and zeal, my son, the scribes of the Temple in the Holy City keep the names of the newly born, that every son of Israel may trace his line of ancestry to its beginning, though it antedate the patriarchs. My fathers—may the recollection of them be green forever!—did not think it sinful to borrow the idea, and apply it to their dumb servants. See these tablets!"

Ben-Hur took the rings, and separating the tablets saw they bore rude hieroglyphs in Arabic burned on the smooth surface by a sharp point of heated metal.

"Canst thou read them, O son of Israel?"

"No. Thou must tell me their meaning."

"Know thou, then, each tablet records the name of a foal of the pure blood born to my fathers through the hundreds of years passed; and also the names of sire and dam. Take them, and note their age, that thou mayst the more readily believe."

Some of the tablets were nearly worn away. All were yellow with age.

"In the chest there, I can tell thee now, I have the perfect history; perfect because certified as history seldom is — showing of what stock all these are sprung—this one, and that now supplicating thy notice and caress; and as they come to us here, their sires, even the furthest removed in time, came to my sires,

under a tent-roof like this of mine, to eat their
measure of barley from the open hand, and be
talked to as children; and as children kiss the
thanks they have not speech to express. And
now, O son of Israel, thou mayst believe my
declaration—if I am a lord of the Desert, be-
hold my ministers! Take them from me, and
I become as a sick man left by the caravan to
die. Thanks to them, age hath not diminished
the terror of me on the highways between
cities; and it will not while I have strength to
go with them. Ha, ha, ha! I could tell thee
marvels done by their ancestors. In a favoring
time I may do so; for the present, enough that
they were never overtaken in retreat; nor, by
the sword of Solomon, did they ever fail in
pursuit! That, mark you, on the sands and
under saddle; but now—I do not know—I am
afraid, for they are under yoke the first time,
and the conditions of success are so many.
They have the pride and the speed and the en-
durance. If I find them a master, they will
win. Son of Israel! so thou art the man, I
swear it shall be a happy day that brought
thee thither. Of thyself now speak."

"I know now," said Ben-Hur, "why it is
that in the love of an Arab his horse is next
to his children; and I know, also, why the
Arab horses are the best in the world; but,
good sheik, I would not have you judge me
by words alone; for, as you know, all promises
of men sometimes fail. Give me the trial first
on some plain hereabout, and put the four in
my hand to-morrow."

Ilderim's face beamed again, and he would have spoken.

"A moment, good sheik, a moment!" said Ben-Hur. "Let me say further. From the masters in Rome I learned many lessons, little thinking they would serve me in a time like this. I tell thee these thy sons of the Desert, though they have separately the speed of eagles and the endurance of lions, will fail if they are not trained to run together under the yoke. For bethink thee, sheik, in every four there is one the slowest and one the swiftest; and while the race is always to the slowest, the trouble is always with the swiftest. It was so to-day; the driver could not reduce the best to harmonious action with the poorest. My trial may have no better result; but if so, I will tell thee of it: that I swear. Wherefore, in the same spirit I say, can I get them to run together, moved by my will, the four as one, thou shalt have the sestertii and the crown, and I my revenge. What sayest thou?"

Ilderim listened, combing his beard the while. At the end he said, with a laugh, "I think better of thee, son of Israel. We have a saying in the Desert, 'If you will cook the meal with words, I will promise an ocean of butter.' Thou shalt have the horses in the morning."

At that moment there was a stir at the rear entrance to the tent.

"The supper—it is here! and yonder my friend Balthasar, whom thou shalt know. He hath a story to tell which an Israelite should never tire of hearing."

And to the servants he added,
"Take the records away, and return my jewels to their apartment."
And they did as he ordered.

F the reader will return now to the repast of the wise men at their meeting in the desert, he will understand the preparations for the supper in Ilderim's tent. The differences were chiefly such as were incident to ampler means and better service.

Three rugs were spread on the carpet within the space so nearly enclosed by the divan; a table not more than a foot in height was brought and set within the same place, and covered with a cloth. Off to one side a portable earthenware oven was established under the presidency of a woman whose duty it was to keep the company in bread, or, more precisely, in hot cakes of flour from the handmills grinding with constant sound in a neighboring tent.

Meanwhile Balthasar was conducted to the divan, where Ilderim and Ben-Hur received him standing. A loose black gown covered his person; his step was feeble, and his whole movement slow and cautious, apparently dependent upon a long staff and the arm of a servant.

"Peace to you, my friend," said Ilderim, re
spectfully. "Peace and welcome."

The Egyptian raised his head and replied,
"And to thee, good sheik—to thee and thine,
peace and the blessing of the One God—God
the true and loving."

The manner was gentle and devout, and im-
pressed Ben-Hur with a feeling of awe; besides
which the blessing included in the answering
salutation had been partly addressed to him,
and while that part was being spoken, the eyes
of the aged guest, hollow yet luminous, rested
upon his face long enough to stir an emotion
new and mysterious, and so strong that he
again and again during the repast scanned the
much-wrinkled and bloodless face for its mean-
ing; but always there was the expression bland,
placid, and trustful as a child's. A little later
he found that expression habitual.

"This is he, O Balthasar," said the sheik,
laying his hand on Ben-Hur's arm, "who will
break bread with us this evening."

The Egyptian glanced at the young man,
and looked again surprised and doubting; see-
ing which the sheik continued, "I have prom-
ised him my horses for trial to-morrow; and
if all goes well, he will drive them in the
Circus."

Balthasar continued his gaze.

"He came well recommended," Ilderim pur-
sued, much puzzled. "You may know him as
the son of Arrius, who was a noble Roman
sailor, though"—the sheik hesitated, then re-
sumed, with a laugh—"though he declares

407

himself an Israelite of the tribe of Judah; and,
by the splendor of God, I believe that he tells
me!"

Balthasar could no longer withhold explana-
tion.

"To-day, O most generous sheik, my life
was in peril, and would have been lost had
not a youth, the counterpart of this one — if,
indeed, he be not the very same — intervened
when all others fled, and saved me." Then he
addressed Ben-Hur directly, "Art thou not he?"

"I cannot answer so far," Ben-Hur replied,
with modest deference. "I am he who stopped
the horses of the insolent Roman when they
were rushing upon thy camel at the Fountain
of Castalia. Thy daughter left a cup with me."

From the bosom of his tunic he produced
the cup and gave it to Balthasar.

A glow lighted the faded countenance of
the Egyptian.

"The Lord sent thee to me at the Fountain
to-day," he said, in a tremulous voice, stretch-
ing his hand towards Ben-Hur; "and he sends
thee to me now. I give him thanks; and praise
him thou, for of his favor I have wherewith
to give thee great reward, and I will. The cup
is thine; keep it."

Ben-Hur took back the gift, and Balthasar,
seeing the inquiry upon Ilderim's face, related
the occurrence at the Fountain.

"What!" said the sheik to Ben-Hur. "Thou
saidst nothing of this to me, when better rec-
ommendation thou couldst not have brought.
Am I not an Arab, and sheik of my tribe of

tens of thousands? And is not he my guest?
And is it not in my guest-bond that the good
or evil thou dost him is good or evil done to
me? Whither shouldst thou go for reward
but here? And whose the hand to give it but
mine?"

His voice at the end of the speech rose to
cutting shrillness.

"Good sheik, spare me, I pray. I came not
for reward, great or small; and that I may be
acquitted of the thought, I say the help I gave
this excellent man would have been given as
well to thy humblest servant."

"But he is my friend, my guest—not my
servant; and seest thou not in the difference
the favor of Fortune?" Then to Balthasar
the sheik subjoined, "Ah, by the splendor of
God! I tell thee again he is not a Roman."

With that he turned away, and gave atten-
tion to the servants, whose preparations for the
supper were about complete.

The reader who recollects the history of Bal-
thasar as given by himself at the meeting in
the desert will understand the effect of Ben-
Hur's assertion of disinterestedness upon that
worthy. In his devotion to men there had
been, it will be remembered, no distinctions;
while the redemption which had been prom-
ised him in the way of reward—the redemp-
tion for which he was waiting—was universal.
To him, therefore, the assertion sounded some-
what like an echo of himself. He took a step
nearer Ben-Hur, and spoke to him in the child-
like way.

"How did the sheik say I should call you?
It was a Roman name, I think."

"Arrius, the son of Arrius."

"Yet thou art not a Roman?"

"All my people were Jews."

"Were, saidst thou? Are they not living?"

The question was subtle as well as simple;
but Ilderim saved Ben-Hur from reply.

"Come," he said to them, "the meal is
ready."

Ben-Hur gave his arm to Balthasar and con-
ducted him to the table, where shortly they
were all seated on their rugs Eastern fashion.
The lavers were brought them, and they wash-
ed and dried their hands; then the sheik made
a sign, the servants stopped, and the voice of
the Egyptian arose tremulous with holy feel-
ing.

"Father of All—God! What we have is of
thee; take our thanks, and bless us, that we
may continue to do thy will."

It was the grace the good man had said
simultaneously with his brethren Gaspar the
Greek and Melchior the Hindoo, the utterance
in diverse tongues out of which had come the
miracle attesting the Divine Presence at the
meal in the desert years before.

The table to which they immediately ad-
dressed themselves was, as may be thought,
rich in the substantials and delicacies favorite
in the East—in cakes hot from the oven, veg-
etables from the gardens, meats singly, com-
pounds of meats and vegetables, milk of kine,
and honey and butter—all eaten or drunk, it

410

should be remarked, without any of the modern accessories—knives, forks, spoons, cups, or plates; and in this part of the repast but little was said, for they were hungry. But when the dessert was in course it was otherwise. They laved their hands again, had the lapcloths shaken out, and with a renewed table and the sharp edge of their appetites gone they were disposed to talk and listen.

With such a company—an Arab, a Jew, and an Egyptian, all believers alike in one God—there could be at that age but one subject of conversation; and of the three, which should be speaker but he to whom the Deity had been so nearly a personal appearance, who had seen him in a star, had heard his voice in direction, had been led so far and so miraculously by his Spirit? And of what should he talk but that of which he had been called to testify?

CHAPTER XV
BALTHASAR IMPRESSES BEN-HUR

THE shadows cast over the Orchard of Palms by the mountains at set of sun left no sweet margin time of violet sky and drowsing earth between the day and night. The latter came early and swift; and against its glooming in the tent this evening the servants brought four candlesticks of brass and set them by the corners of the table. To each candlestick there were four branches, and on each branch a lighted silver

411

lamp and a supply cup of olive-oil. In light
ample, even brilliant, the group at dessert con-
tinued their conversation, speaking in the Syr-
iac dialect, familiar to all peoples in that part
of the world.

The Egyptian told his story of the meeting
of the three in the desert, and agreed with the
sheik that it was in December, twenty-seven
years before, when he and his companions, flee-
ing from Herod, arrived at the tent praying
shelter. The narrative was heard with intense
interest; even the servants lingering when they
could to catch its details. Ben-Hur received
it as became a man listening to a revela-
tion of deep concern to all humanity, and to
none of more concern than the people of Is-
rael. In his mind, as we shall presently see,
there was crystallizing an idea which was to
change his course of life, if not absorb it ab-
solutely.

As the recital proceeded, the impression
made by Balthasar upon the young Jew in-
creased; at its conclusion, his feeling was too
profound to permit a doubt of its truth; in-
deed, there was nothing left him desirable in
the connection but assurances, if such were to
be had, pertaining exclusively to the conse-
quences of the amazing event.

And now there is wanting an explanation
which the very discerning may have heretofore
demanded; certainly it can be no longer de-
layed. Our tale begins, in point of date not
less than fact, to trench close upon the open-
ing of the ministry of the Son of Mary, whom

we have seen but once since this same Balthasar left him worshipfully in his mother's lap in the cave by Bethlehem. Henceforth to the end the mysterious Child will be a subject of continual reference ; and slowly though surely the current of events with which we are dealing will bring us nearer and nearer to him, until finally we see him a man—we would like, if armed contrariety of opinion would permit it, to add — A MAN WHOM THE WORLD COULD NOT DO WITHOUT. Of this declaration, apparently so simple, a shrewd mind inspired by faith will make much—and in welcome. Before his time, and since, there have been men indispensable to particular people and periods ; but his indispensability was to the whole race, and for all time—a respect in which it is unique, solitary, divine.

To Sheik Ilderim the story was not new. He had heard it from the three wise men together under circumstances which left no room for doubt ; he had acted upon it seriously, for the helping a fugitive escape from the anger of the first Herod was dangerous. Now one of the three sat at his table again, a welcome guest and revered friend. Sheik Ilderim certainly believed the story ; yet, in the nature of things, its mighty central fact could not come home to him with the force and absorbing effect it came to Ben-Hur. He was an Arab, whose interest in the consequences was but general ; on the other hand, Ben-Hur was an Israelite and a Jew, with more than a special interest in —if the solecism can be pardoned—the truth

413

of the fact. He laid hold of the circumstance with a purely Jewish mind.

From his cradle, let it be remembered, he had heard of the Messiah; at the colleges he had been made familiar with all that was known of that Being at once the hope, the fear, and the peculiar glory of the chosen people; the prophets from the first to the last of the heroic line foretold him; and the coming had been, and yet was, the theme of endless exposition with the rabbis — in the synagogues, in the schools, in the Temple, of fast-days and feast-days, in public and in private, the national teachers expounded and kept expounding until all the children of Abraham, wherever their lots were cast, bore the Messiah in expectation, and by it literally, and with iron severity, ruled and moulded their lives.

Doubtless, it will be understood from this that there was much argument among the Jews themselves about the Messiah, and so there was; but the disputation was all limited to one point, and one only—when would he come?

Disquisition is for the preacher; whereas the writer is but telling a tale, and that he may not lose his character, the explanation he is making requires notice merely of a point connected with the Messiah about which the unanimity among the chosen people was matter of marvellous astonishment; he was to be, when come, the KING OF THE JEWS—their political King, their Cæsar. By their instrumentality he was to make armed conquest of the earth, and then, for their profit and in the

414

name of God, hold it down forever. On this faith, dear reader, the Pharisees or Separatists — the latter being rather a political term — in the cloisters and around the altars of the Temple, built an edifice of hope far overtopping the dream of the Macedonian. His but covered the earth; theirs covered the earth and filled the skies; that is to say, in their bold, boundless fantasy of blasphemous egotism, God the Almighty was in effect to suffer them for their uses to nail him by the ear to a door in sign of eternal servitude.

Returning directly to Ben-Hur, it is to be observed now that there were two circumstances in his life the result of which had been to keep him in a state comparatively free from the influence and hard effects of the audacious faith of his Separatist countrymen.

In the first place, his father followed the faith of the Sadducees, who may, in a general way, be termed the Liberals of their time. They had some loose opinions in denial of the soul. They were strict constructionists and rigorous observers of the Law as found in the books of Moses; but they held the vast mass of Rabbinical addenda to those books in derisive contempt. They were unquestionably a sect, yet their religion was more a philosophy than a creed; they did not deny themselves the enjoyments of life, and saw many admirable methods and productions among the Gentile divisions of the race. In politics they were the active opposition of the Separatists. In the natural order of things, these circumstances

and conditions, opinions and peculiarities, would have descended to the son as certainly and really as any portion of his father's estate; and, as we have seen, he was actually in course of acquiring them when the second saving event overtook him.

Upon a youth of Ben-Hur's mind and temperament the influence of five years of affluent life in Rome can be appreciated best by recalling that the great city was then, in fact, the meeting-place of the nations — their meeting-place politically and commercially, as well as for the indulgence of pleasure without restraint. Round and round the golden mile-stone in front of the Forum — now in gloom of eclipse, now in unapproachable splendor — flowed all the active currents of humanity. If excellences of manner, refinements of society, attainments of intellect, and glory of achievement made no impression upon him, how could he, as the son of Arrius, pass day after day, through a period so long, from the beautiful villa near Misenum into the receptions of Cæsar, and be wholly uninfluenced by what he saw there of kings, princes, ambassadors, hostages, and delegates, suitors all of them from every known land, waiting humbly the yes or no which was to make or unmake them? As mere assemblages, to be sure, there was nothing to compare with the gatherings at Jerusalem in celebration of the Passover; yet when he sat under the purple velaria of the Circus Maximus one of three hundred and fifty thousand spectators, he must have been visited by the thought that

416

possibly there might be some branches of the
family of man worthy divine consideration, if
not mercy, though they were of the uncircum-
cised—some, by their sorrows, and, yet worse,
by their hopelessness in the midst of sorrows,
fitted for brotherhood in the promises to his
countrymen.

That he should have had such a thought
under such circumstances was but natural; we
think so much, at least, will be admitted; but
when the reflection came to him, and he gave
himself up to it, he could not have been blind
to a certain distinction. The wretchedness of
the masses, and their hopeless condition, had
no relation whatever to religion; their mur-
murs and groans were not against their gods
or for want of gods. In the oak-woods of
Britain the Druids held their followers; Odin
and Freya maintained their godships in Gaul
and Germany and among the Hyperboreans;
Egypt was satisfied with her crocodiles and
Anubis; the Persians were yet devoted to Or-
muzd and Ahriman, holding them in equal
honor; in hope of the Nirvana, the Hindoos
moved on patient as ever in the rayless paths
of Brahm; the beautiful Greek mind, in pauses
of philosophy, still sang the heroic gods of
Homer; while in Rome nothing was so com-
mon and cheap as gods. According to whim,
the masters of the world, because they were
masters, carried their worship and offerings in-
differently from altar to altar, delighted in the
pandemonium they had erected. Their dis-
content, if they were discontented, was with the

number of gods; for, after borrowing all the divinities of the earth, they proceeded to deify their Cæsars, and vote them altars and holy service. No, the unhappy condition was not from religion, but misgovernment and usurpations and countless tyrannies. The Avernus men had been tumbled into, and were praying to be relieved from, was terribly but essentially political. The supplication—everywhere alike, in Lodinum, Alexandria, Athens, Jerusalem— was for a king to conquer with, not a god to worship.

Studying the situation after two thousand years, we can see and say that religiously there was no relief from the universal confusion except some God could prove himself a true God, and a masterful one, and come to the rescue; but the people of the time, even the discerning and philosophical, discovered no hope except in crushing Rome; that done, the relief would follow in restorations and reorganizations; therefore they prayed, conspired, rebelled, fought, and died, drenching the soil today with blood, to-morrow with tears—and always with the same result.

It remains to be said now that Ben-Hur was in agreement with the mass of men of his time not Romans. The five years' residence in the capital served him with opportunity to see and study the miseries of the subjugated world; and in full belief that the evils which afflicted it were political, and to be cured only by the sword, he was going forth to fit himself for a part in the day of resort to the heroic remedy.

POOL OF BETHSEDA

By practice of arms he was a perfect soldier;
but war has its higher fields, and he who would
move successfully in them must know more
than to defend with shield and thrust with
spear. In those fields the general finds his
tasks, the greatest of which is the reduction of
the many into one, and that one himself; the
consummate captain is a fighting-man armed
with an army. This conception entered into
the scheme of life to which he was further
swayed by the reflection that the vengeance
he dreamed of, in connection with his individ-
ual wrongs, would be more surely found in
some of the ways of war than in any pursuit of
peace.

The feelings with which he listened to Bal-
thasar can be now understood. The story
touched two of the most sensitive points of
his being so they rang within him. His heart
beat fast—and faster still when, searching him-
self, he found not a doubt either that the re-
cital was true in every particular, or that the
Child so miraculously found was the Messiah.
Marvelling much that Israel rested so dead to
the revelation, and that he had never heard of
it before that day, two questions presented
themselves to him as centring all it was at that
moment further desirable to know:

Where was the Child then?

And what was his mission?

With apologies for the interruptions, he pro-
ceeded to draw out the opinions of Balthasar,
who was in nowise loath to speak.

CHAPTER XVI
CHRIST IS COMING—BALTHASAR

F I could answer you," Balthasar said, in his simple, earnest, devout way —"oh, if I knew where he is, how quickly I would go to him! The seas should not stay me, nor the mountains."

"You have tried to find him, then?" asked Ben-Hur.

A smile flitted across the face of the Egyptian.

"The first task I charged myself with after leaving the shelter given me in the desert"— Balthasar cast a grateful look at Ilderim—"was to learn what became of the Child. But a year had passed, and I dared not go up to Judea in person, for Herod still held the throne bloody-minded as ever. In Egypt, upon my return, there were a few friends to believe the wonderful things I told them of what I had seen and heard—a few who rejoiced with me that a Redeemer was born—a few who never tired of the story. Some of them came up for me looking after the Child. They went first to Bethlehem, and found there the khan and the cave; but the steward—he who sat at the gate the night of the birth, and the night we came following the star—was gone. The king had taken him away, and he was no more seen."

"But they found some proofs, surely," said Ben-Hur, eagerly.

420

"Yes, proofs written in blood—a village in
mourning; mothers yet crying for their little
ones. You must know, when Herod heard of
our flight, he sent down and slew the youngest-
born of the children of Bethlehem. Not one
escaped. The faith of my messengers was con-
firmed; but they came to me saying the Child
was dead, slain with the other innocents."

"Dead!" exclaimed Ben-Hur, aghast. "Dead,
sayest thou?"

"Nay, my son, I did not say so. I said they,
my messengers, told me the Child was dead.
I did not believe the report then; I do not be-
lieve it now."

"I see—thou hast some special knowledge."

"Not so, not so," said Balthasar, dropping
his gaze. "The Spirit was to go with us no
farther than to the Child. When we came out
of the cave, after our presents were given and
we had seen the babe, we looked first thing for
the star; but it was gone, and we knew we were
left to ourselves. The last inspiration of the
Holy One — the last I can recall — was that
which sent us to Ilderim for safety."

"Yes," said the sheik, fingering his beard
nervously. "You told me you were sent to
me by a Spirit—I remember it."

"I have no special knowledge," Balthasar
continued, observing the dejection which had
fallen upon Ben-Hur; "but, my son, I have
given the matter much thought—thought con-
tinuing through years, inspired by faith, which,
I assure you, calling God for witness, is as
strong in me now as in the hour I heard the

voice of the Spirit calling me by the shore of the lake. If you will listen, I will tell you why I believe the Child is living."

Both Ilderim and Ben-Hur looked assent, and appeared to summon their faculties that they might understand as well as hear. The interest reached the servants, who drew near to the divan, and stood listening. Throughout the tent there was the profoundest silence.

"We three believe in God."

Balthasar bowed his head as he spoke.

"And he is the Truth," he resumed. "His word is God. The hills may turn to dust, and the seas be drunk dry by south winds; but his word shall stand, because it is the Truth."

The utterance was in a manner inexpressibly solemn.

"The voice, which was his, speaking to me by the lake, said, 'Blessed art thou, O son of Mizraim! The Redemption cometh. With two others from the remotenesses of the earth, thou shalt see the Saviour.' I have seen the Saviour — blessed be his name! — but the Redemption, which was the second part of the promise, is yet to come. Seest thou now? If the Child be dead, there is no agent to bring the Redemption about, and the word is naught, and God—nay, I dare not say it!"

He threw up both hands in horror.

"The Redemption was the work for which the Child was born; and so long as the promise abides, not even death can separate him from his work until it is fulfilled, or at least in the way of fulfilment. Take you that now as one

reason for my belief; then give me further attention."

The good man paused.

"Wilt thou not taste the wine? It is at thy hand—see," said Ilderim, respectfully.

Balthasar drank, and, seeming refreshed, continued:

"The Saviour I saw was born of woman, in nature like us, and subject to all our ills—even death. Let that stand as the first proposition. Consider next the work set apart to him. Was it not a performance for which only a man is fitted?—a man wise, firm, discreet—a man, not a child? To become such he had to grow as we grow. Bethink you now of the dangers his life was subject to in the interval—the long interval between childhood and maturity. The existing powers were his enemies; Herod was his enemy; and what would Rome have been? And as for Israel—that he should not be accepted by Israel was the motive for cutting him off. See you now. What better way was there to take care of his life in the helpless growing time than by passing him into obscurity? Wherefore I say to myself, and to my listening faith, which is never moved except by yearning of love—I say he is not dead, but lost; and, his work remaining undone, he will come again. There you have the reasons for my belief. Are they not good?"

Ilderim's small Arab eyes were bright with understanding, and Ben-Hur, lifted from his dejection, said heartily, "I, at least, may not gainsay them. What further, pray?"

"Hast thou not enough, my son? Well," he began, in calmer tone, "seeing that the reasons were good—more plainly, seeing it was God's will that the Child should not be found—I settled my faith into the keeping of patience, and took to waiting." He raised his eyes, full of holy trust, and broke off abstractedly—" I am waiting now. He lives, keeping well his mighty secret. What though I cannot go to him, or name the hill or the vale of his abiding-place? He lives—it may be as the fruit in blossom, it may be as the fruit just ripening; but by the certainty there is in the promise and reason of God, I know he lives."

A thrill of awe struck Ben-Hur—a thrill which was but the dying of his half-formed doubt.

"Where thinkest thou he is?" he asked, in a low voice, and hesitating, like one who feels upon his lips the pressure of a sacred silence.

Balthasar looked at him kindly, and replied, his mind not entirely freed from its abstraction,

"In my house on the Nile, so close to the river that the passers-by in boats see it and its reflection in the water at the same time—in my house, a few weeks ago, I sat thinking. A man thirty years old, I said to myself, should have his fields of life all ploughed, and his planting well done; for after that it is summer-time, with space scarce enough to ripen his sowing. The Child, I said further, is now twenty-seven—his time to plant must be at hand. I asked myself, as you here asked me, my son, and answered by coming hither, as to

a good resting-place close by the land thy fathers had from God. Where else should he appear, if not in Judea? In what city should he begin his work if not in Jerusalem? Who should be first to receive the blessings he is to bring, if not the children of Abraham, Isaac, and Jacob; in love, at least, the children of the Lord? If I were bidden go seek him, I would search well the hamlets and villages on the slopes of the mountains of Judea and Galilee falling eastwardly into the valley of the Jordan. He is there now. Standing in a door or on a hill-top, only this evening he saw the sun set one day nearer the time when he himself shall become the light of the world."

Balthasar ceased, with his hand raised and finger pointing as if at Judea. All the listeners, even the dull servants outside the divan, affected by his fervor, were startled as if by a majestic presence suddenly apparent within the tent. Nor did the sensation die away at once: of those at the table, each sat awhile thinking. The spell was finally broken by Ben-Hur.

"I see, good Balthasar," he said, "that thou hast been much and strangely favored. I see, also, that thou art a wise man indeed. It is not in my power to tell how grateful I am for the things thou hast told me. I am warned of the coming of great events, and borrow somewhat from thy faith. Complete the obligation, I pray thee, by telling further of the mission of him for whom thou art waiting, and for whom from this night I too shall wait as becomes a believing son of Judah. He is to be a Saviour,

thou saidst; is he not to be King of the Jews also?"

"My son," said Balthasar, in his benignant way, "the mission is yet a purpose in the bosom of God. All I think about it is wrung from the words of the Voice in connection with the prayer to which they were in answer. Shall we refer to them again?"

"Thou art the teacher."

"The cause of my disquiet," Balthasar began, calmly—"that which made me a preacher in Alexandria and in the villages of the Nile; that which drove me at last into the solitude where the Spirit found me—was the fallen condition of men, occasioned, as I believed, by loss of the knowledge of God. I sorrowed for the sorrows of my kind—not of one class, but all of them. So utterly were they fallen it seemed to me there could be no Redemption unless God himself would make it his work; and I prayed him to come, and that I might see him. 'Thy good works have conquered. The Redemption cometh; thou shalt see the Saviour'—thus the Voice spake; and with the answer I went up to Jerusalem rejoicing. Now, to whom is the Redemption? To all the world. And how shall it be? Strengthen thy faith, my son! Men say, I know, that there will be no happiness until Rome is razed from her hills. That is to say, the ills of the time are not, as I thought them, from ignorance of God, but from the misgovernment of rulers. Do we need to be told that human governments are never for the sake of religion? How many kings have

426

you heard of who were better than their subjects? Oh no, no! The Redemption cannot be for a political purpose—to pull down rulers and powers, and vacate their places merely that others may take and enjoy them. If that were all of it, the wisdom of God would cease to be surpassing. I tell you, though it be but the saying of blind to blind, he that comes is to be a Saviour of souls; and the Redemption means God once more on earth, and righteousness, that his stay here may be tolerable to himself."

Disappointment showed plainly on Ben-Hur's face—his head drooped; and if he was not convinced, he yet felt himself incapable that moment of disputing the opinion of the Egyptian. Not so Ilderim.

"By the splendor of God!" he cried, impulsively, "the judgment does away with all custom. The ways of the world are fixed, and cannot be changed. There must be a leader in every community clothed with power, else there is no reform."

Balthasar received the burst gravely.

"Thy wisdom, good sheik, is of the world; and thou dost forget that it is from the ways of the world we are to be redeemed. Man as a subject is the ambition of a king; the soul of a man for its salvation is the desire of a God."

Ilderim, though silenced, shook his head, unwilling to believe. Ben-Hur took up the argument for him.

"Father—I call thee such by permission,"

he said—"for whom wert thou required to ask at the gates of Jerusalem?"

The sheik threw him a grateful look.

"I was to ask of the people," said Balthasar, quietly, "where is he that is born King of the Jews?"

"And you saw him in the cave by Bethlehem?"

"We saw and worshipped him, and gave him presents — Melchior, gold; Gaspar, frankincense; and I, myrrh."

"When thou dost speak of fact, O father, to hear thee is to believe," said Ben-Hur; "but in the matter of opinion, I cannot understand the kind of king thou wouldst make of the Child —I cannot separate the ruler from his powers and duties."

"Son," said Balthasar, "we have the habit of studying closely the things which chance to lie at our feet, giving but a look at the greater objects in the distance. Thou seest now but the title — King of the Jews; wilt thou lift thine eyes to the mystery beyond it, the stumbling-block will disappear. Of the title, a word. Thy Israel hath seen better days—days in which God called thy people endearingly his people, and dealt with them through prophets. Now, if in those days he promised them the Saviour I saw—promised him as King of the Jews—the appearance must be according to the promise, if only for the word's sake. Ah, thou seest the reason of my question at the gate!—thou seest, and I will no more of it, but pass on. It may be, next, thou art regarding

the dignity of the Child; if so, bethink thee—what is it to be a successor of Herod?—by the world's standard of honor, what? Could not God better by his beloved? If thou canst think of the Almighty Father in want of a title, and stooping to borrow the inventions of men, why was I not bidden ask for a Cæsar at once? Oh, for the substance of that whereof we speak, look higher, I pray thee! Ask rather of what he whom we await shall be king; for I do tell, my son, that is the key to the mystery, which no man shall understand without the key."

Balthasar raised his eyes devoutly.

"There is a kingdom on the earth, though it is not of it—a kingdom of wider bounds than the earth—wider than the sea and the earth, though they were rolled together as finest gold and spread by the beating of hammers. Its existence is a fact as our hearts are facts, and we journey through it from birth to death without seeing it; nor shall any man see it until he hath first known his own soul; for the kingdom is not for him, but for his soul. And in its dominion there is glory such as hath not entered imagination—original, incomparable, impossible of increase."

"What thou sayest, father, is a riddle to me," said Ben-Hur. "I never heard of such a kingdom."

"Nor did I," said Ilderim.

"And I may not tell more of it," Balthasar added, humbly dropping his eyes. "What it is, what it is for, how it may be reached, none

can know until the Child comes to take possession of it as his own. He brings the key of the viewless gate, which he will open for his beloved, among whom will be all who love him, for of such only the redeemed will be."

After that there was a long silence, which Balthasar accepted as the end of the conversation.

"Good sheik," he said, in his placid way, "to-morrow or the next day I will go up to the city for a time. My daughter wishes to see the preparations for the games. I will speak further about the time of our going. And, my son, I will see you again. To you both, peace and good-night."

They all arose from the table. The sheik and Ben-Hur remained looking after the Egyptian until he was conducted out of the tent.

"Sheik Ilderim," said Ben-Hur then, "I have heard strange things to-night. Give me leave, I pray, to walk by the lake that I may think of them."

"Go; and I will come after you."

They washed their hands again; after which, at a sign from the master, a servant brought Ben-Hur his shoes, and directly he went out.

CHAPTER XVII
THE KINGDOM—SPIRITUAL OR POLITICAL?

UP a little way from the dowar there was a cluster of palms which threw its shade half in the water, half on the land. A bulbul sang from the branches a song of invitation. Ben-Hur stopped beneath to listen. At any other time the notes of the bird would have driven thought away ; but the story of the Egyptian was a burden of wonder, and he was a laborer carrying it, and, like other laborers, there was to him no music in the sweetest music until mind and body were happily attuned by rest.

The night was quiet. Not a ripple broke upon the shore. The old stars of the old East were all out, each in its accustomed place ; and there was summer everywhere—on land, on lake, in the sky.

Ben-Hur's imagination was heated, his feelings aroused, his will all unsettled.

So the palms, the sky, the air, seemed to him of the far south zone into which Balthasar had been driven by despair for men ; the lake, with its motionless surface, was a suggestion of the Nilotic mother by which the good man stood praying when the Spirit made its radiant appearance. Had all these accessories of the miracle come to Ben-Hur? or had he been transferred to them? And what if the miracle

should be repeated—and to him? He feared, yet wished, and even waited for the vision. When at last his feverish mood was cooled, permitting him to become himself, he was able to think.

His scheme of life has been explained. In all reflection about it heretofore there had been one hiatus which he had not been able to bridge or fill up—one so broad he could see but vaguely to the other side of it. When, finally, he was graduated a captain as well as a soldier, to what object should he address his efforts? Revolution he contemplated, of course; but the processes of revolution have always been the same, and to lead men into them there have always been required, first, a cause or pretence to enlist adherents; second, an end, or something as a practical achievement. As a rule he fights well who has wrongs to redress; but vastly better fights he who, with wrongs as a spur, has also steadily before him a glorious result in prospect—a result in which he can discern balm for wounds, compensation for valor, remembrance and gratitude in the event of death.

To determine the sufficiency of either the cause or the end, it was needful that Ben-Hur should study the adherents to whom he looked when all was ready for action. Very naturally, they were his countrymen. The wrongs of Israel were to every son of Abraham, and each one was a cause vastly holy, vastly inspiring.

Aye, the cause was there; but the end—what should it be?

The hours and days he had given this branch of his scheme were past calculation—all with the same conclusion—a dim, uncertain, general idea of national liberty. Was it sufficient? He could not say no, for that would have been the death of his hope; he shrank from saying yes, because his judgment taught him better. He could not assure himself even that Israel was able single-handed to successfully combat Rome. He knew the resources of that great enemy; he knew her art was superior to her resources. A universal alliance might suffice, but, alas! that was impossible, except—and upon the exception how long and earnestly he had dwelt!—except a hero would come from one of the suffering nations, and by martial successes accomplish a renown to fill the whole earth. What glory to Judea could she prove the Macedonia of the new Alexander! Alas, again! Under the rabbis valor was possible, but not discipline. And then the taunt of Messala in the garden of Herod—"All you conquer in the six days, you lose on the seventh."

So it happened he never approached the chasm thinking to surmount it but he was beaten back; and so incessantly had he failed in the object that he had about given it over, except as a thing of chance. The hero might be discovered in his day or he might not. God only knew. Such his state of mind, there need be no lingering upon the effect of Malluch's skeleton recital of the story of Balthasar. He heard it with a bewildering satisfaction—a feeling that here was the solution of the trouble—

here was the requisite hero found at last; and
he a son of the Lion tribe, and King of the
Jews! Behind the hero, lo! the world in arms.

The king implied a kingdom; he was to be
a warrior glorious as David, a ruler wise and
magnificent as Solomon; the kingdom was to
be a power against which Rome was to dash
itself to pieces. There would be colossal war,
and the agonies of death and birth — then
peace, meaning, of course, Judean dominion
forever.

Ben-Hur's heart beat hard as for an instant
he had a vision of Jerusalem the capital of the
world, and Zion, the site of the throne of the
Universal Master.

It seemed to the enthusiast rare fortune that
the man who had seen the king was at the
tent to which he was going. He could see
him there, and hear him, and learn of him what
all he knew of the coming change, especially
all he knew of the time of its happening. If
it were at hand, the campaign with Maxentius
should be abandoned; and he would go and
set about organizing and arming the tribes,
that Israel might be ready when the great day
of the restoration began to break.

Now, as we have seen, from Balthasar him-
self Ben-Hur had the marvellous story. Was
he satisfied?

There was a shadow upon him deeper than
that of the cluster of palms—the shadow of a
great uncertainty, which—take note, O reader!
which pertained more to the kingdom than
the king.

"What of this kingdom? And what is it to be?" Ben-Hur asked himself in thought.

Thus early arose the questions which were to follow the Child to his end, and survive him on earth—incomprehensible in his day, a dispute in this—an enigma to all who do not or cannot understand that every man is two in one—a deathless Soul and a mortal Body.

"What is it to be?" he asked.

For us, O reader, the Child himself has answered; but for Ben-Hur there were only the words of Balthasar, "On the earth, yet not of it—not for men, but for their souls—a dominion, nevertheless, of unimaginable glory."

What wonder the hapless youth found the phrases but the darkening of a riddle?

"The hand of man is not in it," he said, despairingly. "Nor has the king of such a kingdom use for men; neither toilers, nor councillors, nor soldiers. The earth must die, or be made anew, and for government new principles must be discovered—something besides armed hands — something in place of Force. But what?"

Again, O reader!

That which we will not see, he could not. The power there is in Love had not yet occurred to any man; much less had one come saying directly that for government and its objects—peace and order—Love is better and mightier than Force.

In the midst of his reverie a hand was laid upon his shoulder.

"I have a word to say, O son of Arrius,"

said Ilderim, stopping by his side—" A word, and then I must return, for the night is going."

" I give you welcome, sheik."

" As to the things you have heard but now," said Ilderim, almost without pause, "take in belief all save that relating to the kind of kingdom the Child will set up when he comes; as to so much keep virgin mind until you hear Simonides the merchant—a good man here in Antioch, to whom I will make you known. The Egyptian gives you coinage of his dreams which are too good for the earth; Simonides is wiser; he will ring you the sayings of your prophets, giving book and page, so you cannot deny that the Child will be King of the Jews in fact — aye, by the splendor of God! a king as Herod was, only better and far more magnificent. And then, see you, we will taste the sweetness of vengeance. I have said. Peace to you!"

" Stay—sheik!"

If Ilderim heard his call, he did not stay.

" Simonides again!" said Ben-Hur, bitterly. " Simonides here, Simonides there; from this one now, then from that! I am like to be well ridden by my father's servant, who knows at least to hold fast that which is mine; wherefore he is richer, if indeed he be not wiser, than the Egyptian. By the covenant! it is not to the faithless a man should go to find a faith to keep—and I will not. But, hark! singing— and the voice a woman's—or an angel's? It comes this way."

Down the lake towards the dowar came a woman singing. Her voice floated along the

436

hushed water melodious as a flute, and louder growing each instant. Directly the dipping of oars was heard in slow measure; a little later the words were distinguishable—words in purest Greek, best fitted of all the tongues of the day for the expression of passionate grief.

THE LAMENT.

(*Egyptian.*)

"I sigh as I sing for the story land
　　Across the Syrian sea.
The odorous winds from the musky sand
　　Were breaths of life to me.
They play with the plumes of the whispering palm
　　For me, alas! no more;
No more does the Nile in the moonlit calm
　　Moan past the Memphian shore.

"O Nilus! thou god of my fainting soul!
　　In dreams thou comest to me;
And, dreaming, I play with the lotus bowl,
　　And sing old songs to thee;
And hear from afar the Memnonian strain,
　　And calls from dear Simbel;
And wake to a passion of grief and pain
　　That e'er I said—Farewell!"

At the conclusion of the song the singer was past the cluster of palms. The last word—farewell—floated past Ben-Hur weighted with all the sweet sorrow of parting. The passing of the boat was as the passing of a deeper shadow into the deeper night.

Ben-Hur drew a long breath hardly distinguishable from a sigh.

"I know her by the song—the daughter of

437

Balthasar. How beautiful it was! And how beautiful is she!"

He recalled her large eyes curtained slightly by the drooping lids, the cheeks oval and rosy rich, the lips full and deep with dimpling in the corners, and all the grace of the tall, lithe figure.

"How beautiful she is!" he repeated.

And his heart made answer by a quickening of its movement.

Then, almost the same instant, another face, younger and quite as beautiful—more childlike and tender, if not so passionate—appeared as if held up to him out of the lake.

"Esther!" he said, smiling. "As I wished, a star has been sent to me."

He turned, and passed slowly back to the tent.

His life had been crowded with griefs and with vengeful preparations—too much crowded for love. Was this the beginning of a happy change?

And if the influence went with him into the tent, whose was it?

Esther had given him a cup.

So had the Egyptian.

And both had come to him at the same time under the palms.

Which?

438

VOLUME TWO

TABLE OF CONTENTS

VOLUME II

BOOK FIFTH

BOOK SEVENTH

BOOK EIGHTH

FULL-PAGE ILLUSTRATIONS

VOLUME II

THE ILLUSTRATED BEN-HUR

BOOK FIFTH

"*Only the actions of the just
Smell sweet and blossom in the dust.*"
SHIRLEY.

"*And, through the heat of conflict, keeps the law,
In calmness made, and sees what he foresaw.*"
WORDSWORTH.

CHAPTER I

MESSALA DOFFS HIS CHAPLET

THE morning after the bacchanalia in the saloon of the palace, the divan was covered with young patricians. Maxentius might come, and the city throng to receive him; the legion might descend from Mount Sulpius in glory of arms and armor; from Nymphæum to Omphalus there might be ceremonial splendors to shame the most notable ever before seen or heard of in the gorgeous East; yet would the many continue to sleep ignominiously on the divan where they had fallen or been carelessly tumbled by the indifferent slaves; that they would be able to take part in the reception that day was about as possible as for the lay-figures in the studio of a modern artist to rise and go bonneted and plumed through the one, two, three of a waltz.

Not all, however, who participated in the orgy were in the shameful condition. When dawn began to peer through the skylights of the saloon, Messala arose, and took the chaplet from his head, in sign that the revel was at an end; then he gathered his robe about him, gave a last look at the scene, and, without a word, departed for his quarters. Cicero could not have retired with more gravity from a night-long senatorial debate.

Three hours afterwards two couriers entered

his room, and from his own hand received each
a despatch, sealed and in duplicate, and con-
sisting chiefly of a letter to Valerius Gratus,
the procurator, still resident in Cæsarea. The
importance attached to the speedy and certain
delivery of the paper may be inferred. One
courier was to proceed overland, the other by
sea; both were to make the utmost haste.

It is of great concern now that the reader
should be fully informed of the contents of the
letter thus forwarded, and it is accordingly
given:

"ANTIOCH, *XII. Kal. Jul.*

"Messala to Gratus.

"O my Midas!

"I pray thou take no offence at the address, see-
ing it is one of love and gratitude, and an admission
that thou art most fortunate among men; seeing,
also, that thy ears are as they were derived from thy
mother, only proportionate to thy matured condition.

"O my Midas!

"I have to relate to thee an astonishing event,
which, though as yet somewhat in the field of con-
jecture, will, I doubt not, justify thy instant consid-
eration.

"Allow me first to revive thy recollection. Re-
member, a good many years ago, a family of a prince
of Jerusalem, incredibly ancient and vastly rich—by
name Ben-Hur. If thy memory have a limp or ail-
ment of any kind, there is, if I mistake not, a wound
on thy head which may help thee to a revival of the
circumstance.

"Next, to arouse thy interest. In punishment of
the attempt upon thy life—for dear repose of con-
science, may all the gods forbid it should ever prove
to have been an accident!—the family were seized
and summarily disposed of, and their property con-

456

fiscated. And inasmuch, O my Midas! as the action had the approval of our Cæsar, who was as just as he was wise — be there flowers upon his altar forever!—there should be no shame in referring to the sums which were realized to us respectively from that source, for which it is not possible I can ever cease to be grateful to thee, certainly not while I continue, as at present, in the uninterrupted enjoyment of the part which fell to me.

"In vindication of thy wisdom — a quality for which, as I am now advised, the son of Gordius, to whom I have boldly likened thee, was never distinguished among men or gods—I recall further that thou didst make disposition of the family of Hur, both of us at the time supposing the plan hit upon to be the most effective possible for the purposes in view, which were silence and delivery over to inevitable but natural death. Thou wilt remember what thou didst with the mother and sister of the malefactor; yet, if now I yield to a desire to learn whether they be living or dead, I know, from knowing the amiability of thy nature, O my Gratus, that thou wilt pardon me as one scarcely less amiable than thyself.

"As more immediately essential to the present business, however, I take the liberty of inviting to thy remembrance that the actual criminal was sent to the galleys a slave for life—so the precept ran; and it may serve to make the event which I am about to relate the more astonishing by saying here that I saw and read the receipt for his body delivered in course to the tribune commanding a galley.

"Thou mayst begin now to give me more especial heed, O my most excellent Phrygian!

"Referring to the limit of life at the oar, the outlaw thus justly disposed of should be dead, or, better speaking, some one of the three thousand Oceanides should have taken him to husband at least five years ago. And if thou wilt excuse a momentary weakness, O most virtuous and tender of men! inasmuch as I loved him in childhood, and also because he was very handsome — I used in much admiration to call

457

him my Ganymede—he ought in right to have fallen
into the arms of the most beautiful daughter of the
family. Of opinion, however, that he was certainly
dead, I have lived quite five years in calm and inno-
cent enjoyment of the fortune for which I am in a
degree indebted to him. I make the admission of
indebtedness without intending it to diminish my ob-
ligation to thee.

"Now I am at the very point of interest.

"Last night, while acting as master of the feast
for a party just from Rome—their extreme youth
and inexperience appealed to my compassion—I
heard a singular story. Maxentius, the consul, as
you know, comes to-day to conduct a campaign
against the Parthians. Of the ambitious who are to
accompany him there is one, a son of the late duum-
vir Quintus Arrius. I had occasion to inquire about
him particularly. When Arrius set out in pursuit of
the pirates, whose defeat gained him his final honors,
he had no family; when he returned from the expe-
dition, he brought back with him an heir. Now be
thou composed as becomes the owner of so many tal-
ents in ready sestertii! The son and heir of whom I
speak is he whom thou didst send to the galleys—the
very Ben-Hur who should have died at his oar five
years ago—returned now with fortune and rank, and
possibly as a Roman citizen, to— Well, thou art too
firmly seated to be alarmed, but I, O my Midas! I
am in danger—no need to tell thee of what. Who
should know, if thou dost not?

"Sayest thou to all this, tut-tut?

"When Arrius, the father, by adoption, of this
apparition from the arms of the most beautiful of the
Oceanides (see above my opinion of what she should
be), joined battle with the pirates, his vessel was
sunk, and but two of all her crew escaped drowning
—Arrius himself and this one, his heir.

"The officers who took them from the plank on
which they were floating say the associate of the fort-
unate tribune was a young man who, when lifted to
the deck, was in the dress of a galley slave.

"This should be convincing, to say least; but lest

thou say tut-tut again, I tell thee, O my Midas! that yesterday, by good chance—I have a vow to Fortune in consequence—I met the mysterious son of Arrius face to face; and I declare now that, though I did not then recognize him, he is the very Ben-Hur who was for years my playmate; the very Ben-Hur who, if he be a man, though of the commonest grade, must this very moment of my writing be thinking of vengeance—for so would I were I he—vengeance not to be satisfied short of life; vengeance for country, mother, sister, self, and—I say it last, though thou mayst think it would be first—for fortune lost.

"By this time, O good my benefactor and friend! my Gratus! in consideration of thy sestertii in peril, their loss being the worst which could befall one of thy high estate—I quit calling thee after the foolish old King of Phrygia—by this time, I say (meaning after having read me so far), I have faith to believe thou hast ceased saying tut-tut, and art ready to think what ought to be done in such emergency.

"It were vulgar to ask thee now what shall be done. Rather let me say I am thy client; or, better yet, thou art my Ulysses whose part it is to give me sound direction.

"And I please myself thinking I see thee when this letter is put into thy hand. I see thee read it once, thy countenance all gravity, and then again with a smile; then, hesitation ended, and thy judgment formed, it is this, or it is that; wisdom like Mercury's, promptitude like Cæsar's.

"The sun is now fairly risen. An hour hence two messengers will depart from my door, each with a sealed copy hereof; one of them will go by land, the other by sea, so important do I regard it that thou shouldst be early and particularly informed of the appearance of our enemy in this part of our Roman world.

"I will await thy answer here.

"Ben-Hur's going and coming will of course be regulated by his master, the consul, who, though he exert himself without rest day and night, cannot get away under a month. Thou knowest what work it

is to assemble and provide for an army destined to
operate in a desolate, townless country.

"I saw the Jew yesterday in the Grove of Daphne;
and if he be not there now, he is certainly in the
neighborhood, making it easy for me to keep him in
eye. Indeed, wert thou to ask me where he is now,
I should say, with the most positive assurance, he is
to be found at the old Orchard of Palms, under the
tent of the traitor Sheik Ilderim, who cannot long
escape our strong hand. Be not surprised if Maxen-
tius, as his first measure, places the Arab on the ship
for forwarding to Rome.

"I am so particular about the whereabouts of the
Jew because it will be important to thee, O illustri-
ous! when thou comest to consider what is to be
done; for already I know, and by the knowledge I
flatter myself I am growing in wisdom, that in every
scheme involving human action there are three ele-
ments always to be taken in account—time, place,
and agency.

"If thou sayest this is the place, have thou then
no hesitancy in trusting the business to thy most lov-
ing friend, who would be thy aptest scholar as well.
"MESSALA."

CHAPTER II
ILDERIM'S ARABS UNDER THE YOKE

ABOUT the time the couriers depart-
ed from Messala's door with the
despatches (it being yet the early
morning hour), Ben-Hur entered Il-
derim's tent. He had taken a plunge into the
lake, and breakfasted, and appeared now in an
under-tunic, sleeveless, and with skirt scarcely
reaching to the knee.

The sheik saluted him from the divan.

"I give thee peace, son of Arrius," he said,

with admiration, for, in truth, he had never seen a more perfect illustration of glowing, powerful, confident manhood. " I give thee peace and good-will. The horses are ready, I am ready. And thou ?"

" The peace thou givest me, good sheik, I give thee in return. I thank thee for so much good-will. I am ready."

Ilderim clapped his hands.

" I will have the horses brought. Be seated."

" Are they yoked ?"

" No."

" Then suffer me to serve myself," said Ben-Hur. " It is needful that I make the acquaintance of thy Arabs. I must know them by name, O sheik, that I may speak to them singly: nor less must I know their temper, for they are like men; if bold, the better of scolding; if timid, the better of praise and flattery. Let the servants bring me the harness."

" And the chariot ?" asked the sheik.

" I will let the chariot alone to-day. In its place, let them bring me a fifth horse, if thou hast it; he should be barebacked, and fleet as the others."

Ilderim's wonder was aroused, and he summoned a servant immediately.

" Bid them bring the harness for the four," he said—" the harness for the four, and the bridle for Sirius."

Ilderim then arose.

" Sirius is my love, and I am his, O son of Arrius. We have been comrades for twenty years—in tent, in battle, in all stages of the

461

desert we have been comrades. I will show him to you."

Going to the division curtain, he held it, while Ben-Hur passed under. The horses came to him in a body. One with a small head, luminous eyes, neck like the segment of a bended bow, and mighty chest, curtained thickly by a profusion of mane soft and wavy as a damsel's locks, nickered low and gladly at sight of him.

"Good horse," said the sheik, patting the dark-brown cheek. "Good horse, good-morning." Turning then to Ben-Hur, he added, "This is Sirius, father of the four here. Mira, the mother, awaits our return, being too precious to be hazarded in a region where there is a stronger hand than mine. And much I doubt," he laughed as he spoke — "much I doubt, O son of Arrius, if the tribe could endure her absence. She is their glory; they worship her; did she gallop over them, they would laugh. Ten thousand horsemen, sons of the desert, will ask to-day, 'Have you heard of Mira?' And to the answer, 'She is well,' they will say, 'God is good! blessed be God!'"

"Mira—Sirius—names of stars, are they not, O sheik?" asked Ben-Hur, going to each of the four, and to the sire, offering his hand.

"And why not?" replied Ilderim. "Wert thou ever abroad on the desert at night?"

"No."

"Then thou canst not know how much we Arabs depend upon the stars. We borrow their names in gratitude, and give them in love. My fatners all had their Miras, as I have mine:

and these children are stars no less. There, see thou, is Rigel, and there Antares; that one is Atair, and he whom thou goest to now is Aldebaran, the youngest of the brood, but none the worse of that—no, not he! Against the wind he will carry thee till it roar in thy ears like Akaba; and he will go where thou sayest, son of Arrius—aye, by the glory of Solomon! he will take thee to the lion's jaws, if thou darest so much."

The harness was brought. With his own hands Ben-Hur equipped the horses; with his own hands he led them out of the tent, and there attached the reins.

"Bring me Sirius," he said.

An Arab could not have better sprung to seat on the courser's back.

"And now the reins."

They were given him, and carefully separated.

"Good sheik," he said, "I am ready. Let a guide go before me to the field, and send some of thy men with water."

There was no trouble at starting. The horses were not afraid. Already there seemed a tacit understanding between them and the new driver, who had performed his part calmly, and with the confidence which always begets confidence. The order of going was precisely that of driving, except that Ben-Hur sat upon Sirius instead of standing in the chariot. Ilderim's spirit arose. He combed his beard, and smiled with satisfaction as he muttered, "He is not a Roman, no, by the splendor of God!" He followed on foot, the entire tenantry of the

dowar—men, women, and children—pouring after him, participants all in his solicitude, if not in his confidence.

The field, when reached, proved ample and well fitted for the training, which Ben-Hur began immediately by driving the four at first slowly, and in perpendicular lines, and then in wide circles. Advancing a step in the course, he put them next into a trot; again progressing, he pushed into a gallop; at length he contracted the circles, and yet later drove eccentrically here and there, right, left, forward, and without a break. An hour was thus occupied. Slowing the gait to a walk, he drove up to Ilderim.

"The work is done, nothing now but practice," he said. "I give you joy, Sheik Ilderim, that you have such servants as these. See," he continued, dismounting and going to the horses, "see, the gloss of their red coats is without spot; they breathe lightly as when I began. I give thee great joy, and it will go hard if"—he turned his flashing eyes upon the old man's face—"if we have not the victory and our—"

He stopped, colored, bowed. At the sheik's side he observed, for the first time, Balthasar, leaning upon his staff, and two women closely veiled. At one of the latter he looked a second time, saying to himself, with a flutter about his heart, "'Tis she—'tis the Egyptian!" Ilderim picked up his broken sentence—

"The victory, and our revenge!" Then he said aloud "I am not afraid; I am glad. Son

of Arrius, thou art the man. Be the end like the beginning, and thou shalt see of what stuff is the lining of the hand of an Arab who is able to give."

"I thank thee, good sheik," Ben-Hur returned, modestly. "Let the servants bring drink for the horses."

With his own hands he gave the water.

Remounting Sirius, he renewed the training, going as before from walk to trot, from trot to gallop; finally, he pushed the steady racers into the run, gradually quickening it to full speed. The performance then became exciting; and there were applause for the dainty handling of the reins, and admiration for the four, which were the same, whether they flew forward or wheeled in varying curvature. In their action there were unity, power, grace, pleasure, all without effort or sign of labor. The admiration was unmixed with pity or reproach, which would have been as well bestowed upon swallows in their evening flight.

In the midst of the exercises, and the attention they received from all the by-standers, Malluch came upon the ground, seeking the sheik.

"I have a message for you, O sheik," he said, availing himself of a moment he supposed favorable for the speech —"a message from Simonides, the merchant."

"Simonides!" ejaculated the Arab. "Ah! tis well. May Abaddon take all his enemies!"

"He bade me give thee first the holy peace of God," Malluch continued; "and then this

despatch, with prayer that thou read it the instant of receipt."

Ilderim, standing in his place, broke the sealing of the package delivered to him, and from a wrapping of fine linen took two letters, which he proceeded to read.

[No. 1.]

" Simonides to Sheik Ilderim.

" O friend!

" Assure thyself first of a place in my inner heart.

" Then—

" There is in thy dowar a youth of fair presence, calling himself the son of Arrius; and such he is by adoption.

" He is very dear to me.

" He hath a wonderful history, which I will tell thee; come thou to-day or to-morrow, that I may tell thee the history, and have thy counsel.

" Meantime, favor all his requests, so they be not against honor. Should there be need of reparation, I am bound to thee for it.

" That I have interest in this youth, keep thou private.

" Remember me to thy other guest. He, his daughter, thyself, and all whom thou mayst choose to be of thy company, must depend upon me at the Circus the day of the games. I have seats already engaged.

" To thee and all thine, peace.

" What should I be, O my friend, but thy friend?

" SIMONIDES."

[No. 2.]

" Simonides to Sheik Ilderim.

" O friend!

" Out of the abundance of my experience, I send you a word.

" There is a sign which all persons not Romans,

and who have moneys or goods subject to despoilment, accept as warning—that is, the arrival at a seat of power of some high Roman official charged with authority.

"To-day comes the Consul Maxentius.

"Be thou warned!

"Another word of advice.

"A conspiracy, to be of effect against thee, O friend, must include the Herods as parties; thou hast great properties in their dominions.

"Wherefore keep thou watch.

"Send this morning to thy trusty keepers of the roads leading south from Antioch, and bid them search every courier going and coming; if they find private despatches relating to thee or thine affairs, thou shouldst see them.

"You should have received this yesterday, though it is not too late, if you act promptly.

"If couriers left Antioch this morning, your messengers know the by-ways, and can get before them with your orders.

"Do not hesitate.

"Burn this after reading.

"O my friend! thy friend, SIMONIDES."

Ilderim read the letters a second time, and refolded them in the linen wrap, and put the package under his girdle.

The exercises in the field continued but a little longer—in all about two hours. At their conclusion, Ben-Hur brought the four to a walk, and drove to Ilderim.

"With leave, O sheik," he said, "I will return thy Arabs to the tent, and bring them out again this afternoon."

Ilderim walked to him as he sat on Sirius, and said, "I give them to you, son of Arrius, to do with as you will until after the games.

You have done with them in two hours what the Roman—may jackals gnaw his bones flesh-less!—could not in as many weeks. We will win—by the splendor of God, we will win!"

At the tent Ben-Hur remained with the horses while they were being cared for; then, after a plunge in the lake and a cup of arrack with the sheik, whose flow of spirits was roy-ally exuberant, he dressed himself in his Jew-ish garb again, and walked with Malluch on into the Orchard.

There was much conversation between the two, not all of it important. One part, how-ever, must not be overlooked. Ben-Hur was speaking.

"I will give you," he said, "an order for my property stored in the khan this side the river by the Seleucian Bridge. Bring it to me to-day, if you can. And, good Malluch—if I do not overtask you—"

Malluch protested heartily his willingness to be of service.

"Thank you, Malluch, thank you," said Ben-Hur. "I will take you at your word, remem-bering that we are brethren of the old tribe, and that the enemy is a Roman. First, then —as you are a man of business, which I much fear Sheik Ilderim is not—"

"Arabs seldom are," said Malluch, gravely.

"Nay, I do not impeach their shrewdness, Malluch. It is well, however, to look after them. To save all forfeit or hinderance in con-nection with the race, you would put me per-fectly at rest by going to the office of the Cir-

cus, and seeing that he has complied with every preliminary rule; and if you can get a copy of the rules, the service may be of great avail to me. I would like to know the colors I am to wear, and particularly the number of the crypt I am to occupy at the starting; if it be next Messala's on the right or left, it is well; if not, and you can have it changed so as to bring me next the Roman, do so. Have you good memory, Malluch?"

"It has failed me, but never, son of Arrius, where the heart helped it as now."

"I will venture, then, to charge you with one further service. I saw yesterday that Messala was proud of his chariot, as he might be, for the best of Cæsar's scarcely surpass it. Can you not make its display an excuse which will enable you to find if it be light or heavy? I would like to have its exact weight and measurements — and, Malluch, though you fail in all else, bring me exactly the height his axle stands above the ground. You understand, Malluch? I do not wish him to have any actual advantage of me. I do not care for his splendor; if I beat him, it will make his fall the harder, and my triumph the more complete. If there are advantages really important, I want them."

"I see, I see!" said Malluch. "A line dropped from the centre of the axle is what you want."

"Thou hast it; and be glad, Malluch—it is the last of my commissions. Let us return to the dowar."

At the door of the tent they found a servant replenishing the smoke-stained bottles of leben freshly made, and stopped to refresh themselves. Shortly afterwards Malluch returned to the city.

During their absence, a messenger well mounted had been despatched with orders as suggested by Simonides. He was an Arab, and carried nothing written.

CHAPTER III
THE ARTS OF CLEOPATRA

"RAS, the daughter of Balthasar, sends me with salutation and a message," said a servant to Ben-Hur, who was taking his ease in the tent.

" Give me the message."

"Would it please you to accompany her upon the lake ?"

"I will carry the answer myself. Tell her so."

His shoes were brought him, and in a few minutes Ben-Hur sallied out to find the fair Egyptian. The shadow of the mountains was creeping over the Orchard of Palms in advance of night. Afar through the trees came the tinkling of sheep-bells, the lowing of cattle, and the voices of the herdsmen bringing their charges home. Life at the Orchard, it should be remembered, was in all respects as pastoral as life on the scantier meadows of the desert.

Sheik Ilderim had witnessed the exercises of the afternoon, being a repetition of those of

the morning; after which he had gone to the city in answer to the invitation of Simonides; he might return in the night; but, considering the immensity of the field to be talked over with his friend, it was hardly possible. Ben-Hur, thus left alone, had seen his horses cared for; cooled and purified himself in the lake; exchanged the field garb for his customary vestments, all white, as became a Sadducean of the pure blood; supped early; and, thanks to the strength of youth, was well recovered from the violent exertion he had undergone.

It is neither wise nor honest to detract from beauty as a quality. There cannot be a refined soul insensible to its influence. The story of Pygmalion and his statue is as natural as it is poetical. Beauty is of itself a power; and it was now drawing Ben-Hur.

The Egyptian was to him a wonderfully beautiful woman — beautiful of face, beautiful of form. In his thought she always appeared to him as he saw her at the fountain; and he felt the influence of her voice, sweeter because in tearful expression of gratitude to him, and of her eyes—the large, soft, black, almond-shaped eyes declarative of her race—eyes which looked more than lies in the supremest wealth of words to utter; and recurrences of the thought of her were returns just so frequent of a figure tall, slender, graceful, refined, wrapped in rich and floating drapery, wanting nothing but a fitting mind to make her, like the Shulamite, and in the same sense, terrible as an army with banners. In other words, as she returned to

his fancy, the whole passionate Song of Solomon came with her, inspired by her presence. With this sentiment and that feeling, he was going to see if she actually justified them. It was not love that was taking him, but admiration and curiosity, which might be the heralds of love.

The landing was a simple affair, consisting of a short stair-way, and a platform garnished by some lamp-posts; yet at the top of the steps he paused, arrested by what he beheld.

There was a shallop resting upon the clear water lightly as an egg-shell. An Ethiop—the camel-driver at the Castalian fount—occupied the rower's place, his blackness intensified by a livery of shining white. All the boat aft was cushioned and carpeted with stuffs brilliant with Tyrian red. On the rudder seat sat the Egyptian herself, sunk in Indian shawls and a very vapor of most delicate veils and scarfs. Her arms were bare to the shoulders; and, not merely faultless in shape, they had the effect of compelling attention to them—their pose, their action, their expression; the hands, the fingers even, seemed endowed with graces and meaning; each was an object of beauty. The shoulders and neck were protected from the evening air by an ample scarf, which yet did not hide them.

In the glance he gave her, Ben-Hur paid no attention to these details. There was simply an impression made upon him; and, like strong light, it was a sensation, not a thing of sight or enumeration. Thy lips are like a thread of

scarlet; thy temples are like a piece of pomegranate within thy locks. Rise up, my love, my fair one, and come away; for, lo! the winter is past, the rain is over and gone; the flowers appear on the earth; the time of the singing of birds is come, and the voice of the turtle is heard in the land—such was the impression she made upon him translated into words.

"Come," she said, observing him stop, "come, or I shall think you a poor sailor."

The red of his cheek deepened. Did she know anything of his life upon the sea? He descended to the platform at once.

"I was afraid," he said, as he took the vacant seat before her.

"Of what?"

"Of sinking the boat," he replied, smiling.

"Wait until we are in deeper water," she said, giving a signal to the black, who dipped the oars, and they were off.

If love and Ben-Hur were enemies, the latter was never more at mercy. The Egyptian sat where he could not but see her; she, whom he had already engrossed in memory as his ideal of the Shulamite. With her eyes giving light to his, the stars might come out, and he not see them; and so they did. The night might fall with unrelieved darkness everywhere else; her look would make illumination for him. And then, as everybody knows, given youth and such companionship, there is no situation in which the fancy takes such complete control as upon tranquil waters under a calm night sky, warm with summer. It is so easy at such time to glide

imperceptibly out of the commonplace into the ideal.

"Give me the rudder," he said.

"No," she replied, "that were to reverse the relation. Did I not ask you to ride with me? I am indebted to you, and would begin payment. You may talk and I will listen, or I will talk and you will listen: that choice is yours; but it shall be mine to choose where we go, and the way thither."

"And where may that be?"

"You are alarmed again."

"O fair Egyptian, I but asked you the first question of every captive."

"Call me Egypt."

"I would rather call you Iras."

"You may think of me by that name, but call me Egypt."

"Egypt is a country, and means many people."

"Yes, yes! And such a country!"

"I see; it is to Egypt we are going."

"Would we were! I would be so glad."

She sighed as she spoke.

"You have no care for me, then," he said.

"Ah, by that I know you were never there."

"I never was."

"Oh, it is the land where there are no unhappy people, the desired of all the rest of the earth, the mother of all the gods, and therefore supremely blest. There, O son of Arrius, there the happy find increase of happiness, and the wretched, going, drink once of the sweet water of the sacred river, and laugh and sing, rejoicing like children."

ACELDAMA, THE FIELD OF BLOOD

Are not the very poor with you there as elsewhere ?"

"The very poor in Egypt are the very simple in wants and ways," she replied. "They have no wish beyond enough, and how little that is a Greek or a Roman cannot know."

"But I am neither Greek nor Roman."

She laughed.

"I have a garden of roses, and in the midst of it is a tree, and its bloom is the richest of all. Whence came it, think you ?"

"From Persia, the home of the rose."

"No."

"From India, then."

"No."

"Ah ! one of the isles of Greece."

"I will tell you," she said : "a traveller found it perishing by the road-side on the plain of Rephaim."

"Oh, in Judea !"

"I put it in the earth left bare by the receding Nile, and the soft south wind blew over the desert and nursed it, and the sun kissed it in pity ; after which it could not else than grow and flourish. I stand in its shade now, and it thanks me with much perfume. As with the roses, so with the men of Israel. Where shall they reach perfection but in Egypt ?"

"Moses was but one of millions."

"Nay, there was a reader of dreams. Will you forget him ?"

"The friendly Pharaohs are dead."

"Ah, yes ! The river by which they dwelt sings to them in their tombs ; yet the same

sun tempers the same air to the same people."

"Alexandria is but a Roman town."

"She has but exchanged sceptres. Cæsar took from her that of the sword, and in its place left that of learning. Go with me to the Brucheium, and I will show you the college of nations; to the Serapeion, and see the perfection of architecture; to the Library, and read the immortals; to the theatre, and hear the heroics of the Greeks and Hindoos; to the quay, and count the triumphs of commerce; descend with me into the streets, O son of Arrius, and, when the philosophers have dispersed, and taken with them the masters of all the arts, and all the gods have home their votaries, and nothing remains of the day but its pleasures, you shall hear the stories that have amused men from the beginning, and the songs which will never, never die."

As he listened, Ben-Hur was carried back to the night when, in the summer-house in Jerusalem, his mother, in much the same poetry of patriotism, declaimed the departed glories of Israel.

"I see now why you wish to be called Egypt. Will you sing me a song if I call you by that name? I heard you last night."

"That was a hymn of the Nile," she answered, "a lament which I sing when I would fancy I smell the breath of the desert, and hear the surge of the dear old river; let me rather give you a piece of the Indian mind. When we get to Alexandria, I will take you to the corner of

476

the street where you can hear it from the
daughter of the Ganga, who taught it to me.
Kapila, you should know, was one of the most
revered of the Hindoo sages."

Then, as if it were a natural mode of ex-
pression, she began the song.

KAPILA.

I.

Kapila, Kapila, so young and true,
 I yearn for a glory like thine,
And hail thee from battle to ask anew,
 Can ever thy Valor be mine?

Kapila sat on his charger dun,
 A hero never so grave:
Who loveth all things hath fear of none,
 'Tis love that maketh me brave.
A woman gave me her soul one day,
The soul of my soul to be alway;
 Thence came my Valor to me,
 Go try it—try it—and see.'

II.

Kapila, Kapila, so old and gray,
 The queen is calling for me;
But ere I go hence, I wish thou wouldst say,
 How Wisdom first came to thee.

Kapila stood in his temple door,
 A priest in eremite guise:
' It did not come as men get their lore,
 'Tis faith that maketh me wise.
A woman gave me her heart one day,
The heart of my heart to be alway;
 Thence came my Wisdom to me,
 Go try it—try it—and see.' "

Ben-Hur had not time to express his thanks

for the song before the keel of the boat grated upon the underlying sand, and, next moment, the bow ran upon the shore.

"A quick voyage, O Egypt!" he cried.

"And a briefer stay!" she replied, as, with a strong push, the black sent them shooting into the open water again.

"You will give me the rudder now."

"Oh, no," said she, laughing. "To you, the chariot; to me, the boat. We are merely at the lake's end, and the lesson is that I must not sing any more. Having been to Egypt, let us now to the Grove of Daphne."

"Without a song on the way?" he said, in deprecation.

"Tell me something of the Roman from whom you saved us to-day," she asked.

The request struck Ben-Hur unpleasantly.

"I wish this were the Nile," he said, evasively. "The kings and queens, having slept so long, might come down from their tombs, and ride with us."

"They were of the colossi, and would sink our boat. The pygmies would be preferable. But tell me of the Roman. He is very wicked, is he not?"

"I cannot say."

"Is he of noble family, and rich?"

"I cannot speak of his riches."

"How beautiful his horses were! and the bed of his chariot was gold, and the wheels ivory. And his audacity! The by-standers laughed as he rode away; they, who were so nearly under his wheels!"

478

She laughed at the recollection.

"They were rabble," said Ben-Hur, bitterly.

"He must be one of the monsters who are said to be growing up in Rome—Apollos ravenous as Cerberus. Does he reside in Antioch?"

"He is of the East somewhere."

"Egypt would suit him better than Syria."

"Hardly," Ben-Hur replied. "Cleopatra is dead."

That instant the lamps burning before the door of the tent came into view.

"The dowar!" she cried.

"Ah, then, we have not been to Egypt. I have not seen Karnak or Philæ or Abydos. This is not the Nile. I have but heard a song of India, and been boating in a dream."

"Philæ—Karnak. Mourn rather that you have not seen the Rameses at Aboo Simbel, looking at which makes it so easy to think of God, the maker of the heavens and earth. Or why should you mourn at all? Let us go on to the river; and if I cannot sing"—she laughed—"because I have said I would not, yet I can tell you stories of Egypt."

"Go on! Aye, till morning comes, and the evening, and the next morning!" he said, vehemently.

"Of what shall my stories be? Of the mathematicians?"

"Oh, no."

"Of the philosophers?"

"No, no."

"Of the magicians and genii?"

"If you will."

"Of war?"

"Yes."

"Of love?"

"Yes."

"I will tell you a cure for love. It is the story of a queen. Listen reverently. The papyrus from which it was taken by the priests of Philæ was wrested from the hand of the heroine herself. It is correct in form, and must be true:

NE-NE-HOFRA.

I.

"There is no parallelism in human lives.

"No life runs a straight line.

"The most perfect life develops as a circle, and terminates in its beginning, making it impossible to say, This is the commencement, that the end.

"Perfect lives are the treasures of God; of great days he wears them on the ring-finger of his heart hand."

II.

"Ne-ne-hofra dwelt in a house close by Essouan, yet closer to the first cataract—so close, indeed, that the sound of the eternal battle waged there between river and rocks was of the place a part.

"She grew in beauty day by day, so that it was said of her, as of the poppies in her father's garden, What will she not be in the time of blooming?

"Each year of her life was the beginning of a new song more delightful than any of those which went before.

"Child was she of a marriage between the North, bounded by the sea, and the South, bounded by the desert beyond the Luna mountains; and one gave her its passion, the other its genius; so when they

beheld her, both laughed, saying, not meanly, 'She is mine,' but generously, 'Ha, ha! she is ours.'

"All excellences in nature contributed to her perfection and rejoiced in her presence. Did she come or go, the birds ruffled their wings in greeting; the unruly winds sank to cooling zephyrs; the white lotus rose from the water's depth to look at her; the solemn river loitered on its way; the palm-trees, nodding, shook all their plumes; and they seemed to say, this one, I gave her of my grace; that, I gave her of my brightness; the other, I gave her of my purity: and so each as it had a virtue to give.

"At twelve, Ne-ne-hofra was the delight of Essouan; at sixteen, the fame of her beauty was universal; at twenty, there was never a day which did not bring to her door princes of the desert on swift camels, and lords of Egypt in gilded barges; and, going away disconsolate, they reported everywhere, 'I have seen her, and she is not a woman, but Athor herself.'"

III.

"Now of the three hundred and thirty successors of good King Menes, eighteen were Ethiopians, of whom Orætes was one hundred and ten years old. He had reigned seventy-six years. Under him the people thrived, and the land groaned with fatness of plenty. He practised wisdom because, having seen so much, he knew what it was. He dwelt in Memphis, having there his principal palace, his arsenals, and his treasure-house. Frequently he went down to Butos to talk with Latona.

"The wife of the good king died. Too old was she for perfect embalmment; yet he loved her, and mourned as the inconsolable; seeing which, a colchyte presumed one day to speak to him.

"'O Orætes, I am astonished that one so wise and great should not know how to cure a sorrow like this.'

"'Tell me a cure,' said the king.

"Three times the colchyte kissed the floor, and then he replied, knowing the dead could not hear

481

him, 'At Essouan lives Ne-ne-hofra, beautiful as
Athor the beautiful. Send for her. She has re-
fused all the lords and princes, and I know not how
many kings; but who can say no to Orætes?'"

IV.

"Ne-ne-hofra descended the Nile in a barge rich-
er than any ever before seen, attended by an army in
barges each but a little less fine. All Nubia and
Egypt, and a myriad from Libya, and a host of Trog-
lodytes, and not a few Macrobii from beyond the
Mountains of the Moon, lined the tented shores to
see the cortége pass, wafted by perfumed winds and
golden oars.

"Through a dromos of sphinxes and couchant
double-winged lions she was borne, and set down
before Orætes sitting on a throne specially erected
at the sculptured pylon of the palace. He raised
her up, gave her place by his side, clasped the uræus
upon her arm, kissed her, and Ne-ne-hofra was queen
of all queens.

"That was not enough for the wise Orætes; he
wanted love, and a queen happy in his love. So he
dealt with her tenderly, showing her his possessions,
cities, palaces, people; his armies, his ships: and
with his own hand he led her through his treasure-
house, saying, 'O Ne-ne-hofra! but kiss me in love,
and they are all thine.'

"And, thinking she could be happy, if she was not
then, she kissed him once, twice, thrice—kissed him
thrice, his hundred and ten years notwithstanding.

"The first year she was happy, and it was very
short; the third year she was wretched, and it was
very long; then she was enlightened: that which she
thought love of Orætes was only daze of his power.
Well for her had the daze endured! Her spirits
deserted her; she had long spells of tears, and her
women could not remember when they heard her
laugh; of the roses on her cheeks only ashes remain-
ed; she languished and faded gradually, but certain-
ly. Some said she was haunted by the Erinnyes for

cruelty to a lover; others, that she was stricken by
some god envious of Oraetes. Whatever the cause of
her decline, the charms of the magicians availed not
to restore her, and the prescript of the doctor was
equally without virtue. Ne-ne-hofra was given over
to die.

"Oraetes chose a crypt for her up in the tombs of
the queens; and, calling the master sculptors and
painters to Memphis, he set them to work upon de-
signs more elaborate than any even in the great gal-
leries of the dead kings.

"'O thou beautiful as Athor herself, my queen!'
said the king, whose hundred and thirteen years did
not lessen his ardor as a lover, 'Tell me, I pray, the
ailment of which, alas! thou art so certainly perish-
ing before my eyes.'

"'You will not love me any more if I tell you,'
she said, in doubt and fear.

"'Not love you! I will love you the more. I
swear it, by the genii of Amente! by the eye of Osi-
ris, I swear it! Speak!' he cried, passionate as a
lover, authoritative as a king.

"'Hear, then,' she said. 'There is an anchorite,
the oldest and holiest of his class, in a cave near Es-
souan. His name is Menopha. He was my teacher
and guardian. Send for him, O Oraetes, and he will
tell you that you seek to know; he will also help you
find the cure for my affliction.'

"Oraetes arose rejoicing. He went away in spirit
a hundred years younger than when he came."

V.

"'Speak!' said Oraetes to Menopha, in the palace
at Memphis.

"And Menopha replied, 'Most mighty king, if you
were young, I should not answer, because I am yet
pleased with life; as it is, I will say the queen, like
any other mortal, is paying the penalty of a crime.'

"'A crime!' exclaimed Oraetes, angrily.

"Menopha bowed very low.

"'Yes; to herself.'

483

" ' I am not in mood for riddles,' said the king.

" ' What I say is not a riddle, as you shall hear. Ne-ne-hofra grew up under my eyes, and confided every incident of her life to me; among others, that she loved the son of her father's gardener, Barbec by name.'

" Oraetes's frown, strangely enough, began to dissipate.

" ' With that love in her heart, O king, she came to you; of that love she is dying.'

" ' Where is the gardener's son now?' asked Oraetes.

" ' In Essouan.'

" The king went out and gave two orders. To one oeris he said, ' Go to Essouan and bring hither a youth named Barbec. You will find him in the garden of the queen's father:' to another, 'Assemble workmen and cattle and tools, and construct for me in Lake Chemmis an island, which, though laden with a temple, a palace, and a garden, and all manner of trees bearing fruit, and all manner of vines, shall nevertheless float about as the winds may blow it. Make the island, and let it be fully furnished by the time the moon begins to wane.'

" Then to the queen he said,

" ' Be of cheer. I know all, and have sent for Barbec.'

" Ne-ne-hofra kissed his hands.

" ' You shall have him to yourself, and he you to himself; nor shall any disturb your loves for a year.'

" She kissed his feet; he raised her, and kissed her in return; and the rose came back to her cheek, the scarlet to her lips, and the laughter to her heart."

VI.

" For one year Ne-ne-hofra and Barbec the gardener floated as the winds blew on the island of Chemmis, which became one of the wonders of the world; never a home of love more beautiful; one year, seeing no one and existing for no one but themselves. Then she returned in state to the palace in Memphis.

484

" 'Now whom lovest thou best?' asked the king.

"She kissed his cheek and said, 'Take me back, O good king, for I am cured.'

"Orætes laughed, none the worse, that moment, of his hundred and fourteen years.

" 'Then it is true, as Menopha said: ha, ha, ha! it is true, the cure of love is love.'

" 'Even so,' she replied.

"Suddenly his manner changed, and his look became terrible.

" 'I did not find it so,' he said.

"She shrank affrighted.

" 'Thou guilty!' he continued. 'Thy offence to Orætes the man he forgives; but thy offence to Orætes the king remains to be punished.'

"She cast herself at his feet.

" 'Hush!' he cried. 'Thou art dead!'

"He clapped his hands, and a terrible procession came in—a procession of parachistes, or embalmers, each with some implement or material of his loathsome art.

"The king pointed to Ne-ne-hofra.

" 'She is dead. Do thy work well.'"

VII.

"Ne-ne-hofra the beautiful, after seventy-two days, was carried to the crypt chosen for her the year before, and laid with her queenly predecessors; yet there was no funeral procession in her honor across the sacred lake."

At the conclusion of the story, Ben-Hur was sitting at the Egyptian's feet, and her hand upon the tiller was covered by his hand.

"Menopha was wrong," he said.

"How?"

"Love lives by loving."

"Then there is no cure for it?"

"Yes. Orætes found the cure."

" What was it ?"

" Death."

" You are a good listener, O son of Arrius."

And so with conversation and stories, they whiled the hours away. As they stepped ashore, she said,

" To-morrow we go to the city."

" But you will be at the games ?" he asked.

" Oh yes."

" I will send you my colors."

With that they separated.

CHAPTER IV

MESSALA ON GUARD

ILDERIM returned to the dowar next day about the third hour. As he dismounted, a man whom he recognized as of his own tribe came to him and said, " O sheik, I was bidden give thee this package, with request that thou read it at once. If there be answer, I was to wait thy pleasure."

Ilderim gave the package immediate attention. The seal was already broken. The address ran, " To Valerius Gratus at Cæsarea."

" Abaddon take him !" growled the sheik, at discovering a letter in Latin.

Had the missive been in Greek or Arabic, he could have read it ; as it was, the utmost he could make out was the signature in bold Roman letters — MESSALA — whereat his eyes twinkled.

486

"Where is the young Jew?" he asked.

"In the field with the horses," a servant replied.

The sheik replaced the papyrus in its envelopes, and, tucking the package under his girdle, remounted the horse. That moment a stranger made his appearance, coming, apparently, from the city.

"I am looking for Sheik Ilderim, surnamed the Generous," the stranger said.

His language and attire bespoke him a Roman.

What he could not read, he yet could speak; so the old Arab answered, with dignity, "I am Sheik Ilderim."

The man's eyes fell; he raised them again, and said, with forced composure, "I heard you had need of a driver for the games."

Ilderim's lip under the white mustache curled contemptuously.

"Go thy way," he said. "I have a driver."

He turned to ride away, but the man, lingering, spoke again.

"Sheik, I am a lover of horses, and they say you have the most beautiful in the world."

The old man was touched; he drew rein, as if on the point of yielding to the flattery, but finally replied, "Not to-day, not to-day; some other time I will show them to you. I am too busy just now."

He rode to the field, while the stranger betook himself to town again with a smiling countenance. He had accomplished his mission.

And every day thereafter, down to the great

day of the games, a man—sometimes two or three men—came to the sheik at the Orchard, pretending to seek an engagement as driver.

In such manner Messala kept watch over Ben-Hur.

<div align="center">

CHAPTER V

ILDERIM AND BEN-HUR DELIBERATE

</div>

THE sheik waited, well satisfied, until Ben-Hur drew his horses off the field for the forenoon—well satisfied, for he had seen them, after being put through all the other paces, run full speed in such manner that it did not seem there were one the slowest and another the fastest—run, in other words, as if the four were one.

"This afternoon, O sheik, I will give Sirius back to you." Ben-Hur patted the neck of the old horse as he spoke. "I will give him back, and take to the chariot."

"So soon?" Ilderim asked.

"With such as these, good sheik, one day suffices. They are not afraid; they have a man's intelligence, and they love the exercise. This one," he shook a rein over the back of the youngest of the four—"you called him Aldebaran, I believe—is the swiftest; in once round a stadium he would lead the others thrice his length."

Ilderim pulled his beard, and said, with twinkling eyes, "Aldebaran is the swiftest; but what of the slowest?"

"This is he." Ben-Hur shook the rein over

<div align="center">488</div>

Antares. "This is he: but he will win, for, look you, sheik, he will run his utmost all day —all day; and, as the sun goes down, he will reach his swiftest."

"Right again," said Ilderim.

"I have but one fear, O sheik."

The sheik became doubly serious.

"In his greed of triumph, a Roman cannot keep honor pure. In the games—all of them, mark you—their tricks are infinite; in chariot-racing their knavery extends to everything— from horse to driver, from driver to master. Wherefore, good sheik, look well to all thou hast; from this till the trial is over, let no stranger so much as see the horses. Would you be perfectly safe, do more — keep watch over them with armed hand as well as sleep-less eye; then I will have no fear of the end."

At the door of the tent they dismounted.

"What you say shall be attended to. By the splendor of God, no hand shall come near them except it belong to one of the faithful. To-night I will set watches. But, son of Arrius" —Ilderim drew forth the package, and opened it slowly, while they walked to the divan and seated themselves—"son of Arrius, see thou here, and help me with thy Latin."

He passed the despatch to Ben-Hur.

"There; read—and read aloud, rendering what thou findest into the tongue of thy fathers. Latin is an abomination."

Ben-Hur was in good spirits, and began the reading carelessly. "Messala to Gratus!" He

paused. A premonition drove the blood to his heart. Ilderim observed his agitation.

"Well, I am waiting."

Ben-Hur prayed pardon, and recommenced the paper, which, it is sufficient to say, was one of the duplicates of the letter despatched so carefully to Gratus by Messala the morning after the revel in the palace.

The paragraphs in the beginning were remarkable only as proof that the writer had not outgrown his habit of mockery; when they were passed, and the reader came to the parts intended to refresh the memory of Gratus, his voice trembled, and twice he stopped to regain his self-control. By a strong effort he continued. "'I recall further,'" he read, "'that thou didst make disposition of the family of Hur'"—there the reader again paused and drew a long breath—"'both of us at the time supposing the plan hit upon to be the most effective possible for the purposes in view, which were silence and delivery over to inevitable but natural death.'"

Here Ben-Hur broke down utterly. The paper fell from his hands, and he covered his face.

"They are dead—dead. I alone am left."

The sheik had been a silent but not unsympathetic witness of the young man's suffering: now he arose and said, "Son of Arrius, it is for me to beg thy pardon. Read the paper by thyself. When thou art strong enough to give the rest of it to me, send word, and I will return."

He went out of the tent, and nothing in all his life became him better.

Ben-Hur flung himself on the divan and gave way to his feelings. When somewhat recovered, he recollected that a portion of the letter remained unread, and, taking it up, he resumed the reading. "Thou wilt remember," the missive ran, "what thou didst with the mother and sister of the malefactor; yet, if now I yield to a desire to learn if they be living or dead"—Ben-Hur started, and read again, and then again, and at last broke into exclamation. "He does not know they are dead; he does not know it! Blessed be the name of the Lord! there is yet hope." He finished the sentence, and was strengthened by it, and went on bravely to the end of the letter.

"They are not dead," he said, after reflection; "they are not dead, or he would have heard of it."

A second reading, more careful than the first, confirmed him in the opinion. Then he sent for the sheik.

"In coming to your hospitable tent, O sheik," he said, calmly, when the Arab was seated and they were alone, "it was not in my mind to speak of myself further than to assure you I had sufficient training to be intrusted with your horses. I declined to tell you my history. But the chances which have sent this paper to my hand and given it to me to be read are so strange that I feel bidden to trust you with everything. And I am the more inclined to

do so by knowledge here conveyed that we are both of us threatened by the same enemy, against whom it is needful that we make common cause. I will read the letter and give you explanation; after which you will not wonder I was so moved. If you thought me weak or childish, you will then excuse me."

The sheik held his peace, listening closely, until Ben-Hur came to the paragraph in which he was particularly mentioned: "'I saw the Jew yesterday in the Grove of Daphne;'" so ran the part, "'and if he be not there now, he is certainly in the neighborhood, making it easy for me to keep him in eye. Indeed, wert thou to ask me where he is now, I should say, with the most positive assurance, he is to be found at the old Orchard of Palms.'"

"A—h!" exclaimed Ilderim, in such a tone one might hardly say he was more surprised than angry; at the same time, he clutched his beard.

"'At the old Orchard of Palms,'" Ben-Hur repeated, "'under the tent of the traitor Sheik Ilderim.'"

"Traitor!—I?" the old man cried, in his shrillest tone, while lip and beard curled with ire, and on his forehead and neck the veins swelled and beat as they would burst.

"Yet a moment, sheik," said Ben-Hur, with a deprecatory gesture. "Such is Messala's opinion of you. Hear his threat." And he read on—"'under the tent of the traitor Sheik Ilderim, who cannot long escape our strong hand. Be not surprised if Maxentius, as his

492

first measure, places the Arab on ship for forwarding to Rome.' "

" To Rome ! Me — Ilderim — sheik of ten thousand horsemen with spears—me to Rome !"

He leaped rather than rose to his feet, his arms outstretched, his fingers spread and curved like claws, his eyes glittering like a serpent's.

" O God ! — nay, by all the gods except of Rome ! —when shall this insolence end ? A freeman am I ; free are my people. Must we die slaves ? Or, worse, must I live a dog, crawling to a master's feet ? Must I lick his hand lest he lash me ? What is mine is not mine ; I am not my own ; for breath of body I must be beholden to a Roman. Oh, if I were young again ! Oh, could I shake off twenty years—or ten—or five !"

He ground his teeth and shook his hands overhead ; then, under the impulse of another idea, he walked away and back again to Ben-Hur swiftly, and caught his shoulder with a strong grasp.

" If I were as thou, son of Arrius—as young, as strong, as practised in arms; if I had a motive hissing me to revenge — a motive, like thine, great enough to make hate holy— Away with disguise on thy part and on mine ! Son of Hur, son of Hur, I say—"

At that name all the currents of Ben-Hur's blood stopped; surprised, bewildered, he gazed into the Arab's eyes, now close to his, and fiercely bright.

" Son of Hur, I say, were I as thou, with half thy wrongs, bearing about with me memories

493

like thine, I would not, I could not, rest." Never pausing, his words following each other torrent-like, the old man swept on. "To all my grievances, I would add those of the world, and devote myself to vengeance. From land to land I would go firing all mankind. No war for freedom but should find me engaged; no battle against Rome in which I would not bear a part. I would turn Parthian, if I could not better. If men failed me, still I would not give over the effort—ha, ha, ha! By the splendor of God! I would herd with wolves, and make friends of lions and tigers, in hope of marshalling them against the common enemy. I would use every weapon. So my victims were Romans, I would rejoice in slaughter. Quarter I would not ask; quarter I would not give. To the flames everything Roman; to the sword every Roman born. Of nights I would pray the gods, the good and the bad alike, to lend me their special terrors—tempests, drought, heat, cold, and all the nameless poisons they let loose in air, all the thousand things of which men die on sea and on land. Oh, I could not sleep. I—I—"

The sheik stopped for want of breath, panting, wringing his hands. And, sooth to say, of all the passionate burst Ben-Hur retained but a vague impression wrought by fiery eyes, a piercing voice, and a rage too intense for coherent expression.

For the first time in years, the desolate youth heard himself addressed by his proper name. One man, at least, knew him, and acknowledged

it without demand of identity; and he an Arab fresh from the desert!

How came the man by his knowledge? The letter? No. It told the cruelties from which his family had suffered; it told the story of his own misfortunes, but it did not say he was the very victim whose escape from doom was the theme of the heartless narrative. That was the point of explanation he had notified the sheik would follow the reading of the letter. He was pleased, and thrilled with hope restored, yet kept an air of calmness.

"Good sheik, tell me how you came by this letter."

"My people keep the roads between cities," Ilderim answered, bluntly. "They took it from a courier."

"Are they known to be thy people?"

"No. To the world they are robbers, whom it is mine to catch and slay."

"Again, sheik. You call me son of Hur—my father's name. I did not think myself known to a person on earth. How came you by the knowledge?"

Ilderim hesitated; but, rallying, he answered, "I know you, yet I am not free to tell you more."

"Some one holds you in restraint?"

The sheik closed his mouth, and walked away; but, observing Ben-Hur's disappointment, he came back, and said, "Let us say no more about the matter now. I will go to town; when I return, I may talk to you fully. Give me the letter."

Ilderim rolled the papyrus carefully, restored

495

it to its envelopes, and became once more all
energy.

"What sayest thou?" he asked, while wait-
ing for his horse and retinue. "I told what I
would do, were I thou, and thou hast made no
answer."

"I intended to answer, sheik, and I will."
Ben-Hur's countenance and voice changed with
the feeling invoked. "All thou hast said, I
will do—all at least in the power of a man. I
devoted myself to vengeance long ago. Every
hour of the five years passed I have lived with
no other thought. I have taken no respite. I
have had no pleasures of youth. The blandish-
ments of Rome were not for me. I wanted
her to educate me for revenge. I resorted to
her most famous masters and professors—not
those of rhetoric or philosophy: alas! I had
no time for them. The arts essential to a
fighting-man were my desire. I associated
with gladiators, and with winners of prizes in
the Circus; and they were my teachers. The
drill-masters in the great camp accepted me as
a scholar, and were proud of my attainments
in their line. O sheik, I am a soldier; but the
things of which I dream require me to be a
captain. With that thought, I have taken part
in the campaign against the Parthians; when
it is over, then, if the Lord spare my life and
strength—then"—he raised his clenched hands,
and spoke vehemently—"then I will be an en-
emy Roman-taught in all things; then Rome
shall account to me in Roman lives for her ills.
You have my answer, sheik."

Ilderim put an arm over his shoulder, and kissed him, saying, passionately, " If thy God favor thee not, son of Hur, it is because he is dead. Take thou this from me—sworn to, if so thy preference run : thou shalt have my hands, and their fulness—men, horses, camels, and the desert for preparation. I swear it! For the present, enough. Thou shalt see or hear from me before night."

Turning abruptly off, the sheik was speediiy on the road to the city.

HE intercepted letter was conclusive upon a number of points of great interest to Ben-Hur. It had all the effect of a confession that the writer was a party to the putting-away of the family with murderous intent ; that he had sanctioned the plan adopted for the purpose ; that he had received a portion of the proceeds of the confiscation, and was yet in enjoyment of his part ; that he dreaded the unexpected appearance of what he was pleased to call the chief malefactor, and accepted it as a menace ; that he contemplated such further action as would secure him in the future, and was ready to do whatever his accomplice in Cæsarea might advise.

And, now that the letter had reached the hand of him really its subject, it was notice of danger to come, as well as a confession of guilt.

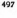

So when Ilderim left the tent, Ben-Hur had much to think about, requiring immediate action. His enemies were as adroit and powerful as any in the East. If they were afraid of him, he had greater reason to be afraid of them. He strove earnestly to reflect upon the situation, but could not; his feelings constantly overwhelmed him. There was a certain qualified pleasure in the assurance that his mother and sister were alive; and it mattered little that the foundation of the assurance was a mere inference. That there was one person who could tell him where they were seemed to his hope so long deferred as if discovery were now close at hand. These were mere causes of feeling; underlying them, it must be confessed he had a superstitious fancy that God was about to make ordination in his behalf, in which event faith whispered him to stand still.

Occasionally, referring to the words of Ilderim, he wondered whence the Arab derived his information about him; not from Malluch certainly; nor from Simonides, whose interests, all adverse, would hold him dumb. Could Messala have been the informant? No, no: disclosure might be dangerous in that quarter. Conjecture was vain; at the same time, often as Ben-Hur was beaten back from the solution, he was consoled with the thought that whoever the person with the knowledge might be, he was a friend, and, being such, would reveal himself in good time. A little more waiting—a little more patience. Possibly the errand of the sheik was to see the worthy;

possibly the letter might precipitate a full disclosure.

And patient he would have been if only he could have believed Tirzah and his mother were waiting for him under circumstances permitting hope on their part strong as his; if, in other words, conscience had not stung him with accusations respecting them.

To escape such accusations, he wandered far through the Orchard, pausing now where the date-gatherers were busy, yet not too busy to offer him of their fruit and talk with him; then, under the great trees, to watch the nesting birds, or hear the bees swarming about the berries bursting with honeyed sweetness, and filling all the green and golden spaces with the music of their beating wings.

By the lake, however, he lingered longest. He might not look upon the water and its sparkling ripples, so like sensuous life, without thinking of the Egyptian and her marvellous beauty, and of floating with her here and there through the night, made brilliant by her songs and stories; he might not forget the charm of her manner, the lightness of her laugh, the flattery of her attention, the warmth of her little hand under his upon the tiller of the boat. From her it was for his thought but a short way to Balthasar, and the strange things of which he had been witness, unaccountable by any law of nature; and from him, again, to the King of the Jews, whom the good man, with such pathos of patience, was holding in holy promise, the distance was even nearer. And

there his mind stayed, finding in the mysteries
of that personage a satisfaction answering well
for the rest he was seeking. Because, it may
have been, nothing is so easy as denial of an
idea not agreeable to our wishes, he rejected
the definition given by Balthasar of the king-
dom the king was coming to establish. A king-
dom of souls, if not intolerable to his Saddu-
cean faith, seemed to him but an abstraction
drawn from the depths of a devotion too fond
and dreamy. A kingdom of Judea, on the other
hand, was more than comprehensible : such
had been, and, if only for that reason, might be
again. And it suited his pride to think of a
new kingdom broader of domain, richer in
power, and of a more unapproachable splendor
than the old one ; of a new king wiser and
mightier than Solomon—a new king, under
whom, especially, he could find both service
and revenge. In that mood he returned to the
dowar.

The mid-day meal disposed of, still further
to occupy himself, Ben-Hur had the chariot
rolled out into the sunlight for inspection.
The word but poorly conveys the careful study
the vehicle underwent. No point or part of it
escaped him. With a pleasure which will be
better understood hereafter, he saw the pattern
was Greek, in his judgment preferable to the
Roman in many respects; it was wider between
the wheels, and lower and stronger, and the
disadvantage of greater weight would be more
than compensated by the greater endurance of
his Arabs. Speaking generally, the carriage-

makers of Rome built for the games almost
solely, sacrificing safety to beauty, and durabil-
ity to grace ; while the chariots of Achilles and
"the king of men," designed for war and all its
extreme tests, still ruled the tastes of those who
met and struggled for the crowns Isthmian
and Olympic.

Next he brought the horses, and, hitching
them to the chariot, drove to the field of exer-
cise, where, hour after hour, he practised them
in movement under the yoke. When he came
away in the evening, it was with restored spirit,
and a fixed purpose to defer action in the mat-
ter of Messala until the race was won or lost.
He could not forego the pleasure of meeting
his adversary under the eyes of the East ; that
there might be other competitors seemed not
to enter his thought. His confidence in the
result was absolute ; no doubt of his own skill ;
and as to the four, they were his full partners
in the glorious game.

"Let him look to it, let him look to it! Ha,
Antares—Aldebaran ! Shall he not, O honest
Rigel ? And thou, Atair, king among coursers,
shall he not beware of us ? Ha, ha! good
hearts !"

So in rests he passed from horse to horse,
speaking, not as a master, but the senior of as
many brethren.

After nightfall, Ben-Hur sat by the door of
the tent waiting for Ilderim, not yet returned
from the city. He was not impatient, or vexed,
or doubtful. The sheik would be heard from,
at least. Indeed, whether it was from satis-

faction with the performance of the four, or
the refreshment there is in cold water succeed-
ing bodily exercise, or supper partaken with
royal appetite, or the reaction which, as a kind-
ly provision of nature, always follows depres-
sion, the young man was in good-humor verg-
ing upon elation. He felt himself in the hands
of Providence no longer his enemy. At last
there was a sound of horse's feet coming rap-
idly, and Malluch rode up.

"Son of Arrius," he said, cheerily, after sal-
utation, " I salute you for Sheik Ilderim, who
requests you to mount and go to the city. He
is waiting for you."

Ben-Hur asked no questions, but went in
where the horses were feeding. Aldebaran
came to him, as if offering his service. He
played with him lovingly, but passed on, and
chose another, not of the four—they were sa-
cred to the race. Very shortly the two were
on the road, going swiftly and in silence.

Some distance below the Seleucian Bridge,
they crossed the river by a ferry, and, riding
far round on the right bank, and recrossing by
another ferry, entered the city from the west.
The detour was long, but Ben-Hur accepted
it as a precaution for which there was good
reason.

Down to Simonides' landing they rode, and
in front of the great warehouse, under the
bridge, Malluch drew rein.

"We are come," he said. "Dismount."

Ben-Hur recognized the place.

"Where is the sheik?" he asked.

FOUNTAIN AT NAZARETH

"Come with me. I will show you."

A watchman took the horses, and almost before he realized it Ben-Hur stood once more at the door of the house up on the greater one, listening to the response from within — " In God's name, enter."

MALLUCH stopped at the door; Ben-Hur entered alone.

The room was the same in which he had formerly interviewed Simonides, and it had been in nowise changed, except now, close by the arm-chair, a polished brazen rod, set on a broad wooden pedestal, arose higher than a tall man, holding lamps of silver on sliding arms, half a dozen or more in number, and all burning. The light was clear, bringing into view the panelling on the walls, the cornice with its row of gilded balls, and the dome dully tinted with violet mica.

Within, a few steps, Ben-Hur stopped.

Three persons were present, looking at him —Simonides, Ilderim, and Esther.

He glanced hurriedly from one to another, as if to find answer to the question half formed in his mind, What business can these have with me? He became calm, with every sense on the alert, for the question was succeeded by another, Are they friends or enemies?

At length his eyes rested upon Esther.

The men returned his look kindly; in her face there was something more than kindness —something too spirituel for definition, which yet went to his inner consciousness without definition.

Shall it be said, good reader? Back of his gaze there was a comparison in which the Egyptian arose and set herself over against the gentle Jewess; but it lived an instant, and as is the habit of such comparisons, passed away without a conclusion.

"Son of Hur—"

The guest turned to the speaker.

"Son of Hur," said Simonides, repeating the address slowly, and with distinct emphasis, as if to impress all its meaning upon him most interested in understanding it, "take thou the peace of the Lord God of our fathers—take it from me." He paused, then added, "From me and mine."

The speaker sat in his chair; there were the royal head, the bloodless face, the masterful air, under the influence of which visitors forgot the broken limbs and distorted body of the man. The full black eyes gazed out under the white brows steadily, but not sternly. A moment thus, then he crossed his hands upon his breast.

The action, taken with the salutation, could not be misunderstood, and was not.

"Simonides," Ben-Hur answered, much moved, "the holy peace you tender is accepted. As son to father, I return it to you. Only let there be perfect understanding between us."

Thus delicately he sought to put aside the submission of the merchant, and, in place of the relation of master and servant, substitute one higher and holier.

Simonides let fall his hands, and, turning to Esther, said, "A seat for the master, daughter."

She hastened, and brought a stool, and stood, with suffused face, looking from one to the other—from Ben-Hur to Simonides, from Simonides to Ben-Hur; and they waited, each declining the superiority direction would imply. When at length the pause began to be embarrassing, Ben-Hur advanced, and gently took the stool from her, and, going to the chair, placed it at the merchant's feet.

" I will sit here," he said.

His eyes met hers—an instant only; but both were better of the look. He recognized her gratitude, she his generosity and forbearance.

Simonides bowed his acknowledgment.

" Esther, child, bring me the paper," he said, with a breath of relief.

She went to a panel in the wall, opened it, took out a roll of papyri, and brought and gave it to him.

" Thou saidst well, son of Hur," Simonides began, while unrolling the sheets. " Let us understand each other. In anticipation of the demand—which I would have made hadst thou waived it—I have here a statement covering everything necessary to the understanding required. I could see but two points involved —the property first, and then our relation. The

505

statement is explicit as to both. Will it please thee to read it now?"

Ben-Hur received the papers, but glanced at Ilderim.

"Nay," said Simonides, "the sheik shall not deter thee from reading. The account—such thou wilt find it—is of a nature requiring a witness. In the attesting place at the end thou wilt find, when thou comest to it, the name—Ilderim, Sheik. He knows all. He is thy friend. All he has been to me, that will he be to thee also."

Simonides looked at the Arab, nodding pleasantly, and the latter gravely returned the nod, saying, "Thou hast said."

Ben-Hur replied, "I know already the excellence of his friendship, and have yet to prove myself worthy of it." Immediately he continued, "Later, O Simonides, I will read the papers carefully ; for the present, do thou take them, and if thou be not too weary, give me their substance."

Simonides took back the roll.

"Here, Esther, stand by me and receive the sheets, lest they fall into confusion."

She took place by his chair, letting her right arm fall lightly across his shoulder, so, when he spoke, the account seemed to have rendition from both of them jointly.

"This," said Simonides, drawing out the first leaf, "shows the money I had of thy father's, being the amount saved from the Romans ; there was no property saved, only money, and that the robbers would have secured but for

our Jewish custom of bills of exchange. The amount saved, being sums I drew from Rome, Alexandria, Damascus, Carthage, Valentia, and elsewhere within the circle of trade, was one hundred and twenty talents Jewish money."

He gave the sheet to Esther, and took the next one.

"With that amount—one hundred and twenty talents—I charged myself. Hear now my credits. I use the word, as thou wilt see, with reference rather to the proceeds gained from the use of the money."

From separate sheets he then read footings, which, fractions omitted, were as follows:

"Cr.
By ships................... 60 talents.
" goods in store............ 110 "
" cargoes in transit........ 75 "
" camels, horses, etc........ 20 "
" warehouses.............. 10 "
" bills due................. 54 "
" money on hand and subject
 to draft............... 224 "
 Total................. 553 " "

"To these now, to the five hundred and fifty-three talents gained, add the original capital I had from thy father, and thou hast SIX HUNDRED AND SEVENTY-THREE TALENTS!—and all thine—making thee, O son of Hur, the richest subject in the world."

He took the papyri from Esther, and, reserving one, rolled them and offered them to Ben-Hur. The pride perceptible in his manner was not offensive; it might have been from a sense

of duty well done; it might have been for Ben-Hur without reference to himself.

"And there is nothing," he added, dropping his voice, but not his eyes—"there is nothing now thou mayst not do."

The moment was one of absorbing interest to all present. Simonides crossed his hands upon his breast again; Esther was anxious; Ilderim nervous. A man is never so on trial as in the moment of excessive good-fortune.

Taking the roll, Ben-Hur arose, struggling with emotion.

"All this is to me as a light from heaven, sent to drive away a night which has been so long I feared it would never end, and so dark I had lost the hope of seeing," he said, with a husky voice. "I give first thanks to the Lord, who has not abandoned me, and my next to thee, O Simonides. Thy faithfulness outweighs the cruelty of others, and redeems our human nature. 'There is nothing I cannot do:' be it so. Shall any man in this my hour of such mighty privilege be more generous than I? Serve me as a witness now, Sheik Ilderim. Hear thou my words as I shall speak them—hear and remember. And thou, Esther, good angel of this good man! hear thou also."

He stretched his hand with the roll to Simonides.

"The things these papers take into account —all of them: ships, houses, goods, camels, horses, money; the least as well as the greatest—give I back to thee, O Simonides, making

them all thine, and sealing them to thee and thine forever."

Esther smiled through her tears; Ilderim pulled his beard with rapid motion, his eyes glistening like beads of jet. Simonides alone was calm.

"Sealing them to thee and thine forever," Ben-Hur continued, with better control of himself, "with one exception, and upon one condition."

The breath of the listeners waited upon his words.

"The hundred and twenty talents which were my father's thou shalt return to me."

Ilderim's countenance brightened.

"And thou shalt join me in search of my mother and sister, holding all thine subject to the expense of discovery, even as I will hold mine."

Simonides was much affected. Stretching out his hand, he said, "I see thy spirit, son of Hur, and I am grateful to the Lord that he hath sent thee to me such as thou art. If I served well thy father in life, and his memory afterwards, be not afraid of default to thee; yet must I say the exception cannot stand."

Exhibiting, then, the reserved sheet, he continued,

"Thou hast not all the account. Take this and read—read aloud."

Ben-Hur took the supplement, and read it.

"Statement of the servants of Hur, rendered by Simonides, steward of the estate.

"1. Amrah, Egyptian, keeping the palace in Jeru-
salem.

"2. Simonides, the steward, in Antioch.

"3. Esther, daughter of Simonides."

Now, in all his thoughts of Simonides, not
once had it entered Ben-Hur's mind that, by
the law, a daughter followed the parent's con-
dition. In all his visions of her, the sweet-
faced Esther had figured as the rival of the
Egyptian, and an object of possible love. He
shrank from the revelation so suddenly brought
him, and looked at her blushing; and, blush-
ing, she dropped her eyes before him. Then he
said, while the papyrus rolled itself together,

"A man with six hundred talents is indeed
rich, and may do what he pleases; but, rarer
than the money, more priceless than the prop-
erty, is the mind which amassed the wealth, and
the heart it could not corrupt when amassed.
O Simonides—and thou, fair Esther—fear not.
Sheik Ilderim here shall be witness that in the
same moment ye were declared my servants,
that moment I declared ye free; and what I
declare, that will I put in writing. Is it not
enough? Can I do more?"

"Son of Hur," said Simonides, "verily thou
dost make servitude lightsome. I was wrong;
there are some things thou canst not do: thou
canst not make us free in law. I am thy serv-
ant forever, because I went to the door with
thy father one day, and in my ear the awl-
marks yet abide."

"Did my father that?"

"Judge him not," cried Simonides, quickly.

"He accepted me a servant of that class because I prayed him to do so. I never repented the step. It was the price I paid for Rachel, the mother of my child here; for Rachel, who would not be my wife unless I became what she was."

"Was she a servant forever?"

"Even so."

Ben-Hur walked the floor in pain of impotent wish.

"I was rich before," he said, stopping suddenly. "I was rich with the gifts of the generous Arrius; now comes this greater fortune, and the mind which achieved it. Is there not a purpose of God in it all? Counsel me, O Simonides! Help me to see the right and do it. Help me to be worthy my name, and what thou art in law to me, that will I be to thee in fact and deed. I will be thy servant forever."

Simonides' face actually glowed.

"O son of my dead master! I will do better than help; I will serve thee with all my might of mind and heart. Body, I have not; it perished in thy cause; but with mind and heart I will serve thee. I swear it, by the altar of our God, and the gifts upon the altar! Only make me formally what I have assumed to be."

"Name it," said Ben-Hur, eagerly.

"As steward the care of the property will be mine."

"Count thyself steward now; or wilt thou have it in writing?"

"Thy word simply is enough; it was so with the father, and I will not more from the son.

And now, if the understanding be perfect "—
Simonides paused.

"It is with me," said Ben-Hur.

"And thou, daughter of Rachel, speak!" said
Simonides, lifting her arm from his shoulder.

Esther, left thus alone, stood a moment
abashed, her color coming and going; then she
went to Ben-Hur, and said, with a womanliness
singularly sweet, "I am not better than my
mother was; and, as she is gone, I pray you, O
my master, let me care for my father."

Ben-Hur took her hand, and led her back
to the chair, saying, "Thou art a good child.
Have thy will."

Simonides replaced her arm upon his neck,
and there was silence for a time in the room.

<div align="center">

CHAPTER VIII

SPIRITUAL OR POLITICAL?—SIMONIDES
ARGUES

</div>

SIMONIDES looked up, none the less
a master.

"Esther," he said, quietly, "the
night is going fast; and, lest we be-
come too weary for that which is before us, let
the refreshments be brought."

She rang a bell. A servant answered with
wine and bread, which she bore round.

"The understanding, good my master," con-
tinued Simonides, when all were served, "is
not perfect in my sight. Henceforth our lives
will run on together like rivers which have met

<div align="center">

512

</div>

and joined their waters. I think their flowing
will be better if every cloud is blown from the
sky above them. You left my door the other
day with what seemed a denial of the claims
which I have just allowed in the broadest terms;
but it was not so, indeed it was not. Esther is
witness that I recognized you; and that I did
not abandon you, let Malluch say."

"Malluch!" exclaimed Ben-Hur.

"One bound to a chair, like me, must have
many hands far-reaching, if he would move the
world from which he is so cruelly barred. I
have many such, and Malluch is one of the best
of them. And, sometimes "—he cast a grate-
ful glance at the sheik—"sometimes I borrow
from others good of heart, like Ilderim the
Generous — good and brave. Let him say if I
either denied or forgot you."

Ben-Hur looked at the Arab.

"This is he, good Ilderim, this is he who told
you of me?"

Ilderim's eyes twinkled as he nodded his
answer.

"How, O my master," said Simonides, "may
we without trial tell what a man is? I knew
you; I saw your father in you; but the kind
of man you were I did not know. There are
people to whom fortune is a curse in disguise.
Were you of them? I sent Malluch to find out
for me, and in the service he was my eyes and
ears. Do not blame him. He brought me
report of you which was all good."

"I do not," said Ben-Hur, heartily. "There
was wisdom in your goodness."

"The words are very pleasant to me," said the merchant, with feeling, "very pleasant. My fear of misunderstanding is laid. Let the rivers run on now as God may give them direction."

After an interval he continued:

"I am compelled now by truth. The weaver sits weaving, and, as the shuttle flies, the cloth increases, and the figures grow, and he dreams dreams meanwhile; so to my hands the fortune grew, and I wondered at the increase, and asked myself about it many times. I could see a care not my own went with the enterprises I set going. The simooms which smote others on the desert jumped over the things which were mine. The storms which heaped the sea-shore with wrecks did but blow my ships the sooner into port. Strangest of all, I, so dependent upon others, fixed to a place like a dead thing, had never a loss by an agent—never. The elements stooped to serve me, and all my servants, in fact, were faithful."

"It is very strange," said Ben-Hur.

"So I said, and kept saying. Finally, O my master, finally I came to be of your opinion—God was in it—and, like you, I asked, What can his purpose be? Intelligence is never wasted; intelligence like God's never stirs except with design. I have held the question in heart, lo! these many years, watching for an answer. I felt sure, if God were in it, some day, in his own good time, in his own way, he would show me his purpose, making it clear as a whited house upon a hill. And I believe he has done so."

Ben-Hur listened with every faculty intent.

"Many years ago, with my people—thy mother was with me, Esther, beautiful as morning over old Olivet—I sat by the way-side out north of Jerusalem, near the Tombs of the Kings, when three men passed by riding great white camels, such as had never been seen in the Holy City. The men were strangers, and from far countries. The first one stopped and asked me a question. 'Where is he that is born King of the Jews?' As if to allay my wonder, he went on to say, 'We have seen his star in the east, and have come to worship him.' I could not understand, but followed them to the Damascus Gate; and of every person they met on the way—of the guard at the Gate, even —they asked the question. All who heard it were amazed like me. In time I forgot the circumstance, though there was much talk of it as a presage of the Messiah. Alas, alas! What children we are, even the wisest! When God walks the earth, his steps are often centuries apart. You have seen Balthasar?"

"And heard him tell his story," said Ben-Hur.

"A miracle!—a very miracle!" cried Simonides. "As he told it to me, good my master, I seemed to hear the answer I had so long waited; God's purpose burst upon me. Poor will the King be when he comes—poor and friendless; without following, without armies, without cities or castles; a kingdom to be set up, and Rome reduced and blotted out. See, see, O my master! thou flushed with strength,

thou trained to arms, thou burdened with riches; behold the opportunity the Lord hath sent thee! Shall not his purpose be thine? Could a man be born to a more perfect glory?"

Simonides put his whole force in the appeal.

"But the kingdom, the kingdom!" Ben-Hur answered, eagerly. "Balthasar says it is to be of souls."

The pride of the Jew was strong in Simonides, and therefore the slightly contemptuous curl of the lip with which he began his reply:

"Balthasar has been a witness of wonderful things—of miracles, O my master; and when he speaks of them, I bow with belief, for they are of sight and sound personal to him. But he is a son of Mizraim, and not even a proselyte. Hardly may he be supposed to have special knowledge by virtue of which we must bow to him in a matter of God's dealing with our Israel. The prophets had their light from Heaven directly, even as he had his—many to one, and Jehovah the same forever. I must believe the prophets.—Bring me the Torah, Esther."

He proceeded without waiting for her.

"May the testimony of a whole people be slighted, my master? Though you travel from Tyre, which is by the sea in the north, to the capital of Edom, which is in the desert south, you will not find a lisper of the Shema, an alms-giver in the Temple, or any one who has ever eaten of the lamb of the Passover, to tell you the kingdom the King is coming to build for us, the children of the covenant, is other

than of this world, like our father David's. Now where got they the faith, ask you? We will see presently."

Esther here returned, bringing a number of rolls carefully enveloped in dark-brown linen lettered quaintly in gold.

"Keep them, daughter, to give to me as I call for them," the father said, in the tender voice he always used in speaking to her, and continued his argument:

"It were long, good my master—too long, indeed—for me to repeat to you the names of the holy men who, in the providence of God, succeeded the prophets, only a little less favored than they—the seers who have written and the preachers who have taught since the Captivity; the very wise who borrowed their lights from the lamp of Malachi, the last of his line, and whose great names Hillel and Shammai never tired of repeating in the colleges. Will you ask them of the kingdom? Thus, the Lord of the sheep in the Book of Enoch —who is he? Who but the King of whom we are speaking? A throne is set up for him; he smites the earth, and the other kings are shaken from their thrones, and the scourges of Israel flung into a cavern of fire flaming with pillars of fire. So also the singer of the Psalms of Solomon—'Behold, O Lord, and raise up to Israel their king, the son of David, at the time thou knowest, O God, to rule Israel, thy children. . . . And he will bring the peoples of the heathen under his yoke to serve him. . . . And he shall be a righteous king taught of

517

God, . . . for he shall rule all the earth by the word of his mouth forever.' And last, though not least, hear Ezra, the second Moses, in his visions of the night, and ask him who is the lion with human voice that says to the eagle —which is Rome—'Thou hast loved liars, and overthrown the cities of the industrious, and razed their walls, though they did thee no harm. Therefore, begone, that the earth may be refreshed, and recover itself, and hope in the justice and piety of him who made her.' Whereat the eagle was seen no more. Surely, O my master, the testimony of these should be enough! but the way to the fountain's head is open. Let us go up to it at once.—Some wine, Esther, and then the Torah."

"Dost thou believe the prophets, master?" he asked, after drinking. "I know thou dost, for of such was the faith of all thy kindred.— Give me, Esther, the book which hath in it the visions of Isaiah."

He took one of the rolls which she had unwrapped for him, and read, "'The people that walked in darkness have seen a great light: they that dwell in the land of the shadow of death, upon them hath the light shined. . . . For unto us a child is born, unto us a son is given: and the government shall be upon his shoulder. . . . Of the increase of his government and peace there shall be no end, upon the throne of David, and upon his kingdom, to order it, and to establish it with judgment and with justice from henceforth even forever.'— Believest thou the prophets, O my master?

—Now, Esther, the word of the Lord that came to Micah."

She gave him the roll he asked.

"'But thou,'" he began reading—"'but thou, Bethlehem Ephrath, though thou be little among the thousands of Judah, yet out of thee shall he come forth unto me that is to be ruler in Israel.'—This was he, the very child Balthasar saw and worshipped in the cave. Believest thou the prophets, O my master?—Give me, Esther, the words of Jeremiah."

Receiving that roll, he read as before, "'Behold, the days come, saith the Lord, that I will raise unto David a righteous branch, and a king shall reign and prosper, and shall execute judgment and justice in the earth. In his days Judah shall be saved, and Israel shall dwell safely.' As a king he shall reign—as a king, O my master! Believest thou the prophets?—Now, daughter, the roll of the sayings of that son of Judah in whom there was no blemish."

She gave him the book of Daniel.

"Hear, my master," he said: "'I saw in the night visions, and behold, one like the Son of man came with the clouds of heaven.... And there was given him dominion, and glory, and a kingdom, that all people, nations, and languages should serve him; his dominion is an everlasting dominion, which shall not pass away, and his kingdom that which shall not be destroyed.'—Believest thou the prophets, O my master?"

"It is enough. I believe," cried Ben-Hur.

"What then?" asked Simonides. "If the

King come poor, will not my master, of his abundance, give him help?"

"Help him? To the last shekel and the last breath. But why speak of his coming poor?"

"Give me, Esther, the word of the Lord as it came to Zechariah," said Simonides.

She gave him one of the rolls.

"Hear how the King will enter Jerusalem." Then he read, "'Rejoice greatly, O daughter of Zion. . . . Behold, thy King cometh unto thee with justice and salvation; lowly, and riding upon an ass, and upon a colt, the foal of an ass.'"

Ben-Hur looked away.

"What see you, O my master?"

"Rome!" he answered, gloomily—"Rome, and her legions. I have dwelt with them in their camps. I know them."

"Ah!" said Simonides. "Thou shalt be a master of legions for the King, with millions to choose from."

"Millions!" cried Ben-Hur.

Simonides sat a moment thinking.

"The question of power should not trouble you," he next said.

Ben-Hur looked at him inquiringly.

"You were seeing the lowly King in the act of coming to his own," Simonides answered—"seeing him on the right hand, as it were, and on the left the brassy legions of Cæsar, and you were asking, What can he do?"

"It was my very thought."

"O my master!" Simonides continued. "You do not know how strong our Israel is. You

think of him as a sorrowful old man weeping by the rivers of Babylon. But go up to Jerusalem next Passover, and stand on the Xystus or in the Street of Barter, and see him as he is. The promise of the Lord to father Jacob coming out of Padan-Aram was a law under which our people have not ceased multiplying — not even in captivity; they grew under foot of the Egyptian; the clench of the Roman has been but wholesome nurture to them; now they are indeed 'a nation, and a company of nations.' Nor that only, my master; in fact, to measure the strength of Israel—which is, in fact, measuring what the King can do — you shall not bide solely by the rule of natural increase, but add thereto the other—I mean the spread of the faith, which will carry you to the far and near of the whole known earth. Further, the habit is, I know, to think and speak of Jerusalem as Israel, which may be likened to our finding an embroidered shred, and holding it up as a magisterial robe of Cæsar's. Jerusalem is but a stone of the Temple, or the heart in the body. Turn from beholding the legions, strong though they be, and count the hosts of the faithful waiting the old alarm, 'To your tents, O Israel!' —count the many in Persia, children of those who chose not to return with the returning; count the brethren who swarm the marts of Egypt and Farther Africa; count the Hebrew colonists eking profit in the West—in Lodinum and the trade-courts of Spain; count the pure of blood and the proselytes in Greece and in the isles of the sea, and over in Pontus, and

here in Antioch, and, for that matter, those of
that city lying accursed in the shadow of the
unclean walls of Rome herself; count the wor-
shippers of the Lord dwelling in tents along
the deserts next us, as well as in the deserts
beyond the Nile: and in the regions across the
Caspian, and up in the old lands of Gog and
Magog even; separate those who annually send
gifts to the Holy Temple in acknowledgment
of God—separate them, that they may be count-
ed also. And when you have done counting,
lo! my master, a census of the sword hands that
await you; lo! a kingdom ready fashioned for
him who is to do 'judgment and justice in the
whole earth'—in Rome not less than in Zion.
Have then the answer, What Israel can do,
that can the King."

The picture was fervently given.

Upon Ilderim it operated like the blowing of
a trumpet. "Oh that I had back my youth!"
he cried, starting to his feet.

Ben-Hur sat still. The speech, he saw, was
an invitation to devote his life and fortune to
the mysterious Being who was palpably as much
the centre of a great hope with Simonides as
with the devout Egyptian. The idea, as we
have seen, was not a new one, but had come to
him repeatedly; once while listening to Mal-
luch in the Grove of Daphne; afterwards more
distinctly while Balthasar was giving his con-
ception of what the kingdom was to be; still
later, in the walk through the old Orchard, it
had risen almost, if not quite, into a resolve. At
such times it had come and gone only an idea,

attended with feelings more or less acute. Not so now. A master had it in charge, a master was working it up; already he had exalted it into a cause brilliant with possibilities and infinitely holy. The effect was as if a door theretofore unseen had suddenly opened flooding Ben-Hur with light, and admitting him to a service which had been his one perfect dream —a service reaching far into the future, and rich with the rewards of duty done, and prizes to sweeten and soothe his ambition. One touch more was needed.

"Let us concede all you say, O Simonides," said Ben-Hur—"that the King will come, and his kingdom be as Solomon's; say also I am ready to give myself and all I have to him and his cause; yet more, say that I should do as was God's purpose in the ordering of my life and in your quick amassment of astonishing fortune; then what? Shall we proceed like blind men building? Shall we wait till the King comes? Or until he sends for me? You have age and experience on your side. Answer."

Simonides answered at once.

"We have no choice; none. This letter"— he produced Messala's despatch as he spoke— "this letter is the signal for action. The alliance proposed between Messala and Gratus we are not strong enough to resist; we have not the influence at Rome nor the force here. They will kill you if we wait. How merciful they are, look at me and judge."

He shuddered at the terrible recollection.

"O good my master," he continued, recover-

ing himself; "how strong are you—in purpose, I mean?"

Ben-Hur did not understand him.

"I remember how pleasant the world was to me in my youth," Simonides proceeded.

"Yet," said Ben-Hur, "you were capable of a great sacrifice."

"Yes; for love."

"Has not life other motives as strong?"

Simonides shook his head.

"There is ambition."

"Ambition is forbidden a son of Israel."

"What, then, of revenge?"

The spark dropped upon the inflammable passion; the man's eyes gleamed; his hands shook; he answered, quickly, "Revenge is a Jew's of right; it is the law."

"A camel, even a dog, will remember a wrong," cried Ilderim.

Directly Simonides picked up the broken thread of his thought.

"There is a work, a work for the King, which should be done in advance of his coming. We may not doubt that Israel is to be his right hand; but, alas! it is a hand of peace, without cunning in war. Of the millions, there is not one trained band, not a captain. The mercenaries of the Herods I do not count, for they are kept to crush us. The condition is as the Roman would have it; his policy has fruited well for his tyranny; but the time of change is at hand, when the shepherd shall put on armor, and take to spear and sword, and the feeding flocks be turned to fighting lions. Some one,

524

my son, must have place next the King at his right hand. Who shall it be if not he who does this work well?"

Ben-Hur's face flushed at the prospect, though he said, "I see; but speak plainly. A deed to be done is one thing; how to do it is another."

Simonides sipped the wine Esther brought him, and replied,

"The sheik, and thou, my master, shall be principals, each with a part. I will remain here, carrying on as now, and watchful that the spring go not dry. Thou shalt betake thee to Jerusalem, and thence to the wilderness, and begin numbering the fighting-men of Israel, and telling them into tens and hundreds, and choosing captains and training them, and in secret places hoarding arms, for which I shall keep thee supplied. Commencing over in Perea, thou shalt go then to Galilee, whence it is but a step to Jerusalem. In Perea, the desert will be at thy back, and Ilderim in reach of thy hand. He will keep the roads, so that nothing shall pass without thy knowledge. He will help thee in many ways. Until the ripening time no one shall know what is here contracted. Mine is but a servant's part. I have spoken to Ilderim. What sayest thou?"

Ben-Hur looked at the sheik.

"It is as he says, son of Hur," the Arab responded. "I have given my word, and he is content with it; but thou shalt have my oath, binding me, and the ready hands of my tribe, and whatever serviceable thing I have."

The three—Simonides, Ilderim, Esther—
gazed at Ben-Hur fixedly.

"Every man," he answered, at first sadly, "has
a cup of pleasure poured for him, and soon or
late it comes to his hand, and he tastes and
drinks—every man but me. I see, Simonides,
and thou, O generous sheik!—I see whither the
proposal tends. If I accept, and enter upon
the course, farewell peace, and the hopes which
cluster around it. The doors I might enter and
the gates of quiet life shut behind me, never
to open again, for Rome keeps them all; and
her outlawry will follow me, and her hunters;
and in the tombs near cities and the dismal
caverns of remotest hills, I must eat my crust
and take my rest."

The speech was broken by a sob. All turned
to Esther, who hid her face upon her father's
shoulder.

"I did not think of you, Esther," said Simon-
ides, gently, for he was himself deeply moved.

"It is well enough, Simonides," said Ben-
Hur. "A man bears a hard doom better, know-
ing there is pity for him. Let me go on."

They gave him ear again.

"I was about to say," he continued, "I have
no choice, but take the part you assign me;
and as remaining here is to meet an ignoble
death, I will to the work at once."

"Shall we have writings?" asked Simonides,
moved by his habit of business.

"I rest upon your word," said Ben-Hur.

"And I," Ilderim answered.

Thus simply was effected the treaty which

was to alter Ben-Hur's life. And almost immediately the latter added,

"It is done, then."

"May the God of Abraham help us!" Simonides exclaimed.

"One word now, my friends," Ben-Hur said, more cheerfully. "By your leave, I will be my own until after the games. It is not probable Messala will set peril on foot for me until he has given the procurator time to answer him, and that cannot be in less than seven days from the despatch of his letter. The meeting him in the Circus is a pleasure I would buy at whatever risk."

Ilderim, well pleased, assented readily, and Simonides, intent on business, added, "It is well; for look you, my master, the delay will give me time to do you a good part. I understood you to speak of an inheritance derived from Arrius. Is it in property?"

"A villa near Misenum, and houses in Rome."

"I suggest, then, the sale of the property, and safe deposit of the proceeds. Give me an account of it, and I will have authorities drawn, and despatch an agent on the mission forthwith. We will forestall the imperial robbers at least this once."

"You shall have the account to-morrow."

"Then, if there be nothing more, the work of the night is done," said Simonides.

Ilderim combed his beard complacently, saying, "And well done."

"The bread and wine again, Esther. Sheik

Ilderim will make us happy by staying with us till to-morrow, or at his pleasure; and thou, my master—"

"Let the horses be brought," said Ben-Hur. "I will return to the Orchard. The enemy will not discover me if I go now, and "—he glanced at Ilderim—" the four will be glad to see me."

As the day dawned, he and Malluch dismounted at the door of the tent.

CHAPTER IX
ESTHER AND BEN-HUR

NEXT night, about the fourth hour, Ben-Hur stood on the terrace of the great warehouse with Esther. Below them, on the landing, there was much running about, and shifting of packages and boxes, and shouting of men, whose figures, stooping, heaving, hauling, looked, in the light of the crackling torches kindled in their aid, like the laboring genii of the fantastic Eastern tales. A galley was being laden for instant departure. Simonides had not yet come from his office, in which, at the last moment, he would deliver to the captain of the vessel instructions to proceed without stop to Ostia, the seaport of Rome, and, after landing a passenger there, continue more leisurely to Valentia, on the coast of Spain.

The passenger is the agent going to dispose of the estate derived from Arrius the duumvir.

528

When the lines of the vessel are cast off, and she is put about, and her voyage begun, Ben-Hur will be committed irrevocably to the work undertaken the night before. If he is disposed to repent the agreement with Ilderim, a little time is allowed him to give notice and break it off. He is master, and has only to say the word.

Such may have been the thought at the moment in his mind. He was standing with folded arms, looking upon the scene in the manner of a man debating with himself. Young, handsome, rich, but recently from the patrician circles of Roman society, it is easy to think of the world besetting him with appeals not to give more to onerous duty or ambition attended with outlawry and danger. We can even imagine the arguments with which he was pressed; the hopelessness of contention with Cæsar, the uncertainty veiling everything connected with the King and his coming; the ease, honors, state, purchasable like goods in market, and, strongest of all, the sense newly acquired of home, with friends to make it delightful. Only those who have been wanderers long desolate can know the power there was in the latter appeal.

Let us add now, the world — always cunning enough of itself; always whispering to the weak, Stay, take thine ease; always presenting the sunny side of life—the world was in this instance helped by Ben-Hur's companion.

" Were you ever at Rome ?" he asked.

" No," Esther replied.

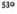

"Would you like to go?"

"I think not."

"Why?"

"I am afraid of Rome," she answered, with a perceptible tremor of the voice.

He looked at her then—or rather down upon her, for at his side she appeared little more than a child. In the dim light he could not see her face distinctly; even the form was shadowy. But again he was reminded of Tirzah, and a sudden tenderness fell upon him—just so the lost sister stood with him on the house-top the calamitous morning of the accident to Gratus. Poor Tirzah! Where was she now? Esther had the benefit of the feeling evoked. If not his sister, he could never look upon her as his servant; and that she was his servant in fact would make him always the more considerate and gentle towards her.

"I cannot think of Rome," she continued, recovering her voice, and speaking in her quiet, womanly way—"I cannot think of Rome as a city of palaces and temples, and crowded with people; she is to me a monster which has possession of one of the beautiful lands, and lies there luring men to ruin and death—a monster which it is not possible to resist—a ravenous beast gorging with blood. Why—"

She faltered, looked down, stopped.

"Go on," said Ben-Hur, reassuringly.

She drew closer to him, looked up again, and said, "Why must you make her your enemy? Why not rather make peace with her, and be at rest? You have had many ills and borne

530

them; you have survived the snares laid for you by foes. Sorrow has consumed your youth, is it well to give it the remainder of your days?"

The girlish face under his eyes seemed to come nearer and get whiter as the pleading went on; he stooped towards it, and asked, softly, "What would you have me do, Esther?"

She hesitated a moment, then asked, in return, "Is the property near Rome a residence?"

"Yes."

"And pretty?"

"It is beautiful—a palace in the midst of gardens and shell-strewn walks; fountains without and within; statuary in the shady nooks; hills around covered with vines, and so high that Neapolis and Vesuvius are in sight, and the sea an expanse of purpling blue dotted with restless sails. Cæsar has a country-seat near by, but in Rome they say the old Arrian villa is the prettiest."

"And the life there, is it quiet?"

"There was never a summer day, never a moonlit night, more quiet, save when visitors come. Now that the old owner is gone, and I am here, there is nothing to break its silence— nothing, unless it be the whispering of servants, or the whistling of happy birds, or the noise of fountains at play; it is changeless, except as day by day old flowers fade and fall, and new ones bud and bloom, and the sunlight gives place to the shadow of a passing cloud. The life, Esther, was all too quiet for me. It made me restless by keeping always present a feeling

531

that I, who have so much to do, was dropping
into idle habits, and tying myself with silken
chains, and after a while—and not a long while
either—would end with nothing done."

She looked off over the river.

"Why did you ask?" he said.

"Good my master—"

"No, no, Esther—not that. Call me friend—
brother, if you will ; I am not your master, and
will not be. Call me brother."

He could not see the flush of pleasure which
reddened her face, and the glow of the eyes
that went out lost in the void above the river.

"I cannot understand," she said, " the nature
which prefers the life you are going to—a life—"

"Of violence, and it may be of blood," he
said, completing the sentence.

"Yes," she added, " the nature which could
prefer that life to such as might be in the beau-
tiful villa."

"Esther, you mistake. There is no preference.
Alas ! the Roman is not so kind. I am going
of necessity. To stay here is to die ; and if I
go there, the end will be the same—a poisoned
cup, a bravo's blow. or a judge's sentence ob-
tained by perjury. Messala and the procura-
tor Gratus are rich with plunder of my father's
estate, and it is more important to them to
keep their gains now than was their getting in
the first instance. A peaceable settlement is
out of reach, because of the confession it would
imply. And then—then— Ah, Esther, if I
could buy them, I do not know that I would.
I do not believe peace possible to me ; no, not

even in the sleepy shade and sweet air of the
marble porches of the old villa—no matter
who might be there to help me bear the bur-
dens of the days, nor by what patience of love
she made the effort. Peace is not possible to
me while my people are lost, for I must be
watchful to find them. If I find them, and
they have suffered wrong, shall not the guilty
suffer for it? If they are dead by violence, shall
the murderers escape? Oh, I could not sleep
for dreams! Nor could the holiest love, by any
stratagem, lull me to a rest which conscience
would not strangle."

"Is it so bad then?" she asked, her voice
tremulous with feeling. "Can nothing, nothing,
be done?"

Ben-Hur took her hand.

"Do you care so much for me?"

"Yes," she answered, simply.

The hand was warm, and in the palm of his
it was lost. He felt it tremble. Then the
Egyptian came, so the opposite of this little
one; so tall, so audacious, with a flattery so
cunning, a wit so ready, a beauty so wonderful,
a manner so bewitching. He carried the hand
to his lips and gave it back.

"You shall be another Tirzah to me, Esther."

"Who is Tirzah?"

"The little sister the Roman stole from me,
and whom I must find before I can rest or be
happy."

Just then a gleam of light flashed athwart
the terrace and fell upon the two; and, look-
ing round, they saw a servant roll Simonides

533

in his chair out of the door. They went to the merchant, and in the after-talk he was principal.

Immediately the lines of the galley were cast off, and she swung round, and, midst the flashing of torches and the shouting of joyous sailors, hurried off to the sea—leaving Ben-Hur committed to the cause of the KING WHO WAS TO COME.

CHAPTER X
POSTED FOR THE RACE

THE day before the games, in the afternoon, all Ilderim's racing property was taken to the city, and put in quarters adjoining the Circus. Along with it the good man carried a great deal of property not of that class; so with servants, retainers mounted and armed, horses in leading, cattle driven, camels laden with baggage, his outgoing from the Orchard was not unlike a tribal migration. The people along the road failed not to laugh at his motley procession; on the other side, it was observed that, with all his irascibility, he was not in the least offended by their rudeness. If he was under surveillance, as he had reason to believe, the informer would describe the semi-barbarous show with which he came up to the races. The Romans would laugh; the city would be amused; but what cared he? Next morning the pageant would be far on the road to the desert, and going with it would be every movable thing of value belonging to the Orchard—everything save such

as were essential to the success of his four. He was, in fact, started home; his tents were all folded; the dowar was no more; in twelve hours all would be out of reach, pursue who might. A man is never safer than when he is under the laugh; and the shrewd old Arab knew it.

Neither he nor Ben-Hur overestimated the influence of Messala; it was their opinion, however, that he would not begin active measures against them until after the meeting in the Circus; if defeated there, especially if defeated by Ben-Hur, they might instantly look for the worst he could do; he might not even wait for advices from Gratus. With this view, they shaped their course, and were prepared to betake themselves out of harm's way. They rode together now in good spirits, calmly confident of success on the morrow.

On the way, they came upon Malluch in waiting for them. The faithful fellow gave no sign by which it was possible to infer any knowledge on his part of the relationship so recently admitted between Ben-Hur and Simonides, or of the treaty between them and Ilderim. He exchanged salutations as usual, and produced a paper, saying to the sheik, " I have here the notice of the editor of the games, just issued, in which you will find your horses published for the race. You will find in it also the order of exercises. Without waiting, good sheik, I congratulate you upon your victory."

He gave the paper over, and, leaving the worthy to master it, turned to Ben-Hur.

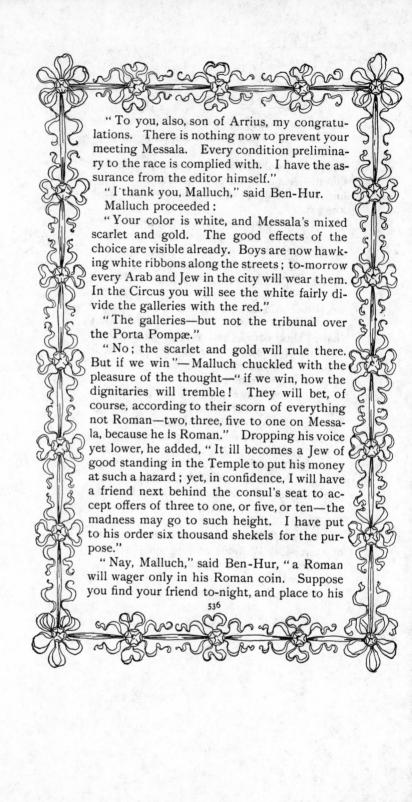

"To you, also, son of Arrius, my congratulations. There is nothing now to prevent your meeting Messala. Every condition preliminary to the race is complied with. I have the assurance from the editor himself."

"I thank you, Malluch," said Ben-Hur.

Malluch proceeded:

"Your color is white, and Messala's mixed scarlet and gold. The good effects of the choice are visible already. Boys are now hawking white ribbons along the streets; to-morrow every Arab and Jew in the city will wear them. In the Circus you will see the white fairly divide the galleries with the red."

"The galleries—but not the tribunal over the Porta Pompæ."

"No; the scarlet and gold will rule there. But if we win"—Malluch chuckled with the pleasure of the thought—"if we win, how the dignitaries will tremble! They will bet, of course, according to their scorn of everything not Roman—two, three, five to one on Messala, because he is Roman." Dropping his voice yet lower, he added, "It ill becomes a Jew of good standing in the Temple to put his money at such a hazard; yet, in confidence, I will have a friend next behind the consul's seat to accept offers of three to one, or five, or ten—the madness may go to such height. I have put to his order six thousand shekels for the purpose."

"Nay, Malluch," said Ben-Hur, "a Roman will wager only in his Roman coin. Suppose you find your friend to-night, and place to his

order sestertii in such amount as you choose.
And look you, Malluch—let him be instructed
to seek wagers with Messala and his support-
ers; Ilderim's four against Messala's."

Malluch reflected a moment.

"The effect will be to centre interest upon
your contest."

"The very thing I seek, Malluch."

"I see, I see."

"Aye, Malluch; would you serve me perfectly,
help me to fix the public eye upon our race—
Messala's and mine."

Malluch spoke quickly—"It can be done."

"Then let it be done," said Ben-Hur.

"Enormous wagers offered will answer; if
the offers are accepted, all the better."

Malluch turned his eyes watchfully upon
Ben-Hur.

"Shall I not have back the equivalent of
his robbery?" said Ben-Hur, partly to himself.
"Another opportunity may not come. And
if I could break him in fortune as well as in
pride! Our father Jacob could take no of-
fence."

A look of determined will knit his hand-
some face, giving emphasis to his further
speech.

"Yes, it shall be. Hark, Malluch! Stop
not in thy offer of sestertii. Advance them to
talents, if any there be who dare so high. Five,
ten, twenty talents; aye, fifty, so the wager be
with Messala himself."

"It is a mighty sum," said Malluch. "I
must have security."

"So thou shalt. Go to Simonides, and tell him I wish the matter arranged. Tell him my heart is set on the ruin of my enemy, and that the opportunity hath such excellent promise that I choose such hazards. On our side be the God of our fathers. Go, good Malluch. Let this not slip."

And Malluch, greatly delighted, gave him parting salutation, and started to ride away, but returned presently.

"Your pardon," he said to Ben-Hur. "There was another matter. I could not get near Messala's chariot myself, but I had another measure it; and, from his report, its hub stands quite a palm higher from the ground than yours."

"A palm! So much?" cried Ben-Hur, joyfully.

Then he leaned over to Malluch.

"As thou art a son of Judah, Malluch, and faithful to thy kin, get thee a seat in the gallery over the Gate of Triumph. down close to the balcony in front of the pillars, and watch well when we make the turns there; watch well, for if I have favor at all, I will— Nay, Malluch, let it go unsaid! Only get thee there, and watch well."

At that moment a cry burst from Ilderim.

"Ha! By the splendor of God! what is this?"

He drew near Ben-Hur with a finger pointing on the face of the notice.

"Read," said Ben-Hur.

"No; better thou."

Ben-Hur took the paper, which, signed by the prefect of the province as editor, performed the office of a modern programme, giving particularly the several divertisements provided for the occasion. It informed the public that there would be first a procession of extraordinary splendor; that the procession would be succeeded by the customary honors to the god Consus, whereupon the games would begin; running, leaping, wrestling, boxing, each in the order stated. The names of the competitors were given, with their several nationalities and schools of training, the trials in which they had been engaged, the prizes won, and the prizes now offered; under the latter head the sums of money were stated in illuminated letters, telling of the departure of the day when the simple chaplet of pine or laurel was fully enough for the victor, hungering for glory as something better than riches, and content with it.

Over these parts of the programme Ben-Hur sped with rapid eyes. At last he came to the announcement of the race. He read it slowly. Attending lovers of the heroic sports were assured they would certainly be gratified by an Orestean struggle unparalleled in Antioch. The city offered the spectacle in honor of the consul. One hundred thousand sestertii and a crown of laurel were the prizes. Then followed the particulars. The entries were six in all—fours only permitted; and, to further interest in the performance, the competitors would be turned into the course together. Each four then received description.

539

"I. A four of Lysippus the Corinthian—two grays, a bay, and a black; entered at Alexandria last year, and again at Corinth, where they were winners. Lysippus, driver. Color, yellow.

"II. A four of Messala of Rome—two white, two black; victors of the Circensian as exhibited in the Circus Maximus last year. Messala, driver. Colors, scarlet and gold.

"III. A four of Cleanthes the Athenian—three gray, one bay; winners at the Isthmian last year. Cleanthes, driver. Color, green.

"IV. A four of Dicæus the Byzantine—two black, one gray, one bay; winners this year at Byzantium. Dicæus, driver. Color, black.

"V. A four of Admetus the Sidonian—all grays. Thrice entered at Cæsarea, and thrice victors. Admetus, driver. Color, blue.

"VI. A four of Ilderim, sheik of the Desert. All bays; first race. Ben-Hur, a Jew, driver. Color, white."

Ben-Hur, a Jew, driver!

Why that name instead of Arrius?

Ben-Hur raised his eyes to Ilderim. He had found the cause of the Arab's outcry. Both rushed to the same conclusion.

The hand was the hand of Messala!

CHAPTER XI

MAKING THE WAGERS

VENING was hardly come upon Antioch, when the Omphalus, nearly in the centre of the city, became a troubled fountain from which in every direction, but chiefly down to the Nymphæum and east and west along the Colonnade of Herod, flowed currents of people, for the time given up to Bacchus and Apollo.

For such indulgence anything more fitting cannot be imagined than the great roofed streets, which were literally miles on miles of porticos wrought of marble, polished to the last degree of finish, and all gifts to the voluptuous city by princes careless of expenditure where, as in this instance, they thought they were eternizing themselves. Darkness was not permitted anywhere; and the singing, the laughter, the shouting, were incessant, and in compound like the roar of waters dashing through hollow grots, confused by a multitude of echoes.

The many nationalities represented, though they might have amazed a stranger, were not peculiar to Antioch. Of the various missions of the great empire, one seems to have been the fusion of men and the introduction of strangers to each other; accordingly, whole peoples rose up and went at pleasure, taking with them their costumes, customs, speech, and gods; and

where they chose, they stopped, engaged in business, built houses, erected altars, and were what they had been at home.

There was a peculiarity, however, which could not have failed the notice of a looker-on this night in Antioch. Nearly everybody wore the colors of one or other of the charioteers announced for the morrow's race. Sometimes it was in form of a scarf, sometimes a badge; often a ribbon or a feather. Whatever the form, it signified merely the wearer's partiality; thus, green published a friend of Cleanthes the Athenian, and black an adherent of the Byzantine. This was according to a custom, old probably as the day of the race of Orestes—a custom, by the way, worthy of study as a marvel of history, illustrative of the absurd yet appalling extremities to which men frequently suffer their follies to drag them.

The observer abroad on this occasion, once attracted to the wearing of colors, would have very shortly decided that there were three in predominance — green, white, and the mixed scarlet and gold.

But let us from the streets to the palace on the island.

The five great chandeliers in the saloon are freshly lighted. The assemblage is much the same as that already noticed in connection with the place. The divan has its corps of sleepers and burden of garments, and the tables yet resound with the rattle and clash of dice. Yet the greater part of the company are not doing anything. They walk about, or

yawn tremendously, or pause as they pass each
other to exchange idle nothings. Will the
weather be fair to-morrow? Are the prepa-
rations for the games complete? Do the laws
of the Circus in Antioch differ from the laws
of the Circus in Rome? Truth is, the young
fellows are suffering from ennui. Their heavy
work is done; that is, we would find their tab-
lets, could we look at them, covered with mem-
oranda of wagers—wagers on every contest;
on the running, the wrestling, the boxing; on
everything but the chariot-race.

And why not on that?

Good reader, they cannot find anybody who
will hazard so much as a denarius with them
against Messala.

There are no colors in the saloon but his.

No one thinks of his defeat.

Why, they say, is he not perfect in his train-
ing? Did he not graduate from an imperial
lanista? Were not his horses winners at the
Circensian in the Circus Maximus? And then
—ah, yes! he is a Roman!

In a corner, at ease on the divan, Messala
himself may be seen. Around him, sitting or
standing, are his courtierly admirers, plying
him with questions. There is, of course, but
one topic.

Enter Drusus and Cecilius.

"Ah!" cries the young prince, throwing him-
self on the divan at Messala's feet, "Ah, by
Bacchus, I am tired!"

"Whither away?" asks Messala.

"Up the street; up to the Omphalus, and

beyond — who shall say how far? Rivers of
people; never so many in the city before. They
say we will see the whole world at the Circus
to-morrow."

Messala laughed scornfully.

"The idiots! Perpol! They never beheld
a Circensian with Cæsar for editor. But, my
Drusus, what found you?"

"Nothing."

"O—ah! You forget," said Cecilius.

"What?" asked Drusus.

"The procession of whites."

"Mirabile!" cried Drusus, half rising. "We
met a faction of whites, and they had a ban-
ner. But—ha, ha, ha!"

He fell back indolently.

"Cruel Drusus—not to go on," said Messala.

"Scum of the desert were they, my Messala,
and garbage-eaters from the Jacob's Tem-
ple in Jerusalem. What had I to do with
them?"

"Nay," said Cecilius, "Drusus is afraid of a
laugh, but I am not, my Messala."

"Speak thou, then."

"Well, we stopped the faction, and—"

"Offered them a wager," said Drusus, relent-
ing, and taking the word from the shadow's
mouth. "And—ha, ha, ha!—one fellow with
not enough skin on his face to make a worm
for a carp stepped forth, and—ha, ha, ha!—said
yes. I drew my tablets. 'Who is your man?'
I asked. 'Ben-Hur, the Jew,' said he. Then
I: 'What shall it be? How much?' He an·
swered, 'A—a—' Excuse me, Messala. By

Jove's thunder, I cannot go on for laughter!
Ha, ha, ha!"

The listeners leaned forward.

Messala looked to Cecilius.

"A shekel," said the latter.

"A shekel! A shekel!"

A burst of scornful laughter ran fast upon
the repetition.

"And what did Drusus?" asked Messala.

An outcry over about the door just then oc-
casioned a rush to that quarter; and, as the
noise there continued, and grew louder, even
Cecilius betook himself off, pausing only to say,
"The noble Drusus, my Messala, put up his
tablets and—lost the shekel."

"A white! A white!"

"Let him come!"

"This way, this way!"

These and like exclamations filled the saloon,
to the stoppage of other speech. The dice-
players quit their games; the sleepers awoke,
rubbed their eyes, drew their tablets, and hur-
ried to the common centre.

"I offer you—"

"And I—"

"I—"

The person so warmly received was the re-
spectable Jew, Ben-Hur's fellow-voyager from
Cyprus. He entered grave, quiet, observant.
His robe was spotlessly white; so was the cloth
of his turban. Bowing and smiling at the wel-
come, he moved slowly towards the central ta-
ble. Arrived there, he drew his robe about him
in a stately manner, took seat, and waved his

hand. The gleam of a jewel on a finger helped him not a little to the silence which ensued.

"Romans — most noble Romans — I salute you!" he said.

"Easy, by Jupiter! Who is he?" asked Drusus.

"A dog of Israel—Sanballat by name—purveyor for the army; residence, Rome; vastly rich; grown so as a contractor of furnishments which he never furnishes. He spins mischiefs, nevertheless, finer than spiders spin their webs. Come—by the girdle of Venus! let us catch him!"

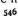

Messala arose as he spoke, and, with Drusus, joined the mass crowded about the purveyor.

"It came to me on the street," said that person, producing his tablets, and opening them on the table with an impressive air of business, "that there was great discomfort in the palace because offers on Messala were going without takers. The gods, you know, must have sacrifices; and here am I. You see my color; let us to the matter. Odds first, amounts next. What will you give me?"

The audacity seemed to stun his hearers.

"Haste!" he said. "I have an engagement with the consul."

The spur was effective.

"Two to one," cried half a dozen in a voice.

"What!" exclaimed the purveyor, astonished. "Only two to one, and yours a Roman!"

"Take three, then."

"Three say you—only three—and mine but a dog of a Jew! Give me four."

546

"Four it is," said a boy, stung by the taunt.

"Five—give me five," cried the purveyor, instantly.

A profound stillness fell on the assemblage.

"The consul — your master and mine — is waiting for me."

The inaction became awkward to the many.

"Give me five—for the honor of Rome, five."

"Five let it be," said one in answer.

There was a sharp cheer—a commotion—and Messala himself appeared.

"Five let it be," he said.

And Sanballat smiled, and made ready to write.

"If Cæsar die to-morrow," he said, "Rome will not be all bereft. There is at least one other with spirit to take his place. Give me six."

"Six be it," answered Messala.

There was another shout louder than the first.

"Six be it," repeated Messala. "Six to one —the difference between a Roman and a Jew. And, having found it, now, O redemptor of the flesh of swine, let us on. The amount—and quickly. The consul may send for thee, and I will then be bereft."

Sanballat took the laugh against him coolly, and wrote, and offered the writing to Messala.

"Read, read!" everybody demanded.

And Messala read:

"MEM.—Chariot-race. Messala of Rome, in wager with Sanballat, also of Rome, says he will beat Ben-Hur, the Jew. Amount of wager, twenty talents. Odds to Sanballat, six to one.

"Witnesses: SANBALLAT."

There was no noise, no motion. Each person seemed held in the pose the reading found him. Messala stared at the memorandum, while the eyes which had him in view opened wide, and stared at him. He felt the gaze, and thought rapidly. So lately he stood in the same place, and in the same way hectored the countrymen around him. They would remember it. If he refused to sign, his heroship was lost. And sign he could not; he was not worth one hundred talents, nor the fifth part of the sum. Suddenly his mind became a blank; he stood speechless; the color fled his face. An idea at last came to his relief.

"Thou Jew!" he said, "Where hast thou twenty talents? Show me."

Sanballat's provoking smile deepened.

"There," he replied, offering Messala a paper.

"Read, read!" arose all around.

Again Messala read:

> "At ANTIOCH, Tammuz 16th day.
>
> "The bearer, Sanballat of Rome, hath now to his order with me fifty talents, coin of Cæsar.
> "SIMONIDES."

"Fifty talents, fifty talents!" echoed the throng, in amazement.

Then Drusus came to the rescue.

"By Hercules!" he shouted, "the paper lies, and the Jew is a liar. Who but Cæsar hath fifty talents at order? Down with the insolent white!"

The cry was angry, and it was angrily repeated; yet Sanballat kept his seat, and his

548

smile grew more exasperating the longer he waited. At length Messala spoke.

"Hush! One to one, my countrymen—one to one, for love of our ancient Roman name."

The timely action recovered him his ascendency.

"O thou circumcised dog!" he continued, to Sanballat, "I gave thee six to one, did I not?"

"Yes," said the Jew, quietly.

"Well, give me now the fixing of the amount."

"With reserve, if the amount be trifling, have thy will," answered Sanballat.

"Write, then, five in place of twenty."

"Hast thou so much?"

"By the mother of the gods, I will show you receipts."

"Nay, the word of so brave a Roman must pass. Only make the sum even—six make it, and I will write."

"Write it so."

And forthwith they exchanged writings.

Sanballat immediately arose and looked around him, a sneer in place of his smile. No man better than he knew those with whom he was dealing.

"Romans," he said, "another wager, if you dare! Five talents against five talents that the white will win. I challenge you collectively."

They were again surprised.

"What!" he cried, louder. "Shall it be said in the Circus to-morrow that a dog of Israel went into the saloon of the palace full of Roman nobles—among them the scion of a Cæsar —and laid five talents before them in chal-

lenge, and they had not the courage to take it up?"

The sting was unendurable.

"Have done, O insolent!" said Drusus, "write the challenge, and leave it on the table; and to-morrow, if we find thou hast indeed so much money to put at such hopeless hazard, I, Drusus, promise it shall be taken."

Sanballat wrote again, and, rising, said, unmoved as ever, "See, Drusus, I leave the offer with you. When it is signed, send it to me any time before the race begins. I will be found with the consul in a seat over the Porta Pompæ. Peace to you; peace to all."

He bowed and departed, careless of the shout of derision with which they pursued him out of the door.

In the night the story of the prodigious wager flew along the streets and over the city; and Ben-Hur, lying with his four, was told of it, and also that Messala's whole fortune was on the hazard.

And he slept never so soundly.

TOMB OF LAZARUS

CHAPTER XII
THE CIRCUS

THE Circus at Antioch stood on the south bank of the river nearly opposite the island, differing in no respect from the plan of such buildings in general.

In the purest sense, the games were a gift to the public; consequently, everybody was free to attend; and, vast as the holding capacity of the structure was, so fearful were the people, on this occasion, lest there should not be room for them, that, early the day before the opening of the exhibition, they took up all the vacant spaces in the vicinity, where their temporary shelter suggested an army in waiting.

At midnight the entrances were thrown wide, and the rabble, surging in, occupied the quarters assigned to them, from which nothing less than an earthquake or an army with spears could have dislodged them. They dozed the night away on the benches, and breakfasted there; and there the close of the exercises found them, patient and sight-hungry as in the beginning.

The better people, their seats secured, began moving towards the Circus about the first hour of the morning, the noble and very rich among them distinguished by litters and retinues of liveried servants.

By the second hour, the efflux from the city was a stream unbroken and innumerable.

Exactly as the gnomon of the official dial up in the citadel pointed the second hour half gone, the legion, in full panoply, and with all its standards on exhibit, descended from Mount Sulpius ; and when the rear of the last cohort disappeared in the bridge, Antioch was literally abandoned—not that the Circus could hold the multitude, but that the multitude was gone out to it, nevertheless.

A great concourse on the river shore witnessed the consul come over from the island in a barge of state. As the great man landed, and was received by the legion, the martial show for one brief moment transcended the attraction of the Circus.

At the third hour, the audience, if such it may be termed, was assembled ; at last, a flourish of trumpets called for silence, and instantly the gaze of over a hundred thousand persons was directed towards a pile forming the eastern section of the building.

There was a basement first, broken in the middle by a broad arched passage, called the Porta Pompæ, over which, on an elevated tribunal magnificently decorated with insignia and legionary standards, the consul sat in the place of honor. On both sides of the passage the basement was divided into stalls termed carceres, each protected in front by massive gates swung to statuesque pilasters. Over the stalls next was a cornice crowned by a low balustrade ; back of which the seats arose in theatre

552

arrangement, all occupied by a throng of dignitaries superbly attired. The pile extended the width of the Circus, and was flanked on both sides by towers, which, besides helping the architects give grace to their work, served the velaria, or purple awnings, stretched between them so as to throw the whole quarter in a shade that became exceedingly grateful as the day advanced.

This structure, it is now thought, can be made useful in helping the reader to a sufficient understanding of the arrangement of the rest of the interior of the Circus. He has only to fancy himself seated on the tribunal with the consul, facing to the west, where everything is under his eye.

On the right and left, if he will look, he will see the main entrances, very ample, and guarded by gates hinged to the towers.

Directly below him is the arena — a level plane of considerable extent, covered with a fine white sand. There all the trials will take place except the running.

Looking across this sanded arena westwardly still, there is a pedestal of marble supporting three low conical pillars of gray stone, much carven. Many an eye will hunt for those pillars before the day is done, for they are the first goal, and mark the beginning and end of the race-course. Behind the pedestal, leaving a passage-way and space for an altar, commences a wall ten or twelve feet in breadth and five or six in height, extending thence exactly two hundred yards, or one Olympic stadium.

At the farther, or westward, extremity of the wall there is another pedestal, surmounted with pillars which mark the second goal.

The racers will enter the course on the right of the first goal, and keep the wall all the time to their left. The beginning and ending points of the contest lie, consequently, directly in front of the consul across the arena; and for that reason his seat was admittedly the most desirable in the Circus.

Now if the reader, who is still supposed to be seated on the consular tribunal over the Porta Pompæ, will look up from the ground arrangement of the interior, the first point to attract his notice will be the marking of the outer boundary-line of the course—that is, a plain-faced, solid wall, fifteen or twenty feet in height, with a balustrade on its cope, like that over the carceres, or stalls, in the east. This balcony, if followed round the course, will be found b. oken in three places to allow passages of exit and entrance, two in the north and one in the west; the latter very ornate, and called the Gate of Triumph, because, when all is over, the victors will pass out that way, crowned, and with triumphal escort and ceremonies.

At the west end the balcony encloses the course in the form of a half-circle, and is made to uphold two great galleries.

Directly behind the balustrade on the coping of the balcony is the first seat, from which ascend the succeeding benches, each higher than the one in front of it; giving to view a spectacle of surpassing interest—the spectacle

of a vast space ruddy and glistening with human faces, and rich with vari-colored costumes.

The commonalty occupy quarters over in the west, beginning at the point of termination of an awning, stretched, it would seem, for the accommodation of the better classes exclusively.

Having thus the whole interior of the Circus under view at the moment of the sounding of the trumpets, let the reader next imagine the multitude seated and sunk to sudden silence, and motionless in its intensity of interest.

Out of the Porta Pompæ over in the east rises a sound mixed of voices and instruments harmonized. Presently, forth issues the chorus of the procession with which the celebration begins; the editor and civic authorities of the city, givers of the games, follow in robes and garlands; then the gods, some on platforms borne by men, others in great four-wheel carriages gorgeously decorated; next them, again, the contestants of the day, each in costume exactly as he will run, wrestle, leap, box, or drive.

Slowly crossing the arena, the procession proceeds to make circuit of the course. The display is beautiful and imposing. Approval runs before it in a shout, as the water rises and swells in front of a boat in motion. If the dumb, figured gods make no sign of appreciation of the welcome, the editor and his associates are not so backward.

The reception of the athletes is even more demonstrative, for there is not a man in the assemblage who has not something in wager upon them, though but a mite or farthing. And

it is noticeable, as the classes move by, that the favorites among them are easily singled out : either their names are loudest in the uproar, or they are more profusely showered with wreaths and garlands tossed to them from the balcony.

If there is a question as to the popularity with the public of the several games, it is now put to rest. To the splendor of the chariots and the superexcellent beauty of the horses, the charioteers add the personality necessary to perfect the charm of their display. Their tunics, short, sleeveless, and of the finest woollen texture, are of the assigned colors. A horseman accompanies each one of them except Ben-Hur, who, for some reason—possibly distrust—has chosen to go alone; so, too, they are all helmeted but him. As they approach, the spectators stand upon the benches, and there is a sensible deepening of the clamor, in which a sharp listener may detect the shrill piping of women and children ; at the same time, the things roseate flying from the balcony thicken into a storm, and, striking the men, drop into the chariot-beds, which are threatened with filling to the tops. Even the horses have a share in the ovation ; nor may it be said they are less conscious than their masters of the honors they receive.

Very soon, as with the other contestants, it is made apparent that some of the drivers are more in favor than others ; and then the discovery follows that nearly every individual on the benches, women and children as well as men, wears a color, most frequently a ribbon

upon the breast or in the hair : now it is green, now yellow, now blue; but, searching the great body carefully, it is manifest that there is a preponderance of white and scarlet and gold.

In a modern assemblage called together as this one is, particularly where there are sums at hazard upon the race, a preference would be decided by the qualities or performance of the horses ; here, however, nationality was the rule. If the Byzantine and Sidonian found small support, it was because their cities were scarcely represented on the benches. On their side, the Greeks, though very numerous, were divided between the Corinthian and the Athenian, leaving but a scant showing of green and yellow. Messala's scarlet and gold would have been but little better had not the citizens of Antioch, proverbially a race of courtiers, joined the Romans by adopting the color of their favorite. There were left then the country people, or Syrians, the Jews, and the Arabs ; and they, from faith in the blood of the sheik's four, blended largely with hate of the Romans, whom they desired, above all things, to see beaten and humbled, mounted the white, making the most noisy, and probably the most numerous, faction of all.

As the charioteers move on in the circuit, the excitement increases; at the second goal, where, especially in the galleries, the white is the ruling color, the people exhaust their flowers and rive the air with screams.

" Messala ! Messala !"

" Ben-Hur ! Ben-Hur !"

Such are the cries.

Upon the passage of the procession, the factionists take their seats and resume conversation.

"Ah, by Bacchus! was he not handsome?" exclaims a woman, whose Romanism is betrayed by the colors flying in her hair.

"And how splendid his chariot!" replies a neighbor, of the same proclivities. "It is all ivory and gold. Jupiter grant he wins!"

The notes on the bench behind them were entirely different.

"A hundred shekels on the Jew!"

The voice is high and shrill.

"Nay, be thou not rash," whispers a moderating friend to the speaker. "The children of Jacob are not much given to Gentile sports, which are too often accursed in the sight of the Lord."

"True, but saw you ever one more cool and assured? And what an arm he has!"

"And what horses!" says a third.

"And for that," a fourth one adds, "they say he has all the tricks of the Romans."

A woman completes the eulogium:

"Yes, and he is even handsomer than the Roman."

Thus encouraged, the enthusiast shrieks again, "A hundred shekels on the Jew!"

"Thou fool!" answers an Antiochian, from a bench well forward on the balcony. "Knowest thou not there are fifty talents laid against him, six to one, on Messala? Put up thy shekels, lest Abraham rise and smite thee."

"Ha, ha! thou ass of Antioch! Cease thy bray. Knowest thou not it was Messala betting on himself?"

Such the reply.

And so ran the controversy, not always good-natured.

When at length the march was ended and the Porta Pompæ received back the procession, Ben-Hur knew he had his prayer.

The eyes of the East were upon his contest with Messala.

CHAPTER XIII

THE START

ABOUT three o'clock, speaking in modern style, the programme was concluded except the chariot-race. The editor, wisely considerate of the comfort of the people, chose that time for a recess. At once the vomitoria were thrown open, and all who could hastened to the portico outside where the restaurateurs had their quarters. Those who remained yawned, talked, gossiped, consulted their tablets, and, all distinctions else forgotten, merged into but two classes—the winners, who were happy, and the losers, who were grum and captious.

Now, however, a third class of spectators, composed of citizens who desired only to witness the chariot-race, availed themselves of the recess to come in and take their reserved seats; by so doing they thought to attract the least attention and give the least offence. Among

these were Simonides and his party, whose places were in the vicinity of the main entrance on the north side, opposite the consul.

As the four stout servants carried the merchant in his chair up the aisle, curiosity was much excited. Presently some one called his name. Those about caught it and passed it on along the benches to the west; and there was hurried climbing on seats to get sight of the man about whom common report had coined and put in circulation a romance so mixed of good-fortune and bad that the like had never been known or heard of before.

Ilderim was also recognized and warmly greeted; but nobody knew Balthasar or the two women who followed him closely veiled.

The people made way for the party respectfully, and the ushers seated them in easy speaking distance of each other down by the balustrade overlooking the arena. In providence of comfort, they sat upon cushions and had stools for foot-rests.

The women were Iras and Esther.

Upon being seated, the latter cast a frightened look over the Circus, and drew the veil closer about her face; while the Egyptian, letting her veil fall upon her shoulders, gave herself to view, and gazed at the scene with the seeming unconsciousness of being stared at, which, in a woman, is usually the result of long social habitude.

The new-comers generally were yet making their first examination of the great spectacle, beginning with the consul and his attendants,

when some workmen ran in and commenced
to stretch a chalked rope across the arena from
balcony to balcony in front of the pillars of the
first goal.

About the same time, also, six men came in
through the Porta Pompæ and took post, one in
front of each occupied stall; whereat there was
a prolonged hum of voices in every quarter.

"See, see! The green goes to number four
on the right; the Athenian is there."

"And Messala—yes, he is in number two."

"The Corinthian—"

"Watch the white! See, he crosses over, he
stops; number one it is—number one on the
left."

"No, the black stops there, and the white at
number two."

"So it is."

These gate-keepers, it should be understood,
were dressed in tunics colored like those of the
competing charioteers; so, when they took
their stations, everybody knew the particular
stall in which his favorite was that moment
waiting.

"Did you ever see Messala?" the Egyptian
asked Esther.

The Jewess shuddered as she answered no.
If not her father's enemy, the Roman was Ben-
Hur's.

"He is beautiful as Apollo."

As Iras spoke, her large eyes brightened and
she shook her jewelled fan. Esther looked at
her with the thought, "Is he, then, so much
handsomer than Ben-Hur?" Next moment

she heard Ilderim say to her father, "Yes, his stall is number two on the left of the Porta Pompæ;" and, thinking it was of Ben-Hur he spoke, her eyes turned that way. Taking but the briefest glance at the wattled face of the gate, she drew the veil close and muttered a little prayer.

Presently Sanballat came to the party.

"I am just from the stalls, O sheik," he said, bowing gravely to Ilderim, who began combing his beard, while his eyes glittered with eager inquiry. "The horses are in perfect condition."

Ilderim replied simply, "If they are beaten, I pray it be by some other than Messala."

Turning then to Simonides, Sanballat drew out a tablet, saying, "I bring you also something of interest. I reported, you will remember, the wager concluded with Messala last night, and stated that I left another which, if taken, was to be delivered to me in writing to-day before the race began. Here it is."

Simonides took the tablet and read the memorandum carefully.

"Yes," he said, "their emissary came to ask me if you had so much money with me. Keep the tablet close. If you lose, you know where to come; if you win "—his face knit hard—"if you win—ah, friend, see to it! See the signers escape not; hold them to the last shekel. That is what they would with us."

"Trust me," replied the purveyor.

"Will you not sit with us?" asked Simonides.

"You are very good," the other returned;

"but if I leave the consul, young Rome yonder will boil over. Peace to you; peace to all."

At length the recess came to an end.

The trumpeters blew a call at which the absentees rushed back to their places. At the same time, some attendants appeared in the arena, and, climbing upon the division-wall, went to an entablature near the second goal at the west end, and placed upon it seven wooden balls; then returning to the first goal, upon an entablature there they set up seven other pieces of wood hewn to represent dolphins.

"What shall they do with the balls and fishes, O sheik?" asked Balthasar.

"Hast thou never attended a race?"

"Never before; and hardly know I why I am here."

"Well, they are to keep the count. At the end of each round run thou shalt see one ball and one fish taken down."

The preparations were now complete, and presently a trumpeter in gaudy uniform arose by the editor, ready to blow the signal of commencement promptly at his order. Straightway the stir of the people and the hum of their conversation died away. Every face near by, and every face in the lessening perspective, turned to the east, as all eyes settled upon the gates of the six stalls which shut in the competitors.

The unusual flush upon his face gave proof that even Simonides had caught the universal excitement. Ilderim pulled his beard fast and furious.

"Look now for the Roman," said the fair Egyptian to Esther, who did not hear her, for, with close-drawn veil and beating heart, she sat watching for Ben-Hur.

The structure containing the stalls, it should be observed, was in form of the segment of a circle, retired on the right so that its central point was projected forward, and midway the course, on the starting side of the first goal. Every stall, consequently, was equally distant from the starting-line or chalked rope above mentioned.

The trumpet sounded short and sharp; whereupon the starters, one for each chariot, leaped down from behind the pillars of the goal, ready to give assistance if any of the fours proved unmanageable.

Again the trumpet blew, and simultaneously the gate-keepers threw the stalls open.

First appeared the mounted attendants of the charioteers, five in all, Ben-Hur having rejected the service. The chalked line was lowered to let them pass, then raised again. They were beautifully mounted, yet scarcely observed as they rode forward; for all the time the trampling of eager horses, and the voices of drivers scarcely less eager, were heard behind in the stalls, so that one might not look away an instant from the gaping doors.

The chalked line up again, the gate-keepers called their men; instantly the ushers on the balcony waved their hands, and shouted with all their strength, "Down! down!"

As well have whistled to stay a storm.

564

Forth from each stall, like missiles in a volley from so many great guns, rushed the six fours; and up the vast assemblage arose, electrified and irrepressible, and, leaping upon the benches, filled the Circus and the air above it with yells and screams. This was the time for which they had so patiently waited!—this the moment of supreme interest treasured up in talk and dreams since the proclamation of the games!

"He is come—there—look!" cried Iras, pointing to Messala.

"I see him," answered Esther, looking at Ben-Hur.

The veil was withdrawn. For an instant the little Jewess was brave. An idea of the joy there is in doing an heroic deed under the eyes of a multitude came to her, and she understood ever after how, at such times, the souls of men, in the frenzy of performance, laugh at death or forget it utterly.

The competitors were now under view from nearly every part of the Circus, yet the race was not begun; they had first to make the chalked line successfully.

The line was stretched for the purpose of equalizing the start. If it were dashed upon, discomfiture of man and horses might be apprehended; on the other hand, to approach it timidly was to incur the hazard of being thrown behind in the beginning of the race; and that was certain forfeit of the great advantage always striven for—the position next the division-wall on the inner line of the course.

This trial, its perils and consequences, the
spectators knew thoroughly; and if the opin-
ion of old Nestor, uttered what time he handed
the reins to his son, were true—

"It is not strength, but art, obtained the prize,
And to be swift is less than to be wise"—

all on the benches might well look for warning
of the winner to be now given, justifying the
interest with which they breathlessly watched
for the result.

The arena swam in a dazzle of light; yet
each driver looked first thing for the rope, then
for the coveted inner line. So, all six aiming
at the same point and speeding furiously, a
collision seemed inevitable; nor that merely.
What if the editor, at the last moment, dissat-
isfied with the start, should withhold the signal
to drop the rope? Or if he should not give it
in time?

The crossing was about two hundred and
fifty feet in width. Quick the eye, steady the
hand, unerring the judgment required. If now
one look away! or his mind wander! or a rein
slip! And what attraction in the ensemble of
the thousands over the spreading balcony!
Calculating upon the natural impulse to give
one glance—just one—in sooth of curiosity or
vanity, malice might be there with an artifice;
while friendship and love, did they serve the
same result, might be as deadly as malice.

The divine last touch in perfecting the beau-
tiful is animation. Can we accept the saying,

566

then these latter days, so tame in pastime and
dull in sports, have scarcely anything to com-
pare to the spectacle offered by the six con-
testants. Let the reader try to fancy it; let
him first look down upon the arena, and see it
glistening in its frame of dull-gray granite walls;
let him then, in this perfect field, see the char-
iots, light of wheel, very graceful, and ornate
as paint and burnishing can make them—Mes-
sala's rich with ivory and gold ; let him see the
drivers, erect and statuesque, undisturbed by
the motion of the cars, their limbs naked, and
fresh and ruddy with the healthful polish of the
baths—in their right hands goads, suggestive
of torture dreadful to the thought—in their left
hands, held in careful separation, and high, that
they may not interfere with view of the steeds,
the reins passing taut from the fore ends of the
carriage-poles ; let him see the fours, chosen
for beauty as well as speed ; let him see them
in magnificent action, their masters not more
conscious of the situation and all that is asked
and hoped from them—their heads tossing,
nostrils in play, now distended, now contract-
ed—limbs too dainty for the sand which they
touch but to spurn—limbs slender, yet with im-
pact crushing as hammers—every muscle of
the rounded bodies instinct with glorious life,
swelling, diminishing, justifying the world in
taking from them its ultimate measure of force;
finally, along with chariots, drivers, horses, let
the reader see the accompanying shadows fly ;
and, with such distinctness as the picture comes,
he may share the satisfaction and deeper pleas-

ure of those to whom it was a thrilling fact,
not a feeble fancy. Every age has its plenty
of sorrows; Heaven help where there are no
pleasures!

The competitors having started each on the
shortest line for the position next the wall,
yielding would be like giving up the race; and
who dared yield? It is not in common nature to
change a purpose in mid-career; and the cries
of encouragement from the balcony were indis-
tinguishable and indescribable: a roar which
had the same effect upon all the drivers.

The fours neared the rope together. Then
the trumpeter by the editor's side blew a sig-
nal vigorously. Twenty feet away it was not
heard. Seeing the action, however, the judges
dropped the rope, and not an instant too soon,
for the hoof of one of Messala's horses struck
it as it fell. Nothing daunted, the Roman
shook out his long lash, loosed the reins, leaned
forward, and, with a triumphant shout, took the
wall.

"Jove with us! Jove with us!" yelled all the
Roman faction, in a frenzy of delight.

As Messala turned in, the bronze lion's head
at the end of his axle caught the fore-leg of the
Athenian's right-hand trace-mate, flinging the
brute over against its yoke-fellow. Both stag-
gered, struggled, and lost their head-way. The
ushers had their will at least in part. The
thousands held their breath with horror; only
up where the consul sat was there shouting.

"Jove with us!" screamed Drusus, franti-
cally.

"He wins! Jove with us!" answered his associates, seeing Messala speed on.

Tablet in hand, Sanballat turned to them; a crash from the course below stopped his speech, and he could not but look that way.

Messala having passed, the Corinthian was the only contestant on the Athenian's right, and to that side the latter tried to turn his broken four; and then, as ill-fortune would have it, the wheel of the Byzantine, who was next on the left, struck the tail-piece of his chariot, knocking his feet from under him. There was a crash, a scream of rage and fear, and the unfortunate Cleanthes fell under the hoofs of his own steeds: a terrible sight, against which Esther covered her eyes.

On swept the Corinthian, on the Byzantine, on the Sidonian.

Sanballat looked for Ben-Hur, and turned again to Drusus and his coterie.

"A hundred sestertii on the Jew!" he cried.

"Taken!" answered Drusus.

"Another hundred on the Jew!" shouted Sanballat.

Nobody appeared to hear him. He called again; the situation below was too absorbing, and they were too busy shouting, "Messala! Messala! Jove with us!"

When the Jewess ventured to look again, a party of workmen were removing the horses and broken car; another party were taking off the man himself; and every bench upon which there was a Greek was vocal with execrations and prayers for vengeance. Suddenly she

dropped her hands; Ben-Hur, unhurt, was to
the front, coursing freely forward along with
the Roman! Behind them, in a group, follow-
ed the Sidonian, the Corinthian, and the Byz-
antine.

The race was on; the souls of the racers
were in it; over them bent the myriads.

CHAPTER XIV
THE RACE

HEN the dash for position began,
Ben-Hur, as we have seen, was on
the extreme left of the six. For a
moment, like the others, he was half
blinded by the light in the arena; yet he man-
aged to catch sight of his antagonists and di-
vine their purpose. At Messala, who was more
than an antagonist to him, he gave one search-
ing look. The air of passionless hauteur char-
acteristic of the fine patrician face was there
as of old, and so was the Italian beauty, which
the helmet rather increased; but more—it may
have been a jealous fancy, or the effect of the
brassy shadow in which the features were at
the moment cast, still the Israelite thought
he saw the soul of the man as through a glass,
darkly: cruel, cunning, desperate; not so ex-
cited as determined—a soul in a tension of
watchfulness and fierce resolve.

In a time not longer than was required to
turn to his four again, Ben-Hur felt his own
resolution harden to a like temper. At what-

ever cost, at all hazards, he would humble this enemy! Prize, friends, wagers, honor—everything that can be thought of as a possible interest in the race was lost in the one deliberate purpose. Regard for life even should not hold him back. Yet there was no passion, on his part; no blinding rush of heated blood from heart to brain, and back again; no impulse to fling himself upon Fortune: he did not believe in Fortune; far otherwise. He had his plan, and, confiding in himself, he settled to the task, never more observant, never more capable. The air about him seemed aglow with a renewed and perfect transparency.

When not half-way across the arena, he saw that Messala's rush would, if there was no collision, and the rope fell, give him the wall; that the rope would fall, he ceased as soon to doubt; and, further, it came to him, a sudden flash-like insight, that Messala knew it was to be let drop at the last moment (prearrangement with the editor could safely reach that point in the contest); and it suggested, what more Roman-like than for the official to lend himself to a countryman who, besides being so popular, had also so much at stake? There could be no other accounting for the confidence with which Messala pushed his four forward the instant his competitors were prudentially checking their fours in front of the obstruction—no other except madness.

It is one thing to see a necessity and another to act upon it. Ben-Hur yielded the wall for the time.

The rope fell, and all the fours but his sprang
into the course under urgency of voice and
lash. He drew head to the right, and, with all
the speed of his Arabs, darted across the trails
of his opponents, the angle of movement being
such as to lose the least time and gain the
greatest possible advance. So, while the spec-
tators were shivering at the Athenian's mishap,
and the Sidonian, Byzantine, and Corinthian
were striving, with such skill as they possessed,
to avoid involvement in the ruin, Ben-Hur
swept around and took the course neck and
neck with Messala, though on the outside. The
marvellous skill shown in making the change
thus from the extreme left across to the right
without appreciable loss did not fail the sharp
eyes upon the benches : the Circus seemed to
rock and rock again with prolonged applause.
Then Esther clasped her hands in glad sur-
prise ; then Sanballat, smiling, offered his hun-
dred sestertii a second time without a taker;
and then the Romans began to doubt, thinking
Messala might have found an equal, if not a
master, and that in an Israelite !

And now, racing together side by side, a nar-
row interval between them, the two neared the
second goal.

The pedestal of the three pillars there, viewed
from the west, was a stone wall in the form of
a half-circle, around which the course and op-
posite balcony were bent in exact parallelism.
Making this turn was considered in all respects
the most telling test of a charioteer ; it was, in
fact, the very feat in which Orestes failed. As

an involuntary admission of interest on the
part of the spectators, a hush fell over all the
Circus, so that for the first time in the race the
rattle and clang of the cars plunging after the
tugging steeds were distinctly heard. Then, it
would seem, Messala observed Ben-Hur, and
recognized him; and at once the audacity of
the man flamed out in an astonishing manner.

"Down Eros, up Mars!" he shouted, whirl-
ing his lash with practised hand—"Down Eros,
up Mars!" he repeated, and caught the well-
doing Arabs of Ben-Hur a cut the like of which
they had never known.

The blow was seen in every quarter, and the
amazement was universal. The silence deep-
ened; up on the benches behind the consul the
boldest held his breath, waiting for the out-
come. Only a moment thus: then, involun-
tarily, down from the balcony, as thunder falls,
burst the indignant cry of the people.

The four sprang forward affrighted. No hand
had ever been laid upon them except in love;
they had been nurtured ever so tenderly; and
as they grew, their confidence in man became
a lesson to men beautiful to see. What should
such dainty natures do under such indignity
but leap as from death?

Forward they sprang as with one impulse, and
forward leaped the car. Past question, every
experience is serviceable to us. Where got
Ben-Hur the large hand and mighty grip which
helped him now so well? Where but from the
oar with which so long he fought the sea? And
what was this spring of the floor under his feet

to the dizzy eccentric lurch with which in the old time the trembling ship yielded to the beat of staggering billows, drunk with their power? So he kept his place, and gave the four free rein, and called to them in soothing voice, trying merely to guide them round the dangerous turn; and before the fever of the people began to abate, he had back the mastery. Nor that only: on approaching the first goal, he was again side by side with Messala, bearing with him the sympathy and admiration of every one not a Roman. So clearly was the feeling shown, so vigorous its manifestation, that Messala, with all his boldness, felt it unsafe to trifle further.

As the cars whirled round the goal, Esther caught sight of Ben-Hur's face—a little pale, a little higher raised, otherwise calm, even placid.

Immediately a man climbed on the entablature at the west end of the division-wall, and took down one of the conical wooden balls. A dolphin on the east entablature was taken down at the same time.

In like manner, the second ball and second dolphin disappeared.

And then the third ball and third dolphin.

Three rounds concluded: still Messala held the inside position; still Ben-Hur moved with him side by side; still the other competitors followed as before. The contest began to have the appearance of one of the double races which became so popular in Rome during the later Cæsarian period—Messala and Ben-Hur in the first, the Corinthian, Sidonian, and Byzantine in the second. Meantime the ushers succeed-

ed in returning the multitude to their seats,
though the clamor continued to run the rounds,
keeping, as it were, even pace with the rivals
in the course below.

In the fifth round the Sidonian succeeded in
getting a place outside Ben-Hur, but lost it
directly.

The sixth round was entered upon without
change of relative position.

Gradually the speed had been quickened—
gradually the blood of the competitors warmed
with the work. Men and beasts seemed to
know alike that the final crisis was near, bring-
ing the time for the winner to assert himself.

The interest which from the beginning had
centred chiefly in the struggle between the Ro-
man and the Jew, with an intense and general
sympathy for the latter, was fast changing to
anxiety on his account. On all the benches
the spectators bent forward motionless, except
as their faces turned following the contestants.
Ilderim quitted combing his beard, and Esther
forgot her fears.

"A hundred sestertii on the Jew!" cried San-
ballat to the Romans under the consul's awning.

There was no reply.

"A talent—or five talents, or ten; choose ye!"

He shook his tablets at them defiantly.

" I will take thy sestertii," answered a Roman
youth, preparing to write.

" Do not so," interposed a friend.

" Why ?"

" Messala hath reached his utmost speed.
See him lean over his chariot-rim, the reins

loose as flying ribbons. Look then at the Jew."

The first one looked.

"By Hercules!" he replied, his countenance falling. "The dog throws all his weight on the bits. I see, I see! If the gods help not our friend, he will be run away with by the Israelite. No, not yet. Look! Jove with us, Jove with us!"

The cry, swelled by every Latin tongue, shook the velaria over the consul's head.

If it were true that Messala had attained his utmost speed, the effort was with effect; slowly but certainly he was beginning to forge ahead. His horses were running with their heads low down; from the balcony their bodies appeared actually to skim the earth; their nostrils showed blood-red in expansion; their eyes seemed straining in their sockets. Certainly the good steeds were doing their best! How long could they keep the pace? It was but the commencement of the sixth round. On they dashed. As they neared the second goal, Ben-Hur turned in behind the Roman's car.

The joy of the Messala faction reached its bound: they screamed and howled, and tossed their colors; and Sanballat filled his tablets with wagers of their tendering.

Malluch, in the lower gallery over the Gate of Triumph, found it hard to keep his cheer. He had cherished the vague hint dropped to him by Ben-Hur of something to happen in the turning of the western pillars. It was the fifth round, yet the something had not come;

and he had said to himself, the sixth will bring
it; but, lo! Ben - Hur was hardly holding a
place at the tail of his enemy's car.

Over in the east end, Simonides' party held
their peace. The merchant's head was bent
low. Ilderim tugged at his beard, and dropped
his brows till there was nothing of his eyes but
an occasional sparkle of light. Esther scarcely
breathed. Iras alone appeared glad.

Along the home-stretch—sixth round—Mes-
sala leading, next him Ben-Hur, and so close
it was the old story:

> "First flew Eumelus on Pheretian steeds;
> With those of Tros bold Diomed succeeds;
> Close on Eumelus' back they puff the wind,
> And seem just mounting on his car behind;
> Full on his neck he feels the sultry breeze,
> And, hovering o'er, their stretching shadow sees."

Thus to the first goal, and round it. Mes-
sala, fearful of losing his place, hugged the
stony wall with perilous clasp; a foot to the
left, and he had been dashed to pieces; yet,
when the turn was finished, no man, looking
at the wheel - tracks of the two cars, could
have said, here went Messala, there the Jew.
They left but one trace behind them.

As they whirled by, Esther saw Ben-Hur's
face again, and it was whiter than before.

Simonides, shrewder than Esther, said to Il-
derim, the moment the rivals turned into the
course, " I am no judge, good sheik, if Ben-Hur
be not about to execute some design. His face
hath that look."

577

To which Ilderim answered, "Saw you how clean they were and fresh? By the splendor of God, friend, they have not been running! But now watch!"

One ball and one dolphin remained on the entablatures; and all the people drew a long breath, for the beginning of the end was at hand.

First, the Sidonian gave the scourge to his four, and, smarting with fear and pain, they dashed desperately forward, promising for a brief time to go to the front. The effort ended in promise. Next, the Byzantine and Corinthian each made the trial with like result, after which they were practically out of the race. Thereupon, with a readiness perfectly explicable, all the factions except the Romans joined hope in Ben-Hur, and openly indulged their feeling.

"Ben-Hur! Ben-Hur!" they shouted, and the blended voices of the many rolled overwhelmingly against the consular stand.

From the benches above him as he passed, the favor descended in fierce injunctions.

"Speed thee, Jew!"

"Take the wall now!"

"On! loose the Arabs! Give them rein and scourge!"

"Let him not have the turn on thee again. Now or never!"

Over the balustrade they stooped low, stretching their hands imploringly to him.

Either he did not hear, or could not do better, for half-way round the course and he was

still following; at the second goal even still no change!

And now, to make the turn, Messala began to draw in his left-hand steeds, an act which necessarily slackened their speed. His spirit was high; more than one altar was richer of his vows; the Roman genius was still president. On the three pillars only six hundred feet away were fame, increase of fortune, promotions, and a triumph ineffably sweetened by hate, all in store for him! That moment Malluch, in the gallery, saw Ben-Hur lean forward over his Arabs, and give them the reins. Out flew the many-folded lash in his hand; over the backs of the startled steeds it writhed and hissed, and hissed and writhed again and again; and though it fell not, there were both sting and menace in its quick report; and as the man passed thus from quiet to resistless action his face suffused, his eyes gleaming, along the reins he seemed to flash his will; and instantly not one, but the four as one, answered with a leap that landed them alongside the Roman's car. Messala, on the perilous edge of the goal, heard, but dared not look to see what the awakening portended. From the people he received no sign. Above the noises of the race there was but one voice, and that was Ben-Hur's. In the old Aramaic, as the sheik himself, he called to the Arabs,

"On, Atair! On, Rigel! What, Antares! dost thou linger now? Good horse—oho, Aldebaran! I hear them singing in the tents. I hear the children singing and the women—

singing of the stars, of Atair, Antares, Rigel, Aldebaran, victory!—and the song will never end. Well done! Home to-morrow, under the black tent—home! On, Antares! The tribe is waiting for us, and the master is waiting! 'Tis done! 'tis done! Ha, ha! We have overthrown the proud. The hand that smote us is in the dust. Ours the glory! Ha, ha!—steady! The work is done—soho! Rest!"

There had never been anything of the kind more simple; seldom anything so instantaneous.

At the moment chosen for the dash, Messala was moving in a circle round the goal. To pass him, Ben-Hur had to cross the track, and good strategy required the movement to be in a forward direction; that is, on a like circle limited to the least possible increase. The thousands on the benches understood it all: they saw the signal given—the magnificent response; the four close outside Messala's outer wheel, Ben-Hur's inner wheel behind the other's car—all this they saw. Then they heard a crash loud enough to send a thrill through the Circus, and, quicker than thought, out over the course a spray of shining white and yellow flinders flew. Down on its right side toppled the bed of the Roman's chariot. There was a rebound as of the axle hitting the hard earth; another and another; then the car went to pieces; and Messala, entangled in the reins, pitched forward headlong.

To increase the horror of the sight by making death certain, the Sidonian, who had the

wall next behind, could not stop or turn out. Into the wreck full speed he drove; then over the Roman, and into the latter's four, all mad with fear. Presently, out of the turmoil, the fighting of horses, the resound of blows, the murky cloud of dust and sand, he crawled, in time to see the Corinthian and Byzantine go on down the course after Ben-Hur, who had not been an instant delayed.

The people arose, and leaped upon the benches, and shouted and screamed. Those who looked that way caught glimpses of Messala, now under the trampling of the fours, now under the abandoned cars. He was still, they thought him dead; but far the greater number followed Ben-Hur in his career. They had not seen the cunning touch of the reins by which, turning a little to the left, he caught Messala's wheel with the iron-shod point of his axle, and crushed it; but they had seen the transformation of the man, and themselves felt the heat and glow of his spirit, the heroic resolution, the maddening energy of action with which, by look, word, and gesture, he so suddenly inspired his Arabs. And such running! It was rather the long leaping of lions in harness; but for the lumbering chariot, it seemed the four were flying. When the Byzantine and Corinthian were half-way down the course, Ben-Hur turned the first goal.

And the race was WON!

The consul arose; the people shouted themselves hoarse; the editor came down from his seat, and crowned the victors.

The fortunate man among the boxers was a low-browed, yellow-haired Saxon, of such brutalized face as to attract a second look from Ben-Hur, who recognized a teacher with whom he himself had been a favorite at Rome. From him the young Jew looked up and beheld Simonides and his party on the balcony. They waved their hands to him. Esther kept her seat; but Iras arose, and gave him a smile and a wave of her fan—favors not the less intoxicating to him because we know, O reader, they would have fallen to Messala had he been the victor.

The procession was then formed, and, midst the shouting of the multitude which had had its will, passed out of the Gate of Triumph.

And the day was over.

CHAPTER XV

THE INVITATION OF IRAS

EN-HUR tarried across the river with Ilderim; for at midnight, as previously determined, they would take the road which the caravan, then thirty hours out, had pursued.

The sheik was happy; his offers of gifts had been royal; but Ben-Hur had refused everything, insisting that he was satisfied with the humiliation of his enemy. The generous dispute was long continued.

"Think," the sheik would say, "what thou hast done for me. In every black tent down

to the Akaba and to the ocean, and across to the Euphrates, and beyond to the sea of the Scythians, the renown of my Mira and her children will go; and they who sing of them will magnify me, and forget that I am in the wane of life; and all the spears now masterless will come to me, and my sword-hands multiply past counting. Thou dost not know what it is to have sway of the Desert such as will now be mine. I tell thee it will bring tribute incalculable from commerce, and immunity from kings. Aye, by the sword of Solomon! doth my messenger seek favor for me of Cæsar, that will he get. Yet nothing—nothing?"

And Ben-Hur would answer,

"Nay, sheik, have I not thy hand and heart? Let thy increase of power and influence inure to the King who comes. Who shall say it was not allowed thee for him? In the work I am going to, I may have great need. Saying no now will leave me to ask of thee with better grace hereafter."

In the midst of a controversy of the kind, two messengers arrived—Malluch and one unknown. The former was admitted first.

The good fellow did not attempt to hide his joy over the event of the day.

"But, coming to that with which I am charged," he said, "the master Simonides sends me to say that, upon the adjournment of the games, some of the Roman faction made haste to protest against payment of the money prize."

Ilderim started up, crying, in his shrillest tones,

"By the splendor of God! the East shall decide whether the race was fairly won."

"Nay, good sheik," said Malluch, "the editor has paid the money."

"'Tis well."

"When they said Ben-Hur struck Messala's wheel, the editor laughed, and reminded them of the blow the Arabs had at the turn of the goal."

"And what of the Athenian?"

"He is dead."

"Dead!" cried Ben-Hur.

"Dead!" echoed Ilderim. "What fortune these Roman monsters have! Messala escaped?"

"Escaped — yes, O sheik, with life; but it shall be a burden to him. The physicians say he will live, but never walk again."

Ben-Hur looked silently up to heaven. He had a vision of Messala, chair-bound like Simonides, and, like him, going abroad on the shoulders of servants. The good man had abode well; but what would this one with his pride and ambition?

"Simonides bade me say, further," Malluch continued, "Sanballat is having trouble. Drusus, and those who signed with him, referred the question of paying the five talents they lost to the Consul Maxentius, and he has referred it to Cæsar. Messala also refused his losses, and Sanballat, in imitation of Drusus, went to the consul, where the matter is still in advisement. The better Romans say the protestants shall not be excused; and all the adverse fac-

tions join with them. The city rings with the scandal."

"What says Simonides?" asked Ben-Hur.

"The master laughs, and is well pleased. If the Roman pays, he is ruined; if he refuses to pay, he is dishonored. The imperial policy will decide the matter. To offend the East would be a bad beginning with the Parthians; to offend Sheik Ilderim would be to antagonize the Desert, over which lie all Maxentius's lines of operation. Wherefore Simonides bade me tell you to have no disquiet; Messala will pay."

Ilderim was at once restored to his good-humor.

"Let us be off now," he said, rubbing his hands. "The business will do well with Simonides. The glory is ours. I will order the horses."

"Stay," said Malluch. "I left a messenger outside. Will you see him?"

"By the splendor of God! I forgot him."

Malluch retired, and was succeeded by a lad of gentle manners and delicate appearance, who knelt upon one knee, and said, winningly, "Iras, the daughter of Balthasar, well known to good Sheik Ilderim, hath intrusted me with a message to the sheik, who, she saith, will do her great favor so he receive her congratulations on account of the victory of his four."

"The daughter of my friend is kind," said Ilderim, with sparkling eyes. "Do thou give her this jewel, in sign of the pleasure I have from her message."

He took a ring from his finger as he spoke.

"I will as thou sayest, O sheik," the lad replied, and continued, "The daughter of the Egyptian charged me further. She prays the good Sheik Ilderim to send word to the youth Ben-Hur that her father hath taken residence for a time in the palace of Idernee, where she will receive the youth after the fourth hour to-morrow. And if, with her congratulations, Sheik Ilderim will accept her gratitude for this other favor done, she will be ever so pleased."

The sheik looked at Ben-Hur, whose face was suffused with pleasure.

"What will you?" he asked.

"By your leave, O sheik, I will see the fair Egyptian."

Ilderim laughed, and said, "Shall not a man enjoy his youth?"

Then Ben-Hur answered the messenger.

"Say to her who sent you that I, Ben-Hur, will see her at the palace of Idernee, wherever that may be, to-morrow at noon."

The lad arose, and, with silent salute, departed.

At midnight Ilderim took the road, having arranged to leave a horse and a guide for Ben-Hur, who was to follow him.

CHAPTER XVI

IN THE PALACE OF IDERNEE

GOING next day to fill his appointment with Iras, Ben-Hur turned from the Omphalus, which was in the heart of the city, into the Colonnade of Herod, and came shortly to the palace of Idernee.

From the street he passed first into a vestibule, on the sides of which were stair-ways under cover, leading up to a portico. Winged lions sat by the stairs; in the middle there was a gigantic ibis spouting water over the floor; the lions, ibis, wall, and floor were reminders of the Egyptians: everything, even the balustrading of the stairs, was of massive gray stone.

Above the vestibule, and covering the landing of the steps, arose the portico, a pillared grace, so light, so exquisitely proportioned, it was at that period hardly possible of conception except by a Greek. Of marble snowy white, its effect was that of a lily dropped carelessly upon a great bare rock.

Ben-Hur paused in the shade of the portico to admire its tracery and finish, and the purity of its marble; then he passed on into the palace. Ample folding-doors stood open to receive him. The passage into which he first entered was high, but somewhat narrow; red tiling formed the floor, and the walls were

tinted to correspond. Yet this plainness was a warning of something beautiful to come.

He moved on slowly, all his faculties in repose. Presently he would be in the presence of Iras; she was waiting for him; waiting with song and story and badinage, sparkling, fanciful, capricious—with smiles which glorified her glance, and glances which lent voluptuous suggestion to her whisper. She had sent for him the evening of the boat-ride on the lake in the Orchard of Palms; she had sent for him now; and he was going to her in the beautiful palace of Idernee. He was happy and dreamful rather than thoughtless.

The passage brought him to a closed door, in front of which he paused; and, as he did so, the broad leaves began to open of themselves, without creak or sound of lock or latch, or touch of foot or finger. The singularity was lost in the view that broke upon him.

Standing in the shade of the dull passage, and looking through the door-way, he beheld the atrium of a Roman house, roomy and rich to a fabulous degree of magnificence.

How large the chamber was cannot be stated, because of the deceit there is in exact proportions; its depth was vista-like, something never to be said of an equal interior. When he stopped to make survey, and looked down upon the floor, he was standing upon the breast of a Leda, represented as caressing a swan; and, looking farther, he saw the whole floor was similarly laid in mosaic pictures of mythological subjects. And there were stools and

chairs, each a separate design, and a work of
art exquisitely composed, and tables much
carven, and here and there couches which were
invitations of themselves. The articles of fur-
niture, which stood out from the walls, were
duplicated on the floor distinctly as if they
floated upon unrippled water; even the pan-
elling of the walls, the figures upon them in
painting and bass-relief, and the fresco of the
ceiling were reflected on the floor. The ceil-
ing curved up towards the centre, where there
was an opening through which the sunlight
poured without hinderance, and the sky, ever
so blue, seemed in hand-reach; the impluvium
under the opening was guarded by bronzed
rails; the gilded pillars supporting the roof at
the edges of the opening shone like flame
where the sun struck them, and their reflec-
tions beneath seemed to stretch to infinite
depth. And there were candelabra quaint and
curious, and statuary and vases; the whole
making an interior that would have befitted
well the house on the Palatine Hill which Cic-
ero bought of Crassus, or that other, yet more
famous for extravagance, the Tusculan villa of
Scaurus.

Still in his dreamful mood, Ben-Hur saun-
tered about, charmed by all he beheld, and
waiting. He did not mind a little delay; when
Iras was ready, she would come or send a serv-
ant. In every well-regulated Roman house
the atrium was the reception chamber for vis-
itors.

Twice, thrice, he made the round. As often

he stood under the opening in the roof, and pondered the sky and its azure depth; then, leaning against a pillar, he studied the distribution of light and shade and its effects; here a veil diminishing objects, there a brilliance exaggerating others; yet nobody came. Time, or rather the passage of time, began at length to impress itself upon him, and he wondered why Iras stayed so long. Again he traced out the figures upon the floor, but not with the satisfaction the first inspection gave him. He paused often to listen: directly impatience blew a little fevered breath upon his spirit; next time it blew stronger and hotter; and at last he woke to a consciousness of the silence which held the house in thrall, and the thought of it made him uneasy and distrustful. Still he put the feeling off with a smile and a promise. "Oh, she is giving the last touch to her eyelids, or she is arranging a chaplet for me; she will come presently, more beautiful of the delay!" He sat down then to admire a candelabrum—a bronze plinth on rollers, filigree on the sides and edges; the post at one end, and on the end opposite it an altar and a female celebrant; the lamp-rests swinging by delicate chains from the extremities of drooping palm-branches; altogether a wonder in its way. But the silence would obtrude itself: he listened even as he looked at the pretty object—he listened, but there was not a sound; the palace was still as a tomb.

There might be a mistake. No, the messenger had come from the Egyptian, and this was

the palace of Idernee. Then he remembered
how mysteriously the door had opened, so
soundlessly, so of itself. He would see!

He went to the same door. Though he
walked ever so lightly, the sound of his step-
ping was loud and harsh, and he shrank from
it. He was getting nervous. The cumbrous
Roman lock resisted his first effort to raise it;
and the second—the blood chilled in his cheeks
—he wrenched with all his might: in vain—
the door was not even shaken. A sense of
danger seized him, and for a moment he stood
irresolute.

Who in Antioch had the motive to do him
harm?

Messala!

And this palace of Idernee? He had seen
Egypt in the vestibule, Athens in the snowy
portico; but here, in the atrium, was Rome;
everything about him betrayed Roman owner-
ship. True, the site was on the great thorough-
fare of the city, a very public place in which to
do him violence; but for that reason it was
more accordant with the audacious genius of
his enemy. The atrium underwent a change;
with all its elegance and beauty, it was no more
than a trap. Apprehension always paints in
black.

The idea irritated Ben-Hur.

There were many doors on the right and left
of the atrium, leading, doubtless, to sleeping-
chambers; he tried them, but they were all
firmly fastened. Knocking might bring re-
sponse. Ashamed to make outcry, he betook

himself to a couch, and, lying down, tried to reflect.

All too plainly he was a prisoner; but for what purpose? and by whom?

If the work were Messala's! He sat up, looked about, and smiled defiantly. There were weapons in every table. But birds had been starved in golden cages; not so would he— the couches would serve him as battering-rams; and he was strong, and there was such increase of might in rage and despair!

Messala himself could not come. He would never walk again; he was a cripple like Simonides; still he could move others. And where were there not others to be moved by him? Ben-Hur arose, and tried the doors again. Once he called out; the room echoed so that he was startled. With such calmness as he could assume, he made up his mind to wait a time before attempting to break a way out.

In such a situation the mind has its ebb and flow of disquiet, with intervals of peace between. At length—how long, though, he could not have said—he came to the conclusion that the affair was an accident or mistake. The palace certainly belonged to somebody; it must have care and keeping: and the keeper would come; the evening or the night would bring him. Patience!

So concluding, he waited.

Half an hour passed—a much longer period to Ben-Hur—when the door which had admitted him opened and closed noiselessly as before, and without attracting his attention.

The moment of the occurrence he was sitting at the farther end of the room. A footstep startled him.

"At last she has come!" he thought, with a throb of relief and pleasure, and arose.

The step was heavy, and accompanied with the gride and clang of coarse sandals. The gilded pillars were between him and the door; he advanced quietly, and leaned against one of them. Presently he heard voices—the voices of men—one of them rough and guttural. What was said he could not understand, as the language was not of the East or South of Europe.

After a general survey of the room the strangers crossed to their left, and were brought into Ben-Hur's view—two men, one very stout, both tall, and both in short tunics. They had not the air of masters of the house or domestics. Everything they saw appeared wonderful to them; everything they stopped to examine they touched. They were vulgarians. The atrium seemed profaned by their presence. At the same time their leisurely manner and the assurance with which they proceeded pointed to some right or business; if business, with whom?

With much jargon they sauntered this way and that, all the time gradually approaching the pillar by which Ben-Hur was standing. Off a little way, where a slanted gleam of the sun fell with a glare upon the mosaic of the floor, there was a statue which attracted their notice. In examining it they stopped in the light.

The mystery surrounding his own presence in

the palace tended, as we have seen, to make Ben-Hur nervous; so now, when in the tall, stout stranger he recognized the Northman whom he had known in Rome, and seen crowned only the day before in the Circus as the winning pugilist; when he saw the man's face, scarred with the wounds of many battles, and imbruted by ferocious passions; when he surveyed the fellow's naked limbs, very marvels of exercise and training, and his shoulders of Herculean breadth, a thought of personal danger started a chill along every vein. A sure instinct warned him that the opportunity for murder was too perfect to have come by chance; and here now were the myrmidons, and their business was with him. He turned an anxious eye upon the Northman's comrade — young, black-eyed, black-haired, and altogether Jewish in appearance; he observed, also, that both the men were in costume exactly such as professionals of their class were in the habit of wearing in the arena. Putting the several circumstances together, Ben-Hur could not be longer in doubt: he had been lured into the palace with design. Out of reach of aid, in this splendid privacy, he was to die!

At a loss what to do, he gazed from man to man, while there was enacted within him that miracle of mind by which life is passed before us in awful detail, to be looked at by ourselves as if it were another's; and from the evolvement, from a hidden depth, cast up, as it were, by a hidden hand, he was given to see that he had entered upon a new life, different from the

594

old one in this: whereas, in that, he had been the victim of violences done to him, henceforth he was to be the aggressor. Only yesterday he had found his first victim! To the purely Christian nature the presentation would have brought the weakness of remorse. Not so with Ben-Hur; his spirit had its emotions from the teachings of the first law-giver, not the last and greatest one. He had dealt punishment, not wrong, to Messala. By permission of the Lord, he had triumphed; and he derived faith from the circumstance—faith the source of all rational strength, especially strength in peril.

Nor did the influence stop there. The new life was made appear to him a mission just begun, and holy as the King to come was holy, and certain as the coming of the King was certain—a mission in which force was lawful if only because it was unavoidable. Should he, on the very threshold of such an errand, be afraid?

He undid the sash around his waist, and, baring his head and casting off his white Jewish gown, stood forth in an undertunic not unlike those of the enemy, and was ready, body and mind. Folding his arms, he placed his back against the pillar, and calmly waited.

The examination of the statue was brief. Directly the Northman turned, and said something in the unknown tongue; then both looked at Ben-Hur. A few more words, and they advanced towards him.

"Who are you?" he asked in Latin.

The Northman fetched a smile which did

not relieve his face of its brutalism, and answered,

"Barbarians."

"This is the palace of Idernee. Whom seek you? Stand and answer."

The words were spoken with earnestness. The strangers stopped; and in his turn the Northman asked, "Who are you?"

"A Roman."

The giant laid his head back upon his shoulders.

"Ha, ha, ha! I have heard how a god once came from a cow licking a salted stone; but not even a god can make a Roman of a Jew."

The laugh over, he spoke to his companion again, and they moved nearer.

"Hold!" said Ben-Hur, quitting the pillar. "One word."

They stopped again.

"A word!" replied the Saxon, folding his immense arms across his breast, and relaxing the menace beginning to blacken his face. "A word! Speak."

"You are Thord the Northman."

The giant opened his blue eyes.

"You were lanista in Rome."

Thord nodded.

"I was your scholar."

"No," said Thord, shaking his head. "By the beard of Irmin, I had never a Jew to make a fighting-man of."

"But I will prove my saying."

"How?"

"You came here to kill me."

596

"That is true."

"Then let this man fight me singly, and I will make the proof on his body."

A gleam of humor shone in the Northman's face. He spoke to his companion, who made answer; then he replied with the naïveté of a diverted child,

"Wait till I say begin."

By repeated touches of his foot, he pushed a couch out on the floor, and proceeded leisurely to stretch his burly form upon it; when perfectly at ease, he said, simply, "Now begin."

Without ado, Ben-Hur walked to his antagonist.

"Defend thyself," he said.

The man, nothing loath, put up his hands.

As the two thus confronted each other in approved position, there was no discernible inequality between them; on the contrary, they were as like as brothers. To the stranger's confident smile, Ben-Hur opposed an earnestness which, had his skill been known, would have been accepted fair warning of danger. Both knew the combat was to be mortal.

Ben-Hur feinted with his right hand. The stranger warded, slightly advancing his left arm. Ere he could return to guard, Ben-Hur caught him by the wrist in a grip which years at the oar had made terrible as a vice. The surprise was complete, and no time given. To throw himself forward; to push the arm across the man's throat and over his right shoulder, and turn him left side front; to strike surely with the ready left hand; to strike the bare

neck under the ear—were but petty divisions of the same act. No need of a second blow. The myrmidon fell heavily, and without a cry, and lay still.

Ben-Hur turned to Thord.

"Ha! What! By the beard of Irmin!" the latter cried, in astonishment, rising to a sitting posture. Then he laughed.

"Ha, ha, ha! I could not have done it better myself."

He viewed Ben-Hur coolly from head to foot, and, rising, faced him with undisguised admiration.

"It was my trick—the trick I have practised for ten years in the schools of Rome. You are not a Jew. Who are you?"

"You knew Arrius the duumvir?"

"Quintus Arrius? Yes, he was my patron."

"He had a son."

"Yes," said Thord, his battered features lighting dully. "I knew the boy; he would have made a king gladiator. Cæsar offered him his patronage. I taught him the very trick you played on this one here—a trick impossible except to a hand and arm like mine. It has won me many a crown."

"I am that son of Arrius."

Thord drew nearer, and viewed him carefully; then his eyes brightened with genuine pleasure, and, laughing, he held out his hand.

"Ha, ha, ha! He told me I would find a Jew here—a Jew—a dog of a Jew—killing whom was serving the gods."

CEDARS OF LEBANON

"Who told you so?" asked Ben-Hur, taking the hand.

"He—Messala—ha, ha, ha!"

"When, Thord?"

"Last night."

"I thought he was hurt."

"He will never walk again. On his bed he told me between groans."

A very vivid portrayal of hate in a few words; and Ben-Hur saw that the Roman, if he lived, would still be capable and dangerous, and follow him unrelentingly. Revenge remained to sweeten the ruined life ; therefore the clinging to fortune lost in the wager with Sanballat. Ben-Hur ran the ground over, with a distinct foresight of the many ways in which it would be possible for his enemy to interfere with him in the work he had undertaken for the King who was coming. Why not he resort to the Roman's methods. The man hired to kill him could be hired to strike back. It was in his power to offer higher wages. The temptation was strong ; and, half yielding, he chanced to look down at his late antagonist lying still, with white upturned face, so like himself. A light came to him, and he asked, " Thord, what was Messala to give you for killing me?"

"A thousand sestertii."

"You shall have them yet ; and so you do now what I tell you, I will add three thousand more to the sum."

The giant reflected aloud.

"I won five thousand yesterday ; from the Roman one—six. Give me four, good Arrius

—four more—and I will stand firm for you, though old Thor, my namesake, strike me with his hammer. Make it four, and I will kill the lying patrician, if you say so. I have only to cover his mouth with my hand—thus."

He illustrated the process by clapping his hand over his own mouth.

"I see," said Ben-Hur; "ten thousand sestertii is a fortune. It will enable you to return to Rome, and open a wine-shop near the Great Circus, and live as becomes the first of the lanistæ."

The very scars on the giant's face glowed afresh with the pleasure the picture gave him.

"I will make it four thousand," Ben-Hur continued; "and in what you shall do for the money there will be no blood on your hands, Thord. Hear me now. Did not your friend here look like me?"

"I would have said he was an apple from the same tree."

"Well, if I put on his tunic, and dress him in these clothes of mine, and you and I go away together, leaving him here, can you not get your sestertii from Messala all the same? You have only to make him believe it me that is dead."

Thord laughed till the tears ran into his mouth.

"Ha, ha, ha! Ten thousand sestertii were never won so easily. And a wine-shop by the Great Circus!—all for a lie without blood in it! Ha, ha, ha! Give me thy hand, O son of Arrius. Get on now, and—ha, ha, ha!—if ever you come to Rome, fail not to ask for the wine-

shop of Thord the Northman. By the beard
of Irmin, I will give you the best, though I bor-
row it from Cæsar!"

They shook hands again; after which the
exchange of clothes was effected. It was ar-
ranged then that a messenger should go at
night to Thord's lodging-place with the four
thousand sestertii. When they were done, the
giant knocked at the front door; it opened to
him; and, passing out of the atrium, he led
Ben-Hur into a room adjoining, where the lat-
ter completed his attire from the coarse gar-
ments of the dead pugilist. They separated
directly in the Omphalus.

"Fail not, O son of Arrius, fail not the wine-
shop near the Great Circus! Ha, ha, ha! By
the beard of Irmin, there was never fortune
gained so cheap. The gods keep you!"

Upon leaving the atrium, Ben-Hur gave a
last look at the myrmidon as he lay in the Jew-
ish vestments, and was satisfied. The likeness
was striking. If Thord kept faith, the cheat
was a secret to endure forever.

· · · · · · · ·

At night, in the house of Simonides, Ben-
Hur told the good man all that had taken
place in the palace of Idernee; and it was
agreed that, after a few days, public inquiry
should be set afloat for the discovery of the
whereabouts of the son of Arrius. Eventually
the matter was to be carried boldly to Maxen-
tius; then, if the mystery came not out, it was
concluded that Messala and Gratus would be
at rest and happy, and Ben-Hur free to betake

himself to Jerusalem, to make search for his
lost people.

At the leave-taking, Simonides sat in his
chair out on the terrace overlooking the river,
and gave his farewell and the peace of the Lord
with the impressment of a father. Esther went
with the young man to the head of the steps.

"If I find my mother, Esther, thou shalt go
to her at Jerusalem, and be a sister to Tirzah."

And with the words he kissed her.

Was it only a kiss of peace?

He crossed the river next to the late quar-
ters of Ilderim, where he found the Arab who
was to serve him as guide. The horses were
brought out.

"This one is thine," said the Arab.

Ben-Hur looked, and, lo! it was Aldebaran,
the swiftest and brightest of the sons of Mira,
and, next to Sirius, the beloved of the sheik;
and he knew the old man's heart came to him
along with the gift.

The corpse in the atrium was taken up and
buried by night; and, as part of Messala's plan,
a courier was sent off to Gratus to make him
at rest by the announcement of Ben-Hur's
death—this time past question.

Ere long a wine-shop was opened near the
Circus Maximus, with inscription over the
door:

THORD THE NORTHMAN.

BOOK SIXTH

"*Is that a Death? and are there two?*
Is Death that woman's mate?

Her skin was white as leprosy,
The Nightmare Life-in-Death was she,
Who thicks man's blood with cold."

COLERIDGE.

CHAPTER I

THE TOWER OF ANTONIA—CELL NO. VI

UR story moves forward now thirty days from the night Ben-Hur left Antioch to go out with Sheik Ilderim into the desert.

A great change has befallen—great, at least, as respects the fortunes of our hero. Valerius Gratus has been succeeded by Pontius Pilate!

The removal, it may be remarked, cost Simonides exactly five talents Roman money in hand paid to Sejanus, who was then in height of power as imperial favorite ; the object being to help Ben-Hur, by lessening his exposure while in and about Jerusalem attempting discovery of his people. To such pious use the faithful servant put the winnings from Drusus and his associates ; all of whom, having paid their wagers, became at once and naturally the enemies of Messala, whose repudiation was yet an unsettled question in Rome.

Brief as the time was, already the Jews knew the change of rulers was not for the better.

The cohorts sent to relieve the garrison of Antonia made their entry into the city by night ; next morning the first sight that greeted the people resident in the neighborhood was the walls of the old Tower decorated with military ensigns, which unfortunately consisted of

busts of the emperor mixed with eagles and globes. A multitude, in passion, marched to Cæsarea, where Pilate was lingering, and implored him to remove the detested images. Five days and nights they beset his palace gates; at last he appointed a meeting with them in the Circus. When they were assembled, he encircled them with soldiers; instead of resisting, they offered him their lives, and conquered. He recalled the images and ensigns to Cæsarea, where Gratus, with more consideration, had kept such abominations housed during the eleven years of his reign.

The worst of men do once in a while vary their wickednesses by good acts; so with Pilate. He ordered an inspection of all the prisons in Judea, and a return of the names of the persons in custody, with a statement of the crimes for which they had been committed. Doubtless the motive was the one so common with officials just installed—dread of entailed responsibility; the people, however, in thought of the good which might come of the measure, gave him credit, and, for a period, were comforted. The revelations were astonishing. Hundreds of persons were released against whom there were no accusations; many others came to light who had long been accounted dead; yet more amazing, there was opening of dungeons not merely unknown at the time by the people, but actually forgotten by the prison authorities. With one instance of the latter kind we have now to deal; and, strange to say, it occurred in Jerusalem.

The Tower of Antonia, which will be remembered as occupying two-thirds of the sacred area on Mount Moriah, was originally a castle built by the Macedonians. Afterwards, John Hyrcanus erected the castle into a fortress for the defence of the Temple, and in his day it was considered impregnable to assault; but when Herod came with his bolder genius, he strengthened its walls and extended them, leaving a vast pile which included every appurtenance necessary for the stronghold he intended it to be forever; such as offices, barracks, armories, magazines, cisterns, and last, though not least, prisons of all grades. He levelled the solid rock, and tapped it with deep excavations, and built over them; connecting the whole great mass with the Temple by a beautiful colonnade, from the roof of which one could look down over the courts of the sacred structure. In such condition the Tower fell at last out of his hands into those of the Romans, who were quick to see its strength and advantages, and convert it to uses becoming such masters. All through the administration of Gratus it had been a garrisoned citadel and underground prison terrible to revolutionists. Woe when the cohorts poured from its gates to suppress disorder! Woe not less when a Jew passed the same gates going in under arrest!

With this explanation we hasten to our story.

.

The order of the new procurator requiring a report of the persons in custody was received

at the Tower of Antonia, and promptly execut-
ed ; and two days have gone since the last un-
fortunate was brought up for examination. The
tabulated statement, ready for forwarding, lies
on the table of the tribune in command ; in
five minutes more it will be on the way to
Pilate, sojourning in the palace up on Mount
Zion.

The tribune's office is spacious and cool, and
furnished in a style suitable to the dignity of
the commandant of a post in every respect so
important. Looking in upon him about the
seventh hour of the day, the officer appears
weary and impatient; when the report is de-
spatched, he will to the roof of the colonnade
for air and exercise, and the amusement to be
had watching the Jews over in the courts of
the Temple. His subordinates and clerks share
his impatience.

In the spell of waiting a man appeared in a
door-way leading to an adjoining apartment.
He rattled a bunch of keys, each heavy as a
hammer, and at once attracted the chief's at-
tention.

"Ah, Gesius! come in," the tribune said.

As the new-comer approached the table be-
hind which the chief sat in an easy-chair, every-
body present looked at him, and, observing a
certain expression of alarm and mortification
on his face, became silent that they might hear
what he had to say.

"O tribune!" he began, bending low, "I fear
to tell what now I bring you."

"Another mistake—ha, Gesius?"

"If I could persuade myself it is but a mistake, I would not be afraid."

"A crime then—or, worse, a breach of duty. Thou mayst laugh at Cæsar, or curse the gods, and live; but if the offence be to the eagles—ah, thou knowest, Gesius—go on!"

"It is now about eight years since Valerius Gratus selected me to be keeper of prisoners here in the Tower," said the man, deliberately. "I remember the morning I entered upon the duties of my office. There had been a riot the day before, and fighting in the streets. We slew many Jews, and suffered on our side. The affair came, it was said, of an attempt to assassinate Gratus, who had been knocked from his horse by a tile thrown from a roof. I found him sitting where you now sit, O tribune, his head swathed in bandages. He told me of my selection, and gave me these keys, numbered to correspond with the numbers of the cells; they were the badges of my office, he said, and not to be parted with. There was a roll of parchment on the table. Calling me to him, he opened the roll. 'Here are maps of the cells,' said he. There were three of them. 'This one,' he went on, 'shows the arrangement of the upper floor; this second one gives you the second floor; and this last is of the lower floor. I give them to you in trust.' I took them from his hand, and he said, further, 'Now you have the keys and the maps; go immediately, and acquaint yourself with the whole arrangement; visit each cell, and see to its condition. When anything is needed for the se-

curity of a prisoner, order it according to your judgment, for you are the master under me, and no other.'

"I saluted him, and turned to go away; he called me back. 'Ah, I forgot,' he said. 'Give me the map of the third floor.' I gave it to him, and he spread it upon the table. 'Here, Gesius,' he said, 'see this cell.' He laid his finger on the one numbered V. 'There are three men confined in that cell, desperate characters, who by some means got hold of a state secret, and suffer for their curiosity, which'—he looked at me severely—'in such matters is worse than a crime. Accordingly, they are blind and tongueless, and are placed there for life. They shall have nothing but food and drink, to be given them through a hole, which you will find in the wall covered by a slide. Do you hear, Gesius?' I made him answer. 'It is well,' he continued. 'One thing more which you shall not forget, or'—he looked at me threateningly— 'The door of their cell—cell Number V. on the same floor—this one, Gesius' —he put his finger on the particular cell to impress my memory—'shall never be opened for any purpose, neither to let one in nor out, not even yourself.' 'But if they die?' I asked. 'If they die,' he said, 'the cell shall be their tomb. They were put there to die, and be lost. The cell is leprous. Do you understand?' With that he let me go."

Gesius stopped, and from the breast of his tunic drew three parchments, all much yellowed by time and use; selecting one of them, he

spread it upon the table before the tribune, saying, simply, " This is the lower floor."

The whole company looked at

		Passage.		
V	IV	III	II	I

" This is exactly, O tribune, as I had it from Gratus. See, there is cell Number V.," said Gesius.

" I see," the tribune replied. " Go on now. The cell was leprous, he said."

" I would like to ask you a question," remarked the keeper, modestly.

The tribune assented.

" Had I not a right, under the circumstances, to believe the map a true one?"

" What else couldst thou?"

" Well, it is not a true one."

The chief looked up surprised.

" It is not a true one," the keeper repeated.

" It shows but five cells upon that floor, while there are six."

" Six, sayest thou?"

" I will show you the floor as it is—or as I believe it to be."

Upon a page of his tablets Gesius drew the following diagram, and gave it to the tribune:

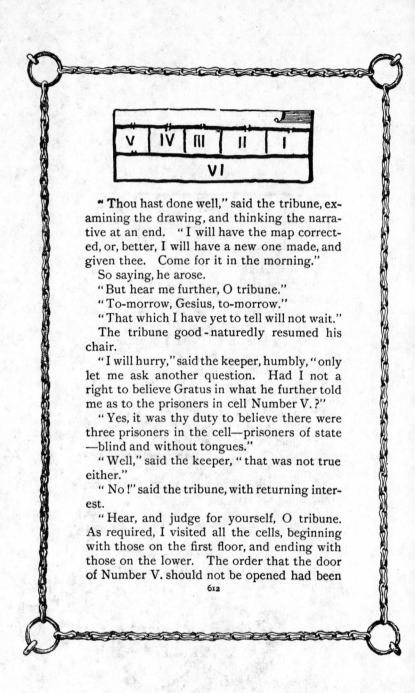

"Thou hast done well," said the tribune, examining the drawing, and thinking the narrative at an end. "I will have the map corrected, or, better, I will have a new one made, and given thee. Come for it in the morning."

So saying, he arose.

"But hear me further, O tribune."

"To-morrow, Gesius, to-morrow."

"That which I have yet to tell will not wait."

The tribune good-naturedly resumed his chair.

"I will hurry," said the keeper, humbly, "only let me ask another question. Had I not a right to believe Gratus in what he further told me as to the prisoners in cell Number V.?"

"Yes, it was thy duty to believe there were three prisoners in the cell—prisoners of state —blind and without tongues."

"Well," said the keeper, "that was not true either."

"No!" said the tribune, with returning interest.

"Hear, and judge for yourself, O tribune. As required, I visited all the cells, beginning with those on the first floor, and ending with those on the lower. The order that the door of Number V. should not be opened had been

respected; through all the eight years food and drink for three men had been passed through a hole in the wall. I went to the door yesterday, curious to see the wretches who, against all expectation, had lived so long. The locks refused the key. We pulled a little, and the door fell down, rusted from its hinges. Going in, I found but one man, old, blind, tongueless, and naked. His hair dropped in stiffened mats below his waist. His skin was like the parchment there. He held his hands out, and the finger-nails curled and twisted like the claws of a bird. I asked him where his companions were. He shook his head in denial. Thinking to find the others, we searched the cell. The floor was dry; so were the walls. If three men had been shut in there, and two of them had died, at least their bones would have endured."

"Wherefore thou thinkest—"

"I think, O tribune, there has been but one prisoner there in the eight years."

The chief regarded the keeper sharply, and said, "Have a care; thou art more than saying Valerius lied."

Gesius bowed, but said, "He might have been mistaken."

"No, he was right," said the tribune, warmly. "By thine own statement he was right. Didst thou not say but now that for eight years food and drink had been furnished three men?"

The by-standers approved the shrewdness of their chief; yet Gesius did not seem discomfited.

"You have but half the story, O tribune. When you have it all, you will agree with me. You know what I did with the man: that I sent him to the bath, and had him shorn and clothed, and then took him to the gate of the Tower, and bade him go free. I washed my hands of him. To-day he came back and was brought to me. By signs and tears he at last made me understand he wished to return to his cell, and I so ordered. As they were leading him off, he broke away and kissed my feet, and, by piteous dumb imploration, insisted I should go with him; and I went. The mystery of the three men stayed in my mind. I was not satisfied about it. Now I am glad I yielded to his entreaty."

The whole company at this point became very still.

"When we were in the cell again, and the prisoner knew it, he caught my hand eagerly, and led me to a hole like that through which we were accustomed to pass him his food. Though large enough to push your helmet through, it escaped me yesterday. Still holding my hand, he put his face to the hole and gave a beast-like cry. A sound came faintly back. I was astonished, and drew him away, and called out, 'Ho, here!' At first there was no answer. I called again, and received back these words, 'Be thou praised, O Lord!' Yet more astonishing, O tribune, the voice was a woman's. And I asked, 'Who are you?' and had reply, 'A woman of Israel, entombed here with her daughter. Help us quickly, or we die.'

I told them to be of cheer, and hurried here
to know your will."

The tribune arose hastily.

"Thou wert right, Gesius," he said, "and I
see now. The map was a lie, and so was the
tale of the three men. There have been better
Romans than Valerius Gratus."

"Yes," said the keeper. "I gleaned from the
prisoner that he had regularly given the women
of the food and drink he had received."

"It is accounted for," replied the tribune,
and observing the countenances of his friends,
and reflecting how well it would be to have
witnesses, he added, "Let us rescue the women.
Come all."

Gesius was pleased.

"We will have to pierce the wall," he said.
"I found where a door had been, but it was fill-
ed solidly with stones and mortar."

The tribune stayed to say to a clerk, "Send
workmen after me with tools. Make haste;
but hold the report, for I see it will have to be
corrected."

In a short time they were gone.

CHAPTER II
THE LEPERS

WOMAN of Israel, entombed here with her daughter. Help us quickly, or we die."

Such was the reply Gesius, the keeper, had from the cell which appears on his amended map as VI. The reader, when he observed the answer, knew who the unfortunates were, and, doubtless, said to himself, "At last the mother of Ben-Hur, and Tirzah, his sister!"

And so it was.

The morning of their seizure, eight years before, they had been carried to the Tower, where Gratus proposed to put them out of the way. He had chosen the Tower for the purpose as more immediately in his own keeping, and Cell VI. because, first, it could be better lost than any other; and, secondly, it was infected with leprosy; for these prisoners were not merely to be put in a safe place, but in a place to die. They were, accordingly, taken down by slaves in the night-time, when there were no witnesses of the deed; then, in completion of the savage task, the same slaves walled up the door, after which they were themselves separated, and sent away never to be heard of more. To save accusation, and, in the event of discovery, to leave himself such justification as might be allowed in a distinction between the

infliction of a punishment and the commission of a double murder, Gratus preferred sinking his victims where natural death was certain, though slow. That they might linger along, he selected a convict who had been made blind and tongueless, and sank him in the only connecting cell, there to serve them with food and drink. Under no circumstances could the poor wretch tell the tale or identify either the prisoners or their doomsman. So, with a cunning partly due to Messala, the Roman, under color of punishing a brood of assassins, smoothed a path to confiscation of the estate of the Hurs, of which no portion ever reached the imperial coffers.

As the last step in the scheme, Gratus summarily removed the old keeper of the prisons; not because he knew what had been done—for he did not—but because, knowing the underground floors as he did, it would be next to impossible to keep the transaction from him. Then, with masterly ingenuity, the procurator had new maps drawn for delivery to a new keeper, with the omission, as we have seen, of Cell VI. The instructions given the latter, taken with the omission on the map, accomplished the design—the cell and its unhappy tenants were all alike lost.

What may be thought of the life of the mother and daughter during the eight years must have relation to their culture and previous habits. Conditions are pleasant or grievous to us according to our sensibilities. It is not extreme to say, if there was a sudden exit of

all men from the world, heaven, as prefigured
in the Christian idea, would not be a heaven to
the majority ; on the other hand, neither would
all suffer equally in the so-called Tophet. Cul-
tivation has its balances. As the mind is made
intelligent, the capacity of the soul for pure en-
joyment is proportionally increased. Well,
therefore, if it be saved ! If lost, however, alas
that it ever had cultivation ! its capacity for en-
joyment in the one case is the measure of its
capacity to suffer in the other. Wherefore re-
pentance must be something more than mere
remorse for sins ; it comprehends a change of
nature befitting heaven.

We repeat, to form an adequate idea of the
suffering endured by the mother of Ben-Hur,
the reader must think of her spirit and its sen-
sibilities as much as, if not more than, of the
conditions of the immurement ; the question
being, not what the conditions were, but how
she was affected by them. And now we may
be permitted to say it was in anticipation of
this thought that the scene in the summer-
house on the roof of the family palace was
given so fully in the beginning of the Second
Book of our story. So, too, to be helpful when
the inquiry should come up, we ventured the
elaborate description of the palace of the Hurs.

In other words, let the serene, happy, luxu-
rious life in the princely house be recalled and
contrasted with this existence in the lower
dungeon of the Tower of Antonia ; then if the
reader, in his effort to realize the misery of the
woman, persists in mere reference to conditions

618

physical, he cannot go amiss; as he is a lover
of his kind, tender of heart, he will be melted
with much sympathy. But will he go further;
will he more than sympathize with her; will
he share her agony of mind and spirit; will
he at least try to measure it—let him recall
her as she discoursed to her son of God and
nations and heroes; one moment a philoso-
pher, the next a teacher, and all the time a
mother.

Would you hurt a man keenest, strike at his
self-love; would you hurt a woman worst, aim
at her affections.

With quickened remembrance of these un-
fortunates—remembrance of them as they were
— let us go down and see them as they are.

The Cell VI. was in form as Gesius drew it
on his map. Of its dimensions but little idea
can be had; enough that it was a roomy, rough-
ened interior, with ledged and broken walls
and floors.

In the beginning, the site of the Macedonian
Castle was separated from the site of the Tem-
ple by a narrow but deep cliff somewhat in
shape of a wedge. The workmen, wishing to
hew out a series of chambers, made their entry
in the north face of the cleft, and worked in,
leaving a ceiling of the natural stone; delving
farther, they executed the cells V., IV., III., II.,
I., with no connection with Number VI. except
through Number V. In like manner, they con-
structed the passage and stairs to the floor
above. The process of the work was precisely
that resorted to in carving out the Tombs of

the Kings, yet to be seen a short distance north of Jerusalem; only when the cutting was done, cell VI. was enclosed on its outer side by a wall of prodigious stones, in which, for ventilation, narrow apertures were left bevelled like modern port-holes. Herod, when he took hold of the Temple and Tower, put a facing yet more massive upon this outer wall, and shut up all the apertures but one, which yet admitted a little vitalizing air, and a ray of light not nearly strong enough to redeem the room from darkness.

Such was Cell VI.

Startle not now!

The description of the blind and tongueless wretch just liberated from Cell V. may be accepted to break the horror of what is coming.

The two women are grouped close by the aperture; one is seated, the other is half-reclining against her; there is nothing between them and the bare rock. The light, slanting upward, strikes them with ghastly effect, and we cannot avoid seeing they are without vesture or covering. At the same time we are helped to the knowledge that love is there yet, for the two are in each other's arms. Riches take wings, comforts vanish, hope withers away, but love stays with us. Love is God.

Where the two are thus grouped the stony floor is polished shining-smooth. Who shall say how much of the eight years they have spent in that space there in front of the aperture, nursing their hope of rescue by that timid yet friendly ray of light? When the bright-

ness came creeping in, they knew it was dawn; when it began to fade, they knew the world was hushing for the night, which could not be anywhere so long and utterly dark as with them. The world! Through that crevice, as if it were broad and high as a king's gate, they went to the world in thought, and passed the weary time going up and down as spirits go, looking and asking, the one for her son, the other for her brother. On the seas they sought him, and on the islands of the seas; to-day he was in this city, to-morrow in that other; and everywhere, and at all times, he was a flitting sojourner; for, as they lived waiting for him, he lived looking for them. How often their thoughts passed each other in the endless search, his coming, theirs going! It was such sweet flattery for them to say to each other, "While he lives, we shall not be forgotten; so long as he remembers us, there is hope!" The strength one can eke from little, who knows till he has been subjected to the trial?

Our recollections of them in former days enjoin us to be respectful; their sorrows clothe them with sanctity. Without going too near, across the dungeon, we see they have undergone a change of appearance not to be accounted for by time or long confinement. The mother was beautiful as a woman, the daughter beautiful as a child; not even love could say so much now. Their hair is long, unkempt, and strangely white; they make us shrink and shudder with an indefinable repulsion, though the effect may be from an illusory glossing of

the light glimmering dismally through the unhealthy murk; or they may be enduring the tortures of hunger and thirst, not having had to eat or drink since their servant, the convict, was taken away—that is, since yesterday.

Tirzah, reclining against her mother in half embrace, moans piteously.

"Be quiet, Tirzah. They will come. God is good. We have been mindful of him, and forgotten not to pray at every sounding of the trumpets over in the Temple. The light, you see, is still bright; the sun is standing in the south sky yet, and it is hardly more than the seventh hour. Somebody will come to us. Let us have faith. God is good."

Thus the mother. The words were simple and effective, although, eight years being now to be added to the thirteen she had attained when last we saw her, Tirzah was no longer a child.

"I will try and be strong, mother," she said. "Your suffering must be great as mine; and I do so want to live for you and my brother! But my tongue burns, my lips scorch. I wonder where he is, and if he will ever, ever find us!"

There is something in the voices that strikes us singularly—an unexpected tone, sharp, dry, metallic, unnatural.

The mother draws the daughter closer to her breast, and says, "I dreamed about him last night, and saw him as plainly, Tirzah, as I see you. We must believe in dreams, you know, because our fathers did. The Lord spoke to them so often in that way. I thought we were

in the Women's Court just before the Gate Beautiful; there were many women with us; and he came and stood in the shade of the Gate, and looked here and there, at this one and that. My heart beat strong. I knew he was looking for us, and stretched my arms to him, and ran, calling him. He heard me and saw me, but he did not know me. In a moment he was gone."

"Would it not be so, mother, if we were to meet him in fact? We are so changed."

"It might be so; but—" The mother's head droops, and her face knits as with a wrench of pain; recovering, however, she goes on—"but we could make ourselves known to him."

Tirzah tossed her arms, and moaned again.

"Water, mother, water, though but a drop."

The mother stares around in blank helplessness. She has named God so often, and so often promised in his name, the repetition is beginning to have a mocking effect upon herself. A shadow passes before her dimming the dim light, and she is brought down to think of death as very near, waiting to come in as her faith goes out. Hardly knowing what she does, speaking aimlessly, because speak she must, she says again,

"Patience, Tirzah; they are coming—they are almost here."

She thought she heard a sound over by the little trap in the partition-wall through which they held all their actual communication with the world. And she was not mistaken. A moment, and the cry of the convict rang through

the cell. Tirzah heard it also; and they both arose, still keeping hold of each other.

"Praised be the Lord forever!" exclaimed the mother, with the fervor of restored faith and hope.

"Ho, there!" they heard next; and then, "Who are you?"

The voice was strange. What matter? Except from Tirzah, they were the first and only words the mother had heard in eight years. The revulsion was mighty—from death to life—and so instantly.

"A woman of Israel, entombed here with her daughter. Help us quickly, or we die."

"Be of cheer. I will return."

The women sobbed aloud. They were found; help was coming. From wish to wish hope flew as the twittering swallows fly. They were found; they would be released. And restoration would follow—restoration to all they had lost—home, society, property, son and brother! The scanty light glossed them with the glory of day, and, forgetful of pain and thirst and hunger, and of the menace of death, they sank upon the floor and cried, keeping fast hold of each other the while.

And this time they had not long to wait. Gesius, the keeper, told his tale methodically, but finished it at last. The tribune was prompt.

"Within there!" he shouted through the trap.

"Here!" said the mother, rising.

Directly she heard another sound in another place, as of blows on the wall—blows quick,

ringing, and delivered with iron tools. She did not speak, nor did Tirzah, but they listened, well knowing the meaning of it all—that a way to liberty was being made for them. So men a long time buried in deep mines hear the coming of rescuers, heralded by thrust of bar and beat of pick, and answer gratefully with heart-throbs, their eyes fixed upon the spot whence the sounds proceed; and they cannot look away, lest the work should cease, and they be returned to despair.

The arms outside were strong, the hands skilful, the will good. Each instant the blows sounded more plainly; now and then a piece fell with a crash; and liberty came nearer and nearer. Presently the workmen could be heard speaking. Then—O happiness!—through a crevice flashed a red ray of torches. Into the darkness it cut incisive as diamond brilliance, beautiful as if from a spear of the morning.

"It is he, mother, it is he! He has found us at last!" cried Tirzah, with the quickened fancy of youth.

But the mother answered, meekly, "God is good!"

A block fell inside, and another—then a great mass, and the door was open. A man grimed with mortar and stone-dust stepped in, and stopped, holding a torch over his head. Two or three others followed with torches, and stood aside for the tribune to enter.

Respect for women is not all a conventionality, for it is the best proof of their proper

nature. The tribune stopped, because they fled from him—not with fear, be it said, but shame; nor yet, O reader, from shame alone! From the obscurity of their partial hiding he heard these words, the saddest, most dreadful, most utterly despairing of the human tongue:

"Come not near us—unclean, unclean!"

The men flared their torches while they stared at each other.

"Unclean, unclean!" came from the corner again, a slow tremulous wail, exceedingly sorrowful. With such a cry we can imagine a spirit vanishing from the gates of Paradise, looking back the while.

So the widow and mother performed her duty, and in the moment realized that the freedom she had prayed for and dreamed of, fruit of scarlet and gold seen afar, was but an apple of Sodom in the hand.

She and Tirzah were—LEPERS!

Possibly the reader does not know all the word means. Let him be told it with reference to the Law of that time, only a little modified in this.

"These four are accounted as dead — the blind, the leper, the poor, and the childless." Thus the Talmud.

That is, to be a leper was to be treated as dead—to be excluded from the city as a corpse; to be spoken to by the best beloved and most loving only at a distance; to dwell with none but lepers; to be utterly unprivileged; to be denied the rites of the Temple and the synagogue; to go about in rent garments and with

covered mouth, except when crying, "Unclean, unclean!" to find home in the wilderness or in abandoned tombs; to become a materialized spectre of Hinnom and Gehenna; to be at all times less a living offence to others than a breathing torment to self; afraid to die, yet without hope except in death.

Once—she might not tell the day or the year, for down in the haunted hell even time was lost—once the mother felt a dry scurf in the palm of her right hand, a trifle which she tried to wash away. It clung to the member pertinaciously; yet she thought but little of the sign till Tirzah complained that she, too, was attacked in the same way. The supply of water was scant, and they denied themselves drink that they might use it as a curative. At length the whole hand was attacked; the skin cracked open, the finger-nails loosened from the flesh. There was not much pain withal, chiefly a steadily increasing discomfort. Later their lips began to parch and seam. One day the mother, who was cleanly to godliness, and struggled against the impurities of the dungeon with all ingenuity, thinking the enemy was taking hold on Tirzah's face, led her to the light, and, looking with the inspiration of a terrible dread, lo! the young girl's eyebrows were white as snow.

Oh, the anguish of that assurance!

The mother sat a while speechless, motionless, paralyzed of soul, and capable of but one thought—leprosy, leprosy!

When she began to think, mother-like, it

was not of herself, but her child, and, mother-
like, her natural tenderness turned to courage,
and she made ready for the last sacrifice of
perfect heroism. She buried her knowledge
in her heart; hopeless herself, she redoubled
her devotion to Tirzah, and with wonderful in-
genuity — wonderful chiefly in its very inex-
haustibility—continued to keep the daughter
ignorant of what they were beset with, and
even hopeful that it was nothing. She repeat-
ed her little games, and retold her stories, and
invented new ones, and listened with ever so
much pleasure to the songs she would have
from Tirzah, while on her own wasting lips the
psalms of the singing king of their race served
to bring soothing of forgetfulness, and keep
alive in them both the recollection of the God
who would seem to have abandoned them—
the world not more lightly or utterly.

Slowly, steadily, with horrible certainty, the
disease spread, after a while bleaching their
heads white, eating holes in their lips and eye-
lids, and covering their bodies with scales;
then it fell to their throats, shrilling their
voices, and to their joints, hardening the tis-
sues and cartilages—slowly, and, as the mother
well knew, past remedy, it was affecting their
lungs and arteries and bones, at each advance
making the sufferers more and more loath-
some; and so it would continue till death,
which might be years before them.

Another day of dread at length came—the
day the mother, under impulsion of duty, at
last told Tirzah the name of their ailment;

and the two, in agony of despair, prayed that the end might come quickly.

Still, as is the force of habit, these so afflicted grew in time not merely to speak composedly of their disease; they beheld the hideous transformation of their persons as of course, and in despite clung to existence. One tie to earth remained to them; unmindful of their own loneliness, they kept up a certain spirit by talking and dreaming of Ben-Hur. The mother promised reunion with him to the sister, and she to the mother, not doubting, either of them, that he was equally faithful to them, and would be equally happy of the meeting. And with the spinning and respinning of this slender thread they found pleasure, and excused their not dying. In such manner as we have seen, they were solacing themselves the moment Gesius called them, at the end of twelve hours' fasting and thirst.

The torches flashed redly through the dungeon, and liberty was come. "God is good," the widow cried—not for what had been, O reader, but for what was. In thankfulness for present mercy, nothing so becomes us as losing sight of past ills.

The tribune came directly; then in the corner to which she had fled, suddenly a sense of duty smote the elder of the women, and straightway the awful warning—

"Unclean, unclean!"

Ah, the pang the effort to acquit herself of that duty cost the mother! Not all the selfishness of joy over the prospect could keep

her blind to the consequences of release, now that it was at hand. The old happy life could never be again. If she went near the house called home, it would be to stop at the gate and cry, "Unclean, unclean!" She must go about with the yearnings of love alive in her breast strong as ever, and more sensitive even, because return in kind could not be. The boy of whom she had so constantly thought, and with all sweet promises such as mothers find their purest delight in, must, at meeting her, stand afar off. If he held out his hands to her, and called "Mother, mother," for very love of him she must answer, "Unclean, unclean!" And this other child, before whom, in want of other covering, she was spreading her long, tangled locks, bleached unnaturally white — ah! that she was she must continue, sole partner of her blasted remainder of life. Yet, O reader, the brave woman accepted the lot, and took up the cry which had been its sign immemorially, and which thenceforward was to be her salutation without change—" Unclean, unclean!"

The tribune heard it with a tremor, but kept his place.

"Who are you?" he asked.

"Two women dying of hunger and thirst. Yet"—the mother did not falter—"come not near us, nor touch the floor or the wall. Unclean, unclean!"

"Give me thy story, woman—thy name, and when thou wert put here, and by whom, and for what."

"There was once in this city of Jerusalem a Prince Ben-Hur, the friend of all generous Romans, and who had Cæsar for his friend. I am his widow, and this one with me is his child. How may I tell you for what we were sunk here, when I do not know, unless it was because we were rich? Valerius Gratus can tell you who our enemy was, and when our imprisonment began. I cannot. See to what we have been reduced—oh, see, and have pity!"

The air was heavy with the pest and the smoke of the torches, yet the Roman called one of the torch-bearers to his side, and wrote the answer nearly word for word. It was terse and comprehensive, containing at once a history, an accusation, and a prayer. No common person could have made it, and he could not but pity and believe.

"Thou shalt have relief, woman," he said, closing the tablets. "I will send thee food and drink."

"And raiment, and purifying water, we pray you, O generous Roman!"

"As thou wilt," he replied.

"God is good," said the widow, sobbing. "May his peace abide with you!"

"And, further," he added, "I cannot see thee again. Make preparation, and to-night I will have thee taken to the gate of the Tower, and set free. Thou knowest the law. Farewell."

He spoke to the men, and went out the door.

Very shortly some slaves came to the cell with a large gurglet of water, a basin and nap-

kins, a platter with bread and meat, and some
garments of women's wear; and, setting them
down within reach of the prisoners, they ran
away.

About the middle of the first watch, the two
were conducted to the gate, and turned into
the street. So the Roman quit himself of them,
and in the city of their fathers they were once
more free.

Up to the stars, twinkling merrily as of old,
they looked; then they asked themselves,
"What next? and where to?"

<div align="center">

CHAPTER III

JERUSALEM AGAIN

</div>

ABOUT the hour Gesius, the keeper,
made his appearance before the trib-
une in the Tower of Antonia, a foot-
man was climbing the eastern face of
Mount Olivet. The road was rough and dusty,
and vegetation on that side burned brown, for
it was the dry season in Judea. Well for the
traveller that he had youth and strength, not
to speak of the cool, flowing garments with
which he was clothed.

He proceeded slowly, looking often to his
right and left; not with the vexed, anxious ex-
pression which marks a man going forward un-
certain of the way, but rather the air with which
one approaches an old acquaintance after a
long separation — half of pleasure, half of in-
quiry; as if he were saying, "I am glad to be

with you again; let me see in what you are changed."

As he arose higher, he sometimes paused to look behind him over the gradually widening view terminating in the mountains of Moab; but when at length he drew near the summit, he quickened his step, unmindful of fatigue, and hurried on without pause or turning of the face. On the summit — to reach which he bent his steps somewhat right of the beaten path—he came to a dead stop, arrested as if by a strong hand. Then one might have seen his eyes dilate, his cheeks flush, his breath quicken, effects all of one bright, sweeping glance at what lay before him.

The traveller, good reader, was no other than Ben-Hur; the spectacle Jerusalem.

Not the Holy City of to-day, but the Holy City as left by Herod—the Holy City of the Christ. Beautiful yet, as seen from old Olivet, what must it have been then?

Ben-Hur betook him to a stone and sat down, and, stripping his head of the close white handkerchief which served it for covering, made the survey at leisure.

The same has been done often since by a great variety of persons, under circumstances surpassingly singular—by the son of Vespasian, by the Islamite, by the Crusader, conquerors all of them; by many a pilgrim from the great New World, which waited discovery nearly fifteen hundred years after the time of our story; but of the multitude probably not one has taken that view with sensations more keenly poignant,

633

more sadly sweet, more proudly bitter, than Ben-Hur. He was stirred by recollections of his countrymen, their triumphs and vicissitudes, their history the history of God. The city was of their building, at once a lasting testimony of their crimes and devotion, their weakness and genius, their religion and their irreligion. Though he had seen Rome to familiarity, he was gratified. The sight filled a measure of pride which would have made him drunk with vainglory but for the thought, princely as the property was, it did not any longer belong to his countrymen; the worship in the Temple was by permission of strangers; the hill where David dwelt was a marbled cheat—an office in which the chosen of the Lord were wrung and wrung for taxes, and scourged for very deathlessness of faith. These, however, were pleasures and griefs of patriotism common to every Jew of the period; in addition, Ben-Hur brought with him a personal history which would not out of mind for other consideration whatever, which the spectacle served only to freshen and vivify.

A country of hills changes but little; where the hills are of rock, it changes not at all. The scene Ben-Hur beheld is the same now, except as respects the city. The failure is in the handiwork of man alone.

The sun dealt more kindly by the west side of Olivet than by the east, and men were certainly more loving towards it. The vines with which it was partially clad, and the sprinkling of trees, chiefly figs and old wild olives, were

634

comparatively green. Down to the dry bed of
the Cedron the verdure extended, a refresh-
ment to the vision; there Olivet ceased and
Moriah began—a wall of bluff boldness, white
as snow, founded by Solomon, completed by
Herod. Up, up the wall the eye climbed course
by course of the ponderous rocks composing
it—up to Solomon's Porch, which was as the
pedestal of the monument, the hill being the
plinth. Lingering there a moment, the eye re-
sumed its climbing, going next to the Gentiles'
Court, then to the Israelites' Court, then to the
Women's Court, then to the Court of the Priests,
each a pillared tier of white marble, one above
the other in terraced retrocession; over them
all a crown of crowns infinitely sacred, infinite-
ly beautiful, majestic in proportions, effulgent
with beaten gold—lo! the Tent, the Tabernacle,
the Holy of Holies. The Ark was not there,
but Jehovah was—in the faith of every child of
Israel he was there a personal Presence. As
a temple, as a monument, there was nowhere
anything of man's building to approach that
superlative apparition. Now, not a stone of it
remains above another. Who shall rebuild
that building? When shall the rebuilding be
begun? So asks every pilgrim who has stood
where Ben-Hur was—he asks, knowing the an-
swer is in the bosom of God, whose secrets are
not least marvellous in their well-keeping. And
then the third question, What of him who fore-
told the ruin which has so certainly befallen?
God? Or man of God? Or—enough that the
question is for us to answer.

And still Ben-Hur's eyes climbed on and up—
up over the roof of the Temple, to the hill Zion,
consecrated to sacred memories, inseparable
from the anointed kings. He knew the Cheese-
monger's Valley dipped deep down between
Moriah and Zion; that it was spanned by the
Xystus; that there were gardens and palaces
in its depths; but over them all his thoughts
soared with his vision to the great grouping on
the royal hill—the house of Caiaphas, the Cen-
tral Synagogue, the Roman Prætorium, Hip-
picus the eternal, and the sad but mighty ceno-
taphs Phasælus and Mariamne—all relieved
against Gareb, purpling in the distance. And
when midst them he singled out the palace of
Herod, what could he but think of the King
Who Was Coming, to whom he was himself
devoted, whose path he had undertaken to
smooth, whose empty hands he dreamed of fill-
ing? And forward ran his fancy to the day the
new King should come to claim his own and
take possession of it—of Moriah and its Tem-
ple; of Zion and its towers and palaces; of An-
tonia, frowning darkly there just to the right
of the Temple; of the new unwalled city of
Bezetha; of the millions of Israel to assemble
with palm-branches and banners, to sing re-
joicing because the Lord had conquered and
given them the world.

Men speak of dreaming as if it were a phe-
nomenon of night and sleep. They should
know better. All results achieved by us are
self-promised, and all self-promises are made
in dreams awake. Dreaming is the relief of

labor, the wine that sustains us in act. We learn to love labor, not for itself, but for the opportunity it furnishes for dreaming, which is the great under-monotone of real life, unheard, unnoticed, because of its constancy. Living is dreaming. Only in the grave are there no dreams. Let no one smile at Ben-Hur for doing that which he himself would have done at that time and place under the same circumstances.

The sun stooped low in its course. Awhile the flaring disk seemed to perch itself on the far summit of the mountains in the west, brazening all the sky above the city, and rimming the walls and towers with the brightness of gold. Then it disappeared as with a plunge. The quiet turned Ben-Hur's thought homeward. There was a point in the sky a little north of the peerless front of the Holy of Holies upon which he fixed his gaze ; under it, straight as a lead-line would have dropped, lay his father's house, if yet the house endured.

The mellowing influences of the evening mellowed his feelings, and, putting his ambitions aside, he thought of the duty that was bringing him to Jerusalem.

Out in the desert while with Ilderim, looking for strong places and acquainting himself with it generally, as a soldier studies a country in which he has projected a campaign, a messenger came one evening with the news that Gratus was removed, and Pontius Pilate sent to take his place.

Messala was disabled and believed him dead ;

Gratus was powerless and gone; why should Ben-Hur longer defer the search for his mother and sister? There was nothing to fear now. If he could not himself see into the prisons of Judea, he could examine them with the eyes of others. If the lost were found, Pilate could have no motive in holding them in custody—none, at least, which could not be overcome by purchase. If found, he would carry them to a place of safety, and then, in calmer mind, his conscience at rest, this one first duty done, he could give himself more entirely to the King Who Was Coming. He resolved at once. That night he counselled with Ilderim, and obtained his assent. Three Arabs came with him to Jericho, where he left them and the horses, and proceeded alone and on foot. Malluch was to meet him in Jerusalem.

Ben-Hur's scheme, be it observed, was as yet a generality.

In view of the future, it was advisable to keep himself in hiding from the authorities, particularly the Romans. Malluch was shrewd and trusty; the very man to charge with the conduct of the investigation.

Where to begin was the first point. He had no clear idea about it. His wish was to commence with the Tower of Antonia. Tradition not of long standing planted the gloomy pile over a labyrinth of prison-cells, which, more even than the strong garrison, kept it a terror to the Jewish fancy. A burial, such as his people had been subjected to, might be possible there. Besides, in such a strait, the nat-

ural inclination is to start search at the place where the loss occurred, and he could not forget that his last sight of the loved ones was as the guard pushed them along the street in the direction to the Tower. If they were not there now, but had been, some record of the fact must remain, a clew which had only to be followed faithfully to the end.

Under this inclination, morever, there was a hope which he could not forego. From Simonides he knew Amrah, the Egyptian nurse, was living. It will be remembered, doubtless, that the faithful creature, the morning the calamity overtook the Hurs, broke from the guard and ran back into the palace, where, along with other chattels, she had been sealed up. During the years following, Simonides kept her supplied; so she was there now, sole occupant of the great house, which, with all his offers, Gratus had not been able to sell. The story of its rightful owners sufficed to secure the property from strangers, whether purchasers or mere occupants. People going to and fro passed it with whispers. Its reputation was that of a haunted house; derived probably from the infrequent glimpses of poor old Amrah, sometimes on the roof, sometimes in a latticed window. Certainly no more constant spirit ever abided than she; nor was there ever a tenement so shunned and fitted for ghostly habitation. Now, if he could get to her, Ben-Hur fancied she could help him to knowledge which, though faint, might yet be serviceable. Anyhow, sight of her in that

place, so endeared by recollection, would be to him a pleasure next to finding the objects of his solicitude.

So, first of all things, he would go to the old house, and look for Amrah.

Thus resolved, he arose shortly after the going-down of the sun, and began descent of the Mount by the road which, from the summit, bends a little north of east. Down nearly at the foot, close by the bed of the Cedron, he came to the intersection with the road leading south to the village of Siloam and the pool of that name. There he fell in with a herdsman driving some sheep to market. He spoke to the man, and joined him, and in his company passed by Gethsemane on into the city through the Fish Gate.

CHAPTER IV
BEN-HUR AT HIS FATHER'S GATE

T was dark when, parting with the drover inside the gate, Ben-Hur turned into a narrow lane leading to the south. A few of the people whom he met saluted him. The bowldering of the pavement was rough. The houses on both sides were low, dark, and cheerless; the doors all closed: from the roofs, occasionally, he heard women crooning to children. The loneliness of his situation, the night, the uncertainty cloaking the object of his coming, all affected him cheerlessly. With feelings sinking lower and lower, he came directly to the

deep reservoir now known as the Pool of Bethesda, in which the water reflected the overpending sky. Looking up, he beheld the northern wall of the Tower of Antonia, a black frowning heap reared into the dim steel-gray sky. He halted as if challenged by a threatening sentinel.

The Tower stood up so high, and seemed so vast, resting apparently upon foundations so sure, that he was constrained to acknowledge its strength. If his mother were there in living burial, what could he do for her? By the strong hand, nothing! An army might beat the stony face with ballista and ram, and be laughed at. Against him alone the gigantic south-east turret looked down in the self-containment of a hill. And he thought, cunning is so easily baffled; and God, always the last resort of the helpless—God is sometimes so slow to act!

In doubt and misgiving, he turned into the street in front of the Tower and followed it slowly on to the west.

Over in Bezetha he knew there was a khan, where it was his intention to seek lodging while in the city; but just now he could not resist the impulse to go home. His heart drew him that way.

The old formal salutation which he received from the few people who passed him had never sounded so pleasantly. Presently all the eastern sky began to silver and shine, and objects before invisible in the west—chiefly the tall towers on Mount Zion—emerged as from a

shadowy depth, and put on spectral distinctness, floating, as it were, above the yawning blackness of the valley below, very castles in the air.

He came, at length, to his father's house.

Of those who read this page, some there will be to divine his feelings without prompting. They are such as had happy homes in their youth, no matter how far that may have been back in time—homes which are now the starting-points of all recollection; paradises from which they went forth in tears, and which they would now return to, if they could, as little children; places of laughter and singing, and associations dearer than any or all the triumphs of after-life.

At the gate on the north side of the old house Ben-Hur stopped. In the corners the wax used in the sealing-up was still plainly seen, and across the valves was the board with the inscription—

" This is the Property of
THE EMPEROR."

Nobody had gone in or out the gate since the dreadful day of the separation. Should he knock as of old ? It was useless, he knew; yet he could not resist the temptation. Amrah might hear, and look out of one of the windows on that side. Taking a stone, he mounted the broad stone step, and tapped three times. A dull echo replied. He tried again, louder than before ; and again, pausing each time to listen. The silence was mocking.

Retiring into the street, he watched the windows; but they, too, were lifeless. The parapet on the roof was defined sharply against the brightening sky; nothing could have stirred upon it unseen by him, and nothing did stir.

From the north side he passed to the west, where there were four windows which he watched long and anxiously, but with as little effect. At times his heart swelled with impotent wishes; at others, he trembled at the deceptions of his own fancy. Amrah made no sign—not even a ghost stirred.

Silently, then, he stole round to the south. There, too, the gate was sealed and inscribed. The mellow splendor of the August moon, pouring over the crest of Olivet, since termed the Mount of Offence, brought the lettering boldly out; and he read, and was filled with rage. All he could do was to wrench the board from its nailing, and hurl it into the ditch. Then he sat upon the step, and prayed for the New King, and that his coming might be hastened. As his blood cooled, insensibly he yielded to the fatigue of long travel in the summer heat, and sank down lower, and, at last, slept.

About that time two women came down the street from the direction of the Tower of Antonia, approaching the palace of the Hurs. They advanced stealthily, with timid steps, pausing often to listen. At the corner of the rugged pile, one said to the other, in a low voice,

"This is it, Tirzah!"

And Tirzah, after a look, caught her mother's hand, and leaned upon her heavily, sobbing, but silent.

"Let us go on, my child, because"—the mother hesitated and trembled; then, with an effort to be calm, continued—"because when morning comes they will put us out of the gate of the city to—return no more."

Tirzah sank almost to the stones.

"Ah, yes!" she said, between sobs; "I forgot. I had the feeling of going home. But we are lepers, and have no homes; we belong to the dead!"

The mother stooped and raised her tenderly, saying, "We have nothing to fear. Let us go on."

Indeed, lifting their empty hands, they could have run upon a legion and put it to flight.

And, creeping in close to the rough wall, they glided on, like two ghosts, till they came to the gate, before which they also paused. Seeing the board, they stepped upon the stone in the scarce cold tracks of Ben-Hur, and read the inscription—"This is the Property of the Emperor."

Then the mother clasped her hands, and, with upraised eyes, moaned in unutterable anguish.

"What now, mother? You scare me!"

And the answer was, presently, "Oh, Tirzah, the poor are dead! He is dead!"

"Who, mother?"

"Your brother! They took everything from him—everything—even this house!"

" Poor !" said Tirzah, vacantly.

" He will never be able to help us."

"And then, mother ?"

" To-morrow—to-morrow, my child, we must
find a seat by the way-side, and beg alms as the
lepers do ; beg, or—"

Tirzah leaned upon her again, and said, whis-
pering, " Let us—let us die !"

" No !" the mother said, firmly. " The Lord
has appointed our times, and we are believers
in the Lord. We will wait on him even in this.
Come away !"

She caught Tirzah's hand as she spoke, and
hastened to the west corner of the house, keep-
ing close to the wall. No one being in sight
there, they kept on to the next corner, and
shrank from the moonlight, which lay exceed-
ingly bright over the whole south front, and
along a part of the street. The mother's will
was strong. Casting one look back and up to
the windows on the west side, she stepped out
into the light, drawing Tirzah after her; and
the extent of their affliction was then to be
seen—on their lips and cheeks, in their bleared
eyes, in their cracked hands ; especially in the
long, snaky locks, stiff with loathsome ichor,
and, like their eyebrows, ghastly white. Nor
was it possible to have told which was mother,
which daughter ; both alike seemed witch-like
old.

" Hist !" said the mother. " There is some
one lying upon the step—a man. Let us go
round him."

They crossed to the opposite side of the street

quickly, and, in the shade there, moved on till before the gate, where they stopped.

" He is asleep, Tirzah !"

The man was very still.

" Stay here, and I will try the gate."

So saying, the mother stole noiselessly across, and ventured to touch the wicket; she never knew if it yielded, for that moment the man sighed, and, turning restlessly, shifted the handkerchief on his head in such manner that the face was left upturned and fair in the broad moonlight. She looked down at it and started; then looked again, stooping a little, and arose and clasped her hands and raised her eyes to heaven in mute appeal. An instant so, and she ran back to Tirzah.

"As the Lord liveth, the man is my son—thy brother !" she said, in an awe-inspiring whisper.

" My brother?—Judah?"

The mother caught her hand eagerly.

"Come !" she said, in the same enforced whisper, " let us look at him together—once more —only once—then help thou thy servants, Lord !"

They crossed the street hand in hand ghostly-quick, ghostly-still. When their shadows fell upon him, they stopped. One of his hands was lying out upon the step palm up. Tirzah fell upon her knees, and would have kissed it; but the mother drew her back.

" Not for thy life; not for thy life! Unclean, unclean !" she whispered.

Tirzah shrank from him, as if he were the leprous one.

TOMB OF ABSOLOM

Ben-Hur was handsome as the manly are. His cheeks and forehead were swarthy from exposure to the desert sun and air; yet under the light mustache the lips were red, and the teeth shone white, and the soft beard did not hide the full roundness of chin and throat. How beautiful he appeared to the mother's eyes! How mightily she yearned to put her arms about him, and take his head upon her bosom and kiss him, as had been her wont in his happy childhood! Where got she the strength to resist the impulse! From her love, O reader!— her mother-love, which, if thou wilt observe well, hath this unlikeness to any other love: tender to the object, it can be infinitely tyrannical to itself, and thence all its power of self-sacrifice. Not for restoration to health and fortune, not for any blessing of life, not for life itself, would she have left her leprous kiss upon his cheek! Yet touch him she must; in that instant of finding him she must renounce him forever! How bitter, bitter hard it was, let some other mother say! She knelt down, and, crawling to his feet, touched the sole of one of his sandals with her lips, yellow though it was with the dust of the street—and touched it again and again; and her very soul was in the kisses.

He stirred, and tossed his hand. They moved back, but heard him mutter in his dream,

"Mother! Amrah! Where is—"

He fell off into the deep sleep.

Tirzah stared wistfully. The mother put her face in the dust, struggling to suppress a sob so

deep and strong it seemed her heart was bursting. Almost she wished he might waken.

He had asked for her; she was not forgotten; in his sleep he was thinking of her. Was it not enough?

Presently the mother beckoned to Tirzah, and they arose, and taking one more look, as if to print his image past fading, hand in hand they recrossed the street. Back in the shade of the wall there, they retired and knelt, looking at him, waiting for him to wake —waiting some revelation, they knew not what. Nobody has yet given us a measure for the patience of a love like theirs.

By-and-by, the sleep being yet upon him, another woman appeared at the corner of the palace. The two in the shade saw her plainly in the light; a small figure, much bent, dark-skinned, gray-haired, dressed neatly in servant's garb, and carrying a basket full of vegetables.

At sight of the man upon the step the new-comer stopped; then, as if decided, she walked on—very lightly as she drew near the sleeper. Passing round him, she went to the gate, slid the wicket latch easily to one side, and put her hand in the opening. One of the broad boards in the left valve swung ajar without noise. She put the basket through, and was about to follow, when, yielding to curiosity, she lingered to have one look at the stranger whose face was below her in open view.

The spectators across the street heard a low exclamation, and saw the woman rub her eyes as if to renew their power, bend closer down,

clasp her hands, gaze wildly around, look at the sleeper, stoop and raise the outlying hand, and kiss it fondly—that which they wished so mightily to do, but dared not.

Awakened by the action, Ben-Hur instinctively withdrew the hand; as he did so, his eyes met the woman's.

"Amrah! O Amrah, is it thou?" he said.

The good heart made no answer in words, but fell upon his neck crying for joy.

Gently he put her arms away, and, lifting the dark face wet with tears, kissed it, his joy only a little less than hers. Then those across the way heard him say,

"Mother—Tirzah—O Amrah, tell me of them! Speak, speak, I pray thee!"

Amrah only cried afresh.

"Thou hast seen them, Amrah. Thou knowest where they are; tell me they are at home."

Tirzah moved, but the mother, divining her purpose, caught her and whispered, "Do not go—not for life. Unclean, unclean!"

Her love was in tyrannical mood. Though both their hearts broke, he should not become what they were; and she conquered.

Meantime Amrah, so entreated, only wept the more.

"Wert thou going in?" he asked, presently, seeing the board swung back. "Come, then. I will go with thee." He arose as he spoke. "The Romans—be the curse of the Lord upon them!—the Romans lied. The house is mine. Rise, Amrah, and let us go in."

A moment and they were gone, leaving the

two in the shade to behold the gate staring
blankly at them—the gate which they might
not ever enter more. They nestled together in
the dust.

They had done their duty.

Their love was proven.

Next morning they were found, and driven
out the city with stones.

"Begone! Ye are of the dead; go to the
dead!"

With the doom ringing in their ears, they
went forth.

<center>CHAPTER V</center>

<center>THE TOMB ABOVE THE KING'S GARDEN</center>

OWADAYS travellers in the Holy
Land looking for the famous place
with the beautiful name, the King's
Garden, descend the bed of the Ce-
dron or the curve of Gihon and Hinnom as far
as the old well En-rogel, take a drink of the
sweet living water, and stop, having reached
the limit of the interesting in that direction.
They look at the great stones with which the
well is curbed, ask its depth, smile at the prim-
itive mode of drawing the purling treasure, and
waste some pity on the ragged wretch who pre-
sides over it; then, facing about, they are en-
raptured with the mounts Moriah and Zion,
both of which slope towards them from the
north, one terminating in Ophel, the other in
what used to be the site of the city of David.
In the background, up far in the sky, the gar-

<center>650</center>

niture of the sacred places is visible: here the
Haram, with its graceful dome; yonder the
stalwart remains of Hippicus, defiant even in
ruins. When that view has been enjoyed, and
is sufficiently impressed upon the memory, the
travellers glance at the Mount of Offence stand-
ing in rugged stateliness at their right hand,
and then at the Hill of Evil Counsel over on the
left, in which, if they be well up in Scriptural
history and in the traditions rabbinical and
monkish, they will find a certain interest not to
be overcome by superstitious horror.

It were long to tell all the points of interest
grouped around that hill; for the present pur-
pose, enough that its feet are planted in the
veritable orthodox Hell of the moderns—the
Hell of brimstone and fire—in the old nomen-
clature Gehenna; and that now, as in the days
of Christ, its bluff face opposite the city on
the south and south-east is seamed and pitted
with tombs which have been immemorially
the dwelling-places of lepers, not singly, but
collectively. There they set up their govern-
ment and established their society; there they
founded a city and dwelt by themselves, avoid-
ed as the accursed of God.

The second morning after the incidents of
the preceding chapter, Amrah drew near the
well En-rogel, and seated herself upon a stone.
One familiar with Jerusalem, looking at her,
would have said she was the favorite servant
of some well-to-do family. She brought with
her a water-jar and a basket, the contents of
the latter covered with a snow-white napkin.

Placing them on the ground at her side, she loosened the shawl which fell from her head, knit her fingers together in her lap, and gazed demurely up to where the hill drops steeply down into Aceldama and the Potter's Field.

It was very early, and she was the first to arrive at the well. Soon, however, a man came bringing a rope and a leathern bucket. Saluting the little dark-faced woman, he undid the rope, fixed it to the bucket, and waited customers. Others who chose to do so might draw water for themselves; he was a professional in the business, and would fill the largest jar the stoutest woman could carry for a gerah.

Amrah sat still, and had nothing to say. Seeing the jar, the man asked after a while if she wished it filled, she answered him civilly, "Not now;" whereupon he gave her no more attention. When the dawn was fairly defined over Olivet, his patrons began to arrive, and he had all he could do to attend to them. All the time she kept her seat, looking intently up at the hill.

The sun made its appearance, yet she sat watching and waiting; and while she thus waits let us see what her purpose is.

Her custom had been to go to market after nightfall. Stealing out unobserved, she would seek the shops in the Tyropœon, or those over by the Fish Gate in the east, make her purchases of meat and vegetables, and return and shut herself up again.

The pleasure she derived from the presence of Ben-Hur in the old house once more may

be imagined. She had nothing to tell him of her mistress or Tirzah—nothing. He would have had her move to a place not so lonesome; she refused. She would have had him take his own room again, which was just as he had left it; but the danger of discovery was too great, and he wished above all things to avoid inquiry. He would come and see her often as possible. Coming in the night, he would also go away in the night. She was compelled to be satisfied, and at once occupied herself contriving ways to make him happy. That he was a man now did not occur to her; nor did it enter her mind that he might have put by or lost his boyish tastes; to please him, she thought to go on her old round of services. He used to be fond of confections; she remembered the things in that line which delighted him most, and resolved to make them, and have a supply always ready when he came. Could anything be happier? So next night, earlier than usual, she stole out with her basket, and went over to the Fish Gate Market. Wandering about, seeking the best honey, she chanced to hear a man telling a story.

What the story was the reader can arrive at with sufficient certainty when told that the narrator was one of the men who had held torches for the commandant of the Tower of Antonia when, down in Cell VI., the Hurs were found. The particulars of the finding were all told, and she heard them, with the names of the prisoners, and the widow's account of herself.

The feelings with which Amrah listened to the recital were such as became the devoted creature she was. She made her purchases, and returned home in a dream. What a happiness she had in store for her boy! She had found his mother.

She put the basket away, now laughing, now crying. Suddenly she stopped and thought. It would kill him to be told that his mother and Tirzah were lepers. He would go through the awful city over on the Hill of Evil Counsel — into each infected tomb he would go without rest, asking for them, and the disease would catch him, and their fate would be his. She wrung her hands. What should she do?

Like many a one before her, and many a one since, she derived inspiration, if not wisdom, from her affection, and came to a singular conclusion.

The lepers, she knew, were accustomed of mornings to come down from their sepulchral abodes in the hill, and take a supply of water for the day from the well En-Rogel. Bringing their jars, they would set them on the ground and wait, standing afar until they were filled. To that the mistress and Tirzah must come; for the law was inexorable, and admitted no distinction. A rich leper was no better than a poor one.

So Amrah decided not to speak to Ben-Hur of the story she had heard, but go alone to the well and wait. Hunger and thirst would drive the unfortunates thither, and she believed she

could recognize them at sight; if not, they might recognize her.

Meantime Ben-Hur came, and they talked much. To-morrow Malluch would arrive; then the search should be immediately begun. He was impatient to be about it. To amuse himself he would visit the sacred places in the vicinity. The secret, we may be sure, weighed heavily on the woman, but she held her peace.

When he was gone she busied herself in the preparation of things good to eat, applying her utmost skill to the work. At the approach of day, as signalled by the stars, she filled the basket, selected a jar, and took the road to En-Rogel, going out by the Fish Gate which was earliest open, and arriving as we have seen.

Shortly after sunrise, when business at the well was most pressing, and the drawer of water most hurried; when, in fact, half a dozen buckets were in use at the same time, everybody making haste to get away before the cool of the morning melted into the heat of the day, the tenantry of the hill began to appear and move about the doors of their tombs. Somewhat later they were discernible in groups, of which not a few were children so young that they suggested the holiest relation. Numbers came momentarily around the turn of the bluff —women with jars upon their shoulders, old and very feeble men hobbling along on staffs and crutches. Some leaned upon the shoulders of others; a few—the utterly helpless— lay, like heaps of rags, upon litters. Even that

community of superlative sorrow had its love-light to make life endurable and attractive. Distance softened without entirely veiling the misery of the outcasts.

From her seat by the well Amrah kept watch upon the spectral groups. She scarcely moved. More than once she imagined she saw those she sought. That they were there upon the hill she had no doubt; that they must come down and near she knew; when the people at the well were all served they would come.

Now, quite at the base of the bluff there was a tomb which had more than once attracted Amrah by its wide gaping. A stone of large dimensions stood near its mouth. The sun looked into it through the hottest hours of the day, and altogether it seemed uninhabitable by anything living, unless, perchance, by some wild dogs returning from scavenger duty down in Gehenna. Thence, however, and great-ly to her surprise, the patient Egyptian beheld two women come, one half supporting, half leading, the other. They were both white-haired; both looked old; but their garments were not rent, and they gazed about them as if the locality were new. The witness below thought she even saw them shrink terrified at the spectacle offered by the hideous assem-blage of which they found themselves part. Slight reasons, certainly, to make her heart beat faster, and draw her attention to them exclusively; but so they did.

The two remained by the stone awhile; then

they moved slowly, painfully, and with much
fear towards the well, whereat several voices
were raised to stop them; yet they kept on.
The drawer of water picked up some pebbles,
and made ready to drive them back. The
company cursed them. The greater company
on the hill shouted shrilly, "Unclean, unclean!"

"Surely," thought Amrah of the two, as
they kept coming—"surely, they are strangers
to the usage of lepers."

She arose, and went to meet them, taking
the basket and jar. The alarm at the well im-
mediately subsided.

"What a fool," said one, laughing; "what a
fool to give good bread to the dead in that
way!"

"And to think of her coming so far!" said
another. "I would at least make them meet
me at the gate."

Amrah, with better impulse, proceeded. If
she should be mistaken! Her heart arose into
her throat. And the farther she went the
more doubtful and confused she became. Four
or five yards from where they stood waiting for
her she stopped.

That the mistress she loved! whose hand
she had so often kissed in gratitude! whose
image of matronly loveliness she had treasured
in memory so faithfully! And that the Tir-
zah she had nursed through babyhood! whose
pains she had soothed, whose sports she had
shared! that the smiling, sweet-faced, songful
Tirzah, the light of the great house, the prom-
ised blessing of her old age! Her mistress,

657

her darling—they? The soul of the woman sickened at the sight.

"These are old women," she said to herself. "I never saw them before. I will go back."

She turned away.

"Amrah," said one of the lepers.

The Egyptian dropped the jar, and looked back, trembling.

"Who called me?" she asked.

"Amrah."

The servant's wondering eyes settled upon the speaker's face.

"Who are you?" she cried.

"We are they you are seeking."

Amrah fell upon her knees.

"O my mistress, my mistress! As I have made your God my God, be he praised that he has led me to you!"

And upon her knees the poor overwhelmed creature began moving forward.

"Stay, Amrah! Come not nearer. Unclean, unclean!"

The words sufficed. Amrah fell upon her face, sobbing so loud the people at the well heard her. Suddenly she arose upon her knees again.

"O my mistress, where is Tirzah?"

"Here I am, Amrah, here! Will you not bring me a little water?"

The habit of the servant renewed itself. Putting back the coarse hair fallen over her face, Amrah arose and went to the basket and uncovered it.

"See," she said, "here are bread and meat."

She would have spread the napkin upon the ground, but the mistress spoke again.

"Do not so, Amrah. Those yonder may stone you, and refuse us drink. Leave the basket with me. Take up the jar and fill it, and bring it here. We will carry them to the tomb with us. For this day you will then have rendered all the service that is lawful. Haste, Amrah."

The people under whose eyes all this had passed made way for the servant, and even helped her fill the jar, so piteous was the grief her countenance showed.

"Who are they?" a woman asked.

Amrah meekly answered, "They used to be good to me."

Raising the jar upon her shoulder, she hurried back. In forgetfulness, she would have gone to them, but the cry, "Unclean, unclean! Beware!" arrested her. Placing the water by the basket, she stepped back, and stood off a little way.

"Thank you, Amrah," said the mistress, taking the articles into possession. "This is very good of you."

"Is there nothing more I can do?" asked Amrah.

The mother's hand was upon the jar, and she was fevered with thirst; yet she paused, and, rising, said firmly, "Yes, I know that Judah has come home. I saw him at the gate night before last asleep on the step. I saw you wake him."

Amrah clasped her hands.

"O my mistress! You saw it, and did not come!"

"That would have been to kill him. I can never take him in my arms again. I can never kiss him more. O Amrah, Amrah, you love him, I know!"

"Yes," said the true heart, bursting into tears again, and kneeling. "I would die for him."

"Prove to me what you say, Amrah."

"I am ready."

"Then you shall not tell him where we are or that you have seen us—only that, Amrah."

"But he is looking for you. He has come from afar to find you."

"He must not find us. He shall not become what we are. Hear, Amrah. You shall serve us as you have this day. You shall bring us the little we need—not long now—not long. You shall come every morning and evening thus, and—and"—the voice trembled, the strong will almost broke down—"and you shall tell us of him, Amrah; but to him you shall say nothing of us. Hear you?"

"Oh, it will be so hard to hear him speak of you, and see him going about looking for you —to see all his love, and not tell him so much as that you are alive!"

"Can you tell him we are well, Amrah?"

The servant bowed her head in her arms.

"No," the mistress continued; "wherefore be silent altogether. Go now, and come this evening. We will look for you. Till then, farewell!"

"The burden will be heavy, O my mistress,

and hard to bear," said Amrah, falling upon her face.

"How much harder would it be to see him as we are," the mother answered, as she gave the basket to Tirzah. "Come again this evening," she repeated; taking up the water, and starting for the tomb.

Amrah waited kneeling until they had disappeared; then she took the road sorrowfully home.

In the evening she returned; and thereafter it became her custom to serve them in the morning and evening, so that they wanted for nothing needful. The tomb, though ever so stony and desolate, was less cheerless than the cell in the Tower had been. Daylight gilded its door, and it was in the beautiful world. Then, one can wait death with so much more faith out under the open sky.

CHAPTER VI

A TRICK OF PILATE'S—THE COMBAT

THE morning of the first day of the seventh month—Tishri in the Hebrew, October in English—Ben-Hur arose from his couch in the khan ill-satisfied with the whole world.

Little time had been lost in consultation upon the arrival of Malluch. The latter began the search at the Tower of Antonia, and began it boldly, by a direct inquiry of the tribune commanding. He gave the officer a history of the

Hurs, and all the particulars of the accident to Gratus, describing the affair as wholly without criminality. The object of the quest now, he said, was if any of the unhappy family were discovered alive to carry a petition to the feet of Cæsar, praying restitution of the estate and return to their civil rights. Such a petition, he had no doubt, would result in an investigation by the imperial order, a proceeding of which the friends of the family had no fear.

In reply the tribune stated circumstantially the discovery of the women in the Tower, and permitted a reading of the memorandum he had taken of their account of themselves; when leave to copy it was prayed, he even permitted that.

Malluch thereupon hurried to Ben-Hur.

It were useless to attempt description of the effect the terrible story had upon the young man. The pain was not relieved by tears or passionate outcries; it was too deep for any expression. He sat still a long time, with pallid face and laboring heart. Now and then, as if to show the thoughts which were most poignant, he muttered,

"Lepers, lepers! They—my mother and Tirzah—they lepers! How long, how long, O Lord!"

One moment he was torn by a virtuous rage of sorrow, next by a longing for vengeance which, it must be admitted, was scarcely less virtuous.

At length he arose.

"I must look for them. They may be dying."

662

"Where will you look?" asked Malluch.

"There is but one place for them to go."

Malluch interposed, and finally prevailed so far as to have the management of the further attempt intrusted to him. Together they went to the gate over on the side opposite the Hill of Evil Counsel, immemorially the lepers' begging-ground. There they stayed all day, giving alms, asking for the two women, and offering rich rewards for their discovery. So they did in repetition day after day through the remainder of the fifth month, and all the sixth. There was diligent scouring of the dread city on the hill by lepers to whom the rewards offered were mighty incentives, for they were only dead in law. Over and over again the gaping tomb down by the well was invaded, and its tenants subjected to inquiry; but they kept their secret fast. The result was failure. And now, the morning of the first day of the seventh month, the extent of the additional information gained was that not long before two leprous women had been stoned from the Fish Gate by the authorities. A little pressing of the clew, together with some shrewd comparison of dates, led to the sad assurance that the sufferers were the Hurs, and left the old question darker than ever. Where were they? And what had become of them?

"It was not enough that my people should be made lepers," said the son, over and over again, with what intensity of bitterness the reader may imagine; "that was not enough.

Oh, no! They must be stoned from their native city! My mother is dead! she has wandered to the wilderness! she is dead! Tirzah is dead! I alone am left. And for what? How long, O God, thou Lord God of my fathers, how long shall this Rome endure?"

Angry, hopeless, vengeful, he entered the court of the khan, and found it crowded with people come in during the night. While he ate his breakfast, he listened to some of them. To one party he was specially attracted. They were mostly young, stout, active, hardy men, in manner and speech provincial. In their look, the certain indefinable air, the pose of the head, glance of the eye, there was a spirit which did not, as a rule, belong to the outward seeming of the lower orders of Jerusalem ; the spirit thought by some to be a peculiarity of life in mountainous districts, but which may be more surely traced to a life of healthful freedom. In a short time he ascertained they were Galileans, in the city for various purposes, but chiefly to take part in the Feast of Trumpets, set for that day. They became to him at once objects of interest, as hailing from the region in which he hoped to find readiest support in the work he was shortly to set about.

While observing them, his mind running ahead in thought of achievements possible to a legion of such spirits disciplined after the severe Roman style, a man came into the court, his face much flushed, his eyes bright with excitement.

"Why are you here?" he said to the Gali-

leans. "The rabbis and elders are going from the Temple to see Pilate. Come, make haste, and let us go with them."

They surrounded him in a moment.

"To see Pilate! For what?"

"They have discovered a conspiracy. Pilate's new aqueduct is to be paid for with money of the Temple."

"What, with the sacred treasure?"

They repeated the question to each other with flashing eyes.

"It is Corban—money of God. Let him touch a shekel of it if he dare!"

"Come," cried the messenger. "The procession is by this time across the bridge. The whole city is pouring after. We may be needed. Make haste!"

As if the thought and the act were one, there was quick putting away of useless garments, and the party stood forth bareheaded, and in the short sleeveless under-tunics they were used to wearing as reapers in the field and boatmen on the lake—the garb in which they climbed the hills following the herds, and plucked the ripened vintage, careless of the sun. Lingering only to tighten their girdles, they said, "We are ready."

Then Ben-Hur spoke to them.

"Men of Galilee," he said, "I am a son of Judah. Will you take me in your company?"

"We may have to fight," they replied.

"Oh, then, I will not be the first to run away!"

They took the retort in good-humor, and

665

the messenger said, "You seem stout enough. Come along."

Ben-Hur put off his outer garments.

"You think there may be fighting?" he asked, quietly, as he tightened his girdle.

"Yes."

"With whom?"

"The guard."

"Legionaries?"

"Whom else can a Roman trust?"

"What have you to fight with?"

They looked at him silently.

"Well," he continued, "we will have to do the best we can; but had we not better choose a leader? The legionaries always have one, and so are able to act with one mind."

The Galileans stared more curiously, as if the idea were new to them.

"Let us at least agree to stay together," he said. "Now I am ready, if you are."

"Yes, let us go."

The khan, it should not be forgotten, was in Bezetha, the new town; and to get to the Prætorium, as the Romans resonantly styled the palace of Herod on Mount Zion, the party had to cross the lowlands north and west of the Temple. By streets—if they may be so called —trending north and south, with intersections hardly up to the dignity of alleys, they passed rapidly round the Akra district to the Tower of Mariamne, from which the way was short to the grand gate of the walled heights. In going, they overtook, or were overtaken by, people like themselves stirred to wrath by news of

the proposed desecration. When, at length, they reached the gate of the Prætorium, the procession of elders and rabbis had passed in with a great following, leaving a greater crowd clamoring outside.

A centurion kept the entrance with a guard drawn up full armed under the beautiful marble battlements. The sun struck the soldiers fervidly on helm and shield; but they kept their ranks indifferent alike to its dazzle and to the mouthings of the rabble. Through the open bronze gates a current of citizens poured in, while a much lesser one poured out.

"What is going on?" one of the Galileans asked an outcomer.

"Nothing," was the reply. "The rabbis are before the door of the palace asking to see Pilate. He has refused to come out. They have sent one to tell him they will not go away till he has heard them. They are waiting."

"Let us go in," said Ben-Hur, in his quiet way, seeing what his companions probably did not, that there was not only a disagreement between the suitors and the governor, but an issue joined, and a serious question as to who should have his will.

Inside the gate there was a row of trees in leaf, with seats under them. The people, whether going or coming, carefully avoided the shade cast gratefully upon the white, clean-swept pavement; for, strange as it may seem, a rabbinical ordinance, alleged to have been derived from the law, permitted no green thing to be grown within the walls of Jerusalem.

Even the wise king, it was said, wanting a garden for his Egyptian bride, was constrained to found it down in the meeting-place of the valleys above En-Rogel.

Through the tree-tops shone the outer fronts of the palace. Turning to the right, the party proceeded a short distance to a spacious square, on the west side of which stood the residence of the governor. An excited multitude filled the square. Every face was directed towards a portico built over a broad door-way which was closed. Under the portico there was another array of legionaries.

The throng was so close the friends could not well have advanced if such had been their desire; they remained therefore in the rear, observers of what was going on. About the portico they could see the high turbans of the rabbis, whose impatience communicated at times to the mass behind them; a cry was frequent to the effect " Pilate, if thou be a governor, come forth, come forth !"

Once a man coming out pushed through the crowd, his face red with anger.

"Israel is of no account here," he said, in a loud voice. "On this holy ground we are no better than dogs of Rome."

"Will he not come out, think you?"

"Come? Has he not thrice refused?"

"What will the rabbis do?"

"As at Cæsarea — camp here till he gives them ear."

"He will not dare touch the treasure, will he?" asked one of the Galileans.

"Who can say? Did not a Roman profane
the Holy of Holies? Is there anything sacred
from Romans?"

An hour passed, and though Pilate deigned
them no answer, the rabbis and crowd remain-
ed. Noon came, bringing a shower from the
west, but no change in the situation, except
that the multitude was larger and much noisier,
and the feeling more decidedly angry. The
shouting was almost continuous, Come forth,
come forth! The cry was sometimes with dis-
respectful variations. Meanwhile Ben-Hur held
his Galilean friends together. He judged the
pride of the Roman would eventually get the
better of his discretion, and that the end could
not be far off. Pilate was but waiting for the
people to furnish him an excuse for resort to
violence.

And at last the end came. In the midst of
the assemblage there was heard the sound of
blows, succeeded instantly by yells of pain and
rage, and a most furious commotion. The ven-
erable men in front of the portico faced about
aghast. The common people in the rear at first
pushed forward; in the centre, the effort was
to get out; and for a short time the pressure
of opposing forces was terrible. A thousand
voices made inquiry, raised all at once; as no
one had time to answer, the surprise speedily
became a panic.

Ben-Hur kept his senses.

"You cannot see?" he said to one of the Gali-
leans.

"No."

"I will raise you up."

He caught the man about the middle, and lifted him bodily.

"What is it?"

"I see now," said the man. "There are some armed with clubs, and they are beating the people. They are dressed like Jews."

"Who are they?"

"Romans, as the Lord liveth! Romans in disguise. Their clubs fly like flails! There, I saw a rabbi struck down—an old man! They spare nobody!"

Ben-Hur let the man down.

"Men of Galilee," he said, "it is a trick of Pilate's. Now, will you do what I say, we will get even with the club-men."

The Galilean spirit arose.

"Yes, yes!" they answered.

"Let us go back to the trees by the gate, and we may find the planting of Herod, though unlawful, has some good in it after all. Come!"

They ran back all of them fast as they could; and, by throwing their united weight upon the limbs, tore them from the trunks. In a brief time they, too, were armed. Returning, at the corner of the square they met the crowd rushing madly for the gate. Behind, the clamor continued — a medley of shrieks, groans, and execrations.

"To the wall!" Ben-Hur shouted. "To the wall!—and let the herd go by!"

So, clinging to the masonry at their right hand, they escaped the might of the rush, and

little by little made head-way until, at last, the
square was reached.

"Keep together now, and follow me!"

By this time Ben-Hur's leadership was per-
fect; and as he pushed into the seething mob
his party closed after him in a body. And when
the Romans, clubbing the people and making
merry as they struck them down, came hand
to hand with the Galileans, lithe of limb, eager
for the fray, and equally armed, they were in
turn surprised. Then the shouting was close
and fierce; the crash of sticks rapid and deadly;
the advance furious as hate could make it. No
one performed his part as well as Ben-Hur,
whose training served him admirably; for, not
merely he knew to strike and guard; his long
arm, perfect action, and incomparable strength
helped him, also, to success in every encounter.
He was at the same time fighting-man and
leader. The club he wielded was of goodly
length and weighty, so he had need to strike a
man but once. He seemed, moreover, to have
eyes for each combat of his friends, and the fac-
ulty of being at the right moment exactly where
he was most needed. In his fighting cry there
were inspiration for his party and alarm for his
enemies. Thus surprised and equally matched,
the Romans at first retired, but finally turned
their backs and fled to the portico. The im-
petuous Galileans would have pursued them to
the steps, but Ben-Hur wisely restrained them.

"Stay, my men!" he said. "The centurion
yonder is coming with the guard. They have
swords and shields; we cannot fight them.

We have done well; let us get back and out of the gate while we may."

They obeyed him, though slowly; for they had frequently to step over their countrymen lying where they had been felled; some writhing and groaning, some praying help, others mute as the dead. But the fallen were not all Jews. In that there was consolation.

The centurion shouted to them as they went off; Ben-Hur laughed at him, and replied in his own tongue, " If we are dogs of Israel, you are jackals of Rome. Remain here, and we will come again."

The Galileans cheered, and laughing went on.

Outside the gate there was a multitude the like of which Ben-Hur had never seen, not even in the circus at Antioch. The house-tops, the streets, the slope of the hill, appeared densely covered with people wailing and praying. The air was filled with their cries and imprecations.

The party were permitted to pass without challenge by the outer guard. But hardly were they out before the centurion in charge at the portico appeared, and in the gate-way called to Ben-Hur.

" Ho, insolent! Art thou a Roman or a Jew?"

Ben-Hur answered, " I am a son of Judah, born here. What wouldst thou with me?"

" Stay and fight."

" Singly ?"

" As thou wilt."

Ben-Hur laughed derisively.

"O brave Roman! Worthy son of the bastard Roman Jove! I have no arms."

"Thou shalt have mine," the centurion answered. "I will borrow of the guard here."

The people in hearing of the colloquy became silent; and from them the hush spread afar. But lately Ben-Hur had beaten a Roman under the eyes of Antioch and the Farther East; now, could he beat another one under the eyes of Jerusalem, the honor might be vastly profitable to the cause of the New King. He did not hesitate. Going frankly to the centurion, he said, "I am willing. Lend me thy sword and shield."

"And the helm and breastplate?" asked the Roman.

"Keep them. They might not fit me."

The arms were as frankly delivered, and directly the centurion was ready. All this time the soldiers in rank close by the gate never moved; they simply listened. As to the multitude, only when the combatants advanced to begin the fight the question sped from mouth to mouth, "Who is he?" And no one knew.

Now the Roman supremacy in arms lay in three things—submission to discipline, the legionary formation of battle, and a peculiar use of the short sword. In combat, they never struck or cut; from first to last they thrust— they advanced thrusting, they retired thrusting; and generally their aim was at the foeman's face. All this was well known to Ben-Hur. As they were about to engage he said, "I told thee I was a son of Judah; but I did

673

not tell that I am lanista-taught. Defend thy-
self!"

At the last word Ben-Hur closed with his
antagonist. A moment, standing foot to foot,
they glared at each other over the rims of their
embossed shields; then the Roman pushed
forward and feinted an under-thrust. The Jew
laughed at him. A thrust at the face followed.
The Jew stepped lightly to the left; quick as
the thrust was, the step was quicker. Under
the lifted arm of the foe he slid his shield, ad-
vancing it until the sword and sword-arm were
both caught on its upper surface; another step,
this time forward and left, and the man's whole
right side was offered to the point. The cen-
turion fell heavily on his breast, clanging the
pavement, and Ben-Hur had won. With his
foot upon his enemy's back, he raised his shield
overhead after a gladiatorial custom, and sa-
luted the imperturbable soldiers by the gate.

When the people realized the victory, they
behaved like mad. On the houses far as the
Xystus, fast as the word could fly, they waved
their shawls and handkerchiefs and shouted;
and if he had consented, the Galileans would
have carried Ben-Hur off upon their shoulders.

To a petty officer who then advanced from
the gate he said, "Thy comrade died like a sol-
dier. I leave him undespoiled. Only his sword
and shield are mine."

With that, he walked away. Off a little he
spoke to the Galileans.

"Brethren, you have behaved well. Let us
now separate, lest we be pursued. Meet me to-

night at the khan in Bethany. I have something to propose to you of great interest to Israel."

"Who are you?" they asked him.

"A son of Judah," he answered, simply.

A throng eager to see him surged around the party.

"Will you come to Bethany?" he asked.

"Yes, we will come."

"Then bring with you this sword and shield that I may know you."

Pushing brusquely through the increasing crowd, he speedily disappeared.

At the instance of Pilate, the people went up from the city, and carried off their dead and wounded, and there was much mourning for them; but the grief was greatly lightened by the victory of the unknown champion, who was everywhere sought, and by every one extolled. The fainting spirit of the nation was revived by the brave deed; insomuch that in the streets and up in the Temple even, amid the solemnities of the feast, old tales of the Maccabees were told again, and thousands shook their heads whispering wisely,

"A little longer, only a little longer, brethren, and Israel will come to her own. Let there be faith in the Lord, and patience."

In such manner Ben-Hur obtained hold on Galilee, and paved the way to greater services in the cause of the King Who Was Coming.

And with what result we shall see.

BOOK SEVENTH

"*And, waking, I beheld her there
Sea-dreaming in the moted air,
A siren lithe and debonair,
With wristlets woven of scarlet weeds,
And oblong lucent amber beads
Of sea-kelp shining in her hair.*"

THOMAS BAILEY ALDRICH.

CHAPTER I

JERUSALEM GOES OUT TO A PROPHET

THE meeting took place in the khan of Bethany as appointed. Thence Ben-Hur went with the Galileans into their country, where his exploits up in the old Market-place gave him fame and influence. Before the winter was gone he raised three legions, and organized them after the Roman pattern. He could have had as many more, for the martial spirit of that gallant people never slept. The proceeding, however, required careful guarding as against both Rome and Herod Antipas. Contenting himself for the present with the three, he strove to train and educate them for systematic action. For that purpose he carried the officers over into the lava-beds of Trachonitis, and taught them the use of arms, particularly the javelin and sword, and the manœuvring peculiar to the legionary formation; after which he sent them home as teachers. And soon the training became a pastime of the people.

As may be thought, the task called for patience, skill, zeal, faith, and devotion on his part—qualities into which the power of inspiring others in matters of difficulty is always resolvable; and never man possessed them in greater degree or used them to better effect. How he labored! And with utter denial of

self! Yet withal he would have failed but for
the support he had from Simonides, who fur-
nished him arms and money, and from Ilderim,
who kept watch and brought him supplies.
And still he would have failed but for the
genius of the Galileans.

Under that name were comprehended the
four tribes — Asher, Zebulon, Issachar, and
Naphthali — and the districts originally set
apart to them. The Jew born in sight of the
Temple despised these brethren of the north;
but the Talmud itself has said, "The Galilean
loves honor, and the Jew money."

Hating Rome fervidly as they loved their
own country, in every revolt they were first in
the field and last to leave it. One hundred
and fifty thousand Galilean youths perished in
the final war with Rome. For the great festal
days they went up to Jerusalem marching and
camping like armies; yet they were liberal in
sentiment, and even tolerant to heathenism.
In Herod's beautiful cities, which were Roman
in all things, in Sepphoris and Tiberias espe-
cially, they took pride, and in the building
them gave loyal support. They had for fel-
low-citizens men from the outside world every-
where, and lived in peace with them. To the
glory of the Hebrew name they contributed
poets like the singer of the Song of Songs, and
prophets like Hosea.

Upon such a people, so quick, so proud, so
brave, so devoted, so imaginative, a tale like
that of the coming of the King was all-power-
ful. That he was coming to put Rome down

would have been sufficient to enlist them in
the scheme proposed by Ben-Hur; but when,
besides, they were assured he was to rule the
world, more mighty than Cæsar, more magnif-
icent than Solomon, and that the rule was to
last forever, the appeal was irresistible, and
they vowed themselves to the cause body and
soul. They asked Ben-Hur his authority for
the sayings, and he quoted the prophets, and
told them of Balthasar in waiting over in An-
tioch; and they were satisfied, for it was the
old much-loved legend of the Messiah, familar
to them almost as the name of the Lord: the
long-cherished dream with a time fixed for its
realization. The King was not merely coming
now; he was at hand.

So with Ben-Hur the winter months rolled
by, and spring came; with gladdening showers
blown over from the summering sea in the
west; and by that time so earnestly and suc-
cessfully had he toiled that he could say to
himself and his followers, "Let the good King
come. He has only to tell us where he will
have his throne set up. We have the sword-
hands to keep it for him."

And in all his dealings with the many men
they knew him only as a son of Judah, and by
that name.

.

One evening, over in Trachonitis, Ben-Hur
was sitting with some of his Galileans at the
mouth of the cave in which he quartered, when
an Arab courier rode to him, and delivered a
letter. Breaking the package, he read,

"Jerusalem, Nisan IV.

"A prophet has appeared who men say is Elias.
He has been in the wilderness for years, and to our
eyes he is a prophet ; and such also is his speech, the
burden of which is of one much greater than himself,
who, he says, is to come presently, and for whom he
is now waiting on the eastern shore of the River Jor-
dan. I have been to see and hear him, and the one
he is waiting for is certainly the King you are await-
ing. Come and judge for yourself.

"All Jerusalem is going out to the prophet, and
with many people else the shore on which he abides
is like Mount Olivet in the last days of the Passover.
"Malluch."

Ben-Hur's face flushed with joy.

"By this word, O my friends," he said—"by
this word, our waiting is at end. The herald
of the King has appeared and announced him."

Upon hearing the letter read, they also re-
joiced at the promise it held out.

"Get ready now," he added, "and in the
morning set your faces homeward ; when ar-
rived there, send word to those under you,
and bid them be ready to assemble as I may
direct. For myself and you, I will go see if
the King be indeed at hand, and send you re-
port. Let us, in the mean time, live in the
pleasure of the promise."

Going into the cave, he addressed a letter to
Ilderim, and another to Simonides, giving no-
tice of the news received, and of his purpose
to go up immediately to Jerusalem. The let-
ters he despatched by swift messengers. When
night fell, and the stars of direction came out,
he mounted, and with an Arab guide set out
for the Jordan, intending to strike the track

of the caravans between Rabbath-Ammon and Damascus.

The guide was sure, and Aldebaran swift; so by midnight the two were out of the lava fastness speeding southward.

CHAPTER II
NOONING BY THE POOL—IRAS

IT was Ben-Hur's purpose to turn aside at the break of day, and find a safe place in which to rest; but the dawn overtook him while out in the Desert, and he kept on, the guide promising to bring him afterwhile to a vale shut in by great rocks, where there were a spring, some mulberry-trees, and herbage in plenty for the horses.

As he rode thinking of the wondrous events so soon to happen, and of the changes they were to bring about in the affairs of men and nations, the guide, ever on the alert, called attention to an appearance of strangers behind them. Everywhere around the Desert stretched away in waves of sand, slowly yellowing in the growing light, and without any green thing visible. Over on the left, but still far off, a range of low mountains extended, apparently interminable. In the vacancy of such a waste an object in motion could not long continue a mystery.

"It is a camel with riders," the guide said, directly.

"Are there others behind ?" said Ben-Hur.

"It is alone. No, there is a man on horse-back—the driver, probably."

A little later Ben-Hur himself could see the camel was white and unusually large, remind-ing him of the wonderful animal he had seen bring Balthasar and Iras to the fountain in the Grove of Daphne. There could be no other like it. Thinking then of the fair Egyptian, in-sensibly his gait became slower, and at length fell into the merest loiter, until finally he could discern a curtained houdah, and two persons seated within it. If they were Balthasar and Iras! Should he make himself known to them? But it could not be: this was the Desert—and they were alone. But while he debated the question, the long swinging stride of the camel brought its riders up to him. He heard the ringing of the tiny bells, and beheld the rich housings which had been so attractive to the crowd at the Castalian fount. He beheld, also, the Ethiopian, always attendant upon the Egyp-tians. The tall brute stopped close by his horse, and Ben-Hur, looking up, lo! Iras her-self under the raised curtain looking down at him, her great swimming eyes bright with as-tonishment and inquiry!

"The blessing of the true God upon you!" said Balthasar, in his tremulous voice.

"And to thee and thine be the peace of the Lord," Ben-Hur replied.

"My eyes are weak with years," said Baltha-sar; "but they approve you that son of Hur whom lately I knew an honored guest in the tent of Ilderim the Generous."

"And thou art that Balthasar, the wise Egyptian, whose speech concerning certain holy things in expectation is having so much to do with the finding me in this waste place. What dost thou here?"

"He is never alone who is where God is—and God is everywhere," Balthasar answered, gravely; "but in the sense of your asking, there is a caravan short way behind us going to Alexandria; and as it is to pass through Jerusalem, I thought best to avail myself of its company as far as the Holy City, whither I am journeying. This morning, however, in discontent with its slow movement—slower because of a Roman cohort in attendance upon it—we rose early, and ventured thus far in advance. As to robbers along the way, we are not afraid, for I have here a signet of Sheik Ilderim; against beasts of prey, God is our sufficient trust."

Ben-Hur bowed and said, "The good sheik's signet is a safeguard wherever the wilderness extends, and the lion shall be swift that overtakes this king of his kind."

He patted the neck of the camel as he spoke.

"Yet," said Iras, with a smile which was not lost upon the youth, whose eyes, it must be admitted, had several times turned to her during the interchange of speeches with the elder— "Yet even he would be better if his fast were broken. Kings have hunger and headaches. If you be, indeed, the Ben-Hur of whom my father has spoken, and whom it was my pleasure to have known as well, you will be happy,

685

I am sure, to show us some near path to living water, that with its sparkle we may grace a morning's meal in the Desert."

Ben-Hur, nothing loath, hastened to answer.

"Fair Egyptian, I give you sympathy. Can you bear suffering a little longer, we will find the spring you ask for, and I promise that its draught shall be as sweet and cooling as that of the more famous Castalia. With leave, we will make haste."

"I give you the blessing of the thirsty," she replied; "and offer you in return a bit of bread from the city ovens, dipped in fresh butter from the dewy meadows of Damascus."

"A most rare favor! Let us go on."

So saying, Ben-Hur rode forward with the guide, one of the inconveniences of travelling with camels being that it is necessarily an interdiction of polite conversation.

Afterwhile the party came to a shallow wady, down which, turning to the right hand, the guide led them. The bed of the cut was somewhat soft from recent rains, and quite bold in its descent. Momentarily, however, it widened; and erelong the sides became bluffs ribbed with rocks much scarred by floods rushing to lower depths ahead. Finally, from a narrow passage, the travellers entered a spreading vale which was very delightful; but come upon suddenly from the yellow, unrelieved, verdureless plain, it had the effect of a freshly discovered Paradise. The water-channels winding here and there, definable by crisp white shingling,

appeared like threads tangled among islands green with grasses and fringed with reeds. Up from the final depths of the valley of the Jordan some venturous oleanders had crept, and with their large bloom now starred the sunken place. One palm-tree arose in royal assertion. The bases of the boundary-walls were cloaked with clambering vines, and under a leaning cliff over on the left the mulberry grove had planted itself, proclaiming the spring which the party were seeking. And thither the guide conducted them, careless of whistling partridges and lesser birds of brighter hues roused whirring from the reedy coverts.

The water started from a crack in the cliff which some loving hand had enlarged into an arched cavity. Graven over it in bold Hebraic letters was the word GOD. The graver had no doubt drunk there, and tarried many days, and given thanks in that durable form. From the arch the stream ran merrily over a flag spotted with bright moss, and leaped into a pool glassy clear; thence it stole away between grassy banks, nursing the trees before it vanished in the thirsty sand. A few narrow paths were noticeable about the margin of the pool; otherwise the space around was untrodden turf, at sight of which the guide was assured of rest free from intrusion by men. The horses were presently turned loose, and from the kneeling camel the Ethiopian assisted Balthasar and Iras; whereupon the old man, turning his face to the east, crossed his hands reverently upon his breast and prayed.

"Bring me a cup," Iras said, with some impatience.

From the houdah the slave brought her a crystal goblet; then she said to Ben-Hur,

"I will be your servant at the fountain."

They walked to the pool together. He would have dipped the water for her, but she refused his offer, and, kneeling, held the cup to be filled by the stream itself; nor yet content, when it was cooled and overrunning, she tendered him the first draught.

"No," he said, putting the graceful hand aside, and seeing only the large eyes half hidden beneath the arches of the upraised brows, "be the service mine, I pray."

She persisted in having her way.

"In my country, O son of Hur, we have a saying, 'Better a cup-bearer to the fortunate than minister to a king.'"

"Fortunate!" he said.

There were both surprise and inquiry in the tone of his voice and in his look, and she said quickly,

"The gods give us success as a sign by which we may know them on our side. Were you not winner in the Circus?"

His cheeks began to flush.

"That was one sign. There is another. In a combat with swords you slew a Roman."

The flush deepened — not so much for the triumphs themselves as the flattery there was in the thought that she had followed his career with interest. A moment, and the pleasure was succeeded by a reflection. The combat,

688

he knew, was a matter of report throughout the East; but the name of the victor had been committed to a very few — Malluch, Ilderim, and Simonides. Could they have made a confidante of the woman? So with wonder and gratification he was confused; and seeing it, she arose and said, holding the cup over the pool,

"O gods of Egypt! I give thanks for a hero discovered—thanks that the victim in the Palace of Idernee was not my king of men. And so, O holy gods, I pour and drink."

Part of the contents of the cup she returned to the stream, the rest she drank. When she took the crystal from her lips, she laughed at him.

"O son of Hur, is it a fashion of the very brave to be so easily overcome by a woman? Take the cup now, and see if you cannot find a happy word in it for me."

He took the cup, and stooped to refill it.

"A son of Israel has no gods whom he can libate," he said, playing with the water to hide his amazement, now greater than before. What more did the Egyptian know about him? Had she been told of his relations with Simonides? And there was the treaty with Ilderim—had she knowledge of that also? He was struck with mistrust. Somebody had betrayed his secrets, and they were serious. And, besides, he was going to Jerusalem, just then of all the world the place where such intelligence possessed by an enemy might be most dangerous to him, his associates, and the cause. But was

she an enemy? It is well for us that, while
writing is slow, thought is instantaneous.
When the cup was fairly cooled, he filled it
and arose, saying, with indifference well af-
fected,

"Most fair, were I an Egyptian or a Greek
or a Roman, I would say"—he raised the gob-
let overhead as he spoke—"O ye better gods!
I give thanks that there are yet left to the world,
despite its wrongs and sufferings, the charm of
beauty and the solace of love, and I drink to
her who best represents them—to Iras, loveliest
of the daughters of the Nile!"

She laid her hand softly upon his shoulder.

"You have offended against the law. The
gods you have drunk to are false gods. Why
shall I not tell the rabbis on you!"

"Oh!" he replied, laughing, "that is very
little to tell for one who knows so much else
that is really important."

"I will go further—I will go to the little Jew-
ess who makes the roses grow and the shadows
flame in the house of the great merchant over
in Antioch. To the rabbis I will accuse you
of impenitence; to her—"

"Well, to her?"

"I will repeat what you have said to me un-
der the lifted cup, with the gods for witnesses."

He was still a moment, as if waiting for the
Egyptian to go on. With quickened fancy he
saw Esther at her father's side listening to the
despatches he had forwarded—sometimes read-
ing them. In her presence he had told Simon-
ides the story of the affair in the Palace of

Idernee. She and Iras were acquainted; this one was shrewd and worldly; the other was simple and affectionate, and therefore easily won. Simonides could not have broken faith —nor Ilderim—for if not held by honor, there was no one, unless it might be himself, to whom the consequences of exposure were more serious and certain. Could Esther have been the Egyptian's informant? He did not accuse her; yet a suspicion was sown with the thought, and suspicions, as we all know, are weeds of the mind which grow of themselves, and most rapidly when least wanted. Before he could answer the allusion to the little Jewess, Balthasar came to the pool.

"We are greatly indebted to you, son of Hur," he said, in his grave manner. "This vale is very beautiful; the grass, the trees, the shade, invite us to stay and rest, and the spring here has the sparkle of diamonds in motion, and sings to me of a loving God. It is not enough to thank you for the enjoyment we find; come sit with us, and taste our bread."

"Suffer me first to serve you."

With that Ben-Hur filled the goblet, and gave it to Balthasar, who lifted his eyes in thanksgiving.

Immediately the slave brought napkins; and after laving their hands and drying them, the three seated themselves in Eastern style under the tent which years before had served the Wise Men at the meeting in the Desert. And they ate heartily of the good things taken from the camel's pack.

CHAPTER III
THE LIFE OF A SOUL

HE tent was cosily pitched beneath a tree where the gurgle of the stream was constantly in ear. Overhead the broad leaves hung motionless on their stems; the delicate reed-stalks off in the pearly haze stood up arrowy-straight; occasionally a home-returning bee shot humming athwart the shade, and a partridge creeping from the sedge drank, whistled to his mate, and ran away. The restfulness of the vale, the freshness of the air, the garden beauty, the Sabbath stillness, seemed to have affected the spirits of the elder Egyptian; his voice, gestures, and whole manner were unusually gentle; and often as he bent his eyes upon Ben-Hur conversing with Iras, they softened with pity.

"When we overtook you, son of Hur," he said, at the conclusion of the repast, "it seemed your face was also turned towards Jerusalem. May I ask, without offence, if you are going so far?"

"I am going to the Holy City."

"For the great need I have to spare myself prolonged toil, I will further ask you, Is there a shorter road than that by Rabbath-Ammon?"

"A rougher route, but shorter, lies by Gerasa and Rabbath-Gilead. It is the one I design taking."

692

"I am impatient," said Balthasar. "Latterly my sleep has been visited by dreams—or rather by the same dream in repetition. A voice—it is nothing more—comes and tells me, 'Haste —arise! He whom thou hast so long awaited is at hand.'"

"You mean he that is to be King of the Jews?" Ben-Hur asked, gazing at the Egyptian in wonder.

"Even so."

"Then you have heard nothing of him?"

"Nothing except the words of the voice in the dream."

"Here, then, are tidings to make you glad as they made me."

From his gown Ben-Hur drew the letter received from Malluch. The hand the Egyptian held out trembled violently. He read aloud, and as he read his feelings increased; the limp veins in his neck swelled and throbbed. At the conclusion he raised his suffused eyes in thanksgiving and prayer. He asked no questions, yet had no doubts.

"Thou hast been very good to me, O God," he said. "Give me, I pray thee, to see the Saviour again, and worship him, and thy servant will be ready to go in peace."

The words, the manner, the singular personality of the simple prayer, touched Ben-Hur with a sensation new and abiding. God never seemed so actual and so near by; it was as if he were there bending over them or sitting at their side—a Friend whose favors were to be had by the most unceremonious asking

—a Father to whom all his children were alike in love—Father, not more of the Jew than of the Gentile—the universal Father, who needed no intermediates, no rabbis, no priests, no teachers. The idea that such a God might send mankind a Saviour instead of a king appeared to Ben-Hur in a light not merely new, but so plain that he could almost discern both the greater want of such a gift and its greater consistency with the nature of such a Deity. So he could not resist asking,

"Now that he has come, O Balthasar, you still think he is to be a Saviour, and not a king?"

Balthasar gave him a look thoughtful as it was tender.

"How shall I understand you?" he asked, in return. "The Spirit, which was the Star that was my guide of old, has not appeared to me since I met you in the tent of the good sheik; that is to say, I have not seen or heard it as formerly. I believe the voice that spoke to me in my dreams was it; but other than that I have no revelation."

"I will recall the difference between us," said Ben-Hur, with deference. "You were of opinion that he would be a king, but not as Cæsar is; you thought his sovereignty would be spiritual, not of the world."

"Oh yes," the Egyptian answered; "and I am of the same opinion now. I see the divergence in our faith. You are going to meet a king of men, I a Saviour of souls."

He paused with the look often seen when

NAIN

people are struggling, with introverted effort, to disentangle a thought which is either too high for quick discernment or too subtle for simple expression.

"Let me try, O son of Hur," he said, directly, "and help you to a clear understanding of my belief; then it may be, seeing how the spiritual kingdom I expect him to set up can be more excellent in every sense than anything of mere Cæsarean splendor, you will better understand the reason of the interest I take in the mysterious person we are going to welcome.

"I cannot tell you when the idea of a Soul in every man had its origin. Most likely the first parents brought it with them out of the garden in which they had their first dwelling. We all do know, however, that it has never perished entirely out of mind. By some peoples it was lost, but not by all; in some ages it dulled and faded; in others it was overwhelmed with doubts; but, in great goodness, God kept sending us at intervals mighty intellects to argue it back to faith and hope.

"Why should there be a Soul in every man? Look, O son of Hur—for one moment look at the necessity of such a device. To lie down and die, and be no more—no more forever—time never was when man wished for such an end; nor has the man ever been who did not in his heart promise himself something better. The monuments of the nations are all protests against nothingness after death; so are statues and inscriptions; so is history. The greatest

of our Egyptian kings had his effigy cut out of a hill of solid rock. Day after day he went with a host in chariots to see the work; at last it was finished, never effigy so grand, so enduring: it looked like him — the features were his, faithful even in expression. Now may we not think of him saying in that moment of pride, 'Let Death come; there is an after-life for me!' He had his wish. The statue is there yet.

"But what is the after-life he thus secured? Only a recollection by men—a glory unsubstantial as moonshine on the brow of the great bust; a story in stone—nothing more. Meantime what has become of the king? There is an embalmed body up in the royal tombs which once was his—an effigy not so fair to look at as the other out in the Desert. But where, O son of Hur, where is the king himself? Is he fallen into nothingness? Two thousand years have gone since he was a man alive as you and I are. Was his last breath the end of him?

"To say yes would be to accuse God; let us rather accept his better plan of attaining life after death for us—actual life, I mean—the something more than a place in mortal memory; life with going and coming, with sensation, with knowledge, with power and all appreciation; life eternal in term though it may be with changes of condition.

"Ask you what God's plan is? The gift of a Soul to each of us at birth, with this simple law—there shall be no immortality except

through the Soul. In that law see the necessity of which I spoke.

"Let us turn from the necessity now. A word as to the pleasure there is in the thought of a Soul in each of us. In the first place, it robs death of its terrors by making dying a change for the better, and burial but the planting of a seed from which there will spring a new life. In the next place, behold me as I am — weak, weary, old, shrunken in body, and graceless; look at my wrinkled face, think of my failing senses, listen to my shrilled voice. Ah! what happiness to me in the promise that when the tomb opens, as soon it will, to receive the worn-out husk I call myself, the now viewless doors of the universe, which is but the palace of God, will swing wide ajar to receive me, a liberated immortal Soul!

"I would I could tell the ecstasy there must be in that life to come! Do not say I know nothing about it. This much I know, and it is enough for me—the being a Soul implies conditions of divine superiority. In such a being there is no dust, nor any gross thing; it must be finer than air, more impalpable than light, purer than essence—it is life in absolute purity.

"What now, O son of Hur? Knowing so much, shall I dispute with myself or you about the unnecessaries—about the form of my soul? Or where it is to abide? Or whether it eats and drinks? Or is winged, or wears this or that? No. It is more becoming to trust in God. The beautiful in this world is all from his hand

declaring the perfection of taste; he is the author of all form; he clothes the lily, he colors the rose, he distils the dew-drop, he makes the music of nature; in a word, he organized us for this life, and imposed its conditions; and they are such guaranty to me that, trustful as a little child, I leave to him the organization of my Soul, and every arrangement for the life after death. I know he loves me."

The good man stopped and drank, and the hand carrying the cup to his lips trembled; and both Iras and Ben-Hur shared his emotion and remained silent. Upon the latter a light was breaking. He was beginning to see, as never before, that there might be a spiritual kingdom of more import to men than any earthly empire; and that after all a Saviour would indeed be a more godly gift than the greatest king.

"I might ask you now," said Balthasar, continuing, "whether this human life, so troubled and brief, is preferable to the perfect and everlasting life designed for the Soul? But take the question, and think of it for yourself, formulating thus: Supposing both to be equally happy, is one hour more desirable than one year? From that then advance to the final inquiry, what are threescore and ten years on earth to all eternity with God? By-and-by, son of Hur, thinking in such manner, you will be filled with the meaning of the fact I present you next, to me the most amazing of all events, and in its effects the most sorrowful; it is that the very idea of life as a Soul is a light almost

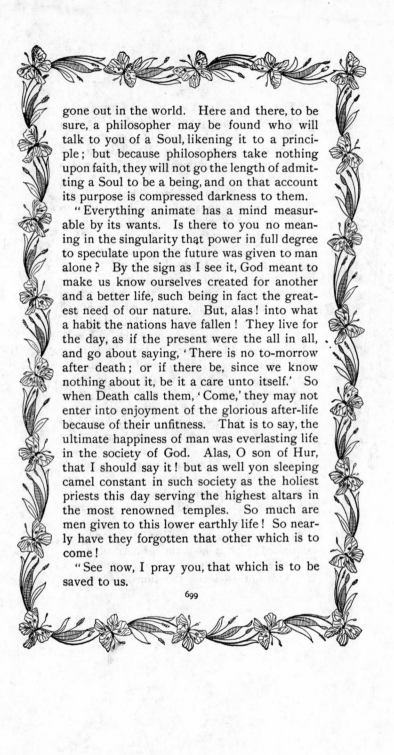

gone out in the world. Here and there, to be
sure, a philosopher may be found who will
talk to you of a Soul, likening it to a princi-
ple; but because philosophers take nothing
upon faith, they will not go the length of admit-
ting a Soul to be a being, and on that account
its purpose is compressed darkness to them.

"Everything animate has a mind measur-
able by its wants. Is there to you no mean-
ing in the singularity that power in full degree
to speculate upon the future was given to man
alone? By the sign as I see it, God meant to
make us know ourselves created for another
and a better life, such being in fact the great-
est need of our nature. But, alas! into what
a habit the nations have fallen! They live for
the day, as if the present were the all in all,
and go about saying, 'There is no to-morrow
after death; or if there be, since we know
nothing about it, be it a care unto itself.' So
when Death calls them, 'Come,' they may not
enter into enjoyment of the glorious after-life
because of their unfitness. That is to say, the
ultimate happiness of man was everlasting life
in the society of God. Alas, O son of Hur,
that I should say it! but as well yon sleeping
camel constant in such society as the holiest
priests this day serving the highest altars in
the most renowned temples. So much are
men given to this lower earthly life! So near-
ly have they forgotten that other which is to
come!

"See now, I pray you, that which is to be
saved to us.

699

"For my part, speaking with the holiness of truth, I would not give one hour of life as a Soul for a thousand years of life as a man."

Here the Egyptian seemed to become unconscious of companionship and fall away into abstraction.

"This life has its problems," he said, "and there are men who spend their days trying to solve them; but what are they to the problems of the hereafter? What is there like knowing God? Not a scroll of the mysteries, but the mysteries themselves would for that hour at least lie before me revealed; even the innermost and most awful—the power which now we shrink from thought of—which rimmed the void with shores, and lighted the darkness, and out of nothing appointed the universe. All places would be opened. I would be filled with divine knowledge; I would see all glories, taste all delights; I would revel in being. And if, at the end of the hour, it should please God to tell me, 'I take thee into my service forever,' the furthest limit of desire would be passed; after which the attainable ambitions of this life, and its joys of whatever kind, would not be so much as the tinkling of little bells."

Balthasar paused as if to recover from very ecstasy of feeling; and to Ben-Hur it seemed the speech had been the delivery of a Soul speaking for itself.

"I pray pardon, son of Hur," the good man continued, with a bow the gravity of which was relieved by the tender look that followed it, "I meant to leave the life of a Soul, its

conditions, pleasures, superiority, to your own reflection and finding out. The joy of the thought has betrayed me into much speech. I set out to show, though ever so faintly, the reason of my faith. It grieves me that words are so weak. But help yourself to truth. Consider first the excellence of the existence which was reserved for us after death, and give heed to the feelings and impulses the thought is sure to awaken in you—heed them, I say, because they are your own Soul astir, doing what it can to urge you in the right way. Consider next that the after-life has become so obscured as to justify calling it a lost light. If you find it, rejoice, O son of Hur—rejoice as I do, though in beggary of words. For then, besides the great gift which is to be saved to us, you will have found the need of a Saviour so infinitely greater than the need of a king; and he we are going to meet will not longer hold place in your hope a warrior with a sword or a monarch with a crown.

"A practical question presents itself—How shall we know him at sight? If you continue in your belief as to his character—that he is to be a king as Herod was—of course you will keep on until you meet a man clothed in purple and with a sceptre. On the other hand, he I look for will be one poor, humble, undistinguished—a man in appearance as other men; and the sign by which I will know him will be never so simple. He will offer to show me and all mankind the way to the eternal life; the beautiful pure Life of the Soul."

The company sat a moment in silence which was broken by Balthasar.

"Let us arise now," he said—"let us arise and set forward again. What I have said has caused a return of impatience to see him who is ever in my thought; and if I seem to hurry you, O son of Hur—and you, my daughter—be that my excuse."

At his signal the slave brought them wine in a skin bottle; and they poured and drank, and shaking the lap-cloths out arose.

While the slave restored the tent and wares to the box under the houdah, and the Arab brought up the horses, the three principals laved themselves in the pool.

In a little while they were retracing their steps back through the wady, intending to overtake the caravan if it had passed them by.

CHAPTER IV
BEN-HUR KEEPS WATCH WITH IRAS

THE caravan, stretched out upon the Desert, was very picturesque; in motion, however, it was like a lazy serpent. By-and-by its stubborn dragging became intolerably irksome to Balthasar, patient as he was; so, at his suggestion, the party determined to go on by themselves.

If the reader be young, or if he has yet a sympathetic recollection of the romanticisms of his youth, he will relish the pleasure with which Ben-Hur, riding near the camel of the

Egyptians, gave a last look at the head of the straggling column almost out of sight on the shimmering plain.

To be definite as may be, and perfectly confidential, Ben-Hur found a certain charm in Iras's presence. If she looked down upon him from her high place, he made haste to get near her; if she spoke to him, his heart beat out of its usual time. The desire to be agreeable to her was a constant impulse. Objects on the way, though ever so common, became interesting the moment she called attention to them; a black swallow in the air pursued by her pointing finger went off in a halo; if a bit of quartz or a flake of mica was seen to sparkle in the drab sand under kissing of the sun, at a word he turned aside and brought it to her; and if she threw it away in disappointment, far from thinking of the trouble he had been put to, he was sorry it proved so worthless, and kept a lookout for something better — a ruby, perchance a diamond. So the purple of the far mountains became intensely deep and rich if she distinguished it with an exclamation of praise; and when, now and then, the curtain of the houdah fell down, it seemed a sudden dulness had dropped from the sky bedraggling all the landscape. Thus disposed, yielding to the sweet influence, what shall save him from the dangers there are in days of the close companionship with the fair Egyptian incident to the solitary journey they were entered upon?

For that there is no logic in love, nor the least mathematical element, it is simply natural

that she shall fashion the result who has the wielding of the influence.

To quicken the conclusion, there were signs, too, that she well knew the influence she was exercising over him. From some place under hand she had since morning drawn a caul of golden coins, and adjusted it so the gleaming strings fell over her forehead and upon her cheeks, blending lustrously with the flowing of her blue-black hair. From the same safe deposit she had also produced articles of jewelry —rings for finger and ear, bracelets, a necklace of pearls—also, a shawl embroidered with threads of fine gold—the effect of all which she softened with a scarf of Indian lace skilfully folded about her throat and shoulders. And so arrayed she plied Ben-Hur with countless coquetries of speech and manner; showering him with smiles; laughing in flute-like tremolo —and all the while following him with glances, now melting-tender, now sparkling-bright. By such play Antony was weaned from his glory; yet she who wrought his ruin was really not half so beautiful as this her countrywoman.

And so to them the nooning came, and the evening.

The sun at its going down behind a spur of the old Bashan left the party halted by a pool of clear water of the rains out in the Abilene Desert. There the tent was pitched, the supper eaten, and preparations made for the night.

The second watch was Ben-Hur's; and he was standing, spear in hand, within arm-reach of the dozing camel, looking a while at the

stars, then over the veiled land. The stillness
was intense; only after long spells a warm
breath of wind would sough past, but without
disturbing him, for yet in thought he enter-
tained the Egyptian, recounting her charms,
and sometimes debating how she came by his
secrets, the uses she might make of them, and
the course he should pursue with her. And
through all the debate Love stood off but a
little way—a strong temptation, the stronger
of a gleam of policy behind. At the very mo-
ment he was most inclined to yield to the al-
lurement a hand, very fair even in the moon-
less gloaming, was laid softly upon his shoulder.
The touch thrilled him; he started, turned—
and she was there.

"I thought you asleep," he said, presently.

"Sleep is for old people and little children,
and I came out to look at my friends, the stars
in the south—those now holding the curtains
of midnight over the Nile. But confess your-
self surprised!"

He took the hand which had fallen from
his shoulder, and said, "Well, was it by an
enemy?"

"Oh no! To be an enemy is to hate, and
hating is a sickness which Isis will not suffer
to come near me. She kissed me, you should
know, on the heart when I was a child."

"Your speech does not sound in the least
like your father's. Are you not of his faith?"

"I might have been"—and she laughed low
—"I might have been had I seen what he
has. I may be when I get old like him. There

705

should be no religion for youth, only poetry
and philosophy; and no poetry except such
as is the inspiration of wine and mirth and
love, and no philosophy that does not nod ex-
cuse for follies which cannot outlive a season.
My father's God is too awful for me. I failed
to find him in the Grove of Daphne. He was
never heard of as present in the atria of Rome.
But, son of Hur, I have a wish."

"A wish! Where is he who could say it
no?"

"I will try you."

"Tell it then."

"It is very simple. I wish to help you."

She drew closer as she spoke.

He laughed, and replied, lightly, "O Egypt!
—I came near saying dear Egypt!—does not
the sphinx abide in your country?"

"Well?"

"You are one of its riddles. Be merciful,
and give me a little clew to help me under-
stand you. In what do I need help? And
how can you help me?"

She took her hand from him, and, turning
to the camel, spoke to it endearingly, and pat-
ted its monstrous head as it were a thing of
beauty.

"O thou last and swiftest and stateliest of
the herds of Job! Sometimes thou, too, goest
stumbling, because the way is rough and stony
and the burden grievous. How is it thou know-
est the kind intent by a word, and always mak-
est answer gratefully, though the help offered
is from a woman? I will kiss thee, thou royal

brute !"— she stooped and touched its broad forehead with her lips, saying immediately, " because in thy intelligence there is no suspicion !"

And Ben-Hur, restraining himself, said calmly, "The reproach has not failed its mark, O Egypt! I seem to say thee no; may it not be because I am under seal of honor, and by my silence cover the lives and fortunes of others?"

"May be !" she said, quickly. "It is so."

He shrank a step, and asked, his voice sharp with amazement, " What all knowest thou?"

She answered, after a laugh,

" Why do men deny that the senses of women are sharper than theirs? Your face has been under my eyes all day. I had but to look at it to see you bore some weight in mind; and to find the weight, what had I to do more than recall your debates with my father? Son of Hur !"—she lowered her voice with singular dexterity, and, going nearer, spoke so her breath was warm upon his cheek — "son of Hur! he thou art going to find is to be King of the Jews, is he not?"

His heart beat fast and hard.

"A King of the Jews like Herod, only greater," she continued.

He looked away—into the night, up to the stars; then his eyes met hers, and lingered there; and her breath was on his lips, so near was she.

"Since morning," she said, further, "we have been having visions. Now if I tell you mine, will you serve me as well? What! silent still?"

She pushed his hand away, and turned as if to go; but he caught her, and said, eagerly, "Stay—stay and speak!"

She went back, and with her hand upon his shoulder, leaned against him; and he put his arm around her, and drew her close, very close; and in the caress was the promise she asked.

"Speak, and tell me thy visions, O Egypt, dear Egypt! A prophet—nay, not the Tishbite, not even the Law-giver—could have refused an asking of thine. I am at thy will. Be merciful—merciful, I pray."

The entreaty passed apparently unheard, for looking up and nestling in his embrace, she said, slowly, "The vision which followed me was of magnificent war—war on land and sea —with clashing of arms and rush of armies, as if Cæsar and Pompey were come again, and Octavius and Antony. A cloud of dust and ashes arose and covered the world, and Rome was not any more; all dominion returned to the East; out of the cloud issued another race of heroes; and there were vaster satrapies and brighter crowns for giving away than were ever known. And, son of Hur, while the vision was passing, and after it was gone, I kept asking myself, 'What shall he not have who served the King earliest and best?'"

Again Ben-Hur recoiled. The question was the very question which had been with him all day. Presently he fancied he had the clew he wanted.

"So," he said, "I have you now. The satrapies and crowns are the things to which you

would help me. I see, I see! And there never
was such queen as you would be, so shrewd, so
beautiful, so royal—never! But, alas, dear
Egypt! by the vision as you show it me the
prizes are all of war, and you are but a woman,
though Isis did kiss you on the heart. And
crowns are starry gifts beyond your power of
help, unless, indeed, you have a way to them
more certain than that of the sword. If so, O
Egypt, Egypt, show it me, and I will walk in
it, if only for your sake."

She removed his arm, and said, "Spread
your cloak upon the sand—here, so I can rest
against the camel. I will sit, and tell you a
story which came down the Nile to Alexandria,
where I had it."

He did as she said, first planting the spear
in the ground near by.

"And what shall I do?" he said, ruefully,
when she was seated. "In Alexandria is it
customary for the listeners to sit or stand?"

From the comfortable place against the old
domestic she answered, laughing, "The audi-
ences of story-tellers are wilful, and sometimes
they do as they please."

Without more ado he stretched himself upon
the sand, and put her arm about his neck.

"I am ready," he said.

And directly she began:

HOW THE BEAUTIFUL CAME TO THE EARTH.

"You must know, in the first place, that Isis was
—and, for that matter, she may yet be—the most
beautiful of deities; and Osiris, her husband, though

709

wise and powerful, was sometimes stung with jealousy of her, for only in their loves are the gods like mortals.

"The palace of the Divine Wife was of silver, crowning the tallest mountain in the moon, and thence she passed often to the sun, in the heart of which, a source of eternal light, Osiris kept his palace of gold too shining for men to look at.

"One time—there are no days with the gods— while she was full pleasantly with him on the roof of the golden palace, she chanced to look, and afar, just on the line of the universe, saw Indra passing with an army of simians, all borne upon the backs of flying eagles. He, the Friend of Living Things—so with much love is Indra called—was returning from his final war with the hideous Rakshakas—returning victorious ; and in his suite were Rama, the hero, and Sita, his bride, who, next to Isis herself, was the very most beautiful. And Isis arose, and took off her girdle of stars, and waved it to Sita—to Sita, mind you—waved it in glad salute. And instantly, between the marching host and the two on the golden roof, a something as of night fell, and shut out the view ; but it was not night—only the frown of Osiris.

"It happened the subject of his speech that moment was such as none else than they could think of ; and he arose, and said, majestically, 'Get thee home. I will do the work myself. To make a perfectly happy being I do not need thy help. Get thee gone.'

"Now Isis had eyes large as those of the white cow which in the temple eats sweet grasses from the hands of the faithful even while they say their prayers ; and her eyes were the color of the cow's, and quite as tender. And she too arose and said, smiling as she spoke, so her look was little more than the glow of the moon in the hazy harvest-month, 'Farewell, good my lord. You will call me presently, I know ; for without me you cannot make the perfectly happy creature of which you were thinking, any more '—and she stopped to laugh, knowing well the truth of the saying—'any more, my lord, than you yourself can be perfectly happy without me.'

"'We will see,' he said.

"And she went her way, and took her needles and her chair, and on the roof of the silver palace sat watching and knitting.

"And the will of Osiris, at labor in his mighty breast, was as the sound of the mills of all the other gods grinding at once, so loud that the near stars rattled like seeds in a parched pod; and some dropped out and were lost. And while the sound kept on she waited and knit; nor lost she ever a stitch the while.

"Soon a spot appeared in the space over towards the sun; and it grew until it was great as the moon, and then she knew a world was intended; but when, growing and growing, at last it cast her planet in the shade, all save the little point lighted by her presence, she knew how very angry he was; yet she knit away, assured that the end would be as she had said.

"And so came the earth, at first but a cold gray mass hanging listless in the hollow void. Later she saw it separate into divisions; here a plain, there a mountain, yonder a sea, all as yet without a sparkle. And then, by a river-bank, something moved; and she stopped her knitting for wonder. The something arose, and lifted its hands to the sun in sign of knowledge whence it had its being. And this First Man was beautiful to see. And about him were the creations we call nature—the grass, the trees, birds, beasts, even the insects and reptiles.

"And for a time the man went about happy in his life: it was easy to see how happy he was. And in the lull of the sound of the laboring will Isis heard a scornful laugh, and presently the words, blown across from the sun,

"'Thy help, indeed! Behold a creature perfectly happy!'

"And Isis fell to knitting again, for she was patient as Osiris was strong; and if he could work, she could wait; and wait she did, knowing that mere life is not enough to keep anything content.

"And sure enough. Not long until the Divine Wife could see a change in the man. He grew listless, and kept to one place prone by the river, and

looked up but seldom, and then always with a moody face. Interest was dying in him. And when she made sure of it, even while she was saying to herself, 'The creature is sick of his being,' there was a roar of the creative will at work again, and in a twinkling the earth, theretofore all a thing of coldest gray, flamed with colors; the mountains swam in purple, the plains bearing grass and trees turned green, the sea blue, and the clouds varied infinitely. And the man sprang up and clapped his hands, for he was cured and happy again.

"And Isis smiled, and knit away, saying to herself, 'It was well thought, and will do a little while; but mere beauty in a world is not enough for such a being. My lord must try again.'

"With the last word, the thunder of the will at work shook the moon, and, looking, Isis dropped her knitting and clapped her hands; for theretofore everything on the earth but the man had been fixed to a given place; now all living, and much that was not living, received the gift of Motion. The birds took to wing joyously; beasts great and small went about, each in its way: the trees shook their verdurous branches, nodding to the enamoured winds; the rivers ran to the seas, and the seas tossed in their beds and rolled in crested waves, and with surging and ebbing painted the shores with glistening foam; and over all the clouds floated like sailed ships unanchored.

"And the man rose up happy as a child; whereat Osiris was pleased, so that he shouted, 'Ha, ha! See how well I am doing without thee!'

"The good wife took up her work, and answered ever so quietly, 'It was well thought, my lord—ever so well thought—and will serve a while.'

"And as before, so again. The sight of things in motion became to the man as of course. The birds in flight, the rivers running, the seas in tumult of action, ceased to amuse him, and he pined again even worse.

"And Isis waited, saying to herself, 'Poor creature! He is more wretched than ever.'

"And, as if he heard the thought, Osiris stirred,

712

and the noise of his will shook the universe ; the sun
in its central seat alone stood firm. And Isis looked,
but saw no change ; then, while she was smiling, as-
sured that her lord's last invention was sped, sudden-
ly the creature arose, and seemed to listen ; and his
face brightened, and he clapped his hands for joy, for
Sounds were heard the first time on earth—sounds
dissonant, sounds harmonious. The winds murmured
in the trees ; the birds sang, each kind a song of its
own, or chattered in speech ; the rivulets running to
the rivers became so many harpers with harps of sil-
ver strings all tinkling together ; and the rivers run-
ning to the seas surged on in solemn accord, while
the seas beat the land to a tune of thunder. There
was music, music everywhere, and all the time ; so
the man could not but be happy.

" Then Isis mused, thinking how well, how won-
drous well, her lord was doing ; but presently she
shook her head : Color, Motion, Sound—and she re-
peated them slowly—there was no element else of
beauty except Form and Light, and to them the
earth had been born. Now, indeed, Osiris was done ;
and if the creature should again fall off into wretch-
edness, her help must be asked ; and her fingers flew
—two, three, five, even ten stitches she took at once.

" And the man was happy a long time — longer
than ever before ; it seemed, indeed, he would never
tire again. But Isis knew better ; and she waited
and waited, nor minded the many laughs flung at her
from the sun ; she waited and waited, and at last saw
signs of the end. Sounds became familiar to him,
and in their range, from the chirruping of the cricket
under the roses to the roar of the seas and the bel-
low of the clouds in storm, there was not anything un-
usual. And he pined and sickened, and sought his
place of moping by the river, and at last fell down
motionless.

" Then Isis in pity spoke.

" ' My lord,' she said, ' the creature is dying.'

" But Osiris, though seeing it all, held his peace ;
he could do no more.

" ' Shall I help him ?' she asked.

713

"Osiris was too proud to speak.

"Then Isis took the last stitch in her knitting, and gathering her work in a roll of brilliance flung it off —flung it so it fell close to the man. And he, hearing the sound of the fall so near by, looked up, and lo ! a Woman—the First Woman—was stooping to help him ! She reached a hand to him ; he caught it and arose ; and nevermore was miserable, but evermore happy."

"Such, O son of Hur! is the genesis of the beautiful, as they tell it on the Nile."

She paused.

"A pretty invention, and cunning," he said, directly; "but it is imperfect. What did Osiris afterwards?"

"Oh, yes," she replied. "He called the Divine Wife back to the sun, and they went on all pleasantly together, each helping the other."

"And shall I not do as the first man?"

He carried the hand resting upon his neck to his lips. "In love—in love!" he said.

His head dropped softly into her lap.

"You will find the King," she said, placing her other hand caressingly upon his head. "You will go on and find the King and serve him. With your sword you will earn his richest gifts ; and his best soldier will be my hero."

He turned his face, and saw hers close above. In all the sky there was that moment nothing so bright to him as her eyes, enshadowed though they were. Presently he sat up, and put his arms about her, and kissed her passionately, saying, "O Egypt, Egypt ! If the King has crowns in gift, one shall be mine ; and I will

bring it and put it here over the place my lips'
have marked. You shall be a queen—my queen
—no one more beautiful ! And we will be ever,
ever so happy !"

"And you will tell me everything, and let
me help you in all?" she said, kissing him in
return.

The question chilled his fervor.

"Is it not enough that I love you?" he asked.

"Perfect love means perfect faith," she re-
plied. "But never mind—you will know me
better."

She took her hand from him and arose.

"You are cruel," he said.

Moving away, she stopped by the camel, and
touched its front face with her lips.

"O thou noblest of thy kind !—that, because
there is no suspicion in thy love."

An instant, and she was gone.

<div align="center">

CHAPTER V

AT BETHABARA

</div>

THE third day of the journey the party
nooned by the river Jabbok, where
there were a hundred or more men,
mostly of Peræa, resting themselves
and their beasts. Hardly had they dismounted,
before a man came to them with a pitcher of
water and a bowl, and offered them drink ; as
they received the attention with much courtesy,
he said, looking at the camel, " I am returning
from the Jordan, where just now there are many

<div align="center">715</div>

people from distant parts, travelling as you are, illustrious friend; but they had none of them the equal of your servant here. A very noble animal. May I ask of what breed he is sprung?"

Balthasar answered, and sought his rest; but Ben-Hur, more curious, took up the remark.

"At what place on the river are the people?" he asked.

"At Bethabara."

"It used to be a lonesome ford," said Ben-Hur. "I cannot understand how it can have become of such interest."

"I see," the stranger replied; "you, too, are from abroad, and have not heard the good tidings."

"What tidings?"

"Well, a man has appeared out of the wilderness—a very holy man—with his mouth full of strange words, which take hold of all who hear them. He calls himself John the Nazarite, son of Zacharias, and says he is the messenger sent before the Messiah."

Even Iras listened closely while the man continued:

"They say of this John that he has spent his life from childhood in a cave down by En-Gedi, praying and living more strictly than the Essenes. Crowds go to hear him preach. I went to hear him with the rest."

"Have all these, your friends, been there?"

"Most of them are going; a few are coming away."

"What does he preach?"

"A new doctrine—one never before taught

in Israel, as all say. He calls it repentance
and baptism. The rabbis do not know what
to make of him; nor do we. Some have asked
him if he is the Christ, others if he is Elias;
but to them all he has the answer,' I am the
voice of one crying in the wilderness, Make
straight the way of the Lord!'"

At this point the man was called away by
his friends; as he was going, Balthasar spoke.

"Good stranger!" he said, tremulously, " tell
us if we shall find the preacher at the place
you left him."

"Yes, at Bethabara."

" Who should this Nazarite be?" said Ben-
Hur to Iras, "if not the herald of our King?"

In so short a time he had come to regard
the daughter as more interested in the myste-
rious personage he was looking for than the
aged father! Nevertheless, the latter, with a
positive glow in his sunken eyes, half arose,
and said,

" Let us make haste. I am not tired."

They turned away to help the slave.

There was little conversation between the
three at the stopping-place for the night west
of Ramoth-Gilead.

" Let us arise early, son of Hur," said the old
man. "The Saviour may come, and we not
there."

"The King cannot be far behind his herald,"
Iras whispered, as she prepared to take her
place on the camel.

" To-morrow we will see!" Ben-Hur replied,
kissing her hand.

Next day about the third hour, out of the pass through which, skirting the base of Mount Gilead, they had journeyed since leaving Ramoth, the party came upon the barren steppe east of the sacred river. Opposite them they saw the upper limit of the old palm lands of Jericho, stretching off to the hill-country of Judea. Ben-Hur's blood ran quickly, for he knew the ford was close at hand.

"Content you, good Balthasar," he said, "we are almost there."

The driver quickened the camel's pace. Soon they caught sight of booths and tents and tethered animals; and then of the river, and a multitude collected down close by the bank, and yet another multitude on the western shore. Knowing that the preacher was preaching, they made greater haste; yet, as they were drawing near, suddenly there was a commotion in the mass, and it began to break up and disperse.

They were too late!

"Let us stay here," said Ben-Hur to Balthasar, who was wringing his hands. "The Nazarite may come this way."

The people were too intent upon what they had heard, and too busy in discussion, to notice the new-comers. When some hundreds were gone by, and it seemed the opportunity to so much as see the Nazarite was lost to the latter, up the river not far away they beheld a person coming towards them of such singular appearance they forgot all else.

Outwardly the man was rude and uncouth,

even savage. Over a thin, gaunt visage of the hue of brown parchment, over his shoulders and down his back below the middle, in witch-like locks, fell a covering of sun-scorched hair. His eyes were burning-bright. All his right side was naked, and of the color of his face, and quite as meagre; a shirt of the coarsest camel's hair—coarse as Bedouin tent-cloth—clothed the rest of his person to the knees, being gathered at the waist by a broad girdle of untanned leather. His feet were bare. A scrip, also of untanned leather, was fastened to the girdle. He used a knotted staff to help him forward. His movement was quick, de-cided, and strangely watchful. Every little while he tossed the unruly hair from his eyes, and peered round as if searching for somebody.

The fair Egyptian surveyed the son of the Desert with surprise, not to say disgust. Pres-ently, raising the curtain of the houdah, she spoke to Ben-Hur, who sat his horse near by.

"Is that the herald of thy King?"

"It is the Nazarite," he replied, without look-ing up.

In truth, he was himself more than disap-pointed. Despite his familiarity with the ascetic colonists in En-Gedi—their dress, their indif-ference to all worldly opinion, their constancy to vows which gave them over to every imagin-able suffering of body, and separated them from others of their kind as absolutely as if they had not been born like them—and notwithstanding, he had been notified on the way to look for a Nazarite whose simple description of himself

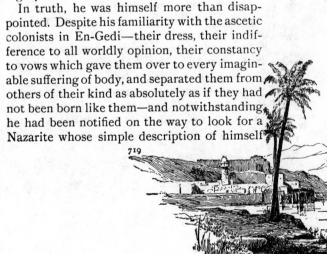

was a Voice from the Wilderness—still Ben-
Hur's dream of the King who was to be so
great and do so much had colored all his
thought of him, so that he never doubted to
find in the forerunner some sign or token of
the goodliness and royalty he was announcing.
Gazing at the savage figure before him, the
long trains of courtiers whom he had been used
to see in the thermæ and imperial corridors at
Rome arose before him, forcing a comparison.
Shocked, shamed, bewildered, he could only
answer,

"It is the Nazarite."

With Balthasar it was very different. The
ways of God, he knew, were not as men would
have them. He had seen the Saviour a child
in a manger, and was prepared by his faith for
the rude and simple in connection with the Di-
vine reappearance. So he kept his seat, his
hands crossed upon his breast, his lips moving
in prayer. He was not expecting a king.

In this time of such interest to the new-
comers, and in which they were so differently
moved, another man had been sitting by him-
self on a stone at the edge of the river, think-
ing yet, probably, of the sermon he had been
hearing. Now, however, he arose, and walked
slowly up from the shore, in a course to take
him across the line the Nazarite was pursuing
and bring him near the camel.

And the two—the preacher and the stranger
—kept on until they came, the former within
twenty yards of the animal, the latter within
ten feet. Then the preacher stopped, and flung

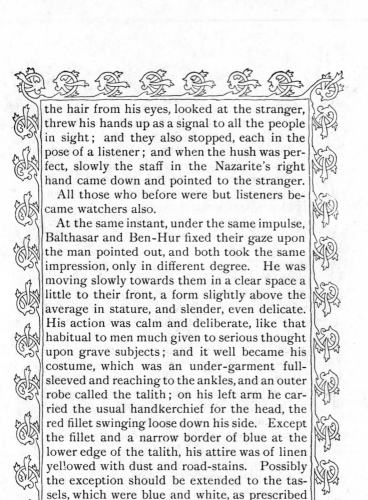

the hair from his eyes, looked at the stranger, threw his hands up as a signal to all the people in sight; and they also stopped, each in the pose of a listener; and when the hush was perfect, slowly the staff in the Nazarite's right hand came down and pointed to the stranger.

All those who before were but listeners became watchers also.

At the same instant, under the same impulse, Balthasar and Ben-Hur fixed their gaze upon the man pointed out, and both took the same impression, only in different degree. He was moving slowly towards them in a clear space a little to their front, a form slightly above the average in stature, and slender, even delicate. His action was calm and deliberate, like that habitual to men much given to serious thought upon grave subjects; and it well became his costume, which was an under-garment full-sleeved and reaching to the ankles, and an outer robe called the talith; on his left arm he carried the usual handkerchief for the head, the red fillet swinging loose down his side. Except the fillet and a narrow border of blue at the lower edge of the talith, his attire was of linen yellowed with dust and road-stains. Possibly the exception should be extended to the tassels, which were blue and white, as prescribed by law for rabbis. His sandals were of the simplest kind. He was without scrip or girdle or staff.

These points of appearance, however, the three beholders observed briefly, and rather as accessaries to the head and face of the man,

which — especially the latter — were the real
sources of the spell they caught in common
with all who stood looking at him.

The head was open to the cloudless light,
except as it was draped with hair long and
slightly waved, and parted in the middle, and
auburn in tint, with a tendency to reddish
golden where most strongly touched by the
sun. Under a broad, low forehead, under
black well-arched brows, beamed eyes dark-
blue and large, and softened to exceeding ten-
derness by lashes of the great length some-
times seen on children, but seldom, if ever, on
men. As to the other features, it would have
been difficult to decide whether they were
Greek or Jewish. The delicacy of the nostrils
and mouth was unusual to the latter type; and
when it was taken into account with the gen-
tleness of the eyes, the pallor of the complex-
ion, the fine texture of the hair, and the soft-
ness of the beard, which fell in waves over his
throat to his breast, never a soldier but would
have laughed at him in encounter, never a
woman who would not have confided in him
at sight, never a child that would not, with
quick instinct, have given him its hand and
whole artless trust; nor might any one have
said he was not beautiful.

The features, it should be further said, were
ruled by a certain expression which, as the
viewer chose, might with equal correctness
have been called the effect of intelligence, love,
pity, or sorrow; though, in better speech, it
was a blending of them all — a look easy to

fancy as a mark of a sinless soul doomed to the sight and understanding of the utter sinfulness of those among whom it was passing; yet withal no one could have observed the face with a thought of weakness in the man; so, at least, would not they who know that the qualities mentioned — love, sorrow, pity — are the results of a consciousness of strength to bear suffering oftener than strength to do; such has been the might of martyrs and devotees and the myriads written down in saintly calendars. And such, indeed, was the air of this one.

Slowly he drew near—nearer the three.

Now Ben-Hur, mounted and spear in hand, was an object to claim the glance of a king; yet the eyes of the man approaching were all the time raised above him—and not to Iras, whose loveliness has been so often remarked, but to Balthasar, the old and unserviceable.

The hush was profound.

Presently the Nazarite, still pointing with his staff, cried, in a loud voice,

"Behold the Lamb of God, which taketh away the sin of the world!"

The many standing still, arrested by the action of the speaker, and listening for what might follow, were struck with awe by words so strange and past their understanding; upon Balthasar they were overpowering. He was there to see once more the Redeemer of men. The faith which had brought him the singular privileges of the time long gone abode yet in his heart; and if now it gave him a power of

vision above that of his fellows—a power to
see and know him for whom he was looking
—better than calling the power a miracle, let
it be thought of as the faculty of a soul not yet
entirely released from the divine relations to
which it had been formerly admitted, or as the
fitting reward of a life in that age so without
examples of holiness—a life itself a miracle.
The ideal of his faith was before him, perfect
in face, form, dress, action, age; and he was in
its view, and the view was recognition. Ah,
now if something should happen to identify
the stranger beyond all doubt!

And that was what did happen.

Exactly at the fitting moment, as if to as-
sure the trembling Egyptian, the Nazarite re-
peated the outcry.

"Behold the Lamb of God, which taketh
away the sin of the world!"

Balthasar fell upon his knees. For him
there was no need of explanation; and as if
the Nazarite knew it, he turned to those more
immediately about him staring in wonder, and
continued:

"This is he of whom I said, After me com-
eth a man which is preferred before me; for
he was before me. And I knew him not: but
that he should be manifest to Israel, therefore
am I come baptizing with water. I saw the
Spirit descending from heaven like a dove,
and it abode upon him. And I knew him not:
but he that sent me to baptize with water, the
same said unto me, Upon whom thou shalt see
the Spirit descending and remaining on him,

the same is he which baptizeth with the Holy
Ghost. And I saw and bare record, that this "
—he paused, his staff still pointing at the
stranger in the white garments, as if to give a
more absolute certainty to both his words and
the conclusions intended—" I bare record, that
this is the SON OF GOD !"

"It is he, it is he !" Balthasar cried, with up-
raised tearful eyes. Next moment he sank
down insensible.

In this time, it should be remembered, Ben-
Hur was studying the face of the stranger,
though with an interest entirely different. He
was not insensible to its purity of feature, and
its thoughtfulness, tenderness, humility, and
holiness ; but just then there was room in his
mind for but one thought—Who is this man ?
And what ? Messiah or king ? Never was ap-
parition more unroyal. Nay, looking at that
calm, benignant countenance, the very idea of
war and conquest, and lust of dominion, smote
him like a profanation. He said, as if speak-
ing to his own heart, Balthasar must be right
and Simonides wrong. This man has not
come to rebuild the throne of Solomon ; he
has neither the nature nor the genius of Her-
od ; king he may be, but not of another and
greater than Rome.

It should be understood now that this was
not a conclusion with Ben - Hur, but an im-
pression merely; and while it was forming,
while yet he gazed at the wonderful counte-
nance, his memory began to throe and strug-
gle. "Surely," he said to himself, "I have

seen the man; but where and when?" That
the look, so calm, so pitiful, so loving, had
somewhere in a past time beamed upon him
as that moment it was beaming upon Balthasar
became an assurance. Faintly at first, at last
a clear light, a burst of sunshine the scene by
the well at Nazareth what time the Roman
guard was dragging him to the galleys re-
turned, and all his being thrilled. Those hands
had helped him when he was perishing. The
face was one of the pictures he had carried in
mind ever since. In the effusion of feeling
excited, the explanation of the preacher was
lost by him, all but the last words—words so
marvellous that the world yet rings with them:
"—this is the SON OF GOD!"

Ben-Hur leaped from his horse to render
homage to his benefactor; but Iras cried to
him, "Help, son of Hur, help, or my father
will die!"

He stopped, looked back, then hurried to
her assistance. She gave him a cup; and
leaving the slave to bring the camel to its
knees, he ran to the river for water. The
stranger was gone when he came back.

At last Balthasar was restored to conscious-
ness. Stretching forth his hands he asked,
feebly, "Where is he?"

"Who?" asked Iras.

An intense instant interest shone upon the
good man's face, as if a last wish had been
gratified, and he answered,

"He—the Redeemer—the Son of God, whom
I have seen again."

726

"Believest thou so?" Iras asked in a low voice of Ben-Hur.

"The time is full of wonders; let us wait," was all he said.

And next day while the three were listening to him, the Nazarite broke off in mid-speech, saying, reverently, "Behold the Lamb of God!"

Looking to where he pointed, they beheld the stranger again. As Ben-Hur surveyed the slender figure, and holy beautiful countenance compassionate to sadness, a new idea broke upon him.

"Balthasar is right—so is Simonides. May not the Redeemer be a king also?"

And he asked one at his side, "Who is the man walking yonder?"

The other laughed mockingly, and replied,

"He is the son of a carpenter over in Nazareth."

BOOK EIGHTH

"*Who could resist? Who in this universe?*
She did so breathe ambrosia, so immerse
My fine existence in a golden clime.
She took me like a child of suckling-time,
And cradled me in roses. Thus condemn'd,
The current of my former life was stemm'd,
And to this arbitrary queen of sense
ı bow'd a tranced vassal."—KEATS, *Endymion.*

"*I am the resurrection and the life.*"

CHAPTER I

GUESTS IN THE HOUSE OF HUR

"ESTHER—Esther! Speak to the servant below that he may bring me a cup of water."

"Would you not rather have wine, father?"

"Let him bring both."

This was in the summer-house upon the roof of the old palace of the Hurs of Jerusalem. From the parapet overlooking the court-yard Esther called to a man in waiting there; at the same moment another man-servant came up and saluted respectfully.

"A package for the master," he said, giving her a letter enclosed in linen cloth, tied and sealed.

For the satisfaction of the reader, we stop to say that it is the twenty-first day of March, nearly three years after the annunciation of the Christ at Bethabara.

In the mean while, Malluch, acting for Ben-Hur, who could no longer endure the emptiness and decay of his father's house, had bought it from Pontius Pilate; and, in process of repair, gates, courts, lewens, stair-ways, terraces, rooms, and roof had been cleansed and thoroughly restored; not only was there no reminder left of the tragic circumstances so ruinous to the family, but the refurnishment was

731

in a style richer than before. At every point, indeed, a visitor was met by evidences of the higher tastes acquired by the young proprietor during his years of residence in the villa by Misenum and in the Roman capital.

Now it should not be inferred from this explanation that Ben-Hur had publicly assumed ownership of the property. In his opinion, the hour for that was not yet come. Neither had he yet taken his proper name. Passing the time in the labors of preparation in Galilee, he waited patiently the action of the Nazarene, who became daily more and more a mystery to him, and by prodigies done, often before his eves, kept him in a state of anxious doubt both as to his character and mission. Occasionally he came up to the Holy City, stopping at the paternal house; always, however, as a stranger and a guest.

These visits of Ben-Hur, it should also be observed, were far more than mere rest from labor. Balthasar and Iras made their home in the palace; and the charm of the daughter was still upon him with all its original freshness, while the father, though feebler in body, held him an unflagging listener to speeches of astonishing power, urging the divinity of the wandering miracle-worker of whom they were all so expectant.

As to Simonides and Esther, they had arrived from Antioch only a few days before this their reappearance—a wearisome journey to the merchant, borne, as he had been, in a palanquin swung between two camels, which, in their

careening, did not always keep the same step.
But now that he was come, the good man, it
seemed, could not see enough of his native
land. He delighted in the perch upon the roof,
and spent most of his day hours there seated
in an arm-chair, the duplicate of that one kept
for him in the cabinet over the storehouse by
the Orontes. In the shade of the summer-
house he could drink fully of the inspiring air
lying lightly upon the familiar hills; he could
better watch the sun rise, run its course, and
set as it used to in the far-gone, not a habit lost;
and with Esther by him it was so much easier
up there close to the sky, to bring back the
other Esther, his love in youth, his wife, dearer
growing with the passage of years. And yet
he was not unmindful of business. Every day
a messenger brought him a despatch from San-
ballat, in charge of the big commerce behind;
and every day a despatch left him for Sanballat
with directions of such minuteness of detail as
to exclude all judgment save his own, and all
chances except those the Almighty has refused
to submit to the most mindful of men.

As Esther started in return to the summer-
house, the sunlight fell softly upon the dustless
roof, showing her a woman now—small, grace-
ful in form, of regular features, rosy with youth
and health, bright with intelligence, beautiful
with the outshining of a devoted nature—a
woman to be loved because loving was a habit
of life irrepressible with her.

She looked at the package as she turned,
paused, looked at it a second time more closely

than at first; and the blood rose reddening her
cheeks—the seal was Ben-Hur's. With quick-
ened steps she hastened on.

Simonides held the package a moment while
he also inspected the seal. Breaking it open,
he gave her the roll it contained.

"Read," he said.

His eyes were upon her as he spoke, and in-
stantly a troubled expression fell upon his own
face.

"You know who it is from, I see, Esther."

"Yes—from—our master."

Though the manner was halting, she met his
gaze with modest sincerity. Slowly his chin
sank into the roll of flesh puffed out under it
like a cushion.

"You love him, Esther," he said, quietly.

"Yes," she answered.

"Have you thought well of what you do?"

"I have tried not to think of him, father,
except as the master to whom I am dutifully
bound. The effort has not helped me to
strength."

"A good girl, a good girl, even as thy mother
was," he said, dropping into reverie, from which
she roused him by unrolling the paper.

"The Lord forgive me, but—but thy love
might not have been vainly given had I kept
fast hold of all I had, as I might have done—
such power is there in money?"

"It would have been worse for me had you
done so, father; for then I had been unworthy
a look from him, and without pride in you.
Shall I not read now?"

734

"In a moment," he said. "Let me, for your sake, my child, show you the worst. Seeing it with me may make it less terrible to you. His love, Esther, is all bestowed."

"I know it," she said, calmly.

"The Egyptian has him in her net," he continued. "She has the cunning of her race, with beauty to help her—much beauty, great cunning; but, like her race again, no heart. The daughter who despises her father will bring her husband to grief."

"Does she that?"

Simonides went on:

"Balthasar is a wise man who has been wonderfully favored for a Gentile, and his faith becomes him; yet she makes a jest of it. I heard her say, speaking of him yesterday, 'The follies of youth are excusable; nothing is admirable in the aged except wisdom, and when that goes from them, they should die.' A cruel speech, fit for a Roman. I applied it to myself, knowing a feebleness like her father's will come to me also—nay, it is not far off. But you, Esther, will never say of me—no, never—'It were better he were dead.' No, your mother was a daughter of Judah."

With half-formed tears, she kissed him, and said, "I am my mother's child."

"Yes, and my daughter—my daughter, who is to me all the Temple was to Solomon.

After a silence, he laid his hand upon her shoulder, and resumed: "When he has taken the Egyptian to wife, Esther, he will think of you with repentance and much calling of the

spirit; for at last he will awake to find himself but the minister of her bad ambition. Rome is the centre of all her dreams. To her he is the son of Arrius the duumvir, not the son of Hur, Prince of Jerusalem."

Esther made no attempt to conceal the effect of these words.

"Save him, father! It is not too late!" she said, entreatingly.

He answered, with a dubious smile, "A man drowning may be saved; not so a man in love."

"But you have influence with him. He is alone in the world. Show him his danger. Tell him what a woman she is."

"That might save him from her. Would it give him to you, Esther? No," and his brows fell darkly over his eyes. "I am a servant, as my fathers were for generations; yet I could not say to him, 'Lo, master, my daughter! She is fairer than the Egyptian, and loves thee better!' I have caught too much from years of liberty and direction. The words would blister my tongue. The stones upon the old hills yonder would turn in their beds for shame when I go out to them. No, by the patriarchs, Esther, I would rather lay us both with your mother to sleep as she sleeps!"

A blush burned Esther's whole face.

"I did not mean you to tell him so, father. I was concerned for him alone—for his happiness, not mine. Because I have dared love him, I shall keep myself worthy his respect; so only can I excuse my folly. Let me read his letter now."

"Yes, read it."

She began at once, in haste to conclude the distasteful subject.

"Nisan, 8th day.

"On the road from Galilee to Jerusalem.

"The Nazarene is on the way also. With him, though without his knowledge, I am bringing a full legion of mine. A second legion follows. The Passover will excuse the multitude. He said upon setting out, 'We will go up to Jerusalem, and all things that are written by the prophets concerning me shall be accomplished.'

"Our waiting draws to an end.

"In haste.

"Peace to thee, Simonides. BEN-HUR."

Esther returned the letter to her father, while a choking sensation gathered in her throat. There was not a word in the missive for her—not even in the salutation had she a share—and it would have been so easy to have written "and to thine, peace." For the first time in her life she felt the smart of a jealous sting.

"The eighth day," said Simonides, "the eighth day; and this, Esther, this is the—"

"The ninth," she replied.

"Ah, then, they may be in Bethany now."

"And possibly we may see him to-night," she added, pleased into momentary forgetfulness.

"It may be, it may be! To-morrow is the Feast of Unleavened Bread, and he may wish to celebrate it; so may the Nazarene; and we may see him—we may see both of them, Esther."

737

At this point the servant appeared with the wine and water. Esther helped her father, and in the midst of the service Iras came upon the roof.

To the Jewess the Egyptian never appeared so very, very beautiful as at that moment. Her gauzy garments fluttered about her like a little cloud of mist; her forehead, neck, and arms glittered with the massive jewelry so affected by her people. Her countenance was suffused with pleasure. She moved with buoyant steps, and self-conscious, though without affectation. Esther at the sight shrank within herself, and nestled closer to her father.

"Peace to you, Simonides, and to the pretty Esther peace," said Iras, inclining her head to the latter. "You remind me, good master—if I may say it without offence—you remind me of the priests in Persia who climb their temples at the decline of day to send prayers after the departing sun. Is there anything in the worship you do not know, let me call my father. He is Magian-bred."

"Fair Egyptian," the merchant replied, nodding with grave politeness, "your father is a good man who would not be offended if he knew I told you his Persian lore is the least part of his wisdom."

Iras's lip curled slightly.

"To speak like a philosopher, as you invite me," she said, "the least part always implies a greater. Let me ask what you esteem the greater part of the rare quality you are pleased to attribute to him."

738

Simonides turned upon her somewhat sternly.

"Pure wisdom always directs itself towards God; the purest wisdom is knowledge of God; and no man of my acquaintance has it in higher degree, or makes it more manifest in speech and act, than the good Balthasar."

To end the parley, he raised the cup and drank.

The Egyptian turned to Esther a little testily.

"A man who has millions in store, and fleets of ships at sea, cannot discern in what simple women like us find amusement. Let us leave him. By the wall yonder we can talk."

They went to the parapet then, stopping at the place where, years before, Ben-Hur loosed the broken tile upon the head of Gratus.

"You have not been to Rome?" Iras began, toying the while with one of her unclasped bracelets.

"No," said Esther, demurely.

"Have you not wished to go?"

"No."

"Ah, how little there has been of your life!"

The sigh that succeeded the exclamation could not have been more piteously expressive had the loss been the Egyptian's own. Next moment her laugh might have been heard in the street below; and she said, "Oh, oh, my pretty simpleton! The half-fledged birds nested in the ear of the great bust out on the Memphian sands know nearly as much as you."

Then, seeing Esther's confusion, she changed

739

her manner, and said in a confiding tone, "You must not take offence. Oh no! I was playing. Let me kiss the hurt, and tell you what I would not to any other—not if Simbel himself asked it of me, offering a lotus-cup of the spray of the Nile!"

Another laugh, masking excellently the look she turned sharply upon the Jewess, and she said, "The King is coming."

Esther gazed at her in innocent surprise.

"The Nazarene," Iras continued—"he whom our fathers have been talking about so much, whom Ben-Hur has been serving and toiling for so long"—her voice dropped several tones lower—"the Nazarene will be here to-morrow, and Ben-Hur to-night."

Esther struggled to maintain her composure, but failed: her eyes fell, the tell-tale blood surged to her cheek and forehead, and she was saved sight of the triumphant smile that passed, like a gleam, over the face of the Egyptian.

"See, here is his promise."

And from her girdle she took a roll.

"Rejoice with me, O my friend! He will be here to-night! On the Tiber there is a house, a royal property, which he has pledged to me; and to be its mistress is to be—"

A sound of some one walking swiftly along the street below interrupted the speech, and she leaned over the parapet to see. Then she drew back, and cried, with hands clasped above her head, "Now blessed be Isis! 'Tis he—Ben-Hur himself! That he should appear while I had such thought of him! There are no gods

if it be not a good omen. Put your arms about me, Esther—and a kiss !"

The Jewess looked up. Upon each cheek there was a glow; her eyes sparkled with a light more nearly of anger than ever her nature emitted before. Her gentleness had been too roughly overridden. It was not enough for her to be forbidden more than fugitive dreams of the man she loved ; a boastful rival must tell her in confidence of her better success, and of the brilliant promises which were its rewards. Of her, the servant of a servant, there had been no hint of remembrance; this other could show his letter, leaving her to imagine all it breathed. So she said,

"Dost thou love him so much, then, or Rome so much better."

The Egyptian drew back a step; then she bent her haughty head quite near the questioner.

"What is he to thee, daughter of Simonides?"

Esther, all thrilling, began, " He is my—"

A thought blasting as lightning stayed the words: she paled, trembled, recovered, and answered,

"He is my father's friend."

Her tongue had refused to admit her servile condition.

Iras laughed more lightly than before.

"Not more than that?" she said. "Ah, by the lover-gods of Egypt, thou mayst keep thy kisses—keep them. Thou hast taught me but

now that there are others vastly more esti-
mable waiting me here in Judea; and "—she
turned away, looking back over her shoulder
—" I will go get them. Peace to thee."

Esther saw her disappear down the steps,
when, putting her hands over her face, she
burst into tears so they ran scalding through
her fingers—tears of shame and choking pas-
sion. And, to deepen the paroxysm to her
even temper so strange, up with a new mean-
ing of withering force rose her father's words
—" Thy love might not have been vainly given
had I kept fast hold of all I had, as I might
have done."

And all the stars were out, burning low
above the city and the dark wall of mountains
about it, before she recovered enough to go
back to the summer-house, and in silence take
her accustomed place at her father's side,
humbly waiting his pleasure. To such duty it
seemed her youth, if not her life, must be given.
And, let the truth be said, now that the pang
was spent, she went not unwillingly back to
the duty.

BAZAAR TOWARDS EVENING

N hour or thereabouts after the scene upon the roof, Balthasar and Simonides, the latter attended by Esther, met in the great chamber of the palace ; and while they were talking, Ben-Hur and Iras came in together.

The young Jew, advancing in front of his companion, walked first to Balthasar, and saluted him, and received his reply ; then he turned to Simonides, but paused at sight of Esther.

It is not often we have hearts roomy enough for more than one of the absorbing passions at the same time ; in its blaze the others may continue to live, but only as lesser lights. So with Ben-Hur, much study of possibilities, indulgence of hopes and dreams, influences born of the condition of his country, influences more direct — that of Iras, for example — had made him in the broadest worldly sense ambitious ; and as he had given the passion place, allowing it to become a rule, and finally an imperious governor, the resolves and impulses of former days faded imperceptibly out of being, and at last almost out of recollection. It is at best so easy to forget our youth ; in his case it was but natural that his own sufferings and the mystery darkening the fate of his family should

743

move him less and less as, in hope at least, he approached nearer and nearer the goals which occupied all his visions. Only let us not judge him too harshly.

He paused in surprise at seeing Esther a woman now, and so beautiful; and as he stood looking at her a still voice reminded him of broken vows and duties undone: almost his oid seif returned.

For an instant he was startled; but recovering, he went to Esther, and said, "Peace to thee, sweet Esther—peace; and thou, Simonides"—he looked to the merchant as he spoke —"the blessing of the Lord be thine, if only because thou hast been a good father to the fatherless."

Esther heard him with downcast face; Simonides answered,

"I repeat the welcome of the good Balthasar, son of Hur—welcome to thy father's house and sit, and tell us of thy travels, and of thy work, and of the wonderful Nazarene — who he is, and what. If thou art not at ease here, who shall be? Sit, I pray—there, between us, that we may all hear."

Esther stepped out quickly and brought a covered stool, and set it for him.

"Thanks," he said to her, gratefully.

When seated, after some other conversation, he addressed himself to the men.

"I have come to tell you of the Nazarene."

The two became instantly attentive.

"For many days now I have followed him with such watchfulness as one may give an-

744

other upon whom he is waiting so anxiously. I have seen him under all circumstances said to be trials and tests of men; and while I am certain he is a man as I am, not less certain am I that he is something more."

"What more?" asked Simonides.

"I will tell you—"

Some one coming into the room interrupted him; he turned, and arose with extended hands.

"Amrah! Dear old Amrah!" he cried.

She came forward; and they, seeing the joy in her face, thought not once how wrinkled and tawny it was. She knelt at his feet, clasped his knees, and kissed his hands over and over; and when he could he put the lank gray hair from her cheeks, and kissed them, saying, "Good Amrah, have you nothing, nothing of them—not a word—not one little sign?"

Then she broke into sobbing which made him answer plainer even than the spoken word.

"God's will has been done," he next said, solemnly, in a tone to make each listener know he had no hope more of finding his people. In his eyes there were tears which he would not have them see, because he was a man.

When he could again, he took seat, and said, "Come, sit by me, Amrah—here. No? then at my feet; for I have much to say to these good friends of a wonderful man come into the world."

But she went off, and stooping with her back to the wall, joined her hands before her knees, content, they all thought, with seeing him.

Then Ben-Hur, bowing to the old men, began again:

"I fear to answer the question asked me about the Nazarene without first telling you some of the things I have seen him do; and to that I am the more inclined, my friends, because to-morrow he will come to the city, and go up into the Temple, which he calls his father's house, where, it is further said, he will proclaim himself. So, whether you are right, O Balthasar, or you, Simonides, we and Israel shall know to-morrow."

Balthasar rubbed his hands tremulously together, and asked, "Where shall I go to see him?"

"The pressure of the crowd will be very great. Better, I think, that you all go upon the roof above the cloisters—say upon the porch of Solomon."

"Can you be with us?"

"No," said Ben-Hur, "my friends will require me, perhaps, in the procession."

"Procession!" exclaimed Simonides. "Does he travel in state?"

Ben-Hur saw the argument in mind.

"He brings twelve men with him, fishermen, tillers of the soil, one a publican, all of the humbler class; and he and they make their journeys on foot, careless of wind, cold, rain, or sun. Seeing them stop by the way-side at nightfall to break bread or lie down to sleep, I have been reminded of a party of shepherds going back to their flocks from market, not of nobles and kings. Only when he lifts the corners of his handkerchief to look at some one

746

or shake the dust from his head, I am made know he is their teacher as well as their companion—their superior not less than their friend.

"You are shrewd men," Ben-Hur resumed, after a pause. "You know what creatures of certain master motives we are, and that it has become little less than a law of our nature to spend life in eager pursuit of certain objects; now, appealing to that law as something by which we may know ourselves, what would you say of a man who could be rich by making gold of the stones under his feet, yet is poor of choice?"

"The Greeks would call him a philosopher," said Iras.

"Nay, daughter," said Balthasar, "the philosophers had never the power to do such thing."

"How know you this man has?"

Ben-Hur answered quickly, "I saw him turn water into wine."

"Very strange, very strange," said Simonides; "but it is not so strange to me as that he should prefer to live poor when he could be so rich. Is he so poor?"

"He owns nothing, and envies nobody his owning. He pities the rich. But passing that, what would you say to see a man multiply seven loaves and two fishes, all his store, into enough to feed five thousand people, and have full baskets over? That I saw the Nazarene do."

"You saw it?" exclaimed Simonides.

"Aye, and ate of the bread and fish."

"More marvellous still," Ben-Hur contin-

ued, " what would you say of a man in whom there is such healing virtue that the sick have but to touch the hem of his garment to be cured, or cry to him afar? That, too, I witnessed, not once, but many times. As we came out of Jericho two blind men by the way-side called to the Nazarene, and he touched their eyes, and they saw. So they brought a palsied man to him, and he said merely, ' Go unto thy house,' and the man went away well. What say you to these things ?"

The merchant had no answer.

" Think you now, as I have heard others argue, that what I have told you are tricks of jugglery? Let me answer by recalling greater things which I have seen him do. Look first to that curse of God—comfortless, as you all know, except by death—leprosy."

At these words Amrah dropped her hands to the floor, and in her eagerness to hear him half arose.

" What would you say," said Ben-Hur, with increased earnestness—" what would you say to have seen that I now tell you? A leper came to the Nazarene while I was with him down in Galilee, and said, 'Lord, if thou wilt, thou canst make me clean.' He heard the cry, and touched the outcast with his hand, saying, ' Be thou clean ;' and forthwith the man was himself again, healthful as any of us who beheld the cure, and we were a multitude."

Here Amrah arose, and with her gaunt fingers held the wiry locks from her eyes. The brain of the poor creature had long since gone

to heart, and she was troubled to follow the speech.

"Then, again," said Ben-Hur, without stop, "ten lepers came to him one day in a body, and, falling at his feet, called out—I saw and heard it all—called out, ' Master, Master, have mercy upon us !' He told them, 'Go, show yourselves to the priest, as the law requires ; and before you are come there ye shall be healed.' "

"And were they ?"

"Yes. On the road going their infirmity left them, so that there was nothing to remind us of it except their polluted clothes."

"Such thing was never heard before—never in all Israel !" said Simonides, in undertone.

And then, while he was speaking, Amrah turned away, and walked noiselessly to the door, and went out ; and none of the company saw her go.

"The thoughts stirred by such things done under my eyes I leave you to imagine," said Ben-Hur, continuing ; "but my doubts, my misgivings, my amazement, were not yet at the full. The people of Galilee are, as you know, impetuous and rash ; after years of waiting their swords burned their hands ; nothing would do them but action. 'He is slow to declare himself ; let us force him,' they cried to me. And I too became impatient. If he is to be king, why not now ? The legions are ready. So as he was once teaching by the sea-side we would have crowned him whether or not ; but he disappeared, and was next seen

749

on a ship departing from the shore. Good
Simonides, the desires that make other men
mad — riches, power, even kingships offered
out of great love by a great people — move this
one not at all. What say you?"

The merchant's chin was low upon his breast;
raising his head, he replied, resolutely, "The
Lord liveth, and so do the words of the proph-
ets. Time is in the green yet; let to-morrow
answer."

"Be it so," said Balthasar, smiling.

And Ben-Hur said, "Be it so." Then he
went on : "But I have not yet done. From
these things, not too great to be above sus-
picion by such as did not see them in perform-
ance as I did, let me carry you now to others in-
finitely greater, acknowledged since the world
began to be past the power of man. Tell me,
has any one to your knowledge ever reached
out and taken from Death what Death has
made his own? Who ever gave again the
breath of a life lost? Who but—"

"God!" said Balthasar, reverently.

Ben-Hur bowed.

"O wise Egyptian! I may not refuse the
name you lend me. What would you—or you,
Simonides—what would you either or both
have said had you seen as I did, a man, with
few words and no ceremony, without effort
more than a mother's when she speaks to
wake her child asleep, undo the work of
Death? It was down at Nain. We were
about going into the gate, when a company
came out bearing a dead man. The Nazarene

stopped to let the train pass. There was a woman among them crying. I saw his face soften with pity. He spoke to her, then went and touched the bier, and said to him who lay upon it dressed for burial, 'Young man, I say unto thee, Arise!' And instantly the dead sat up and talked."

"God only is so great," said Balthasar to Simonides.

"Mark you," Ben-Hur proceeded, " I do but tell you things of which I was a witness, together with a cloud of other men. On the way hither I saw another act still more mighty. In Bethany there was a man named Lazarus, who died and was buried; and after he had lain four days in a tomb, shut in by a great stone, the Nazarene was shown to the place. Upon rolling the stone away, we beheld the man lying inside bound and rotting. There were many people standing by, and we all heard what the Nazarene said, for he spoke in a loud voice: 'Lazarus, come forth!' I cannot tell you my feelings when in answer, as it were, the man arose and came out to us with all his cerements about him. 'Loose him,' said the Nazarene next—'loose him, and let him go.' And when the napkin was taken from the face of the resurrected, lo, my friends! the blood ran anew through the wasted body, and he was exactly as he had been in life before the sickness that took him off. He lives yet, and is hourly seen and spoken to. You may go see him to-morrow. And now, as nothing more is needed for the purpose, I ask you that which

I came to ask, it being but a repetition of what
you asked me, O Simonides, What more than
a man is this Nazarene?"

The question was put solemnly, and long
after midnight the company sat and debated
it; Simonides being yet unwilling to give up
his understanding of the sayings of the proph-
ets, and Ben-Hur contending that the elder
disputants were both right — that the Naza-
rene was the Redeemer, as claimed by Baltha-
sar, and also the destined king the merchant
would have.

"To-morrow we will see. Peace to you all."

So saying, Ben-Hur took his leave, intend-
ing to return to Bethany.

CHAPTER III
THE LEPERS LEAVE THEIR TOMB

HE first person to go out of the city
upon the opening of the Sheep's
Gate next morning was Amrah, bas-
ket on arm. No questions were ask-
ed her by the keepers, since the morning itself
had not been more regular in coming than she;
they knew her somebody's faithful servant, and
that was enough for them.

Down the eastern valley she took her way.
The side of Olivet, darkly green, was spotted
with white tents recently put up by people at-
tending the feasts; the hour, however, was too
early for the strangers to be abroad; still, had
it not been so, no one would have troubled

her. Past Gethsemane; past the tombs at the meeting of the Bethany roads: past the sepulchral village of Siloam she went. Occasionally the decrepit little body staggered; once she sat down to get her breath; rising shortly, she struggled on with renewed haste. The great rocks on either hand, if they had had ears, might have heard her mutter to herself; could they have seen, it would have been to observe how frequently she looked up over the Mount, reproving the dawn for its promptness; if it had been possible for them to gossip, not improbably they would have said to each other, "Our friend is in a hurry this morning; the mouths she goes to feed must be very hungry."

When at last she reached the King's Garden she slackened her gait; for then the grim city of the lepers was in view, extending far round the pitted south hill of Hinnom.

As the reader must by this time have surmised, she was going to her mistress, whose tomb, it will be remembered, overlooked the well En-Rogel.

Early as it was, the unhappy woman was up and sitting outside, leaving Tirzah asleep within. The course of the malady had been terribly swift in the three years. Conscious of her appearance, with the refined instincts of her nature, she kept her whole person habitually covered. Seldom as possible she permitted even Tirzah to see her.

This morning she was taking the air with bared head, knowing there was no one to be

shocked by the exposure. The light was not full, but enough to show the ravages to which she had been subject. Her hair was snow-white and unmanageably coarse, falling over her back and shoulders like so much silver wire. The eyelids, the lips, the nostrils, the flesh of the cheeks, were either gone or reduced to fetid rawness. The neck was a mass of ash-colored scales. One hand lay outside the folds of her habit rigid as that of a skeleton; the nails had been eaten away; the joints of the fingers, if not bare to the bone, were swollen knots crusted with red secretion. Head, face, neck, and hand indicated all too plainly the condition of the whole body. Seeing her thus, it was easy to understand how the once fair widow of the princely Hur had been able to maintain her incognito so well through such a period of years.

When the sun would gild the crest of Olivet and the Mount of Offence with light sharper and more brilliant in that old land than in the West, she knew Amrah would come, first to the well, then to a stone midway the well and the foot of the hill on which she had her abode, and that the good servant would there deposit the food she carried in the basket, and fill the water-jar afresh for the day. Of her former plenitude of happiness, that brief visit was all that remained to the unfortunate. She could then ask about her son, and be told of his welfare, with such bits of news concerning him as the messenger could glean. Usually the information was meagre enough, yet comforting;

at times she heard he was at home; then she
would issue from her dreary cell at break of
day, and sit till noon, and from noon to set of
sun, a motionless figure draped in white, look-
ing, statue-like, invariably to one point—over
the Temple to the spot under the rounded sky
where the old house stood, dear in memory,
and dearer because he was there. Nothing else
was left her. Tirzah she counted of the dead;
and as for herself, she simply waited the end,
knowing every hour of life was an hour of dy-
ing—happily, of painless dying.

The things of nature about the hill to keep
her sensitive to the world's attractions were
wretchedly scant; beasts and birds avoided
the place as if they knew its history and
present use; every green thing perished in its
first season; the winds warred upon the shrubs
and venturous grasses, leaving to drought such
as they could not uproot. Look where she
would, the view was made depressingly sug-
gestive by tombs—tombs above her, tombs be-
low, tombs opposite her own tomb—all now
freshly whitened in warning to visiting pil-
grims. In the sky—clear, fair, inviting—one
would think she might have found some re-
lief to her ache of mind; but, alas! in making
the beautiful elsewhere the sun served her
never so unfriendly—it did but disclose her
growing hideousness. But for the sun she
would not have been the horror she was to her-
self, nor been waked so cruelly from dreams of
Tirzah as she used to be. The gift of seeing
can be sometimes a dreadful curse.

755

Does one ask why she did not make an end to her sufferings?

THE LAW FORBADE HER!

A Gentile may smile at the answer; but so will not a son of Israel.

While she sat there peopling the dusky solitude with thoughts even more cheerless, suddenly a woman came up the hill staggering and spent with exertion.

The widow arose hastily, and, covering her head, cried, in a voice unnaturally harsh, "Unclean, unclean!"

In a moment, heedless of the notice, Amrah was at her feet. All the long-pent love of the simple creature burst forth: with tears and passionate exclamations she kissed her mistress's garments, and for a while the latter strove to escape from her; then, seeing she could not, she waited till the violence of the paroxysm was over.

"What have you done, Amrah?" she said. "Is it by such disobedience you prove your love for us? Wicked woman! You are lost; and he—your master—you can never, never go back to him."

Amrah grovelled sobbing in the dust.

"The ban of the Law is upon you, too; you cannot return to Jerusalem. What will become of us? Who will bring us bread? O wicked, wicked Amrah! We are all, all undone alike!"

"Mercy, mercy!" Amrah answered, from the ground.

"You should have been merciful to yourself, and by so doing been most merciful to us. Now

756

where can we fly? There is no one to help us.
O false servant! The wrath of the Lord was
already too heavy upon us."

Here Tirzah, awakened by the noise, appear-
ed at the door of the tomb. The pen shrinks
from the picture she presented. In the half-clad
apparition, patched with scales, lividly seamed,
nearly blind, its limbs and extremities swollen
to grotesque largeness, familiar eyes however
sharpened by love could not have recognized
the creature of childish grace and purity we
first beheld her.

"Is it Amrah, mother?"

The servant tried to crawl to her also.

"Stay, Amrah!" the widow cried, imperious-
ly. "I forbid you touching her. Rise, and get
you gone before any at the well see you here.
Nay, I forgot—it is too late! You must remain
now and share our doom. Rise, I say!"

Amrah rose to her knees, and said, brokenly
and with clasped hands, "O good mistress! I
am not false—I am not wicked. I bring you
good tidings."

"Of Judah?" and as she spoke, the widow
half withdrew the cloth from her head.

"There is a wonderful man," Amrah contin-
ued, "who has power to cure you. He speaks
a word, and the sick are made well, and even
the dead come to life. I have come to take
you to him."

"Poor Amrah!" said Tirzah, compassionately.

"No," cried Amrah, detecting the doubt un-
derlying the expression—"no, as the Lord lives,
even the Lord of Israel, my God as well as

yours, I speak the truth. Go with me, I pray, and lose no time. This morning he will pass by on his way to the city. See! the day is at hand. Take the food here—eat, and let us go."

The mother listened eagerly. Not unlikely she had heard of the wonderful man, for by this time his fame had penetrated every nook in the land.

"Who is he?" she asked.

"A Nazarene."

"Who told you about him?"

"Judah."

"Judah told you? Is he at home?"

"He came last night."

The widow, trying to still the beating of her heart, was silent a while.

"Did Judah send you to tell us this?" she next asked.

"No. He believes you dead."

"There was a prophet once who cured a leper," the mother said thoughtfully to Tirzah; "but he had his power from God." Then addressing Amrah, she asked, "How does my son know this man so possessed?"

"He was travelling with him, and heard the lepers call, and saw them go away well. First there was one man; then there were ten; and they were all made whole."

The elder listener was silent again. The skeleton hand shook. We may believe she was struggling to give the story the sanction of faith, which is always an absolutist in demand, and that it was with her as with the men of the day, eye-witnesses of what was done by the Christ,

758

as well as the myriads who have succeeded them. She did not question the performance, for her own son was the witness testifying through the servant; but she strove to comprehend the power by which work so astonishing could be done by a man. Well enough to make inquiry as to the fact; to comprehend the power, on the other hand, it is first necessary to comprehend God; and he who waits for that will die waiting. With her, however, the hesitation was brief. To Tirzah she said, "This must be the Messiah !"

She spoke not coldly, like one reasoning a doubt away, but as a woman of Israel familiar with the promises of God to her race—a woman of understanding, ready to be glad over the least sign of the realization of the promises.

"There was a time when Jerusalem and all Judea were filled with a story that he was born. I remember it. By this time he should be a man. It must be—it is he. Yes," she said to Amrah, "we will go with you. Bring the water which you will find in the tomb in a jar, and set the food for us. We will eat and be gone."

The breakfast, partaken under excitement, was soon despatched, and the three women set out on their extraordinary journey. As Tirzah had caught the confident spirit of the others, there was but one fear that troubled the party. Bethany, Amrah said, was the town the man was coming from; now from that to Jerusalem there were three roads, or rather paths—one over the first summit of Olivet, a second at its base, a third between the second

summit and the Mount of Offence. The three
were not far apart; far enough, however, to
make it possible for the unfortunates to miss
the Nazarene if they failed the one he chose
to come by.

A little questioning satisfied the mother
that Amrah knew nothing of the country be-
yond the Cedron, and even less of the inten-
tions of the man they were going to see, if
they could. She discerned, also, that both
Amrah and Tirzah—the one from confirmed
habits of servitude, the other from natural de-
pendency—looked to her for guidance; and
she accepted the charge.

"We will go first to Bethphage," she said to
them. "There, if the Lord favor us, we may
learn what else to do."

They descended the hill to Tophet and the
King's Garden, and paused in the deep trail
furrowed through them by centuries of way-
faring.

"I am afraid of the road," the matron said.
"Better that we keep to the country among
the rocks and trees. This is feast-day, and on
the hill-sides yonder I see signs of a great mul-
titude in attendance. By going across the
Mount of Offence here we may avoid them."

Tirzah had been walking with great diffi-
culty; upon hearing this her heart began to
fail her.

"The mount is steep, mother; I cannot
climb it."

"Remember, we are going to find health
and life. See, my child, how the day bright-

ens around us! And yonder are women coming this way to the well. They will stone us if we stay here. Come, be strong this once."

Thus the mother, not less tortured herself, sought to inspire the daughter; and Amrah came to her aid. To this time the latter had not touched the persons of the afflicted, nor they her; now, in disregard of consequences as well as of command, the faithful creature went to Tirzah, and put her arm over her shoulder, and whispered, "Lean on me. I am strong, though I am old; and it is but a little way off. There—now we can go."

The face of the hill they essayed to cross was somewhat broken with pits and ruins of old structures; but when at last they stood upon the top to rest, and looked at the spectacle presented them over in the north-west— at the Temple and its courtly terraces, at Zion, at the enduring towers white beetling into the sky beyond — the mother was strengthened with a love of life for life's sake.

"Look, Tirzah," she said — "look at the plates of gold on the Gate Beautiful. How they give back the flames of the sun, brightness for brightness! Do you remember we used to go up there? Will it not be pleasant to do so again? And think—home is but a little way off. I can almost see it over the roof of the Holy of Holies; and Judah will be there to receive us!"

From the side of the middle summit, garnished green with myrtle and olive trees, they saw, upon looking that way next, thin columns

of smoke rising lightly and straight up into the pulseless morning, each a warning of restless pilgrims astir, and of the flight of the pitiless hours, and the need of haste.

Though the good servant toiled faithfully to lighten the labor in descending the hill-side, not sparing herself in the least, the girl moaned at every step; sometimes in extremity of anguish she cried out. Upon reaching the road—that is, the road between the Mount of Offence and the middle or second summit of Olivet—she fell down exhausted.

"Go on with Amrah, mother, and leave me here," she said, faintly.

"No, no, Tirzah. What would the gain be to me if I were healed and you not? When Judah asks for you, as he will, what would I have to say to him were I to leave you?"

"Tell him I loved him."

The elder leper arose from bending over the fainting sufferer, and gazed about her with that sensation of hope perishing which is more nearly like annihilation of the soul than anything else. The supremest joy of the thought of cure was inseparable from Tirzah, who was not too old to forget, in the happiness of healthful life to come, the years of misery by which she had been so reduced in body and broken in spirit. Even as the brave woman was about leaving the venture they were engaged in to the determination of God, she saw a man on foot coming rapidly up the road from the east.

"Courage, Tirzah! Be of cheer," she said.

"Yonder I know is one to tell us of the Nazarene."

Amrah helped the girl to a sitting posture, and supported her while the man advanced.

"In your goodness, mother, you forget what we are. The stranger will go around us; his best gift to us will be a curse, if not a stone."

"We will see."

There was no other answer to be given, since the mother was too well and sadly acquainted with the treatment outcasts of the class to which she belonged were accustomed to at the hands of her countrymen.

As has been said, the road at the edge of which the group was posted was little more than a worn path or trail, winding crookedly through tumuli of limestone. If the stranger kept it, he must meet them face to face; and he did so, until near enough to hear the cry she was bound to give. Then, uncovering her head, a further demand of the law, she shouted shrilly,

"Unclean, unclean!"

To her surprise, the man came steadily on.

"What would you have?" he asked, stopping opposite them not four yards off.

"Thou seest us. Have a care," the mother said, with dignity.

"Woman, I am the courier of him who speaketh but once to such as thou and they are healed. I am not afraid."

"The Nazarene?"

"The Messiah," he said.

"Is it true that he cometh to the city to-day?"

"He is now at Bethphage."

"On what road, master?"

"This one."

She clasped her hands, and looked up thankfully.

"For whom takest thou him?" the man asked, with pity.

"The Son of God," she replied.

"Stay thou here, then; or, as there is a multitude with him, take thy stand by the rock yonder, the white one under the tree; and as ne goeth by fail not to call to him; call, and fear not. If thy faith but equal thy knowledge, he will hear thee though all the heavens thunder. I go to tell Israel, assembled in and about the city, that he is at hand, and to make ready to receive him. Peace to thee and thine, woman."

The stranger moved on.

"Did you hear, Tirzah? Did you hear? The Nazarene is on the road, on this one, and he will hear us. Once more, my child—oh, only once! and let us to the rock. It is but a step."

Thus encouraged, Tirzah took Amrah's hand and arose; but as they were going, Amrah said, "Stay; the man is returning." And they waited for him.

"I pray your grace, woman," he said, upon overtaking them. "Remembering that the sun will be hot before the Nazarene arrives, and tnat the city is near by to give me refreshment snould I need it, I thought this water would do thee better than it will me. Take it and be of good cheer. Call to him as he passes."

He followed the words by offering her a gourd full of water, such as foot-travellers sometimes carried with them in their journeys across the hills; and instead of placing the gift on the ground for her to take up when he was at a safe distance, he gave it into her hand.

"Art thou a Jew?" she asked, surprised.

"I am that, and better; I am a disciple of the Christ who teacheth daily by word and example this thing which I have done unto you. The world hath long known the word charity without understanding it. Again I say peace and good cheer to thee and thine."

He went on, and they went slowly to the rock he had pointed out to them, high as their heads, and scarcely thirty yards from the road on the right. Standing in front of it, the mother satisfied herself they could be seen and heard plainly by passers-by whose notice they desired to attract. There they cast themselves under the tree in its shade, and drank of the gourd, and rested refreshed. Ere long Tirzah slept, and fearing to disturb her, the others held their peace.

THE MIRACLE

URING the third hour the road in front of the resting-place of the lepers became gradually more and more frequented by people going in the direction of Bethphage and Bethany; now, however, about the commencement of the fourth hour, a great crowd appeared over the crest of Olivet, and as it defiled down the road thousands in number, the two watchers noticed with wonder that every one in it carried a palm-branch freshly cut. As they sat absorbed by the novelty, the noise of another multitude approaching from the east drew their eyes that way. Then the mother awoke Tirzah.

"What is the meaning of it all?" the latter asked.

"He is coming," answered the mother. "These we see are from the city going to meet him; those we hear in the east are his friends bearing him company; and it will not be strange if the processions meet here before us."

"I fear, if they do, we cannot be heard."

The same thought was in the elder's mind.

"Amrah," she asked, "when Judah spoke of the healing of the ten, in what words did he say they called to the Nazarene?"

"Either they said, 'Lord, have mercy upon us,' or 'Master, have mercy. ''

"Only that?"

"No more that I heard."

"Yet it was enough," the mother added, to herself.

"Yes," said Amrah, "Judah said he saw them go away well."

Meantime the people in the east came up slowly. When at length the foremost of them were in sight, the gaze of the lepers fixed upon a man riding in the midst of what seemed a chosen company which sang and danced about him in extravagance of joy. The rider was bareheaded and clad all in white. When he was in distance to be more clearly observed, these, looking anxiously, saw an olive-hued face shaded by long chestnut hair slightly sun-burned and parted in the middle. He looked neither to the right nor left. In the noisy abandon of his followers he appeared to have no part; nor did their favor disturb him in the least, or raise him out of the profound melancholy into which, as his countenance showed, he was plunged. The sun beat upon the back of his head, and lighting up the floating hair gave it a delicate likeness to a golden nimbus. Behind him the irregular procession, pouring forward with continuous singing and shouting, extended out of view. There was no need of any one to tell the lepers that this was he—the wonderful Nazarene!

"He is here, Tirzah," the mother said; "he is here. Come, my child."

As she spoke she glided in front of the white rock and fell upon her knees.

Directly the daughter and servant were by her side. Then at sight of the procession in the west, the thousands from the city halted, and began to wave their green branches, shouting, or rather chanting (for it was all in one voice),

"Blessed is the King of Israel that cometh in the name of the Lord!"

And all the thousands who were of the rider's company, both those near and those afar, replied so the air shook with the sound, which was as a great wind threshing the side of the hill. Amidst the din, the cries of the poor lepers were not more than the twittering of dazed sparrows.

The moment of the meeting of the hosts was come, and with it the opportunity the sufferers were seeking; if not taken, it would be lost forever, and they would be lost as well.

"Nearer, my child—let us get nearer. He cannot hear us," said the mother.

She arose, and staggered forward. Her ghastly hands were up, and she screamed with horrible shrillness. The people saw her—saw her hideous face, and stopped awe-struck—an effect for which extreme human misery, visible as in this instance, is as potent as majesty in purple and gold. Tirzah, behind her a little way, fell down too faint and frightened to follow farther.

"The lepers! the lepers!"

"Stone them!"

"The accursed of God! Kill them!"

These, with other yells of like import, broke in upon the hosannas of the part of the multitude too far removed to see and understand the cause of the interruption. Some there were, however, near by familiar with the nature of the man to whom the unfortunates were appealing — some who, by long intercourse with him, had caught somewhat of his divine compassion: they gazed at him, and were silent while, in fair view, he rode up and stopped in front of the woman. She also beheld his face—calm, pitiful, and of exceeding beauty, the large eyes tender with benignant purpose.

And this was the colloquy that ensued:

"O Master, Master! Thou seest our need; thou canst make us clean. Have mercy upon us—mercy!"

"Believest thou I am able to do this?" he asked.

"Thou art he of whom the prophets spake —thou art the Messiah!" she replied.

His eyes grew radiant, his manner confident.

"Woman," he said, "great is thy faith; be it unto thee even as thou wilt."

He lingered an instant after, apparently unconscious of the presence of the throng—an instant—then he rode away.

To the heart divinely original, yet so human in all the better elements of humanity, going with sure prevision to a death of all the inventions of men the foulest and most cruel, breathing even then in the forecast shadow of

the awful event, and still as hungry and thirsty
for love and faith as in the beginning, how
precious and ineffably soothing the farewell
exclamation of the grateful woman:

"To God in the highest, glory! Blessed,
thrice blessed, the Son whom he hath given
us!"

Immediately both the hosts, that from the
city and that from Bethphage, closed around
him with their joyous demonstrations, with ho-
sannas and waving of palms, and so he passed
from the lepers forever. Covering her head,
the elder hastened to Tirzah, and folded her
in her arms, crying, "Daughter, look up! I
have his promise; he is indeed the Messiah.
We are saved—saved!" And the two remain-
ed kneeling while the procession, slowly go-
ing, disappeared over the mount. When the
noise of its singing afar was a sound scarcely
heard the miracle began.

There was first in the hearts of the lepers a
freshening of the blood; then it flowed faster
and stronger, thrilling their wasted bodies with
an infinitely sweet sense of painless healing.
Each felt the scourge going from her; their
strength revived; they were returning to be
themselves. Directly, as if to make the puri-
fication complete, from body to spirit the
quickening ran, exalting them to a very fervor
of ecstasy. The power possessing them to this
good end was most nearly that of a draught of
swift and happy effect; yet it was unlike and
superior in that its healing and cleansing were
absolute, and not merely a delicious conscious-

ness while in progress, but the planting, grow-
ing, and maturing all at once of a recollection
so singular and so holy that the simple thought
of it should be of itself ever after a formless
yet perfect thanksgiving.

To this transformation—for such it may be
called quite as properly as a cure—there was
a witness other than Amrah. The reader will
remember the constancy with which Ben-Hur
had followed the Nazarene throughout his
wanderings; and now, recalling the conversa-
tion of the night before, there will be little sur-
prise at learning that the young Jew was pres-
ent when the leprous woman appeared in the
path of the pilgrims. He heard her prayer,
and saw her disfigured face; he heard the an-
swer also, and was not so accustomed to inci-
dents of the kind, frequent as they had been,
as to have lost interest in them. Had such
thing been possible with him, still the bitter
disputation always excited by the simplest dis-
play of the Master's curative gift would have
sufficed to keep his curiosity alive. Besides
that, if not above it as an incentive, his hope
to satisfy himself upon the vexed question of
the mission of the mysterious man was still
upon him strong as in the beginning; we
might indeed say even stronger, because of a
belief that now quickly, before the sun went
down, the man himself would make all known
by public proclamation. At the close of the
scene, consequently, Ben-Hur had withdrawn
from the procession, and seated himself upon
a stone to wait its passage.

771

From his place he nodded recognition to many of the people—Galileans in his league, carrying short swords under their long abbas. After a little a swarthy Arab came up leading two horses; at a sign from Ben-Hur he also drew out.

"Stay here," the young master said, when all were gone by, even the laggards. "I wish to be at the city early, and Aldebaran must do me service."

He stroked the broad forehead of the horse, now in his prime of strength and beauty, then crossed the road towards the two women.

They were to him, it should be borne in mind, strangers in whom he felt interest only as they were subjects of a superhuman experiment, the result of which might possibly help him to solution of the mystery that had so long engaged him. As he proceeded, he glanced casually at the figure of the little woman over by the white rock, standing there her face hidden in her hands.

"As the Lord liveth, it is Amrah!" he said to himself.

He hurried on, and passing by the mother and daughter, still without recognizing them, he stopped before the servant.

"Amrah," he said to her, "Amrah, what do you here?"

She rushed forward, and fell upon her knees before him, blinded by her tears, nigh speechless with contending joy and fear.

"O master, master! Thy God and mine, how good he is!"

The knowledge we gain from much sympathy with others passing through trials is but vaguely understood; strangely enough, it enables us, among other things, to merge our identity into theirs often so completely that their sorrows and their delights become our own. So poor Amrah, aloof and hiding her face, knew the transformation the lepers were undergoing without a word spoken to her—knew it, and shared all their feeling to the full. Her countenance, her words, her whole manner, betrayed her condition; and with swift presentiment he connected it with the women he had just passed: he felt her presence there at that time was in some way associated with them, and turned hastily as they arose to their feet. His heart stood still; he became rooted in his tracks—dumb past outcry—awe-struck.

The woman he had seen before the Nazarene was standing with her hands clasped and eyes streaming, looking towards heaven. The mere transformation would have been a sufficient surprise; but it was the least of the causes of his emotion. Could he be mistaken? Never was there in life a stranger so like his mother; and like her as she was the day the Roman snatched her from him. There was but one difference to mar the identity—the hair of this person was a little streaked with gray; yet that was not impossible of reconcilement, since the intelligence which had directed the miracle might have taken into consideration the natural effects of the passage of years. And who was it by her side, if not Tirzah?—fair, beauti-

ful, perfect, more mature, but in all other respects exactly the same in appearance as when she looked with him over the parapet the morning of the accident to Gratus. He had given them over as dead, and time had accustomed him to the bereavement; he had not ceased mourning for them, yet, as something distinguishable, they had simply dropped out of his plans and dreams. Scarcely believing his senses, he laid his hand upon the servant's head, and asked, tremulously,

"Amrah, Amrah—my mother! Tirzah! tell me if I see aright."

"Speak to them, O master, speak to them!" she said.

He waited no longer, but ran, with outstretched arms, crying, "Mother! mother! Tirzah! Here I am!"

They heard his call, and with a cry as loving started to meet him. Suddenly the mother stopped, drew back, and uttered the old alarm,

"Stay, Judah, my son; come not nearer. Unclean, unclean!"

The utterance was not from habit, grown since the dread disease struck her, as much as fear; and the fear was but another form of the ever-thoughtful maternal love. Though they were healed in person, the taint of the scourge might be in their garments ready for communication. He had no such thought. They were before him; he had called them, they had answered. Who or what should keep them from him now? Next moment the three, so

774

long separated, were mingling their tears in each other's arms.

The first ecstasy over, the mother said, "In this happiness, O my children, let us not be ungrateful. Let us begin life anew by acknowledgment of him to whom we are all so indebted."

They fell upon their knees, Amrah with the rest; and the prayer of the elder outspoken was as a psalm.

Tirzah repeated it word for word; so did Ben-Hur, but not with the same clear mind and questionless faith; for when they were risen, he asked,

"In Nazareth, where the man was born, mother, they call him the son of a carpenter. What is he?"

Her eyes rested upon him with all their old tenderness, and she answered as she had answered the Nazarene himself—

"He is the Messiah."

"And whence has he his power?"

"We may know by the use he makes of it. Can you tell me any ill he has done?"

"No."

"By that sign, then, I answer, He has his power from God."

It is not an easy thing to shake off in a moment the expectations nurtured through years until they have become essentially a part of us; and though Ben-Hur asked himself what the vanities of the world were to such a one, his ambition was obdurate and would not down. He persiated as men do yet every day in meas-

775

uring the Christ by himself. How much better if we measured ourselves by the Christ!

Naturally, the mother was the first to think of the cares of life.

"What shall we do now, my son? Where shall we go?"

Then Ben-Hur, recalled to duty, observed how completely every trace of the scourge had disappeared from his restored people; that each had back her perfection of person; that, as with Naaman when he came up out of the water, their flesh had come again like unto the flesh of a little child; and he took off his cloak, and threw it over Tirzah.

"Take it," he said, smiling; "the eye of the stranger would have shunned you before, now it shall not offend you."

The act exposed a sword belted to his side.

"Is it a time of war?" asked the mother, anxiously.

"No."

"Why, then, are you armed?"

"It may be necessary to defend the Nazarene."

Thus Ben-Hur evaded the whole truth.

"Has he enemies? Who are they?"

"Alas, mother, they are not all Romans!"

"Is he not of Israel, and a man of peace?"

"There was never one more so; but in the opinion of the rabbis and teachers he is guilty of a great crime."

"What crime?"

"In his eyes the uncircumcised Gentile is as

worthy favor as a Jew of the strictest habit. He preaches a new dispensation."

The mother was silent, and they moved to the shade of the tree by the rock. Calming his impatience to have them home again and hear their story, he showed them the necessity of obedience to the law governing in cases like theirs, and in conclusion called the Arab, bidding him take the horses to the gate by Bethesda and await him there; whereupon they set out by the way of the Mount of Offence. The return was very different from the coming; they walked rapidly and with ease, and in good time reached a tomb newly made near that of Absalom, overlooking the depths of Cedron. Finding it unoccupied, the women took possession, while he went on hastily to make the preparations necessary for their new condition.

CHAPTER V
PILGRIMS TO THE PASSOVER

BEN-HUR pitched two tents out on the Upper Cedron east a short space of the Tombs of the Kings, and furnished them with every comfort at his command; and thither, without loss of time, he conducted his mother and sister, to remain until the examining priest could certify their perfect cleansing.

In course of the duty, the young man had subjected himself to such serious defilement as to debar him from participation in the cere-

monies of the great feast, then near at hand.
He could not enter the least sacred of the courts
of the Temple. Of necessity, not less than
choice, therefore, he stayed at the tents with
his beloved people. There was a great deal to
hear from them, and a great deal to tell them
of himself.

Stories such as theirs—sad experiences ex-
tending through a lapse of years, sufferings of
body, acuter sufferings of mind—are usually
long in the telling, the incidents seldom follow-
ing each other in threaded connection. He lis-
tened to the narrative and all they told him,
with outward patience masking inward feeling.
In fact, his hatred of Rome and Romans reach-
ed a higher mark than ever; his desire for
vengeance became a thirst which attempts at
reflection only intensified. In the almost sav-
age bitterness of his humor many mad impulses
took hold of him. The opportunities of the
highways presented themselves with singular
force of temptation; he thought seriously of
insurrection in Galilee; even the sea, ordinarily
a retrospective horror to him, stretched itself
map-like before his fancy, laced and interlaced
with lines of passage crowded with imperial
plunder and imperial travellers; but the better
judgment matured in calmer hours was happily
too firmly fixed to be supplanted by present
passion however strong. Each mental venture
in reach of new expedients brought him back
to the old conclusion—that there could be no
sound success except in a war involving all Is-
rael in solid union; and all musing upon the

subject, all inquiry, all hope, ended where they
began—in the Nazarene and his purposes.

At odd moments the excited schemer found
a pleasure in fashioning a speech for that per-
son:

"Hear, O Israel! I am he, the promised of
God, born King of the Jews—come to you with
the dominion spoken of by the prophets. Rise
now, and lay hold on the world!"

Would the Nazarene but speak these few
words, what a tumult would follow! How many
mouths performing the office of trumpets would
take them up and blow them abroad for the
massing of armies!

Would he speak them?

And eager to begin the work, and answering
in the worldly way, Ben-Hur lost sight of the
double nature of the man, and of the other
possibility, that the divine in him might tran-
scend the human. In the miracle of which Tir-
zah and his mother were the witnesses even
more nearly than himself, he saw and set apart
and dwelt upon a power ample enough to raise
and support a Jewish crown over the wrecks of
the Italian, and more than ample to remodel
society, and convert mankind into one purified
happy family; and when that work was done,
could any one say the peace which might then
be ordered without hinderance was not a mis-
sion worthy a son of God? Could any one then
deny the Redeemership of the Christ? And
discarding all consideration of political conse-
quences, what unspeakable personal glory there
would then be to him as a man! It was not

in the nature of any mere mortal to refuse such
a career.

Meantime down the Cedron, and in towards
Bezetha, especially on the road-sides quite up to
the Damascus Gate, the country filled rapidly
with all kinds of temporary shelters for pil-
grims to the Passover. Ben-Hur visited the
strangers, and talked with them ; and return-
ing to his tents, he was each time more and
more astonished at the vastness of their num-
bers. And when he further discovered that
every part of the world was represented among
them—cities upon both shores of the Mediter-
ranean far off as the Pillars of the West, river-
towns in distant India, provinces in northern-
most Europe, and that, though they frequently
saluted him with tongues unacquainted with a
syllable of the old Hebrew of the fathers, these
representatives had all the same object—cele-
bration of the notable feast—an idea tinged
mistily with superstitious fancy forced itself
upon him. Might he not after all have misun-
derstood the Nazarene ? Might not that person
by patient waiting be covering silent prepara-
tion, and proving his fitness for the glorious
task before him ? How much better this time
for the movement than that other when, by
Gennesaret, the Galileans would have forced
assumption of the crown ! Then the support
would have been limited to a few thousands;
now his proclamation would be responded to
by millions—who could say how many ? Pur-
suing this theory to its conclusions, Ben-Hur
moved amid brilliant promises, and glowed

<center>780</center>

with the thought that the melancholy man, under gentle seeming and wondrous self-denial, was in fact carrying in disguise the subtlety of a politician and the genius of a soldier.

Several times, also, in the mean while, low-set, brawny men, bareheaded and black-bearded, came and asked for Ben-Hur at the tent; his interviews with them were always apart; and to his mother's question who they were he answered,

"Some good friends of mine from Galilee."

Through them he kept informed of the movements of the Nazarene, and of the schemes of the Nazarene's enemies, Rabbinical and Roman. That the good man's life was in danger, he knew; but that there were any bold enough to attempt to take it at that time he could not believe. It seemed too securely intrenched in a great fame and an assured popularity. The very vastness of the attendance in and about the city brought with it a seeming guarantee of safety. And yet, to say truth, Ben-Hur's confidence rested most certainly upon the miraculous power of the Christ. Pondering the subject in the purely human view, that the master of such authority over life and death, used so frequently for the good of others, would not exert it in care of himself was simply as much past belief as it was past understanding.

Nor should it be forgotten that all these were incidents of occurrence between the twenty-first day of March—counting by the modern calendar—and the twenty-fifth. The evening

of the latter day Ben-Hur yielded to his impatience, and rode to the city, leaving behind him a promise to return in the night.

The horse was fresh, and, choosing his own gait, sped swiftly. The eyes of the clambering vines winked at the rider from the garden fences on the way; there was nothing else to see him, nor child nor woman nor man. Through the rocky float in the hollows of the road the agate hoofs drummed, ringing like cups of steel; but without notice from any stranger. In the houses passed there were no tenants; the fires by the tent-doors were out; the road was deserted; for this was the first Passover eve, and the hour "between the evenings" when the visiting millions crowded the city, and the slaughter of lambs in offering reeked the forecourts of the Temple, and the priests in ordered lines caught the flowing blood and carried it swiftly to the dripping altars—when all was haste and hurry, racing with the stars fast coming with the signal after which the roasting and the eating and the singing might go on, but not the preparation more.

Through the great northern gate the rider rode, and lo! Jerusalem before the fall, in ripeness of glory, illuminated for the Lord.

EN-HUR alighted at the gate of the khan from which the three Wise Men more than thirty years before departed, going down to Bethlehem. There, in keeping of his Arab followers, he left the horse, and shortly after was at the wicket of his father's house, and in a yet briefer space in the great chamber. He called for Malluch first; that worthy being out, he sent a salutation to his friends the merchant and the Egyptian. They were being carried abroad to see the celebration. The latter, he was informed, was very feeble, and in a state of deep dejection.

Young people of that time who were supposed hardly to know their own hearts indulged the habit of politic indirection quite as much as young people in the same condition indulge it in this time; so when Ben-Hur inquired for the good Balthasar, and with grave courtesy desired to know if he would be pleased to see him, he really addressed the daughter a notice of his arrival. While the servant was answering for the elder, the curtain of the doorway was drawn aside, and the younger Egyptian came in, and walked—or floated, upborne in a white cloud of the gauzy raiment she so loved and lived in—to the centre of the cham-

783

ber, where the light cast by lamps from the seven-armed brazen stick planted upon the floor was the strongest. With her there was no fear of light.

The servant left the two alone.

In the excitement occasioned by the events of the few days past Ben-Hur had scarcely given a thought to the fair Egyptian. If she came to his mind at all, it was merely as a briefest pleasure, a suggestion of a delight which could wait for him, and was waiting.

But now the influence of the woman revived with all its force the instant Ben-Hur beheld her. He advanced to her eagerly, but stopped and gazed. Such a change he had never seen!

Theretofore she had been a lover studious to win him—in manner all warmth, each glance an admission, each action an avowal. She had showered him with incense of flattery. While he was present, she had impressed him with her admiration; going away, he carried the impression with him to remain a delicious expectancy hastening his return. It was for him the painted eyelids drooped lowest over the lustrous almond eyes; for him the love-stories caught from the professionals abounding in the streets of Alexandria were repeated with emphasis and lavishment of poetry; for him endless exclamations of sympathy, and smiles, and little privileges with hand and hair and cheek and lips, and songs of the Nile, and displays of jewelry, and subtleties of lace in veils and scarfs, and other subtleties not less exquisite in flosses of Indian silk. The idea, old as the

oldest of peoples, that beauty is the reward of the hero had never such realism as she contrived for his pleasure; insomuch that he could not doubt he was her hero; she avouched it in a thousand artful ways as natural with her as her beauty—winsome ways reserved, it would seem, by the passionate genius of old Egypt for its daughters.

Such the Egyptian had been to Ben-Hur from the night of the boat-ride on the lake in the Orchard of Palms. But now!

Elsewhere in this volume the reader may have observed a term of somewhat indefinite meaning used reverently in a sacred connection; we repeat it now with a general application. There are few persons who have not a double nature, the real and the acquired; the latter a kind of addendum resulting from education, which in time often perfects it into a part of the being as unquestionable as the first. Leaving the thought to the thoughtful, we proceed to say that now the real nature of the Egyptian made itself manifest.

It was not possible for her to have received a stranger with repulsion more incisive: yet she was apparently as passionless as a statue, only the small head was a little tilted, the nostrils a little drawn, and the sensuous lower lip pushed the upper the least bit out of its natural curvature.

She was the first to speak.

"Your coming is timely, O son of Hur," she said, in a voice sharply distinct. "I wish to thank you for hospitality; after to-mor-

row I may not have the opportunity to do so."

Ben-Hur bowed slightly without taking his eyes from her.

"I have heard of a custom which the dice-players observe with good result among themselves," she continued. "When the game is over, they refer to their tablets and cast up their accounts; then they libate the gods and put a crown upon the happy winner. We have had a game—it has lasted through many days and nights. Why, now that it is at an end, shall not we see to which the chaplet belongs?"

Yet very watchful, Ben-Hur answered, lightly, "A man may not balk a woman bent on having her way."

"Tell me," she continued, inclining her head, and permitting the sneer to become positive—"tell me, O prince of Jerusalem, where is he, that son of the carpenter of Nazareth, and son not less of God, from whom so lately such mighty things were expected?"

He waved his hand impatiently, and replied, "I am not his keeper."

The beautiful head sank forward yet lower.

"Has he broken Rome to pieces?"

Again, but with anger, Ben-Hur raised his hand in deprecation.

"Where has he seated his capital?" she proceeded. "Cannot I go see his throne and its lions of bronze? And his palace—he raised the dead; and to such a one, what is it to raise a golden house? He has but to stamp his foot

786

and say the word, and the house is, pillared
like Karnak, and wanting nothing."

There was by this time slight ground left to
believe her playing; the questions were offen-
sive, and her manner pointed with unfriendli-
ness; seeing which, he on his side became more
wary, and said, with good-humor, "O Egypt, let
us wait another day, even another week, for
him, the lions, and the palace."

She went on without noticing the suggestion.

"And how is it I see you in that garb? Such
is not the habit of governors in India or vice-
kings elsewhere. I saw the satrap of Teheran
once, and he wore a turban of silk and a cloak
of cloth of gold, and the hilt and scabbard of
his sword made me dizzy with their splendor
of precious stones. I thought Osiris had lent
him a glory from the sun. I fear you have not
entered upon your kingdom — the kingdom I
was to share with you."

"The daughter of my wise guest is kinder
than she imagines herself; she is teaching me
that Isis may kiss a heart without making it
better."

Ben-Hur spoke with cold courtesy, and Iras,
after playing with the pendent solitaire of her
necklace of coins, rejoined, "For a Jew, the son
of Hur is clever. I saw your dreaming Cæsar
make his entry into Jerusalem. You told us he
would that day proclaim himself King of the
Jews from the steps of the Temple. I beheld
the procession descend the mountain bringing
him. I heard their singing. They were beau-
tiful with palms in motion. I looked everywhere

787

among them for a figure with a promise of royalty—a horseman in purple, a chariot with a driver in shining brass, a stately warrior behind an orbed shield, rivalling his spear in stature. I looked for his guard. It would have been pleasant to have seen a prince of Jerusalem and a cohort of the legions of Galilee."

She flung her listener a glance of provoking disdain, then laughed heartily, as if the ludicrousness of the picture in her mind were too strong for contempt.

"Instead of a Sesostris returning in triumph or a Cæsar helmed and sworded—ha, ha, ha!—I saw a man with a woman's face and hair, riding an ass's colt, and in tears. The King! the Son of God! the Redeemer of the World! Ha, ha, ha!"

In spite of himself, Ben-Hur winced.

"I did not quit my place, O prince of Jerusalem," she said, before he could recover. "I did not laugh. I said to myself, 'Wait. In the Temple he will glorify himself as becomes a hero about to take possession of the world.' I saw him enter the Gate of Shushan and the Court of the Women. I saw him stop and stand before the Gate Beautiful. There were people with me on the porch and in the courts, and on the cloisters and on the steps of the three sides of the Temple there were other people—I will say a million of people, all waiting breathlessly to hear his proclamation. The pillars were not more still than we. Ha, ha, ha! I fancied I heard the axles of the mighty Roman machine begin to crack. Ha, ha, ha! O prince,

by the soul of Solomon, your King of the World
drew his gown about him and walked away,
and out by the farthest gate, nor opened his
mouth to say a word; and—the Roman ma-
chine is running yet!"

In simple homage to a hope that instant
lost—a hope which, as it began to fall and
while it was falling, he unconsciously followed
with a parting look down to its disappearance
—Ben-Hur lowered his eyes.

At no previous time, whether when Baltha-
sar was plying him with arguments, or when
miracles were being done before his face, had
the disputed nature of the Nazarene been so
plainly set before him. The best way, after all,
to reach an understanding of the divine is by
study of the human. In the things superior
to men we may always look to find God. So
with the picture given by the Egyptian of the
scene when the Nazarene turned from the Gate
Beautiful; its central theme was an act utterly
beyond performance by a man under control
of merely human inspirations. A parable to
a parable-loving people, it taught what the
Christ had so often asserted—that his mission
was not political. There was not much more
time for thought of all this than that allowed
for a common respiration; yet the idea took
fast hold of Ben-Hur, and in the same instant
he followed his hope of vengeance out of sight,
and the man with the woman's face and hair,
and in tears, came near to him—near enough
to leave something of his spirit behind.

"Daughter of Balthasar," he said, with dig-

nity, "if this be the game of which you spoke
to me, take the chaplet—I accord it yours.
Only let us make an end of words. That you
have a purpose I am sure. To it, I pray, and
I will answer you; then let us go our several
ways, and forget we ever met. Say on; I will
listen, but not to more of that which you have
given me."

She regarded him intently a moment, as if
determining what to do—possibly she might
have been measuring his will—then she said,
coldly, "You have my leave—go."

"Peace to you," he responded, and walked
away.

As he was about passing out of the door she
called to him.

"A word."

He stopped where he was and looked back.

"Consider all I know about you."

"O most fair Egyptian," he said, returning,
"what all do you know about me?"

She looked at him absently.

"You are more of a Roman, son of Hur, than
any of your Hebrew brethren."

"Am I so unlike my countrymen?" he asked,
indifferently.

"The demi-gods are all Roman now," she
rejoined.

"And therefore you will tell me what more
you know about me?"

"The likeness is not lost upon me. It might
induce me to save you."

"Save me!"

The pink-stained fingers toyed daintily with

GATE OF ST. STEPHEN

the lustrous pendant at the throat, and her voice was exceeding low and soft; only a tapping on the floor with her silken sandal admonished him to have a care.

"There was a Jew, an escaped galley-slave, who killed a man in the Palace of Idernee," she began, slowly.

Ben-Hur was startled.

"The same Jew slew a Roman soldier before the Market-place here in Jerusalem; the same Jew has three trained legions from Galilee to seize the Roman governor to-night; the same Jew has alliances perfected for war upon Rome, and Ilderim the Sheik is one of his partners."

Drawing nearer to him, she almost whispered,

"You have lived in Rome. Suppose these things repeated in ears we know of. Ah! you change color."

He drew back from her with somewhat of the look which may be imagined upon the face of a man who, thinking to play with a kitten, has run upon a tiger; and she proceeded:

"You are acquainted in the antechamber, and know the Lord Sejanus. Suppose it were told him with the proofs in hand—or without the proofs—that the same Jew is the richest man in the East—nay, in all the empire. The fishes of the Tiber would have fattening other than that they dig out of its ooze, would they not? And while they were feeding—ha! son of Hur!—what splendor there would be on exhibition in the Circus! Amusing the Roman people is a fine art; getting the money to keep

them amused is another art even finer; and was there ever an artist the equal of the Lord Sejanus?"

Ben-Hur was not too much stirred by the evident baseness of the woman for recollection. Not unfrequently when all the other faculties are numb and failing memory does its offices with the greatest fidelity. The scene at the spring on the way to the Jordan reproduced itself; and he remembered thinking then that Esther had betrayed him, and thinking so now, he said calmly as he could,

"To give you pleasure, daughter of Egypt, I acknowledge your cunning, and that I am at your mercy. It may also please you to hear me acknowledge I have no hope of your favor. I could kill you, but you are a woman. The Desert is open to receive me; and though Rome is a good hunter of men, there she would follow long and far before she caught me, for in its heart there are wildernesses of spears as well as wildernesses of sand, and it is not unlovely to the unconquered Parthian. In the toils as I am — dupe that I have been — yet there is one thing my due: who told you all you know about me? In flight or captivity, dying even, there will be consolation in leaving the traitor the curse of a man who has lived knowing nothing but wretchedness. Who told you all you know about me?"

It might have been a touch of art, or might have been sincere — that as it may — the expression of the Egyptian's face became sympathetic.

"There are in my country, O son of Hur,"
she said, presently, "workmen who make pict-
ures by gathering vari-colored shells here and
there on the sea-shore after storms, and cut-
ting them up, and patching the pieces as in-
laying on marble slabs. Can you not see the
hint there is in the practice to such as go
searching for secrets? Enough that from this
person I gathered a handful of little circum-
stances, and from that other yet another hand-
ful, and that afterwhile I put them together,
and was happy as a woman can be who has at
disposal the fortune and life of a man whom"
—she stopped, and beat the floor with her foot,
and looked away as if to hide a sudden emo-
tion from him; with an air of even painful
resolution she presently finished the sentence
—"whom she is at loss what to do with."

"No, it is not enough," Ben-Hur said, un-
moved by the play—"it is not enough. To-
morrow you will determine what to do with
me. I may die."

"True," she rejoined quickly and with em-
phasis, "I had something from Sheik Ilderim
as he lay with my father in a grove out in the
Desert. The night was still, very still, and the
walls of the tent, sooth to say, were poor ward
against ears outside listening to—birds and
beetles flying through the air."

She smiled at the conceit, but proceeded:

"Some other things—bits of shell for the
picture—I had from—"

"Whom?"

"The son of Hur himself.

"Was there no other who contributed?"

"No, not one."

Hur drew a breath of relief, and said, lightly, "Thanks. It were not well to keep the Lord Sejanus waiting for you. The Desert is not so sensitive. Again, O Egypt, peace!"

To this time he had been standing uncovered; now he took the handkerchief from his arm where it had been hanging, and adjusting it upon his head, turned to depart. But she arrested him; in her eagerness, she even reached a hand to him.

"Stay," she said.

He looked back at her, but without taking the hand, though it was very noticeable for its sparkling of jewels; and he knew by her manner that the reserved point of the scene which was so surprising to him was now to come.

"Stay, and do not distrust me, O son of Hur, if I declare I know why the noble Arrius took you for his heir. And, by Isis! by all the gods of Egypt! I swear I tremble to think of you, so brave and generous, under the hand of the remorseless minister. You have left a portion of your youth in the atria of the great capital; consider, as I do, what the Desert will be to you in contrast of life. Oh, I give you pity— pity! And if you but do what I say, I will save you. That, also, I swear, by our holy Isis!"

Words of entreaty and prayer these, poured forth volubly and with earnestness and the mighty sanction of beauty.

"Almost—almost I believe you," Ben-Hur said, yet hesitatingly, and in a voice low and

indistinct; for a doubt remained with him grumbling against the yielding tendency of the man—a good sturdy doubt, such a one as has saved many a life and fortune.

"The perfect life for a woman is to live in love; the greatest happiness for a man is the conquest of himself; and that, O prince, is what I have to ask of you."

She spoke rapidly, and with animation; indeed, she had never appeared to him so fascinating.

"You had once a friend," she continued. "It was in your boyhood. There was a quarrel, and you and he became enemies. He did you wrong. After many years you met him again in the Circus at Antioch."

"Messala!"

"Yes, Messala. You are his creditor. Forgive the past; admit him to friendship again; restore the fortune he lost in the great wager; rescue him. The six talents are as nothing to you; not so much as a bud lost upon a tree already in full leaf; but to him— Ah, he must go about with a broken body; wherever you meet him he must look up to you from the ground. O Ben-Hur, noble prince! To a Roman descended as he is, beggary is the other most odious name for death. Save him from beggary!"

If the rapidity with which she spoke was a cunning invention to keep him from thinking, either she never knew or else had forgotten that there are convictions which derive nothing from thought, but drop into place without

leave or notice. It seemed to him, when at last she paused to have his answer, that he could see Messala himself peering at him over her shoulder; and in its expression the countenance of the Roman was not that of a mendicant or a friend; the sneer was as patrician as ever, and the fine edge of the hauteur as flawless and irritating.

"The appeal has been decided then, and for once a Messala takes nothing. I must go and write it in my book of great occurrences—a judgment by a Roman against a Roman! But did he—did Messala send you to me with this request, O Egypt?"

"He has a noble nature, and judged you by it."

Ben-Hur took the hand upon his arm.

"As you know him in such friendly way, fair Egyptian, tell me, would he do for me, there being a reversal of the conditions, that he asks of me? Answer, by Isis! Answer, for the truth's sake!"

There was insistence in the touch of his hand, and in his look also.

"Oh!" she began, "he is—"

"A Roman, you were about to say; meaning that I, a Jew, must not determine dues from me to him by any measure of dues from him to me; being a Jew, I must forgive him my winnings because he is a Roman. If you have more to tell me, daughter of Balthasar, speak quickly, quickly; for by the Lord God of Israel, when this heat of blood, hotter waxing, attains its highest, I may not be able longer to see

that you are a woman, and beautiful! I may see but the spy of a master the more hateful because the master is a Roman. Say on, and quickly."

She threw his hand off and stepped back into the full light, with all the evil of her nature collected in her eyes and voice.

"Thou drinker of lees, feeder upon husks! To think I could love thee, having seen Messala! Such as thou were born to serve him. He would have been satisfied with release of the six talents; but I say to the six thou shalt add twenty — twenty, dost thou hear? The kissings of my little finger which thou hast taken from him, though with my consent, shall be paid for; and that I have followed thee with affectation of sympathy, and endured thee so long, enter into the account not less because I was serving him. The merchant here is thy keeper of moneys. If by to-morrow at noon he has not thy order acted upon in favor of my Messala for six-and-twenty talents—mark the sum!—thou shalt settle with the Lord Sejanus. Be wise and—farewell."

As she was going to the door, he put himself in her way.

"The old Egypt lives in you," he said. "Whether you see Messala to-morrow or the next day, here or in Rome, give him this message. Tell him I have back the money, even the six talents, he robbed me of by robbing my father's estate; tell him I survived the galleys to which he had me sent, and in my strength rejoice in his beggary and dishonor; tell him I

think the affliction of body which he has from
my hand is the curse of our Lord God of Israel
upon him more fit than death for his crimes
against the helpless; tell him my mother and
sister, whom he had sent to a cell in Antonia
that they might die of leprosy, are alive and
well, thanks to the power of the Nazarene
whom you so despise; tell him that, to fill my
measure of happiness, they are restored to me,
and that I will go hence to their love, and find
in it more than compensation for the impure
passions which you leave me to take to him;
tell him—this for your comfort, O cunning in-
carnate, as much as his—tell him that when
the Lord Sejanus comes to despoil me he will
find nothing; for the inheritancc I had from
the duumvir, including the villa by Misenum,
has been sold, and the money from the sale is
out of reach, afloat in the marts of the world
as bills of exchange; and that this house and
the goods and merchandise and the ships and
caravans with which Simonides plies his com-
merce with such princely profits are covered
by imperial safeguards—a wise head having
found the price of the favor, and the Lord Se-
janus preferring a reasonable gain in the way
of gift to much gain fished from pools of blood
and wrong; tell him if all this were not so, if
the money and property were all mine, yet
should he not have the least part of it, for
when he finds our Jewish bills, and forces them
to give up their values, there is yet another
resort left me—a deed of gift to Cæsar—so
much, O Egypt, I found out in the atria of the

great capital; tell him that along with my de-
fiance I do not send him a curse in words, but,
as a better expression of my undying hate, I
send him one who will prove to him the sum
of all curses; and when he looks at you repeat-
ing this my message, daughter of Balthasar,
his Roman shrewdness will tell him all I mean.
Go now—and I will go."

He conducted her to the door, and, with
ceremonious politeness, held back the curtain
while she passed out.

"Peace to you," he said, as she disappeared.

CHAPTER VII
BEN-HUR RETURNS TO ESTHER

WHEN Ben-Hur left the guest-chamber
there was not nearly so much life in
his action as when he entered it; his
steps were slower, and he went along
with his head quite upon his breast. Having
made discovery that a man with a broken back
may yet have a sound brain, he was reflecting
upon the discovery.

Forasmuch as it is easy after a calamity has
befallen to look back and see the proofs of its
coming strewn along the way, the thought that
he had not even suspected the Egyptian as in
Messala's interest, but had gone blindly on
through whole years putting himself and his
friends more and more at her mercy, was a
sore wound to the young man's vanity. "I
remember," he said to himself, "she had no

word of indignation for the perfidious Roman at the Fountain of Castalia! I remember she extolled him at the boat-ride on the lake in the Orchard of Palms! And, ah!"—he stopped, and beat his left hand violently with his right —"ah! that mystery about the appointment she made with me at the Palace of Idernee is no mystery now!"

The wound, it should be observed, was to his vanity; and fortunately it is not often that people die of such hurts, or even continue a long time sick. In Ben-Hur's case, moreover, there was a compensation; for presently he exclaimed aloud, " Praised be the Lord God that the woman took not a more lasting hold on me! I see I did not love her."

Then, as if he had already parted with not a little of the weight on his mind, he stepped forward more lightly; and, coming to the place on the terrace where one stair-way led down to the court-yard below, and another ascended to the roof, he took the latter and began to climb. As he made the last step in the flight he stopped again.

" Can Balthasar have been her partner in the long mask she has been playing? No, no. Hypocrisy seldom goes with wrinkled age like that. Balthasar is a good man."

With this decided opinion he stepped upon the roof. There was a full moon overhead, yet the vault of the sky at the moment was lurid with light cast up from the fires burning in the streets and open places of the city, and the chanting and chorusing of the old psalmody of

Israel filled it with plaintive harmonies to which he could not but listen. The countless voices bearing the burden seemed to say, "Thus, O son of Judah, we prove our worshipfulness of the Lord God, and our loyalty to the land he gave us. Let a Gideon appear, or a David, or a Maccabæus, and we are ready."

That seemed an introduction; for next he saw the man of Nazareth.

In certain moods the mind is disposed to mock itself with inapposite fancies.

The tearful woman-like face of the Christ stayed with him while he crossed the roof to the parapet above the street on the north side of the house, and there was in it no sign of war; but rather as the heavens of calm evenings look peace upon everything, so it looked, provoking the old question, What manner of man is he?

Ben-Hur permitted himself one glance over the parapet, then turned and walked mechanically towards the summer-house.

"Let them do their worst," he said, as he went slowly on. "I will not forgive the Roman. I will not divide my fortune with him, nor will I fly from this city of my fathers. I will call on Galilee first, and here make the fight. By brave deeds I will bring the tribes to our side. He who raised up Moses will find us a leader, if I fail. If not the Nazarene, then some other of the many ready to die for freedom."

The interior of the summer-house, when Ben-Hur, slow sauntering, came to it, was murkily

lighted. The faintest of shadows lay along the floor from the pillars on the north and west sides. Looking in, he saw the arm-chair usually occupied by Simonides drawn to a spot from which a view of the city over towards the Market-place could be best had.

"The good man is returned. I will speak with him, unless he be asleep."

He walked in, and with a quiet step approached the chair. Peering over the high back, he beheld Esther nestled in the seat asleep—a small figure snugged away under her father's lap-robe. The hair dishevelled fell over her face. Her breathing was low and irregular. Once it was broken by a long sigh, ending in a sob. Something—it might have been the sigh or the loneliness in which he found her—imparted to him the idea that the sleep was a rest from sorrow rather than fatigue. Nature kindly sends such relief to children, and he was used to thinking Esther scarcely more than a child. He put his arms upon the back of the chair, and thought.

"I will not wake her. I have nothing to tell her—nothing unless—unless it be my love. . . . She is a daughter of Judah, and beautiful, and so unlike the Egyptian; for there it is all vanity, here all truth; there ambition, here duty; there selfishness, here self-sacrifice. . . . Nay, the question is not do I love her, but does she love me? She was my friend from the beginning. The night on the terrace at Antioch, how childlike she begged me not to make Rome my enemy, and had me tell her of the villa by Mise-

num, and of the life there! That she should not see I saw her cunning drift I kissed her. Can she have forgotten the kiss? I have not. I love her. . . . They do not know in the city that I have back my people. I shrank from telling it to the Egyptian; but this little one will rejoice with me over their restoration, and welcome them with love and sweet services of hand and heart. She will be to my mother another daughter; in Tirzah she will find her other self. I would wake her and tell her these things, but—out on the sorceress of Egypt! Of that folly I could not command myself to speak. I will go away, and wait another and a better time. I will wait. Fair Esther, dutiful child, daughter of Judah!"

He retired silently as he came.

CHAPTER VIII
GETHSEMANE—"WHOM SEEK YE?"

THE streets were full of people going and coming, or grouped about the fires roasting meat and feasting and singing and happy. The odor of scorching flesh mixed with the odor of cedarwood aflame and smoking loaded the air; and as this was the occasion when every son of Israel was full brother to every other son of Israel, and hospitality was without bounds, Ben-Hur was saluted at every step, while the groups by the fires insisted, "Stay and partake with us. We are brethren in the love of the

Lord." But with thanks to them he hurried on, intending to take horse at the khan and return to the tents on the Cedron.

To make the place, it was necessary for him to cross the thoroughfare so soon to receive sorrowful Christian perpetuation. There also the pious celebration was at its height. Looking up the street, he noticed the flames of torches in motion streaming out like pennons; then he observed that the singing ceased where the torches came. His wonder rose to its highest, however, when he became certain that amid the smoke and dancing sparks he saw the keener sparkling of burnished spear-tips, arguing the presence of Roman soldiers. What were they, the scoffing legionaries, doing in a Jewish religious procession? The circumstance was unheard of, and he stayed to see the meaning of it.

The moon was shining its best; yet, as if the moon and the torches, and the fires in the street, and the rays streaming from windows and open doors were not enough to make the way clear, some of the processionists carried lighted lanterns; and fancying he discovered a special purpose in the use of such equipments, Ben-Hur stepped into the street so close to the line of march as to bring every one of the company under view while passing. The torches and the lanterns were being borne by servants, each of whom was armed with a bludgeon or a sharpened stave. Their present duty seemed to be to pick out the smoothest paths among the rocks in the street for certain

dignitaries among them — elders and priests; rabbis with long beards, heavy brows, and beaked noses; men of the class potential in the councils of Caiaphas and Hannas. Where could they be going? Not to the Temple, certainly, for the route to the sacred house from Zion, whence these appeared to be coming, was by the Xystus. And their business — if peaceful, why the soldiers?

As the procession began to go by Ben-Hur, his attention was particularly called to three persons walking together. They were well towards the front, and the servants who went before them with lanterns appeared unusually careful in the service. In the person moving on the left of this group he recognized a chief policeman of the Temple; the one on the right was a priest; the middle man was not at first so easily placed, as he walked leaning heavily upon the arms of the others, and carried his head so low upon his breast as to hide his face. His appearance was that of a prisoner not yet recovered from the fright of arrest, or being taken to something dreadful — to torture or death. The dignitaries helping him on the right and left, and the attention they gave him, made it clear that if he were not himself the object moving the party, he was at least in some way connected with the object — a witness or a guide, possibly an informer. So if it could be found who he was the business in hand might be shrewdly guessed. With great assurance, Ben-Hur fell in on the right of the priest, and walked along with him. Now if

the man would lift his head! And presently
he did so, letting the light of the lanterns
strike full in his face, pale, dazed, pinched with
dread; the beard roughed; the eyes filmy,
sunken, and despairing. In much going about
following the Nazarene, Ben-Hur had come to
know his disciples as well as the Master; and
now, at sight of the dismal countenance, he
cried out,

"The 'Scariot!"

Slowly the head of the man turned until his
eyes settled upon Ben-Hur, and his lips moved
as if he were about to speak; but the priest
interfered.

"Who art thou? Begone!" he said to Ben-
Hur, pushing him away.

The young man took the push good-nat-
uredly, and, waiting an opportunity, fell into
the procession again. Thus he was carried
passively along down the street, through the
crowded lowlands between the hill Bezetha
and the Castle of Antonia, and on by the Be-
thesda reservoir to the Sheep Gate. There
were people everywhere, and everywhere the
people were engaged in sacred observances.

It being Passover night, the valves of the
gate stood open. The keepers were off some-
where feasting. In front of the procession as
it passed out unchallenged was the deep gorge
of the Cedron, with Olivet beyond, its dressing
of cedar and olive trees darker of the moon-
light silvering all the heavens. Two roads
met and merged into the street at the gate —
one from the north-east, the other from Beth-

any. Ere Ben-Hur could finish wondering whether he were to go farther, and if so, which road was to be taken, he was led off down into the gorge. And still no hint of the purpose of the midnight march.

Down the gorge and over the bridge at the bottom of it. There was a great clatter on the floor as the crowd, now a straggling rabble, passed over beating and pounding with their clubs and staves. A little farther, and they turned off to the left in the direction of an olive orchard enclosed by a stone wall in view from the road. Ben-Hur knew there was nothing in the place but old gnarled trees, the grass, and a trough hewn out of a rock for the treading of oil after the fashion of the country. While, yet more wonder-struck, he was thinking what could bring such a company at such an hour to a quarter so lonesome, they were all brought to a stand-still. Voices called out excitedly in front; a chill sensation ran from man to man; there was a rapid falling back and a blind stumbling over each other. The soldiers alone kept their order.

It took Ben-Hur but a moment to disengage himself from the mob and run forward. There he found a gate-way without a gate admitting to the orchard, and he halted to take in the scene.

A man in white clothes, and bareheaded, was standing outside the entrance, his hands crossed before him—a slender, stooping figure, with long hair and thin face—in an attitude of resignation and waiting.

It was the Nazarene!

Behind him, next the gate-way, were the disciples in a group; they were excited, but no man was ever calmer than he. The torch-light beat redly upon him, giving his hair a tint ruddier than was natural to it; yet the expression of the countenance was as usual all gentleness and pity.

Opposite this most unmartial figure stood the rabble, gaping, silent, awed, cowering—ready at a sign of anger from him to break and run. And from him to them—then at Judas, conspicuous in their midst—Ben-Hur looked—one quick glance, and the object of the visit lay open to his understanding. Here was the betrayer, there the betrayed; and these with clubs and staves, and the legionaries, were brought to take him.

A man may not always tell what he will do until the trial is upon him. This was the emergency for which Ben-Hur had been for years preparing. The man to whose security he had devoted himself, and upon whose life he had been building so largely, was in personal peril; yet he stood still. Such contradictions are there in human nature! To say truth, O reader, he was not entirely recovered from the picture of the Christ before the Gate Beautiful as it had been given by the Egyptian; and besides that, the very calmness with which the mysterious person confronted the mob held him in restraint by suggesting the possession of a power in reserve more than sufficient for the peril. Peace and good-will, and love and

808

non-resistance, had been the burden of the Nazarene's teaching; would he put his preaching into practice? He was master of life; he could restore it when lost; he could take it at pleasure. What use would he make of the power now? Defend himself? And how? A word—a breath—a thought were sufficient. That there would be some signal exhibition of astonishing force beyond the natural Ben-Hur believed, and in that faith waited. And in all this he was still measuring the Nazarene by himself—by the human standard.

Presently the clear voice of the Christ arose.

"Whom seek ye?"

"Jesus of Nazareth," the priest replied.

"I am he."

At these simplest of words, spoken without passion or alarm, the assailants fell back several steps, the timid among them cowering to the ground; and they might have let him alone and gone away had not Judas walked over to him.

"Hail, master!"

With this friendly speech, he kissed him.

"Judas," said the Nazarene, mildly, "betrayest thou the Son of man with a kiss? Wherefore art thou come?"

Receiving no reply, the Master spoke to the crowd again.

"Whom seek ye?"

"Jesus of Nazareth."

"I have told you that I am he. If, therefore, you seek me, let these go their way."

At these words of entreaty the rabbis ad-

vanced upon him; and, seeing their intent, some of the disciples for whom he interceded drew nearer; one of them cut off a man's ear, but without saving the Master from being taken. And yet Ben-Hur stood still! Nay, while the officers were making ready with their ropes the Nazarene was doing his greatest charity—not the greatest in deed, but the very greatest in illustration of his forbearance, so far surpassing that of men.

"Suffer ye thus far," he said to the wounded man, and healed him with a touch.

Both friends and enemies were confounded —one side that he could do such a thing, the other that he would do it under the circumstances.

"Surely he will not allow them to bind him!"

Thus thought Ben-Hur.

"Put up thy sword into the sheath; the cup which my Father hath given me, shall I not drink it?" From the offending follower, the Nazarene turned to his captors. "Are you come out as against a thief, with swords and staves to take me? I was daily with you in the Temple, and you took me not; but this is your hour, and the power of darkness."

The posse plucked up courage and closed about him; and when Ben-Hur looked for the faithful they were gone—not one of them remained.

The crowd about the deserted man seemed very busy, with tongue, hand, and foot. Over their heads, between the torch-sticks, through the smoke, sometimes in openings between

the restless men, Ben-Hur caught momentary glimpses of the prisoner. Never had anything struck him as so piteous, so unfriended, so forsaken! Yet, he thought, the man could have defended himself — he could have slain his enemies with a breath, but he would not. What was the cup his father had given him to drink? And who was the father to be so obeyed? Mystery upon mystery — not one, but many.

Directly the mob started in return to the city, the soldiers in the lead. Ben-Hur became anxious; he was not satisfied with himself. Where the torches were in the midst of the rabble he knew the Nazarene was to be found. Suddenly he resolved to see him again. He would ask him one question.

Taking off his long outer garment and the handkerchief from his head, he threw them upon the orchard wall, and started after the posse, which he boldly joined. Through the stragglers he made way, and by littles at length reached the man who carried the ends of the rope with which the prisoner was bound.

The Nazarene was walking slowly, his head down, his hands bound behind him; the hair fell thickly over his face, and he stooped more than usual; apparently he was oblivious to all going on around him. In advance a few steps were priests and elders talking and occasionally looking back. When, at length, they were all near the bridge in the gorge, Ben-Hur took the rope from the servant who had it, and stepped past him.

811

"Master, master!" he said, hurriedly, speaking close to the Nazarene's ear. "Dost thou hear, master? A word—one word. Tell me—"

The fellow from whom he had taken the rope now claimed it.

"Tell me," Ben-Hur continued, "goest thou with these of thine own accord?"

The people were come up now, and in his own ears asking angrily, "Who art thou, man?"

"O master," Ben-Hur made haste to say, his voice sharp with anxiety, "I am thy friend and lover. Tell me, I pray thee, if I bring rescue, wilt thou accept it?"

The Nazarene never so much as looked up or allowed the slightest sign of recognition; yet the something which when we are suffering is always telling it to such as look at us, though they be strangers, failed not now. "Let him alone," it seemed to say; "he has been abandoned by his friends; the world has denied him; in bitterness of spirit, he has taken farewell of men; he is going he knows not where, and he cares not. Let him alone."

And to that Ben-Hur was now driven. A dozen hands were upon him, and from all sides there was shouting, "He is one of them. Bring him along; club him—kill him!"

With a gust of passion which gave him many times his ordinary force, Ben-Hur raised himself, turned once about with his arms outstretched, shook the hands off, and rushed through the circle which was fast hemming him in. The hands snatching at him as he

passed tore his garments from his back, so he ran off the road naked; and the gorge, in keeping of the friendly darkness, darker there than elsewhere, received him safe.

Reclaiming his handkerchief and outer garments from the orchard wall, he followed back to the city gate; thence he went to the khan, and on the good horse rode to the tents of his people out by the Tombs of the Kings.

As he rode, he promised himself to see the Nazarene on the morrow — promised it, not knowing that the unfriended man was taken straightway to the house of Hannas to be tried that night.

The heart the young man carried to his couch beat so heavily he could not sleep; for now clearly his renewed Judean kingdom resolved itself into what it was—only a dream. It is bad enough to see our castles overthrown one after another with an interval between in which to recover from the shock, or, at least, let the echoes of the fall die away; but when they go altogether—go as ships sink, as houses tumble in earthquakes—the spirits which endure it calmly are made of stuffs sterner than common, and Ben-Hur's was not of them. Through vistas in the future, he began to catch glimpses of a life serenely beautiful, with a home instead of a palace of state, and Esther its mistress. Again and again through the leaden-footed hours of the night he saw the villa by Misenum, and with his little countrywoman strolled through the garden, and rested in the panelled atrium; overhead the Neapol-

itan sky, at their feet the sunniest of sun-lands
and the bluest of bays.

In plainest speech, he was entering upon a
crisis with which to-morrow and the Nazarene
will have everything to do.

CHAPTER IX
THE GOING TO CALVARY

NEXT morning, about the second hour,
two men rode full speed to the doors
of Ben-Hur's tents, and, dismount-
ing, asked to see him. He was not
yet risen, but gave directions for their admis-
sion.

"Peace to you, brethren," he said, for they
were of his Galileans, and trusted officers.
"Will you be seated?"

"Nay," the senior replied, bluntly, "to sit
and be at ease is to let the Nazarene die. Rise,
son of Judah, and go with us. The judgment
has been given. The tree of the cross is al-
ready at Golgotha."

Ben-Hur stared at them.

"The cross!" was all he could for the mo-
ment say.

"They took him last night, and tried him,"
the man continued. "At dawn they led him
before Pilate. Twice the Roman denied his
guilt; twice he refused to give him over. At
last he washed his hands, and said, 'Be it upon
you then;' and they answered—"

"Who answered?"

"They—the priests and people—'His blood be upon us and our children.'"

"Holy father Abraham!" cried Ben-Hur; "a Roman kinder to an Israelite than his own kin! And if—ah, if he should indeed be the son of God, what shall ever wash his blood from their children? It must not be—'tis time to fight!"

His face brightened with resolution, and he clapped his hands.

"The horses—and quickly!" he said to the Arab who answered the signal. "And bid Amrah send me fresh garments, and bring my sword! It is time to die for Israel, my friends. Tarry without till I come."

He ate a crust, drank a cup of wine, and was soon upon the road.

"Whither would you go first?" asked the Galilean.

"To collect the legions."

"Alas!" the man replied, throwing up his hands.

"Why alas?"

"Master"—the man spoke with shame—"master, I and my friend here are all that are faithful. The rest do follow the priests."

"Seeking what?" and Ben-Hur drew rein.

"To kill him."

"Not the Nazarene?"

"You have said it."

Ben-Hur looked slowly from one man to the other. He was hearing again the question of the night before: "The cup my Father hath given me, shall I not drink it?" In the ear of

the Nazarene he was putting his own question, "If I bring thee rescue, wilt thou accept it?" He was saying to himself, "This death may not be averted. The man has been travelling towards it with full knowledge from the day he began his mission: it is imposed by a will higher than his; whose but the Lord's? If he is consenting, if he goes to it voluntarily, what shall another do?" Nor less did Ben-Hur see the failure of the scheme he had built upon the fidelity of the Galileans; their desertion, in fact, left nothing more of it. But how singular it should happen that morning of all others! A dread seized him. It was possible his scheming, and labor, and expenditure of treasure might have been but blasphemous contention with God. When he picked up the reins and said, "Let us go, brethren," all before him was uncertainty. The faculty of resolving quickly, without which one cannot be a hero in the midst of stirring scenes, was numb within him.

"Let us go, brethren; let us to Golgotha."

They passed through excited crowds of people going south, like themselves. All the country north of the city seemed aroused and in motion.

Hearing that the procession with the condemned might be met with somewhere near the great white towers left by Herod, the three friends rode thither, passing round south-east of Akra. In the valley below the Pool of Hezekiah, passage-way against the multitude became impossible, and they were compelled to

dismount, and take shelter behind the corner
of a house and wait.

The waiting was as if they were on a river
bank, watching a flood go by, for such the peo-
ple seemed.

There are certain chapters in the First Book
of this story which were written to give the
reader an idea of the composition of the Jew-
ish nationality as it was in the time of Christ.
They were also written in anticipation of this
hour and scene; so that he who has read them
with attention can now see all Ben-Hur saw of
the going to the crucifixion — a rare and won-
derful sight!

Half an hour — an hour — the flood surged
by Ben-Hur and his companions, within arm's
reach, incessant, undiminished. At the end of
that time he could have said, "I have seen all
the castes of Jerusalem, all the sects of Judea,
all the tribes of Israel, and all the nationalities
of earth represented by them." The Libyan
Jew went by, and the Jew of Egypt, and the
Jew from the Rhine; in short, Jews from all
East countries and all West countries, and all
islands within commercial connection; they
went by on foot, on horseback, on camels, in
litters and chariots, and with an infinite variety
of costumes, yet with the same marvellous si-
militude of features which to-day particularizes
the children of Israel, tried as they have been
by climates and modes of life; they went by
speaking all known tongues, for by that means
only were they distinguishable group from
group; they went by in haste—eager, anxious,

crowding—all to behold one poor Nazarene die,
a felon between felons.

These were the many, but they were not all.

Borne along with the stream were thousands
not Jews—thousands hating and despising
them—Greeks, Romans, Arabs, Syrians, Afri-
cans, Egyptians, Easterns. So that, studying
the mass, it seemed the whole world was to be
represented, and, in that sense, present at the
crucifixion.

The going was singularly quiet. A hoof-
stroke upon a rock, the glide and rattle of re-
volving wheels, voices in conversation, and now
and then a calling voice, were all the sounds
heard above the rustle of the mighty move-
ment. Yet was there upon every countenance
the look with which men make haste to see
some dreadful sight, some sudden wreck, or
ruin, or calamity of war. And by such signs
Ben-Hur judged that these were the strangers
in the city come up to the Passover, who had
had no part in the trial of the Nazarene, and
might be his friends.

At length, from the direction of the great
towers, Ben-Hur heard, at first faint in the
distance, a shouting of many men.

"Hark! they are coming now," said one of
his friends.

The people in the street halted to hear; but
as the cry rang on over their heads, they looked
at each other, and in shuddering silence moved
along.

The shouting drew nearer each moment;
and the air was already full of it and trembling,

when Ben-Hur saw the servants of Simonides coming with their master in his chair, and Esther walking by his side; a covered litter was next behind them.

"Peace to you, O Simonides—and to you, Esther," said Ben-Hur, meeting them. "If you are for Golgotha, stay until the procession passes; I will then go with you. There is room to turn in by the house here."

The merchant's large head rested heavily upon his breast; rousing himself, he answered, "Speak to Balthasar; his pleasure will be mine. He is in the litter."

Ben-Hur hastened to draw aside the curtain. The Egyptian was lying within, his wan face so pinched as to appear like a dead man's. The proposal was submitted to him.

"Can we see him?" he inquired, faintly.

"The Nazarene? yes; he must pass within a few feet of us."

"Dear Lord!" the old man cried, fervently. "Once more, once more! Oh, it is a dreadful day for the world!"

Shortly the whole party were in waiting under shelter of the house. They said but little, afraid, probably, to trust their thoughts to each other; everything was uncertain, and nothing so much so as opinions. Balthasar drew himself feebly from the litter, and stood supported by a servant; Esther and Ben-Hur kept Simonides company.

Meantime the flood poured along, if anything, more densely than before; and the shouting came nearer, shrill up in the air,

hoarse along the earth, and cruel. At last the procession was up.

"See!" said Ben-Hur, bitterly; "that which cometh now is Jerusalem."

The advance was in possession of an army of boys, hooting and screaming, "The King of the Jews! Room, room for the King of the Jews!"

Simonides watched them as they whirled and danced along, like a cloud of summer insects, and said, gravely, "When these come to their inheritance, son of Hur, alas for the city of Solomon!"

A band of legionaries fully armed followed next, marching in sturdy indifference, the glory of burnished brass about them the while.

Then came the NAZARENE!

He was nearly dead. Every few steps he staggered as if he would fall. A stained gown badly torn hung from his shoulders over a seamless undertunic. His bare feet left red splotches upon the stones. An inscription on a board was tied to his neck. A crown of thorns had been crushed hard down upon his head, making cruel wounds from which streams of blood, now dry and blackened, had run over his face and neck. The long hair, tangled in tne thorns, was clotted thick. The skin, where it could be seen, was ghastly white. His hands were tied before him. Back somewhere in the city he had fallen exhausted under the transverse beam of his cross, which, as a condemned person, custom required him to bear to the place of execution; now a countryman carried

the burden in his stead. Four soldiers went
with him as a guard against the mob, who
sometimes, nevertheless, broke through, and
struck him with sticks, and spit upon him.
Yet no sound escaped him, neither remon-
strance nor groan; nor did he look up until
he was nearly in front of the house sheltering
Ben-Hur and his friends, all of whom were
moved with quick compassion. Esther clung
to her father; and he, strong of will as he was,
trembled. Balthasar fell down speechless.
Even Ben-Hur cried out, "O my God! my
God!" Then, as if he divined their feelings or
heard the exclamation, the Nazarene turned
his wan face towards the party, and looked at
them each one, so they carried the look in
memory through life. They could see he was
thinking of them, not himself, and the dying
eyes gave them the blessing he was not per-
mitted to speak.

"Where are thy legions, son of Hur?" asked
Simonides, aroused.

"Hannas can tell thee better than I."

"What, faithless?"

"All but these two."

"Then all is lost, and this good man must
die!"

The face of the merchant knit convulsively
as he spoke, and his head sank upon his breast.
He had borne his part in Ben-Hur's labors
well, and he had been inspired by the same
hopes, now blown out never to be rekindled.

Two other men succeeded the Nazarene
bearing cross-beams.

"Who are these?" Ben-Hur asked of the Galileans.

"Thieves appointed to die with the Nazarene," they replied.

Next in the procession stalked a mitred figure clad all in the golden vestments of the high-priest. Policemen from the Temple curtained him round about; and after him, in order, strode the sanhedrim, and a long array of priests, the latter in their plain white garments overwrapped by abnets of many folds and gorgeous colors.

"The son-in-law of Hannas," said Ben-Hur, in a low voice.

"Caiaphas! I have seen him," Simonides replied, adding, after a pause during which he thoughtfully watched the haughty pontiff, "And now am I convinced. With such assurance as proceeds from clear enlightenment of the spirit—with absolute assurance—now know I that he who first goes yonder with the inscription about his neck is what the inscription proclaims him—KING OF THE JEWS. A common man, an impostor, a felon, was never thus waited upon. For look! Here are the nations —Jerusalem, Israel. Here is the ephod, here the blue robe with its fringe, and purple pomegranates, and golden bells, not seen in the street since the day Jaddua went out to meet the Macedonian—proofs all that this Nazarene is King. Would I could rise and go after him!"

Ben-Hur listened surprised; and directly, as if himself awakened to his unusual display of feeling, Simonides said, impatiently,

"Speak to Balthasar, I pray you, and let us begone. The vomit of Jerusalem is coming."

Then Esther spoke.

" I see some women there, and they are weeping. Who are they?"

Following the point of her hand, the party beheld four women in tears; one of them leaned upon the arm of a man of aspect not unlike the Nazarene's. Presently Ben-Hur answered,

" The man is the disciple whom the Nazarene loves the best of all; she who leans upon his arm is Mary, the Master's mother; the others are friendly women of Galilee."

Esther pursued the mourners with glistening eyes until the multitude received them out of sight.

It may be the reader will fancy the foregoing snatches of conversation were had in quiet; but it was not so. The talking was, for the most part, like that indulged by people at the sea-side under the sound of the surf; for to nothing else can the clamor of this division of the mob be so well likened.

The demonstration was the forerunner of those in which, scarce thirty years later, under rule of the factions, the Holy City was torn to pieces; it was quite as great in numbers, as fanatical and bloodthirsty; boiled and raved, and had in it exactly the same elements—servants, camel-drivers, market-men, gate-keepers, gardeners, dealers in fruits and wines, proselytes, and foreigners not proselytes, watchmen and menials from the Temple, thieves, robbers, and the myriad not assignable to any class, but

who, on such occasions as this, appeared no one could say whence, hungry and smelling of caves and old tombs—bareheaded wretches with naked arms and legs, hair and beard in uncombed mats, and each with one garment the color of clay; beasts with abysmal mouths, in outcry effective as lions calling each other across desert spaces. Some of them had swords; a greater number flourished spears and javelins; though the weapons of the many were staves and knotted clubs, and slings, for which latter selected stones were stored in scrips, and sometimes in sacks improvised from the foreskirts of their dirty tunics. Among the mass here and there appeared persons of high degree—scribes, elders, rabbis, Pharisees with broad fringing, Sadducees in fine cloaks—serving for the time as prompters and directors. If a throat tired of one cry, they invented another for it; if brassy lungs showed signs of collapse, they set them going again; and yet the clamor, loud and continuous as it was, could have been reduced to a few syllables—King of the Jews!—Room for the King of the Jews!—Defiler of the Temple! —Blasphemer of God!—Crucify him, crucify him! And of these cries the last one seemed in greatest favor, because, doubtless, it was more directly expressive of the wish of the mob, and helped to better articulate its hatred of the Nazarene.

"Come," said Simonides, when Balthasar was ready to proceed—"come, let us forward."

824

Ben-Hur did not hear the call. The appearance of the part of the procession then passing, its brutality and hunger for life, were reminding him of the Nazarene—his gentleness, and the many charities he had seen him do for suffering men. Suggestions beget suggestions; so he remembered suddenly his own great indebtedness to the man; the time he himself was in the hands of a Roman guard going, as was supposed, to a death as certain and almost as terrible as this one of the cross; the cooling drink he had at the well by Nazareth, and the divine expression of the face of him who gave it; the later goodness, the miracle of Palm-Sunday; and with these recollections, the thought of his present powerlessness to give back help for help or make return in kind stung him keenly, and he accused himself. He had not done all he might; he could have watched with the Galileans, and kept them true and ready; and this—ah! this was the moment to strike! A blow well given now would not merely disperse the mob and set the Nazarene free; it would be a trumpet-call to Israel, and precipitate the long-dreamed-of war for freedom. The opportunity was going; the minutes were bearing it away; and if lost! God of Abraham! Was there nothing to be done—nothing?

That instant a party of Galileans caught his eye. He rushed through the press and overtook them.

"Follow me," he said. "I would have speech with you."

The men obeyed him, and when they were under shelter of the house he spoke again:

"You are of those who took my swords, and agreed with me to strike for freedom and the King who was coming. You have the swords now, and now is the time to strike with them. Go, look everywhere, and find our brethren, and tell them to meet me at the tree of the cross making ready for the Nazarene. Haste all of you! Nay, stand not so! The Nazarene is the King, and freedom dies with him."

They looked at him respectfully, but did not move.

"Hear you?" he asked.

Then one of them replied,

"Son of Judah"—by that name they knew him—"son of Judah, it is you who are deceived, not we or our brethren who have your swords. The Nazarene is not the King; neither has he the spirit of a king. We were with him when he came into Jerusalem; we saw him in the Temple; he failed himself and us and Israel; at the Gate Beautiful he turned his back upon God and refused the throne of David. He is not King, and Galilee is not with him. He shall die the death. But hear you, son of Judah. We have your swords, and we are ready now to draw them and strike for freedom! and we will meet you at the tree of the cross."

The sovereign moment of his life was upon Ben-Hur. Could he have taken the offer and said the word, history might have been other than it is; but then it would have been histo-

ry ordered by men, not God—something that never was, and never will be. A confusion fell upon him; he knew not how, though afterwards he attributed it to the Nazarene; for when the Nazarene was risen, he understood the death was necessary to faith in the resurrection, without which Christianity would be an empty husk. The confusion, as has been said, left him without the faculty of decision; he stood helpless—wordless even. Covering his face with his hand, he shook with the conflict between his wish, which was what he would have ordered, and the power that was upon him.

"Come; we are waiting for you," said Simonides, the fourth time.

Thereupon he walked mechanically after the chair and the litter. Esther walked with him. Like Balthasar and his friends, the Wise Men, the day they went to the meeting in the desert, he was being led along the way.

CHAPTER X
THE CRUCIFIXION

WHEN the party—Balthasar, Simonides, Ben-Hur, Esther, and the two faithful Galileans—reached the place of crucifixion, Ben-Hur was in advance leading them. How they had been able to make way through the great press of excited people, he never knew; no more did he know the road by which they came or the time it took them to come. He had walked in total

827

unconsciousness, neither hearing nor seeing anybody or anything, and without a thought of where he was going, or the ghostliest semblance of a purpose in his mind. In such condition a little child could have done as much as he to prevent the awful crime he was about to witness. The intentions of God are always strange to us; but not more so than the means by which they are wrought out, and at last made plain to our belief.

Ben-Hur came to a stop; those following him also stopped. As a curtain rises before an audience, the spell holding him in its sleep-awake rose, and he saw with a clear understanding.

There was a space upon the top of a low knoll rounded like a skull, and dry, dusty, and without vegetation, except some scrubby hyssop. The boundary of the space was a living wall of men, with men behind struggling, some to look over, others to look through it. An inner wall of Roman soldiery held the dense outer wall rigidly to its place. A centurion kept eye upon the soldiers. Up to the very line so vigilantly guarded Ben-Hur had been led; at the line he now stood, his face to the north-west. The knoll was the old· Aramaic Golgotha—in Latin, Calvaria; anglicized, Calvary; translated, The Skull.

On its slopes, in the low places, on the swells and higher hills, the earth sparkled with a strange enamelling. Look where he would outside the walled space, he saw no patch of brown soil, no rock, no green thing; he saw only thou-

sands of eyes in ruddy faces ; off a little way in the perspective only ruddy faces without eyes ; off a little farther only a broad, broad circle, which the nearer view instructed him was also of faces. And this was the ensemble of three millions of people ; under it three millions of hearts throbbing with passionate interest in what was taking place upon the knoll ; indifferent as to the thieves, caring only for the Nazarene, and for him only as he was an object of hate or fear or curiosity—he who loved them all, and was about to die for them.

In the spectacle of a great assemblage of people there are always the bewilderment and fascination one feels while looking over a stretch of sea in agitation, and never had this one been exceeded ; yet Ben-Hur gave it but a passing glance, for that which was going on in the space described would permit no division of his interest.

Up on the knoll so high as to be above the living wall, and visible over the heads of an attending company of notables, conspicuous because of his mitre and vestments and his haughty air, stood the high-priest. Up the knoll still higher, up quite to the round summit, so as to be seen far and near, was the Nazarene, stooped and suffering, but silent. The wit among the guard had complemented the crown upon his head by putting a reed in his hand for a sceptre. Clamors blew upon him like blasts — laughter — execrations — sometimes both together indistinguishably. A man—only a man, O reader, would have charged the blasts with

the remainder of his love for the race, and let
it go forever.

All the eyes then looking were fixed upon
the Nazarene. It may have been pity with
which he was moved; whatever the cause,
Ben-Hur was conscious of a change in his
feelings. A conception of something better
than the best of this life—something so much
better that it could serve a weak man with
strength to endure agonies of spirit as well as
of body; something to make death welcome
—perhaps another life purer than this one—
perhaps the spirit-life which Balthasar held to
so fast, began to dawn upon his mind clearer
and clearer, bringing to him a certain sense
that, after all, the mission of the Nazarene was
that of guide across the boundary for such as
loved him; across the boundary to where his
kingdom was set up and waiting for him.
Then, as something borne through the air out
of the almost forgotten, he heard again, or
seemed to hear, the saying of the Nazarene,

"I AM THE RESURRECTION AND THE LIFE."

And the words repeated themselves over and
over, and took form, and the dawn touched
them with its light, and filled them with a new
meaning. And as men repeat a question to
grasp and fix the meaning, he asked, gazing at
the figure on the hill fainting under its crown,
Who the Resurrection? and who the Life?

"I AM,"

the figure seemed to say—and say it for him;
for instantly he was sensible of a peace such

830

as he had never known—the peace which is the end of doubt and mystery, and the beginning of faith and love and clear understanding.

From this dreamy state Ben-Hur was aroused by the sound of hammering. On the summit of the knoll he observed then what had escaped him before—some soldiers and workmen preparing the crosses. The holes for planting the trees were ready, and now the transverse beams were being fitted to their places.

"Bid the men make haste," said the high-priest to the centurion. "These "—and he pointed to the Nazarene—"must be dead by the going-down of the sun, and buried that the land may not be defiled. Such is the Law."

With a better mind, a soldier went to the Nazarene and offered him something to drink, but he refused the cup. Then another went to him and took from his neck the board with the inscription upon it, which he nailed to the tree of the cross—and the preparation was complete.

"The crosses are ready," said the centurion to the pontiff, who received the report with a wave of the hand and the reply,

"Let the blasphemer go first. The Son of God should be able to save himself. We will see."

The people to whom the preparation in its several stages was visible, and who to this time had assailed the hill with incessant cries of impatience, permitted a lull which directly became a universal hush. The part of the infliction most shocking, at least to the thought,

was reached — the men were to be nailed to their crosses. When for that purpose the soldiers laid their hands upon the Nazarene first, a shudder passed through the great concourse; the most brutalized shrank with dread. Afterwards there were those who said the air suddenly chilled and made them shiver.

"How very still it is!" Esther said, as she put her arm about her father's neck.

And remembering the torture he himself had suffered, he drew her face down upon his breast, and sat trembling.

"Avoid it, Esther, avoid it!" he said. "I know not but all who stand and see it—the innocent as well as the guilty—may be cursed from this hour."

Balthasar sank upon his knees.

"Son of Hur," said Simonides, with increasing excitement — "son of Hur, if Jehovah stretch not forth his hand, and quickly, Israel is lost—and we are lost."

Ben-Hur answered, calmly, "I have been in a dream, Simonides, and heard in it why all this should be, and why it should go on. It is the will of the Nazarene—it is God's will. Let us do as the Egyptian here—let us hold our peace and pray."

As he looked up on the knoll again, the words were wafted to him through the awful stillness—

"I AM THE RESURRECTION AND THE LIFE."

He bowed reverently as to a person speaking.

Up on the summit meantime the work went

on. The guard took the Nazarene's clothes from him; so that he stood before the millions naked. The stripes of the scourging he had received in the early morning were still bloody upon his back; yet he was laid pitilessly down, and stretched upon the cross—first, the arms upon the transverse beam; the spikes were sharp—a few blows, and they were driven through the tender palms; next, they drew his knees up until the soles of his feet rested flat upon the tree; then they placed one foot upon the other, and one spike fixed both of them fast. The dulled sound of the hammering was heard outside the guarded space; and such as could not hear, yet saw the hammer as it fell, shivered with fear. And withal not a groan, or cry, or word of remonstrance from the sufferer: nothing at which an enemy could laugh; nothing a lover could regret.

"Which way wilt thou have him faced?" asked a soldier, bluntly.

"Towards the Temple," the pontiff replied. "In dying I would have him see the holy house hath not suffered by him."

The workmen put their hands to the cross, and carried it, burden and all, to the place of planting. At a word, they dropped the tree into the hole; and the body of the Nazarene also dropped heavily, and hung by the bleeding hands. Still no cry of pain — only the exclamation divinest of all recorded exclamations,

"Father, forgive them, for they know not what they do."

The cross, reared now above all other objects, and standing singly out against the sky, was greeted with a burst of delight; and all who could see and read the writing upon the board over the Nazarene's head made haste to decipher it. Soon as read, the legend was adopted by them and communicated, and presently the whole mighty concourse was ringing the salutation from side to side, and repeating it with laughter and groans,

"King of the Jews! Hail, King of the Jews!"

The pontiff, with a clearer idea of the import of the inscription, protested against it, but in vain; so the titled King, looking from the knoll with dying eyes, must have had the city of his fathers at rest below him—she who had so ignominiously cast him out.

The sun was rising rapidly to noon; the hills bared their brown breasts lovingly to it; the more distant mountains rejoiced in the purple with which it so regally dressed them. In the city, the temples, palaces, towers, pinnacles, and all points of beauty and prominence seemed to lift themselves into the unrivalled brilliance, as if they knew the pride they were giving the many who from time to time turned to look at them. Suddenly a dimness began to fill the sky and cover the earth—at first no more than a scarce perceptible fading of the day; a twilight out of time; an evening gliding in upon the splendors of noon. But it deepened, and directly drew attention; whereat the noise of the shouting and laughter fell off, and men, doubting their senses, gazed at

834

each other curiously : then they looked to the sun again ; then at the mountains, getting farther away ; at the sky and the near landscape, sinking in shadow ; at the hill upon which the tragedy was enacting ; and from all these they gazed at each other again, and turned pale, and held their peace.

"It is only a mist or passing cloud," Simonides said, soothingly, to Esther, who was alarmed. "It will brighten presently."

Ben-Hur did not think so.

"It is not a mist or a cloud," he said. "The spirits who live in the air—the prophets and saints—are at work in mercy to themselves and nature. I say to you, O Simonides, truly as God lives, he who hangs yonder is the Son of God."

And leaving Simonides lost in wonder at such a speech from him, he went where Balthasar was kneeling near by, and laid his hand upon the good man's shoulder.

"O wise Egyptian, hearken ! Thou alone wert right—the Nazarene is indeed the Son of God."

Balthasar drew him down to him, and replied, feebly, "I saw him a child in the manger where he was first laid ; it is not strange that I knew him sooner than thou ; but oh that I should live to see this day ! Would I had died with my brethren ! Happy Melchior ! Happy, happy Gaspar !"

"Comfort thee !" said Ben-Hur. "Doubtless they, too, are here."

The dimness went on deepening into ob-

scurity, and that into positive darkness, but without deterring the bolder spirits upon the knoll. One after the other the thieves were raised on their crosses, and the crosses planted. The guard was then withdrawn, and the people set free closed in upon the height, and surged up it, like a converging wave. A man might take a look, when a new-comer would push him on, and take his place, to be in turn pushed on—and there were laughter and ribaldry and revilements, all for the Nazarene.

"Ha, ha! If thou be King of the Jews, save thyself," a soldier shouted.

"Aye," said a priest, "if he will come down to us now, we will believe in him."

Others wagged their heads wisely, saying, "He would destroy the Temple, and rebuild it in three days, but cannot save himself."

Others still: "He called himself the Son of God; let us see if God will have him."

What all there is in prejudice no one has ever said. The Nazarene had never harmed the people; far the greater part of them had never seen him except in this his hour of calamity; yet—singular contrariety!—they loaded him with their curses, and gave their sympathy to the thieves.

The supernatural night, dropped thus from the heavens, affected Esther as it began to affect thousands of others braver and stronger.

"Let us go home," she prayed—twice, three times—saying, "It is the frown of God, father. What other dreadful things may happen, who can tell? I am afraid."

Simonides was obstinate. He said little, but was plainly under great excitement. Observing, about the end of the first hour, that the violence of the crowding up on the knoll was somewhat abated, at his suggestion the party advanced to take position nearer the crosses. Ben-Hur gave his arm to Balthasar; yet the Egyptian made the ascent with difficulty. From their new stand, the Nazarene was imperfectly visible, appearing to them not more than a dark suspended figure. They could hear him, however—hear his sighing, which showed an endurance or exhaustion greater than that of his fellow-sufferers; for they filled every lull in the noises with their groans and entreaties.

The second hour after the suspension passed like the first one. To the Nazarene they were hours of insult, provocation, and slow dying. He spoke but once in the time. Some women came and knelt at the foot of his cross. Among them he recognized his mother with the beloved disciple.

"Woman," he said, raising his voice, "behold thy son!" And to the disciple, "Behold thy mother!"

The third hour came, and still the people surged round the hill, held to it by some strange attraction, with which, in probability, the night in mid-day had much to do. They were quieter than in the preceding hour; yet at intervals they could be heard off in the darkness shouting to each other, multitude calling unto multitude. It was noticeable, also, that coming now to the Nazarene, they approached his

cross in silence, took the look in silence, and so departed. This change extended even to the guard, who so shortly before had cast lots for the clothes of the crucified; they stood with their officers a little apart, more watchful of the one convict than of the throngs coming and going. If he but breathed heavily, or tossed his head in a paroxysm of pain, they were instantly on the alert. Most marvellous of all, however, was the altered behavior of the high-priest and his following, the wise men who had assisted him in the trial in the night, and, in the victim's face, kept place by him with zealous approval. When the darkness began to fall, they began to lose their confidence. There were among them many learned in astronomy, and familiar with the apparitions so terrible in those days to the masses; much of the knowledge was descended to them from their fathers far back; some of it had been brought away at the end of the Captivity; and the necessities of the Temple service kept it all bright. These closed together when the sun commenced to fade before their eyes, and the mountains and hills to recede; they drew together in a group around their pontiff, and debated what they saw. "The moon is at its full," they said, with truth, "and this cannot be an eclipse." Then, as no one could answer the question common with them all—as no one could account for the darkness, or for its occurrence at that particu-lar time, in their secret hearts they associated it with the Nazarene, and yielded to an alarm which the long continuance of the phenome-

SUMMIT OF MOUNT OF OLIVES

non steadily increased. In their place behind the soldiers, they noted every word and motion of the Nazarene, and hung with fear upon his sighs, and talked in whispers. The man might be the Messiah, and then— But they would wait and see!

In the mean time Ben-Hur was not once visited by the old spirit. The perfect peace abode with him. He prayed simply thát the end might be hastened. He knew the condition of Simonides' mind — that he was hesitating on the verge of belief. He could see the massive face weighed down by solemn reflection. He noticed him casting inquiring glances at the sun, as seeking the cause of the darkness. Nor did he fail to notice the solicitude with which Esther clung to him, smothering her fears to accommodate his wishes.

"Be not afraid," he heard him say to her; "but stay and watch with me. Thou mayst live twice the span of my life, and see nothing of human interest equal to this; and there may be revelations more. Let us stay to the close."

When the third hour was about half gone, some men of the rudest class—wretches from the tombs about the city—came and stopped in front of the centre cross.

"This is he, the new King of the Jews," said one of them.

The others cried, with laughter, "Hail, all hail, King of the Jews!"

Receiving no reply, they went closer.

"If thou be King of the Jews, or Son of God, come down," they said, loudly.

At this, one of the thieves quit groaning, and called to the Nazarene, "Yes, if thou be Christ, save thyself and us."

The people laughed and applauded; then, while they were listening for a reply, the other felon was heard to say to the first one, "Dost thou not fear God? We receive the due rewards of our deeds; but this man hath done nothing amiss."

The by-standers were astonished; in the midst of the hush which ensued, the second felon spoke again, but this time to the Nazarene:

"Lord," he said, "remember me when thou comest into thy kingdom."

Simonides gave a great start. "When thou comest into thy kingdom!" It was the very point of doubt in his mind; the point he had so often debated with Balthasar.

"Didst thou hear?" said Ben-Hur to him. "The kingdom cannot be of this world. Yon witness saith the King is but going to his kingdom; and, in effect, I heard the same in my dream."

"Hush!" said Simonides, more imperiously than ever before in speech to Ben-Hur. "Hush, I pray thee! If the Nazarene should answer—"

And as he spoke, the Nazarene did answer, in a clear voice, full of confidence:

"Verily I say unto thee, To-day shalt thou be with me in Paradise!"

Simonides waited to hear if that were all; then he folded his hands and said, "No more, no more, Lord! The darkness is gone; I see

with other eyes—even as Balthasar, I see with eyes of perfect faith."

The faithful servant had at last his fitting reward. His broken body might never be restored; nor was there riddance of the recollection of his sufferings, or recall of the years imbittered by them; but suddenly a new life was shown him, with assurance that it was for him—a new life lying just beyond this one—and its name was Paradise. There he would find the Kingdom of which he had been dreaming, and the King. A perfect peace fell upon him.

Over the way, in front of the cross, however, there were surprise and consternation. The cunning casuists there put the assumption underlying the question and the admission underlying the answer together. For saying through the land that he was the Messiah, they had brought the Nazarene to the cross; and, lo! on the cross, more confidently than ever, he had not only reasserted himself, but promised enjoyment of his Paradise to a malefactor. They trembled at what they were doing. The pontiff, with all his pride, was afraid. Where got the man his confidence except from Truth? And what should the Truth be but God? A very little now would put them all to flight.

The breathing of the Nazarene grew harder; his sighs became great gasps. Only three hours upon the cross, and he was dying!

The intelligence was carried from man to man, until every one knew it; and then every-

841

thing hushed; the breeze faltered and died;
a stifling vapor loaded the air; heat was super-
added to darkness; nor might any one un-
knowing the fact have thought that off the
hill, out under the overhanging pall, there
were three millions of people waiting awe-
struck what should happen next—they were
so still!

Then there went out through the gloom,
over the heads of such as were on the hill
within hearing of the dying man, a cry of de-
spair, if not reproach:

"My God! my God! why hast thou for-
saken me?"

The voice startled all who heard it. One it
touched uncontrollably,

The soldiers in coming had brought with
them a vessel of wine and water, and set it
down a little way from Ben-Hur. With a
sponge dipped into the liquor, and put on the
end of a stick, they could moisten the tongue
of a sufferer at their pleasure. Ben-Hur
thought of the draught he had had at the well
near Nazareth; an impulse seized him; catch-
ing up the sponge, he dipped it into the vessel,
and started for the cross.

"Let him be!" the people in the way shout-
ed, angrily. "Let him be!"

Without minding them, he ran on, and put
the sponge to the Nazarene's lips.

Too late, too late!

The face then plainly seen by Ben-Hur,
bruised and black with blood and dust as it
was, lighted nevertheless with a sudden glow;

the eyes opened wide, and fixed upon some one visible to them alone in the far heavens; and there were content and relief, even triumph, in the shout the victim gave.

"It is finished! It is finished!"

So a hero, dying in the doing a great deed, celebrates his success with a last cheer.

The light in the eyes went out; slowly the crowned head sank upon the laboring breast. Ben-Hur thought the struggle over; but the fainting soul recollected itself, so that he and those around him caught the other and last words, spoken in a low voice, as if to one listening close by:

"Father, into thy hands I commend my spirit."

A tremor shook the tortured body; there was a scream of fiercest anguish, and the mission and the earthly life were over at once. The heart, with all its love, was broken; for of that, O reader, the man died!

Ben-Hur went back to his friends, saying, simply, "It is over; he is dead."

In a space incredibly short the multitude was informed of the circumstance. No one repeated it aloud; there was a murmur which spread from the knoll in every direction; a murmur that was little more than a whispering, "He is dead! he is dead!" and that was all. The people had their wish; the Nazarene was dead; yet they stared at each other aghast. His blood was upon them! And while they stood staring at each other, the ground commenced to shake; each man took hold of his

neighbor to support himself; in a twinkling
the darkness disappeared, and the sun came
out; and everybody, as with the same glance,
beheld the crosses upon the hill all reeling
drunken-like in the earthquake. They beheld
all three of them; but the one in the centre
was arbitrary; it alone would be seen; and
for that it seemed to extend itself upward, and
lift its burden, and swing it to and fro higher
and higher in the blue of the sky. And every
man among them who had jeered at the Naz-
arene; every one who had struck him; every
one who had voted to crucify him; every one
who had marched in the procession from the
city; every one who had in his heart wished
him dead, and they were as ten to one, felt
that he was in some way individually singled
out from the many, and that if he would live
he must get away quickly as possible from that
menace in the sky. They started to run;
they ran with all their might; on horseback,
and camels, and in chariots they ran, as well
as on foot; but then, as if it were mad at them
for what they had done, and had taken up the
cause of the unoffending and friendless dead,
the earthquake pursued them, and tossed them
about, and flung them down, and terrified them
yet more by the horrible noise of great rocks
grinding and rending beneath them. They
beat their breasts and shrieked with fear. His
blood was upon them! The home-bred and
the foreign, priest and layman, beggar, Saddu-
cee, Pharisee, were overtaken in the race, and
tumbled about indiscriminately. If they called

on the Lord, the outraged earth answered for him in fury, and dealt them all alike. It did not even know wherein the high-priest was better than his guilty brethren; overtaking him, it tripped him up also, and smirched the fringing of his robe, and filled the golden bells with sand, and his mouth with dust. He and his people were alike in the one thing at least —the blood of the Nazarene was upon them all!

When the sunlight broke upon the crucifixion, the mother of the Nazarene, the disciple, and the faithful women of Galilee, the centurion and his soldiers, and Ben-Hur and his party, were all who remained upon the hill. These had not time to observe the flight of the multitude; they were too loudly called upon to take care of themselves.

"Seat thyself here," said Ben-Hur to Esther, making a place for her at her father's feet. "Now cover thine eyes, and look not up; but put thy trust in God, and the spirit of yon just man so foully slain."

"Nay," said Simonides, reverently, "let us henceforth speak of him as the Christ."

"Be it so," said Ben-Hur.

Presently a wave of the earthquake struck the hill. The shrieks of the thieves upon the reeling crosses were terrible to hear. Though giddy with the movements of the ground, Ben-Hur had time to look at Balthasar, and beheld him prostrate and still. He ran to him and called—there was no reply. The good man was dead! Then Ben-Hur remembered to

have heard a cry in answer, as it were, to the scream of the Nazarene in his last moment; but he had not looked to see from whom it had proceeded; and ever after he believed the spirit of the Egyptian accompanied that of his Master over the boundary into the kingdom of Paradise. The idea rested not only upon the cry heard, but upon the exceeding fitness of the distinction. If faith were worthy reward in the person of Gaspar, and love in that of Melchior, surely he should have some special meed who through a long life had so excellently illustrated the three virtues in combination—Faith, Love, and Good Works.

The servants of Balthasar had deserted their master; but when all was over, the two Galileans bore the old man in his litter back to the city.

It was a sorrowful procession that entered the south gate of the palace of the Hurs about the set of sun that memorable day. About the same hour the body of the Christ was taken down from the cross.

The remains of Balthasar were carried to the guest-chamber. All the servants hastened weeping to see him; for he had the love of every living thing with which he had in anywise to do; but when they beheld his face, and the smile upon it, they dried their tears, saying, "It is well. He is happier this evening than when he went out in the morning."

Ben-Hur would not trust a servant to inform Iras what had befallen her father. He went himself to see her and bring her to the

body. He imagined her grief; she would now be alone in the world; it was a time to forgive and pity her. He remembered he had not asked why she was not of the party in the morning, or where she was; he remembered he had not thought of her; and, from shame, he was ready to make any amends, the more so as he was about to plunge her into such acute grief.

He shook the curtains of her door; and though he heard the ringing of the little bells echoing within, he had no response; he called her name, and again he called — still no answer. He drew the curtain aside and went into the room; she was not there. He ascended hastily to the roof in search of her; nor was she there. He questioned the servants; none of them had seen her during the day. After a long quest everywhere through the house, Ben-Hur returned to the guest-chamber, and took the place by the dead which should have been hers; and he bethought him there how merciful the Christ had been to his aged servant. At the gate of the kingdom of Paradise happily the afflictions of this life, even its desertions, are left behind and forgotten by those who go in and rest.

When the gloom of the burial was nigh gone, on the ninth day after the healing, the law being fulfilled, Ben-Hur brought his mother and Tirzah home; and from that day, in that house the most sacred names possible of utterance by men were always coupled worshipfully together,

GOD THE FATHER AND CHRIST THE SON.

847

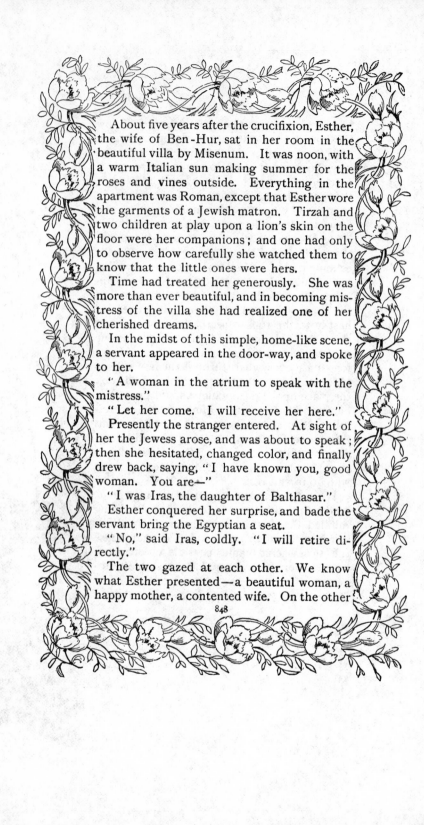

About five years after the crucifixion, Esther,
the wife of Ben-Hur, sat in her room in the
beautiful villa by Misenum. It was noon, with
a warm Italian sun making summer for the
roses and vines outside. Everything in the
apartment was Roman, except that Esther wore
the garments of a Jewish matron. Tirzah and
two children at play upon a lion's skin on the
floor were her companions; and one had only
to observe how carefully she watched them to
know that the little ones were hers.

Time had treated her generously. She was
more than ever beautiful, and in becoming mis-
tress of the villa she had realized one of her
cherished dreams.

In the midst of this simple, home-like scene,
a servant appeared in the door-way, and spoke
to her.

"A woman in the atrium to speak with the
mistress."

"Let her come. I will receive her here."

Presently the stranger entered. At sight of
her the Jewess arose, and was about to speak;
then she hesitated, changed color, and finally
drew back, saying, "I have known you, good
woman. You are—"

"I was Iras, the daughter of Balthasar."

Esther conquered her surprise, and bade the
servant bring the Egyptian a seat.

"No," said Iras, coldly. "I will retire di-
rectly."

The two gazed at each other. We know
what Esther presented—a beautiful woman, a
happy mother, a contented wife. On the other

843

side, it was very plain that fortune had not dealt so gently with her former rival. The tall figure remained with some of its grace; but an evil life had tainted the whole person. The face was coarse; the large eyes were red and pursed beneath the lower lids; there was no color in her cheeks. The lips were cynical and hard, and general neglect was leading rapidly to premature old age. Her attire was ill-chosen and draggled. The mud of the road clung to her sandals. Iras broke the painful silence.

"These are thy children?"

Esther looked at them, and smiled.

"Yes. Will you not speak to them?"

"I would scare them," Iras replied. Then she drew closer to Esther, and, seeing her shrink, said, "Be not afraid. Give thy husband a message for me. Tell him his enemy is dead, and that for the much misery he brought me I slew him."

"His enemy!"

"The Messala. Further, tell thy husband that for the harm I sought to do him I have been punished until even he would pity me."

Tears arose in Esther's eyes, and she was about to speak.

"Nay," said Iras, "I do not want pity or tears. Tell him, finally, I have found that to be a Roman is to be a brute. Farewell."

She moved to go. Esther followed her.

"Stay, and see my husband. He has no feeling against you. He sought for you everywhere. He will be your friend. I will be your friend. We are Christians."

849

The other was firm.

"No; I am what I am of choice. It will be over shortly."

"But"—Esther hesitated—"have we nothing you would wish; nothing to—to—"

The countenance of the Egyptian softened; something like a smile played about her lips. She looked at the children upon the floor.

"There is something," she said.

Esther followed her eyes, and with quick perception answered, "It is yours."

Iras went to them, and knelt on the lion's skin, and kissed them both. Rising slowly, she looked at them; then passed to the door and out of it without a parting word. She walked rapidly, and was gone before Esther could decide what to do.

Ben-Hur, when he was told of the visit, knew certainly what he had long surmised—that on the day of the crucifixion Iras had deserted her father for Messala. Nevertheless, he set out immediately and hunted for her vainly; they never saw her more, or heard of her. The blue bay, with all its laughing under the sun, has yet its dark secrets. Had it a tongue, it might tell us of the Egyptian.

Simonides lived to be a very old man. In the tenth year of Nero's reign, he gave up the business so long centred in the warehouse at Antioch. To the last he kept a clear head and a good heart, and was successful.

One evening, in the year named, he sat in his arm-chair on the terrace of the warehouse.

Ben-Hur and Esther, and their three children, were with him. The last of the ships swung at mooring in the current of the river; all the rest had been sold. In the long interval between this and the day of the crucifixion but one sorrow had befallen them : that was when the mother of Ben-Hur died; and then and now their grief would have been greater but for their Christian faith.

The ship spoken of had arrived only the day before, bringing intelligence of the persecution of Christians begun by Nero in Rome, and the party on the terrace were talking of the news when Malluch, who was still in their service, approached and delivered a package to Ben-Hur.

"Who brings this?" the latter asked, after reading.

"An Arab."

"Where is he?"

"He left immediately."

"Listen," said Ben-Hur to Simonides.

He read then the following letter :

"I, Ilderim, the son of Ilderim the Generous, and sheik of the tribe of Ilderim, to Judah, son of Hur.

"Know, O friend of my father's, how my father loved you. Read what is herewith sent, and you will know. His will is my will; therefore what he gave is thine.

"All the Parthians took from him in the great battle in which they slew him I have retaken—this writing, with other things, and vengeance, and all the brood of that Mira who in his time was mother of so many stars.

"Peace be to you and all yours.

"This voice out of the desert is the voice of
"ILDERIM, Sheik."

Ben-Hur next unrolled a scrap of papyrus yellow as a withered mulberry leaf. It required the daintiest handling. Proceeding, he read:

"Ilderim, surnamed the Generous, sheik of the tribe of Ilderim, to the son who succeeds me.

"All I have, O son, shall be thine in the day of thy succession, except that property by Antioch known as the Orchard of Palms; and it shall be to the son of Hur who brought us such glory in the Circus—to him and his forever.

"Dishonor not thy father.

"ILDERIM THE GENEROUS, Sheik."

"What say you?" asked Ben-Hur, of Simonides.

Esther took the papers pleased, and read them to herself. Simonides remained silent. His eyes were upon the ship; but he was thinking. At length he spoke.

"Son of Hur," he said, gravely, "the Lord has been good to you in these later years. You have much to be thankful for. Is it not time to decide finally the meaning of the gift of the great fortune now all in your hand, and growing?"

"I decided that long ago. The fortune was meant for the service of the Giver; not a part, Simonides, but all of it. The question with me has been, How can I make it most useful in his cause? And of that tell me, I pray you."

Simonides answered,

"The great sums you have given to the Church here in Antioch, I am witness to. Now, instantly almost with this gift of the generous

852

sheik's, comes the news of the persecution of the brethren in Rome. It is the opening of a new field. The light must not go out in the capital."

"Tell me how I can keep it alive."

"I will tell you. The Romans, even this Nero, hold two things sacred—I know of no others they so hold—they are the ashes of the dead and all places of burial. If you cannot build temples for the worship of the Lord above ground, then build them below the ground; and to keep them from profanation, carry to them the bodies of all who die in the faith."

Ben-Hur arose excitedly.

"It is a great idea," he said. "I will not wait to begin it. Time forbids waiting. The ship that brought the news of the suffering of our brethren shall take me to Rome. I will sail to-morrow."

He turned to Malluch.

"Get the ship ready, Malluch, and be thou ready to go with me."

"It is well," said Simonides.

"And thou, Esther, what sayest thou?" asked Ben-Hur.

Esther came to his side, and put her hand on his arm, and answered,

"So wilt thou best serve the Christ. O my husband, let me not hinder, but go with thee and help."

.

If any of my readers, visiting Rome, will make the short journey to the Catacomb of

San Calixto, which is more ancient than that of San Sebastiano, he will see what became of the fortune of Ben-Hur, and give him thanks. Out of that vast tomb Christianity issued to supersede the Cæsars.